Jack Cooke had to defend his wife, Marion, and his 11-year-old boy, Ricky, against the nightmare enveloping them.

He had to fight the strange, inhuman cold that had descended on the island and would not relax its death grip.

He had to fight the wolf packs that somehow had lost their fear of humans, and now attacked with increasing boldness.

He had to fight the horde of criminally insane inmates who had turned their prison into an orgiastic slaughter house.

And finally, in a world gone mad, Jack Cooke would have to fight its new master . . .

ICEFIRE

"A story of intense horror, compellingly told"

—WASHINGTON POST

Berkley books by Robert C. Wilson

ICEFIRE

ROBERT C. WILSON

This Berkley book contains the complete
text of the original hardcover edition.
It has been completely reset in a typeface
designed for easy reading, and has been printed from new film.

ICEFIRE

A Berkley Book / published by arrangement with
G. P. Putnam's Sons

PRINTING HISTORY
G. P. Putnam's edition / February 1984
Berkley edition / December 1984

ISBN: 0-425-07323-8

A BERKLEY BOOK ® TM 757,375
Berkley Books are published by The Berkley Publishing Group,
200 Madison Avenue, New York, New York 10016.
The name "BERKLEY" and the stylized "B" with design
are trademarks belonging to Berkley Publishing Corporation.
PRINTED IN THE UNITED STATES OF AMERICA

Acknowledgments

Scales Psychiatric Facility does not exist, nor are any of the characters in *Icefire* real or based on actual figures. But for a glimpse into the inner workings of what such a facility would be like, I am deeply indebted to Lawrence Levey, Dr. Dennis Jurzsak, and Dr. Robert Ort, all of the Michigan Department of Corrections.

For their encouragement and valuable insight, I am particularly grateful to Ralph Slovenko, Professor of Law and Psychiatry, Wayne State University, and Dr. Bruce Greyson, Professor of Psychiatry, University of Michigan.

I am also grateful to Dr. William Prychodko, of the Wayne State University School of Medicine, for sharing with me his knowledge and research on the effect of cold on the human body.

Leon Guzinski and Don Grant of the Michigan Department of Natural Resources and Dr. Charles Olson of the University of Michigan provided valuable assistance regarding forest and peat fires, and I wish to thank them.

The following people gave freely of their time, knowledge, and expertise and I especially appreciate their help: The Honorable Patricia Boyle and Terrance Boyle, Dr. Samuel C. Brooks, Meteorologist Lyle Brosche, Greg Carron, Dr. Carl Christensen, Brian Cleary, my agent Diane Cleaver, Kathy Coccia, Jeanne Corombos, Dr. George Dean, David Gentile, Vic Norris, Paul Travalini, Tim Watts, Andrew F. Wilson, and Mike Young.

Any factual inaccuracies are, or course, solely my own.

For Jeanne

PROLOGUE

Standing in the recess of the building, the man knew he could not be seen from the sidewalk, much less from across the street. If it weren't for the scuffing of his shoes on the pavement as he tried to keep himself warm, there would be no hint of his presence at all.

Only one overhead light burned on the block, and that toward the next cross street. The others had been broken by young sharpshooters the hot summer before. Across from where he stood was a flower shop, the lone splash of color in the otherwise barren area, stubbornly resistant to the blight of the grayed paintless wood that covered many of the other storefronts. Inside, beyond the silhouettes of potted plants and fresh-cut flowers, he could see a woman moving about the shop.

Viola Fantuzzi was returning the vases to the glass-doored refrigerator along the wall. It was part of a familiar routine she did that night and had done at the close of every business day for the past twenty-six years, exactly half her lifetime. A dozen reflections of her in the front window, a sheet of glass fragmented by spreading cracks and held in place by yellowed tape, followed her as she walked across the room. Dark eyes sunk deep in her head were like pinpoints of coal in her pale face, made all the starker by luxuriant, cream-white hair.

The wet chill outside had stiffened the man's arms and legs, had penetrated to his body through the flimsy suede jacket that he wore. But despite the cold, despite the winter drizzle that fell unbuffeted in the windless night, he stood resolutely on his vigil, staring across at the lighted interior of the flower shop. His thoughts had been almost totally a swirl of images from the past, but as he watched the woman readying to leave, they became consumed by her actions and what he was going to do. He felt a confusion of emotions kindling in the pit of his stomach. The fear was there, to be sure; but there was also a certain anticipation, a growing urgency that was alive with expectation. The feelings stirred a warmth inside him that gradually touched his skin. His shoulders unhunched, and he loosened his grip on the front of his jacket.

The man stepped away from the building, into the light but steady rain. The water beaded on his oily brown hair and trickled onto his shoulders and down his back. As the wetness touched him, an involuntary tremble rippled through his skin. A plume of vapor gushed from his mouth as he exhaled. Slowly his face turned skyward toward the hazy umbrella of illumination that hovers over a city at night. The rain seemed to come not from the clouds but from this dirty brown mass that is neither light nor dark. The rain touched his face, slowly accumulated, and then began to run down his cheeks like miniature rivulets meandering across mud-choked flats. The water felt good, washing across his face. A tremor of excitement began to build within him. His lips parted, and the water began to drip into his mouth.

Viola stepped into a small room behind the counter where her coat hung on a peg from the wall. A low-wattage bare light bulb hung from a single cord in the ceiling. In its dim glow she bent down to a cast-iron safe and spun the silver knob, shiny from years of touching. The thick door swung open, and from inside the narrow compartment she retrieved her purse. Locking it there during the day was a precaution urged on her by the local precinct. It wasn't something she thought necessary since she had never been robbed in the shop, though it had been burglarized at night before.

Placing one hand on the open metal door, she pushed herself to her feet. Then stopped. There was a distinct crack, perhaps from the front room. It couldn't be a customer. The door was locked. She had locked it, hadn't she? Viola peered around the door jamb. Nothing. No one was there.

She dismissed her momentary twinge of fear and turned back to the room. She had decided long ago that if she were to continue at the shop, she would have to ignore the creaks and whines and unexplained noises of the old building and, at times, of her imagination. Otherwise she would have been driven away years earlier.

She slipped into her tan, fleece-lined raincoat, then pulled the segmented metal chain dangling from the light fixture. As she walked through the front room, her eyes swept over the corners and behind the display tables.

A partially peeled decal by the light switch next to the front door carried a slogan that reappeared outside in faded lettering above the front window: "The most beautiful arrangements in the neighborhood." It was an accurate but hollow boast made meaningless by the deterioration of the entire area.

Viola's hand paused on the light switch, and she said a silent prayer to St. Christopher. She had never been mugged or even had her purse snatched on the lonely walk home. It wasn't because of the respect held for her in the neighborhood, she knew, because modern thieves know no such chivalry. It was because of her prayers.

Outside, the rain continued its steady drizzle. An inner warmth had been ignited within the man, and it burned through the cold. As he stood with his neck angled back and his face stretched toward the sky, the shadows seemed to deform his features. His cheeks looked as though they had been scooped out of what should be a fuller face. High cheekbones formed a ridge below his eyes, and his skin sank into a skeletonlike depression that ended at his narrowly squared chin. His angled nose was razor-thin, and when he breathed, the air whistled noisily through nostrils that bulged as they gulped for more oxygen. With his lanky frame standing motionless in front of the decrepit building, his hair matted in oily wet tufts, he looked as though he were at the brink of all that is human, nourished just enough to stay alive.

The corners of his lips were turned upward in a slight smile. The exhilaration he felt he knew from before, a sensation that took root in his body then spread, captured his thoughts, enlivened his soul. He was unaware of the cold, of the water soaking through to his skin, unaware of everything but the growing excitement, and the dry cold of the steel pressing against his thigh. Concealed down the left side of his leg, its hilt resting at his waistband, was a carbon-edged dagger.

The door of the flower shop opened, and the inside light

blinked out. The woman stepped onto a deserted sidewalk. At the slam of the door the man's head jerked down and his eyes snapped open. The tension returned. The anticipation was still there, but the dangers aroused familiar fears and quickened his pulse.

Viola saw a man standing in the rain on the other side of the street. Or at least she thought there was a man. Not looking again she walked away from the shop and down the street. If he was there, what was he doing standing in the rain? Maybe what she thought was a man was only a blend of shadows and an imagination nurtured by modern horror stories the media and her friends seemed to relish telling her. Like the imagined noise she heard a few moments before when she was in the back room, the shape could have been nothing more than her fears crystallizing into a three-dimensional figure.

The rain tapped its consistent pattern on the plastic scarf knotted tightly under her chin. Her eyes were cast downward, watchful for the spreading cracks and depressions now filled with water. The rain deadened the sound, and Viola did not hear the footsteps from across the street.

The man kept pace with the woman, all the while watching her, gauging her step, studying her movement. Moving calmed his nerves, but there was still that barely restrained tingle, prickling his skin like an electric charge sparking through frayed wire, ready to surge uncontrolled at any moment. The surroundings, the rain, the shimmer of the lone streetlight on the wet asphalt seemed to shrink into the darkness beyond his cone of concentration. His vision tunneled past the leafless elm, scarred at the trunk by countless bumpers, and through the graffiti-smeared bus-stop shelter with its once-clear plastic walls now smudged with grime and yellowed with age, and focused exclusively on the woman. Nothing else mattered. Not the rain, the danger, the possibility of a police car on patrol. He stepped off the curb and crossed the street.

Viola was nearing the corner. She pulled the lapel of her raincoat up and kept her fist clenched at the fold. The wind seemed to come from nowhere bending the vertical sheet of rain into a gentle arc. As the air came alive, the old streetlight with a shade like a doughboy's helmet swung on its fragile tether, casting spidery shadows that jittered nervously across the ground and then up the storefront walls.

She didn't know what made her do it, but she looked to her left and then behind. She brought her eyes forward again, but seared in her vision was the hunched figure walking as if to overtake her. Was he after her, or just another drunk stumbling directionless in the rain, his eyes seeing no farther than the ever-present red blur? She searched the vision in her memory for a clue. But the swelling anxiety blurred the sight. Eyes darting, intense, her hearing alert for any sounds, she glanced again toward the figure.

In the brief moment she allowed herself to look, Viola could see he was tall. A suede jacket, shiny in spots with age and lack of care, draped from his bony shoulders. His left arm remained rigidly attached to his side as he walked. Though his eyes were lost in the deep recesses of his face, she could see that they were fixed directly on her.

Viola's fist clenched tighter at her collar. She stepped faster. As she did, a chilling realization settled with numbing confusion in her thoughts: he was not a wine-sodden tramp. His steps were strong and direct. And he was pursuing her.

She was at the corner, but she didn't know which way to turn. Her mind was wiped blank by the danger that threatened. She tried to repress the fear, but it wasn't like before when it was just atmosphere, horror stories in the press coming back to haunt her, or her imagination. This time it was real. Someone was there. And he was getting closer.

At the corner she looked down the side street. The closest lit window was halfway down the block. Ahead of her was another row of abandoned or closed businesses, and she knew there was no help to be found there. But would the house open its doors? Would someone come if she called? As the thoughts began to tumble one upon another, as the indecision began to pulse in her mind, the chill inside her gave way. The blank pall that had enveloped her thoughts cracked like an aged sunscreen stretched across glass, and a fiery panic burned through.

Her hand left her collar, and her lapel flapped open. She gasped for breath, then turned to her right toward the houses. At least there were people there. They would help. They would have to.

Viola looked back again at the man. He was at the corner she had left moments before. Ahead the lighted house was a hundred yards away. With every ounce of reserve she possessed, she resisted breaking into a run. The distance between them had narrowed, but at a gradual pace. She felt that he was like a wild dog approaching its prey carefully, not wishing to arouse it by a sudden lunge, but ready to disregard caution and bolt ahead at the first sign of attempted escape. If they were running, Viola knew the man would narrow the gap much faster. Please, Jesus, she prayed, keep him away, don't let this happen.

A crumpled snack-food package blew like urban tumbleweed by her feet, while above and near the curb a no-parking sign hanging from rusted links rattled in a sudden gust of wind. Terror welled up within her. She glanced toward her pursuer again and stepped into a puddle of water dimpled with droplets of the steady rain. The fear gasped from her, the fear she had been trying to keep from him. The inky blots of his eyes, hidden by the shadows, recognized the panic, sensed her terror. His path would intersect with hers before she reached the alley. She turned and headed back toward the business street. His footsteps became louder.

The excitement, the anticipation pounded noisily through his temples, drowning out the distant hum of cars racing through a ditchlike expressway carved through the old neighborhood. The woman's fear crackled unimpeded through the dense air, electrifying his nerves, tensing his muscles, focusing his thoughts. Suddenly she turned back toward the street they had come from.

He followed. As his legs moved higher, the sharp edge of the knife blade pressed painfully into his thigh. With his left hand he tried to keep it flush against his skin, but emotions stronger than the pain guided his actions, and he stepped faster.

Viola could hear him almost upon her. Her thoughts raced incoherently through her mind, the fear, the surging terror preventing all rational order. His breath! She could hear his labored breathing. Viola turned to face him, stumbling backward against a chipped red-brick wall. Her lips quivered in an effort to speak, but all that she could do was whimper. He stopped several paces away, his left arm still clutched to his side, his chest pumping wildly. Viola's back pressed against the wall. Her purse slipped from her fingers and thudded to the pavement. She swallowed and with concentration was finally able to bring words to her mouth. "It's all that I have," she said. "You can have it. You can take it all." Her voice was nervous. He was moving slowly toward her, but she could talk to him now. She felt encouraged. Hopeful.

The man stepped by the dropped purse as if it weren't there. Viola's hand, pressed flat against the building, groped ahead of her, feeling the cold brick, slimy with the rain and the grime of the city. The tightness in her stomach returned. The man's steely approach, the unyielding glare of the dark holes in the center of his face signaled Viola it was not her money but herself he was after. A near despair descended upon her, smothering the glimmer of hope of a moment before and bringing a kind of resignation, an inner wish that it all be over in a hurry. "Please, please leave me alone." Her voice was plaintive, beseeching. "I've done nothing to you. And you can't get anything from me. I have nothing."

Buffeted by the wind, the streetlight balanced in the middle of the intersection suddenly cast its light toward Viola and her pursuer. She looked into his face, into the sunken eyes that seemed to flame with black fire, a gaze that scorched through her resignation, her acquiescence to her fate. She saw the madness in his expression, the undirected rage focused for this brief moment on her, and she felt a horror, a deep, wrenching dread that screamed throughout her body, that eclipsed all reason, all feeling within her. As she stood immobilized in his death glare, the scream erupted from her lungs, bursting into the heavy air.

The man moved rapidly at her scream, grabbing her throat with his right hand. Her cries died quickly in his suffocating grasp. He pushed her along the wall to the corner. Viola struggled against him, against his grip on her throat. She clawed at his hand, then suddenly, as she kicked at his legs, she found herself crashing to the pavement. She was at the door of an abandoned store; the glass from the entrance was in scattered fragments on the ground, jabbing into her back. But she could breathe. The air surged through her throat in a dizzying rush. Her voice returned. "Help! Please, somebody help me!"

The man picked her up by the collar and forced her backward through the door into the gutted building. Her screams continued, echoing answerless in the abandoned street, calling out in blind desperation for someone to bring an end to the assault. But if any heard, none responded.

Outside, the rain continued as it had been, neither harder nor softer, expressing neither revulsion nor approval. Its steady drizzle and the constant, repetitive splashing on the pavement quickly brought the street back to what it was before as if the rain had washed the violence away.

The cigarette butt, burned nearly to the filter, hissed as it landed on the pavement. Among the soggy litter and scattered windblown shreds of paper now seemingly pasted to the cement by the wetness, it was indistinguishable.

Detective James McDaniel slipped a pack of Winstons from his pocket, flicked his wrist, and pulled one out by the filter with his lips. Then he leaned forward, his face frozen for a moment as if in a silent convulsion before the tobacco cough came. It was a phlegmy sound, rattling in the back of his throat.

"You should watch yourself in this weather, Lieutenant." Behind McDaniel and studying him stood a younger detective, Aaron Simpson, a man whose background was as different from his partner's as the color of their skin.

"Yeah, I'd better." Though the words acknowledged the sentiment, his tone made it clear he couldn't care less about his health. The lingering cough was a part of living, like taking a shit or shaving his face, just another inconvenience he had to put up with and that he couldn't do anything about.

Though McDaniel's eyes followed the pattern of the small mounds of brown dirt that collected at the cracks in the cement and snaked across the sidewalk, his thoughts were a continent and two decades away. He thought of the tropical terrain, the steamy heat that hovered almost visibly in the air, sapping his strength as fast as it dulled his sense of adventure. The memories were the first things that had come to mind when he and Simpson had arrived an hour earlier, and they were what came back to him now as the evidence techs finished their work inside.

The precinct had called Squad 7 in Homicide after investigating the anonymous call, and McDaniel and Simpson had arrived before dawn. The two-story corner building had been vacant for years and left to a gradual destruction by age, neighborhood juveniles, and transients. The inside walls had been ripped away from the studs and, combined with the similarly bared ceiling beams, created the illusion of being inside the skeleton of some long dead and rotted behemoth.

Stretched and tacked between the wooden studs and beams was electrical cord that led not to light fixtures, but to frayed ends that dangled impotently in the air. The crackling life that had surged through the wire ensuring the necessary functioning of the business was gone, leaving little more than an ugly tangle of useless copper and cloth. It was some of this electrical cord that had been yanked from its moorings and looped under the body's arms, holding it suspended from the ceiling rafters.

Except for her tan raincoat that lay crumpled amid tufts of scattered mattress stuffing and broken glass, the woman was fully clothed. Below her dangling feet a large pool of her blood was now sticky to the touch. Deep vertical slashes scarred her face. Yet it was not the disfigurement that had aroused the detectives' interest and had touched their disbelief, a disbelief long tempered by similar scenes of brutality and horror. It was the bare human footprint in the blood.

With an occasional flash from the police camera shooting arcs of light through the slants of the boarded front window, McDaniel seemed as removed from his partner as he was from the investigation. He was thinking about the Congo during the early sixties, about his stint as a mercenary for Tshombe. Simpson knew of his past and had listened to bits and pieces of it before. He would just start talking, as if the memory was yesterday, not twenty years ago.

"You know what I feared most, over there?"

"No, I don't."

"A cat. A lousy, stinking cat. A leopard. That's what

I feared most.'' McDaniel coughed again, and he brought his fist to his mouth as if trying to force it to stop. As he waited for his lungs to still, he looked out at the street, at the gray sky gradually getting lighter, at the glossy black pavement that was patched and repatched with bulbous globs of tar that appeared like some awful, festering slime oozing from the bowels of the city. They were permanent scabs clinging to skin already dead.

Then he continued, turning to face Simpson. ''There was a village we attacked, then them, then us again. It went on for weeks, then right in the middle of it everything stopped. It stopped because there was a leopard that at night started killing people. Us, them, it didn't make any difference. It went nuts, like it was fighting its own private war.

''I remember I used to think it wasn't supposed to happen that way. I wasn't supposed to die because of a cat. I had seen one of the guys it did get, and after that, his face was the only one I thought of at night, in the jungle. The guys killed by the fighting, and even those we found that had been tortured, never bothered me, or not so much that I woke up sweating about it. This one stuck with me, though.'' He took a long drag of his cigarette. ''I guess it must have been something about this guy being killed by a wild animal that affected me.''

The orange flashing light atop the medical examiner's truck appeared at the far end of the block. ''The leopard had raked the guy across the face with its claws. His skin was slashed in four vertical lines and his eyes were still open, like he must have died of fright before the cat actually touched him.'' McDaniel nipped his cigarette butt to the pavement and watched as the truck approached. ''He looked just like the woman hanging up in there.''

Simpson stared silently at McDaniel's back for a while, then looked where he did at the truck, and watched as it arrived, then backed up to the corner. He pulled a notebook from his shirt pocket and began walking toward the driver's-side door. As he did, his thoughts were on his partner and his story. He wondered what haunted him now—the memory or the present.

The woman's mouth was round in a scream, a scream he did not hear but could sense from the trembling of her body and the fear emblazoned in her eyes, pinpoints of coal below stark white hair. Beyond her, water streaming from the gutterless roof fell in a ragged curtain at the open door leading to the alley. It was only in his mind that he could hear the gentle trickling of water as it splashed on the hard surface.

He felt a kind of exhilaration, at first creeping, now surging throughout his veins. His entire body pulsed with the sensation, bringing a burning sweat to his skin. The surroundings—the skeletal frame of the dying structure, the chill in the air, her struggle and calls for help, for mercy, all seemed to melt away. The only thing in his thoughts, in his narrow vision became the blade in his hand.

As the glinting steel moved closer to the woman, a slight smile froze on his face. He was deadened to sound and feeling. Then suddenly a scream pierced his shrouded hearing like a narrow ray of light streaking through a crypt.

He awoke with the violence of his thoughts, of the tortured shriek sparking through his nerves. His back was as rigid as a plank and raised an inch from the bed. His fingers clenched the sides of the skinny mattress with the tautness that gripped his entire body. His chest pounded with the events of the dream and the sudden rush of fright that came from waking. The hot sweat quickly turned icy. Around him the close white walls of the small cubicle brought recognition and a return to reality.

Reuker Stilkes flung the soggy sheet to the side and sprang from his bed to a small barred window in the door. His moist hands gripped the steel as he listened intently. His heart still racing from the relived murder, his thoughts still racing from the fear, he could hear only the silence.

Very gradually, when he realized no one had heard, that the noise and voices of the dream were in his mind only, his grip on the bars relaxed. Slowly a calmness, an inner peace he knew so rarely settled over him. It was the same peace he had felt five years before when he had walked out of the vacant building into the rain.

PART I

SCALES

1

"The fire, she lives. I say it's so. She lives!" His face was white and dry, as if the Lake Superior cold had permanently iced his cheeks, leaving only little flecks of dried skin to flake away like wind-hardened crystals of snow. Crinkled lines webbed out from the corners of his eyes, forever etched by the squinting glare of the winter sun.

"He musta had the sun burn his good eye, like it did the other."

"That or his brain this time."

The old man slammed his open palm to the table, and the glasses rattled on the heavy wood surface. One of the others snatched his tottering beer and downed it in one swift gulp as if afraid it might not survive the next burst of anger. "I seen it good and I heard it," the old man said, his stubby fingers touching an ear that folded inward like a wilted flower. "The ground weren't alight today. The sun's not been seen for days. And my thoughts are as clear as the ice." The last was said with a touch of a different kind of anger, and with a glare that challenged the others to question his faculties again. Then with a mixture of disgust and indifference, the glare softened and he sank back into his chair. "Aw, I don't care what you think. I know what I seen an' I seen that moose go down into the snow an' it burnt to a gawddamn cinder. There was a fire down there, under the ice, and the moose fell smack-dab into it. An' its howl stayed with me 'til I crossed o'er the ridge."

"I garner now what's for real into him. It's the wolves; they thieved his moose."

"That's not true! A man would be crazy to poach a moose in the snow other side Blackstone."

"You never been accused a bein' a whole lot sane."

The fire from the brew flared in the old man's eyes, but his voice was lost in a chorus of raucous disbelief.

A gap of several stools separated the men at the table from the curve of the bar, where a lone drinker sat isolated from the rest as a stray wolf keeps its distance from the pack. Standing, he would be tall with squared shoulders and back that, like the others, had spent time hauling lines and cutting wood. But hunched as he was over the bar, his posture belied his strength. He was younger than they, but his face, coarsened by winters that seemed to last a lifetime, by a wind that bit into a man's skin the same as it gnawed the rocky cliffs of the island, this face displayed his kinship with the others.

"Hey there, Jack. What do you say?" The old man broke the unwritten rule of the tavern that a person at the end of the bar wasn't to be disturbed. But it was a rule broken frequently, whenever an argument was in danger of being lost. And the old man knew that Jack Cooke would never call a friend of his father's a liar.

Jack swirled his sudsless draft in the bottom of the glass before downing the last swallow. His face was dark as if genetically smudged with the grime and dust of the copper mine that lured his grandfather from Cornwall to Lake Superior. His thin brown hair, interspersed with a few strands of gray, splayed to the side from a middle part to just over the tops of his ears, and in back down to his collar. His Pendleton shirt was open at the neck revealing the hexagonal pattern of thermal underwear. As he swiveled to face the men, he could not contain his smile. He knew well the old man's ploy. "I don't know, Tom. I never heard of a forest fire in the winter. But if you say you saw what you say you saw, I guess maybe we got one now."

Tom whacked his friend seated next to him on the fleshy bicep of his arm. "Get behind your bar and draw him another shell. Only man on the island with enough sense to take my word."

"I'm one of the only men on the island, period. Like the rest of you." What Jack said wasn't true. There were perhaps more men than ever on the island, but that included the institution, and none of the men even thought to count them.

Their laughs resounded in the otherwise empty room,

a room that before the whitefish and lake trout were fished to near depletion, held a noisy crew every night of the off-season.

Jack moved to their table and sat with them and joined in the warmth of their conversation. All around, the cold hung heavy on the building, creeping in at the windows and the cracks in the old wood structure.

The beer finished, Jack hefted his parka from the rack at the wall and slipped into it. As he stepped outside, he pulled his wool cap snug into what had become a semi-permanent wave in his hair where the cap perched so frequently. His first breath crystallized in his nose as he hunched forward, his arms held tightly to his sides. The cold settled like an immense weight on his shoulders.

Walking away from the tavern and the small cluster of wood frame buildings, he could hear the distant crashing of waves on the faulted ice line far from shore. Rising in the shadows behind the buildings were scattered houses, darkened and mostly abandoned, and beyond them the sloping black of the ridge.

The town fronted on a cove that during summer was a protected harbor, but now, except for a line of rotting wood posts—reminders of the pier—that jutted up at crazy angles, and a haphazard pattern of treaded snowmobile tracks, it was an unbroken expanse of white. Across the harbor, bathed in a yellowish glow of mercury vapor lights, was the institution.

Jack walked onto the ice and followed a furrowed path toward the shore at the end of the cove. The still air seemed to add a tonal crispness to the screech-crunch of each step on the hard packed subzero snow. The huge floodlights surrounding the Facility's grounds blotted out the night sky and tinted the pervading white a dull yellow, like dried tape in an old photo album. It didn't require a great leap of imagination to view the unnatural glow hanging in the air as not coming from the electric lamps of the institution, but rather emanating from the men locked inside. They were men as much removed from reality as their crimes were from civilized behavior.

Amid the distant might of the waves and the squeaking wheeze of the snow under his steps, Jack thought of those men locked inside and his job working with them. They were the same thoughts that had driven him to the tavern, to his stool at the end of the bar.

To the inmates, he was one of the imprisoners, one of their tormentors, just another person at the end of a long chain of people whose medical reports and legal decisions were the reasons for their imprisonment.

The other MCAs, the Medical Corrections Aides, did not seem to be affected by that suffocating atmosphere in the wards. Only he nearly succumbed to the pervasive hate. The others were used to it, Jack thought. They had all transferred from other correctional facilities in the state, and most were there for a limited time. He was the only outsider, the only islander, along with Marion, to work there.

The path angled up the steep rock embankment. As he climbed to solid ground, he could hear the delicate jangling of swirled wire atop the chain-link fence that surrounded the compound. Ahead, halfway between Gulletston and the hospital and settled amid a stand of pines that had grown to maturity around it, was his cabin. An orange glow flickered through the windows, and from the chimney thin wisps of heat rose straight into the air. Jack's shoulders relaxed at the thought of the warmth.

He knocked the snow off his feet before stepping inside where a log fire burned low in the glass-doored iron fireplace. Jack kicked off his boots and placed them under his coat hanging near the door. He walked past the fire and down a hallway near the back of the house. He paused at the doorway to an open room and peered inside. In the dark he couldn't see his son, but he could hear his steady breathing. It was smooth, content. Jack thought of the time four years ago when Ricky was seven and asked him why all his friends were leaving the island. Jack tried to explain how most of the families felt about the institution, but to Ricky it just seemed to highlight his isolation, his feeling that somehow they were different. There were a few kids who came to the island with their parents when they transferred to the new facility, but Ricky, like his father, felt out of place. His best friend was now sixty-three-year-old Philip Tardif, whose love for the wilderness had enveloped Ricky and taken his mind off his lost friends, and turned his isolation into a wonderful and unique experience filled with adventure and new discoveries on every trip into the wilds. But the adventure would grow stale, Jack knew, and the wonder would turn to loneliness in just a few years when his growing up revealed different mysteries.

Backing away from the doorway, Jack turned and stepped back to the front room and closed the metal doors over the fire. In the bedroom his eyes adjusted to the snow-reflected light filtering in through the windows.

Marion stirred under the Traverse Bay blanket and down comforter. She was not awake, but not quite asleep either, and she roused to the quiet noises of her husband in the room. The barely discernible light softened her already soft features, and Jack paused for a moment next to the bed to stare at her face. God, you're beautiful, he thought. As he stared down at her, he felt happy, grateful that she was still so much in love with him after twelve years, and he with her. But with the joy came a paradoxical emptiness brought on by a fear of what changes the institution would inevitably make in him, and in them together. He felt strangely distant from her, as if his uncertainties created a vacuum in which he floated, equidistant from the borders of the vacuum and just beyond his reach.

He undressed and slid under the covers as gently as he could. Marion rolled toward him and pulled herself close to his body. Her arm rested lightly across his chest, her head on his shoulder. "Oh," she moaned drowsily, "you're so cold."

The warmth from her body flowed into him, warming his skin and soothing his thoughts. "I missed you tonight," Jack said.

"No you didn't," she said, her eyes still gently shut. "You love that stinky old place."

Jack laughed. It was so easy for her, he thought, to make him feel comfortable.

"You see?" She tilted her head to look into his face. Her blond hair, made all the blonder by the darkness of his skin, fell across his arm and lay rumpled on the sheet. "You *do* love going to that stinky bar."

"I still missed you tonight."

Marion's head nestled once again on his shoulder. "Was Tom there?"

"Of course. He said he saw a moose fall into a fire beneath the snow yesterday."

"I bet the only thing that got burned yesterday is between his ears."

Smiling, Jack said, "That's just about what everybody thought."

Marion was wide awake now, and her eyes, though they flitted about the empty spaces in the room, saw only the past. "Remember the bonfire you built for me on the ice?" She had been nineteen then, and Jack had been thirty, though he was acting like a teenager.

Until he met Marion just out of high school, Jack's life had been toiling on a Lake Superior fishing schooner, then as a deckhand in the Great Lakes Merchant Marine. All that miraculously changed in Marquette when he met the young Marion Rissanen, whose great-grandparents had come from Finland to work Michigan's northern mines much as his grandparents had been lured from Cornwall. "Yes," he said tenderly. "I remember."

"Everybody thought you were crazy then. My mom, my sister, the police . . ."

"And you?"

"Me? I thought you were a stark raving loony. I was sure the fire would burn a hole to the water and we'd end up just a couple of ice cubes in the lake."

Jack laughed and rolled to his side, his back toward Marion. "You liked it though. You brought the marshmallows."

"I must have been touched by your craziness."

"Am I still crazy?" Jack asked, lifting his head from the pillow and looking over his shoulder.

"No. You're too old to be crazy."

Jack turned quickly back to face her. "Forty-two is not old."

Marion laughed out loud and pulled him down to her with both arms squeezing his chest tightly to her breast. "You're so easy," she said.

Jack resisted for just a moment before letting himself sink down into her softness as they both sank into the old mattress. Piled high with the wool blanket and the airy comforter, it was hard to tell they were even under there. Jack let his mind wander and the memories fade. As he did, as the quiet seconds grew to minutes, he could feel her grip lessening, her strength ebbing away to the darkness. As she drifted away from him and back into sleep, he was left alone with his thoughts. The tenseness returned, the same tenseness that he would awake with in the morning, tired from a fitful sleep. It was a tenseness that recurred every time the knowledge settled in that he had to go back to the institution again the next morning.

Like a dread that reveals neither terror nor release, there was no end to the apprehension, the concern, the fear of being inside those walls.

2

Daylight rarely came unequivocally to Scale Island during the winter. The sky changed from a dark gray to a heavy white, the color of old snow, until finally there was a semblance of day. Maybe by midafternoon the sun could be glimpsed trying, but never fully succeeding, to burn through the even layer of clouds that arced across the sky in an unbroken but subtly churning dome.

Under that dome, against the sky, the island was a minuscule slash of rock surrounded by the inland sea called Lake Superior. It was really an archipelago about fifty miles long, the main island split halfway up the middle wishbonelike as if two mighty basaltic battleships rammed each other at 45 degrees. Skerries intermittently paralleled the shore and trailed off into the lake from the ends of the island like flotsam bobbing close to wreckage at sea.

Though prehistoric mining sites dotted the craggy surface of the island, where long-forgotten and unknown peoples gouged pure copper from rocky outcroppings centuries before metals became common in other civilizations, the later-arriving Ojibwa avoided the superstition-shrouded land. They called it Kitcheta Beka, scaled serpent, partly because of the flinty, weathered rocks that seemed to emerge everywhere through the thin soil, eroded in places to leave huge overlapping slabs of granite and basalt like the irregular armor plating of an extinct dinosaur. Its appearance alone seemed to justify its name, at least to the French voyageurs who translated the Ojibwa into *Serpent Isle*. But the Ojibwa name represented a deeper perspective. From either side of the two ridges that extended from a common center out each arm of the wishbone, if one was far enough out to observe its silhouette, the island appeared to be the scaly spine of a serpent arching its back in a dive into the icy waters. The Ojibwa believed it was the serpent that made the lake so black and cold and treacherous. They felt that the island was an evil place, that if a man chanced stepping on its rocky shore, he risked losing his virility, and a woman, the baby in her womb.

Scale Island seemed such a primitive, unfair sobriquet for a land whose spectacular wilderness beauty was matched only by its ruggedness.

His crepe-rubber–soled moccasin-style shoes silenced his steps down the hall of the Administration Building. He wore a white medical jacket that was unbuttoned, revealing a red-and-white–checked Western shirt with imitation pearl snaps for buttons, open at the collar. A sallow-faced, expressionless photo of himself, affixed to an identification card, was clipped to the jacket's breast pocket. The card identified him as Dr. Michael Huxley.

As he neared a doorway with CENTRAL FILE lettered on the glass window of its upper half, Huxley slowed and peered inside. There was no one at the desk, nor at the table along the wall. The overhead fluorescent lights were not on.

He fished the ever-present keys from his pocket. The second master key he tried opened the door. He entered quickly, and the latch clicked behind him.

The early morning grayness filtering in through the windows gave him just enough light to see. He stepped to the file bank that lined one wall of the room, and flicked on a flexible-necked lamp that hovered out of the file bank's counter like a cobra enraptured by a fakir's pipe. He opened a red-bound, three-ring binder tabbed with alphabetical dividers, swung the tab marked s to the left, noted a number, then twisted the teardrop-shaped shade of the lamp toward the files.

Huxley depressed a button, and the file bank came noisily to life. The shelves rotated on a large drum with no more than two shelves visible at any one time in an open vertical slot. The first two numbers of the identifying tabs changed from 82 to 81, then after a few more shelves passed, to 80. At 79, Huxley lifted his finger from the button, checked the range of the files, then raised one more shelf.

He stopped suddenly and listened. Down the hallway a door opened and shut. Then a muffled conversation drifted in through the vent. Damn, he thought. Somebody was early. He located the file and pulled it out. Where it left the divided shelf, a plastic yellow marker sprang up, indicating at a glance a missing file. Huxley looked at the sign-out sheet left in the slot. The only signature followed by TIME OUT and TIME IN notations was the illegible scrawl of Dr. Neil Lummer.

In bold print on the expandable, plasticized paper folder was the number 79–031. Beneath it, in smaller lettering, was the name Reuker Stilkes.

Huxley's fingertips brushed across the letters of the name as if a blind man reading Braille. A breathless tremor fluttered in his throat, a function of the tension and of the excitement. Since coming to Scales the previous June, anytime he had heard the name Reuker Stilkes, it was said invariably with a glance over a shoulder or with an unmistakable dread, as if the syllables of his name were a forbidden incantation, secret words that beckoned deadly forces.

In an environment of the abnormal, Stilkes was unique. Even to the other patients, he was something different. Something special. Something to be feared.

From the beginning Huxley's curiosity was aroused, and over time his interest had turned to a fascination—an irresistible desire to find out what was it about Stilkes that caused the reaction he did. It became a need to understand the intangible Stilkes controlled that made tangible hidden fears in others.

Like a collector seeking a rare specimen, a naturalist with a biological anomaly, Huxley had taken to watching him—when he could—trying to catch a glimpse of him at the cafeteria, in the halls, at recreation. He observed, yet it was all from a distance. To know him better he had to get into the man's file. The file assigned to Dr. Lummer.

Huxley moved to a Xerox machine in the corner and turned the power switch on. The panel flashed a red warning, NOT READY. The machine whirred in a steady rhythm, like the nervous chorus in *Equus* humming "Beware" to the play's protagonist. His armpits dampened, and he felt a chattering impatience uncomfortably churn in his stomach. "Damn it," he breathed angrily. He was angry not so much at finding himself in what another doctor might call a compromising situation, but at being nervous about it. Then just as quickly as the anger arose, it was vented, as it normally was, to someone else. Lummer's only interest, Huxley thought, was seeing his name in print every now and then when someone from the press would call about Stilkes. He didn't care as a scientist and even less as a doctor. And if it weren't for Lummer, he wouldn't have to be sneaking around stealing files.

It wasn't the first time events and personalities had forced Huxley into an unorthodox course of action. It was in Chicago where he had brought about the early retirement of the revered Dr. Leonard Stoughton. He had gone eagerly to work for him at the Chicago Mental Health and Psychiatric Institute, near the University. But he wasn't there long before the frustrations began to mount.

The vaunted Institute was really no different from New York General or any other large hospital. There were the same procedures, the same deputies not to affront, and the same colleagues who wouldn't know an original thought if it were to aneurize in their brains. Worst of all, there was Stoughton himself.

Once he had decided that Dr. Leonard Stoughton should leave the Institute, it really wasn't as difficult to arrange as he had thought. He leaked misleading information to the press that hinted at mismanagement, then followed that with incomplete files regarding a well-publicized patient suicide. Questions were raised in the minds of scandal-conscious directors, and an investigation followed. Stoughton was eventually vindicated, but the vindication was months too late. Leonard Stoughton had resigned to protect the prestige of the Institute.

Huxley had been convinced that he could have been the new chief of staff within a few years. But that wasn't what he wanted. He hadn't gone into psychiatry to treat menopausal women and insecure men frustrated with their careers, so he looked for new challenges. He went to Denver to work at its Forensic Center, but rumors of what he had done dogged him to Colorado. He knew he wasn't trusted, but to him the petty professional worries of his colleagues were their problems, not his.

The consistent purr of the Xerox machine died. Huxley assembled the pages in a manila file and slipped it into the accordionlike folder, among several similar files. Each covered a particular aspect of Stilkes's background, his family, his treatment.

The thickest manila file contained a sheaf of newspaper clippings, Huxley knew. He pulled it out and opened it. The clips were mostly from the Detroit papers, but there were also several from North Carolina and Oregon, some from various cities around the country, a few from *The New York Times*, and even a glossy half page from *Time*.

The headlines screamed from the yellowed newsprint. MUTILATED CORPSE FOUND. MURDER VICTIM HUNG FROM PIPES. Then bolder. MISSING WOMAN VICTIM OF SLASHER. A piece from the Charlotte *Observer* was headlined: LINVILLE GORGE SLAYING TIED TO MICHIGAN KILLINGS. The stories chronicled the grotesque murders, the capture of a suspect, Stilkes's trial and defense of insanity, his conviction, and finally his commitment to Scales Psychiatric Facility, or as it was commonly and simply referred to, Scales.

Huxley found himself drawn through one article, then the next. He was drawn by his curiosity, by an intellectual wonder that was not challenged often enough. As he read, though he felt the stimulation, he would deny that something beyond a doctor's concern for the ill had been pricked. He would deny that it was possible that a challenge posed by a patient's psychological mystery could ever come to dominate him.

A soft electronic whine was followed by the metallic clank of the door's locks automatically opening. Reuker

Stilkes was already awake lying with his arms up, his wrists balanced across his forehead. He glanced toward the door, then back at the ceiling. Through the small barred window he heard the sounds of other men stirring.

His mouth was dry, the consistency of crisp paper tacky with globs of rubber cement. He didn't swallow; he had given up on trying to keep moisture there long ago. Since coming to this place, and even before when the Prolixin started, the dryness, the parched throat, the difficulty in swallowing were a permanent condition. And so was the slowness.

It seemed at times as though everything moved in slow motion, or maybe it was his own perceptions dragging behind what he saw as if some imperceptible yet unshakable weights held him back. When he tried to link thoughts together, invariably the chain would break, and the next thought would glimmer just out of reach so he could almost but never quite say it. The thought, the words on his lips would disappear as if snatched from his mind by some jealous demon who survived by devouring those images. When they disappeared like that, they were as though forgotten, and only straining to concentrate could he bring them back. Usually it wasn't worth it, and the images faded and thoughts never formed and the words broke off in midsentence.

Except in his dreams. Whether Stilkes was awake or asleep, the demon's talons could not reach into his dreams.

Stilkes savored the calmness of the morning, the mellow emptiness that filled him like an immaculate white void. Sometimes he wished he'd never have to move again. But it was not always like this. Most times, during wakefulness, the one constant was the skein of wet yarn that was his stomach being twisted and tugged by unseen and unrelenting forces. The jangling of his nerves was muted by the synthetic hormones of the medicine, but it was not extinguished. Only after the dreams did he feel truly at peace.

The door swung open, and Arnie Johnson, wearing the green-slacks, white-shirt uniform of the Medical Corrections Aides, stepped inside. His eyes never seemed wider than an Army reservist's might be on night guard duty during his two-week stint in a hot Alabama summer. His heavy jowls pulled the skin on his head tight over his skull. His bulk took up almost the entire opening of the doorway.

"C'mon, Stilkes. Get your ass out of bed. We ain't gonna hold breakfast just for you."

Slowly, always slowly, Stilkes's wrists came away from his forehead, and he rested them against his sides. He saw the fat guard blotting out the opening to the hallway. His lips were moving, but Stilkes did not hear.

"You think this is the Holiday's Inn?" Johnson's voice badgered.

Though it would be a while before words penetrated Stilkes's head, he knew what the guard wanted. It was the same every morning and would be the same every day for the rest of his life. Stilkes raised himself to his elbows and swung one foot to the matted throw rug that covered a tiny portion of his tile-floored cell. Already the peace he had been feeling was marred.

Johson watched Stilkes climb out of his bed and stand naked except for his baggy white boxer shorts. He seemed to sway, as if struggling to decide what to do next. His chest seemed pitted in all the wrong places, and he was as close to a sexless creature as Johnson had ever seen. His short brown hair was in tufts angling in every direction, and if a comb ever touched his head, Johnson was sure it would not be long before the tufts would fall into their own disarray.

Stilkes had deep, dark eye sockets, and when his head was down, as it was now, Johnson could not tell where he was looking. It made him nervous. Angrily, he pushed Stilkes at the shoulder. "Let's go. You know I don't like waitin'."

Finally dressed, Stilkes followed the swaying form of Arnie Johnson down the hall. The guard's legs thrust to either side with each step, and from behind he appeared to waddle as much as walk.

Coming toward them, a slightly built short inmate scurried to the side as Johnson brushed by. He stared up at the guard, then looked toward Stilkes. He stepped out and grabbed his arm with both hands.

"Pool? You wanna play pool? Come on, let's play some pool." His voice had the high-pitched, insistent tone of a nagging adolescent. He had been the first through the cafeteria line, as he was every morning, and now was on his way back to his room. Stilkes tried to shake him off, but he had a good grip. He looked down at him, his large nose like the point of an arrow that was his face. He had no chin and a forehead that slanted back to a receding hairline.

"Lemme go, Squirrel," Stilkes said.

"Come on. We'll shoot some pool."

It was all he ever wanted to do, Stilkes thought. It was like he was retarded, not crazy, and that made Stilkes nervous. "Get outa here," he said, trying again to free his arm.

Johnson had turned, watching. "Squirrel," he barked. "Didn't you hear the man? Leave him alone. He's gotta eat."

"Sure, Arnie, sure. I didn't mean nothin'." His bony hands sprang loose from Stilkes's biceps. "Go ahead, Reuker. You go on. We'll play pool later." He scurried away from them and hurried down the hallway.

Stilkes continued after Johnson. He could hear the guard chuckling to himself, as if to him there was no difference between Squirrel and him, just two nuts jabbering at each other. That wasn't true, Stilkes seethed. He was like none of the others.

The calm he had awakened into was rippled by an unwanted wave.

Markus slipped the key into the CENTRAL FILE office door and swung it open. Out of the corner of his eye a figure moved by the files, and Markus jumped. There was a shuffling of papers, and by the time he flicked the overhead light on, the figure had slipped a folder back into the shelf. As the white-jacketed man turned around, recognition brought a heavy whoosh from Markus.

"Jeez, Doc. You scared me half to death."

"Yeah, sorry," Huxley said. "You scared me too." He laughed nervously, slipping a rolled-up stack of papers under his arm.

"I thought you were one of the nu . . . one of the residents. You know."

"That's okay. I don't blame you. I should've had the light on. Sorry. Just had to check something in a file."

You stupid shit, Huxley could have shouted to himself. Why did he sound so lame-brained? Markus was just a clerk. But, goddamn it, he should have left. Markus is just like them, like all the rest of them here. Lummer will find out. Huxley tried to slip by Markus to the door.

"Can I help you with anything?" he offered.

"No, I'm okay. All set." He was by him and moving out the door. He said "Thanks," and was gone.

Markus stared at the open doorway for an awkward moment. As the embarrassment faded, he said aloud to himself, "Jesus, he's an odd bugger." He shook his head and started toward his desk, then stopped. Just like the rumors, he thought. He glanced at the Xerox machine in the corner. He could see the power was off, but he stepped to it and lifted the opaque cover. The glass underneath was still warm.

3

There were five living quarters within the compound. One housed most of the MCAs, another contained the apartments for the medical and administrative staff, and the remaining three residential buildings were the barracks for the inmates of Scales—thirty men to a floor, two floors to a barracks.

The men had a degree of freedom within their barracks. When not at therapy, or work, or outside, they were allowed to roam anywhere on their floor. They could stay in their rooms, visit one another, or come to the lounge.

In the corner of the lounge on the first floor of A-Barracks, a television set was anchored to the wall at head level with steel brackets and two chains taut from the ceiling. Directly opposite the TV was a three-sided observation room, kept secure by three Plexiglas panels that made it resemble a living room bay window. Black-and-white video screens monitored the hallway and the shower room; each cell had its own toilet.

About half the floor's thirty permanent residents were in the room, some playing cards, some just sitting, none watching the interference-marred reception of the television. Squirrel was in continual motion circling and bobbing around the pool table, pausing only to strike the cue ball with his stick, sometimes before it came to rest. All the while he maintained a running commentary on his play. No one else was near him.

The door to the observation triangle was open, and one of the MCAs stood in the entrance talking to two other guards. Jack Cooke idly watched the inmates while Arnie Johnson and Eric Creegan did most of the talking.

"They were supposed to be here last week," Creegan said. He meant the representatives from the State Senate Corrections Committee. "I wish to hell they'd make up their minds."

"It was a close vote, one of them said." Arnie didn't seem to care one way or the other.

"Yeah. Even the dogcatcher's bill comes before us."

The ceramic crack of the pool balls echoed continuously in the tile-floored room. Jack watched as one of the inmates stood motionless staring out the window, his face mere inches from the glass.

"Would you rather have them here more often?" Arnie asked.

"No. I just don't like having to get ready for them, then having to do it all over again a week later. It's hard enough getting these assholes in line once. Especially when it's too cold to keep 'em outside very long."

"They'll only be here for a day," Arnie observed. Then he added with a smile, "I think they're afraid to spend the night."

"I wish they'd come in the summer."

"They couldn't do that. They're not in session then." They both laughed, but Jack remained impassive, as if the Plexiglas of the booth were between them.

Creegan slapped him on the arm with the back of his hand. "Hey, lighten up. You look like you've been slipped one of their prescriptions." Their small, isolated fraternity required singleness of thought, mutuality of behavior. They were hated by the prisoners, distrusted by the doctors. A wall as impervious as the barriers around the institution was necessary to some to keep their own sanity.

Jack smiled hollowly. They weren't all drugged. Most were, though they reacted differently to the different drugs and different doses. Some it helped, most it controlled. With others, no amount of chemicals could veil that special glare of madness and violence that shone from their eyes. "Do I?" he said simply.

Creegan's grin betrayed an uncertainty, a tiny crack through which Jack's doubts could become his. "Naw," he assured. "Just kiddin'. Everybody's down sometimes. These guys may look human, but they don't have feelings like us. They're zombies."

Zombies? Now Jack's laugh was genuine. The perfect description for Reuker Stilkes, the living skeleton blankly staring out the window, dead of feeling, of emotion, of sentience. "Sorry. I just can't seem to get used to zombies like Stilkes."

"You will," Creegan said. "Just takes time." But he thought to himself that Cooke had had plenty of time. What the hell was wrong with him?

"Stilkes is no zombie," Arnie broke in. "You can see it in his eyes. He may not move much, but there's something always going on in that head."

Outside, the white was everywhere, covering the buildings, the yard, the ground beyond the fences, the foliage of the trees, the sky. Wherever Stilkes looked, the purity of the scene grasped his mind, enraptured his soul. The brightness was almost blinding, and if an object was not covered by snow, it was nonetheless practically lost, as if swallowed up in the frosty haze. Dancing, swirling, jittering against this backdrop were images and willowy figures that Stilkes alone could see.

A little girl darted across the field of snow, disappearing behind a spot of glare each time Stilkes tried to focus on her. She had fluffy blond hair, that much he could tell, and wore a blue-and-white patterned blouse. But her face remained as blank as the scene she drifted across. If he had pull himself from his reverie, where the injections seemed to make it so easy for him to hide, he would have seen the girl's face, he would have recognized the blue-

and-white blouse, he would have known why she darted from hiding place to hiding place. It seemed like long minutes—was it hours?—before the girl tired of her game and dissolved into the background, consumed by the glare.

The glow grew brighter, until Stilkes's deep, sunken eyes squinted from its brilliance. Suddenly it was aflame. The blinding whiteness turned yellow as a ragged sheet of fire streaked skyward. Stilkes watched as the flame flared closer to the window, closer to his eyes. He could feel the heat radiating through the windows; slick icicles just beyond the plate of glass dripped with moisture. There was something inside the flame. For a moment it looked as if it were an upraised arm, its fingers clawed in a desperate grasp for relief from the scorching inferno; yet as he watched, he could see the thin dark line grow more distant. It wasn't an arm. It was simply a wooden branch, a staff, a long straight stick that resisted the furious consumption of the fire. Indeed, it seemed to draw shape from the fire, and as it grew clearer, he could see one end was carved to a crude point. The wood sucked the fire into it until the last tongues of flame, flaring out as if to escape the draft of the stick, flickered out. Then the stick was gone.

Somewhere behind him Stilkes heard the carom of a pool ball as it cracked like a gunshot off another ball. To his left, the constant sound of the TV droned on. He remembered the stick. And he remembered the boy. As he thought of him, the image of the boy began to take shape in his mind.

As he pictured him, the boy was eleven years old. Judging by his height, he could have been older, but few would have made that mistake. He had that pudgy cheekiness that in a few years the changing hormones within him would cause to melt away or become firmer. He wore a dirty, striped T-shirt—the same one he usually wore when Reuker thought of him—with spreading holes at the shoulder seams near the collar. His nails were crescents of black at the tips of his fingers. That's one of the things Reuker had always liked about Billy: his dirty fingernails. Somehow that had seemed to symbolize the differences between himself and his cousin.

The woods had suddenly appeared, taking the place of

the snow. It was summer, and Billy was marching through the ferns. There was a second boy with him, leaner and smaller with deep, dark eyes not unlike his own—they were his own! Reuker was nine years old, and he followed his cousin through the woods, and as the illusion grew stronger, Stilkes felt that same fascination, that same forbidden wonder that he had known as a child. Billy would turn occasionally and say something over his shoulder. The boy was carrying on a rambling discourse on the woods, the dangers of the animals, the stinking kids at school, Reuker's good fortune at having an older cousin like him to watch out for him—anything at all that occurred to him would leap from his brain to his lips like an electric spark between two conductors.

He didn't know how long his mind drifted with thoughts of Billy and summers long ago, but just as easily as the memories drifted in, they drifted away. Stilkes watched the skateless hockey players chase around the rubber ball that substituted for a puck on the rink in the yard. Skates had disappeared from the rink a couple winters before after missing blades began turning up in shakedowns as knives honed in the shop or on concrete to a deadly sharpness.

Wherever the ball went, the players followed, without any strategy or holding of positions. As Stilkes watched this directionless mob slipping and sliding on the ice, pulled around its slick surface by the erratic path of the ball, he felt an anger flare in his stomach, an anger that hurt him as much as it threatened the others. He wasn't one of them, and as the thought gouged deeper into his stomach, his arms drew tightly to his chest, and he squeezed as though to smother the sharp pain that invariably would follow. He shouldn't be here, among them. The realization only made it worse, made the feeling inside become tauter.

A door slammed. It was a wooden door, and Reuker felt himself propelled away from it, as if he were falling into an abyss and this stark, mocking door solidly refused to open. But he wasn't falling, he was stumbling down a staircase, a broad pine staircase painted dark gray. Dark, deep-set eyes, like his own yet ablaze with fury, stared at him from the face of a woman. Her hair was circled around her head like some misshapen and dirty halo. Instinctively, Stilkes stared at his hands. Like before, like always before, they were covered with some unspeakable grime. Stilkes tried to turn away from the stench. He turned slowly from the window, yet the smell stuck with him the same as the grime on his hands. Then he saw the bugs, narrow half-inch shiny-backed bugs the color of a lake at midnight, scamper across his fingers. He tried to look away, but his hands were frozen in front of his face. The bugs filled his palms, darted across his wrists, up his arms. He spun faster, farther away from the window, into the middle of the room.

Suddenly, his arms were in the vise grip of another, and his hands were pulled away from his stare, pulled behind his back. The woman? Though he stopped spinning, the room continued to whirl. A sickly, phlegmy slime collected in his mouth. The thought of the bugs, which now for sure must be swarming over his chest, caused him to shudder. As he felt them at his neck, he stretched his chin outward, the shudder now becoming audible. Someone's hands lightly touched his shoulder. He could see a figure taking shape in front of him. He was talking, yet the words only hurt his ears. One of the white-shirted devils! Stilkes spat at the face in front of him.

Jack Cooke jerked away, brought his hand to his cheek, and quickly wiped the spit off. He stared into Stilkes's face, into an expression filled with a viciousness he rarely saw. Stilkes's arms were pinned behind him by Arnie Johnson, who had first noticed him spinning away from the window in a fit. Jack had followed Arnie across the room, and Creegan had stepped back into the Plexiglas observation area and locked the door.

Now, standing in front of the restrained but threatening Stilkes, he was aware of the other men in the room watching him. They had moved closer, forming a circle around the two guards and Stilkes, and were now silently watching as he rubbed the back of his hand on his pants. The crack of the pool balls had stilled.

Once before Jack had seen a man spit in the face of another. It had been in a bar that was near the docks in Erie, Pennsylvania. The kind of place where the stickiness of spilled drinks on unscrubbed tables eventually wore away leaving a layer of grime everywhere that would scrape off like the velvet skin of a young plant.

"Hit 'im," Arnie breathed, the forced whisper coming through clenched teeth. The other inmates watched, not intervening. Behind them all, in the glass booth, Creegan lifted a plastic box hinged to the counter and held his hand poised over a yellow button it concealed.

The guy who had been spat upon in the bar had been accused of cheating on some money owed, or screwing a woman he shouldn't have, Jack could not remember which. He struck back by beating him half to death, maddened, Jack had thought, not by outrage at the insult, but by his shame, as if the spit had singed a guilty mark on his cheek, a brand he knew he deserved.

Arnie spun Stilkes around and slammed his fist into his stomach. He doubled over gasping for breath. The circle around them dissolved, and the men went back to cards and pool. The box over the emergency button in Creegan's booth snapped shut. And Jack got the feeling from Arnie's glare that he would rather have slugged him in the stomach than Stilkes.

"Why didn't you hit him?" Arnie demanded when they were out of the room.

"I'm not sure," Jack said.

"You shoulda hit 'im. You can't take that kinda shit from one of them." The exasperation in his voice was as sharp as the creases in his face. "If they see one getting away with it, they'll all be that way." Jack started to turn away from the hulking Arnie Johnson, but the fat guard grabbed him by the shirt and pulled him closer. "You treat those monsters as if they were human. But let me tell you, they're no way near it. I don't care if the doctors call them patients or residents or whatever their little mind-games tell them to do. They're nothing but filthy scum. Stepping on an ant is no different than crushing a baby's head in their bare hands."

Arnie released the shirt and pointed his finger like a stiff little dagger directly at the center of Jack's chest. "You may be the only one of us who understands this fucked-up iceberg we live on, but inside these walls there's some things you gotta learn. If it's a shiv between your ribs you want, I could care less. But listen, buddy. You and I wear the same shirt, the same pants. To them we're no different. If you let them push you around, they'll do it to all of us. And I guarantee you, it wouldn't take long for that to happen."

Like a shout ricocheting through stone tunnels, word spread fast within Scales. When Jack received a call from one of the doctors after lunch to come see him about Stilkes, he wasn't surprised. Yet as he walked through the underground passage to the Medical Building, he did wonder why it was Huxley, not Lummer.

Huxley closed the door behind Jack, then ushered him to a chair in front of his desk. "From what I heard," he said, moving to the chair behind, "it must have been unnerving. There, in the open, with all the others around."

"It was, and I'm afraid I didn't react too well."

"So what happened, exactly?"

Jack wasn't sure, exactly. Though he had seen and participated, the details meant little because he did not understand why. But he cleared his throat and tried to answer. "He was at the window for a long time. Just standing there, staring out. Then he started to turn away—actually, more like he was jerking away from the window—and he was looking at his hands. He was spinning, as if trying to pull away from something, and that's when I grabbed his shoulders, to try to steady him. Then he looked at me, or through me, and spit in my face."

"Did he say anything?"

"No. The only sound he made was a kind of a moan."

"Did he do anything else? Make any indication of what he had been thinking?" Huxley was leaning forward, and the questions were coming fast.

"No."

"Anything at all he do that give you an idea of what he was up to?"

"No."

"Do you know why he acted like he did?"

"I couldn't say."

Huxley sat poised, his arms resting on the edge of his desk. He was looking straight at Jack, but his eyes seemed to be dancing in time to a secret rhythm, as if not focusing at all on Jack. He was thinking, his thoughts tumbling rapidly within his mind.

Several seconds passed before Huxley's face relaxed, and as it did he settled back in his chair. "I had been meaning to bring you here, Jack, for some time. To talk about Reuker Stilkes. For one reason or another, the time wasn't right. But after I heard about this morning's incident, I decided not to put it off any longer."

Jack sat impassively, waiting for Huxley to continue.

"The man is seriously disturbed, much more so than most of the others. I think you know that"—Jack nodded—"and I think you're the kind of man who wants to help him."

"If there's something I can do for any of them, I try." Jack was noncommittal.

"I know. And that's what makes you different from the other MCAs here, Jack. You could have hit Stilkes today, like the other guard. Lord knows, I've wanted to do that to patients before. But you didn't hit him, and that showed me something about you. It showed me you're not only smart, but you care about them. You care about the patients."

"What is it exactly you want of me?"

Huxley grinned. "I shouldn't beat about the bush with someone like you. So I'll talk to you straight. I want you to help me with Stilkes."

"Is this for you and Dr. Lummer?"

Huxley smiled. "No. Lummer doesn't know I'm looking into this." His eyes were fixed on Jack. He was taking a chance. "But Lummer's my worry. I promise you, you won't be drawn into anything."

"What kind of help do you need from me?"

Huxley settled again, his stare losing its intensity. He swiveled slowly in his chair so he was sideways to Jack, and staring out the window. "I've taken an interest in him," he said. "And I need to know all that I can about him. Oh, I can read the file, but that only goes so far." He swiveled back to face Jack. "I need to know how he lives, day to day, what he says, how he acts. I need you to be my eyes for me."

"Are you writing a book?"

"I don't know, I might." Huxley smiled, a peculiar twist to his lips. "But that's not the main reason for my interest."

"So why, then? What's your interest in this one patient? There are so many others."

"You are a perceptive man, and that's a fair question.

But let me ask you this first: Aren't you ever curious about him?" He paused to let his words sink in, as if to stimulate a curiosity if none existed. "Don't you wonder why he is so different, even from the other patients? What makes him tick? Why did he kill? What does he keep so tightly locked up inside him?"

"Sometimes I wonder, but—"

"But you don't go on. Afraid, maybe?"

"No, I don't think that's it. It's just that some of the men here are beyond us, beyond what we can, or maybe what we should try, to understand."

"That's the concern of the family man in you. But you have an inquisitive mind, I can tell, and no matter what you do, the questions always remain in your head. Am I right?"

Jack only stared at him, neither agreeing nor disagreeing.

"Don't you ever wonder what you can learn about yourself, through them?"

"No. I never thought of it like that."

"Ever see yourself, or part of yourself, in the men?"

"I'm not sure what you mean."

Huxley tented his hands in front of his mouth, his fingertips lightly tapping against each other. "Let me try to explain it this way. The patients here are very complex entities. But the problems they exhibit are simple." Huxley shifted in his chair, leaning forward. "I take that back. Simple is the wrong word. The problems they exhibit are in the *purest* form. And these problems, or neuroses, or whatever you want to call them, are within all of us to some extent. We are subject to the same psychological laws of nature as any of them. But within us, these kinds of things are submerged, and since they are, we cannot identify them as easily. You follow?"

Jack nodded.

"So we study those that exhibit these things most clearly."

"So you want to study Stilkes to learn about yourself?"

Huxley laughed. "Not me, personally. I'm a psychiatrist. It's my life's work to study these kinds of things. And Reuker Stilkes just happens to be the most interesting subject here."

There was something not right about Huxley, Jack felt.

But he wasn't sure, and even if he was, he couldn't quite put his finger on it.

"In some ways," Huxley continued, "Reuker and I *are* alike. And so are you. All three of us. We're alike because we're different from the others. You from the guards, me from the other doctors and staff, and Stilkes from the other patients." He paused, then said, "That's why I chose you to ask for help."

There was little Jack could do but go along. "I'll tell you what I see. For whatever help that is."

Huxley stood and began toward the door. "It will be of vast help. One last thing," he said, his hand on the knob, "until Stilkes is transferred to my care, maybe it would be best to keep our talk to ourselves."

The Medical Building was close to the staff apartments on the southeast side of the compound, opposite A-Barracks. As Jack descended into the tunnels, he was thinking of Huxley, and of Huxley's interest in Stilkes.

The feeling that something wasn't right with Huxley returned. It wasn't right because his study wasn't balanced, Jack thought. The patients may demonstrate the effects of psychological laws in their purest form, but it was the purest form of all that was wrong with human behavior.

It was an uncomfortable thought, and Jack decided not to go directly back to A-Barracks. Instead, he followed the tunnels to the staff apartments where Marion worked in the kitchen. She was finishing straightening up after lunch, before getting ready to go home.

"Anybody sees you here, they're not going to like it," Marion said. "They weren't crazy about hiring both of us to begin with."

"You want me to leave?"

Marion peered around the open door of the refrigerator at Jack. "No." It was a mischievous look she gave him, and then her face, her smile, disappeared back into the refrigerator.

"Busy day?"

The door slammed. "Whew," she said, her eyes rolling to the ceiling. "When isn't it?" She was off, walking quickly over the polished tile floor. Then she stopped abruptly and looked back at Jack. "I hear yours was too."

Jack shrugged. "Busy isn't the word for it."

She nodded, then continued toward a stainless-steel counter that was a rectangular island in the large room. "Eddie," she called to the slight-figured inmate who was at the far side of the kitchen, washing dishes, "Don't forget the cart load near the door."

Jack followed her, then leaned against the counter. "Are you tired of all this yet?"

She was the picture of frenetic activity. Moving, not slowing down. "Are you?"

"I don't know."

"It's the price we have to pay if we want to stay on the island."

Jack smiled and inched his hand along the counter toward her. "I had thought a life in the wilderness would mean long nights with you."

Marion's lips acquired a sly bent. "You already have those. Too many of those." Then she turned and strode back across the room.

Jack followed as she went into a hallway near the pantry. "Sometimes afternoons are better." He was blocking the hall.

Marion's hands were behind her back, untying her apron. She looked sideways at Jack with an expression she would use if her son, Ricky, was in one of his more juvenile moods.

"Isn't it funny how the urge can strike at the oddest times?"

Marion slipped out of her apron and hung it on a peg on the wall. Turning toward Jack, she said, "I didn't think there was ever an odd time for you."

Jack stepped toward her. "You exaggerate."

"It's hard not to with that silly leer on your face."

Jack laughed. "No sillier than your attempt to look above it all."

"Oh, you," she said, and tried to push by him. But Jack wrapped his arms around her and hugged her from behind.

Marion started to laugh. "Jack. Stop it." His lips brushed across her neck, up to her ear. She squirmed, trying to control her laugh. "Not here," she breathed.

Jack's hands rubbed across the front of her blouse, down to her stomach.

She struggled less, her resistance failing. Her head lolled to one side to allow him to kiss her neck more easily, then it rolled back, her eyes closed. "I'm glad you get your urges," she said.

Marion accepted her husband's touch, and she was warmed by it. She was comforted by it, taken away from the activity of the kitchen. Then she opened her eyes, and suddenly she tensed. The blur at the end of the hallway rapidly took shape.

"Jack!"

Jack looked where she did, and standing at the end of the hallway was Eddie Hyland. He was watching. Just standing and watching. Saying nothing.

And they said nothing, staring at him. Until Marion pushed herself from Jack, adjusting her blouse as she did. "You have other things to do, Eddie." He remained where he was, silent and staring. "Go on now." Then slowly he turned and walked away.

It took a few seconds for Jack to get angry. He started to move past Marion, but she grabbed his arm. "It's nothing," she said. "He's harmless. He probably didn't even know what we were doing."

"Don't be ridiculous. You know why he's at Scales."

Marion had recovered and began to walk out of the hallway. "Don't start with that. Now go on. Get back to where you're supposed to be and be glad it was Eddie and not Hagan."

When Jack stepped from the corridor into the open kitchen, Eddie was at the sink with his back to them, washing dishes. He did look harmless. Pathetic, even.

"Go on, Jack. I'll see you later." She came closer, her hand lightly clasping his arm. "I'll be looking forward to one of those long, wilderness nights."

Jack tried to smile but was only half-successful. As he left the kitchen, the same uneasiness he had felt leaving Huxley's office returned. It had lifted after just a few moments with Marion, but now it was back.

He descended into the tunnels and headed back toward A-Barracks. As he walked, nothing seemed right anymore.

Self-doubt can be like a virus—it weakens, then it lays bare the defenses to other sicknesses. It can work on even the strongest of men until everything that happens to him, everything he thinks, is part of the same conspiracy.

Jack stood in the lounge, his back to the men, staring out the window into the yard. It was white and stark and so terribly empty, and he felt trapped within it, within what it represented, as effectively as the residents on his floor. He was imprisoned by his job, by the island, by the vast moat of Lake Superior, and he felt a sickening helplessness as deep as he imagined the most forlorn of convicts must feel. But at least they had an excuse: They had no choice.

As he stood there and thought about himself, about what he was becoming, as he thought of the brand Reuker had burned into his face, across the yard the door of the staff apartments opened and two figures stepped out. Jack's eyes absently followed them, and it wasn't until they were halfway across the open area that he recognized who it was.

He tensed and quickly scanned the far reaches of the yard. No one else was out there. No one except Marion and Eddie Hyland.

Jack watched as Marion staggered, apparently slipping on the hard-packed snow. Eddie caught her by the arm, then helped her until she was nearly to the Administration Building. Then they parted, and Eddie started toward A-Barracks.

Jack went to the observation room and let himself in with his key. He dialed Records and asked if Hyland's status had been changed.

"Yes, as of today."

"You mean he's a trusty?"

"Yes."

"But why? Why *him*?"

"I don't know, Jack. The doctor ordered it. Dr. Huxley."

"Jesus," Jack exhaled, closing his eyes. It's bad enough he's in there with her, now he can saunter about unescorted. He thanked the clerk, then hung up the phone.

At another time, in another frame of mind, he'd know what to do, what to think. But the doubts were still there, and suddenly, he wasn't sure of himself. Was there a reason for legitimate concern for Marion? Or was it simply the conspiracy again, the mutual suspicions that suggested something wrong in everything he saw, that hinted at the worst in everything he thought.

A buzzer electronically whined. Jack punched a code into the computer keyboard, and one of the three video screens showed the outside entrance. It was Eddie Hyland. Jack pushed different keys, and the door unlocked.

Eddie came inside, and took his coat off as he walked down the hall and into the lounge. From the cold his face was splotched a feverish red, which camouflaged his sparse growth of beard that seemed always to be in that unkempt intermediate stage between a decent growth and unshaven stubble. He had thin, dirty hair and a hunch-shouldered gait that suggested a knavish cunning.

As he passed by, Jack noticed the slightly upturned corners of his mouth and a harshness to his eyes that was chilling. His gaze was a vacant stare—a mask of smug aloofness—as if inside he harbored dreams of secret pleasures that would soon be realized. Jack watched him through the glass, and he could not help but feel that inside Eddie Hyland's mind twisted twin skeins of fantasy and desire, and within this knotted disorder he was seeking a way to stretch the tangle taut.

4

The dark stained ribs inside a log cabin give the interior a textured richness of both light and surface. The roll of the wall alternately reflects and absorbs into shadows the light in the room, whether it's the flicker of the fire or the steady glow of the electric lamps. The uneven feel of the logs themselves, their indelible stamp of nature create the illusion of movement, as if the walls stretched and re-tracted with each breath of some imagined life within the wood itself.

Marion maneuvered a charred log in the fireplace with a blackened iron poker, then carefully laid on another piece of wood. A moose stew simmered on the stove in the kitchen, its rich aroma filling every room in the house. Cooking dinner for three seemed like recreation to Marion, compared with the dozens of administrative personnel and doctors in the staff apartments that she and one other woman were responsible for providing with breakfast and lunch. The early meal required her to get up an hour and a half before Jack in the morning, and she was usually home by three.

"No more wood, Mom. It's too hot already," Ricky said, peering from behind a paperback book as he lay on the couch, his feet stretched to the end of the second of three cushions.

"It's not too hot for me," Marion said.

"It's boiling in here. The pages are going to burst into flames in my hands."

"Is that right? Just exactly what are you reading, young man?"

Ricky laughed as he sat up on the couch. "Not one of Dad's books. He put a new lock on that old chest in the attic, remember?"

"Ricky," Marion said, more with surprise than disapproval. She recovered quickly and declared, "You are never to go into that chest. Do you understand?"

He nodded and said, "I won't," but a mischievous glint in his eyes belied his assurance.

Marion walked over and sat on the couch next to her son. "Those books are from your father's sailor days. All the sailors had them back then. But you can be sure he hasn't looked at them in years."

"I know, Mom," Ricky said, grinning from ear to ear. Then he said, in his most innocent way, "When I grow up, can I be a sailor? Just like Dad?"

"Oh, you," Marion said with mock exasperation, and Ricky only grinned more broadly. She looked into that beaming face and saw in it so much of what she loved about Jack.

Impulsively, she put her arms around Ricky's neck and brought his head to her chest. He allowed himself to be hugged for a moment before squirming like any self-respecting eleven-year-old boy would do in the clutches of an older female. "You're suffocating me," he coughed, pulling his head free.

Marion smiled broadly. "Tell me, Ricky. Why is it in the last few days it is suddenly so hot in here all the time?"

" 'Cause it is."

"It seems to have started after your father surveyed the wood and said we've gone through much more than he had planned."

"Must be a coincidence."

"It wouldn't have anything to do with you not wanting to split more logs, would it?"

Ricky reopened his book. "Of course not, Mom," he said, with all the nonchalance he could muster. After suffering under his mother's gaze for several seconds, Ricky glanced over the pages at her and said, "It's a good book."

"Oh? What is it?" she asked, pushing the cover back so she could see. "*Kidnapped*! Can you understand what you're reading?"

"Sure I can."

Marion was proud that her son was expanding his education so rapidly, developing his mind so early, reading real books instead of comics. She curled her legs up catlike on the couch and said, "Tell me what it's about."

"Oh, mainly about a kid who keeps getting himself into trouble with crooks and pirates. Pretty dumb kid, if you ask me. He never seems to do the right thing, what I would do if it was me."

"Wouldn't that scare you to be kidnapped by pirates?"

"Aw, gee, Mom. It'd take more than that to scare me," he said bravely. "Would you be scared?"

"Well, I suppose so. Sure I would. Unless of course, you were there to protect me."

"I'd be there, Mom. You can count on that."

Jack had thought the day would never end. He suffered through the disgusted stares of Arnie and the other MCAs as well as the less contemptuous but more threatening expressions of the inmates. He felt their eyes boring into him as if they had seen his inner doubts, his worries about being on the island, at Scales.

He had left himself exposed, and they had seen deep into his weakness. A man who would let another spit in his face is one who would turn from worse provocations. If he had reacted in some way, even with compassion, it would have given a message to the others. Instead, he had stood there.

"Hi, Dad," Ricky called, his voice carrying the same liveliness as it did every other day when his father came home.

"Hi," he said, conscious of his tired smile.

Marion draped an elbow over the back of the couch. "Hi, honey. Glad you're home."

Jack's smile became easier. "I missed you two today," he said, balancing on one foot as he slipped the other from his boot, the felt liner pulling partway out.

"Any more than usual?" Marion asked.

"Nope. The same as always. Something about you two I guess I like being around."

"Good," Ricky said. "Maybe tomorrow we can all go hiking with Philip up to the ridge."

Jack laughed as he aligned his boots on a mat by the door. Hanging above a little puddle of water were Ricky's hand-fashioned snowshoes put together by Ricky with a little help from Philip Tardif. "I don't miss you so much that I'd like to lose my job," Jack said.

"Philip doesn't work," Ricky observed.

"Philip is retired," Jack said as he walked across the room in his white wool socks, flecked with lint from the felt. "But he used to work, and he worked real hard."

"How was your day?" Marion asked. She meant the *rest* of his day.

The day was over, the unpleasantness behind him. "Great," he said convincingly. Jack fell backward over the back of the couch between Marion and Ricky.

"Hey, you're going to squish me," Ricky shouted.

Marion laughed a hearty laugh as Jack, lying on the couch with his legs up the backrest and his feet dangling over the edge, pulled her and Ricky's heads down to his chest. He kissed her on her forehead and Ricky on the top of his head. To Ricky he said, "A father can squish his child any time he wants. Didn't you know that?"

"Says who?"

"The U.S. Constitution. Right after it says all the things

you can't do, it says 'Child Squishing' is okay." To emphasize the point, Jack squeezed Ricky a little tighter to his chest. The boy laughed with unbridled glee.

Jack couldn't have been more content, his wife in one arm, his son in the other. Arnie Johnson, Reuker Stilkes, and the Michigan Department of Corrections Scales Psychiatric Facility all seemed a world away. It hadn't taken long for the love inside his home to make him forget Scales. It wasn't actually forgotten, of course, but the cloud of uncertainty that shrouded his every move while he was there, the gnawing, relentless concerns, somehow seemed less important.

Jack breathed in deeply, smelling the stew for the first time. "What's that smell?"

"It wasn't me," Ricky giggled.

"That's not what I meant," he said, looking to Marion.

"It wasn't me either," she said.

"Not that kind of smell. The good smell; the food."

"The last of Bullwinkle." To Ricky every moose on the island was Bullwinkle. Suddenly the aroma wasn't as inviting. "Good," Jack said, and they all laughed. They were big animals, and the one Jack had shot in the fall had provided endless meals of moose burgers, moose ribs, moose roast, moose sausage, and moose stew. Moose had a taste that was somewhere between beef and venison, but tougher than both, and after a few months the flavor had a way of losing its appeal.

They were a close family, and though Jack did not like the institution, being in the North Country was so much better for them than it had been down below.

Making Buicks was good money, but for a man used to fresh air and open sky, the unavoidable grime of the plant and the heavy industrial smell of oil, and worst of all, the incessant hammering of steel on steel, was gradually beating out of him the spirit Marion loved.

And for Marion, the wildness of the forest and the rugged coast of Lake Superior had been more a part of her than she realized. The dark, always-cold waters of the lake were forbidding, the weather treacherous, and the stories she heard about it scared her; but to her, the majesty of the lake was enchanting. To sit along the brink of a fjordlike inlet, with her feet dangling high above the foamy crash of waves, or to be braced against the foot of a rising dune that at her back blocked out the world, and to watch the lake was like staring into the heart of a mystery that had no answer, that could never be solved. The only thing that could be understood was what she could feel, an attraction that possessed her like a creed a believer. She was irresistibly drawn to the power and the peace of the lake. The forces it controlled, the history it had lived, the continuing spectacle of its surface were as much a part of Marion as the genes in her blood.

Though the people of Lake Superior didn't talk or act or seem different from people anywhere else, to Marion there was a ruggedness in their core to match the aged escarpment from a past geological era that spined its way through the lake.

When Scales was under construction, Jack and Marion were two of the very few from outside—or inside—the Corrections Department to apply for positions.

Marion's face was just a few inches from Ricky's. They were a pretty silly crew, she thought, the three of them on the couch. Jack upside down and she and Ricky with their heads on his chest. Marion could see that Ricky was watching her and he was feeling the same thing, thinking the same thought. It *was* pretty silly. Marion's smile was quickly matched by his as they shared a conspiratorial chuckle. A kind of innocent, carefree feeling bubbled through her. There was really no rational way to explain the ebullient spirit that took control of her, the joy that she felt. But it indeed was an exhilarating sensation, like the time she and a high school girlfriend had only to sniff the aroma of her father's Canadian Club. Ricky had that intoxicated look as well, and he began to laugh. It didn't take long before the two of them were roaring with laughter.

Jack let himself somersault slowly to the floor. He couldn't figure them out, but the spectacle they created was not unamusing to him. "You know," he said, looking from his wife to his son, both overcome by a paroxysm of merriment, "I work with those nuts all day long, but I don't think any of them are nuttier than you two."

Of course, he just made them laugh all the harder.

"You didn't tell me Eddie was going to be a trusty." The last of the stew had been blotted up with thick slices of bread, and the moose, all of him, was thankfully gone.

"Now don't start anything about him. He's as harmless as a flea."

"Not so harmless he—"

"Jack!" Marion's eyes darted in Ricky's direction, then locked on his.

"He knows the kind of people we deal with in there."

Her eyes flared.

Jack knew of the nightmares Marion had when she was thirteen. An entire family was found murdered at a summer cottage near Grand Marais, and though it had been an isolated act and the killer caught, she had had nightmares for months. It was one thing reading something like that in newspapers, but another learning it happened so close. It was as if the horror took shape and lingered in the air, and since she had been young and impressionable, the shapes had stayed with her, late at night, when she was alone. She didn't want that for Ricky, and whatever crimes the men had committed, she tried to preserve that bit of unreality, that remoteness, so that no matter how real the institution was, and the men behind its fences, to Ricky they would remain no more threatening than a newspaper story of some far-off place.

The silence passed, and she turned to Ricky and asked where he was going with Philip tomorrow.

"Up to the cabin. It might be tomorrow, or maybe the next day. Philip wanted to shovel the roof. And he said if we're lucky, we might see some wolves."

"What about school with Emma?"

"Oh," Ricky said vaguely, eyeing the swirled pattern of congealed grease on his plate, "She said it would be okay."

As they talked, the helplessness returned to Jack. It was all out of his control, he thought. He couldn't even talk about it.

"You're not going near the ice tomorrow, are you?"

"No, not at all."

"And you'll never go out there again?" Marion pressed. Snowshoeing inland was one thing. At least it was on solid ground. But climbing out over the buckled ice that rimmed the island was courting an icy death.

"Aw, Mom. There's nothing dangerous about it."

"You're too young to know if there is or isn't."

"But Philip isn't."

Marion breathed an exasperated sigh. Philip was a wonder, she knew, but sometimes she felt even he let that boyish adventuresome spirit take control of his sixty-three-year-old body.

"Dad. There's really neat ice caves out there. You can climb inside them and everything."

"You're not to go on the ice, Ricky. Do you understand?"

As dejected as he could make his voice, Ricky said, "Yes, I understand." But inside, Ricky thought it very difficult to understand how he could give up exploring the amazing thing he had discovered.

It wasn't until later, after Ricky had gone to bed, that Jack was able to talk to Marion about Eddie Hyland.

"You worry too much. Eddie is very shy and insecure. He may have done things in the past—"

"Marion. You talk as if he's just a juvenile delinquent. He's a rapist. He showed no shyness then."

"That's behind him. He was sick, after all, otherwise they wouldn't have sent him here. Maybe if he had had a decent chance in the past, if he had been treated as a normal human being, he wouldn't have done what he did."

"You can't say that. You don't know the first thing about his background and why he did what he did."

"I know what I see, and I see a pathetic young man who's afraid of his own shadow, and the only worthwhile thing he has ever done in his entire life is wash dishes in that stupid kitchen."

She was strong, always giving, always ready to believe in the good in others. Maybe that was the best way, Jack thought. Maybe she was right. Maybe he had been infected by something in the air at Scales that soured his entire outlook. To a degree that was true. But inside he knew that it all couldn't be explained away by his paranoia.

Jack could see something in Eddie Hyland that Eddie did not show to Marion. And what he saw was ugly, ulcerous; it was what Marion said was behind him. She didn't see it because he kept it hidden from her, and Jack wondered, as they dimmed the lights and prepared for bed, if he would ever be able to get her to see it. Before Eddie showed it to her himself.

5

Dr. Michael Huxley had not stayed at the Denver Forensic Center long. It had seemed an endless procession of Mental Status Exams and testifying at competency hearings, something any psychologist could do. The tests became as routine as the results were predictable. The joke in the courts was that if a defendant was warm, he was competent to stand trial.

But it was while he was there that he read about Scales. It was an ad in a journal that first attracted his attention. He wrote, and the more he learned about it, the more intrigued he became.

It didn't matter that the other doctors would be institutional types, lifers. He had experience in dealing with them. What mattered was that it was a remote island where the doctor-patient relationship was not subject to the whims of attorneys, courts, or a public screaming for vengeance. Nor was he dependent on unpredictable patients not appearing at scheduled appointments. The men were convicted criminals serving long sentences, carefully sorted to include only the mentally ill, or those who did a good job of faking it. It was just the kind of opportunity Huxley had needed.

Huxley unwrapped his flexible, thin-framed metal eyeglasses from around his ears and placed them on the desk. He scrunched his eyes together and pinched the bridge of his nose to ease the strain of reading the stack of papers scattered before him. Fatigue had slowed his studying of the photocopied file, but nothing could diminish his building enthusiasm.

It was as he rested his eyes that Jack Cooke came to his office. It was late afternoon and the first chance Jack had to get away from A-Barracks. Huxley received him expectantly, but he had not come to talk about Stilkes. He had come to talk about Eddie Hyland.

"I never did like him in there, but at least before there was some supervision. He was taken over and back, and an MCA had to be on the floor. But now, he's practically as free as any of us."

"Is there anything wrong with him feeling that, as long as he's here at Scales?"

"If he feels he can do what he wants, he's liable to do anything."

"Oh, I don't think he's ready to revert to his pre-incarceration behavior."

"I'm worried that you might be wrong. You've even got Marion convinced he poses no danger."

"If she's not afraid, why are you?"

"She just doesn't understand the danger."

"Maybe it's you who misunderstands." Jack's anger flared in his eyes. Huxley shifted. "Look. The criteria for dangerousness is not what he did in the past, but how he is now. And Eddie Hyland is a model prisoner. And a model patient, I may add. He needs his therapy."

"Therapy?"

Huxley's voice became louder, as if suddenly nervous, as if trying to cover something. "You know the reason to give them jobs. To make them feel useful. To reduce their sense of inadequacy, their tensions. Make them feel trusted."

Jack sensed there was something more, that Huxley was being dishonest. "Dr. Huxley," he said, eyeing him directly, "I don't trust him in there with her."

Huxley pursed his lips and stared at Jack, rocking in his chair. "Okay," he said after a few moments of thought, "if you'll feel better, I'll change his status. Fair enough?"

Jack nodded. Yet for some reason, he was still wary of the man. He started to get up.

"I've been looking over Reuker's file," Huxley said quickly. "You might be interested."

"I really have to be getting back."

"No. Please stay. It will help our—our arrangement, if you know a little about him."

Jack stood uncertainly by his chair.

Huxley looked to the papers on his desk. "Interesting life he had as a kid. Interesting for us, that is, not him. He was born in Alkmaar, near Grand Rapids, in 1957. He had no brothers, no sisters. His father deserted his mother and him when he was four years old, and apparently Reuker was raised under her thumb. Listen to this—" Huxley raised his eyebrows and looked up at Jack.

Jack resigned himself to staying and sat down.

"He and his mother, Rebecca, lived in a remote farmhouse outside of town, and this is what one investigator wrote in his report. He's quoting a neighbor down the gravel road from them. 'Rebecca was as devoted a mother as they come. She took that boy everywhere with her, never letting him out of her sight. Not like other mothers who leave their kids to fend for themselves when their man leaves them.'" Huxley looked up from the page. "What do you make of that?"

"I don't know."

"Sounds like she was overprotective, right? Having a single, dominant influence can warp a kid faster than anything. Whatever he hears, or learns, is taken out of perspective."

"There's a lot of single kids raised by one parent. He eventually would have had other contacts, if only at school."

"You're right, but look at this." Huxley shuffled through the papers on his desk until he found what he wanted. "Rebecca pulled him out of school after the first week of fourth grade. And he was never reenrolled." He looked at Jack, then repeated himself for emphasis. "Never."

"What about her, then?"

"Good. You're thinking like a psychiatrist. She died in a fire when he was sixteen, so we don't know too much about her. They moved around a lot, after that third-grade year. She never worked anyplace steady, but she must have made money somehow, to keep them going. She was very religious, several people in Burnips, a town near Alkmaar, had said." Huxley fished for another sheet of paper. "They remembered times when she with her little boy in tow had knocked on doors, offering to read the Bible for the old, offering prayers for the sick."

Huxley paused and looked at Jack. The guard said nothing, so he continued. "That first summer after they left Alkmaar, they went to the Upper Peninsula and stayed at—" he glanced at the sheet "—Munising with Rebecca's sister and her husband and two kids. They were there for the summer, and it was probably the only family life Reuker ever had. There was a cousin named Billy two years older, and for a while at least, he had somebody other than Rebecca. Then they moved on. The funny thing about that family, though, is that after his mother died, the Department of Social Services tried to place him with them. But they wouldn't take him." Huxley looked at Jack for his reaction.

"Why?"

"I don't know. Reuker went out on his own, and two years later when he was eighteen the first of the slasher killings occurred."

"Was he tied to that one?"

"Not officially."

"There were more than the four murders in Michigan, weren't there?"

"Two others. One was in North Carolina, the body being found near the rocky Linville Gorge wilderness area, and the other was in Oregon. They never had enough evidence to indict, and after the Michigan convictions, Oregon closed its case, but North Carolina kept theirs open. I guess because they want the death penalty for him."

"How many of the Michigan killings was he convicted of?"

"Two." Huxley looked at the file. "A Margaret Burgholtz, and Viola Fantuzzi. The Fantuzzi case is the odd one, and for us at least, gives us something to think about. It was cold and rainy, but in her blood they found a bare footprint, and it was that print that clinched the case against Stilkes."

Jack appeared puzzled.

"Why?" Huxley answered his own question with a shrug of his shoulders.

Jack found himself carried along by Huxley's curiosity.

"Were they sure the other four were killed by Stilkes?"

"The authorities were. Dead sure. And let me tell you why. Each victim was a woman in her forties or fifties, and each was found bound and suspended from above—ceiling, rafters, tree limb, whatever—with a rope or wire or something under her arms. Then they were methodically stabbed and slashed and drained of virtually all their blood. Now you tell me. Is it a reasonable assumption that whoever did one, did them all?"

"What was his motive for the killings?"

"There was no apparent motive. Not robbery, nor sex, nor revenge."

"But there must have been some reason."

"Oh, there was. Psychologically, nothing is motiveless. Nothing is senseless. And that's what I want to find out. His reasons. His makeup. His medical disability, if that's what it is."

"Did he know any of these women?"

"Aah," Huxley said, smiling. "You *are* thinking like a psychiatrist." He eased back in his chair. "The answer is no. They were apparently random selections. Or so they say. But I agree with your line of approach. I think if I can determine the who, the why will come easier."

After Jack left, Huxley gathered up the scattered papers on his desk and walked to his apartment. From the outside, the staff living quarters was no different from the other buildings of the institution, and even the apartments, though varying in size and amenities, bore a striking resemblance to the cells across the yard of the prisoners. They were constructed of the same brick walls, the same paint, the same windows. The only difference was their view was not obstructed by the chain-link barricade that enclosed the Facility; the double fences came to the ends of the structure making the staff building itself part of the restraining barrier that surrounded the institution.

From his window Huxley had a view of the Lake Superior shoreline. It was a starkly beautiful scene, especially during winter, but it was also a desolate, lonely scene. Huxley was unaffected by either perception.

All that mattered was his work. And he had seemingly limitless energy for it. He was skinny, about five feet eight, with sallow cheeks that gave the impression that his only nourishment came from ideas, not food. When he was on to something, he would race in all directions at once, resembling the composite movements of a colony of silver beetles scattering under a suddenly overturned rock. Even his medium-long curly black hair, now stranded with white, seemed electrified with his energy.

Huxley leafed again through the photocopied medical charts that documented Stilkes's physical and psychological status, as viewed by a string of doctors, since his arrest. The consensus diagnosis was that he was a paranoid schizophrenic. *Paranoid Schizophrenic,* Huxley repeated in his mind. A fairly safe label to attach to a killer like Stilkes, enabling everybody, medical and lay personnel alike, to categorize his particular brand of mental illness and place him in a familiar psychiatric niche known to all and leave it at that. Throw some pills down the gullet of the problem to keep it controlled, then forget about it.

Different characterizations were added in different handwriting styles to the general classification paranoid schizophrenic. Over the months he was variously described as reclusive, impulsive, unpredictable, aggressive, docile, and dissociative. Taken together, it could mean a personality that could single-handedly keep a clinic full of psychologists happily engaged in contradictory analysis for years. To Huxley the labels meant nothing.

Reuker's treatment had been almost exclusively chemical, the records indicated. Mellaril, Thorazine, and most often and most recently, Prolixin. All were potent antipsychotics with powerful side effects, but Prolixin was long-lasting and could be given by injection. Stilkes was given a single shot of 75 milligrams of Prolixin once a week.

The records indicated that precious little in Stilkes's file came directly from him. Where scheduled sessions or meetings with him were listed on the records, the only notes that followed were a scribbled "uncommunicative" or "refuses to cooperate." For the doctor, psychotherapy was difficult, time-consuming, frustrating, and ultimately dangerous. He became vulnerable: His own fears and weaknesses became a target for the patient, and there was the possibility of the transference of the patient's undefined rage onto the therapist. Therapy was avoided; it was far easier to control violence with drugs than to reteach behavior. But Huxley wanted to do more than control Stilkes. He wanted to learn about him. He wanted to study him. He wanted to know him.

Huxley closed his eyes and contemplated the challenges. A key to the psychological mystery of Stilkes was understanding as much as he could about the man. But Huxley knew that the ultimate key was the thoughts Stilkes kept hidden deep within his mind.

6

It had been a day like most others. They all blended together. In the evening, lying in bed with the lights out, Reuker could not remember what had happened during the day, much less the day before. Or perhaps more accurately, he would not expend the energy to fight back the inhibiting drug-induced veil that made everything a little less clear, a little more distant. At times he tried to think back over events, but when he did, he was like a man waving his arms in front of him as he stumbled through a cobwebbed hallway. It was easier to let the memories glimmer unsparked.

Stilkes did not remember staring out the window yesterday afternoon or the shiny bugs that crawled all over him. He did not recall his arms being pinned back or spitting in the guard's face. Yet the dull ache in his stomach was still there, and an unexplained tension lingered within him.

Usually it was no problem surrendering to the consciousness-snapping chemicals, but tonight he could not sleep. He stared at the blank ceiling, rolled to his side and stared at the symmetrical pattern of the cement blocks, then to his back again. Sometimes the chemicals that came from his own body were stronger than those from the shots.

He tried to imagine a scene removed as far as possible from where he found himself now. It was one of his tricks he had learned, and sometimes it worked. A scene would materialize, and suddenly it was not a struggle to remember anymore; he was in it.

"If I wanted to, I could be playing for that team. I'd be their star pitcher, and when I wasn't pitching the coach would have me play shortstop. He wouldn't want to keep my bat out of the lineup, you see." The pudgy, big-for-his-age eleven-year-old boy stopped his whittling and looked over at Reuker, who sat next to him on the half-rotted plank. "But I gotta watch out for you, Roy." Billy always called him Roy and he was the only one who ever did. Reuker liked to be called Roy. "You're my little cousin and they'd never let you play because you're too shrimpy. So I ain't gonna play with 'em either." Billy went back to sharpening the end of the stick with his jack-knife. "You're real lucky to have me around, you know."

"I know," the nine-year-old Reuker said genuinely, his eyes shifting from the blade slicing through the soft wood to the look of determination on his cousin's face. He *was* lucky Billy played with him and showed him how to do things.

"Don't let those creeps get to you. I don't care if you're a little shrimp or not, if I was on the team it wouldn't matter who else was on it. We'd be the U.P. champs and then win easy over all those black kids from down below." Billy continued whittling and talking, the stroke of the knife keeping time to his rambling monologue. "But like I say, I'd never play baseball with them anyway. They're just a bunch of snots."

Reuker knew exactly what Billy meant. They were just like the kids at school in Alkmaar who made fun of his angular nose, or his sunken, pinpointy eyes, or his meat-less frame. "Hey, Reuker, why did the doctor scoop your eyes out with a spoon when you was born?" they'd ask and laugh. Or "Hey, wimp, what's your momma feed you at home? Diet pop and string beans?"

Billy stopped his carving and looked over at Reuker again. "Hey. Let's go get some stuff to eat," he said. And before waiting for an answer, jumped up from the wooden garbage can platform they were sitting on. Two dented cans lay to either side of the platform, their contents spilling out into the alley.

To Reuker *getting stuff to eat* meant going to the grocery store and stuffing candy bars in his pockets while Billy distracted old Mrs. Compton at the counter. Stilkes didn't like doing it, not because of poor Mrs. Compton, but because he was afraid of getting caught. But he sure didn't want to seem ungrateful to Billy for all he did for him.

Billy plunged the stick he so carefully had crafted into a lance through one of the garbage can lids. It pierced the corroded, galvanized metal easily and stuck into the ground. "Got 'im," Billy said, laughing.

Reuker joined in the laugh and followed his cousin. The alley was an unpaved, rutted dirt trail, but it was not messy. Some of the old wooden garages leaned to the left or the right or simply squatted straight down, but all managed to hold themselves gracefully if somewhat precariously. After the thirty or forty or even fifty winters of a couple hundred inches of snow the structures had endured in the northern Michigan town, it was a mystery of physics why they all hadn't collapsed in a ton of splinters under the weight.

On the Lake Superior coastline of the Upper Peninsula, Munising had a short but luxuriant summer. Reuker and his mother had been staying with his Aunt Trudy and Uncle Lester Harvonnen for almost a month, since the middle of May, and he still had all summer to look forward to exploring the woods, climbing along the rocky shoreline, and tramping through the many streams that ribboned the local terrain. The maple and beech and pine forest came right to the edge of the town, surrounding it like an eager moss ready to reclaim the one clear patch of civilization that had seemingly been torn from its thick, green expanse.

"Don't get any caramel bars this time. I hate caramel, it makes me want to puke."

One rut was muddy and the other was taken up by his cousin, so Reuker was forced to walk along the uneven grass median to keep abreast of Billy. "I'll try. But sometimes I . . ."

"I like Snickers bars," Billy continued. "You get some Snickers bars this time and you're all right." Billy plodded along, his calf-high combat boots laced only halfway before being looped around his ankle and tied tight. He had an exaggerated way of lifting each knee high while walking and then stomping his foot down hard. He thought marching around like that made him tougher, more imposing an adversary.

Reuker gave up trying to walk side by side with Billy over the bumpy ground and fell in behind him. "Boy, I can't wait until tonight."

"What for?" Billy said quickly, stopping dead in his tracks and turning to look at Reuker.

"Because of the fight. You know, when you beat up Mark Weller."

Billy glowered, Reuker not sure if at the memory of their earlier confrontation or at the prospect of their scheduled meeting. "That big mouth is in for it, that's for sure."

Though it was said with his typical confidence, something was missing from the usual sharp edge to his voice. Was he afraid? It was the same question that came to Reuker earlier in the day when his cousin and Mark had squared off at the school playground. He had dismissed it then because what Billy had said made sense: "No sense fighting here where the summer school teacher will catch us. We'll meet back here after dinner."

Could it be Mark would be able to beat up Billy? He certainly was big enough. He was the only kid in the fifth grade who was Billy's size, but he did not have Billy's pudginess. He was thinner and more solid. And coincidentally, he did pitch and play shortstop for the Little League team.

"Come on," Billy said when they reached the street. The grocery store was a few blocks to the left, but instead of turning toward it, Billy ran across the street and into the alley. As Reuker hurried to catch up, he didn't notice the seven-year-old girl dash the half block to the alley and sneak after them.

Reuker knew where they were going, and when they neared the back fence of the Weller house, Billy stopped running and approached cautiously. An elderberry tree in bloom was in the corner, and that's what Billy stood behind. The bushlike leafiness of the tree and its tiny white flowers bunched together like paper plates easily concealed them from anyone looking out the back window. But they could see the yard and the house fairly well.

"What are you . . ."

"Ssh!" Billy commanded, staring intently through the leaves. His face was a mask of spiteful excitement. And the excitement quickly infected Reuker as well. He stared at Billy, enthralled with the mind that was feverishly planning, delighted with the anticipation of vengeance he so rarely felt. His cousin's eyes were a flurry of motion, his fat cheeks jiggled, and his lips moved as he talked silently to himself.

Billy's face hardened into undisguised hate, and as it did it brought a stillness to his chest and a firmness unnatural to his cheeks. As the feeling settled over him, Billy leaned against the fence and draped his arms over it so his chin rested on the top crosspiece of the fence. He stayed slumped in this position, studying the house, for several minutes. It was so long that Reuker's initial surge of excitement dissipated and was replaced by an uncertain fear.

When Billy finally did turn to look at him, his expression had changed to a leer. He nodded sideways toward the yard, his smile growing. Reuker looked but didn't see anything different. He returned Billy's gaze and shook his head, "I don't know."

"The cat, stupid," Billy whispered and stood straight.

Reuker looked again and saw the Weller family cat walking lazily toward the back fence, then flop in the sun in the grass and roll over on its back.

"Go get the cat," Billy said.

"No!" Reuker was terrified. "I can't go in there. They'll see me."

"You little chicken shit. Climb the fence and bring that cat over to me."

Reuker swallowed the fear rising in his throat, then looked from Billy to the cat and back to Billy. "I, I can't," he stammered.

Billy's fat little lips disappeared into a tightly clenched pink line. He turned and walked over to the middle of the fence, away from the elderberry tree, and bent down close to the ground. "Kitty. Come here, kitty, kitty, kitty."

The cat rolled upright quietly and peered in his direction. Its tail twitched with annoyance. Billy tried calling the cat again, but it remained where it was. Billy looked around the alley, spied a garbage can, then hurried over to it. The lid came off revealing two grocery bags filled with house refuse and garbage. Billy tore one open and rooted around with his hand until he found a pork chop bone with some meat and fat still attached.

The cat seemed more interested when Billy now tried to coax it over. It approached warily, its tail still flicking with a jerky motion. It stretched its nose through the wire mesh of the fence to sniff the offering. Then it coiled ready to spring to the top of the fence. When it did, Billy dropped the bone and seized a handful of loose skin on its back and yanked it from its momentary perch.

The cat squawked as Billy ran down the alley gripping it like a carpetbag without handles. Reuker hurried after him, propelled by a great rush of relief that they had not been caught. He could hear Billy's giddy laughter, punctuated with heavy breathing, and he was touched with the same giddiness.

Billy's chest rippled like an air mattress on a wavy lake, and his smile was outshone only by the gleam in his eyes. Gone was the hate, the conniving sneer, replaced with a kind of inebriated glow. "I got 'im," he shouted, holding the cat trophylike in his outstretched arm. "I got 'im," he repeated excitedly.

Reuker laughed, as excited as Billy. "Boy, Mark Weller's sure gonna be sorry."

"You're damn right he is," Billy snapped, a nasty edge suddenly back in his voice. Even the cat's mood seemed to change as it slumped silently in the boy's grasp. "He's gonna realize he can't push me around. He sure is."

Billy started walking down the alley again, this time at a steady pace.

Reuker asked, "What are you going to do with it?"

Billy glanced at Reuker with a smile as smug as a smile could be. He said nothing and didn't break his stride.

"Well? What are you going to do with it?" Reuker wanted to know. Billy didn't answer, and his mouth did not open, but Reuker was sure he heard a laugh gurgle somewhere inside him.

With a motion that startled Reuker and brought a howl from the animal, Billy suddenly brought his arm back and flung the cat through the air. Reuker's thought was that it looked like an underinflated football sailing off target toward some imaginary goalposts. The cat tumbled head over heels and crashed to the ground on its feet five yards away. It stood stunned and bewildered, crouched uncertainly, and looked around.

Billy didn't give it a chance. He pounded down the alley toward it and with a banshee scream leaped high in the air, coming down with both of his heavy-booted feet squarely on the cat. It didn't make a sound.

"Billy!" It was not Reuker's voice, but that of a young girl.

Billy's crazed look of satisfaction disappeared as he looked down the alley. His seven-year-old sister had stepped out from behind one of the garages where she had been hiding, watching. She stared at him in total disbelief. Shocked by the sight of her, Billy remained fixed in his squatting position, his feet together as they had landed.

Normally, she would announce her intention to tattle and run off. But what she had just witnessed seemed beyond her ability to explain. "Billy," she repeated, this time lower.

"Come here Karen," Billy said, recovering.

"No."

Billy started walking toward her. "Come here, Kar . . ." She turned and sprinted away from him. "Karen!" he shouted, then began running after her.

"Stay away from me," she called over her shoulder.

"Don't you tell. Don't you tell anybody." Billy sounded frantic.

Billy pounded after his fleet sister, and Reuker walked to the cat lying crushed on the ground. A metamorphic expression of wonder, amazement, awe shimmered in his face. The image of the cat flying through the air and Billy barreling down on it was repeated in slow motion in his mind. It was the most astounding thing he had ever seen, the most marvelous demonstration of power, of total control. And only Billy could have done it, only Billy had the nerve, the outlandish sense of timing, the imagination to devise such an appropriate way to get even. Mark Weller was sure to be sorry now.

A sense of fascination swept over Reuker as he stared at the cat's eyes, and for just a moment, a quick blink of his mind, it was not a cat but a boy's head on the ground, one of the kids from school. Though the illusion was gone as fast as it appeared, the thought lingered, and he wished as he never wished before that the crushed skull and bulging eyes had really been of that boy from Alkmaar. As hope can brighten despair, the wish alone electrified him with happiness.

Reuker grabbed the cat's tail and lifted it from the soft ground of the alley. He would fling it into the Weller backyard where the revenge would for sure not go unnoticed. As he stood, he saw Billy staring at him from a dozen feet away. His puffy cheeks were small white pillows blotched red with the exertion of his unsuccessful chase, and his chest heaved in huge spasms of fear and fatigue. His eyes were round with horror as he stared at Reuker standing in the middle of the alley holding the dead cat by the tail.

Reuker was perplexed by the expression and stood immobilized. Billy slowly regained control and finally looked away from his cousin. "Come on, let's get out'a here," he said.

"Where?"

"Follow me." Billy turned and started running in the opposite direction of the Weller house.

Reuker let the cat drop and followed. "But where are we going?"

Billy slammed through a gate and headed through one of the backyards. Over his shoulder he yelled, "To the Hole."

They ran the few blocks to the woods and didn't slow down until they were perhaps half a mile from the closest road. They still had about another half mile to go, but they walked more deliberately now, the urgency gone from their purpose, and the bent stalks of the ferns rebounded rather than broke, swallowing up behind them the trail they followed. As they got closer to the Hole, they could hear a sound like wind whooshing through treetops. The noise became louder until what had sounded like wind was now unmistakably a torrent of water rushing off a high precipice and splashing in a steady, rhythmless cascade on the rocks below.

It was neither the biggest nor the most spectacular waterfall in the stream-rich and precipitous terrain of the Upper Peninsula. The entire Lake Superior basin was a mammoth syncline, a depression formed by a mass of rock so heavy it sagged into the molten underground sea like a biscuit in gravy. The edges faulted downward forming the rim of a huge bowl, later scoured by glaciers to form the present reservoir of fresh water.

The angle of the layers of basalt that protruded along the coast of the U.P. from this huge and geologically ancient basin was now forty degrees from horizontal. Along and between these faulted layers, cracks and fissures developed as the rock cooled and shifted. Deep in this volcanic mass, the vast pressure heated water far beyond the boiling point, hot enough to bleach from the basalt minute traces of chemicals and minerals. As the hot solution rose toward the surface through the intertwined network of cracks, the dissolved substances became more and more concentrated. When the solution cooled at or near the surface, the chemicals and minerals hardened, filling the cracks with nearly pure caches including copper, silver, quartz, sodium, or calcium. Where the minerals were softer than the basalt, surface erosion would dissolve them away again, leaving the fissure empty and intact. The Hole was one such fissure.

At the bottom of the cascade Billy pulled his dirty, striped T-shirt over his head and dropped it on a rounded boulder. He had the fleshy chest of a pubescent girl, and it jiggled as he took the rest of his clothes off. Reuker sat on a nearby rock and pulled off his shoes, hurrying to follow Billy up the cascade to the bottom of the falls.

The stream was no wider than ten feet upstream from the falls, and at the very brink the water funneled through a worn, two-foot slot in the stone. It sprayed outward forming an uneven foamy curtain before splashing on a flat deck of rock twenty-five feet from the top. From there, the stream coursed down a steep, rock-strewn path before reaching level ground. Above the cascade and behind the free-falling water the outline of a narrow black crevice could just be discerned.

At the flat deck where the water crashed on the rocks, amid the roar of the liquid tumult, Billy shouted, "I'll go first. Then you follow." Without waiting for a reply, Billy stepped into the curtain and disappeared.

Reuker remembered the first time his cousin had brought him here and had told him of a boy who had slipped and fallen into the Hole. In the darkness the eerie tone of his cousin's voice had sounded sinister, older, and not that of anyone he knew. He was frightened as he listened to Billy describe how the boy fell headfirst, sliding all the way to the bottom until his neck twisted and his head wedged solidly into the crevice. "He's still down there," Billy had said ominously, and after allowing just the right amount of time for the thought to sink in, Billy had screamed a dying shriek as horrifying as Reuker imagined the boy's last calls must have been. Reuker had screamed almost as loud as Billy and had pushed madly by him as he tried to escape the dead boy's fate. Only Billy's convulsive laughter calmed him down and convinced him it was all untrue. Nonetheless, Reuker never came to the Hole without thinking about himself sliding headfirst down into the sightless abyss.

"Come on through," Billy called from the other side of the water.

It was just water, a huge natural shower, yet he felt a twinge of fear. It was a fear not of the Hole but of the water, of being unable to breathe, of walking into the shifting curtain and not being able to walk out. He had felt that before, the sensation of air turning solid, of his lungs seemingly imploding in desperate hunger for breath, of blacking out from lack of oxygen that had the feeling he could imagine of an ax handle slamming across the back of his head.

With the fear beginning to mount he felt his body growing colder, his chest tighter. Yet he was determined not to be held back by the old memories. He plunged into the falls and stumbled with closed eyes inside the cove. Whether from the shock of the cold water or the release of the fear, Reuker breathed rapidly and looked around in wide-eyed relief.

From the side Billy swung toward him suspended from a dangling root. A happy shout—a poor imitation of Tarzan's call—bellowed from his cousin as he collided with Reuker, tumbling them both into the shallow pool.

Reuker squirmed, laughing, trying to break Billy's hold. "The intruder has been captured," Billy yelled to imaginary compatriots.

"No, he's not," Reuker answered as he freed himself. He pretended to run through the water but let himself be grabbed and pulled from behind by Billy. Down again he went and more than what he was doing, more than the game they were playing, Reuker was aware of how absolutely good he felt. It was fun being with somebody else, somebody who had fun being with him. A strange, new feeling crept over Reuker as they played in their secret hideaway, the grotto under the falls on the lip of the Hole. It was a feeling of contentment, happiness, of peace with himself and his world. It was comfortable, yet exciting in what it meant for the future. Where happiness in the past had meant only an absence of pain, now there was something else to experience. There was something else besides the taunts of the others and the discipline at home.

Billy climbed out of the pool and up the dirt-smudged rock wall to the tangle of roots that hung into their grotto. Reuker stayed where he was, lying flat on his back along the side of the pool, and stared up and around him in a kind of dazed ecstasy. It was a different world in here and looking out through the waterfall toward the forest; the outside world was distorted and ugly.

Reuker climbed out of the pool and stood facing the falls. A fine mist seemed to hang in the air like cigar smoke in an unventilated room. He felt it on his face, on his body, and it felt wondrous. His eyes barely open, his face uplifted, he stepped closer to the curtain of water. He felt clean, like he was supposed to feel with the water, like his mother had always said he was to feel. He felt fulfilled, like he imagined it would be, yet it was all somehow different. It was different because *she* was not there, and the pain, the suffocating blankness were gone as well.

As he stepped into the white world of the plunging water, he felt the spray, then the water itself, striking him in the face and coursing over his head and the rest of his body like the cascading stream over the rocks below. He imagined himself the stream, as part of the immaculate translucence of the water, as a soul of purity and absolute cleanliness.

Eventually the water numbed him, then it wiped away his grasp of reality. As it did, almost two decades away and seventy-five miles distant, across an open expanse of Lake Superior, Reuker Stilkes fell asleep in his white-walled cell in the Scales Psychiatric Facility. He fell asleep on the brink of other memories, memories more disturbing, more frightful than any imagined horror of slipping headfirst into a sightless, bottomless crevice.

"I want to understand everything that's going on inside that head. I want to open it like a tin can and find out why one human being would slash and stab and mutilate six women for no apparent reason. He's got memories of it all, I'm sure of it. And I'm just as sure he lives some of those memories every day. There's no other way to explain his dissociative states that last sometimes for hours."

"So what if those memories are uncovered? Will he view them any differently out in the open than he does within his own mind? I think not, and worse, I think we'll risk losing control of him."

"Control! What good does that do?" Huxley was sitting on the edge of the chrome-legged, vinyl-covered chair, his wrist balanced on the edge of Hagan's desk. "Maybe we avoid his blowing up for a while, but the only way to keep him totally under control is flat on his back with 50 cc's of Valium every day."

The offices of Dr. Peter Hagan, director of Scales, sprawled over the south end of the upper floor of the Administration Building. Behind him was Gulletston Bay, and through the windows across the room and behind Huxley he could look into the Scales compound.

Even when he was sitting down, it was apparent Hagan was tall, and at well over two hundred pounds, his college football physique was now somewhere between muscle and fat. His straw-blond hair was thin and lay close to his head, curling inward in a slight ridge along his ears and at the back of his neck like a decorative hem at the bottom of a curtain. He had a bulbous lower lip that made him appear to wear an eternal pout, and when he was agitated, his narrow upper lip became tauter, making the lower lip all the more pronounced.

Huxley could see the tension in Hagan's face as the upper lip turned white, and he made an effort to lower his voice. "He'll see things differently in the sessions with me. And in the long run we won't even have to worry about whether we'll lose control of him or not. Don't you see? The more I know about him—the more *he* knows about *himself*—the less of a risk he will become."

Hagan was leaning back in his chair as if trying to increase the distance between himself and Huxley, who hovered at the other side of the desk seemingly ready to spring across at any moment. Though Huxley's voice was suddenly calmer, Hagan sensed it was only a tactic and that, inside, Huxley was still roiling with his peculiar brand of energy. He studied the young psychiatrist across from him, trying to gauge how much trouble he could be, how far he would pursue his request.

Hagan saw himself as a man in the middle of competing interests. His stewardship over the residents was a main concern, but in no way the only one. There were the guards, the doctors, the staff, the townspeople—the few that still remained on the island—and most of all the legislative Corrections Committee in Lansing. It was that group of senators in the state capitol that held the purse strings to his fief, with the same few members who had had grave misgivings about Scales from the very beginning and would like nothing better now than to slash its budget to the bone. It was also the same committee that made its reports and recommendations to a Senate at large that was continually under budget limitations, as well as under pressures from constituents who hated seeing an extra dime spent on convicted criminals. His main job as he saw it, given all the varying interests, was to smother any problems at the institution and, above all, prevent any shock waves from reaching Lansing. It was a visible job, visible to the public via the members of the press when they chose to feature Scales, and eventually visible to the governor, who held Hagan's career by the tenuous thread of political sensitivity.

There would be trouble from Huxley and his inane request to have Reuker Stilkes transferred to his control from Lummer's. Hagan had to decide where that trouble would be least likely to cause reverberations. "What you are asking puts me in a very delicate position," he began. "I don't think Dr. Lummer cares all that much which patients are or are not assigned to him."

"Then what's the problem?"

"On the other hand," Hagan continued, "he is a professional and if I reassigned one of his patients to you without good reason, he might take that as a slap at him personally and professionally."

"Lummer's a castoff like the others on this island. His

feelings are not a concern to me and they shouldn't be to you either. There's more at stake here than the sensibilities of a doctor who doesn't give a damn about Stilkes in the first place." Huxley's anger, fueled by his curious mixture of intolerance and arrogance, flared easily through what passed as his self-control.

"But why not do whatever you want to do with someone else? One of your own patients?"

He was prepared for the question, and he argued, "Stilkes is an enigma, a true psychological mystery. He's not like the guy who gets fired, then divorced, then breaks down and goes nuts with a gun spraying his neighborhood with bullets because he can't cope with the pressures. And he's not like any other of the sorry group of neurotics and depressives that we see so often who go out of whack and wind up in jail. Stilkes is one of the so-called senseless killers that can terrorize an entire city, a state, a nation, by committing acts so horrible they defy any attempt at understanding. He is a true aberration of all that we consider normal behavior. He doesn't lose control of himself for a while and then snap out of it and come back to reality. He operates under a completely different set of standards. And whatever I find out about him, about those standards he operates under, about how he learned his violent behavior and how he adapted to it, I think will help us understand why someone like Stilkes would commit the crimes that he has. And maybe, just maybe, we'll be able to identify others like him before they are permitted to act out their violence."

Hagan had gradually eased forward in his chair, and now he stared at Huxley with just a trace of disbelief in his face. "Your head is in the clouds," he said, shaking his own head with his continuing incredulity. "It really is, I'm afraid. There is no way in hell you could ever get through to that guy, and even if you did, there's nothing that would prove useful to anybody."

Whether it was what he said, or perhaps the mocking lilt to his voice, Huxley was enraged. In his own opinion Dr. Peter Hagan was at best only a notch above Lummer and the rest, and that only because he stayed out of psychiatry and spent his time pushing papers and glad-handing politicians. To hear Hagan condescendingly ridicule him was like a zealot listening to an incendiary speech.

Huxley gripped the edge of the desk and pulled himself slowly out of the chair. "I'm going to have Stilkes," he said evenly, his jaw barely moving. "One way or another, I'm going to have him."

And just then, Hagan decided Huxley would have Stilkes. Staring into the round eyes framed by a crimson face, Hagan sensed that Huxley had the capacity to ignite tremors that would be felt in Lansing. He could deal with Lummer. At least he could be prevailed upon to recognize the precarious position Scales occupied in relation to the state budget. But Huxley was unpredictable, and of course there were always the rumors of what he had done in Chicago. So Hagan signed an order transferring care of patient Reuker Stilkes to Huxley, allowing him to probe as deeply as he wished into the mind of Reuker Stilkes.

7

The gently falling snow appeared to hang in the dead air. It was a light snowfall, the kind that this winter seemed to be ever-present, either the lingering reminder of an earlier storm, or the prelude to another. As layer upon layer had covered the ground, the normal winter attrition of browsing animals became even more severe, and because of that, the ranks of the predators were thinned. For the wolves of Scale Island it was a desperate year, a season of hypercold that forced them beyond the ridges and closer to the southeast end of the island.

For a wolf to be alone, in the best of times, survival was a dangerous gamble. In a harsh winter it meant slow but certain starvation. Driven away from the packs by the dominant males, such an animal was deprived of the only hunting strategy it knew well, a tactic that required several wolves chasing and surrounding and attacking from all angles. By itself, a wolf was reduced to scavenging what if anything was left of the pack's kills, or struggling after smaller and lighter prey through deep snow.

Since dawn, the lone wolf had not covered much territory. It had shaken the night's dusting of snow from its fur as it awakened in its temporary den under the sagging branches of a spruce and had walked slowly, always slowly, up to the unfamiliar territory of the ridge. Instincts had always prevented it from approaching so close to the smell and sight of the unnatural structure that sat at the crest of the ridge, yet with desperation comes a loosening of instinctual dictates.

The wolf stood within a hundred feet of the square, snow-heaped structure, studying it through the trees, before it moved closer, angling down the foreign side of the ridge. It had to rest, as it did more and more frequently, and though the nearby building was unknown to its experiences, it was alive with the scent of danger. Though wolves had not been hunted for decades, fear of man learned by its ancestors was still deeply ingrained in the animal. But now, hunched in the snow, it was too hungry to be afraid.

Ricky's whole world was the island, and his circle of friendships was but a corral around a single individual. Philip Tardif was the grandfather he didn't know, the young companions he didn't have. Ricky saw Philip's life as what he was going to be, a kind of preview of what lay in store for him. To ask Philip about his past was to glimpse his own future.

"You've always lived on the island, haven't you, Philip?" Neither had spoken for a while, the exertion of each snowshoed step up the steady grade stealing the oxygen from their lungs.

With almost every word punctuated by a heavy breath, Philip replied, "No. I lived for a while down below. In Detroit."

"You did? I didn't know that. How long were you there?"

Philip let the crosshatched lacing of his shoes sink into the snow as he halted his shuffling progress along the trail. Gulletston was four and a half miles behind them, and it was not much farther to the cabin. Even so, the ridge got steeper the closer to the top they came, and it was time to rest. "I was there for just about four years."

"Did you like the big city?" Ricky had leaned against a tree opposite Philip, his posture a mirror image of the older man's.

Philip laughed. "It's been forty years, Ricky. I don't remember much about it now. And I'm sure it's changed a lot since then."

"It's different than here, though. Isn't it?"

"Oh, yes. It's different."

"What's different about it? The living part, I mean."

"You'll find out, someday. You'll leave here in a few years and find out what living in the city is all about."

"I'm never going to leave here," Ricky declared.

"Oh, you will. You will," Tardif said as he pushed himself away from the tree. "But you'll never leave the things you've learned while you were here."

"No, I'm not, Philip. I'm going to be just like you and live here all my life."

Tardif smiled as he looped a pillowy, parka-padded arm around Ricky's head and squeezed him to his side. "I don't know what I did to deserve a good friend like you."

Ricky wiggled his head free and said, "I'm glad you're my friend, Philip. You're the best friend I've ever had."

They were rested, and the cold was just beginning to get through to them again. It was time to move on, and they did, in the slow, shuffle-stepping manner required by the snowshoes.

The wolf lay under the protective sweep of a dense matting of spruce branches, its belly square to the ground. Except for its alert eyes, and an occasional quick movement of its head, the wolf was motionless. It would normally do most of its hunting and scavenging during the night, but in recent weeks, just to stay alive, it had had to be ready virtually every waking moment to take advantage of whatever food opportunity came its way.

An island, like Scales, tended to support more animals than similar terrain on the mainland, simply because there was a limit to how far they could spread. It was an overabundance of moose on Scales that lured a pack of wolves in 1941 into abandoning its hunting territory on the mainland to come to the island to stay. They had crossed an ice bridge that covered the twenty-six miles of open water between the island and the Upper Peninsula shores, an ice bridge that had formed only twice during the past century. The lake could freeze over only if there was the combination of a long spell of extreme cold and a rare stillness to the water.

The only other ice bridge of the last hundred years was in 1906, and it was this avenue maybe a dozen moose had followed across to the island. They were the first of their kind on Scales, and with no predators and with hundreds of thousands of acres of unspoiled browse, by 1941 the moose herd had grown to over two thousand animals. Then the wolves came, and over the years an equilibrium of sorts was established. There were now three wolf packs with a total of about thirty-five wolves, plus a few assorted strays, supported primarily by a moose population of about a thousand.

But to the solitary wolf, alone near where the ridges split, Blackstone angling to the northwest and Greenstone Ridge almost due north, the moose population could have been at its 1941 peak, and it still would be near starvation. Without the tactical advantage of a pack, the wolf did not have the slightest chance of bringing down one of the massive, 1,000-pound creatures. Instead, whatever hunting it did was restricted to beaver, hare, squirrel, and other more vulnerable animals.

Ricky unzipped his parka a few inches down the front. The last thing he wanted was to work up a sweat during the climb, then stand around in the cold and wind at the cabin pushing snow off the roof.

Tardif huffed along in front of him, his shoes leaving a series of overlapping tear-shaped imprints in the snow. He felt the heat of exertion and pulled his wool cap from his head and let it dangle from his gloved fingertips.

His dark hair, more than a little gray, was short like a brush cut, yet it lay as flat across his scalp as a tuft of swamp grass just after the spring thaw. He had a mobile face, an actor's face, not simply because he was handsome, but because it had a certain elasticity, able to shift into a smile without the least effort. Like the faces of many who had spent a lifetime on the rocky archipelago, exposed to a climate that, whatever the season, seemed to erode flesh as it did soil, Tardif's skin seemed weathered more than it did aged. It gave his face a raspy quality, like it had been planed with sandpaper, and it left a pattern of squares like a dried mud puddle embedded at the corners of his eyes.

Tardif had been the Department of Natural Resources man on the island. He had spent thirty-three years monitoring the wildlife and forests, hiking the twin backbones of the ridges and the bowl between them, and had spent innumerable nights, weeks, and sometimes months at the cabin that sat at the highest point on the island, 1,593 feet above sea level and 801 feet above the surface of Lake Superior.

When he retired, there was no replacement. Instead, the DNR presence on the island was reduced to an occasional fly-over during dry seasons by a mainland-based ranger looking for smoke. It was almost as though the DNR, like most of the former residents of Gulletston, had given up on Scales when the institution was built.

"We're almost there, Ricky," Tardif said. He could see the clearing at the mostly treeless crest where the cabin was.

The surface snow at the top was firmer, crusted by the wind, and they walked easily across it. A leafless, stunted oak flanked the cabin to the north, and the only other trees at this highest point on the island were a few pines, much older than their size indicated and all with branches swept away from the west.

With the snow curling over the edge of the roof, and layered a few feet on the ground, the cabin appeared as though it had already partially collapsed. Snow spilled over each eastside corner of the roof and stretched in narrowing columns toward the ground like taffy frozen in midpull.

It was a small structure, leveled on cement blocks, with a wood-plank front porch that extended the width of the cabin. To open the front door they had to shovel drifted snow away from it. Inside it seemed colder than it was out.

The furniture in the one-room interior was handmade, not by Tardif but by a woodsman who had preceded him as the DNR ranger on the island. The chairs were narrow pieces of ash steam-bent into shape and laced with leather strips. They were made by the same technique, and the same materials, as the snowshoes of the era. Over the straight-back wood-frame couch was draped a moose hide, tanned and supple enough to be used as a blanket. On the wall, near the only bed in the cabin, were two wolf pelts taken from animals already poached by a couple hunters Tardif had tracked down fifteen years before. Philip twisted the flue open on the metal-pipe chimney that rose through the ceiling from a potbelly iron stove. He lit a fire, then they went outside.

The snow was packed and heavy, but because of the steep incline of the roof, Philip and Ricky were able to let gravity do most of the work. Once they broke the crust and started it moving, large sections of the snow would avalanche over the edge and pile up in huge heaps on the ground.

After twenty-five minutes, half the roof was cleared of the heavy accumulation, and Philip rested. To his right, he could see the white apron of ice that enlarged the surface area of the island in winter, and beyond that stretched Lake Superior, its blackness textured with ragged white lines of breaking water like a tattered lace tablecloth over polished mahogany.

"It's okay to slide, isn't it?" Ricky was already poised to schuss down the roof and over the edge.

Tardif glanced at the piled snow below. "It looks all right. Don't bury yourself, though."

With a boyish shout Ricky sent himself skidding over the slick surface and was airborne for just a moment before landing in the cottony drift. As Philip watched the boy struggle to climb out of the deep snow, smoke and minute particles of wood ash from the chimney swirled between them. As he watched, he gazed beyond the boy to the crusted drifts and beyond them to the first of the hardy trees that somehow survived the brunt of the wind and weather. If it hadn't been for the smoke rising from the chimney, Philip might have noticed the little puffs of vapor that came from just below the dangling branches of the first spruce.

The hot chocolate they had shared in the cabin had coursed through Ricky's system like water through a mountain sluice. "I gotta take a leak, okay?" he called up to Philip after freeing himself from the snow.

"You expect me to say no?" Ricky only giggled. "Go on, but make sure you're away from the cabin. It attracts animals."

Ricky was feeling good without the least sense of danger as he turned away from the cabin and began walking alone toward the trees.

It was what the wolf had been waiting for. The smaller of the two upright animals was separated from the larger, and he was walking straight toward the wolf.

A deep pain tumbled hollowly in its stomach. A wolf is always hungry, always ready to gorge itself, for it is never sure when the next hunt will prove successful. And if several days had passed, the hunger became a pain that controlled its thoughts, guided its actions, dominated its instincts. It was weak, but its jaws could still exert an incredible 1,500 pounds per square inch, twice the crushing pressure of the largest German shepherd, and powerful enough to crack open the massive leg bones of the moose.

The scent the wolf had always steered clear of was almost overpowering, yet this time the wolf made no move to get away.

As he watched Ricky walk toward the trees, Philip was struck with one of those thoughts that seem to strike at the most unlikely of times, a thought bred as much of emotion as a realization of the small blessings one enjoys. He wondered what his life would be like without the boy, the grandson he never had. He always would have the island, but since his retirement, sharing it with someone else had made his special relationship with the land and the waters all the better. With every trip into the wilderness and every time he explained what a pipsissewa bush was to Ricky or pointed out a Kirkland warbler, it was as if he were rediscovering all these wonders himself.

He was indeed a lucky man, Philip thought, as he swiveled around, draping his legs over the other side of the roof, and looked out over his island.

Ricky was without his snowshoes as he walked toward the tree line. The exposed surface snow was crusted by the wind and blown into miniature drifts that resembled lake waves that had somehow been frozen instantly in place. For the most part it supported his weight, but when he did break through, as he did every four or five steps, he sank up to his thigh. Then it was like trying to climb to the top of a pile of autumn leaves to get back to the surface.

The wolf had paws that acted like natural snowshoes, three times the breadth of the feet of a comparably sized dog. Though it could move easily over this crusted snow, without the pack it had learned it must rely more on surprise than boldness to capture and bring down prey. So it waited and watched as the creature struggled closer toward it.

To his leathery skin the light wind felt invigorating, like tiny pinpricks in his face. No one lived out where Tardif looked, and the land was owned by no one, but perhaps because of his stewardship over it, or because of his intimate knowledge of it, he felt more than a little kinship with the island. He felt at times like it belonged to him.

Blackstone Ridge to his left, and Greenstone Ridge stretching out forty-five miles to his right, were like monumental dikes, bulwarks against the outside world, protecting and isolating the interior V of the island. If it were summer, and he were sitting where he sat now, the ridges would unmistakably resemble the dual scaly backbones the prehistoric Indians imagined them to be. The basaltic lava flows that covered the region formed primarily a very dark rock with a dull luster. But if great heat and pressure combined, and the mineral chlorite was present, the basalt could later metamorphose into greenstone. The ridge to the left had retained its original character, while to the right, Greenstone Ridge had long bands of metamorphic rock easily distinguishable from the black basalt. Both formations, over time, tended to crack into huge segments like the scales of a lizard.

The rock of Scale Island was 3½ billion years old, some of the oldest exposed rock on the face of the globe, and as often as he walked along the ridges, or stared down at them, Tardif was still astonished at their age. To have survived so long, to have witnessed so much, was as much beyond his comprehension now as it was beyond the credulity of a young ranger forty years before who picked away with his fossil ax at the quartz and mineral deposits in the rock. The mountain range that Scale Island had once been part of the bedrock for had been uplifted as high as the Himalayas and eroded away three times when the Appalachians were still a flat underwater plain, and the Rockies a mere distant design of plate tectonics.

Staring out at the primeval landforms, Tardif could not help but imagine what his island had been like before man walked upon it, when the land was ruled by beasts of prey. He thought himself very fortunate to be at a place that had changed so little.

Ricky was no more than twenty feet from the first of the trees when he relieved himself. From where he stood he could see that the snow beyond the trees that was protected from the wind had been disturbed. Tracks? Had an animal been there since the snows the night before?

He felt a tremor of excitement knot in his throat. It was like the time the summer before when Philip and his dad and he had awakened to find a family of moose browsing at their campsite. He had seen moose before, but never so close. It had been a special thrill, and now he had perhaps another chance to view something from up close.

Ricky glanced back at the cabin, but Philip had his back to him, looking out the other way. Carefully he began to creep forward, his eyes intent on any movement. Whatever it was, it must have been fairly large, Ricky thought, based on how the snow was disturbed. Could it be another moose? He could barely contain his excitement.

The wolf was rigidly immobile, its ears forward and erect, its hackles raised. The hunger it felt was now a command, overriding every other instinct the wolf possessed. Its tenseness locked its eyes in an unblinking gaze on the approaching two-legged animal.

The interior of the island was a vast area of lakes and forests and streams and beaver dams and swamps. As he stared out over the varied terrain, it took a few minutes for Tardif to notice it, and even then he wasn't sure. Was there a haze? There seemed to be a thin cloud hanging close to the ground, but as he thought of the possible explanations, he dismissed what he saw. The conditions for fog were absolutely wrong, and it was not cold enough for an ice fog. Yet as he carefully eyed the vale, he was sure there was a shifting, formless haze hugging the ground. It seemed to come and go, but it was there. He stood on the roof, his feet straddling the peak, and balanced himself with the shovel.

As he stared, perplexed by what he saw, he began to notice a faint but discernible odor in the air. It had been there all along, since they reached the ridge, but it had been too faint to notice. But now, looking down at the haze, trying either to explain what it was or to convince himself he didn't see what he indeed saw, Tardif smelled it. It was an acrid odor, and as he became conscious of it, the smell became stronger. It was a distinct smell, as distinct as the aroma of a freshly opened bottle of Scotch whisky, and one that, once sensed, was never forgotten. Standing there, balanced by the shovel, with an aftertaste like unpleasant medicine in the back of his mouth, Tardif realized what it was. And he realized what it could mean for his island.

He felt a sickening feeling in the pit of his stomach, as if something or someone near to his heart had been suddenly snatched away.

Through the short-needled branch came the bursts of vapor from hot breath condensing in the frigid air. Ricky noticed it, and as he did the charge that had been racing through his nerves seemed to freeze on the point of discovery. Something was there!

Ricky turned toward the spruce, and in almost a lunge, bolted for it. At his first step his foot plunged through the thin crust, and he sank to his thigh. With almost a cry of desperation, he struggled to pull his leg free. Then he saw it.

The wolf rose slowly on all fours, pushing its head through the dangling evergreen. It kept its head lower than its shoulders, and its eyes on its prey. Although it was slowly leaning through the encumbrances of the branches, the wolf's control over its body made it appear to be still. The pattern of dark facial fur mixed with the white and the blond and the gray outlined and accentuated its features, making it look all the more menacing.

Ricky stared as though unbelieving at the doglike creature before him. It seemed unreal, as if what he saw was not happening, at least not happening to him, but rather like he was watching something two-dimensional unfold on a screen. He didn't move—he couldn't move—because he was not part of the scene.

The wolf was still several feet away, and it was careful in its approach. It had not had experience with this type of animal before, and did not know how fast it could move away, or how dangerous it could be in resisting. Cautiously it lifted a paw and inched it closer, all the while not lessening the intensity of its gaze.

Ricky was numbed, either from the cold pressing in on his leg from the snow he had sunk into, or from the sight of the wolf before him. Though he was paralyzed, it was not from fright. Indeed, he felt calm, as if bewitched by the wild animal, overcome with a kind of fascination for the wolf, watching, wondering what it was going to do. Ricky was captivated by the grace of the animal, the beauty of its fur, the coiled power of its muscles ready to explode. But most of all, he was captivated by the eyes, the steely, unflinching gaze of the wolf. Ricky stared into the beast's eyes, and it returned his stare.

A tribe of Indians that had lived on the West Coast of North America had had a belief, a story that was at once part of their traditions and their religion. They believed that there was a spirit who became displeased with them, dissatisfied perhaps with their lack of faith or devotion or perhaps their disregard of tribal taboos. To punish them, or to elevate the animals, or to find a worthy replacement—for whatever reason—the manitou decided to change all the animals into men. The task was too great, even for a god, and he failed. But in one small regard, the Indians believed, he succeeded: He had made human the eyes of the wolf.

In the wolf's eyes Ricky could see something he had never seen in an animal before. It was not the nervous darting of a squirrel, or the dull bovinelike blankness of the moose. Rather, in the wolf's uncompromising gaze, in its fixed stare, Ricky saw its intelligence. It was an intelligence that at that very moment, in those circumstances, was greater than his own. He was transfixed by the stare of the wolf and totally within its power.

Its padded feet pulled the wolf slowly closer. A clump of snow, dislodged from the tree above, whumped at its shoulders and disintegrated into a puff of powder. The wolf was undeterred. It was as if in a spell, a trance conjured up by a triumvirate of demons, the sensations of hunger, danger, and uncertainty.

Suddenly the spell was broken as a metallic blast shattered the snow-muffled stillness. The wolf instantly straightened and looked beyond the boy. Ricky turned and looked where the wolf did, back toward Philip atop the cabin. He had crashed the blade of the shovel into the pipelike chimney, and its hollow echo resonated over the ridge.

The hunger of the wolf disappeared as its stomach was suddenly knotted with fear. Replacing it was the danger it had sensed all along, the threat to its safety that had been overcome by its need to eat.

"Get outa here, damn you!" Tardif screamed, his voice like a cannon's roar.

The wolf turned and fled from the clearing back into the cover of the descending slope. Where its forepaws sank into the snow, it bounced effortlessly out again, like a Labrador bounding through chest-deep water. It moved fluidly, its brushlike tail swooping and arching in synchronous movement with its leaps.

As Philip hurried off the roof and pushed his way through the snow toward Ricky, the boy stayed where he was, still thigh-deep in the snow, and watched the graceful retreat of the wolf. He was still without fear.

When it had turned and bolted away, Ricky was able to notice how thin the creature was. Despite its thick fur, he could see how narrow the chest was and how lanky was its frame. He felt sorry for the wolf, and as he watched it disappear behind a wake of scattering snow and thickening trees, he wondered how it would survive. And he wondered if he would ever look into the eyes of such a magnificent animal again.

8

Jack Cooke sat in the observation room in the lounge of A-Barracks. He had just gotten off the phone with Marion and was watching one of the three TV monitors. Jack had set it to receive the feed from a camera in the central hub of the tunnel network.

At the top edge of the screen was a slanted blur—one of the overhanging pipes. The light was bad, and it all appeared dimmer than it really was, as if filmy secretions covered the lens. Because of that filminess, the chipped-rock walls lost their starkness and appeared dull gray, and the checkered pattern of the tile lacked definition. The picture had a strobelike flicker almost too fast to notice, but it tired the eyes, and after watching for a few minutes Jack had to close his momentarily to ease the strain.

In the three or four minutes he watched since he talked to Marion, not a soul had passed under the camera. That wasn't surprising, because the tunnels were merely avenues, not places to congregate, and this time of day—3:35 in the afternoon—there wasn't much traffic. Still it seemed odd to Jack that, sunk just a few feet below a bustling compound of 280 people, there was this vast, empty network of intersecting passages, a series of cold corridors bathed always in a hazy half-light. The tunnels were a perpetual back alley—stark, deserted, and foreboding.

There was no sound, and so Jack did not hear the clicking of heels echoing in the tunnel as Marion approached. Only when she actually appeared on the screen did he know she was there. She stopped directly in the camera's field of vision and looked into its eye. She waved, and Jack flicked one of the monitor's switches off, then on again, and in the tunnel a tiny red light below the lens blinked at Marion. She smiled, then walked on, under the camera and beyond its steady stare.

After she passed, Jack continued to watch the monitor, and for a few moments his mind wandered away from the institution, and from Reuker Stilkes and the other men lingering just beyond the glass of his booth. He thought of Marion, and as he did, he couldn't help but think that her video image on the imperfect screen appeared pale and small and weak. It was a false image, yet for some reason it was what stuck with him.

Jack brought his fingers to the keyboard and began to type a new code for the monitor. He was returning it to the camera focused on the stairs descending from A-Barracks. He glanced again at the screen, and he saw in the far reaches of the camera's focus a flickering of light, like something moving. Jack absently finished coding the instructions into the computer as he watched. It was a figure, and it was approaching fast.

Jack swiveled in his chair to face the screen square. The figure emerged rapidly, like a ghost taking substance from a cloud. Jack felt a flickering unsteadiness to his heart, a beat in time with the strobelike reception. Then the scene abruptly cut to the video snow of black and white and gray dots and blips jittering nervously in an imageless pattern. It held for only an instant, as the screen flashed to the scene of the stairs.

He turned back to the keyboard and started to type in the other code. But he had to stop; he couldn't remember. His mind had locked onto the image of the figure, the picture of him racing through the tunnel, chasing Marion. Come on, come on, what is it? The code!

He finished typing the series, then watched as the screen jumped again to the crazy flecking pattern of black and white and gray dots. Its nervous fluttering became the tempo of his own blood. The screen flickered, and the tunnel appeared. It was where Marion, pale and small and weak, had just waved, where she had just passed through, where he had seen the figure emerge from the darkness like some subliminal horror taking shape in the misty reaches of a dream.

The tunnel was empty. The figure was gone. Eddie Hyland had already passed.

Jack bolted out of his chair. It had happened fast, the figure emerging, then the picture flashing off, but Jack was sure it was Hyland, and he recognized the look on his face. As he pushed through the door of the booth, his mind replayed that expression; it was the same he had seen on Eddie two days before when he had come in from the outside, from walking Marion across the snow.

"Hey!" Creegan called. "What's with you?"
"I have to get to Marion."
"You can't just take off."
But Jack was by him and down the hall and opening the door to the stairs. He pushed through and dashed down the steps. The look he saw in Eddie's face was that secret mask of pleasures unfulfilled, that private fantasy that had incubated for who knows how long in his mind until, finally, it had unleashed itself. And in his face, in Jack's memory of his face, he saw a glint of madness, a hint of Eddie's vicious resolve not to let his opportunity slip by.

Jack thundered through the rock corridor, the ricocheting sound of his steps crashing in his ears, in his mind, echoing within the emptiness in his chest. It was dread, he felt, a sickening, hollow fear that was at once a sense of loss and a sense of horror. Horror at what Eddie Hyland would do to Marion, at what he had done to others in the past. She had said it was behind him, but it wasn't. The evil, the desire, the madness was still there, and he had seen it.

Jack rushed into the hub of the tunnel network, itself a short tunnel with a myriad of diverging spurs. "Marion!" he cried, and he heard his own terrified call rebound to him from a dozen different mouths, each a haunting echo of his own.

Then, "Jack!" It was Marion. He made it to the tunnel leading to the Administration Building. Surely that's where she went, where Eddie had followed. She was on her way home, on her way to exit through the Administration Building.

They were there, in the tunnel, and he had her! "Get away from her!" he screamed, and Eddie stumbled back.

"Jack!" Marion cried.

The pounding of his lungs beat their furious message. Jack pushed by her and after Eddie.

"Jack! Stop it."

Eddie stumbled backward, his face frozen in terror. Then he turned to run, but Jack had him. He grabbed him from behind and spun him around.

"Jack! Jack! Stop it!"

He grabbed Hyland by the shirt, close to the collar, and then Jack felt her, on him. She was pulling at his shoulders. "Let him go," Marion shouted. She pulled, and Jack fell back, releasing Eddie.

"What's wrong with you?" she screamed. He turned to look at her. "What are you doing?"

Jack looked back at Eddie who stood panting, eyeing him fearfully. Then back to Marion.

"My gloves. He brought me my gloves."

Jack looked at her in disbelief, then again at Eddie. Hyland was calmer, no longer ready to break away and run.

Marion stepped by Jack to Eddie and took his arm in a protective gesture. "You've gone too far, Jack. You didn't listen to me the other night, and you went too far."

"I thought . . ."

"You thought wrong."

Jack looked at Eddie, and his face had changed again. And he saw in it a glint of something he couldn't decipher. Was it anger? Amusement? A warning? It was gone in a second, and Marion didn't see it.

It wasn't until he was walking back through the tunnels to A-Barracks that he understood what the quick flash of Eddie's eyes contained. They held his satisfaction, his sense of accomplishment, of domination. In that one glance the eyes told Jack that what he had seen in him was right, and someday the satisfaction would be complete.

That night Marion was quiet, saying only what had to be said. She kept her eyes down, away from Jack, and within the cabin the air seemed heavy and close and hot, as if the iron fireplace radiated heat beyond its capacity and vented its smoke and ash into the room instead of through the chimney. Ricky felt it, and he went to bed early, on his own.

They talked, and gradually Marion came to feel some of Jack's pain, though he tried to keep it from her. But she knew him, and she knew his feelings at times better than he knew them himself. Her anger at him was doomed from the start because of her love, because of her devotion, and because of his for her.

When they were in bed, Marion cried silent tears, and she pulled her husband to her body. She wanted to make love, not for the good reasons, but just to put what happened behind them.

But Jack couldn't. He tried, but he couldn't. And for the first time since he was a kid he felt like crying. He didn't, because he was afraid to, and he kept it locked tight inside.

So they lay there, in each other's arms, until finally they fell asleep. And Jack dreamed. He dreamed of his wife, and a crime, and in this false world he felt the agony he would surely feel if that other world became real.

9

The next few days Jack's world seemed a worsening dream. Though the tension between Marion and him had lifted, their feelings couldn't quite touch at the same level they were used to. Something unpleasant lingered, and it would take time to diminish completely.

And at work Jack was being drawn closer to Reuker Stilkes's world. He was far from understanding him, yet by his observations alone he was unavoidably touched by Stilkes's strangeness. It was a disturbing experience, one that was difficult to explain to Dr. Huxley.

"In some ways," Jack said, "he's not that much different than what you would expect."

"But in other ways?" Huxley prompted.

"He's different. You were right when you said he doesn't fit in. He doesn't talk to the others very much. He doesn't talk hardly at all."

"So tell me what he does do."

"He just stands and stares for hours. Maybe all day. It's the drugs, I know, but there's something else. Like—"

"Like he's thinking about something?"

"Like he's *watching* something. Like he's not just remembering, but he's actually reliving it."

Huxley was fascinated. He wanted to know more, but there was little else Jack could say. He couldn't help but feel frustrated, but the slow pace of discovery was part of his trade. At the least he felt he was nearly prepared enough to meet with Stilkes for the first time himself.

Jack said he couldn't stay any longer, with the senators coming today, and got up to leave. At the door he paused and asked about Eddie Hyland. "Have you taken away his trusty status?"

For just a second a blank pallor came to Huxley's face. But he recovered fast. "Yes. I took care of it. But you know how things are in Records. It takes time. They just got it all changed, and now have to fill out new forms."

Jack understood. "Maybe he could be reassigned to someplace else altogether."

"Maybe," Huxley said. "We'll see."

The single-engine Cessna dipped its wing as it passed by Lake Siskiwit. Amid the spindly, leafless aspen and spruce and pines bowed under the accumulation of snow, it appeared a white meadow that, except for its flatness, was no different from the rock-hard ground of the rest of the island.

From the air, the shifting snow of Scales looked like desert sands slowly burying the last traces of an extinct civilization. Looking down on the island for the first time, Clyde Watson couldn't imagine a more barren place. Though the tiny blower cycled hot air from the engine directly on him, he was chilled. He wondered if there were any act committed that deserved the punishment of a lifetime banished to this island. Whether the others in the plane felt the same, or simply because they were tired after a long flight, no one spoke.

The small craft banked near the ridge and leveled out for a direct approach to Lake Siskiwit. It passed over the trees on the shore without much room to spare, and within a few seconds its skis touched the slick runway. Where it came to a stop at the far end of the narrow lake, one man walked out to meet them.

"Senator Hume, good to see you again." Peter Hagan

had pushed the fur-rimmed hood of his parka back just as the plane door was opening.

"Hello, Peter. I imagine it's good to see anybody up here." Senator James Hume, chairman of the State Senate Corrections Committee, had a grasping handshake that conveyed the power of the man. At six feet three with a chest as broad as a heavyweight boxer's, and the girth of a man used to the finer delicacies of the table, his size alone was intimidating. Though he was sixty years old, his thick black hair revealed not a trace of gray.

Hagan chuckled his diplomatic laugh. "You're right, I suppose. But if I was to have only one visitor, I can't imagine a more stimulating one than you, Senator."

With his full weight behind it, Hume bellowed a guffaw, and as he did, a cloud of vapor erupted from his mouth like the sudden spray of a geyser. Though the flattery was obviously self-serving, the big man enjoyed it nonetheless. "Save your charm for my colleagues, Peter. You may need it."

Turning to the two men who had followed him out of the plane, Hume said, "Clyde Watson, Michael O'Connell, this is the director here, Dr. Peter Hagan."

"Senators," said Hagan, shaking hands with each, "pleased to meet you at last." Unlike Hume, neither had been in the Senate when the issue of improving old facilities versus building a completely new and model psychiatric prison had been debated. Neither was there when Hagan testified and lobbied for what he considered the only workable alternative.

"The pleasure is ours," O'Connell said, and just that fast, Hagan disliked him. He had said it with a kind of smirk, as if the pleasure he spoke of was some secret bullet he had long kept chambered just for him. Instantly Hagan realized O'Connell would be the hardest to impress, requiring the best of his political skills.

"The Sno-Cat's waiting," Hagan said. "Let's get off this frozen lake and in where it's warm."

The rumbling, two-tracked vehicle idled at the edge of the trees. A relatively small, rectangular boxlike cabin sat above and between its oversized treads.

The road to the compound was a narrow swath through the trees just wide enough for the Cat. For once, Hagan was glad the roar of the diesel engine was too loud to talk over. It gave him a chance to think, to sort out the first impressions.

O'Connell, he decided, could be written off. He was obviously there as representative of those who had been against Scales to begin with and who used every opportunity to chisel away at its continued funding.

Hume was safe. A former prosecutor, representing mostly wealthy suburbs of Detroit, he was an old and trusted friend of the Corrections Department. At the Senate hearings seven years ago, Hagan recalled how Hume's sense of timing had superbly defused explosive questions with a joke, or how his seemingly innocuous inquiries led directly into Hagan's strengths.

That left Watson, and Hagan realized he was the key. The conclusions in their collective report to the committee needed only a majority of two, and with Hume already on his side, Watson was the necessary second vote. How was he to get through to him? Since Watson was a black man, did that mean he should stress the rights afforded the inmates, the enlightened sociological awareness of the Scales philosophy? His first temptation was to answer a quick yes, but then again, blacks don't fit into neat issue classifications anymore, he considered. Watson could be a strong law-and-order man, like O'Connell, who, when he sees a convict, sees not just a man behind bars, but a string of victims behind him.

How he handled him would be critical. It was crucial that all he had staked his professional career on not crumble for lack of funding. Hagan realized, of course, that the Senate would never consider defunding Scales completely and closing it down, but without its active support, without budget growth at least as great as inflation and salary increases, without a Senate sensitized to their changing needs and unique problems, the program could die just as surely as if the spigot had been shut completely. In fact, that would be worse, because then the failure would be on him alone, rather than a budget-conscious congressional body.

As the Sno-Cat rumbled out of the trees and into the open, a few hundred yards from the fences, Hagan decided he would just have to play Watson by ear, listening for his interests, alert for his leanings. At the same time he had to keep his distance from O'Connell, not giving him a chance to ask too many questions. He had to isolate O'Connell and his position, making him appear all the more unreasonable to Clyde Watson.

Near the front of the Administration Building, the entrance to Scales, the Cat jerked to a halt. Hagan was the first to jump from the tread to the ground, and whether by chance he was near Watson or not, he reached up his hand to help him down as a few feet away O'Connell was left to climb off the vehicle unaided. It was a small thing, perhaps unintentional, yet Hume noticed it, and when his eye caught Hagan's, he winked. Hagan was fast to pick things up, he mused. He should have run for Congress.

In 1975 Michigan enacted a law that permitted a new verdict in criminal cases when the defense was insanity: Guilty but Mentally Ill. It was this new GMI verdict that led to the construction of Scales Psychiatric Facility.

A 1974 Michigan Supreme Court ruling held unconstitutional the old practice of automatic commitment to a mental hospital for a defendant found Not Guilty by Reason of Insanity. The Guilty but Mentally Ill verdict was enacted partly to respond to the fears that psychotic killers had an easy road back to freedom. Its aim was to provide the courts with an alternative, or a compromise between the extremes of a guilty verdict and an NGRI. A GMI would be convicted and sentenced as any other guilty verdict, but with the stipulation that he was to receive special psychiatric care. It seemed a reasonable solution that avoided incarcerating as criminals the sick, yet at the same time kept them isolated from society while they were being treated.

The problem was that the Michigan Corrections Department had no facilities to guarantee the treatment mandated by the statute. So the Supreme Court ordered that the GMI verdict not be allowed to go to a jury unless and until the legislature granted the Corrections Department the resources to provide the care the new statute intended.

Senator Hume's committee, after extensive hearings, recomended that an entirely new psychiatric facility, under the control of the Department of Corrections, be built.

Hagan suspected Clyde Watson was familiar with the general history of Scales, but he felt a refresher on the rationale for its existence would help put what he was about to see in perspective. Sitting in his office, Gulletston Bay framed by the window behind him, Hagan paused in his oral review of what led to the construction of Scales Psychiatric Facility. He saw in Watson's face a question forming. Leaning back in his chair, he encouraged him with a nod.

"Forgive me for interrupting, Dr. Hagan, but there's something I just can't seem to get off my mind. I suppose it had occurred to me before, but it didn't really hit me until this morning as we flew over." Uncrossing his legs, Watson leaned forward, punctuating his remarks with hand gestures. "Now it seems to me if rehabilitation is a goal here, and I imagine it is for any prison, the key to that is a smooth reintroduction into society. For that to be successful, I would think it is vital for the person to have many contacts to the outside, to have a continuing relationship with his family. And in the treatment of someone who is mentally ill, correct me if I'm wrong, it would seem to be perhaps even more vital to maintain family contacts. But here, isolated on this island in the middle of Lake Superior, it is virtually impossible to have visitors. Isn't that terribly damaging to any therapy you may have? Doesn't it kill from the start any chance of really helping these men?"

"In some cases visitors would be helpful. Without a doubt, it would be nice if we were more accessible."

"Then why was this place chosen in the first place?"

It was the question he hoped Watson would follow with. "Because this is the only place that didn't have the political muscle to say no. To be honest, Scale Island was not my first choice. Senator Hume can tell you that."

"Indeed, indeed," Hume said, the memory of the stormy testimony bringing a smile to him.

"But no one wanted us." Hagan gestured expansively with his arms, as if the frustration was still fresh. "Quite simply," he leaned forward, almost confidentially toward Watson, "I feel it was a matter of discrimination. Discrimination against the sick and the underprivileged. Their opposition based not on compassion or human dignity, or reason, but on deep-seated prejudices that were impossible to alter, and disheartening to have to face." When Watson nodded knowingly, Hagan knew he had scored. He settled back in his chair. "It's a trade-off, Senator Watson. Everything's a trade-off. A little bad with the good."

Just like anything in politics, Watson thought. Always a compromise. Always a little bad with the good.

In another room, in another part of the Facility, things were progressing just as they always did, as if this day were no different from any other. The man's long blond hair cupped around his cheeks, forming a kind of curtain his face was drawn between. If he could have hidden completely within the folds of some imaginary curtain that draped between himself and the outside, he would have. He was that nervous, that insecure, that afraid.

He had always been like that. Jeremy Willet was the eighth of nine children, and his early personality disorders went unrecognized. The only thing different about him was his stutter, and at first it was just a nervous catch in his voice when he got excited. But by the third grade his parents had given the teachers permission to enroll him in special speech therapy classes. It was then that he began to skip school.

In his neighborhood there were drainage ditches that paralleled the streets. Every morning on his way to school Jeremy would pass near a steel pipe that stretched under a crossroad connecting two of the drainage ditches. The pipe was three feet in diameter, and sometimes Jeremy would crawl inside to the middle and just sit, his back rolled up against the cold, corrugated metal surface. He would stay there all day, protected from whatever he feared at school, and do nothing. To overcome the boredom he had trained himself to make his mind go blank, so he didn't even have to face his own thoughts.

Though he was now sixteen years older, his behavior was not that much different from the third-grade boy who used to hide in the sewer all day. Jeremy spent most of his time sitting by himself in the corner of the community room. Despite the distance he maintained from the others, Jeremy had changed. Perhaps it was the familiarity of his routine, or perhaps the drugs had actually helped; whatever the reason, for the first time he wished he had someone to talk to, a friend. His difficulty was, after twenty-four years of avoiding personal contact, normal communication skills and normal methods of showing emotion could not be learned overnight.

The light was not good in the corner. But he sat there shuffling a deck of cards and maneuvering them in seven stacks spread out before him. Every third card of the remaining pile he turned over, and depending on its color and denomination, would either place it on one of the seven stacks or return it to the deck. Intent on his game, he did not notice the fat guard coming from the glass booth in the opposite corner.

"Time to finish up, Jeremy," Arnie Johnson said.

What passed for contentment vanished from Willet's face. The old pain, that churning insecurity, flashed through him. The scheduled group therapy had been the furthest thing from his mind, but now the unwanted realization took exclusive control of his nerves.

"Let's go. It's Thursday, 11 A.M." Arnie sounded bored.

The cards snapped from his fingers in rapid fire to the table. His eyes remained determinedly fixed on the game before him.

"I don't have all day. So let's go."

"I'I d'd'don't wa'wa' to go to th'th'ther', to go." When he got excited, his speech sounded like electronic interference of a play-by-play announcer describing a late-game touchdown.

"Now come on, Jeremy. You know therapy is good for you." He said it in kind of a singsong, sarcastic manner. Arnie didn't think for a minute any of the methods or treatments made a difference one way or another with the men locked in at Scales. They were as beyond hope as Beelzebub beyond baptism.

Jeremy shook his head in a short, negative spasm. He did it as much to emphasize his answer to Arnie Johnson as to shake the image of the therapy session from his thoughts. He hated it, and he could tell that the other three he was seated with at the sessions did not like it either. For Jeremy, it stripped away what little comfort he had managed to sink himself into, and forced him to face everything about himself he hated, everything about himself he wanted to kill.

"Let's go." Arnie's tone was insistent. He tired quickly of playing games with the inmates. As his voice carried through the room, the eyes of most of the others focused on them in the corner.

"I c'c'c' an't."

"Are you going to give me trouble?"

The implied threat increased Jeremy's tension and stiffened his resistance.

Arnie held a special loathing for Jeremy Willet. He didn't like to touch him because of what he had been convicted of, because of what he had done to those two young boys. He was slow to reach his hand to his shoulder. "You're going over. Now."

"No!" Jeremy shouted.

Arnie's reluctance to touch Willet vanished as he grabbed his shoulder and forcibly spun him around in his chair. Jeremy lashed out with his wrist, striking the guard in the crook of his arm.

"Why, you little creep," Arnie spat through clenched teeth, "you've had it!" He pounced on Jeremy and yanked him with two handfuls of shirt out of the chair. He was ready to shake the frail figure and break every bone in his body.

"Johnson!" One of the white-shirted, green-trousered MCAs burst out of the glassed-in booth at the opposite corner. "Let him go," he commanded.

Arnie faced Creegan with Willet still tightly in his grip. He made no effort to let him go; his face flushed and his eyes blazed.

"You can't do anything to him. Not today." Creegan was practically pleading with him. "Don't you remember?"

And quickly Johnson did remember. The senators. The legislative visit. Everything had to run smoothly while they were here. Slowly he loosened his grip on Willet's shirt.

"If he don't want to go today, leave him."

Arnie nodded, allowing a heavy breath to dissipate the adrenaline surge. He glanced at the young, frightened, long-haired blond man whom he had wanted to crush in his bare hands a moment before, then walked away saying nothing.

Jeremy's heart was pounding like a hare's that had just

narrowly escaped the jaws of a fox. Gradually he calmed, and his shoulders slunk down into their usual slouch, his body cupped against the outside. His eyes stole about the room to gauge the reaction of the others, to determine the best way to slink out of their attention. Then something remarkable began to happen. The others were glancing his way, and when their eyes met his, they gave a wink, or a half-smile. They liked what he had done.

It was something Jeremy had never experienced before. A universal expression of approval. He looked from face to face and was not sure how to react to the silent gestures of commendation. The only thing he was sure of was that he felt good. He was elated. And all because of the way he had treated the fat guard.

It was a lesson he was eager to repeat.

From the Administration Building Dr. Peter Hagan led the three senators down a tubular staircase that resembled a precast concrete sewer with steps molded into the bottom. It led to the tunnels, a subterranean network of passages hewn out of the solid rock. The walls and ceiling were the rough-chiseled ancient basalt, while the floor was a contrasting machine-buffed tile.

"You could spend an entire winter without ever going outside," Hagan said, laughing, as he led the visitors through the tunnel network. The passageways were uniform, broad enough to allow two people to pass each other easily, and high enough to permit a series of pipes varying in size to dangle from the ceiling. From an engineer's point of view, the pipes were the real justification for the tunnels, providing an avenue through which the steam pipes could link all the buildings to a single heating plant, as well as keeping the water supply and the electrical and communications lines protected from harsh weather.

Hagan led them through the medical ward and its pharmacy, with shelves stacked from counter to ceiling with pill containers, liquids in bottles, packages of sequels, ampules of yellowish liquid, plastic-sheathed syringes, and all sorts of other medical supplies. The weapons stockade was a well-fortified—and well-removed—room tucked below the MCA Barracks. The only entrance was through an L-shaped tunnel spur at the bottom of the stairs that ascended to the guards' quarters.

During the walk Hagan talked of the computer-controlled override lock system, the video surveillance that covered literally every square inch of the compound, the communications system, the alarm network that alerted nearby stations as it signaled the control center, and every other technical feature that made Scales one of the most advanced facilities of its kind in the country.

When they reached the control center, static like crumpling cellophane burst from radio speakers at the other end of the room. It was followed by a distant voice, "Scale Island, this is Grand Marais. I read you. Over."

As the radioman responded, the director of Scales and his three visitors turned to watch. "Twice a day, at previously determined intervals, we make contact with the mainland," Hagan explained. "The radio avoids any possible technical or climatic interference with the telephone cable which, by the way, carries all the phone service for the island." As he talked, he slowly moved the group toward the radio equipment. "The scheduled contacts are a safeguard against the unthinkable. It's another example of how well all the angles were covered in the planning of Scales. If somehow we did lose control, and I mean total control, there may be no way to get word out. So if that did happen, our mainland contact at the least would know within a matter of hours."

To Watson, that made them seem awfully vulnerable. "Say it's ten hours before Grand Marais realizes something is wrong. Then what can they do?"

"We're never going to lose total control. The system, I think, was designed by a paranoid, so I'd rather not speculate on such an unlikely event. The residents are kept in separate and smaller units, and a series of electronically locking doors divides the floors, and these doors are in each of the staircases that lead into the tunnels. If anything ever did happen in any one unit, our man up here would see it on the monitors and could override any keys or controls for the doors in each unit. We would quickly isolate any disturbance, break out the weapons for our men, and at the worst, sit tight with the problem contained and wait for reinforcements."

"You make it sound so very simple," O'Connell said. "Just a matter of routine."

As Hagan led them from the control center, he was

unquestionably a man in control. "We'll see the cafeteria now," he said. "The men should be having lunch." As he walked down the stairs, there was a lightness to his step. He was feeling good. Everything was going right.

The noisy rattle of silverware and dishes echoed hollowly in the tile-floored room. The inmates from both floors of A-Barracks ate together in the cafeteria, one of the few times that the unit of more than thirty was allowed to mingle.

Squirrel, with the arrowhead profile and a bulging Adam's apple like ball bearings under a tight sheet, had scurried from table to table telling the unlikely story of Jeremy Willet facing down Arnie Johnson. It was one of the rare occasions the others listened to him, and Squirrel reveled in his role.

Jeremy sat with his elbows on the table eating chicken legs with his fingers. As he chewed, he couldn't keep the smile from his face, and little pieces of saliva-covered meat dribbled from his mouth and fell to his shirt. Across from him and leaning over his plate toward him was forty-two-year-old Herman Breitsmann. Black hair was combed straight back over his balding pate, and when he talked excitedly, as he did now, oily black spears of hair fell out of place and spilled to the sides of his forehead. His sport shirt was buttoned tight at the neck with a layer of skin hanging over the collar. He was not overweight so much as he was soft from a lifetime of non-conditioning.

When Jeremy had first come to Scales—two, three years ago? Time seemed to lose its meaning inside the walls—Breitsmann had seen him as someone he had something in common with, someone he could tell his story to. But Jeremy Willet had pulled an impervious shell around himself and, until today, had not emerged.

"You would have liked my grandfather, Jeremy. He was a nice man, a gentle man; he knew how to talk to sweet children. People don't understand the kinds of things that we did. They say we are evil, that what we did was crazy. But at another place, in another time, they wouldn't have thought that at all." Breitsmann spoke softly, a kind of hypnotic wave undulating through his words.

"My grandfather would have understood us, Jeremy. He was a nice man. Do you know what he saw?"

Jeremy was distracted. Too many things were happening to him at once.

"Do you know what he saw?" Breitsmann repeated, louder.

"N'no."

"He saw little children being sold in a butcher shop." Breitsmann leaned back dramatically from the table, his eyes round with emphasis. "That's right. In a butcher shop.

"He told me, he took me on his knee and told me that when he was a young man, he had taken a ship to Hong Kong. There was a famine and people were starving and they had no money to buy anything to eat, if they could find food." Breitsmann had gradually fallen closer to Willet again and leaned toward him over the table. "Children under twelve years old were sold to butchers who cut them up and sold them for food. He said their little behinds were sold as veal because that was the sweetest part." His eyes twinkled, as though he savored the telling of his story. "And you know what? He was right." A conspiratorial laugh seemed to rumble like gargled water deep in his throat, and with a grin fixed on his face he showed brown scum on his teeth at the gumline.

"People don't like to hear what I did. But you're different, Jeremy. You're more like me. You'd like to hear, wouldn't you?"

"Ye'ye'yes," he stammered.

"She was such a sweet thing, you would have liked her. I met her at the playground. She was so pretty, swinging in her little dress, all by herself. I pushed her on the swing for the longest time, and then I brought her home. I said we'd play a game and told her to hide in the basement. Then I took off all my clothes and went down there, but she was scared. She kicked and screamed and bit so I had to paddle her. I paddled her until she stopped."

Not so much the words, but the voice of Breitsmann swirled in a nauseous circle in Jeremy's head. For three years Jeremy had sat alone at every meal, eating by himself unnoticed by everyone else in the room. Yet today it was different. He was the center of everyone's attention, and for once, they weren't all laughing at him.

Little beads of oily sweat formed at the top of Breitsmann's forehead, and under the lights colors shimmered in the drops like a rainbow reflected in an eddy. He continued, as if he had Jeremy's full attention. "It took me seven days to eat her entire body. But I didn't make love to her," he quickly added, as if the thought were repugnant to him, "although I could have. She died a virgin."

Jeremy's gaze wandered about the room as Breitsmann droned on, talking now exclusively for himself. As Jeremy surveyed the other men seated in the cafeteria, he no longer felt afraid of them as he had always felt afraid of any other person. They were not threatening, but supportive. And it had taken so little to feel so good. Without doctors, without drugs, and without therapy.

He felt smug, as if he could do anything, as if Arnie Johnson had been finally put in his place. Across the room from him, standing by the entrance, the fat guard stood watching all of them. He was nothing, Jeremy thought, a man with a little power that has gone to his head. He hated him, and even his hate left untethered by his own inhibitions made him feel better. His loathing of the fat guard was made all the stronger by his accomplishment earlier in the day, by his victory over him. As he stared at Arnie Johnson, he felt sure that the guard would never be the same with him or any of the other men. Jeremy decided he would make sure of that.

Arnie Johnson was alert; he had learned from experience that one test of authority if successful frequently led to another. He was bitter about it, about the system that was more concerned about some hazy rights of convicted killers and rapists than it was about the safety and protection of the men who had to face them every day.

The incident in the recreation room had been just ninety minutes earlier, and the memory was all too vivid. He thought of that spastic cretin who couldn't spit out a complete sentence, who had tied up two boys and had gouged their tongues from their mouths leaving them to drown in their own blood, and he thought of how he had struck him and because some of those outsiders who wrote the laws and moaned to the press about prison reform were at Scales, he couldn't do a thing.

Arnie's turbulent thoughts were a product of his eighteen years in the prison system. He had interned at Jackson, the world's largest walled prison, and was one of 600 guards on duty at any one time among 5,000 hostile enemy. During his time there he had his nose broken three times, his wrist and leg broken in different assaults, and his ribs cracked when pushed down a staircase. But it was at Marquette, Michigan's maximum security facility, that he had almost died. He never saw the man or what kind of homemade weapon was used to stab him in the back, but it punctured his kidney, which during surgery had to be removed. It was also at Marquette that he had killed an inmate. The Prison Review Board ruled it was justifiable self-defense, but it was always there, on his record, for wardens and politicians and newspapermen to see: he had killed someone he was paid to watch. When Scales opened, to hell with seniority and free choice, the department had said, and he was assigned there.

There were footsteps at the doorway, and Arnie jumped. The tension tightened his jaw, and the anger boiling inside bubbled close to the surface. It was Hagan and his visitors.

"The food is quite good, I assure you," the director was saying. "In fact, we have basically the same meals, in our own dining room, of course."

The guard's tension only marginally lessened as Hagan introduced him to the senators. "He's an example of the caliber of men we have here," Hagan said. "With eighteen years' seniority in the system, he's one of our most experienced MCAs."

Hagan moved on toward the kitchen, and O'Connell said, "I'll be right with you. I'd like to have a few words with Mr. Johnson here, if you don't mind."

Hagan paused in midstep, as if his thought froze his movement. With a covert glance toward Arnie, Hagan replied, "No. I don't think that would be a problem."

They left, and O'Connell turned to Arnie. "You don't mind if we chat a bit, do you?"

O'Connell was the kind of man who managed to spark an instant dislike or distrust in those he met. He realized it and survived personally and professionally only by an arrogant self-assertion that paid little regard to the opinions of others. Standing there, smiling at the guard in a posture of friendship, O'Connell could disguise only the nature of his ulterior motives, not that he had them.

While he couldn't retreat physically, Arnie intellectually pulled away from the man. He immediately sensed a threat to his job, and the enemy for just a few moments was not the sixty inmates in the room but this legislator from Lansing. "I don't mind talking," he said at last, "but I don't see what you can learn from me that Dr. Hagan couldn't tell you." Arnie tried to effect a smile; instead, it shriveled and died on his lips.

"Oh, Dr. Hagan has been very helpful, very gracious even. There's not a thing he wouldn't do for us here." The sarcasm was clear to the guard, and Arnie felt resentment. He resented being patronized. "But sometimes," O'Connell continued, "I think Dr. Hagan paints too good a picture. And he should; after all, this has been his baby from cradle to now. The problem with that is, a person can lose his objectivity, and then everybody suffers because of it. You follow?"

"Yes."

"Good, good," O'Connell said, patting Arnie's arm a few times before releasing it. "But a guard—sorry, an MCA—somebody like yourself, probably knows much more about how a place like this really operates. You're so much closer to it, your judgment is not colored by outside considerations. You know what works and what doesn't, what needs improvement, what needs to be changed. Am I right?"

Arnie nodded, distrust evident on his face.

O'Connell questioned and probed, searching for a toehold to discredit the Facility in committee hearings, to reduce its funding and divert the money elsewhere. While they talked, a man seated at one of the tables very deliberately brushed his long blond hair back from his face.

Jeremy Willet was oblivious to everything and everybody around him except for the fat guard. In his mind, all that was wrong with him, that caused him to be different, that brought him to his isolated cubicle on this godforsaken island, somehow crystallized in the obese flesh of that body. And for the first time in his life, he was in control. He was in control of the forces that had always controlled him. He felt certain that as he controlled the fat guard, he controlled his own life.

With Breitsmann's voice a haunting whisper, slowly he

came to his feet, the tray in his hands. He had to prove his control.

"Come on," O'Connell cajoled, "I never heard of a prison—and this is a prison, isn't it? Despite what the shrinks tell us?"

"Yes, it is." Arnie glanced across the room toward Hagan, who returned for just a moment the anxious stare.

"I have never heard of a prison that the inmates did not use good old American ingenuity and fashion an arsenal for themselves. You mean to say that doesn't happen here?"

"Oh, sure, we'll turn up a shiv or two in a shakedown every now and then. Or maybe a toothbrush handle scraped to a sharp point. But nothing like it was at Jacktown. There, a con without some protection was as good as dead. So they all had something."

"So how does it feel that many of them are armed, and you're not?"

"Part of the job, Senator. If I had a gun, anytime a couple of them wanted, wouldn't be nothing to take it from me."

"Doesn't seem fair, somehow. Does it?"

"Nope. It don't."

O'Connell turned sideways to Arnie toward the tables of men. Neither noticed the slight-framed long-haired blond man approach. "How many times has someone tried to break out?"

"Escape? Here? Where the hell they'd go?"

"I don't know. You tell me."

"Nope. Never happened before. There's no escapin' this island. No escapin' for nobody."

"Hey, Arnie," Jeremy shouted from just a few feet away. Both the senator and the guard looked toward him. His posture was a haughty stance, with face thrust forward and the tray held belligerently before him. His mouth parted in a sneer as a laugh trembled in his throat. Slowly, the tray tilted, the dishes slid to the edge, then slipped one by one in a growing crescendo of shattering china. The cavernous room echoed with the noise of the breaking dishes. Every voice stilled, every eye trained on Willet and the guard and the senator.

"Fuck you," Jeremy spat, and his whole body shook with rage at the unseen forces that tormented him, that had labeled him insane, that had kept him encapsulated from the outside world as effectively as the drainage sewer he hid in as a nine-year-old boy. As his insult reverberated in incredulous ears, he laughed again, his voice growing stronger, its tone harsher. The trembling ceased. "Fuck you," he bellowed, and he laughed louder.

Arnie was frozen with surprise, with indecision. Inhibited by the senator standing next to him, the only reaction he knew, the reaction that was urged upon him by his gut emotions, he could not do. He could only stand there, transfixed by the laughing, leering spectacle before him, hypnotized by the peals of laughter pelting his ears. The mocking laughter of other inmates joined Willet's.

"Fuck you," Jeremy screamed again, his laughter now only one of many voices. Then, from somewhere in the room a dish crashed to the floor.

Hagan grabbed Hume and Watson and pushed them toward the doors. As they moved, the sound of breaking dishes exploded in tiny bursts throughout the room like a string of firecrackers. At the door O'Connell joined them, and they hurried into the hallway pursued by a derisive chorus of insults and laughter.

A half dozen MCAs appeared from the recesses of A-Barracks and hurried into the cafeteria. There was nothing they could do but stand back and watch as a cacophony of smashing dishes and glass enveloped them.

Arnie was paralyzed as the laughing, the shouting, the shattering dishes swirled through the room like heat cycloning above a forest fire, spinning faster, growing hotter, drawing flames higher as it feeds upon the havoc it has ignited. At the eye of the fire storm, the vortex of the whirling bedlam in the cafeteria, Arnie stood unmoving. The men's voices, their shouts, their jeers, their taunts circled closer and closer to the fat guard, surrounding him with twiny tendrils of invisible sound. Tighter it squeezed, harder it pressed. Arnie seemed to slump forward, gasping for breath. The air, the noise, were suffocating him.

The hands of Jack Cooke gently but firmly gripped Jeremy Willet's shoulders. At first, in his frenzy, the frail murderer of two young boys did not seem to notice he was in the guard's grip. But as Jack slowly pulled the young man into himself, his shouts and his laughter diminished. Jack put his arms around him and hugged him tight to his chest, and as he did, it seemed to smother the fire raging throughout every fiber of his body. Jeremy went nearly limp, his arms dangling at his sides as if merely an extension of his sweaty, stringy hair. His eyes rolled as the exertion, the emotion, the lingering traces of the drugs in his system all seemed to coalesce in an overpowering sensation of fatigue, and he gave in to the feeling as a dizzy man eventually succumbs to imbalance and falls.

As the turmoil died within him, it slowly died within the others as it had started, with just a few carrying the laughter, and then it was silent.

In the quiet, standing amidst the debris of shattered dishes, each staff member, from Arnie Johnson to Jack Cooke, felt an empty, uncomfortable, sickening sensation within himself. Though order was restored, for several moments they were painfully aware that chaos swept throughout the room, and that they were in a state of total confusion. It showed them and sobered them to how fragile was their control of Scales Psychiatric Facility.

10

Marion Cooke wiped her hands on the apron that hung from her waist. Lettuce was draining from a colander in the sink. In this kitchen, the kitchen for the doctors and administrative staff of the Facility, she and Julia Tucker were unaware of the disturbance in the cafeteria across the yard in A-Barracks. They were busy preparing lunch for Hagan's guests from Lansing.

"Do you think they'll have big portions? The senators?"

"Probably," Marion said. "As long as it's free."

Julia laughed, then she dumped another handful of flat, dry noodles into a pot of boiling water.

From across the room, near another sink, this one full of sudsy water, came a halting, unnatural laugh. Both women looked in that direction, as if surprised someone was even there. It was easy to forget that Eddie Hyland was around, he seemed so innocuous and quiet. But every now and then, he would do something that made them aware he was in the room.

Julia looked quickly away from his stare and began stirring the bubbling pot of noodles. Her shoulders slumped even more than usual, as if she curled inward to protect herself from the inmate who worked with them every day. Her eyes darted nervously toward Marion, and whether it was from the steam or from perspiration, Marion could see moisture collecting on her forehead.

Eddie did not bother her the way he did Julia. If anything, Marion felt sorry for him, especially after seeing him day after day sloshing the breakfast dishes in the soapy water.

Marion smiled at him, and he returned her smile. His face was youthful, and his hair was dark and very thin, so thin that it hung in wispy spears that shifted with the slightest movement. He was not muscular, but he had a lithe, athletic build. In fact, Marion thought, he was quite handsome. And that made the waste seem all the more tragic.

"Could you watch this for me?" Julia said as she laid the wooden spoon on the counter. "I have to step down the hall."

Marion agreed, as she always did. Julia would go to the women's lounge and lie on the couch there, trying to bring calm to her nerves. Marion never complained nor went to the supervisor. But it did make her wonder if that is what working twenty-five years inside prisons would do to a woman.

Eddie Hyland rinsed the silverware mechanically, then placed it in a rack that would take it through a hot-water spray. He watched as Julia left the kitchen, then his eyes were back on Marion. She was so beautiful, he thought, so divinely attractive. Even in her apron that was tied around her waist, and the patterned flannel shirt, her shape was alluring.

The apron shifted as she moved, and to Eddie it seemed to slide open provocatively, as if it were a skirt slipping open revealing her dark underclothes. He swallowed as he felt an excitement prickling within him.

Marion stepped to the shelves along one wall, and Eddie watched her as she did. Her every movement was affected with a sensual grace that captivated his attention, that spiced his imagination. As she reached for a stack of bowls, her shirt pulled taut across her breasts, outlining in tight relief their every curve. He felt himself turning from the sink to stare at her directly.

She placed the bowls on the counter, then bent down to a lower shelf. As she did, the front of her shirt parted and for a fleeting instant, in the billowed opening between the buttons, Eddie could see her breasts. They were covered with the silky, lacy cloth of her bra, and they seemed so exquisitely smooth. A kind of breathlessness came over him, and suddenly he felt light-headed.

Marion glanced at Eddie and smiled again. He seemed so harmless, she wondered how he possibly could have ended up at Scales.

A short hall at the far end of the kitchen led to the pantry where most of the dry goods were stored. Marion took the bowls to the sink where the lettuce sat draining, then she walked to the pantry. It was like a cave, with the windowless concrete block walls lined with shelves that were stocked with cardboard boxes and cans and jars of foodstuffs. There was probably not another place in the building that was as still as in there, and it was comforting, if only for a few moments, to get out of the dish clatter and machine noises of the kitchen. It was so quiet, so peaceful in there.

But today Marion was in a hurry. There were three more people to prepare lunch for, and she was covering for Julia again. She felt a little tight in the stomach, and she thought it must be the rush that made her feel that way. But as she collected what she needed, she had a strange sensation, as if someone were watching her, as if in the stillness she could hear someone breathing.

She turned to leave, then stopped in midstep. "Oh!"

she gasped, startled. Standing squarely in the doorway, blocking any exit, stood Eddie Hyland.

The men of A-Barracks were locked in their rooms and would remain there for at least another hour. There didn't seem to be any resistance to the move, and indeed, it was as if they welcomed it as the mildest of punishments they expected. The gesture in the cafeteria had aroused a collective satisfaction, and, for some, it was a realization that there was really very little the MCAs could do to them.

In the cafeteria a crew was busy sweeping dish fragments. Jack was free for lunch, but he was too keyed up to eat. His head was still racing from the experience, his nerves now suffering that fatigue of release that comes after such intensity. He was going to use his time to see Marion. If only for a few minutes, he knew with her he would feel removed from the atmosphere of Scales.

He slipped on his parka for his walk across the yard. He avoided the tunnels because to him, at this moment, the long narrow tubes seemed nothing more than the living, functioning intestines of the Facility.

"Do I scare you?

"No," she said quickly. Too quickly. Eddie had never caused the least fear in her before, but now, standing before her like he was, he seemed a different person. And it frightened her.

"You don't have to be scared. It doesn't have to be that way, between us."

"I told you I'm not scared. And what do you mean, what doesn't have to be that way?"

"You are a very beautiful woman, Marion. You're the most beautiful woman I've been this close to. I don't suppose you can understand what that does to me."

Marion hesitated, unsure of how to respond, unsure of what he was going to do. "I really must get back to work," she said as she started to walk toward the door. "They'll all be here any minute."

Hyland let himself fall to the side of the door Marion was angling toward. "No they won't. We've got time."

Marion stopped where she was, still several feet separating her from the door and Eddie. Rather than trying to push her way by, she stayed back. It was a gesture that revealed the fear she denied. He noticed it, and he smiled. It was the same expression she had seen on him many times before, the same narrow, mysterious smile that she had thought contributed so much to his appearance. Yet now it gave him a harsh, uncompromising look. She struggled to keep the nervous trembling from her voice as she said, "You're going to get yourself in trouble, Eddie."

He laughed, and suddenly he was like no one she had ever met before. He was hard, even vicious, and he frightened her. "What will they do?" he challenged. "Put me in jail?"

She noticed his hands, what was in his hands, for the first time, and the realization caused her breath to catch in her throat. He had been twisting it in his fingers, but so intent was she on his face and his position blocking the door she hadn't noticed it. But now she did, and her eyes darted nervously from it to his eyes to the passageway beyond him. It was just a dinner knife, a standard blunt piece of stainless steel, but as she recognized it for what it was, a crazy off-the-wall memory popped into her mind. She remembered when she was a kid, her brother saying, in an imaginary battle with an enemy, that he would stab him with a blunt knife and that it would hurt all the more because it would not pierce cleanly. It was a scrap of a child's discarded memory that she had not thought of since, until today, until she stood watching as the blade turned over and over in his hands.

"Do you think I'm attractive?" he said, with as easy a disposition as if he were asking about the weather.

Marion was practically numb, struggling to come up with a plan of defense. Where she was, she knew her voice would travel no farther than the kitchen, if that far.

"Do you?" The transformation was immediate. His eyes flared wide, and an insistent, accusing tone underlined his words.

"Yes, yes," she stammered. "You are, but that doesn't mean anything." And what did she mean by that? She could curse herself for her incoherence.

"It means everything," he said, his voice smooth once again, yet with eyes still gaping from the desire that had been ignited within him. He stepped toward her, and as he did, Marion quickly backed away. She reached the shelves, then began to slide along them, all the while keeping herself facing Hyland. If she could get him farther away from the door, she thought, she had a chance to get by.

"I don't have to hurt you," he said, moving very slowly. "It doesn't have to be like that."

"Nothing can ever happen, between, between us," she said. "It just can't be." The words sounded foreign to her. She couldn't believe she was actually saying them, that she found herself in this situation where she had to say them.

"I dream about you, Marion. About you and me. Together." Eddie mimicked her moves, keeping her always in front of him. He was in the middle of the pantry, away from the door, yet there was no way she could get by him. "Do you want me to tell you about my dream?"

"I'd rather not hear, Eddie."

The anger flashed back in his face with such a fury that it made her wince. But when he spoke, he had changed again. "I dream that you are taking your clothes off, and smiling, like you do. Smiling at me. There is no one else but you and me." He was inching closer toward her, the knife lazily, almost absentmindedly, twisting in his fingers. "You are inviting me to come closer, to come to you, and as I come closer, you so very slowly let your clothes drop to the floor. First your blouse, then your skirt, then your bra. And then you are standing there, naked. Absolutely naked, and you are smiling." He seemed as though in a trance, his eyes unblinking, his voice a soft monotone.

Marion slid with her back against the shelves away from Hyland. Her fingers guided her as her arms were stretched back with her hands gripping the shelf as she moved. Though the fear heaved in her lungs, her mind grew progressively clearer. It was as if the danger brought forth a resolve she didn't know she possessed. She felt a bag, a soft paper bag, and her fingers clenched it.

"Yes, yes. Like that. Your breasts heave like that in my dream from your excitement as you wait for me to touch you."

Eddie lunged toward her, and as he did, Marion spun to the side. He turned again toward her, and his face, the room suddenly exploded in a cloud of powder. Marion had flung a half-empty bag of flour in his eyes, and as he groped and coughed, she pushed by him for the door. She felt a tug at her clothes, at her apron, as blindly he had lashed out and grasped her. She yanked the apron from her waist and stumbled backward out of the room.

"Come back!" he shouted.

Marion tried to wipe the powder from her own eyes as she bounced from side to side of the short hallway. She could hear him just behind, stumbling awkwardly after her. Then suddenly she was grabbed solidly at the wrists.

"Marion!"

It was Jack. "He's got a knife," she shouted and instantly felt herself spinning away from her husband and behind him.

Jack faced the hall. He stripped the parka off and wrapped it around his left hand. Hyland was several feet before him, leaning against the wall. With one hand he wiped the residue of flour from his eyes, and in the other he still clutched the knife. "Drop the blade, Eddie," Jack said evenly.

The smile came back to his face as he stared at the guard. He made no attempt to move, nor to drop the weapon.

"The knife, Eddie. Drop it."

He stood straight, leaning away from the wall, and began to walk slowly toward Jack. He held the knife out in front of him as if it were a delicate instrument, and he wore an expression full of mockery for the uniform Jack had on. Then he let the knife slip through his fingers and clang to the tile. "She doesn't save it just for you anymore," he said. "She gives it to me now, too."

Jack broke toward him, flinging his coat to the floor. He grabbed the inmate's wrist and twisted it behind his back and slammed his chest against the wall.

"Jack! Don't do it!" Marion shouted.

He jerked harder, pushing his arm higher up his back. It was almost to the snapping point, yet all Eddie could do was laugh.

"You'll get yourself in trouble. Let him go."

Jack listened to Marion at last, and he eased the pressure of his hold. Eddie laughed even louder as though enjoying some private victory, as though his laughter were a weapon to flail away at the guard. In a sense it had its effect, as it stayed with Jack even after he made sure

Marion was all right. She wouldn't go home. She said her job was almost done anyway, and she would have to stick it out only a short time longer.

And the laugh continued to ring hollowly in his ears as he led Hyland through the tunnels and back to his cell.

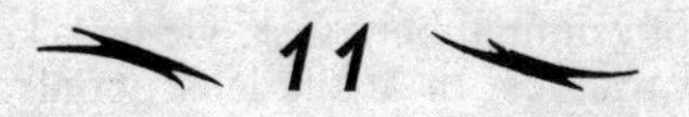

The closer the senators came to their departure, the more relaxed they were. With lunch finished, there remained only a few hours of daylight for the plane safely to lift off the unlit, frozen runway.

Clyde Watson was born in Georgia but had grown up in Black Bottom in Detroit. He had seen poverty, and he had seen crime, but never as a youth had he seen the senseless violence that seemed so common today. Whether the modern criminal was poor or not, there still was no explanation for much of what he did.

Throughout the meal he had liked the straightforward manner of the young Dr. Huxley. He was different from the procession of arch-backed bureaucrats who testified before his committee like eels looking for every available dark crevice in which to hide. And he lacked the politician's habit of weighing everything he said before he spoke.

All that Watson had heard about the Facility, the treatment of the patients, and the costs involved seemed to dissolve into an unimportant and uninteresting mass of data. Looking across the table directly at Huxley, he asked what had increasingly perplexed him as he heard fresh details of the savage crimes committed by the men at Scales. "What makes them do what they do? What makes anyone so terribly and indiscriminately violent?"

"We don't know," Huxley said. "We can't say positively what causes a person to be violent. But in some cases we can trace it to actual physiological breakdowns. Like Charles Whitman, the guy who shot sixteen people from a Texas tower. An autopsy showed he had a malignancy in the temporal lobe area of his brain.

"Or sometimes we can point to exposure to certain long-term environmental or sociological conditions as giving rise to violent patterns of behavior."

"So you can make predictions, in some instances."

"Guesses based on probabilities, not predictions. It's far from an exact science, partly because we're dealing with individuals operating at large in a free society. In the psychiatry of criminal behavior, we lack laboratory control of the variables, or at the least, control where after the fact the variables could be examined scientifically. That situation, that kind of scientific control, has never existed."

"And if it did?"

"Then maybe I could answer your first question: Why are some people so senselessly violent?"

O'Connell could not restrain himself. "They are like that because it is in our nature. Man's nature to be violent." O'Connell glared from Watson to Huxley. "It's in all of us, and is as much a part of us as love or hope or hunger. Most of us control it, as we control our lusts and our desires, because it is wrong, it is against God's moral code. But some people don't care about morality, about the well-being of others, about anything but themselves. God gave man a free will to distinguish him from the lower animals, and there are those that pure and simple choose evil.

"Why do some people love more than others? Why are some more driven? More successful? Why do some give more of themselves for others? They are that way because they make themselves that way. When someone's successful, we give them credit. But when someone's a criminal, all of a sudden they are not responsible for what they do. We wring our hands and try to explain it away, saying it's not what he's really like. It's not his fault. Well, it is his fault. It's his choice. And for those who choose evil, we have to give them the punishment they deserve."

"Like for starters, eliminate all the extra care and

money we lavish on the mentally ill at a place like this?" Huxley was sarcastic, as if privately amused by someone not worth his anger.

O'Connell snorted and looked away from everyone at the table, as if he couldn't care less what any of them thought, his disgust a match for Huxley's arrogance.

Hume shifted toward Neil Lummer, and even as he addressed him, his eyes lingered on O'Connell for a few moments. "Dr. Hagan told us earlier that your treatment focuses on drug therapy. What kind of results have you had with this with your patients?"

Lummer somehow did not look like a doctor. Rather, he appeared dull-witted, like the student in medical school who sat in the corner in the back avoiding eye contact with the lecturer. He wore ordinary black-frame glasses, the kind that were a free optical benefit for a state employee. He had quick, nervous features that seemed to display a lack of confidence in himself, more so than unsettled nerves. He was not someone, Hume thought, to whom he would care to entrust his health.

As he ever so slightly shifted to a more rigid posture, Lummer had to clear his throat. He had been content to sit back and take little part in the conversation. The less he said, the less he could be led into trouble. But with Hume's question, he sensed his role in steering the conversation onto familiar and less controversial grounds.

"Favorable," he said, with a tone that made it sound anything but favorable. As if to compensate, he blurted loudly, "Very favorable, the results have been." He shifted more noticeably in his chair. "The medication, the ah, various phenothiazines like chlorpromazine and trifluoperazine, and the thorazines have been very successful in controlling overt psychoses, and, ah, various cerebral dysfunctions."

"The problem with the drugs," Huxley said, speaking over Lummer as a teacher ignores the ignorant, "is not only an assortment of side effects, from Parkinson's to impotency to dry mouth, but that there is no one drug for the aggressive personality. There are a multitude of etiologies for mental illness, and a drug that's good for a patient one day, may not be good the next. And they treat the symptoms, not the cause of the illness itself."

"But in treating the symptom, they are successful in

controlling aggression." Lummer had never liked Huxley's aloofness, but at least he had learned to live with it. Now he burned inside from Huxley's trying to show him up. And what difference did it make, he thought. Just to impress a couple of senators who couldn't tell psychiatry from witchcraft?

"For a while, maybe. But aggression or violence is not a constant urge. It recurs at unforeseen times. It is impulsive. A dose that might send a patient into apoplexy might have no effect when the impulse is there."

Hagan tried to take the edge off Huxley's remarks. "Dr. Huxley is a strong believer in psychotherapy. Isn't that right, Dr. Huxley?"

"Drugs are fine. Vital, at times. But for the aggressive personality, more so than any other, the psychiatrist must be prepared to look beyond the biochemical processes of the brain. He must not be content merely to control outward manifestations of the illness. He must look inside to the causes, and most importantly he must encourage the patient to see the causes, to understand the problems, to realize the consequences of his behavior. Only when this happens can we hope for something beyond mere sedation of the aggressive personality. Given active participation by the patient, we will be able to reinforce desirable attitudes while countering others. And all of this, I can't emphasize enough, depends on psychotherapy and a strong personal relationship between patient and doctor."

"And that's the danger," Lummer said sharply. "You'll find yourself trapped by his transference."

"And what is that?" Hume asked.

Lummer was quick to take the response from Huxley. "The transfer of the patient's feelings onto something or someone else. In the case of a violent personality, the transfer of the focus of the patient's inner rage onto the doctor. And if it happens, it can defeat the whole purpose of the so-called close relationship Dr. Huxley talks about."

"You're wrong, Lummer. A classic transference of affect might be the best thing. It's one way to draw out the patient, to get him to see some very unpleasant things about himself he had used every psychological device he possessed to keep hidden."

"And what do you end up with? A volatile patient you can't control."

"That, Dr. Lummer, depends on which psychiatrist is handling the situation." Huxley's manner left no mistaking who he felt could handle such a situation, and who could not.

The last bit of coffee was left in cold cups as the lunch broke up and the senators prepared to leave. Hagan had a sinking feeling that the day had turned all wrong. With difficult budget questions facing the state Senate, it would be very easy for the senators to preserve their pet projects at the expense of the Corrections Department. It certainly wouldn't be the first time, and if it came to that, Hagan felt sure it would be Scales the Corrections Committee would recommend be cut back first.

Yet as he stood in the snow along Lake Siskiwit and watched the ski-equipped plane taxi into position to take off, it was not the three senators he was worried about. It was not concern over their report that caused him to linger alone in the cold for several minutes after the plane had cleared the trees and disappeared from his sight. It was the scene from the residents' cafeteria that lingered in his mind; the thought of that screaming, laughing, dish-shattering tumult chilled him more than the Lake Superior winter. It was the realization of how easy it would be for a single spark to land squarely in a tinderbox of volatile emotions.

It had been a long day, and Hagan was tired. All he wanted to do was to go back to his apartment and relax. But there was something else to deal with. Always something else.

Back at his office he was briefed on the incident between one of the trusties and Marion Cooke. He had initialed an order canceling his status, taking away his job, and placing him back in the regular population with all standard restrictions. He thought he was done with it, but one of the MCAs, the woman's husband, was waiting to see him.

Wearily he signaled his secretary to allow him in, then he explained what had already been done. Cooke wasn't satisfied.

To Jack, at last the doubts had taken shape. The formless, graspless concerns were finally real, and he could see them. And he wanted answers. "Why was he of all people, with his criminal record, with his conviction for rape, why was he placed in there with her?"

"It was Dr. Huxley's decision to do that. Eddie Hyland is his patient."

"But you're in charge here. You must have seen what he was doing."

Hagan sighed. He didn't want to be Huxley's defender, but he saw no way around it. It was better he answer the questions than make Jack ask them of Huxley. He cleared his throat and leaned his forearms on the edge of his desk. "Do you know anything about Eddie Hyland?"

"I know what he was convicted of."

"But do you know what caused him to be a criminal sexual offender?"

"Because he couldn't control his impulses like everybody else."

"Yes, but many of us don't have the best self-control. So why was he different? Why did he cross the line in this particular area?"

Jack sat stonily, waiting for him to answer.

"Because he had never learned like everyone else how to deal with his sexuality. And it affected him. When he attacked his victims, he was telling the world of his problems. He may have been reacting to some past rejection, or maybe there was some subconscious demand that he dominate the feelings within him that had so dominated him. I don't know. But the point is, he had never been in a situation, whether at home or school—or on a job—where he dealt with a woman on a one-to-one, normal basis."

"So if you knew all this, why in God's name put him in an unsupervised setting with Marion?"

"Don't you see? That is precisely why he was put there. It was his therapy."

"His what?"

"Dr. Huxley thought it would help him, it would be good therapy to be around a woman, to see women not as objects of mystery and pain, but as normal, living, breathing human beings."

Jack was stunned. "You mean Hyland being there was not just some random assignment?"

"Well, no. Of course not."

"My wife was used to try to teach a rapist to control himself?" The words came slowly, an incredulous wonder rippling through each one.

"Dr. Huxley felt the risk was minimal, and certainly justified in the light of the good it could do for the patient."

"The patient," Jack breathed, slipping forward in his chair. His disbelief turned suddenly to anger, and he shouted, "Why weren't we told? Why wasn't it *our* decision to say what was worth the risk?"

Hagan only shook his head, as if he agreed with him. "I'm sorry. All I can say is, it won't happen again. I signed the order myself dropping his trusty status, and then took away his work privileges."

Jack stared at Hagan, thinking. "You mean nothing had been done about his trusty status before today?"

"Why no. There was no reason to."

"Huxley said he already ordered it dropped."

"He did?" Hagan looked at the file on his desk. "You must be mistaken. There's no such entry at all. If there had been, it would have been changed immediately."

Jack looked beyond Hagan; everything was coming clear. Huxley had been using him, just as he used Marion. He'd say whatever was necessary—or hide whatever he felt he should—to get what he wanted. Anything, to serve his purposes.

As Jack descended into the tunnels, his anger was brewing. He walked straight to the Medical Building, but he wasn't allowed into the corridor to the offices. The woman behind the window said Huxley was seeing a new patient.

Jack turned and walked away, and eventually his anger was to calm. As it did, he was left with other concerns. If Eddie Hyland was an example of Huxley's methods, how would his methods affect his new patient? How would they affect Reuker Stilkes?

After Jack had left the room, Hagan swiveled to face the window. One more crisis over. One more conflict defused. There really wasn't much he could do about Huxley, he thought. Realistically, whatever he wanted to do with his patients was beyond his control.

12

The woman's voice gushed in a whisper, the young boy imagining it to be the warning hiss of a reptile. "This is necessary. You have made it necessary, Reuker, you must feel that is so."

"But, Momma, I didn't do nothing bad."

"You are young. You do not understand. If only you could see as I see, look into people as I do, have the vision that I have, you would see the filth, the evil, the decay, and you would understand."

"Johnny is . . ."

"The Morris boy is a demon from the loins of Satan and the womb of Jezebel. He is a product of their lust and was weaned on rotted milk from his mother's breast. He was taught the ways of hell in that house, by that family, and anything he touches he will leave in ruins. He will feed on your life until there is nothing left but a pitted and blackened soul fit only for the eternal fires."

The six-year-old Reuker Stilkes dropped his chin to his chest and sobbed. For just a moment as tearful spasms radiated throughout his limbs, the numbing cold was forgotten. All he could feel was the loneliness, the desolation, the fear of what his mother said.

"The Lord Jesus Christ has touched so few, the devil so many. And when you touch those who have touched the devil, you must rid yourself of the spot. You must scrape the contamination from your skin, wipe it clean before it burns right into you." Her voice was no longer a haunting whisper but had fallen into a familiar cadence, rising, falling, then rising higher. The words had been spoken before, and the repeated litany brought a comfort to her mind, a confidence to her acts, a stridency to her voice.

Rebecca Stilkes had eyes that were sunk into her face and rimmed with a dark, scaly patch of skin that had never been touched by cosmetics. It was as if her eyes, vulnerable windows to her thoughts, were drawn into the safe recesses of her skull by a disposition filled with mistrust and suspicions. It was the same disposition that had drawn her away from contacts with other people. Yet when she became filled with her spirits, her eyes flamed with righteous fire.

Kneeling on the tile floor, her eyes—those weapons of indignation—trained on her son, her only child, she said, "You, Reuker, you must rely on me to see for you. You cannot see the evil, but I can. I can see into their hearts and I see the talons of the devil clenching them in his eternal grasp. I couldn't always see, but I learned, and, oh, does the learning hurt. If you could see as I do you could see the devil's control, and you would fear them as you fear the devil himself."

Reuker did indeed feel fear, and with his mother's presence hovering over him and her words pelting him, the fear he felt he thought was of the others, of the family that lived down the gravel road from them. He was scared by the suggested image of his skin turning gray and rotting away, eaten by the acid touch of those that were the devil's people.

"Pray! You must pray!" she shouted. "You must thank the Lord for the vision I have, for the care I give you, for the purity I give to your soul."

Reuker's face was streaked with tears, and he shivered in his nakedness. His mother's long black hair, swirled atop her head, made her pale face all the starker, her expression all the sharper. Reuker looked up at her and felt the force of her command.

"Pray!" she cried.

"I pray, I pray, I pray," Reuker screamed and let his chin crash again to his chest. He was kneeling in the bathtub with icy water almost to the rim. The cold numbed him, but worse than the cold was the fear; he was in terror of the shapes, the half-human figures he envisioned coming toward him. In each he saw a flicker of fire where the eyes should be. "Please, Momma, help me," he pleaded as they came closer, their fingers reaching out like jagged knives.

Rebecca was outside the tub on her knees next to him. She leaned closer, and as she did Reuker reacted to the strong smell of her breath. It was like the odor of the cold liquid she rubbed on his legs when they hurt. It was the medicine she drank for her headaches, the throbbing, pulsing headaches that would grip her for days. "You will be cleansed, Reuker, you will be pure once again," she said in her strange, sibilant whisper that was more like steam escaping through a valve than a human's voice.

Her hands crept up his arms, to his shoulders. An involuntary gasp trembled up from deep in his lungs. Resignation settled over him, and he steeled himself for what was to come.

Her fingers gripped the tops of his bony shoulders and Reuker cringed. "No," he moaned. "Please, Momma, don't." His voice was little more than a whimper; it carried his hopelessness, his despair.

"You will feel the cleansing spirit surround you. You will let it wash over you, and you will feel the evil that has touched you vanish. You will feel the good soul spreading throughout your body, you will feel its warming touch." Her grip grew tighter, and as it did, Reuker tensed. He was afraid. He had heard those words before, and he had felt the cleansing spirit, and with it he had felt the pain in his lungs, the deadening sensation it left in his head. He shivered from the cold, the fear, his mother's grip.

"You will be cleansed, Reuker," she said. "You will be purified and it will feel good."

He felt the increase in pressure, and with a terrified expulsion of breath he instinctively pushed his arms to the sides, to the rim of the bathtub. Rebecca raised herself off her knees, and all her strength, her weight, pressed down on Reuker. There was a splash, and he plunged beneath the freezing water; it surged over his chest, his face, his back. He felt consciousness almost slip away. His mother's hands were vises at his shoulders, holding him down, squeezing into his meager flesh, rocking him from side to side.

Under the surface, the slosh of the water in the tub and the sounds of his elbows and hips and legs bumping off the hard porcelain surface were dull thumps in his ears. But over it all, penetrating to his submerged head, was his mother's voice screaming her prayer to her gods, beseeching her spirits to rid the evil from her six-year-old son.

Reuker's breath was gone, and he tried to push himself up, but the pressure of his mother only increased. His lungs seemed to be collapsing, his muscles tightening. He had to force his mouth to stay closed as it yearned to open and gasp for air. Finally he could resist no more, and through his nose he breathed. But it was water that flowed in, blocking his throat, choking him.

Suddenly he was lifted, his head out of the water. But still he could not breathe. He could only gag on the liquid in his throat. Reuker coughed and tried to steady himself to spit out the water, to gasp for air. But he was still in his mother's clutches, and she shook him from side to side, all the while shouting commands to the spirits.

"Purify him! Cleanse him! Remove the filthy stain of the devil's touch from his body. Scrape it from his skin!" Rebecca's fingers dug into Reuker's shoulders as the power of her zealotry surged throughout her muscles. Shaking her son, she cried out to him, "Let the waters come. You must let them come and expunge the filth that has touched you. Whatever sins those who touch the devil have, become yours at their touch. Whatever lusts they have, you lust. Whatever evil deeds are your deeds. Their thoughts are yours, their actions, yours. Your skin becomes like theirs. You must welcome the waters. You must be purified!"

Reuker coughed up phlegm from his throat. His body ached from the gagging, his mind swirled from his mother's words. Suddenly he was being pushed down again. He tried to speak, to plead for her to stop, but his body was wracked with heaving sobs, with gasps for breath. Then he was under again and the cold flooded over his head, and his mother's hands dug painfully into his shoulders, his neck, his back.

He had no strength to resist, no will to fight. He wished for his mother's spirits to come, he wished for the feeling of purity to wash over him, to bring him the goodness his mother called out for him. But it did not come. The pain did not cease. His head pounded from the lack of air. He felt a prickly, incessant heat throbbing in his neck as his throat seemed to burn for breath. The inside fire spread to his lungs, throughout his chest, to his entire body. He twisted in his mother's grip, writhed from side to side, and suddenly he was free, above the water.

"Do you feel it?" his mother shrieked, her voice ricocheting from tile to tile like the screeching of unfitted metal. "Is it good? You must feel their touch leaving. You must feel the goodness!" His mother's shrieks were like needles jabbing into his throbbing head. He could little understand, much less think about her words. He could only fight for the air that did not come fast enough.

Then, without warning, without a last gulp of oxygen, he was pushed down into the water again. Almost immediately the pain was there. The searing cry for breath was in his lungs. A dullness throbbed at the back of his head. It was a dizzy feeling, and as it grew, his mind, then his whole body seemed to swirl with the dizziness. He gulped at the air, but it had turned solid. It slammed into his throat, then his chest like a massive weight had been dropped upon him. His body convulsed in a futile gag, and then there was blackness.

Rebecca screamed as the boy seemed to double over at the waist in her grasp; then he went limp.

"Reuker." The voice was muffled, as if cotton batting covered his ears. "Reuker," the voice repeated gently. "You're all right. You're in a doctor's office."

He was aware of the voice first, and then he noticed the hands. They were at his shoulders, rocking him with only the slightest of force. They touched him like his mother had gripped him in the bathtub, yet it was all very different. There was none of the pain and none of the cold. Reuker Stilkes finally opened his eyes.

"Are you awake now?" Reuker watched the man's lips move, but the words came later. Then he spoke again, his lips treading over the words that Reuker was only just hearing. It was confusing; he did not understand. Reuker looked closely at the man's face, at his round, wire-framed glasses, at his bushy hair that made his head seem so circular. He thought of his mother, and her halo of hair, and he thought of how she had held him in the tub. He suddenly felt a flash of the same terror he had felt then, and his whole body tensed as he looked at the hands on his shoulders.

"It's okay," the man said, releasing his hold. "I'll step back."

As he did, Reuker relaxed in the chair. It wasn't the same as before, and it wasn't his mother. It was someone else.

Reuker watched him step backward to his desk and sit

on the edge of it. As he looked at him, and the desk, and the room, he began to remember it. He remembered the couch opposite him along the wall and the three square-backed wooden chairs with only the slightest of red vinyl padding on the seats. He remembered being brought into the room and being asked where he wanted to sit, and taking the third chair, farthest from the desk. The man in white shirt and green pants then had left him; it was the same man who had come for him in his room in midafternoon and had led him through the tunnels to the Medical Building. The whole trip was out of the routine, the room was someplace he had never been before, and it scared him. It took a while for his apprehension to grow, as it took all his thoughts a while to form since coming to the institution, since the medicine began.

He had been alone in the office, and he had sat there waiting, for what he didn't know. He tried to think of what he had done, of what would have caused him to be brought here. As he tried, the thoughts would seem to pile on top of each other and crumble into confusion before he could see any reason, remember any wrong. But he knew there did not necessarily have to be a reason; he didn't always understand why there was punishment.

An uncomfortable flash of heat had prickled up his back to his neck as he sat there wondering, thinking. The anxiety made it all the harder to remember, to piece together a chain of thoughts. Wherever those thoughts began to lead, there was always a barrier as if someone didn't want him to remember, as if blocks were deliberately placed to frustrate him.

Yet it was not like that in his dreams. There were no barriers. He didn't even try to remember—the thoughts would just come. They would appear effortlessly in his mind and flow in an unbroken series of images and ideas. It was so easy sometimes just to let them come.

Feeling the anxiety of the unfamiliar, Reuker had clasped his hands together and slipped them between his thighs. Slowly, he had begun to rock forward, then backward. The apprehension grew. Uncertainty nurtured the fear. He felt colder, as if an icy shroud were falling down upon him. The nervous warmth that had surged up his spine a moment before turned frigid. It became harder to breathe. It was as if he were suffocating. He rocked forward farther, clenching himself in a tight ball, and he fought the feeling, the labored breathing, the air turning harder. He had felt that before, he had felt it all before . . .

"You are perfectly safe here," the man said. He was leaning against the desk, several feet from Stilkes.

Reuker stared at him trying to discern if what he said was the truth.

"You are safe now. I assure you."

He was slight of build and Reuker guessed in his early thirties. He was not dressed like one of the guards. Finally, Reuker tried to swallow away the dryness in his throat, and he sat straighter, self-consciously drawing his hands back from between his legs.

"I am Dr. Huxley," he said. "I am going to be your doctor now. I'm going to try to help you."

Reuker's hands suddenly clenched his knees as a fragment of someone's voice—"you will be cleansed, you will feel better"—flashed through his mind. The tenseness gripped his entire body, yet he could not sense anything beyond the words. He could visualize no face, recall no name. He tried to remember, but as quickly as the inclination entered his head, the mounting pyramid of thoughts collapsed. The memory, the voice, the tension were gone, and Reuker seemed to slump ever so slightly in his chair.

Huxley had arranged for Stilkes to be brought in and left alone in his office so he could feel comfortable with the new surroundings before meeting his new doctor. It would be one less distraction for Huxley to have to worry about. Staring at him, at the receding wave of tensions, Huxley felt that quickening beat of self-satisfaction that someone anxious for a good first impression feels when the meeting gets off on the right foot. All Stilkes needed was a little time to orient himself. He knew he had to bring him along slowly to nurture the man's trust carefully.

"I can see that you are feeling bad, Reuker. I know what you must be going through." Stilkes gave no indication that he heard, but Huxley continued, "I know that those feelings you have inside must be pretty difficult to live with. What I want to do, what we will do together, is talk about those feelings and try to put them to rest for good. Do you understand me?"

Reuker reacted more to the calm tone of voice than what was being said. Settling back in his chair, he glanced quickly at Huxley, then back to the floor.

"You are afraid. I am too. I am nervous about saying the right thing, doing the right thing. But I don't think I have any reason to fear you, and you don't have any reason to be afraid of me." When he saw Reuker look up at him again and hold his gaze for a few seconds longer, Huxley moved to the chair next to him and sat down.

His breathing had returned to normal, and the anxiety he had felt when he was alone, when the dream had seemed so real, was all but vanished. He looked at the wiry-haired man seated beside him, and as he did, he glimpsed from his past a gallery of portraits, the faces of a number of other doctors he had seen since his arrest. Most were indistinct—it had been years since he had seen any of them, years since he had thought of them. As he tried to focus his thoughts, recall the doctors whose faces he now saw, the picture he had in his mind began to crack into segments like some unassembled mosaic. As always, the thoughts did not linger, the picture never reformed. Quickly, he gave up trying—before *all* his thoughts would dissolve—and looked again toward the floor. "Who . . ." he blurted, not knowing what he wanted to say. "What do you want of me?"

"Time. Just some of your time," Huxley said.

Reuker hunched forward as he tried to assimilate what he heard, as he tried to formulate the uncertainties he felt into questions. But as with his thoughts, the thread of a conversation was an elusive strand to maintain taut between two points. Yet he struggled and was able to force the word, "Why?"

"Because it's time someone gave you the care you're entitled to. It's time someone tried to help you. And I'm going to do it. But to be able to help you, I'll need your help. You will have to cooperate with me, and together we will make progress. I can promise you that we will make progress, if you will promise to help." Reuker's expression seemed to grow increasingly neutral, and Huxley paused to study his new patient. There was no discernible reaction to what he had just said. "Did you hear me?"

The forces that always seemed to be active within his head, the forces that broke apart whatever cohesiveness he was able to build, had overcome him. Though he had wanted to talk, it was easier not to resist. It was easier to succumb to the lure of the emptiness that was his drug-induced peace.

Huxley rested his hand on Stilkes's knee and asked, "What do you remember about the doctor you saw when you first came to Scales?" There was no change in Stilkes's expression. No attempt to respond. "Reuker, do you remember Dr. Lummer at all?" Huxley watched and waited, but there was no response. If anything, he seemed to grow even stiller, even more withdrawn. Huxley tightened his grip on Stilkes's knee. "Do you remember what it was like before the shots, before you started taking the pills? Can you remember what it was like to think what you wanted and say what you felt?"

Reuker sat calmly, in his own private world. It was a world that at the moment consisted of nothing but shadows and echoes. He was aware the doctor was speaking, but the words were too distant or too muffled to understand. And his perception of the doctor's image was that of a silhouette behind frosted glass. He sat there unmoving, staring blankly ahead.

Huxley had seen the blank stare before. He had seen that glassy-eyed vacant gaze on hundreds of patients who existed in an artificial serenity induced by the chlorpromazines. And he knew that the fixed stare saw nothing, that the drug could sap one's thoughts as effectively as exhaustion drains vitality. Prolixin was successful in lessening violent impulses, yet at times it seemed to lessen any impulse for action of any kind. "You're thirsty," Huxley said. "You're always thirsty. No matter what you do you can never rid your throat of that dryness, can you?"

For just a second there was a spark of recognition in Reuker's face.

"You feel like you can't always think straight, that you can't pay attention to something for more than just a few minutes."

Reuker's voice was barely audible. "Yes," he said.

"You try to think, but everything is so confusing. You try to remember something, but if you do, you can't remember why you wanted to think of that thing. You want to talk sometimes, but after a few sentences, you forget how you began. And it all hurts, the frustration gives you headaches. So you don't think. You don't try to do anything."

The glimmer of recognition that had been there a moment before was gone. Any sign that Stilkes acknowledged Huxley's presence was no longer there.

Huxley stood up and walked over to his desk, to the telephone/intercom at the corner of his desk.

To Huxley, physical appearance was a transparent quality as lacking in significance as someone's style of shoes or breed of dog. But as he stood by his desk and stared at the hunched Reuker Stilkes, he could not help but feel a tingling, gripping sensation trying to claw its way through his professionalism, to unseat his grasp of reason. Dark, sunken eye sockets and hollowed cheeks gave his face a skeletal quality, but it was something more than his visage that created a ghastly aura about him. There was a kind of stench, more imagined than real, of decaying flesh. It was a sensation generated by the feeling that, inside, Stilkes was little more than a rotting corpse, a leper from a medieval colony of half-dead, half-alive miscreants, as they were perceived, whose skin putrified and fell off while there was still movement in the body.

Huxley had to turn away from the man, from his image of the man, to let the sensation subside. Though it did, gradually, he was left with a trembling, unsteady vision of his patient that lingered in his thoughts like the aftertaste of bile in a sick man's throat. It was as if he encountered the horrors of the most macabre of fiction, the terrors of a child's nightmare. In Stilkes he saw as close a thing as there could be to a creature the product of some delusional, diseased imagination.

13

The lockup of the inmates in A-Barracks did not last out the afternoon. It was better to get back to the routine fast, the staff had decided, rather than let them think something had changed.

The outside recreation period neared the end of the hour, and the hockey players moved with less energy than they had earlier. A few stood in the snowbank to the side, their chins resting on their hands balanced on their sticks. It was dark, and the mercury vapor lights had been on for a half hour, tinting the snow a sickly yellow.

"Over here," Jeremy Willet shouted, and the ball was passed to him. He swatted at it, and just like that it was in the net.

Though the men were patients deprived of their freedom and living in a climate only the hardiest of them would choose, they reacted to their game the same as schoolkids skating on a frozen pond. As the ball that substituted for a puck rebounded off Willet's stick into the net, his side let out a cheer. Jeremy raised his stick in the typical hockey gesture. And then the play continued.

The spontaneous eruption of emotion quickly died down—it was nothing more than a natural release to a fast and tense game. But to Jeremy the cheer still resounded in his ears. It had been for him, and it was something he had never heard before. The sound of the men's voices ignited a thrilling sensation that rapidly carried throughout his body.

Jeremy stumbled awkwardly after the disorganized and falling band of men chasing the skittering ball across the ice. He felt a happiness he had never felt before. He wasn't thinking of his past troubles, of where he was now, or of the painful emptiness that would come back into him when his euphoria died. His only thoughts were a reaction to the good feelings that were surging through him. His emotions were those that he never thought existed.

"All right. Time to wrap it up." James Enright, one of the MCAs who was spending his first winter at Scales, stood on the snowbank next to the rink and made a sweeping gesture with his right arm.

The ball bounced twice, then skidded the entire length of the ice before rolling into the snow. The mob did not chase after it this time. Instead, one by one the men trooped off the ice and headed over the well-packed snow toward A-Barracks.

Jeremy stood, stick in hand, watching the others leave the game. Everything had been going so well, and now, suddenly, it was over. He didn't want what he was feeling to end.

"Come on. Let's go," Enright said.

Jeremy's eyes were wide, and as his head jerked from watching the men leave, to the guard, and back to the men, his stringy hair jutting out from under his hat flung from side to side like a tattered clump of straw. He fingered the stick in his hands, then took a hesitant step forward.

As he stepped from the ice to the snow, the euphoric high that had elevated his spirits vanished. A sudden rush of uncertainty clouded his thoughts as he moved woodenly after the other men. It would all come back: the loneliness, the isolation, the hollow feeling inside in which he had always suffered. He was scared; he didn't want those feelings to return. And they would, at the door, inside the structure. His legs felt weak, his thoughts were a confused jumble the nearer he came to A-Barracks.

Arnie Johnson was standing close to the door, watching as the men filed by. Jeremy felt a flaring of hatred. He hated him for his power, the control he had, the taunting smirk ever-present on his face. It was the fat guard, Jeremy knew, who wanted to snatch from him all the feelings he had felt today. Arnie Johnson wanted him to slink back into the obscure, voiceless abyss he had inhabited for so long.

Though he had often felt anger before, this time it was very much different. There was none of the frustration, the nervous insecurity that always accompanied his anger before. Instead, it made him stronger, more confident.

Jeremy felt the strength seep back into his legs. He stopped in front of Arnie and stared defiantly into the guard's face.

Arnie watched him, waiting for him to do something,

to say something. But the gaunt inmate simply stood there staring. The others who had not yet filed inside paused and looked back at the two of them.

"You going in?" Arnie said, his voice betraying no emotion.

"No. I'I'm not ready. I'm sta'aying."

Arnie stared at him for a long moment, the others watching him. His expression never altered, and finally he turned from Jeremy and signaled the others to go inside. When the last of the inmates had gone through the entrance, Arnie followed them inside and slammed the heavy steel door behind him. The precision bolts slipped solidly into place.

In the night air, with practically every hard surface sheathed with a thick mantle of snow, the thunderous slam of the door quickly subsided to a muffled echo. To Jeremy it was a distant booming sound, like he was in the middle of a long tunnel and the noise resounded to him from some outside, unseen source.

He was suddenly alone, so totally alone, and the realization caused the breath to freeze in his lungs. The door's window was iced at the corners, but in the middle it was clear, and in the middle was the implacable, stony face of the fat guard. It seemed to be there for just a moment, and then it was gone. No one was there.

Jeremy started to shiver, and as he did, he glanced nervously to the sides, about the yard. The sickly yellow light penetrated the crisp air in all directions with its foglike beams. It was deathy still, as only it can be in winter, and as he stepped toward the door, the hard-packed snow squeaked and wheezed with each footfall. He pressed his face against the window and looked in. The hall was empty.

The sight caused a sudden swell of panic, and he spun around pressing his back against the door. Vaporized breath spewed in rapid bursts from his mouth, and only with effort was he able to swallow the knot that had seemed to tighten in his throat. His eyes searched the yard, his mind searched for what to do. Yet there was nothing he could see, there was nothing he could think of to make it clear what he had to do.

Jeremy wanted to pound on the door, to shout to be let in. But if he did, someone would come and would see him. They would all see him, and he would be singled out in front of them and would be stared at and laughed at, and the acceptance he had felt today would never be there again. It was something he could not bear. It was something he had spent a lifetime hiding from.

Jeremy folded his arms across his chest to ward off the cold, to stifle the emotions he feared would break to the surface in convulsions of self-pity and weeping. Pushing himself away from the door and keeping in the shadows, Jeremy lurched along the wall of the building. The cold air settled more heavily over him, and as it did, it brought a kind of stillness to his chest, an emptiness to his thoughts. He felt hollow, as if nothing was inside of him—no feeling, no desires, no will to live.

The wall cut sharply to the left, and Jeremy followed it to a corner. There were no windows, and the yellow light left crisscrossing shadows just beyond where he stood, in the darkness. From his hidden vantage point, staring out into the starkly lit yard and at the white-mantled buildings, he felt an all-encompassing and, in a way, comforting, isolation. It was like he was in the middle of the drainage sewer that was near the house where he grew up. With a dancer's grace Jeremy slowly slumped to the ground.

He curled his legs to his chest and rested his forehead on his knees. As the cold pressed onto his back, and into his body where it touched the ground, Jeremy withdrew into himself. Mental images and ideas flickered into blankness, and as they did, he retreated further and further from himself. Like in the sewer, where he had learned to deaden his thoughts, to go kind of blank to keep himself from facing the pain, he forced his thinking to cease. After a few minutes, Jeremy was little more than a breathing organism, without feeling, without sentience, without pain.

From the yard, from the buildings, he was all but invisible curled into the shadows at the corner of the building. As he slowly lost sight of himself, there was no one else to see for him.

The office was dark, except for a small desk lamp, and even that cast barely more light than the pale yellow wash that came through the window. Michael Huxley leaned back in his chair, the springs of the rotating mechanism squeaking as he did. The file of Reuker Stilkes lay open on his desk.

After Stilkes had left, Huxley stood numbed by his impressions of his first encounter with him. He had never been affected by anyone in any context as he had been by Stilkes. The numbness brought a twinge of fear, a concern that his new patient would be something beyond his professional capabilities, but that feeling proved to be only a momentary self-doubt that was settled quickly by his usual confidence in himself. Eventually the sensations that had gripped him when Stilkes was in his office subsided and were replaced with his feverish interest in his work.

He was stimulated by the challenge more than he could have imagined. Each previous notation in the file, each scrap of information he greedily pored over again, absorbing everything he possibly could about the psychological mystery that was Stilkes. He stayed late in his office, until he was the only one left on the floor, and all the while his energy felt not the least diminished by his long day.

He noted that other than slight modifications of his prescription, the last entry from Dr. Lummer was over two years ago. Two years! Huxley was as astonished as much this time as when he first read it. The doctor had not done a thing with his patient that was worth even the most meager of file entries.

A normal dose of Prolixin was 25 milligrams injected every two weeks. Fifty milligrams was considered high, even though on rare occasions the recommendation may be as much as 100 milligrams, and Stilkes was at 75 milligrams, not every fourteen days, but every week. It was the most massive dosage of psychotropic medication he had ever seen prescribed.

The chair squeaked as Huxley leaned forward, then stood. Before turning off the desk lamp and going back to his apartment, he stooped over the open file and made his first notation. He ordered that Stilkes's Prolixin injections be ceased immediately, and that he be placed on an oral program of 1-milligram Prolixin tablets twice a day.

* * *

The fire Jack Cooke had stoked high radiated a steady warmth throughout the cabin. Emma Tardif unbuttoned the tan wool cardigan she had knitted fully a decade before as she listened to Ricky tell about his encounter with the wolf.

As he related the story, it was apparent to him it was all a grand adventure. He showed no appreciation of the danger that she imagined she would have felt. Ricky seemed to have enjoyed the experience and would not mind at all repeating it. And that's what scared her. The boy had not learned a thing.

Marion was thinking the same thoughts as she listened to her son holding center stage as he sat on the floor between Jack and Philip, Emma and her. She said, "I still can't believe you were so calm about it with the wolf so close."

"Aw, Mom. He wasn't going to do anything. He was watching me like I was watching him."

"He was watching you because he was hungry."

"But he just ran away when Philip made some noise."

Emma said, "You were lucky. The noise snapped him out of it."

Ricky felt surrounded but undeterred. "Philip says there has *never* been a wolf attack on a person. Nowhere in the United States. Ever!"

Emma's hair was an even mixture of gray and black, and she had it pulled smooth and straight across her temples and tucked in on itself in back. Long bleached of natural oils by the dry winter cold, it still maintained a dull luster. At sixty-one she was two years younger than her husband, and, like him, within her body she possessed the ruggedness of the climate and terrain of Scale Island. It was the full force of this inner strength, through her eyes, that now bore down on her husband.

Philip shifted in his seat, then pulled himself from his chair. "I'm not being unsociable, but if you don't mind I'm going to step outside and enjoy a cigar."

"No need to go out into the cold," Marion said. "Smoke it in here if you want."

"No, he won't," Emma said. "He doesn't smoke those awful things inside at home, and he won't here."

"Thanks, Marion, but it's a nice clear night. And nothing's better than cold, dry air drawn through tobacco. Maybe you can join me, Jack?"

"Sure, I'll step out with you."

It took a few minutes for the men to lace up their insulated boots and adjust their parkas before stepping outside. It was clear and cold, and after Philip lit his cigar, from the vapor they breathed out in the eight-degree air it was impossible to tell who was smoking and who was not. They stood silently for a few moments, acclimating themselves to the cold, and stared out across the ice-covered bay. The new snow that had fallen had already recrystallized, and it glittered like ground glass. In the yellowish glow from the institution, it appeared a meadow of discarded topaz strewn without pattern, nor design.

"Nice night," Jack said, breaking the stillness.

Philip waited a few moments before responding. "We have some problems," he said.

Jack was taken by surprise. Problems? Thoughts of the institution flashed through his mind, but he knew that's not what Philip meant.

Philip stepped a few feet forward and looked along the shoreline as it gradually curved outward, the darkened buildings of Gulletston silhouetted against the snow. "There's a peat fire up in the vale. And I think it's a bad one, too."

"A fire? Is it possible in winter?"

"Yep. Could last all year, or a couple years. It happened in '55, at Seney. Remember?"

Jack did recall the Seney forest fire that raged all summer, and then continued in the ground under the snow during the winter before flaming again the following year. "Yeah, I remember. How do you know we got one now?"

"I smelled it when we were up at the cabin. Could even see a little haze, even though you're not always lucky enough to see smoke above one of those things. It didn't strike me at first, but gradually I noticed the smell, and once I thought about it, I knew just what it was."

Jack rubbed a gloved hand across the back of his neck. "I don't know, Phil. It just doesn't seem possible. Here, anyways."

"Oh, it's possible, and it could be the worst thing that's happened to Scales, depending on the fuel. Once the fire gets in that peat, there's almost total combustion. No smoke, no flame, and darn near impossible to put out."

"What about the snow?"

"Real good insulation. It would keep the fire dry and protected all winter long. Oh, it would melt eventually, but if the fire had a good start in the fall, the coals would be so hot by now any moisture would just steam up and evaporate. Not a drop would touch the coals." Philip stared so intently out across the bay it appeared he was actually seeing what he described. "And if the fire was deep enough and covered with its own ash, the snow would just sit there right on top and you'd never know the difference."

"It can't keep going on forever. If it gets too deep, it'll just burn itself out."

"You'd be surprised. It burns so slow, it hardly needs any oxygen at all. I read reports, scientific ones, of fires in the peat fields of Siberia burning a hundred feet deep before going out. And they can last for years.

"There's a story the Yakuts tell—they're like the Eskimos, but in North Asia—about a peat fire that lasted almost a century. It was there because of the anger of the gods, so they made sacrifices to it. They'd throw their enemies into the fire, and if they didn't suffocate in the ash, they'd burn about as slow as you could burn. They believed the more they screamed, the more the gods were satisfied. And if they ran out of enemies, they'd sacrifice some of their own. I don't know if the legend is true or not, but I suppose a fire like that could happen, if the peat was deep enough."

As Philip related the legend of the Yakuts, somehow, something sounded familiar about it all to Jack. He could picture a snow-strewn flat area, a person, or an animal—a moose—trying to walk across and then suddenly plunging into the coals. As the image played itself out, Jack remembered. It's just what old Tom had seen and had told them all about at the tavern a few nights before. Jack remembered sitting there at the end of the bar, listening to the story, the others disbelieving, and then old Tom asking him his opinion.

Jack told Philip what he had heard, of old Tom saying he saw a moose go down in the snow and burn up, howling in pain for hours. When he was finished, Philip looked away from him and toward the black line that marked the ridge. "It's a bad one, if it could swallow a moose." He drew on his cigar, and then for a moment his face was obscured by a cloud of vapor and smoke. "Of course, it shouldn't be a surprise. Beaver have been up there for 10,000 years making dams and ponds and letting the ponds fill with leaves and twigs and anything else that would sink to the bottom and turn into peat. There's pockets of that stuff all over up there, twenty, thirty, maybe forty feet deep."

"So what has to be done, to put the fires out?"

"We'll have to get pumps and hoses and men—a lot of men—and come spring be ready to pump lake water right down into the ground. It's the only way to get a peat fire—drown it good."

Jack shifted in his stance, not so much against the cold as to be able to look away from Philip. "I'll do whatever I can, you know that."

The way he said it, Philip knew there was something wrong. So he asked, "Is there a problem?"

"Yeah. In a way." Jack turned toward Philip and rested a hand on his shoulder. "We're pulling out."

Philip studied his face in the dusklike light that is omnipresent at night in a land covered with snow. The features were determined. "I don't follow you."

"I'm quitting my job and taking my wife and son off the island. I had hoped to leave by June, or whenever the weather allowed."

"I, I don't know what to say, Jack. I'm surprised. Astounded. Are you firm on this?"

"No, not firm. But pretty sure. I think Marion's ready too."

"Think it over, Jack. A decision like that you gotta let sit for a while and then go with your feelings. The decision makes itself. This isn't an easy place to live, Lord knows. But not many wilderness places left."

"I know. Marion loves it. And so does Ricky. And so do I."

"We've had to put up with a lot, Emma and I. There are certain sacrifices you have to make, long-term sacrifices, I mean."

"It's been a while coming on. I think I've known it was going to come to this. Sooner or later."

"I never noticed anything. You never gave a hint of what you were thinking."

"I know. I thought I could ignore it. That if I did, whatever went on in that place would pass right by me. I was wrong, but I didn't care. Then today something happened to Marion. It was a scare, Phil. A bad one. I thought working where she was, she was safe. But she's not. I don't think there's anyplace safe on Scales anymore. If it was just me I was worried about, like I say, I wouldn't care. If I could stay and earn that good money, I'd do it. But if anything ever happened to Marion or Ricky, I don't know what I'd do."

"You know, it's a funny thing. Just the other day Ricky was telling me he was never going to leave the island. I told him he would, but as I thought about it, I think I was mighty happy to hear him say it. I thought just maybe it would be true, that he'd be here forever." Philip spit on the snow leaving a tobacco-stained mark to melt below the surface. Then he allowed himself a kind of laugh and said, "I guess maybe I was just being selfish."

"You're far from that. You're the best man I've ever known, and you damn well better not forget my son because he'll be back to see you, perhaps more than you'd want him."

Smiling, Philip said, "It'll be good for the boy, to get away. And for you two as well."

"Maybe you and Emma should be thinking about it. About leaving, I mean."

"Leave? Us? No," he said with his gravel-voiced toughness. "We couldn't leave Scales. There's no place else for us. We're going to die here, Jack, and I don't think I'd want it any other way." He spoke with neither sadness nor regret, nor fear of the death he envisioned.

"I wish it could've stayed the same for you, the way it was before they built the institution."

"Yeah. It's changed all right."

Jack suddenly rubbed his hands together and shivered audibly, as if he just noticed the cold for the first time. "I just can't explain what it's like inside that place, Philip, and if I could you wouldn't believe it. Whatever freedom, or spirit, or life, or whatever the hell it is we draw from these old rocks under our feet, is smothered in there. I don't really know what it is, but there's something bad about that place. There's something real bad, and someday it's going to overflow those barracks and squeeze right on through those fences." Jack was surprised how easy it was to talk about what he felt. "Does that sound crazy?"

"Nope. It doesn't sound crazy at all. It reminds me of something the nuns used to tell us as kids. I can't say I remember much of what they taught, but I do remember this old-timer telling us a story once about a man who wanted to trap the devil. He felt if he could somehow just get him behind bars that would solve the world's problems. Well, he did it. Don't ask me how, but the nun said he tracked him down and locked him up. As you might have guessed, the world's problems were not solved. The way she described it, I guess evil seeped out of his cell like slime through an old worm bucket. It was just a story to frighten us kids, to get us to think there was nothing we could do about the devil but pray and go to church every day. But there's some truth to it after all, I suppose, at least where Scales is concerned."

"Maybe so. But in there, it's not just the convicts. It's the guards, the doctors, everybody. Whether their door is locked at night or not, it's all the same. That place is not going to last, and I don't want my family to be around at the end."

From across the cove in A-Barracks, the light in Jack and Marion Cooke's window appeared a solitary mote caught in midair reflection by a carefully targeted beam. To the inmate the light seemed to move as a speck of dust would in a closed room. He stared at the light as in his mind it alternately dipped, then floated, then circled almost in place, buffeted ever so mildly by invisible currents of air.

It was a cold light he stared at, and the chill easily penetrated the flimsy garb he wore. Though he had been standing and staring for a full twenty-five minutes, to him the light itself was little more than a focal point for his eyes he had not been able to close. As he had been all evening, he thought of the skinny kid with the long blond hair out in the yard somewhere, the full force of the frigid air bearing down upon him. It was not an empathetic reaction, rather it was the fear of what could happen to him.

From outside his cell he could hear the sonorous moaning of one of the other patients, from one of the other cells. It was a haunting sound, a constant though varied tone, like the changing chords from a violin bow being drawn slowly across the bass strings.

Whatever provocation the skinny kid had committed was lost on him. The inmate could think only of the cold, of the horror of slowly freezing to death. He imagined what it would be like, and as he did, he could almost feel it happening. His skin seemed to grow tighter as if shrinking on his frame. Then it would crack as it crystallized, and blood would ooze to the surface only to freeze as soon as it was exposed to the air. As he thought of it, he could almost feel his skin burning with the cold, then stinging as it would if brine were rubbed in an open wound. He could almost hear it, his skin cracking and peeling in whitened patches.

He folded his arms across his chest and shuddered as the chill crept throughout his body. The light seemed to grow whiter, colder, like some distant sun as viewed from deep in space. Then suddenly it went out. His focal point was gone.

Everything became quiet. Even the moaning that hovered out in the hall like the buzz of gnats in a swamp ceased. A period of stillness followed, as if every heart on the floor stopped beating, as if every pair of lungs stopped pumping. As if every man in A-Barracks suffered the same anxieties he suffered.

Then, very gradually, the stillness seemed to come alive. It came alive with a shuffled movement behind one door, the squeak of bed springs behind another. And then the insistent, almost melodious droning of the baleful voice returned.

The moaning had a spiral effect as it bore slowly into the thoughts of all who heard it, until finally someone cried, "Shut up! God damn it, shut up!" From inside their cells, no one could tell who cried out, but it could have been any one of them for the way they all felt, from the way their nerves seemed to be alive with fear.

The tension was common to them all, and it produced an uncomfortable churning in their stomachs, a quickness of their eyes, a trembling of their hands. It was a feeling of being finally, totally without control. Their freedom lost behind locked doors, their thoughts manipulated or denied by the arbitrary stroke of a doctor's scrawl on a prescription order, and now their very existence became subject to the whims of their captors.

Each man stood alone, in his cell, and in each was a twisting, tortured anxiety that spun ever faster, ever hotter, with fear. In each, emotions melded with thoughts as if their feelings, their ideas were molten slag in some personal, glowing caldron. If the barriers were breached, if the individual caldrons ran together into a vast communal reservoir, it could be imagined the collective slag would swirl together with such energy that it would create a turbulent, flaming mass, an inferno that would melt, then disintegrate every last scrap of stone and mortar and steel that was the Scales Psychiatric Facility.

14

A clump of snow.

At first he thought the dark mound was a dirty clump of snow that had fallen from the building. Closer he walked, and with each step he became more unsure. He glanced to the roof, and from neither edge was there a gap in the overflowing mantle of white. Yet what else could it be? Windblown trash that had been trapped in the corner of the building, then glazed with ice?

As he walked closer, in the gray midmorning light, it appeared a rumpled mass of rags. But there was shape to it, and what came to mind seemed so out of place, so totally impossible as to be absurd. It reminded him of some discarded effigy from a high school pep rally. It looked that unreal.

He touched it and found that it was solid, not at all

what he expected. He could see the shape of a head resting on what appeared to be knees, with hands fixed to the legs in an unshakable grip. Still, it did not resemble a human being. It was so cold, so hard, so unhuman. Though his mind had yet to grasp what it was, some deep-seated dread had slowly, inexplicably begun to build within him. Then he pushed it and it rolled over, and he realized what it was.

He lurched back, his legs almost failing him, his breath catching in his throat as if the freeze had touched his own chest. Though he wished he could, he could not pull his eyes away from that face. They were fixed on the skin that was as white as the snow heaped around him. It was puffy, yet wrinkled, with deep creases between each swollen patch of skin. The lips were split like a meat cleaver had been taken to them, yet there was no blood. At the eyes, clear ice cemented the lids together.

He did not recognize who it was, but he could tell by the clothes and the hair it was not one of them, one of the MCAs. It was one of the convicts, he thought, and he had tried to escape. That was the thought on his mind, the only rational explanation, as he hurried toward the Administration Building.

Reuker Stilkes had the vacuous expression of a nineteenth-century photographic portrait. He stared beyond Huxley, or through him, never really seeing him. As he was escorted from his office, Huxley watched the perfunctory movements of Stilkes. His legs moved slowly, almost awkwardly, and all the while his expression did not change. It was the same as when he had first sat down, when Huxley had tried to talk with him, and when he was asked to go back to A-Barracks. Nothing had any effect on his face, on the thoughts the face masked. It was as if the mind and the body were not of the same man. They were two distinct entities, neither seeing nor acknowledging the existence of the other.

Huxley had not expected Stilkes to have been more communicative than he was the day before. It would take longer for the decrease in the drug dosage to have an impact on his system. He brought Stilkes to his office to make him feel more comfortable there, to be at ease with him and with the talks he was hoping to establish into a routine.

There was another reason Huxley wanted to see Stilkes again, less than twenty-four hours after the first visit. It was more to do with the needs of the doctor than the patient. Never before in his intellectual career had Huxley had to wait for what he wanted. Whatever academic or professional goal he set for himself, it was simply a matter of drawing on his vast reservoir of energy to attain it. Achievement of a particular goal may have taken time, but it was always in his hands. There was no one else he had to wait for. Until now.

The Stilkes mystery was before him, and so much of the answer he sought depended on his being able to peel away Stilkes's defenses and peer inside the man's thoughts, his motivations, his ideals. And that, Huxley knew, depended on communication between Stilkes and himself.

Huxley pulled the stack of manila folders from Stilkes's bulky file once again. Though ultimately everything depended on waiting for Stilkes to communicate the bits and pieces of his past that would enable Huxley to get a grasp on his violent behavior, Huxley knew he would not have to be merely a passive observer up to that point. He could encourage Stilkes to remember, he would prompt him with what he could glean from the file. The slightest fact, the most inconsequential detail could be the exact spark to start him off. Huxley would not know what it was, and so he felt he had to know everything there was to know about Stilkes and his background and his crimes.

He had pored over all the old newspaper clippings a number of times, but still he found himself drawn to the stark facts and circumstances they described. It was as though jealousy drew him to the stories. He envied the straightforward, journalistic prose that revealed its part of the story with such ease.

MISSING WOMAN FOUND MURDERED read the double-column headline. It was a *Detroit Free Press* article, dated October 7, 1978:

> The body of Dorothy Norvicki was discovered early yesterday morning by mushroom pickers in a

wooded section of Kent Lake Metro Park.

Police cordoned off the area and were keeping an unusually tight lid on the details of the killing, saying only that the 48-year-old mother of three had apparently not been sexually molested.

A source close to the investigation indicated that the body had been mutilated with numerous slashing blows. The police would neither confirm nor deny, saying only that the continuing rains have hampered their investigation by destroying potential clues.

Mrs. Norvicki had been reported missing last Tuesday. . . .

Next to the column of print was a photograph of an obviously younger Mrs. Norvicki, taken at least a decade before. She had a peculiar smile, as if nervously looking just beyond the camera, as if, Huxley imagined, she looked uncertainly at a slender man with deep-set eyes approaching her on the street. Of course she could not have been, Huxley knew, but the thought provoked him, and as he stared at her quavering half-smile, he wondered if there was anything in it that had provoked Stilkes in a different manner.

He wondered what was it about her that had elicited such a response from Stilkes. The way she walked, or spoke, or the clothes she wore? Could she have reminded him of someone, either by appearance or affect, who touched a deep anger within him? The questions tumbled through his mind as he stared at the yellowed news photo, and with each question came the same frustrating response. He just did not know.

Looking for answers, he fingered through the news clipping file. He hoped to find another picture of Mrs. Norvicki, or pictures of other victims. But there were none. He went to the manila folder with POLICE lettered on the index tab. Surely the homicide file would have photos of the victims, if only the morgue shots. He checked, but the file contained only the detectives' summary of the various investigations and a few related documents. It was obvious only a selection of what must have been a voluminous homicide file had been photocopied and included with his psychiatric records.

Huxley shuffled through the papers again. Clipped between two pages was a half-sheet with a photocopy of a photograph. He slipped it from between the pages and looked more closely at it. It appeared a typical snapshot from a family album: a mother with her child. In the margin of the photograph, barely discernible in the copy, they were identified as Rebecca and Reuker Stilkes.

The black-and-white copy was a poor imitation of the photograph, two steps removed from reality. Standing there side by side, their features distorted and made imprecise by the shadows of the machine, they seemed as though pulling away from Huxley. It was as if they revealed only a hint of their true identities. They came close to showing themselves but held back, taunting him with mute deception.

Huxley held the photocopy next to the newspaper picture of Dorothy Norvicki. He shifted them under the light, looking from one to the other, but it was no use trying to compare the two women; one's appearance was all too prophetically real, and the other's a mere ghost of an image.

Though he could discern no significant similarities, nor obvious differences, Huxley began to get the feeling that perhaps he held in his hands a key to explaining the killings. What was the relationship in Reuker's eyes, between the woman so dominant in his early life and the women he later murdered? What effect had Rebecca had on her son that could have led to his later acts? As the questions formed one after another in his head, Huxley sensed a building excitement within himself. He felt a growing exhilaration as his nervous energy propelled him forward, for the moment at least no longer directionless.

But there was an interruption. The guard Jack Cooke wanted to see him, the female voice on the intercom said. Huxley hesitated for a second before saying to show him in.

Jack had been in A-Barracks when Stilkes was led back in from visiting Huxley. Jack watched as he walked past, and there was something different about him. His face still carried his blank stare, but there was something else. Deep in the pits of his eyes. A fear? A tension? A desperation.

He had been waiting for a chance to go see Huxley

himself about Eddie Hyland, but as he walked through the tunnels, it was Stilkes he was thinking about.

"You lied to me about Eddie. You had no intention of changing his—" Jack paused, eyeing him coldly, "—therapy."

Huxley was caught off guard by Jack's directness. "It's not my practice to let other people tell me what's best for my patients."

"You used her as bait. You tempted Hyland with her just so you could see what he'd do. You left her exposed and unprotected."

"My theory was sound. There was no indication he'd be a risk."

Jack maintained his calm, his eyes still locked on Huxley's. "There was every indication. You just refused to see it. You had something you wanted to accomplish, and to hell with anything or anybody else."

"I resent that. I've never exposed anybody to a danger I wouldn't assume myself."

"The difference is you know the danger and if you choose to play with fire, that's up to you. But you have no right making decisions like that for other people."

"If you work in a place like this, you have to accept certain risks."

"Risks that are known, and that you try to minimize. With Marion, you gave Eddie more freedom, increasing the risks deliberately just to see what he would do."

For Huxley it wasn't worth arguing anymore. It was obvious he had lost the guard's cooperation with Stilkes. "I have to get back to my work." He pushed the flat button at the bottom of the intercom and asked that the guard be shown out.

At the door Jack turned back to face him. "You may have thought your treatment was necessary, but you were wrong. I just hope this experience is something you remember."

"Thank you for your input, Mr. Cooke."

After Jack left, Huxley sat staring at the closed door, his fingers tapping out a staccato rhythm on the scattered papers of Stilkes's file. It was a few moments before he could shake the interruption from his mind.

He tried to recapture the same flow of thoughts he had had, just before Jack came in. He shuffled through the papers, the clippings. He looked at the imperfect photographs, then he picked up the phone and through the control center requested a line to the mainland. As he did, he searched again through the police file until he found the name of the officer in charge of the investigation: Lt. James McDaniel. He dialed police headquarters in Detroit and was put through to Homicide.

"No, just missed him," said a voice that sounded like tumbling gravel. "He's out to lunch. Every day, between eleven and twelve. You get regular when you become the inspector."

"I wanted to talk to him about one of his old cases."

"How old?"

"It goes back about five years."

The detective laughed. "Stilkes, right?"

"Yes."

"Why don't you talk to his old partner, Simpson. He's sitting right here."

"No, that's okay. Just have McDaniel call me back."

"You a reporter?"

"No. I'm Dr. Huxley, from the Department of Corrections."

"Uh huh," the voice drawled. "Well, Doc, if I were you I'd call him. He's not so good about returning calls. Try just after noon, before he's had a chance to get into something else."

"All right. I'll do that." Huxley hung up and tapped his fingers nervously on his desk. An hour to wait.

Peter Hagan stood at his office window staring out into the yard. His hands were clasped behind his back, and with the thumb of his left hand he was alternately clicking each of his fingernails. His lower lip puffed outward in his exaggerated pout.

Someone knocked on the door. "Come in," Hagan called without looking around.

Arnie Johnson stepped in, first looking toward the desk, then about the large room until he spied the director at the far window. His back was to him. "You wanted to see me?"

"Yes. Sit down."

Johnson looked around the room, wondering where he should be seated. The chairs facing the desk? Or by the window directly next to Hagan? He chose in between, sitting at a cushiony sofa along the wall.

Though Hagan stood as though barely aware the guard was in the room, he was all too acutely aware he was there. He waited because he wanted to make sure he had total control of himself before turning to face the man. What was on his mind was unsettling.

He had hounded the legislature for three years for the funds to build his model psychiatric facility, and then he succeeded only because of the Supreme Court case that ordered something be done. Then he watched the place get built, and he had run it for the full seven years of its existence. Hagan was fifty-two years old. He knew in all likelihood he wasn't moving up in the department, and he didn't want to. Scales was his, and he had fought hard to keep it alive, to keep it a model psychiatric facility. And no one anywhere had a harder job, considering where they built the place and the people they gave him to staff it. Yet it was working, and in those seven years there had not been one death by other than natural causes at the Facility. It was a record unmatched at any corrections facility of any kind anywhere in the country. But now comes Jeremy Willet.

Yesterday when he had walked the visiting senators to their plane across the ice of Lake Siskiwit, Clyde Watson had apparently sensed Hagan's worries because he had made a point of taking him aside to give his assurances. He had said what really put him behind Scales, despite the outbreak in the cafeteria—and indeed, partly because of that and the way it was handled—was that there was no record of physical violence at the institution. No one had been killed, and that meant, he had said, "that you and your men are doing a good job. If it were any different, though I disagree with about everything he says, on our report I may have been inclined to go along with O'Connell."

As Arnie sat waiting for Hagan, a gumminess thickened at the back of his throat. In the stillness of the room, with the only noise the clicking of Hagan's fingernails, he was afraid to move, afraid to make a sound. He swallowed quietly, but the saliva felt like slime clinging to the inside of his mouth. Finally, he had to clear his throat. And that seemed to jar Hagan from his thoughts.

"So tell me what you know about Willet," Hagan said, hands still clasped behind him, gaze still fixed out the window.

"What about him?"

"You can start with how he died." The words were curt, the tone sharp.

"He froze to death," said Arnie, and he managed a nervous laugh. Hagan turned and glared at him, and the laugh died in his throat. He shifted in his seat, then continued, "I guess it happened like they said. He tried to bust out and didn't make it beyond the fences."

"Where do you think he was going?" Hagan was calmer, in control again.

"I don't know. Maybe to one of the abandoned places across the bay."

"To do what? Set up house?"

Arnie laughed again. "I guess not." He was nervous, and he tried to cover that feeling. "We'll probably never know. It's hard to say what's going on in the heads of some of these crazies. I've been with 'em every day for quite a while now, and I still can't figure them out. They do things that even they couldn't tell you why they did it."

Hagan turned from the window and nodded, as if in agreement with Johnson. "You're right, I suppose, in some cases," he said as he walked across the room. He picked up a straight-backed chair and maneuvered it so it faced the guard. When he sat down, he was slightly higher, and somehow more formal, than Johnson. Arnie shifted again in his seat, uncrossed his legs, and sat straighter.

"What I guess I'd like to know from you is, how the kid could have gotten out of A-Barracks."

"I don't know. I went off duty at six."

"Yes, I know. But I've talked to the other guards that were on duty and they tell me they didn't notice a thing last night. Nobody climbing out windows, asking for the keys. None of that."

The sarcasm in Hagan's voice nipped at Johnson's temper, but he held it. "They must've missed it. That Willet kid was a quiet one. Always felt he was a sneaky son of a bitch."

"That so?" Hagan mused. "Well, why don't you try

to help me figure out how he did it. You've been around lockups a long time, longer than anybody here. You should know all the tricks."

"I know my share, but no way can I keep up with them. I found out at Jackson that when your only thing in life is to dream up a way to get out, even the dumb ones come up with some pretty good ideas."

"Let's just say he was outside all along. He never came in from the exercise period. Is that possible?"

"No, because like I said, I was there until six and was there when he came in. And besides, if somehow a mistake had been made and he was left outside, don't you think he would have banged on the door, or called out for somebody, or gone to another building?"

"You'd think so," Hagan said. "And that's what I thought at first. But then I read his file and it all made sense—him being locked out and then just crawling into a corner to die by himself. In fact, if he had done anything else I would have been surprised. He did exactly as you'd expect."

"Nope. Still couldn't have happened. If he was missing it would have been noticed at the room check at eight."

"I know, and that's a problem, if I am to think he never came in, to escape later, but was outside all the time. But then I thought, what if he was locked out, deliberately. Would one of the other MCAs turn in the guy who did it? One of their friends? Or would they cover for him?" Hagan seemed intent on the inquiry, as if already certain of the conclusion. "What would you do, if it were one of your friends?"

Arnie had that cornered look on his face. He smiled lamely and said, "Well, I don't know. Depends on the situation, I guess."

"Yes, I'm sure it would. And if somebody died, some rotten little creep who you thought was a son of a bitch, you'd cover, wouldn't you?"

"Hey, there's no cause to start talkin' like that to me."

"You know what I think? I think you're responsible for Willet's death."

"You have no proof."

"You locked him outside and let him freeze to death."

"I don't know what you're talkin' about."

"You murdered him as sure as putting a bullet between

his eyes. Only that would have been more humane."

"I don't have to take this crap from you," Arnie said, bolting off the couch.

"You do as long as I'm in charge here."

"You think you're really in charge here, don't you? Well, you don't know shit."

Hagan slowly raised himself out of his chair, all the while his stare fixed on Johnson. His cheeks were flame-red. "I know the difference between discipline and murder."

"If somebody hadn't made a lesson of Willet after what happened, they'd be running this place day after tomorrow, and we'd be the ones in the cells. And then you'd see what inhumane treatment really was."

"You're gone from here, mister."

"In case you didn't know, there ain't no place worse than here."

"You're out of Corrections, completely, and without your pension. You can count on me seeing to that, as soon as I can get you without hurting Scales."

"You can say whatever the fuck you want. But it don't scare me in the least."

Hagan stepped by Johnson and walked to the door. Opening it for the guard, he said, "If I were you, it wouldn't be me I'd be afraid of."

At five after twelve, the control center was a man short, and Huxley had to wait a few minutes to get a line to the mainland. He was irritated with the waiting, and the annoyance from Jack's interruption lingered. When he got through to Homicide, Inspector James McDaniel was at his desk.

"My name is Dr. Huxley, from the Department of Corrections, and I'm calling because I need some information from one of your files."

"What kind of information?"

"Do you remember Reuker Stilkes?"

Except for a high-pitched electronic whine that whistled faintly from some point in the long distance connection, the phone went silent. "McDaniel? You there?" Huxley said.

"Yeah, I know Stilkes. What about him?"

"He's my patient and his treatment requires I have a look at your file."

"His treatment? He coming along well in this . . . this treatment?"

"He will, after I've had a chance to work with him."

McDaniel wheezed as if asthmatic, then broke into his hacking smoker's cough. He made no effort to cover the phone, and Huxley had to listen as the cough rumbled at him from 450 miles away until McDaniel cleared his throat and spit. "I wonder," he said at last, "if he makes progress, might somebody get the idea he's okay to release."

"That's not your concern."

"Why is it exactly you want to see my file?"

"To help me learn why he did it. To get a clearer picture of his episodes of dysfunction. To actually see the photographs of the women he acted out on, to find out what they had in common that caused him to do what he did."

"What *they* had to cause him to do what he did?" McDaniel was so astonished he laughed. "I think you got something backwards. About all they did was be vulnerable."

Huxley snorted. "I didn't call to get into a psychological discussion with you. I doubt very seriously if our communication would be on the same level. I called because I want your file, and sorry if I seem to push, but I want it sent out today."

"Well, don't take too much offense, Dr. Huxley, but I can tell you right now I don't like you." He spoke in a tone that belied his meaning. "But that alone is not why I'm not going to send you my file. I work with people every day I don't especially like, but I deal with them because I have to, and we do operate on the same level. But you're different. I know because I've met hundreds of doctors and lawyers and judges who talk just like you. You think that a guy like Stilkes . . ."

"Now just a minute, McDaniel," Huxley interrupted.

"No, no. Let me finish. Okay?"

There was a pause, then Huxley said, "Go ahead." He really had no other choice.

"You think that Stilkes is not responsible for what he did because something in his head he couldn't control made him do it. A sociologist may have a slightly different excuse than you, but it adds up to the same thing: The people, or maybe even the victim, is to blame. If you've listened to as much of that kind of stuff as I have, you might get to thinking that it's almost as if guys like you enjoy coming up with complicated explanations for things, if only to justify all those diplomas on your wall." McDaniel started to hack again, but he caught himself, forcing himself to go on. His voice was suddenly much raspier. "But believe me, Doc. There's nothing tricky about it. There's no mystery why somebody like Stilkes is the way that he is. They're born that way. They have it in their blood and anytime they can get something out of it, they won't hesitate to kill or maim or torture again and again and again. So if you think I'm going to help you help Stilkes, you can kiss my ass."

"You don't have a choice," Huxley shouted into the receiver. "Stilkes is mine now and I order you to send me whatever you have on him."

"Go to hell," McDaniel said, his quiet tone not disguising his contempt. Then the line went dead.

Huxley sat there with the receiver at his ear, as if disbelieving the detective had hung up on him. Slowly he pulled himself out of his chair as he listened for McDaniel to come back on, but the only thing he heard was the shrill whine of distant cables.

It was the control center that finally broke in. "Need another line, Dr. Huxley?"

He slammed the phone down. Stilkes was his, he thought, and nothing would stop his probing of the man's background, his investigation into his illness. Nothing would stop his manner of treatment of Reuker Stilkes.

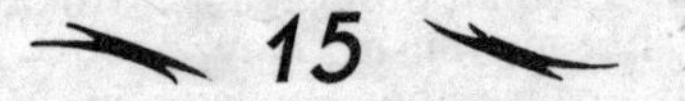

15

Huxley waited two days before bringing Stilkes back to his office. The decrease of the mind drug he hoped would have had a chance to bring about a change in Stilkes. He hoped he would be more lucid in his comments, clearer in his memory.

As the MCA led him down the hallway, Dr. Neil Lummer came out of his office. He watched as Stilkes stepped through Huxley's door, then before the MCA could close it, he pushed his way through.

Huxley reacted quickly, stepping past Stilkes to confront Lummer. "What do you want?"

"I've got something to say to you."

"You can say it outside," Huxley said, gripping Lummer's arm and leading him toward the door.

"Afraid your patient will think less of you? That he'll see you for the conniving bastard you are?"

Outside the office Huxley slammed the door. "So suddenly, after two years, you're concerned about Stilkes."

"It's the way you did it, Huxley. You made me look like a fool."

"That's one thing you can do on your own."

Lummer's eyes flared, then within seconds the fire was gone. A calmness bred of disgust seemed to settle over him. "You're going to fail. You're going to fuck with his head and you're going to end up paying for it."

Lummer is the embodiment of everything that is wrong with psychiatry, Huxley thought. "I don't need a lecture from you on how to deal with a patient." He turned to leave, but Lummer grabbed his arm.

"He was under control. And with Stilkes, that's all you can hope for."

Reuker Stilkes was sitting in the same chair he'd sat in during his two previous visits.

He licked his chapped lips with a moistureless tongue. The dryness was always there, in his mouth and the back of his throat, but for some reason he now seemed to be more aware of it as he sat there, waiting for the doctor to come back. He did not like this place, the office. His mind did not search for reasons he felt that way, it only reacted to the feeling of discomfort, to the very real sensation that the room meant pain. He had known another room like that, a tiled room, and as the memory entered his head, he could picture that room and he could picture himself as a young boy in that room. He pictured himself wet and cold, awakening in an empty tub, with no one around. He didn't remember exactly when it was—there were so many times, they all blended together—but there was a single constant each time he awoke in the drained tub. His head ached with a pain so fierce he could barely walk.

With just a suggestion of that pain returning, Reuker stood abruptly, clasping his arms together against his chest, and he began to pace toward the far wall. As he did, he lost all temporal awareness. The desk seemed to shoot past him on the left, as if he were standing still and the entire room were yanked past him by some unseen yet overwhelming power. The room flashed by him in a blur, like trees pass the window of a speeding train, and he found himself at the wall opposite the bank of chairs.

It had started at breakfast, or perhaps even before, at night, when he had lain in bed filled with restless energy he had grown used to not having. It continued, randomly, throughout the morning. And each time it happened, the experience left him bewildered. His life at Scales had become predictable, routine, and because of that, possessed of a certain peace. Now something different was happening to him, to his world, and it scared him.

In the morning, as he awoke, he felt as he usually did. He arose slowly, leaden limbs anchoring him to the mattress. His mind was blank, his thoughts focused only on what he was seeing and doing at that moment. As always, any effort to remember was fruitless. It would end in frustration or fatigue, and in either case, it was the drugs that prevented him from linking his thoughts together in a series. If he tried, the chain would break and the ideas collapse.

Yet at breakfast, in the cafeteria, he had gone from the line to his table in an instant. And in that instant his vision was a blur, and the voices and kitchen sounds he had always barely noticed before seemed to screech out at him in a deafening racket. Each time the phenomenon recurred, it was the same. He would be moving as though in a dream, then suddenly everything—what he saw, heard, thought—would unaccountably whoosh by him, like a motion picture film speeded beyond the limits that its images can be visualized. Shapes flashed by his eyes, their outlines indistinct yet the colors somehow brighter and more vibrant. Sounds blared inaudibly, and thoughts raced through his mind too fast for him to grasp until the pressure within his head seemed unbearable. Then suddenly, just as it started, it was over. He was left in his own world, but left spinning, confused, frightened. As he tried to think, to piece together what happened, his thoughts would break away from each other like they always had before. Whatever semblance of logic he approached would quickly disintegrate into indistinguishable segments. His concentration failed, and questions that a moment before were frantically posed died in obscurity. The confusion dissolved, and he was again in some manner of drugged peace.

Huxley swung the door open and returned to his office, propelled by his anger with Lummer. When he saw Stilkes standing by the couch, his arms folded protectively against his chest and his face awash with confusion, he stopped in his tracks. Closing the door gently, he said, "Sit down. Please. Wherever you like."

Stilkes appeared lost and indecisive. He looked across the room, at the chairs, then slowly sank to the couch.

"That's good, that's good," Huxley said as he walked past Stilkes to his desk. He punched the record button on a tape recorder, then picked up a spiral note pad. "How are you feeling today?"

"Fine," Stilkes said.

Huxley maneuvered his desk chair closer to the couch and Stilkes. "I'm glad to hear that. I've changed your medicine a little, to try to make you more comfortable. Have you noticed a change?"

Reuker looked across the room at the square-backed chair where he had sat before, and it seemed so far away, so removed from where he was now, like he was peering through the wrong end of a telescope. The doctor's voice warbled in his ears, a nervous tremolo in time with his own anxiety. The doctor, the room, the voice all combined to touch a feeling that had long been dormant: He felt unclean.

Sitting across from him, Huxley watched Stilkes carefully, especially the eyes and the tenseness in the face. The man was more alert—he was sure of it. And Huxley was anxious to break through to him. "We're going to talk today. I'll ask some questions and you'll answer them, or say anything else you like. It's time you started to help me. I know you can, and you will, starting now."

The words spun through a descending tube, as if swirling through a funnel before reaching his ears. He heard and, at last, understood. "What is it you want of me?" he said.

His voice was strong and direct, and because of that, it startled Huxley. It was the first time there was that kind of contact. "I want you to tell me about your mother." The stare did not change; there was no attempt to speak. "What did she look like, your mother? Start by describing her to me."

Reuker looked away, and as he did, he tried to picture her. She was there, in his memory, but somehow distant. He could see her shape and she faced him, but any features were obscured by a darkened veil that was draped between them. She was obscured by its folds and shadows. He opened his mouth to describe what he saw, but as he did, she appeared to pull back, deeper into the dark. He tried to step closer, but she became even less distinct. The image was gone, and as it disappeared he was left groping in the dark, seeing nothing, remembering nothing.

"Reuker. Your mother. What did she look like?" There was no response, and to Huxley he appeared no different from the first two meetings. Huxley grabbed Stilkes's knee and shook it. Reuker reacted with fear, staring at him wide-eyed. "Listen to me." Huxley spoke loudly. "Tell me about her, about you and her. What do you remember most about living with her? What did you like best about her? Or didn't like?" The questions came rapid-fire, Huxley's veneer of patience wearing through.

Stilkes could feel the intensity of Huxley's voice, he could sense the anger. And he could sense the evil. It was the reason, he suddenly realized, for the nervousness he felt coming to this room, for the things that had been happening to him that he did not understand. This man had an aura of evil about him, and it was engulfing those near him, who associated with him. Reuker recoiled into the cushions of the sofa, retreating from the barrage of questions.

Huxley released his grip and leaned back in the chair. Watching Stilkes's reaction, he let himself calm before trying again. "All right," he said after a few moments. "We'll talk about something else. Anything else. Whatever you want. But we will talk."

Reuker watched him carefully. He agreed, he nodded,

anything to keep the man back, to keep the evil from touching him.

"Tell me about that summer after fourth grade, when you were in the U.P. Did you like it in the woods?"

Reuker nodded again. "I did." He was nervous, but rigidly he kept his posture.

"What was it about the woods that you liked?"

"I don't know. I just liked it." He spoke fast, his answers a shield against the man's evil.

"I did too, when I was a kid. I went to summer camp once, in upstate New York. It's a lot like northern Michigan, with lakes and rivers and such. I think I liked the canoeing best, over fast water. Did you do any of that?"

"Yes," he said, then quickly corrected himself. "No, I was never in a canoe, but I liked the river."

"The water always seemed so clear, but cold."

"Yes." Reuker was tense, as though every muscle strained to resist the assault.

"It seemed so peaceful, so quiet in the woods."

Reuker exhaled almost breathlessly, barely able to mouth his agreement. What he said left his thoughts as soon as it left his lips. He was reacting to what the doctor said as if his words were darts aimed for his face. Each inquiry was an intrusive projectile he struggled to divert, by saying something, anything, to keep them away. But the darts came faster.

"You were with Billy, that summer. Weren't you?"

"Yes."

"He was your cousin, wasn't he? A few years older?"

Reuker nodded, then forced himself to say, "Two years older." He was shaking, cold with sweat streaming down his sides. He wanted it to end, to be out of there, but Huxley kept it up. As he talked, his voice seemed to grow louder, his syllables distorted. Reuker began to lose the meaning of the words, and as he did, Huxley seemed to become all the louder, all the more threatening. Stilkes fought a whimper building in his chest.

"Who else was with you, in the woods?" Huxley asked. "Any friends . . . Friends . . . FRIENDS . . .?"

The word flashed in his head like brilliant neon against the night. It blared louder, brighter, and then Huxley suddenly leaned forward again, coming closer. He split in two distinct but identical images, and as he did, just like before, at breakfast, the images shot by him, along either side. Reuker did not move, but Huxley, the desk, the chairs, everything in the room seemed to flash by him in an accelerating blur. It was as if his entire world raced out of control. He was deluged with shapes, words, ideas—each a fragment of some indecipherable whole.

He was frozen in place as each fragment flashed by. Then very gradually the noises, the voices diminished, until he sat in silence. The fragments grew less distinct, losing color, losing their vibrancy. They became like chips, shavings of wood.

Billy sliced through the wood cleanly and quickly, each stroke dropping papery strips into a pile at his feet. The point of the stick grew progressively sharper with each rapid downward thrust of his jackknife. Billy glanced up at his nine-year-old cousin, who was watching him intently. Reuker sat on a fallen tree that was wedged between two others, so that its trunk was held in permanent descent, two feet above the forest floor.

Playing to the younger boy's fascination, Billy whittled faster, with a certain flourish to his strokes. "It's not easy, fashioning a good stick," he said. "You have to choose the right wood, have the right knife, slice without going too deep. That's the hardest part, keeping it even, not going too deep." He paused to examine the tip, twisting it in front of his eyes as a craftsman inspects his art. "It takes a fine touch."

"Can I try?" Reuker was practically beaming.

"Do you have a knife?"

"No."

"You don't expect me to let you use mine?"

"Can I?"

"No. You'd ruin it." Billy quickly rose to his feet, folded the blade, and slipped it into his pocket. "There," he said, holding the stick out in front of him, and in front of his cousin. The oak stake was cleaned of its bark, one inch in diameter, and honed to a pinpoint tip.

Just as Reuker reached for the stick, Billy pulled it back. "Let's go," he said, and was off, talking as he usually did, in his stream-of-consciousness manner. He told Reuker of the need for a good staff in the woods, then he talked of the dangers of the woods, then of the unreliability of other people. "You can trust nobody," Billy said, then he stopped in his tracks to glare accusingly at Reuker. "Least of all those who pretend to be close." Reuker felt a sudden pang of guilt, though for what he did not know, and he protested loudly to Billy, assuring him he trusted him and believed whatever he said. "You'd better," said Billy, "or you would be real sorry. No one else looks out for you like me."

Then he was off again, his tongue flitting to other topics as rapidly as his mind conjured new thoughts. It was too fast for Reuker to keep pace, and because of that, he seemed to be kept continually off guard by his older cousin.

For July it was a cool day, but not terribly unusual for that Upper Peninsula area near Lake Superior. A thunderstorm had blown through the night before, enlivening the sky with its jagged arcs of lightning. The vegetation was coated with moisture, and both boys' pants legs were wet and their shoes glistening. There was a high sky overcast with clouds the color of wet linen, but to them below the trees it made little difference.

Billy waved his stick in front of him as he walked, swishing wet ferns to either side of his path. The path collapsed behind him, the ferns springing back to shower Reuker with a fine spray of droplets.

The topic changed suddenly again as Billy asked, "What are you going to do in the fall?"

"I, I don't know," Reuker said, a tentative catch to his voice. He had preferred not to consider that eventuality, fearing the answer would be a return downstate to Alkmaar and to school.

"You want to go back to your old school?"

"No!"

"Of course you don't. You're much better here." Billy paused to glance over his shoulder at his cousin, then continued forward. "But you'll have to. And you'll be dropped a grade because you skipped all last year. They do that to only the real dumb kids, you know."

"I'm not going back there. I won't."

Billy laughed and glanced over his shoulder again. He turned away, and his laugh erupted even louder, and as it continued, it carried a kind of sadistic, wicked melody. Reuker could feel it, and it hurt. His cousin was laughing so long and so hard that it was obvious he was thinking of something more than what Reuker had just said. "What is it?" Reuker demanded, grabbing Billy on the shoulder. "What do you know about this fall?"

"A secret. I know a secret."

The challenge dropped from Reuker's voice. "What? Am I going back?"

Billy stared into Reuker's eyes, drawing out the moment, as if he enjoyed the touch of panic he saw. Finally he responded. "No. You're not going back," and he turned and resumed his trek.

As Billy turned and continued to push his way through the ferns, Reuker Stilkes was leaving Dr. Huxley's office and on his way back to A-Barracks. Though he moved with languorous ease and did as the MCA instructed, his mind was seventeen years away and his eyes were not really seeing the halls of the Medical Building, the descending steps to the tunnel, and finally the sterile blankness of his cell. During the entire walk he never came out of the safety of his dream.

"How do you know?" he could hear himself saying in the voice of a nine-year-old boy.

"A couple nights ago I listened to my mom talking to yours in your mom's bedroom. She said you're not going back to Alkmaar."

"Then where are we going? Will we stay here?"

"Wouldn't you like to know?"

"Tell me," Reuker pleaded.

"Why should I tell you? You weren't supposed to hear."

"Neither were you, and you did."

"That's different. I was doing it for you."

Reuker sensed a helplessness come over him. "I want to stay here," he said feebly.

"You can't," Billy said. He made no attempt to soften the harsh edge to his voice. "My mom said so. At least, that's what she told your mom."

"Why?"

"She doesn't like you, Reuker. Or maybe it's my dad. He was mad about what you did to Wellers' cat."

"I didn't do that! You did." Reuker sounded frantic.

Billy laughed, then said, "That's not what he thinks." Reuker started to protest, but Billy cut him off. "Ah, so what about what he thinks. He wouldn't hit you; you're not his son. And I think he's afraid of your mom. He thinks she'd put a spell on him. Anyway, he already thinks you're a bad influence on me."

"But I'm not!"

"That's exactly what I've told him before. I've told him I'm helping you, that without me you're lost. But what do you expect? He's just a drunk. He don't understand things."

Reuker fell silent as he trudged along behind Billy, the ferns slapping water all over him. His world seemed in turbulent uncertainty again, and even those he thought cared for him didn't. After a few rare moments of silence with Billy, he summoned the courage to ask, "So what will be happening to me in September?"

It was as if Billy had been waiting for him to ask. He looked back at Reuker and broke into a wide grin. His mouth seemed lost between his fleshy cheeks, but the taunting nature of the expression was unmistakable.

"Tell me, Billy."

The older boy merely laughed, then broke into a run.

"Billy!" Reuker screamed. "Billy, come back!"

But Billy didn't stop. He pushed on, trampling a path through the ferns and dodging around trees. All the while he laughed, and with the exertion, his laugh became higher in pitch until he sounded like the cackling adolescent he was.

Reuker ran after his cousin, shouting for him to stop, to tell him what he knew. Slowly he gained on him, until suddenly he saw that Billy had stopped dead in his tracks. Reuker was up to him in no time. Nearly breathless, Reuker said, "You have to tell me. It's not fair!"

Billy silenced him with an upraised hand. "Look," he said, pointing to the ground near the bottom of a wide-trunked maple. The tree had a large cavity in its base near the ground, Reuker noticed at first, and it seemed to rise partway up the trunk. Then he saw it, just a few feet from the hole. There was a raccoon, fully grown and with grizzled, grayish fur near its snout. It was slumped forward on its chest, both front legs awkwardly buckled underneath it, but it was very much alive. Its glare was razor-sharp as it eyed the boys. Near it was a large fallen branch as wide as some trunks of small trees, and Reuker could see its yellowed and rotted wood where it had torn loose from the maple. Up the trunk, maybe twenty feet from the ground, a scar that matched the end of the branch could be seen.

Billy took a step sideways, and as he did, the raccoon maneuvered itself with its back feet so that it remained facing him. Billy inched closer, and the raccoon hissed, pulling itself ever so slightly backward. The reaction electrified Billy, and he turned quickly to Reuker, his eyes wide and his face wild with excitement. "His legs are busted and he can't move. We got 'im!"

The raccoon snarled in response, recoiling its head close to its body. The creature, though immobile and nearly helpless, was no less defiant.

Billy moved within a few feet and held his stick poised before it. The raccoon's eyes were trained on the sharpened point, its entire body tensed to defend itself. Billy waved the stick in small circles in front of the animal's face, in a tantalizing, hypnotic motion. Suddenly he thrust it forward, and the raccoon reacted instantly. It lurched at the barkless stick and for just a moment had it in its teeth. Billy yanked it back and examined where the raccoon had snapped at it.

"Will you look at this," he said, holding the oak staff out for Reuker to see. Narrow, pinpoint holes were sunk deep into the hard wood, and where the stick had been yanked free, its velvety, exposed skin was torn. Reuker imagined it a gash across Billy's skin, his own skin, and he took a step back from the animal.

The raccoon emitted a guttural hiss like a cat in a fight, and as it did, saliva oozed from its mouth and drooled in a gummy string to the ground. Its mouth was open just enough to bare its rows of tiny, needle-sharp teeth.

"I got an idea," Billy said, dropping his stick. He untied the rope that served as his belt and pulled it from his waist. "If we can get this around his back legs, we'll really have 'im."

"Okay," Reuker said, captivated by the unfolding adventure.

"Good. I'll take his head, you get behind it. Here, take the rope."

Reuker took the length of rope and walked uncertainly around behind the raccoon. As he moved, it watched him, slowly rotating its head to keep him in view.

"Hey," Billy shouted, and the raccoon turned back toward him. He jabbed at it with his stick, and with a spitting snarl it snapped at the thrusting wood. "Go on, get its legs," Billy said as he continued to threaten the raccoon with the stick.

"I don't think I can. I don't know what to do."

"Go on, hurry up, before he gets me."

"I can't."

"Do it. Get the rope around his legs."

Reuker inched forward, bending lower at the knees as he moved, but keeping his upper body rigid and pulled back.

"Hurry," Billy wheezed as he continued to joust with the short but pointed snout of the animal.

Reuker crouched, his knees almost touching the ground. He studied the coiled rear haunches of the raccoon, trying to decide where to grab it. As he did, the churning growl was punctuated by its quick, snapping lurches toward Billy.

"Quit shittin' around and do it," Billy yelled.

The younger boy reached for the animal's legs, but before he touched the fur, the raccoon swirled around and snapped at Reuker's hand. He pulled it away, but the raccoon seemed possessed of a madness. It snapped again, its body flopping on its useless front legs like a seal on ice.

From behind the raccoon Billy jumped forward and braced his staff across the back of its neck. With the animal's head pinned to the ground, Billy shouted for Reuker to get the feet.

Reuker sprang past its head in one fluid movement. He grabbed its legs and tried to pull them back, but the raccoon kicked them free. Its claws were extended and its legs flailed without direction. A trickle of blood appeared on Reuker's hands, and he instinctively pulled his arm back. But there was no pain, and again he grabbed the creature's legs.

"Come on. I can't hold it much longer," Billy warned.

Reuker looped the rope around the legs just above the ankles and tied them tightly together. "Got it," he said excitedly and then jumped back.

Billy leaped to the side, releasing the raccoon's head from under his stick. Freed, the animal lashed its teeth from side to side in a futile show of aggression. With its four limbs immobilized, it could do little but flop around on its stomach like a catfish in the mud.

"What are we going to do with him?" Reuker's voice was almost a whisper, as if a conspiracy had to be concealed.

"I don't know yet," Billy said, then he reached for his stick. "Mean little bastard, isn't he?"

"Yeah." Reuker started to bend down, to look closer, and as he did, Billy suddenly jumped up and spun around.

"What's that?" Reuker said.

"Quiet!"

Reuker was afraid to move, so he stayed where he was, in his half-crouching, half-standing position. He watched Billy who, except for the rapid darting of his eyes, was as still as Reuker. They listened to that special quiet heard only in the forest where all sounds are muffled by the vegetation, and sharp noises die echoless. Overlaying everything is the constant rhythm of the uppermost leaves rubbing their serrated edges together in the breeze.

As they listened, the natural noises of the woods were blotted out. Even the panting of the raccoon seemed to become more controlled, less distracting. Through it all they came to sense more than hear the short, nervous breaths of another, unseen animal. They could almost feel the heavy palpitations of its heart.

The quiet was suddenly shattered. "Karen!" Billy screamed, his anger rushing blood to his face. "Karen!" he screamed again, then took a few steps forward, his eyes madly searching across the ferns, beyond the trees, looking for any movement that would give her position away.

"I know you're there," he shrieked, his voice rising to a panicky rage. He stood still, looking about for just a moment, then he bolted forward a half dozen steps, following the path he and Reuker had followed several minutes before. He waited, then called his sister's name again, "Karen!" His voice cracked on the second syllable, sounding like the screech of sweat-soaked chalk over slate.

Reuker very slowly rose to his feet and started to walk after his cousin. As he did, Billy began to take carefully measured steps forward, all the while checking around himself for his sister.

"I didn't hear her," said Reuker.

"Shut up. She's here."

After a few more steps Billy halted. Reuker looked where he did, toward the dual trunks of two trees that at their base had long ago grown together. Where they began to split, just a few feet from the ground, they glimpsed a shock of blond hair. Then as quickly as it flashed into view, it was gone.

Just as Billy began to head toward the dual-trunked tree, his sister stepped into the open, as if she had sensed her discovery. Though she tried to hide it, her eyes betrayed her fear, and only in a wavering voice was she able to speak. "What are you going to do with that thing?"

"Why did you follow me?" Billy shouted.

As if reacting to the blast of air from his lungs, Karen staggered back. "I can go where I want," she said.

"I told you never to follow me," he screamed and stomped a few steps closer. As he did, Karen retreated by a similar margin but gave no further ground.

"You're going to kill it, aren't you?"

Billy's hands were in tight little fists flexing so rapidly his arms shook. Anger puffed his chest, and he stood there at the brink of losing control. Through clenched teeth he forced the words, "Get out of here!"

"I won't. Not until you let it go."

"I'll do whatever I damn well please to that thing. And if I want to put it out of its misery, I'll God damn well do it!"

Tears erupted from the seven-year-old girl's eyes as she cried, "You're a monster, Billy. You and your scuzzy friend. You can play whatever silly little games you do, and make fun of me, but I won't let you hurt any more animals!"

Until that moment Reuker had always stood apart from any brother/sister rivalry between his two cousins, unmoved by either position. But suddenly Karen was no different from any other child who had taunted him before, and the look she gave him, how she referred to him ignited the same passions that were so familiar to him. The hate he felt for all the other kids who had shown their hate for him came rushing back.

With his sister's outburst Billy became strangely calmer, as a combatant draws strength from the realization of his opponent's weakness. "Don't listen to her, Roy," he said, his fists relaxing and turning his head just slightly in Reuker's direction. "She can't do a thing to us."

"I can and I will. I'll tell everything and this time you won't be able to lie your way out of it." Her tears had left wet streaks down her cheeks, but anger had made her voice strong.

"You do and I'll get you," he said as he started to walk toward her.

"Don't come near me."

"I'll get you," Billy repeated in a hollow, trancelike voice. Then he stepped more quickly in her direction, as if succumbing to the temptation of his threat.

Karen's eyes grew wide with fear, and she turned and bolted away from him. She was faster than her overweight brother, yet the pursuit seemed to grow louder, closer. She could hear the crashing of vegetation gaining on her. She tried to run faster, but there was no extra speed to call upon. And her lungs began to sear with wracking gasps for more air.

As her adrenaline surge began to be overcome by fatigue, she glanced quickly over her shoulder. Behind her, just a few feet, was not her brother but Reuker Stilkes. In the instant that she glimpsed him, his mad visage froze in her mind. His eyes seemed almost to shine, sunk as they were in those dark pits in his face, and his mouth was distorted in a hateful grimace, his lips curled so they revealed teeth solidly clenched. The vision stayed with her, until she could no longer stifle a winded moan of terror.

Then he was on her, and they tumbled to the ground. She twisted and struggled in an attempt to break free, all the while shrieking in panic to the impassive trees. Reuker's bony arms dug deeper into her sides, and she cried out in pain. Her fingers clawed at the dirt, but his grip refused to weaken. She could hear his heavy breath, more the grunting of an animal than the gasping of a nine-year-old boy.

Then she heard her brother wheeze, his voice inflamed with his own rage. "Let her up," he screamed, and Reuker did.

Karen rolled to her side and climbed to her feet. Tiny shreds of decomposing vegetation and dirt stuck to her cheeks where they were wet, and straggles of dead leaves, more veins than leaf, clung to her clothes. As soon as she turned to face her brother, he lashed at her with an unathletic, downward motion. His fist was closed but he struck her with only his middle knuckles and the fleshy heel of his palm. She grabbed her jaw and mouth, where the blow had fallen, and stared at Billy in momentary, silent shock. Then she stumbled backward from him, wailing more from her fear than pain.

"You little brat. You're not going to get me in trouble anymore. Do you hear?"

Karen cried all the louder and clumsily turned to try to get away. But Billy grabbed her by the shoulder and spun her around. Then he pushed more than hit her, and she fell. She cowered there, on the ground, holding herself up by her elbows. Tears and saliva were mixed in muddy streaks on her face.

Watching her, and listening to her sobs that quickly died in the dense woods, Reuker sensed a joyous vindication of past wrongs. Watching her torment, he felt as though, finally, someone who had hated and ridiculed him was made to pay for that contempt. A noiseless laugh distorted his mouth into a grotesque, almost rabid smile.

Billy gripped his sister's face, and twisted it around so that it faced him. She tried to resist, but he overpowered her. His face was just a few inches from hers, and she forced her eyes to the side, away from his glare. "If you tell about anything—*anything*—I'll kill you. You hear me? I'll kill you!"

She gasped in short, terrified spasms, unable to move, to talk, to think. Finally, Billy pushed her face away, and she collapsed fully to the ground. "Believe me," Billy breathed savagely, "I will."

He hovered over her and watched as her chest rose and fell with convulsions of sobbing. She refused to turn and look or try to move away so lost she was in her crying. Billy nodded to Reuker, and the boys backed away, then turned and began walking along what was now a beaten-down path of fallen ferns. As they moved farther away, the sobbing of the girl became muted until they could hear her no more.

The raccoon was still in the same spot. "Give me the rope," Billy snapped. He stood as he imagined a military man would, feet planted firmly to the side with a resolute and unyielding expression.

Reuker picked up the end of the rope and handed it to Billy, who gave it a swift tug. The raccoon gave a brief but piercing cry as it spun on its belly. Then it became silent as if trying to analyze the next move of its adversary.

"Let's go," Billy said and started to tromp off through the woods, carrying his shaved staff in one hand, and dragging the raccoon behind him with the other. Reuker followed for a while, watching the coon that appeared to be watching him. Its eyes penetrated into his thoughts, and he felt its evil creeping into him. He shook the feeling, and then he hurried past the animal and walked next to his cousin.

"This is fun, isn't it?" said Billy.

"It is," Reuker replied, and indeed it was. Inside a special glow began to kindle, bringing a warmth he so rarely felt, a sense of pleasure he only dreamed of.

"Let's take him to the Hole," Billy said, the suggestion immediately solidifying his intent. And suddenly he picked up the pace. The raccoon squealed once at the change, but its protest quickly died.

The river was narrow and strewn with basketball-sized rocks, many of which rose above the surface. It was uniformly shallow and ranged in color from the dark green of the perpetually submerged slippery growth that clung to the bottom to foamy white where it splashed by or over the rocks. They walked upstream along the bank, where they could, and where the bankside vegetation was too lush, they walked in the water.

Gradually they became aware of the falls ahead of them still out of sight but growing appreciably louder every several yards. The noise of the splashing as it filtered through the trees carried a jerking, jittering cadence like the heartbeat of prey suddenly face to face with its hunter, and as it continued, this same nervous pulse of the water became Reuker's pulse. It gripped him, first in the chest then throughout his unsteady limbs. Yet it was not an unpleasant feeling. It was more an expectancy, a sense of building excitement.

At the bottom of the cascades, they took their clothes off and began to climb. The stones were algae-covered and slippery and shifted with the weight of every step. The falls grew louder as they climbed, until it was almost deafening, its flow swollen by the rains the night before.

The tumult of the water pounded inside Reuker as well. The anticipation was there, but for the first time since he came under the influence of the rhythm of the falls, he felt a sense of trepidation enter his mind, weakening his resolve to plunge through the curtain of water to the grotto behind. The cold already numbed his feet, and he imagined that this deadness of feeling would creep up his legs, to his chest, until the dullness entered his head and he was no longer conscious. As he came closer to the falls, the memory of the cold water surging all around him became stronger, more vivid in his mind, and with the memory, a fear. A fear of being unable to breathe, of being trapped under the plunging water as if by some unseen yet powerful hands clasping him at the shoulders.

Reuker shuddered, tears threatening to come to his eyes, as he silently prayed for the fears to leave him in peace, to let him get through the water to the grotto behind. He looked toward the falls, toward the broken sheet of water, and as he did his vision seemed to waver like the shifting curtain before him. His sight grew blurry, and as it did, it allowed his memory to take shape. He was in a bathtub, with his legs curled to his chest and an ache throbbing so painfully in his head that he lay there unmoving, with his eyes tightly shut, waiting for the rhythm of pain to subside. The water had been drained from the tub, but he was still wet and cold. The stained porcelain surface had the same icy feel as packed snow on a roadway.

"We're there!" Billy shouted directly into Reuker's ear. Then his left foot slipped forward, and he had to grab Reuker's shoulder to stop himself from falling.

Billy's mouth turned round in a laugh that Reuker could barely hear. Then Billy moved to the brink of the falls and turned to shout back something else at Reuker, but his voice was totally lost in the crashing of the water. Reuker moved closer, and as he did, he felt first the spray then the splash of water itself. Billy and the raccoon disappeared into the falls, then suddenly, Reuker found himself engulfed by the cold. The water pounded on his head and across his back, and its force was matched by a crazy pounding inside him. He pushed his way into the cove, and though the pounding of the water on his body ceased, the turbulence within him did not die. Yet there was an immediate difference, and the change rushed through him with the same electric speed that his fears sparked throughout his body a moment before. The pounding now brought an ebullient, joyous sensation, and Reuker was free of his fears, free of his memories.

Billy reached for one of the roots that dangled near the ceiling of the grotto and pulled it toward him. He hoisted the raccoon by the rope and struggled to tie it to the root. "Come on, Roy, help me."

It was not as noisy as on the other side of the falls, and Reuker heard his cousin clearly. He grabbed the rope and held the raccoon suspended in the air while Billy fixed the knot. When it was secure, they released it and the root recoiled so the animal dangled just above their heads. From above, the raccoon looked from one boy to the other, the intensity in its eyes no different than when the boys first confronted it in the woods.

Billy stared at the raccoon with a kind of wild-eyed panting wonder, the look of a child gripped by fascination with a new discovery. Yet there was also something very unchildlike to his expression, something harsh, undefinable, evil. Whether it was the way the light reflected in his eyes, or how his parted lips turned upward at the corners, there was something cruel and determined in his face that held Reuker's own sense of wonder and admiration.

He watched as Billy picked up the sharpened stake and held the point in front of the raccoon. His cousin rotated the tip around its face, moving it closer, then away again. The coon could do little but watch as the stake moved tantalizingly just beyond the reach of its jaws. Then suddenly Billy reached it forward and touched the raccoon at the shoulders. It hissed and snapped at the stick, but Billy pulled it away before it could grab it. The coon's mouth was open in a spitting snarl as Billy teased it again by rotating the stick before its eyes. Then again, he jabbed it forward. The raccoon grabbed it in its teeth and tried to tear it away, but Billy was too strong. He yanked it free, and the coon swung in the air from its tether.

Billy looked at Reuker, and they both laughed, and then he poked at the animal again. It hissed its angry, catlike growl, and when it did its lips wrinkled back revealing a tiny row of teeth that to Reuker could well have been the fangs of a demon. His face transformed into a porcelain mask, shaded by swirling images of his past, hardened by his hate. He wasn't sure what Billy was going to do, but of one thing he was sure: He wanted the animal to suffer. And with the wish the pasty hardness of his expression shattered like the minute cracks of old ceramic dishes.

"Get him, Billy," Reuker shouted. "Get him!"

And Billy leaned forward, jabbing his harpoon into the creature. Its defiant little noises melded into one large howl that for just a moment overcame even the sound of the falls. The raccoon swayed in a wide arc and Reuker could see that the tip of the stick was stained red.

As a carnivore would at the smell of blood, Reuker was enveloped by an inner fire that took the water's chill from his body, that brought with it a fine-tuned alertness. He became acutely aware of the sights and smells around him, and each seemed to intensify the sensation that it was all evil, that everything about him was evil, that he lived in a cove surrounded by hate and things that were stuff of this same evil. The tangle of roots above with soil granules trapped by fine root cilia had a musty earth smell that stank of decay, while the pattern of the intertwining roots themselves looked like the twisting, gnarled limbs of the heaps of souls pictured in the Dante book, the book his mother had with pictures of the inferno after death. Yellow green slime coated the moist rock walls and seemed to ooze a pusslike yellow fluid. And at the back of the cove was the jagged slash in the rock that led to the sightless abyss, the crevice that angled deep into the ancient rock. And in the middle of it all howled the angry beast, the furry devil.

"Get him!" Reuker screamed, and Billy did, lancing the animal in its soft belly.

Billy laughed as he thrust again and again. His throat grew raspy giving his laugh an older, sinister tone. As he stabbed at the raccoon, its howl changed to rapid bursts of a high-pitched shriek, and it began to spin on its tether, around and around, propelled by Billy's blows.

As it spun, Reuker began to circle opposite its rotation.

All the while he watched its sharp teeth slashing at the air, its mouth opened in a continuing screech, its devil eyes seemingly without sight. Billy's hands were streaming with the animal's blood, and then Reuker felt it on him. He felt the blood. First in tiny droplets across his forehead, then as it spun faster, as Billy's stick plunged deeper, the blood splattered in his face, on his shoulders. It collected there and then began to run across his chest, and as it did, he felt its warmth seeping into him. The pounding within him for the first time became faster than the rhythm of the falls. Billy's laugh, the shrieking of the raccoon, and the crashing of the water resounded with a shattering effect in his ears, adding to his building frenzy. He was in a state he never experienced before, a state of mind removed from whatever he had known before as reality. The joyous, ebullient feeling that had erupted in him as soon as he had plunged behind the falls now surged brighter, more meaningful, and filled him with a kind of spirited ecstasy so reaching in its impact that he felt as though he were spinning in the air as easily as the creature hanging from the roots of the grotto.

He circled faster, sloshing through the cold pool at his feet, the blood within his veins rushing quicker, hotter, as the blood of the animal collected on his face and coursed over his body. The coon spun faster, Billy's laugh seemed louder, until it all, suddenly, disappeared, until he was climbing out of a tub in a bathroom with walls covered with filth and rust stains streaking down the tile from misfitted fixtures. He recognized the room, and he recognized the tarnished brass doorknob. The pain in his head seemed to have drained all his strength, yet he was able to turn it, he was able to push his way into the hall. It was a memory that had haunted him before, that had ignited his fears as he ascended the cascades several minutes before, but this time it was different. There was no fear, and as he turned into the bedroom, he remembered why the fear was absent this time. He saw her lying on the floor, her head propped against the wall, an incoherent noise gurgling weakly in her throat. It was the woman with the iron-grip fingers and circle of black hair that rimmed her head. Her dress was pulled above her waist and in her hand, limply slung to the side, was a club, a rod, a stick—he did not know which—and there was blood. It was between her legs, streaked down her thighs, and smeared on her stomach. She groaned, and as she did, Reuker realized the pain that the blood meant for her, and the thought lessened his own pain. He felt good, watching her in agony, and he felt that the demons she had screamed of earlier, when she held him in the water, the demons he had prayed would leave, were at last gone. He was cleansed, rid of the evil that encircled him and his world.

The feeling he felt then was the same he felt now as he splashed through the pool at the brink of the Hole. The goodness, the purity of spirit that he had felt then, came rushing back. It washed over him as the waters—the red eternal waters—washed over his skin. The blood was cleansing him, ridding him of the evil that he could not help but touch because it was everywhere, and in everyone.

He felt the contamination his mother had so often told him about, that she said would cling like mold to his skin until, finally, it would burn into his soul, he felt this contamination being scraped away. It dissolved as the warm red liquid ran across his body, and as it did, he felt the presence of something totally pure, something totally fulfilling. It was like she had said it would be, it was like it was supposed to be when she had cried out for her spirits to come. Yet it was all very different. It was better. There was no pain. His head did not throb with the ache that pulsed harder, faster, until he felt it would explode. And he could breathe! He could breathe!

Reuker's chest heaved from the exertion, from his mad circling in the pool, from the thoughts, the feelings that churned within him, that had taken control over him. On the verge of collapse, he stopped, his back to the fissure in the rock. Slowly he brought his hands to his face, barely aware of Billy's laugh that had become little more than vicious, hateful grunting. The raccoon still swung from his thrusts like a pendulum spitting blood. Its blood mixed with Reuker's sweat, and to his touch it had a sticky, peculiar consistency. His touch was gentle, like a blind man's sensing a silk garment with his fingertips, and as Reuker touched his face, touched the blood on his face, the delicacy of his movement seemed to bring a certain calmness to the forces that had been surging within him.

His mouth drooped open, and from it wheezed a tremulous, inarticulate sound of relief, of fulfillment, of peace. Reuker sagged to his knees, his hands caressing himself and smearing the crimson stain all over his body. Above him he could see the lifeless furry shape, and as it died, so died the devil inside it. And so its wicked blood had purified Reuker, scouring the residue of evil that clung to his skin.

Beyond the beast the ragged curtain of water remained unchanged. It beat the stone with the same fury, the same rhythm as it always had, but to Reuker it seemed somehow quieter, tamer, cleaner. He pushed himself to his feet and moved slowly toward it, toward its absolute whiteness, its utter purity.

As he stepped into the falls, he felt as though he were part of it, as fluid and nimble as the water itself. The purity of the water was his.

Reuker Stilkes slumped to the floor of his cell at the Scales Psychiatric Facility. He came to rest in a pile of litter from an overturned basket next to his overturned bed. His shirt was torn open in front revealing a bony chest moist with sweat.

Outwardly he could appear no more at ease, but the peace came only from his fatigue. Deep inside, at the tips of every nerve, a certain tension had been pricked, and even in an unconscious heap on the floor, it continued to vibrate beneath his surface.

Jack couldn't see the tension, but as he peered in through the small opening in the door to Stilkes's cell, he could see what it was doing to him. He could see that some manner of inner torment was scratching at the surface.

He thought of going to Hagan, but the director had already proved himself Huxley's defender. If he did nothing to rein in Huxley after Hyland's attempted rape, he would do nothing now. All Jack could do was hope Reuker did not get worse, and that Huxley would see what Jack saw and have the good sense to back off. There was little else he could do.

Dr. Michael Huxley was leaning back in his chair, the *Guide to Psychopharmacology* open in his lap. Though his fascination with Stilkes grew each time he saw him, his frustration increased by the same increments. He had never seen such rapid changes in a patient before, from coherence to total dissociation.

Huxley felt certain that what he was doing or saying was having an effect on Stilkes, that the patient was not lapsing into a near-comatose state when he dissociated but was very active mentally. And that's why he was frustrated. He was so close, so very close to entering Stilkes's private world, to witnessing the intricate workings of an organism so totally foreign to others of his species, yet he could not make that final breakthrough. There was always something preventing Stilkes from communicating to him.

Though no one knew exactly how Prolixin and the other chlorpromazines worked, Huxley knew well how they affected certain mental processes. It was as if the circuitry of the brain were interrupted, blocking nerve impulses from transferring from one nerve ending to the next. To lessen the effect, the obvious course was to lessen the dosage of the drug. If that brought little change, perhaps he should change the drug altogether. The other antipsychotics would have a similar effect on Stilkes, Huxley knew, and if Prolixin caused problems with his ability to communicate, the others very possibly would as well. But perhaps his reaction was idiosyncratic to Prolixin alone, and another could have a very different effect.

Huxley's finger followed line by line the small print of the *Guide*. Stelazine. Indications: For the management of the manifestations of psychotic disorders. To control excessive anxiety, tension, and agitation as seen in neuroses or associated with somatic conditions. Contraindications: Comatose or greatly depressed states due to central nervous system depressants. Patients who have demonstrated hypersensitivity reaction with a phenothiazine. Warning: May impair mental and/or physical abilities. . . .

He flipped the pages to the thumb tab labeled N. Navane. The warning after the contraindications was the same. Thorazine, Huxley read, was similar in its use and effect.

He looked up Halperdol. First of the series of major tranquilizers. Indications: Indicated for use in the management of manifestations of psychotic disorders. Indicated for use for the control of tics and vocal utterances of Gilles de la Tourette's Syndrome in children and adults. Effective in short-term treatment of hyperactive children who show excessive motor activity with accompanying conduct disorders consisting of some or all of the following symptoms: impulsivity, difficulty sustaining attention, mood lability, and poor frustration tolerance. Contraindications: Severe toxic central nervous system depression, or in patients who have Parkinson's disease. Warning: Ineffective for treatment of severe behavior problems in adults with combative, explosive hyperexcitability.

Huxley ran his finger along the narrow columns of fine print until he came to the suggested dosages for Halperdol. Then he placed the book on his desk and prepared a memo for the pharmacy:

> Re: Stilkes, Reuker. Immediate change in prescription: Cease oral Prolixin.
>
> Substitute Halperdol, 2.5 mg., once daily. Continue Artane at present level.

16

It was three days since Jack had confronted Eddie Hyland in the narrow hallway just off the kitchen where Marion worked. Yet it could have been five minutes ago for how it still stuck in his head. Since then, it hadn't been right between Marion and him, in the bedroom.

As a guard, he always had plenty of time to sit and watch and think. When he was not escorting the men to or from a meal, or exercise, or a medical appointment, his job was just to be there in A-Barracks. He was to be visible. A preventive. It left a lot of time to think.

Jack was walking down the hallway of the barracks, going through the motions of checking on the men who chose to remain in their rooms, then he would check the shower room, then back to the lounge. He was thinking of Marion, of an evening fourteen years ago when they were first falling in love. They were on the beach near Grand Marais.

It was a clear, moonless night, uncharacteristically warm. They lay next to each other in the sand, and as can often happen in the dark, when two people are totally at ease, they shared their thoughts and feelings and closest guarded emotions. It was a free flow, back and forth, for an indeterminable length of time. There were no pretenses and no inhibitions. It was a true baring of the soul, not in a release of tension, but as an expression of trust.

It was only natural that their talk turned to sex. Marion said she wondered what it would be like making love with someone, someday. She said it not as a person with a longing for something, but rather it was a statement of her curiosity, and maybe a little of expectation.

Jack did not see her wonder as an opportunity. He did not instantly couch his words with underlying motives, intent on seizing an advantage. Instead he talked easily, naturally. There was no other way he could have been, on that night. He was not especially eloquent and said the familiar things, probably because if he had thought about it he wouldn't have the faintest idea how an eighteen-year-old girl would experience sex for the first time. He said she'd enjoy it, if it was the right man, someone she cared for more than she thought possible. It would be marvelous, when the time came, and he said it would, so don't worry about missing anything or rushing something with someone just for the experience.

She asked what would it feel like, and Jack laughed. He said he didn't know. It's different for women. But he said he'd been told it was a warm feeling, a strong emotional thing, and maybe something physical like he felt but more intense. He remembered he laughed and said he wished he did know because it sounded like the greatest thing that could be.

Marion laughed, and then they talked of other things. Occasionally they would fall silent, and though nothing may have been said, there still seemed to be the same easy communication. Then they would begin to talk again.

It was during one of the silences that they noticed a spiking of light on the lake's horizon. Over the next twenty minutes the light grew taller, then spread across the sky until it was a shimmering curtain of luminescence. The northern lights were not an infrequent phenomenon during the Lake Superior summer, but some nights were more spectacular than others. And this night the vertical bands of light covered the entire northern sky, coning to a point directly overhead. The celestial curtain seemed to wave, as if shaken slightly at the edge, sending alternating currents of brightness across the sky.

Marion moved closer, allowing herself to be held tighter, and then she asked if he loved her. Jack had been in love before, and when he had told a woman of his love, it was always something that he initiated. But this time, though he had yet to weigh his feelings, the answer came fast. It came fast because he felt it deep inside, like he had for no one. He said yes, and then she pulled herself up so she could look in his eyes and said she wanted to make love with him, now, on the sand.

It took a while, even after they were ready, he being such a big man and she so delicate. And this was her first time, with anyone. And it hurt her, a little.

Finally when he was inside her, he relaxed and lay still for a few moments. She remained as still as he was, until at last she looked up at him with eyes wide and said, "Did we do it?" as if that was all there was to making love.

Even now, sometimes when they were in bed, she would look up at him and smile and say, "Did we do it?" And each time they made love, there was always some of that innocence, some of that wonder that they shared that very first time on the beach of the Grand Sable Dunes.

Eddie Hyland was standing in the hallway, leaning his shoulder against the wall, when Jack finished his rounds and began to walk back toward the lounge area. He stopped when he saw him standing there.

"How's Marion?" he asked.

Since it happened, those were the first words spoken between the two men. Yet every time their eyes met, Jack could see the ridicule in his expression. Until now he had always been able to look away.

"I suppose she misses me," Eddie said. Though he was unshaven, the stubble on his face was sparse, and his cheeks had an oily sheen to them.

Jack's temples twitched as the muscles in his jaw strained, grinding molar against molar. For an attempted rape, with a weapon, the man was restricted to his barracks. Grounded like a teenager. There was no way Jack couldn't be bitter, yet at the same time he realized there was little else that could be done. He was able to maintain his control, and he said, "She doesn't miss you, Eddie. You know perfectly well she doesn't and for whatever reason you have that makes you think like that, you'd better stop. It will only lead to trouble."

The smirk did not alter in the least. He just stared at Jack until Jack started to walk by him. Then he said, "I just thought she must be getting horny, without a man now for a good three days."

Jack turned and grabbed Hyland's shoulder and shoved him through a partially open door into one of the cells. An inmate on the bed scrambled to his knees on the mattress in surprise. "Hey, what's this?" he called.

Jack had Eddie by the throat, and he pushed him against the outside window. Eddie's legs buckled as they hit a chair by the wall, and he dangled awkwardly in the guard's grip. His head was flat against the cold glass. "Watch it," he cried. "The window'll break."

"If ever you touch her, or try to touch her," Jack breathed, his face inches from Hyland's, "by God that'll be the last thing you ever do. You can say what you want about me, but leave Marion out of it. So you can take this as a warning to leave her out of what you say, whatever the hell you think."

"Or what?" he managed to gasp.

Jack twisted his grip of Eddie's shirt and flesh in his hands and squeezed even harder. "I'll break your bloody skull against every wall in this prison."

Eddie couldn't talk. He could only grimace in pain. Propelled as he was by his anger, Jack was oblivious to the other inmate in the room, who knelt still on his bed watching spellbound the scene unfold. Jack was at once infuriated and repelled by what was in this man's head, thoughts that perverted all that was innocent and beautiful about his wife.

Eddie made short, gagging noises, and his hands alternated from maintaining his balance to pawing ineffectually at Jack's grip. Gradually Jack loosened his hold, and Eddie sank to the chair below him, rubbing his neck.

As Jack turned to leave, Eddie croaked in a laryngitic voice, "Give my love to her, will ya?"

At the door Jack looked back at him. His anger spent, he just stared, his glare having no effect at all on Eddie who, though pained, still wore his unmistakable smirk. Then Jack walked away.

The airplane was a single-engine Aeronis Champion, a tandem two-seater with overhead wing bracketed to the fuselage. Behind the cockpit along the side was lettered U.S. MAIL. As its skis glided to a halt at the end of the Lake Siskiwit runway, a snowmobile's engine hacked into gear and sputtered out to meet it.

The pilot swung the flimsy-appearing door back and dropped a canvas bag out onto the snow. Then he jumped out after it. Louis Poiret was a private contractor with the U.S. Postal Service, bringing the mail to Scales and several other places in Michigan's Upper Peninsula. He had taken over the job three years ago at age sixty-five, when he unofficially retired as bush pilot and guide for the hundreds of sportsmen who had him fly them to the remote and unreachable—except by air—lakes of northern Ontario. The retirement was official only in the sense he no longer did it for money, and only with his friends.

Poiret was the kind of guy whose laugh you'd expect to hear frequently and above all others in a crowded bar, and if a fight were to break out, he would be in the middle of it. It took a special nerve to fly in winter over Lake Superior without instruments when a storm could kick up at any time, making eye contact with the surface almost impossible above fifty feet. In that kind of weather, it wasn't unheard of for pilots to lose their bearings and end up flying upside down and, in trying to pull above the weather, drive their planes right into the water. Though he'd had close calls, he was still flying. For him, it would take a special nerve to quit.

The mail run kept his hand in it, but sometimes he felt it was nothing more than driving a bus. An empty bus, with no one to talk to. So when he had the chance, he'd uncork with a line of gab that streamed out of him, more than making up for the time in the air he spent alone.

Paul Chesser pulled the snowmobile up close to the plane before climbing off. He brought a bag of outgoing mail to exchange, and a thermos of coffee, and he and Poiret shared a cup and some laughs before each climbed behind the controls of his own vehicle and continued with his job. The mailbag Chesser brought to the institution contained a package for Dr. Huxley. When it was delivered, Huxley immediately shut himself in his office and opened it. It contained file information and photos from the Homicide Section, Detroit Police Department.

The day after his argument with Inspector McDaniel, Huxley called back. This time he made sure it was close to noon when he knew McDaniel would be out. He asked for Detective Simpson.

Simpson was a different kind of cop, and Huxley was prepared to take a different tack. He said he needed the photos of the victims to complete the picture. "So I can really know what kind of a bastard I'm dealing with up here."

Simpson said sure, he'd have prints made in the photo section.

"One thing, though. I'm in kind of a rush. Could you get on it right away? Like now?"

The detective had paused, his suspicions alerted, though why he wasn't quite sure. "Yeah, I suppose," he had agreed hesitantly.

"Good. I owe you a dinner. Best restaurant on Scales, next time you're up."

The suspicions were allayed, and Simpson laughed. "That's big of you. Listen, do you want the rest of the stuff? Witnesses' statements and such?"

"Sure. If it's no problem."

"Naw. I'll get it out right away."

Huxley spread the new data across his desk. An inner envelope was labeled PHOTOGRAPHS. Inside was a uniform collection of eight-by-ten black-and-white pictures. These he looked at carefully, one at a time, then laid out in front of him. Some were morgue shots while others were reprints of earlier snapshots, enlarged so the dimensions of all the photographs matched.

In his office it seemed deathly still. The stillness was appropriate, staring as he was from picture to picture of the six women, all dead. The morgue shots reflected their utter lifelessness, and he could derive no feeling from them concerning what the women had been like in life. He wasn't sure what he was looking for, but whatever it was, from these particular photographs he did not perceive it. They were no different from pictures in a medical text.

But the snapshots, they were different. They showed movement, a liveliness, a sense of being absent in the other photos. Even the fuzziness from being enlarged beyond the intended capability of the film created an aura of spontaneity, a distinct feeling that behind these two-dimensional portraits was a lifetime of experience, ideals, and goals. Huxley stared intently at the snapshots, as if trying to discern what in life these women had been like, what in life linked them together.

One woman had luxuriant hair, prematurely white. Her smile for the camera was genuine, though not at all a hearty expression. It was more a cautious show of emotion the hardworking might allow themselves to show, their daily struggle to survive never totally off their minds.

Another of the murdered women stood in front of a wood frame house, her arms looped over the shoulders of two early teenage children. Her hair was short, dark, matronly, and from the style, Huxley guessed the photo was taken in the mid-sixties. Then there was the same photo he had seen before in his own file. It was the picture of Dorothy Norvicki, the forty-eight-year-old mother of three with the nervous expression that appeared as if she were looking beyond the camera apprehensively, a prophetic concern on her face.

And then there were the others, one a formal portrait, another with her family, and the last standing before a rhododendron in full June bloom. There was a thread from a common skein that was woven throughout each of their lives, a thread that was immediately apparent to Stilkes, but that Huxley had yet to unravel. He was sure it was there, before him on the table, in some way. A mixture of frustration and excitement alternately interfered with his focus, then honed his thinking.

Though there were differences in basic appearance, there were similarities. Huxley concentrated on the similarities, looking closely at them, his eyes moving from one photo to the next. The age span, he estimated, was no more than fifteen years, and all seemed so totally normal, so completely unspectacular in their looks. Little attention was paid to details of their appearance, though they all looked just fine. Maybe a little makeup, but no more. So very normal-looking, he thought again. They could have just as easily been anybody else. The pictures were so ordinary they could just as easily be a photo on a piano, in a wallet, slipped into the glass corner of a hanging frame, as in a Homicide file. They could have been anyone's mother.

Huxley went back to his original file and fished through the pages until he retrieved the half-sheet he had compared before with the Norvicki photo. It was the photocopy of a photograph of Rebecca and Reuker Stilkes. The quality of the picture was just as imprecise as before, yet this time Huxley felt he could see more clearly. And it was the charcoal-like silhouette of the boy he was drawn to.

From the picture alone and from what he already knew about him, Huxley realized he must have been a lonely boy, with no real companions for most of his childhood. Just his mother. And standing as he was in the photograph in the folds of his mother's dress, because of the shadows of the imperfect image, it appeared to Huxley for a moment as though there was but a single individual standing there. He was always with her; the neighbors had said she took him everywhere with her. She was his eyes on the world, and with no father, and no schooling after the fourth grade, he was totally dependent upon her. The relationship between them must have been incredibly intense, much stronger than the typical parent-child relationship.

And then she died. She deserted him. To Huxley it all began to fit together. He began to get a feel for the motivations for Reuker's later acts. So dependent was he on her for his grip on the world, for his emotional release, he felt betrayed by her desertion, abandoned by her death. He was totally and pathetically lost without her, adrift in a hostile and non-understanding world. The intensity of his feeling for her began to change at her betrayal; it began to shift to a different direction. The total love he felt for her was harshly and unmistakably rejected. In the complex dictates of the mind regarding the expression of the most heartfelt emotions, Huxley knew that a strange metamorphosis could occur, given what the situation must have been. Rejection of extreme feelings of affection and dependence often begets extreme anger. The stronger the love, the greater the hate. It was classic psychiatric theory, and it seemed to fit Stilkes so well.

Huxley swiveled from his chair and nervously paced to the window. Could it be that simple? Feeling abandoned and betrayed, Reuker strikes back with the savagery of his hate that is as all-encompassing and single-minded as were his devotion and dependence on her before. She is dead, so there must be other outlets for his aggression. He kills someone who in some way resembles or reminds him of his betrayer, yet so pervasive is his hate it does not flame out, even after this ultimate retaliation, even after murdering the object of his hate, through unfortunate proxies, again and again.

When Huxley felt he was moving in on one of his goals, he would zero in on it, surround it, devote his boundless energies to attaining that goal. He was capable of unrelenting pressure on himself, on others, on anything, if he had something in his sights. When he was at Chicago and had decided that the esteemed Director Leonard Stoughton had lost touch with modern psychiatric thought and would best be dealt aside, he stopped at nothing until he succeeded. Now he felt close, so very close, to understanding the psychological mystery that was Stilkes, but he knew that that was not enough. In his moment of revelation, there was frustration. The patient still had to see it himself; he must come to terms with his unrequited hate. Only if he saw the things Huxley saw would there be a chance that his rage would be vented at last, safely and completely.

If Huxley had been able to interview Rebecca, if he were able to see into Reuker's mind as clearly as he thought he did and observe the dreams and thoughts that lingered and played themselves out with such regularity in Reuker's head, if somehow he were gifted with powers of analysis beyond the complexities Reuker had to offer, perhaps then he would be able to see the truth. Perhaps he would realize how so terribly wrong he was.

17

The house was a small structure, made all the smaller tucked away among the trees. The only break in the canopy was a narrow road that curved through the woods up to a garage. In the driveway a jeep was parked, a plow attached to the front. Atop the house, and secured by guy wires to the peak and four corners, an antenna rose well above the treetops. The house was five miles east of Grand Marais, and twenty-six miles due south, across the water, from Scale Island.

Inside, Ike Suomi dropped a canvas sack near the door and began to lace up his boots. To the golden retriever the bag was a signal. They were going to check the traps. The dog bounded up to the door and began to rear up on its hind legs in anxious anticipation. It sniffed the rabbit scent on the bag and became even more excited.

"Hold on, Spud. We've got five minutes to wait." He meant for the call from the island. Twice a day it came, at random hours, the time dictated by a two-month schedule sent to him from Scales. Ike was the safety valve the planners of the Facility said they would never need. And they never had, for six years now. But still the procedure was followed at both ends, every day, just to check in. The men in the control center would never say directly that things were okay, and Ike would never ask. It was a superstition between them that if anything was said they would be asking for something to happen. And anyway, nothing had in six years, and the purpose for the routine was something that rarely came to mind.

The dog whined impatiently. It wanted the trek to begin. "As soon as the zealots call, we'll be gone. Okay?"

The *zealots* were the ones on the island. Any of them. In this case, they were the men in the control center. It was part of the local tradition among the Finns that started in 1851, when a man named Gullets brought his religious followers to Scales.

It was a strange and disciplined flock, and it was a combination of their fervent spiritualism and intolerance that chased the independent-minded Finnish immigrants who lived on Scale from their homes. A generation of ill will became over time little more than a historical curiosity that the mainlanders used against the islanders in the same good-natured manner every small town is rival with its neighbor.

The golden retriever lay on its stomach with its head on its paws and its ears perked. Ike Suomi sat as impatiently as his dog at the radio receiver on the desk. It was seven minutes past the hour. It wasn't the first time they were late with the call and certainly wouldn't be the last. To the men in the control center assigned there on their eight-hour shift, a few minutes here or there wasn't critical. But to Suomi it was an inconvenience.

Five more minutes, he decided. That's all he'd wait. Then when they tried to reach him, the beeper on his belt would receive the radio signal, and then they'd have to wait for him to get back to the house to call. He was supposed to contact them if he hadn't heard within fifteen minutes of the appointed hour, but this time he decided he'd make them wait. In fact, he wouldn't even give them the extra five minutes.

"Come on, Spud. We're going." The dog leaped to its feet and was as enthusiastic as a few minutes before. It was then that the signal finally came through.

"It's about time," Suomi shouted into the microphone. "What the hell you doing out there?" He switched the transmit switch to receive in time to hear laughter.

"Dreaming up new rituals." The men in the control center had been quick to take to the popular folk custom of the area.

"Human sacrifice?"

This time the laughter was louder. Mixing with the static, it crackled from the speaker with the sound of mice dancing on tin. "We're zealots here, not pagans."

"What's the difference?"

"Well, one just says you're going to the devil, and the other makes sure you're on your way."

Ike laughed. "I don't know how I've put up with this for six years."

"Hey, it wasn't my fault I missed the hour. Jay had moved the sheet from the file."

"You should tape it to the box."

"Maybe we'll do that. What are you in such a hurry for today?"

"Because, unlike you, I've got other things to do besides sit and watch this stupid box all day."

"You're too much, Suomi."

"I've gotta go. And I suppose you have to get back to your ritualizing."

They signed off, and Suomi pulled on his coat, grabbed the canvas sack, and was out the door. The dog bounded off in front of him. What a lot of nonsense it was, he thought. Waiting for the calls, twice a day, every day, for six years. Oh, he made arrangements when he had to be gone for a few days, but still that was a considerable waste of time, really. Nothing ever happened out there, and nothing ever would. Of that he was sure. It was the kind of confidence that, if he were a military man suddenly faced with a crisis, could lead to gross errors of judgment.

It was after eight o'clock in the evening, but Huxley had arranged for Stilkes to be brought to his office. He felt a breakthrough was about to occur. After studying the photographs throughout the afternoon, and reading more about the specifics of the crimes, he felt he was very close to getting through to his patient. He felt he now had the knowledge that would aid Reuker in seeing himself as clearly as he did. Huxley's excitement had built throughout the day, and now he was confident something was going to happen.

The MCA had been only too happy to leave them. He hadn't wanted to bring him over and had told Huxley he wasn't supposed to leave A-Barracks. It was already understaffed in the evenings. But Huxley had insisted, and now he and Reuker Stilkes were alone.

"Are you feeling better, since we last talked?"

Stilkes looked over at Huxley, half-seated, half-leaning against his desk, then he glanced around the room. He felt different. Was that better?

"You look better. More alert."

"I guess I am. What . . . or, why . . ."

"Why are you changing? Because I've changed your medicine. You were drugged so heavily you couldn't think straight, and barely talk. And that's very important for your treatment, Reuker. Your ability to think and talk. Your ability to remember, and to talk to me."

Reuker swallowed. He felt his shoulders hunching forward, then involuntarily he began rocking in his seat. His hands were squeezed between his thighs. He didn't like this man with the rounded eyeglasses and the relentless stare. He didn't like talking with him. It was like a battle, he remembered from the last time, and he had to struggle continually to fend him off.

Huxley could see the tension. He tried to reassure him. "It's not easy getting well . . ."

But I'm not sick.

". . . and sometimes the cure is painful. In your case I'm sure some of your memories hurt very much. You would just as soon leave them forgotten. And I would too, if I were you. The problem is, they are not forgotten and never will be, at least by your subconscious mind." Huxley paused to let it sink in. Then he asked, "Are you following me?"

Reuker could hear what he was saying, and to him that meant he was following. Understanding was something else. He said, "Yes."

"Good. I thought you were, but I wanted to be sure. If at any time you have any questions of me, just ask. Okay?"

Reuker nodded.

Huxley rubbed his chin thoughtfully as he analyzed the man sitting before him. His patient was ready, he could see, and he felt that he was ready himself. He had a better grasp of how to proceed than he did before, in the earlier sessions when he stumbled blindly through his inquiries.

He continued. "So these things that are in your head subconsciously affect your behavior, whether you want them to or not. And what we're going to do is draw them out because by doing so, we'll—you and I together—we'll be able to get to the cause of your behavior, and only then can we hope to change it. To make you well."

It was as if a different language was being spoken. He could hear and understand what Huxley was trying to say, but it was all nonsense. There was nothing he tried to hide in his head. Did he mean the dreams? But they were good. They were his link to maintaining the purity of his body from the touch of others. They were all he had that kept the evil from leaving its mark.

"You can ask me questions, like I say, but mostly I'm going to ask you things. I want you to talk. Answer my questions however you like. Let them lead you wherever they do."

The discomfort grew in his chest, his limbs, throughout his entire body. He was uncertain of what was coming, uncertain of how to react. He was certain only that he did not want to be here talking to this man. He sought to erect defenses. "I'm not sure if I can."

"Oh, you can. There's no question about that. As long as you ignore that initial pain, the memories may release . . ."

Pain? What kind of pain did he mean? It was the second time he mentioned it. Was it like the pain of the tiled room? Or this room, the office? Reuker thought of how much he disliked being in there, how just stepping inside caused a flood of unpleasant feelings. He wasn't sure why it happened, but it was one thing that lingered after his earlier sessions with Dr. Huxley here.

"You have to remember that I'm here to help you. That I understand how it must be for you. I understand and I care about you."

Reuker folded his arms and leaned back in his seat, then unfolded them and rubbed his hands across his thighs. It was all so fast, he thought. The words were coming at him so fast, and the ideas were jumping out at him from every corner of his brain, the corners that until recently had been fogged with some murky, unexplained darkness. Whereas before, the cloud would settle over his thinking and bring some manner of peace, now the cloud only dissipated.

It had been like this just in the past few days. He had been feeling things he hadn't felt in years, since before coming to the institution, since before the medicine began. It was a paradoxical feeling, an increased awareness was accompanied by growing confusion. He was confused by the pace of it all, by his reintroduction into the world outside his own. It had always been there, on the periphery of his awareness, yet before anything could penetrate much beyond that outer limit, the image would dissolve or the thought collapse. But now it was the wall around himself that seemed to have collapsed. He was like an aged convict who suddenly finds himself at a halfway house receiving brief glimpses of life as a free man. It was when these glimpses became too intense that the *shootings* occurred.

That's what he thought of them as, that's only how they could be described. *Shootings*. He lost all temporal awareness, and he would leap through space and time like the tip of an artillery shell splaying air to the side. He would hear things and see things, but at a greater magnitude, on a level that was almost shattering to him. Then it would crash to a halt, and he would find himself in a bewildered, shaking lump. Like in the cafeteria, or in this very room just prior to the last meeting with Huxley, or any number of times it had happened in the last three days. Was that when the feeling of uncleanliness started? The feeling that clung to his skin like parasitic fingers that leeched whatever purity, whatever peace he had. Or was it because of the others, becoming aware of being forced to be with them?

Reuker thought of the city the first time he arrived there. He remembered finding himself in an area of boarded storefronts and dilapidated, grime-encrusted buildings, and in one of them he spent the first night. Then the first weeks. Worn grooves in the stone steps led to a solid wooden door with the finish rubbed away by the countless hands that had pushed through it. There was an open room with a number of tubular steel cots, all of them taken by snoring, stinking men still dressed in their worn clothes, and on one of these cots he slept. The others around him changed, but each was like the last. They were loathsome creatures who stank of decay and filth and vomit. And he remembered how that evil had touched him, had scarred his skin with its vile marks, until he left one night to find a vessel, an easy vessel, a cleansing vessel.

"I've read that you traveled to different parts of the country several years ago, before you were arrested. Did you like that feeling of freedom?"

"I guess so."

"Where did you go?"

"Everywhere."

"Anywhere stick out more in your mind than others?"

"No."

"How about North Carolina? You were at Linville Gorge, I understand."

"Yes."

"Do you remember why you went there?"

"No."

"What do you remember about it now?"

Reuker glanced at him, then looked away. It was such a long time ago, and so much stood in the way. Yet the doctor hovered above him, his questions insisting he remember what he did not.

Huxley did not want to lose him. When he saw Reuker look away, his face nearly dissolving into the emotionless mask of his past sessions, he pressed him. "What was it like there, in North Carolina?"

Sensing the slight rise in the doctor's tone, Stilkes forced a response. Anything to keep him at bay. "Mountains. And a lot of trees." And the falls, he remembered. The Linville Falls.

"Were you there with anyone?"

"No."

"Do you remember meeting anyone?"

"No," Reuker said quickly.

"Do you remember Jane Anson?"

"I said I didn't meet anyone there."

"I don't suppose you would have known the name. You weren't properly introduced." Huxley selected the photograph of the woman standing in front of a rhododendron and brought it to Stilkes. "Does she register with you?"

"No," he said, barely looking at the picture.

Huxley shifted the eight-by-ten shot so it was before Reuker's eyes again. "You know who she is. I know you know. You killed her."

From Reuker there was no denial and no visible reaction.

Huxley was exasperated. "I'm your doctor, not the prosecuting attorney. I'm not trying to trap you into anything. I'm trying to help you." The man still sat unmoved. Huxley turned away from him and stepped to the center of the room. "I can help you get out of here. You know that, don't you?" On a first-degree murder conviction that wasn't true. Only a pardon by the governor could release him. But that didn't matter to Huxley. What he needed was the man's cooperation.

Stilkes sensed the lie, and he sensed something terribly evil about this man.

Huxley stepped forward and sat on the edge of the chair next to Stilkes. His voice changed again, this time the voice of a man doing his best to sound patient and understanding. "It is important that we study the people like Jane Anson," he said, "because the more we know about them, the more we know about you. Do you see? To understand the victim is to understand you. If we can understand the provocation, we will understand the problem and see its solution. Now I want you to look again at this photograph and tell me when you saw her before.

Reuker looked again at the picture. "I never saw her before . . . before that night."

"I think you did." Huxley came alive. Stilkes had acknowledged *that night*. "What did she do that made you want to hurt her?"

A distant scene flashed through Reuker's mind. He saw a woman with short brown hair at the roadside rest stop. She was alone, and she smiled at him. There was no threat, no insult. Nothing. She seemed so vulnerable.

Huxley repeated the question. "What did she do to you?"

"Nothing."

"Maybe not that night, but before. Long before. What was it that happened?"

Reuker leaned back in his chair, away from the doctor. The nervousness resurfaced, a function of not understanding what Huxley meant. "I never saw her before. I told you that."

Huxley ignored the denial. He was driving toward something, and he was pushing Stilkes ahead of him. He wanted to force the link. "She did something, or something happened. Maybe it was when you were younger. *Think.*"

Reuker didn't understand what was wanted of him. If he knew, he'd give it. Anything to keep him back. Instead, the confusion only increased his discomfort. Added to the nervousness.

It was clicking, Huxley saw. He had to prompt him. He took the photocopy of the picture of Rebecca Stilkes and her son and handed it to him. "Do you recognize her?"

Reuker looked at the picture of his mother and said, "Yes." She appeared ghostlike, exposed as she was under the harsh shadows of the photocopy, and next to her was a representation of himself, cuddled into her dress. As he stared at the likeness, as unworldly as his mother's, the images came to life in his mind, and he pictured that boy with her. What came to him was the memory of them together that was freshest in his mind. She was on the floor, her head propped against the wall. He had recalled that image as he had circled the spiny-toothed beast that spun with Billy's thrusts in the grotto at the edge of the Hole. And now it was that image that came back to him.

"Tell me about her. How she talked, what she looked like to you, what she did."

As the confusion melded with the memory, Reuker felt sick. He tried to stand up to move away, but Huxley grabbed his arm and held him where he was.

"You're going to tell me about her, Reuker. Tonight."

The sickness grew worse, whirring through his head. He saw her, in that memory, lying on the floor. Her lips trembled an incoherent stream of noises, and on her stomach, streaked down her thighs, was the blood.

Huxley shook his arm as if trying to shake the thoughts out of him. "What memory of her lingers in your mind? Something is there, I can see it in your face. Let it out, Reuker. It's the only way."

The sickness congealed. Reuker felt an overwhelming

sense of impurity settle over him. Where it touched him it burned. He pulled away from Huxley, saying, "Stay away. Please."

"She left you when you were sixteen years old, didn't she? She left you alone. But you found her. You found her in the city. Then again in North Carolina, and in Oregon."

"That's not true. It can't be." How could it be? She was dead. The confusion was relentless.

"You're afraid to face her!" Huxley shouted.

"I'm not." There was no reason to fear it.

"You're afraid even to talk about her."

Reuker looked down and away from Huxley. He was evil, Reuker was certain, and his evil would smother him with its decay.

Huxley was sure Stilkes was fighting the thought of her. He could see the only way to get him to see the link between his mother and the women he killed was to force it on him.

He jumped out of his seat and with both hands pinned Reuker's shoulders to the back of the chair. "Tell me how she appears to you, right now. What is it you see her doing to you?"

Reuker was frightened. The last image he had of her flashed into his mind. "She's down. She's lying down."

"And you. Where are you?"

"In front of her."

"And what's she saying?"

"I, I don't know." He could hear only the incoherent, gargling of saliva in her throat. It was what he heard when he had walked in there from the tiled room.

"She's doing what?"

Reuker closed his eyes and turned his head. He saw the blood, on her stomach, streaked across her thighs.

"What's she wearing?" Huxley fought to keep the image alive.

"A dress. A dress, but it's . . ." He clenched his eyes tighter. His teeth were locked together.

"But it's what?"

His eyes opened, and a great gush of air expelled in resignation from his chest. "I don't know."

"It's what?" Huxley shouted.

"It's up, it's pulled up."

Huxley rocked back. His mind blanked momentarily with astonishment. Yet he had to go on. "What's she doing?"

Reuker saw the blood, her legs spread apart, the wooden thing in her hand. "They're open," he gasped. "Her legs, she's got them open . . ."

"And you, Reuker," Huxley blurted, the thoughts crashing furiously in his head, "you are wearing what?"

He remembered the cold. The water enveloping him, then waking on the icy porcelain. He shivered, and the shiver trembled in his voice: "I'm wearing nothing."

"What are you feeling now, standing before her, like that? Tell me your feelings."

Reuker remembered his feeling at the Hole, as he stood there and the raccoon gyrated above him. It was good. The pain she was in, her agony translated into a powerful feeling within him.

"How do you feel?" Huxley screamed.

"Good, I feel good." But it was only in the vision of the past he felt that way. At the present, in the chair, his feelings were a world away. He felt smothered, closed in. He couldn't breathe. He felt the evil, the evil of this man surrounding him. Touching him everywhere. Seeping into him.

The true relationship of Reuker with his mother was clear to Huxley at last. Yet it had to come from Stilkes. "What did you do? What did she do?"

The smothering feeling intensified. The evil became murkier. Thicker. Darker. Still the man pressed. He was leaning over him, his eyes aflame behind round glasses, his face red, spittle spewing in tiny droplets as he shouted. "What happened with her?"

He had shouted the words, yet to Stilkes they were suddenly strangely distant, muffled. Reuker looked at him, and as he did, it happened again. A *shooting*. The face afire with evil loomed suddenly closer, larger, more threatening. It speeded toward him, through him, and then the room flashed by in a roar. Shapes of objects in the room shot by his field of vision. Distorted by the speed, they trailed their colors. It happened so fast that everything lost its distinctiveness, its clarity, its shape. Yet the colors meshed and pulsed brighter, until they hurt his eyes, until they were almost blinding.

He had no physical sensation of movement. It was as if he were still and everything else were shooting by him. As the images continued to flash by, with the colors swirling, he felt dizzy. The feeling persisted until he thought he was going to be sick. But he didn't, the sickness could not be expelled, and it got worse. The noise, the indistinct flashes increased until, suddenly, it stopped. It all screeched to a halt. And it was quiet, except for the pounding in his ears, the thumping of his heart, the surging of his chest. He was gasping, and he found himself leaning over the couch on the far side of the room. With one hand on the arm of the couch and the other braced against the back, he was propping himself up. He felt so tired, so very tired, like he could barely support his weight. With the fatigue sapping his strength, he let himself slowly revolve until he collapsed on the couch.

He sat there, his eyes blankly staring at the floor, his mind blankly trying to settle, until at last his breathing became less frantic. As before, as always before, after a shooting, he felt confused and frightened. But at least his vision slowly returned. And then he saw him. Lying on the floor. Face down.

Reuker immediately stood and walked over by him. He looked down at the unmoving hands, the head tilted to the side and motionless. He did not know how he got there, nor did the possible explanations disturb him. He was afflicted with his own concerns, his own uncertainties.

"They are evil. They are all evil." He heard the words in his head, and as he heard them, he remembered being flung down the steps. The door had just slammed on him and his mother. She had been there to tell the people of the evil that surrounded them, that surrounds us all. And they had cast her aside. Had slammed the door in her face. And she had exploded in a rage and slapped the door, splitting the screen. Where her hand struck, the tiny metal strands left streaks of blood across her fingers and her palm. Then she knocked him down the steps, and where he fell in the grass, his hand skidded in the grime. The awful smell he barely noticed because of the bugs, the narrow half-inch shiny-backed bugs that scampered across his fingers. Frantically he tried to rub it off, but she had him by the collar. "On the steps. Wipe it on the steps,'' and he did. She made him. All the while she screamed at him, at the people inside the house. ''They are like this. They are all like this.'' Then she shouted toward the door, ''You hear me? You are shit. You're all like shit.'' Then turning to Reuker again she told him that he should fear all people. ''No one is to be trusted. No one is safe to be near, because their filth, their decay will touch you and will burn you and will destroy you.'' Then she pulled him away from the steps and toward home, and at home, in the tiled room, like so many other nights, he had to be cleansed.

Feeling the horror of that night, and with the confusion of this night still spinning in his head, Stilkes turned away from Huxley and went for the door. In the hallway, he paused, listening. He heard nothing. Then he walked away from the office and disappeared into the darkness, a darkness as blighted and filth-stained as he felt was smeared across his body.

Roger Wells stood in the dark by the glass-enclosed observation room in the woodworking center of the Vocational Skills Building. A yellowish glow filtered in from the outside mercury vapor lights giving him only partial vision. His suspicion was like that glow: it illuminated his gut feeling that something was wrong; it gave no clear indication of what it was.

He had been watching Dennis Ringly ever since Wells had been assigned to the VSB, and although he felt sure the inmate was manufacturing weapons, he had yet to figure out how.

A short time before, as the evening group of eight inmates was lining up to be searched before returning to A-Barracks, Wells had positioned himself directly in front of Ringly. He had that cocky, infuriating smile, and Wells had grabbed his shirt and pulled his face down to his and said someday that smile was going to change. He would make sure of it.

''I don't think so,'' Ringly had said, the expression not flinching a fraction. ''You're not smart enough to change it.''

''It'll change and it'll change tonight. I'm gonna stay right here in the VSB, for as long as it takes, until I find out what you've been using. And then, Ringly, you'll never be allowed in here again. You'll spend the rest of your time at Scales sitting in that damn lounge listening to those idiots jabber at each other, and at you. Just think how that'll be, Ringly. Just think how it will be, day after day, year after year."

The smile had not vanished, but at the least he froze it on his face. Wells knew that being able to work in the shop was the only way Ringly had to keep his sanity. And losing that privilege was the only effective threat he had to use against him.

As the men filed toward the door, Wells's partner took him aside. "You shouldn't push Ringly so hard. He's a naturally jumpy guy."

"Is that right," Wells said flatly.

"You know what he did on the outside. One day he just up and killed his foreman."

Wells turned to look at the guard. "You afraid to take them back by yourself?"

"No, but—"

"Then get going."

The other guard pulled back from Wells and stared long and hard at him, then he turned and walked to the door. After they left, Wells turned out the lights.

Standing in the dark, he let his eyes roam about the dimly lit room. The silhouetted machines, some totally immersed in shadows, others partially within the rectangular glow from the windows, could easily have been a visionary's concept of metallic creatures from another world. Iron legs supported in stiff silence the agonized contortions of looping saw arms and saber-toothed drill presses. It was an eerie sight, and Wells was not unmoved. He stood there, trying to absorb all that he saw, all that he heard. He sought a new perspective on the room and all that it contained.

As he stood there contemplating the shapes in the darkness, the line of men moved into the central hub of the tunnel network. Ringly was leading, the MCA at the rear.

Ringly could feel a stickiness coming to his skin, a quaking, trembling sensation to his nerves. He thought of Wells's threat, and he was scared. He fingered his waistband, and hidden within the seam he could feel the narrow, flexible band of metal.

Why did he do it? Why did he risk what limited freedom

he had to make weapons for the others? At another time, in a calmer state of mind, he could answer himself. Where respect meant survival, the fashioning of weapons was the currency of power.

As they neared the tunnel spur to A-Barracks, Ringly glanced quickly back. The line was stretched out, the guard still at the end. Ringly rounded the corner, then leaped to the pipes that dangled from the ceiling. He jerked himself up to his waist, then swung his legs above the pipes.

None of the men broke stride, and as the MCA came into the tunnel, Ringly could see him, his white shirt open at the collar. Surely he could see him as well, if he looked up. But he didn't. The MCA walked right underneath and continued to the end of the tunnel, then up the steps and into A-Barracks.

Ringly lay where he was for long minutes after he heard the heavy slam of the door somewhere behind him. There were no other noises. No other voices.

Ringly slid to the side and let his legs drop over pipes. Then he maneuvered himself backward and slowly lowered himself to the floor. He moved quickly to the other intersecting tunnels. From there, it was a familiar path to the VSB.

The lights were on in the VSB, and Wells was searching, for what he wasn't sure. He checked the table saw, the drill press, the jointer, checking every loose screw, looking for missing bolts, missing parts, gerrymandered wiring. Anything.

Whatever Ringly was doing, Wells decided, had to be something that was unexpected, that would appear too difficult. Or wholly innocent. He tried to clear his mind, to think things out. Then he heard it. A noise, like the click of a door latch.

He spun to face the entrance from the tunnels. Had someone just come through the first of the double doors? Or inside the room itself?

Wells felt a touch of panic flicker then die within him. Come on, get a grip on yourself, he heard himself saying. What was he expecting? Inmates working on the night shift? He smiled uncertainly at the thought, at the irrational fears that come so quickly to an unclear head. The fear was a symptom of the tension, and that was all. And the longer he remained quiet, without hearing a thing, the more convinced of that he became. Yet still, the unsteadiness lingered.

He walked slowly toward the shadowboard, as if stepping so as not to disturb the imaginary intruder, then began to examine each outlined tool on the pegs. Some he removed, turned over in his hands as if inspecting for a defect, then replaced on the wall. Others he merely studied from where he was, staring at them as if waiting for revelation to strike. And the funny thing was, the longer he stood there, the more he felt revelation was trying to break through. Something was different, and it was up there, right before his eyes. It wasn't anything he could grasp; just a feeling, a nagging thought that it was not the same. It was a detail—something altered, added, missing—that teased him from just beyond the brink of recognition.

As his eyes swept over the tools, their outlines, the pegs with the band saw blades in the corner, he thought of the first time he was in the room. He tried to visualize that moment. He tried to picture the board then, his impressions as he had stood there. He thought of the tangled mass of drooping saw blades in the corner. He remembered thinking they were overflowing the pegs, that it was probably a nettlesome task just to remove one from the wall. Yet now, it didn't seem like it would be such a task. It wasn't the tangled mess he remembered.

Wells stepped closer to the blades. They were neater. They hung in relative order. There was even room for more.

As he thought, he realized that the saw blades were something—the only thing—they never checked. They didn't because, quite simply, there was no way the spindly metal strips could be fashioned into a weapon. And there was no way their eight-foot lengths could be smuggled out of the building.

But Ringly was a clever one. He could have figured a way to do it. And the more he thought of it, the more convinced he became: If anyone could transform the band saw blades into weapons and smuggle them back to the barracks, it was Dennis Ringly.

Before he could think another thought, the lights went out.

"Hey!" he cried out. "Who's there?"

There was no answer.

"Is this some kind of a joke?" He was angry, and his voice carried his belligerence. But quickly that changed as the absolute darkness wound tighter around him. "Hey, come on. Let's have the lights." He listened, then unable to hold the feelings beginning to churn inside, he breathed in sharply, his breath a shrill whistle through dry lips.

He turned stiff-legged around, as if uncertain of his balance. His nerves flared with heat, and he could feel the warmth growing hotter over his skin. His neck moistened, and sweat collected in his armpits and in the crooks of his elbows. The fear itself was cold. And this time it was real.

He felt weak, as if the darkness had robbed his body of strength. But gradually a semblance of steadiness returned as his eyes grew accustomed to the half-light that filtered in from outside. With partial vision came partial calm. Was the power out to this building? Was there a short? Certainly it was possible, with the demand the machines put on the electrical system day in day out.

Wells began to edge sideways toward the exit into the tunnel, his foot sliding out before him feeling for obstacles on the floor. It seemed so utterly quiet, so deathly still in the room that all he could hear was the sound of his own breathing and the cautious crack of each of his steps. Yet stillness, and darkness, can play tricks on the mind. And it was this that he thought of as he imagined hearing the beating of another heart, the pumping of another's chest.

The drill presses stood like hulking sentries at his flank, poised stoically at attention. Or was it silently, in ambush? They were mere shadows, and shadows have indistinct edges. The fuzziness can even make them appear to move, and to Wells one of them indeed seemed to waver, as if it was not a solid hunk of steel but a papier-mâché replica that shifted with the slightest vibration. Or, as if the shadow had life of its own and could move at will.

He didn't like looking at shapes; he didn't like the feelings they were beginning to stir within him. He turned his head, and when he did, out of the corner of his eye one of the shadows seemed to move all the more. And then he felt it.

It was a kind of a tug at his arm. There was no pain, yet immediately he knew that there should be.

There was a swish of air—it was the same swish that had preceded the tug—and he felt pressure at his shoulder, a pressure that lasted only momentarily. It stretched to his neck, to the bare skin below the ear.

He reached to where he felt the pressure, and where his hand touched his neck, it was wet. He turned toward the drill presses, and he saw the shape. A shape of a man, his arm rearing back, then slashing forward. He heard the whistling sound of the air, and then across the back of his neck and wrapping around his head to his cheek, he felt the pressure. Then the arm pulled back, and he felt a slicing, tearing pain encircling his entire head. It was then that he screamed and held up his arms, but the shape lashed out again, and again. He felt himself falling to the floor, and he felt the ribbony dullness lash across his body. He waved his arms and legs, but they were futile attempts at defense—a blind man flailing away at a circle of attackers.

His voice trailed off into hoarse gasps, and he tired. He knew it would be over soon, and the thought brought a kind of peace. In that peace he was glad that it was dark so he couldn't see what was being done to him.

The shape reached down to the guard's waist, and there was a jangle of keys. To Wells, it was a remote sound, and within moments he lost his ability to hear it altogether.

It was like the sound of a train clanging over aged tracks through a far-off tunnel, the sound he heard. It was a distant noise, and only gradually did he become aware of it, only gradually did he begin to focus on it. It was a persistent noise, an insistent call, and with it came the pain. The louder it became, the more it hurt. And the more alert he became. Until at last he opened his eyes.

Immediately he tried to push himself up, but the throbbing pain in his head almost robbed him of his consciousness. He tried again, more cautiously, and was able to slowly bring himself to his feet.

With the blood rushing through his temples he stood

shakily in the center of the room. He massaged his forehead, and above his right eyebrow he could feel a swollen lump. He looked uncertainly around himself, and when his eyes caught the open door, he felt it meant something. But what?

He tried to steady himself, and gradually he was successful. The woozy incapacity relented. Until finally his mind came clear and with the clarity came the memory of what had happened. His patient was gone!

Reuker Stilkes had knocked him unconscious and left the office.

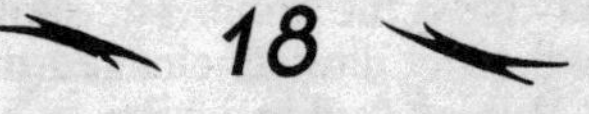

18

Dr. Huxley moved toward the phone on his desk. He was going to call the control center and alert them of Stilkes's disappearance and have a search begun, but as he lifted the receiver something within him told him to wait. To consider it first.

As he did, he realized that it was best not to notify anyone. If he did, restrictions would be placed on Stilkes and on his handling of him. Or worse, they would begin to call into question his manner of treatment, saying that it was too dangerous, that it wasn't working. They might decide to increase the level of psychotropics into his system, and if that happened, Huxley knew his psychotherapy would effectively be at an end.

He would find Stilkes himself and bring him back. It was the only way.

Huxley looked at his watch. It was 9:30. Stilkes had been brought in about 8:00. He wasn't sure how long they talked before he rushed him and knocked him cold. A half hour? An hour? However long, he had had plenty of time to get just about anywhere within the compound. But if he had left the building, Huxley considered, he may well have been seen. And finding him would have led the MCAs back to Huxley's office.

It was likely he was still close by. The thought alone provoked a fluttering nervousness, and Huxley slowly looked around his office, his eyes searching every corner, behind every piece of furniture. Except for himself, the room was empty.

He stepped toward the door and cautiously peered into the hallway. First one way, then the other. It was a silent, gaping tunnel, illuminated with the glow of single fluorescent tubes, one at each end of the corridor. The dimness lent an ethereal quality where darkness dissolved substance and imagination gave shape to shadows.

Huxley stepped into the hall and arbitrarily chose one direction to check first. The office next to his was locked, and so was the door across the hall. He continued down the corridor, trying each door, until he came to one that opened as he twisted the knob. The same, shadowy dimness as the hall, only darker, cloaked the room.

"Reuker," Huxley said in a calm, even tone. He heard no movement, no sounds of life. He stepped into the room, resisting the impulse to turn on the lights—it could draw others to the building. "It's Dr. Huxley, Reuker, and I'm alone." He stood still in the center of the office until he was satisfied no one else was in there. When he left the room he locked the door behind him.

In the hallway again, he heard a noise from behind him. At first he didn't know what it was, but as the sound replayed itself in his mind it became clear what it had been: It was the gentle click of a door being closed very carefully.

Huxley turned and moved in the other direction, past his own office. He tried one door, then another; at each one the knob twisted a little more slowly in his hand, and he hesitated a little more as he tried to open them. Stilkes was there, in one of the rooms, and Huxley knew all too well the savagery he was capable of. The images of the morgue photos flashed through his mind, and as they did, he felt an airy dizziness come over him. He tried to fight the feeling, but it was a sickness he could not control.

Huxley tried another door, and it opened. The stillness

of the room seeped out of the darkness, encircling him in its grip, pulling him into it. He stepped inside, hyperalert to the slightest of noises, the most meager of movements. In the far reaches of his hearing he could hear the rush of air through the vents and the distant rumble of the building's power circulating the steam. As he listened, the air seemed to swish louder, the unseen rumble of the building pulsed with the same rhythm as the throbbing in his forehead.

"Reuker," Huxley tried to say, but his voice caught in a throat made dry by his fear. He swallowed, then said the name again.

Stilkes was there, in the shadows, and he could hear the raspy whisper. And he could see the outline of the figure, his hair forming a fuzzy round image against the light in the hall. It seemed just a few moments before when the doctor was leaning over him, pressing him against the chair. And then had come the rushing confusion of the *shooting*.

Stilkes felt the panic returning. He was coming for him again. Reacting to the fear, he sprang from the shadows.

Huxley heard the movement, then the sound of a table crashing to the floor. It took a second for him to realize what was happening, and another second for the shape to emerge from the dark. It burst from the shadows and lunged toward him.

He staggered back into the hall, and as Stilkes came after him, in his eyes Huxley could see the raging fire of madness. Though he had seen it before, he had never felt threatened by it. It was a glare that transformed Reuker's face into a mask of hate and terror and irrationality. It was a face that in that one, quick instant ignited a terror within Huxley he could not control.

Stilkes pushed by him and dashed down the dim passageway. Huxley continued stumbling backward until he was stopped by the wall. From there he watched as the skeletal figure passed under the meager illumination of the fluorescent bulb, and then around the corner.

It was a few seconds before Huxley could push himself from the wall and start after his patient. As he passed under the single light, he heard the outside door opening, then crashing shut. Huxley rounded the corner in pursuit.

The cold hit Stilkes the same as if he had run straight

into a wall of ice, rather than the outside air. It was ten degrees below zero—cold enough to instantly crinkle his exposed skin and to take his breath away. The heat of terror that fueled his escape turned frigid, and Reuker was able only to stumble awkwardly forward. The snow crunched under his weight as if it were hollow, rather than solid.

The confusion and panic raging within him were deadened by the cold. He slowed, until finally, he collapsed. His face pressed against the hard-packed snow, and as it ground into the icy crystals, the cold intensified. It entered him, surrounded him, smothered him. He remembered the feeling, of being plunged into the icy water, of the hopelessness of trying to resist. The blankness would come. It would be best to let it come.

Huxley reached down and grabbed Stilkes by the shoulders. Reuker was as though unconscious, and Huxley grasped his left arm with both his hands and yanked him to his knees. Then he slipped his shoulder under his arm and pulled him to his feet. As they walked back toward the Medical Building, Reuker staggered along next to Huxley, at times helping, at times seemingly ready to pull the two of them back to the ice.

Outside of the indiscriminate glow of the yellow mercury vapor lights, no other beams were focused on them. It was apparent they had gone unnoticed.

It was with a sense of relief that Huxley pulled Stilkes through the door and back inside the building. The chill of their skin did not change, but at least the oppressive weight of the frigid air was lifted from them. Reuker increasingly walked under his own power, and by the time they reached Huxley's office, he stood alone. Inside, Huxley pointed to a chair and he sat down.

Neither man spoke for a few minutes—Stilkes was in a slouch as expressive as his present thoughts, while Huxley let himself relax. He sat behind his desk, in his fabric-upholstered swivel chair, and stared across at his patient. Even as he allowed the intensity of the events of the evening to dissipate, his mind was feverishly assembling what he had learned. He was not one to yield easily.

It was all coming together, Huxley thought. The relationship between Reuker and Rebecca, and the reasons that bond was so strong. A bond that once broken unleashed a fury that had yet to die.

He leaned forward in his chair, resting his forearms on the desk top. He chose his words carefully. "Sometimes, Reuker, it is easier to see outside of yourself than it is to see within. Sometimes it's easier for someone else to see things about yourself that even you cannot see." Huxley paused briefly as he tried to assess the effect of what he was saying. Then he continued, artfully trying to build his case to draw out Reuker's full cooperation. "I think you understand that, don't you?"

"Yes." Stilkes had no energy to do anything but agree.

"You can't always see what others can partly because you don't want to see those things."

The man was waiting for some kind of acknowledgement, so Reuker nodded.

"But in the end, it's all worthless if the patient does not see what the doctor sees. Despite all that work, and all that pain, not a damn thing will change unless you, Reuker, come to understand what I understand about you."

From the depths of his slouch, Reuker peered over at Huxley. It was an expression that could not be read.

But Huxley felt he could read it. "Yes, I do understand. And I can help you. More than ever, I am sure of that."

Their appearances, and the moods those appearances represented, could not have been more distinct. Huxley rose from his chair, his face once again abeam with its innate confidence, while Stilkes remained slumping where he sat, the contours of his face a mix of pallid and shadow-black creases.

"We'll talk again," Huxley said as he came around the desk. "But I'd like you to think about what I said, because it will take commitment on your part. And as you can realize after what happened tonight, it won't be without a little pain." He smiled, then beckoned him toward the door. "Come on. I'll take you home."

The MCA Paul Mendez quickly brought his feet down from the counter and bolted out of his chair. His partner was in the bathroom. "Sorry," he said to Huxley. "You had him so long I forgot he was gone."

"No problem. We were busy for quite a while."

"Should've called. I'd have come and gotten him."

"I wanted to save you the trouble." The full light of the lounge fell on Huxley for the first time.

"Jesus! You've been outside." His face still carried that rosy cheekiness of the cold.

"No, you're mistaken."

The MCA looked from Huxley to Stilkes and, as if what Huxley said didn't register, said, "You've both been out there. What the hell for? It's ten below."

Anger flashed in Huxley's face. "I just said we weren't outside. Didn't you hear?"

The guard was stung by the force of his words. Though he said he understood, he knew it was a lie.

"Good," Huxley said, then turned and walked back toward the tunnel.

Something had happened, Mendez could tell, and the bastard was trying to hide it.

But not until the next day would he find out. Not until the next day would the body of Roger Wells be found.

The routine for breakfast was always the same—being awakened at the same hour, not being allowed to linger in bed, following the same path to the same wait in line at the cafeteria door, then filing inside to plastic trays and thin silverware and the same unimaginatively rotated menus—and it was this agonizing sameness that was resented. It was a minor thing, so minor that some could not even pinpoint the reason for their irritation. Instead, it was the men in front of them that were annoying, or those pushing from behind, or a dislike for pancakes. But like so many things in a prison, it is the small deprivations of personal liberties that sometimes are resented the most.

The breakfast ritual was one such small deprivation. It was the kind of flashpoint that wardens at the ordinary facility dread, where repressed furies can flare into the open.

But Scales was not ordinary, and neither were its people. They were biochemically controlled. But while tensions were muted, they could never be silenced, and sometimes the warping of reality created new paranoias.

It was this yawning, restless line of thirty men that Jack Cooke stood idly beside. At the front of the column, by the door, stood Arnie Johnson, while Eric Creegan was at the rear. The three guards were as sick of the routine as were their charges. Arnie leaned his bulk against the wall, a smile displaying his private amusement over a resident's aimless shuffling in place. Creegan stood as if at rapt attention, hands draped behind his back, but in actuality he was in his own dream world.

As Jack glanced along the column, only one of the men seemed intent on what he was doing. Jack tried to avoid him, but it was useless. An irresistible loathing kept Eddie Hyland in his mind and the longer they stood there, the more he succumbed to the impulse to move closer to him. It wasn't a conscious desire to provoke a quarrel. It was more an acceptance that inevitably something was going to happen between them, and a secret wish that it would happen soon.

"Jack," Eddie said in an abbreviated greeting.

Jack stood on the opposite side of the hall, looking toward the front, not acknowledging Eddie at all.

"I said hello."

Jack turned and looked at him square. He was a repugnant creature, a reptile that slithered from one decaying pile of muck to another, tailing slime behind him wherever he went. Thin, brownish blond hair clung together in dirty spears, and oils from his hair had run down across his forehead and covered his face with a filmy sheen. His ever-present, three-day growth of beard, sparse and light in color, from more than a few paces looked like splotches of grime.

"Things not going well at home?"

Jack's eyes flashed his anger. At the tips of his resolve something was ignited, and this time, there was no attempt to douse the flame. Like the sparkle of a burning fuse, it traveled in hot spurts along his nerves.

As a pub tenant aims a dart, Eddie said with feigned seriousness, "I miss her, you know."

"What kind of man derives such pleasure from wanting others to hurt?" Outwardly Jack appeared in control, but he was no less volatile than a lit stick of dynamite.

"I'm a student of human nature, that's all. I can see things and feel things, and I know when a woman wants me. It's in how they look at me, and move when they know I'm watching."

"Sex to you is a weapon. You use it on women, and now you're trying to use it on me."

"Ha-hah," he bellowed, exaggerating the last syllable loud enough to turn the heads of the others in line. "You prove my point. You feel threatened by what I say because it is closer to the truth than you care to admit."

"The only person you fool with your fantasies is yourself."

"It's you who live in fantasies, Mr. Medical Corrections Aide. It is you who deny what is obvious to anyone." Muted chortles spread among the men as they were being drawn into the exchange.

Eddie affected a tone of false concern, saying, "I'm afraid you are suffering from delusions and desperately need psychiatric care. Anytime you need my help, I'll be glad to counsel you."

The others broke into open laughter, and Arnie shouted, "Shut up." It was directed as much at Jack as it was to the men, but Jack paid the command no heed. Every muscle, every nerve was on edge. "You can counsel to the end of your sentence for all I care, but you get my wife out of your mind."

Hyland sensed the advantage, and he pressed. "You just don't understand, do you? That the problem is in *your* head, not mine." The line was gradually breaking ranks and swelling in the middle as the men moved closer to Jack and Eddie. "You're a sick man, and the trouble can be traced to your relationship with your wife. You can't control her, and you can't satisfy her. You try, but she's too much for you, and it shows. You are unhappy at home, and here. We can all see that." He gestured, and the others nodded. "And you know what makes it all the worse? Knowing that a punk like me turns your wife on more than you could ever hope in your wildest dreams."

Jack lunged for Hyland and grabbed his shirt and spun him around to the far side of the hall. He crashed him against the cement bricks, but Eddie only laughed. The men pressed forward as Arnie and Eric Creegan pushed through.

"It tears you apart," Eddie went on, "that we made it together, and it was the best thing she ever had."

Jack slammed his fist into Hyland's stomach. Propped against the wall, there was nowhere for Eddie to recoil, so the full brunt of the blow doubled him over and left him gasping for breath. But Jack did not relent. He pulled him up by the shoulder and slugged him in the face. He crashed back against the wall, then fell to the side.

The living wall of men surged closer. Arnie pushed those closest to Jack and Eddie away from them. Neither he nor Creegan made any attempt to stop the assault.

Jack pounced on Eddie, grabbed his collar and began to shake him. In his mind he could see a ravaged Marion and it was this man, in his hands, who had done it. It was as if the crime were a fact, and Jack were under the spell of his vengeance.

Eddie's head flopped up and down like there was no resistance in his neck muscles, but he was not unconscious. His eyes were open and he wheezed a gasping, pained, nonsyllabic moan.

The sight of the head flopping helplessly in his grasp gradually worked its way into Jack's rage. His fingers loosened their grip, and as they did, he suddenly became aware of the muscle pain in his back, the throbbing in his right hand. The fatigue from the exertion quickly rushed over him as if it had collected behind a dam of adrenaline, and now that the rage broke, he was flooded with fatigue, pain, and shame.

He felt Arnie's hand under his arm. "Come on," the guard said quietly. "We have to get him back to his cell. Before they find him like this."

As Jack started to rise, Eddie suddenly clenched his shirt just above the waist. Jack was startled at the strength of his grip. He looked into his face, a face distorted by his loathing more so than the rising bruised skin. Eddie strained to raise his head, then with his eyes fixed on Jack's, gasped, "I'll get to her. Someday. I'll get to her." Then, as had happened to Jack a moment before, his strength quickly drained away, and he slumped back to the floor.

It was the viciousness of how he said it, the timelessness of the threat, that chilled Jack as he let Arnie help him to his feet. The fat guard whispered, "You did it. You finally learned. That's the only way they reason." The encouragement drifted right through him; it was the malevolent determination of Eddie that stuck.

From the end of the hall opposite the cafeteria, one of the MCAs who had been left behind in the glass-enclosed room came walking forward. He moved uncertainly, dazed, as if he were unaware of what he was stumbling into. When he spoke to Arnie and Jack and Creegan, it was with complete disregard that the prisoners were all around.

"They got Wells. He's dead." He said it as though he disbelieved. Then he added, to answer that disbelief, "We just got a call. They killed him."

There was no doubt in anyone's mind who *they* were. The guards could feel the stares, and it was with reluctance that they looked at the tight circle of men surrounding them. They saw a collective look of triumph, of revenge, of warning. They had struck back, quickly and decisively. It was as if they all had had a hand in the murder.

And for Jack they held a special contempt. They believed what Eddie had been telling them, that Jack was an impotent, insecure man, and they watched as he answered his inadequacies by beating a man made defenseless by his status. A man who could easily have been any one of them.

Jack felt their contempt, and he sensed something more. He was inseparably one of the green-trousered, white-shirted custodians of their freedom, but he had always tried to hold himself apart from what he saw as accepted treatment of the residents. Whether they accepted this or not, he was never sure. At the least, he recognized it within himself. Now, looking into their faces, he realized they had seen the difference because in their eyes he could see the accusation of traitor. And the hate for one who betrays a trust is greater than for those who disavowed trust from the very beginning.

Arnie touched his shoulder and motioned for him to help pull Eddie to his feet. He groaned as they did, and leading him back to his cell it was Jack who felt sick to his stomach.

The only man in the hall singularly unmoved by the events was Reuker Stilkes. He stood apart from the intensity, bound tightly with his own tensions.

The news spread fast, and even faster spread the rumors. They worked their unnerving effect on the guards, and a lockdown came into being without any orders being issued. Innocent noises carried ominous messages in the charged air, and the guards' edginess was concealed under only a thin veneer of control.

For the residents of the first floor of A-Barracks, the triumph they had felt proved fleeting, and now, locked in their individual cells, they feared what would begin to happen to them. Natural chemicals within them were released, testing the defensive line of the drugs. As the cranial battlefields grew in intensity, the men suffered.

In the office of the director, Peter Hagan desperately was trying to piece things together. He was shaken by the murder, by the sight of Wells's body on the wood shop floor. When he had seen the multiple slashes across his face and upper chest, he had staggered back. It wasn't the image but the feeling that stuck with him. And now the feeling caused him to feel unsure of himself, that he wasn't asking the right questions, that decisions were coming harder, that he was losing control.

Neil Lummer had been in the office early, and was still there to offer his conclusions and point his fingers. But Hagan knew he had his own reasons to be so quick to assess blame. Jack Cooke came and offered what he knew about how Huxley was pressing Stilkes and how Stilkes had been reacting. What he said began to focus the inquiry, but it wasn't until Paul Mendez—the MCA who had taken Reuker Stilkes to the Medical Building last night—had left the office that Hagan began to feel that at least the mystery of who and how was coming clearer. It was then that he sent for Dr. Huxley.

Huxley nodded to Hagan, then Lummer, as he came into the room. Hagan stood and greeted him, while Lummer remained where he was and looked away.

"Know why you're here?"

"Top-level strategy, I can see," Huxley said with a sarcastic shrug toward Lummer.

"Not exactly," Hagan said, sitting back down. He cleared his throat, and his eyes came reluctantly up from his desk top. "It appears one of your patients is responsible for the murder."

"I suppose Lummer's got it all figured out."

Lummer's voice was a vehement snarl. "You're as much responsible for the killing as he is."

"I'll handle this," Hagan broke in.

Huxley stared at Lummer with amused contempt, a look reserved for the most foolish of adversaries. Then to Hagan he said, "If you mean Stilkes, that's impossible. He was with me."

"All the time?"

"Yes."

"In your office?"

"Of course."

Hagan tented his fingers in front of his mouth. He hadn't intended to set a trap for Huxley, but he hadn't expected such an assured denial. Yet on both accounts it appeared to be turning out that way. He debated, in the few seconds he allowed himself, how to offer an opportunity to retreat. "You may not have been aware of what happened. He may have disappeared and come back without you realizing it."

"Don't be ridiculous. What was I doing, looking out the window while he slipped off the couch?"

"Mendez said you brought him back yourself, and that he was sure you both had been outside."

"That's a lie!"

Lummer slid forward in his chair. "Is the bruise above your eyelid a lie?"

Huxley glared at him, and this time Hagan said nothing. It was apparent Huxley wasn't going to make it easy, and he would just as soon let the challenge come from Lummer.

Lummer didn't wait for Huxley to respond. "You lost control, then you lost him. You may have tracked him down, but after it was too late."

Staring straight at Hagan, Huxley said flatly, "Stilkes did not kill anyone last night."

Hagan was conciliatory. "That may be so. But you must admit, it sure was his style."

"The wounds were wholly inconsistent to Reuker's knife attacks."

Hagan furrowed his brow. "You mean you checked?"

Huxley settled back in his chair. His expression hardened. "He was in the Medical Building the entire time. If he had killed Wells, don't you think he'd be covered with blood?"

"You would think the murderer would be. But no one was found with blood on him."

"It still wasn't his style. Not by a long shot. They were all women, for starters. Didn't that occur to you?"

"He couldn't pick his victim as easily as he did on the streets," Lummer said. "Wells was as close as he could come."

Huxley ran his hand through his hair. Reluctantly he said, "There's a reason why it had to be a woman."

"Why is that?"

"I'm not prepared to discuss it now."

"Oh, shit." Lummer got up, then flapped his arms in a gesture of futility. "He doesn't want us to scoop his book." He moved as if he were going to walk away from him, then suddenly he turned, took one step toward Huxley, planting his foot solidly, then aimed a finger at him as if it were a dagger he clutched. "Not one of those women were abused sexually. Not even touched! So whatever kicks he gets could come from Wells as easily as from Miss America."

Huxley stood to face Lummer. "The extent of your ability, Dr. Lummer, to analyze psychological problems from different perspectives is to decide what color pills to prescribe. So I'm hardly surprised you don't have the foggiest notion of what I'm trying to accomplish."

"I warned you . . ." Lummer shrieked, his voice cracking.

Huxley turned from him and sat down, his move an effective dismissal. To Hagan he said, "It makes absolutely no sense that Reuker Stilkes would kill a thirty-six-year-old male."

Hagan's question came softly. "What he did to those women made sense?"

Huxley was silenced. And the moment of quiet gave Lummer the chance to begin again. "I warned you," he continued, "that if you took him off the drugs you would lose control. I said this would happen . . ."

As Lummer sputtered on and Huxley fended off the barrage, Hagan leaned back in his chair and tried to close them out. His head throbbed, and he massaged his temples with his left hand, his thumb on one side, his fingers on the other. It was a matter of priorities, he told himself. The murder created problems—some greater, some lesser—and each could be dealt with, if handled separately, and in order of importance. What to do about Reuker Stilkes was easy, at least what to do with him for now. But the critical question was how to lessen the impact of the Wells mess on the Senate.

Hagan released his forehead from his pincer grip, and for a moment the ache abated. But it was only temporary relief. Could the death be kept secret from Lansing, he considered, for just a few days? A week perhaps? No, not the death, but perhaps the murder. If the circumstances of the problem could be left uncertain, at least long enough for the whole of the Senate to grind through its appropriations, there would probably be no legislative fallout.

Such a deception—if it indeed was a deception merely to withhold information—would make no difference in the long run. Wells was dead; nothing could change that. And Stilkes could be safely secured. It was no different from a county supervisor with hat in hand in Lansing disguising last year's surplus, or a senator disguising hidden environmental costs in a bill his largest backer desperately wanted. The murder was just one tangential fact, like so many others in the legislative process, kept in the closet until the decision was made.

Of course, no criminal charges could be requested against anyone, until the *investigation* was complete. Hagan leaned forward, feeling somewhat better that things were falling into place, but it had taken its toll. He felt very tired. It wasn't just this morning's discovery, but the last six years. And even before that. All the time spent, the headaches, the uncertainties had a cumulative effect, and with each new problem resolved, he felt a little more tired, a little less enthusiastic about the future. If he were on the outside, if he were retired, it would all be over. It was a wistful thought, and it was the first time retirement occurred to him in just that fashion.

He shook the incipient longing from his mind, then interrupted Lummer and asked him to step outside.

Lummer looked surprised, then defensive, then he settled himself. With a knowing nod to Hagan, he left the office.

"Stilkes will be confined to his cell," Hagan announced to Huxley. "For the time being, at least. He's to stay there and if you want him for medical"—he paused, as if the word stuck in his throat—"reasons, he's to have two escorts and they are to stay with him.'' He regarded Huxley closely, but there was no visible change of expression. He continued. ''I'll have to let the MCAs have their shakedown, and after they do, all restrictions will be off. Except for Stilkes. When I'm sure things are under control, I'll have to take a closer look at Stilkes and how he fits into the Wells things.''

''How long will that be?''

''A day. A week. It depends. In the meantime, the investigation is officially continuing.''

Huxley understood Hagan perfectly. He understood the workings of the bureaucratic mind. As he left the office he knew his time with Stilkes was limited. If something was to happen, it would have to happen soon. And it would, he thought. He would make it happen.

19

The men on both floors in all three resident barracks were taken one by one from their rooms while each cell was systematically searched by teams of guards. It was a methodical process, a shakedown, and this time the guards brought an added thoroughness to the chore. Clothes were dropped on the floor and left there, personal items emptied and left in disarray. The anger that motivated them was only a disguise; it was in poor camouflage for their fear, that unless every corner was searched, every crack examined, the one blade that had killed Wells would be left to kill again.

Mattresses were checked thoroughly, and where a seam looked tampered with, or just worn, it was torn open. Each opening—drains, faucets, vents—was inspected with a light or a probe, the search aided by mirrors mounted on handles. The bottoms of furniture legs were examined for holes, and dressers and desks were emptied. Every book was opened and light bulb unscrewed. No potential hiding place was unchecked.

Before they were taken from their rooms, the men were patted down, then strip-searched, and then their bodily cavities probed. Then they were led to the lounge to wait with the others.

A shakedown has an effect on a prisoner beyond the fear that something incriminating of his may be found. He is left open, vulnerable; his impotence to keep sacred even the privacy of his own body becomes agonizingly clear. Exposed to the caprice of others, he feels naked long after the search is over. Even the most hardened of lifers in a state prison is made to feel insecure and threatened. And when the mind is suffering from incapacities little understood and impossible to gauge, the effect is all the worse.

In the lounge on the first floor of A-Barracks the men shivered, stood alone, talked quietly, chattered mindlessly—whatever to each of them was his way of dealing with his nerves.

In the search several weapons were found, but not by any means were all of them located.

Huxley strode about his office with his restless energy pulsing through every vein, vibrating through every nerve. Stilkes was his obsession, his marvel. His problems, his crimes, his past—his potential—were the sole thoughts that occupied Huxley's mind, that pounded at the limits of his physical endurance.

The swing from a son's abnormal love to his own special loathing because of the desertion, because he was left so utterly alone, was so extreme it had never been diffused. Huxley was astounded beyond belief, and enthralled, by the hate that was so strong that he had killed her six times and still did not feel avenged. It was a rage almost beyond psychiatric comprehension, a sickness that defied traditional treatment. He was a rare find. He would provide valuable insight. If only he would have enough time.

He had called A-Barracks an hour ago, and Jack Cooke had answered. The guard had told him there was no one available to bring the patient to his office, and that they would have to wait until two men were free to stay with him. Those were the orders, regarding Stilkes, he had said.

"Then bring him when you're done. As *soon* as you're done."

Jack said he would see to it, when the shakedown was completed.

So Huxley waited, and the conclusions that had been conjecture, then theory, were now fact. At least to him.

Reuker Stilkes was moved about like a piece of furniture as the guards ransacked his room. When no weapons were found, he was handcuffed and stood in the hall under watch, while his spilled belongings and the entire room were searched again. Every seam was checked for a razor, every crack in the wall's mortar probed carefully. Nothing incriminating was uncovered, and the guards had to give up, returning him to the shambles of his cell.

Reuker leaned his back against the locked door and exhaled a long, quavering breath, as if trying to expel the tensions that knotted within him. Since the night before he had waited for those tensions to unravel, but instead they only grew tighter. He waited for the picture of the doctor to fade, and the memory of last night's *shooting* to slink off into the confused jumble that had always seemed to be there before, ready to dissolve threatening images into a harmless morass. Yet the opposite was happening. His perceptions were becoming clearer. His fears, truer. And the evil that surrounded him was closing in.

With a deductive process he could not command a week before, he traced all that was happening to him, that had jarred him from his protected niche, to Huxley. It was his control that was squeezing ever tighter around him, and it was his touch that had brought the evil that gummed to his skin like a gelatinous acid.

Reuker shuddered and stepped away from the door. He rubbed his hands rapidly over his arms as though chafing against the cold, but it was the mental image of the vile substance of Huxley's evil that he strove to remove. It was on him and around him and in the air he breathed. He spun around, but there was nowhere to pace, nowhere to run. He wished for the drugged peace, but the chemicals were scant in his system.

He sat amid the disarray on the floor and, clenching his

arms tightly to his stomach, began to rock forward, then back, doubling over at the waist as though struggling to contain an ulcerous pain in his stomach. He sought the cleansing, in his dreams he sought the cleansing. He closed his eyes and called on the memories to appear, as they had before, to take him away.

Visual fragments of his past shot in, then out of his mind like celluloid on a fast reel. The more he fought to call the images to some kind of order, to bring the peace of the cleansing, the more harried they became. A tortured face of a woman, the high-pitched whine of a siren, the dagger teeth of a fur-snouted demon, the shriek of the halo-encircled priestess. There was no order, no peace, no way to turn.

He lurched up on his knees, his breath catching in a whistling gasp in his throat. He was in a hole—a grave?—in the ground. His lungs were stilled as he fought to gain the image. Yet it was dark, and heavy earth surrounded him, loomed above him, threatened to smother him. His paralysis squeezed his chest, and the old pain of suffocation began to burn within. He couldn't move, not even so much as to breathe. And it only grew worse. The searing call for breath, the ache that burned in his throat, the throb at the back of his head.

He started to shake, and then, like a claustrophobic's fever breaking, it all gushed out of him, and he collapsed on his side to the floor. As he did, he fell into the memory.

The distortions of his dream were gone. He could see it clearly now—at least as well as the descending darkness allowed. The days were much shorter at the end of the summer, and for Billy and Reuker, they were racing the night.

The hole was four feet deep and just wide enough to enable Reuker to leverage the shovel to the ground before lifting the dirt and tossing it to the side. They had been at it since midafternoon, and it had been a hard and long job. Spongy topsoil gave way to a dense matting of roots, some that broke with the weight of the shovel, some that needed blows of an ax. But now the surface of the ground was just above Reuker's head, and he was hot and sweaty and tired, and it was getting darker. Reuker looked up at his cousin. "Don't you think we should head back? And finish tomorrow?"

"No. I'm doing my part. Now you can finish yours."

"We won't be able to see to get back."

"Hey! Who knows these woods like the back of his hand? Have I ever gotten you lost?" When Reuker did not answer him, Billy went back to sharpening the stake, a signal for his cousin to resume working as well. "It won't be much more," Billy said.

After only a few more strokes of his knife Billy stopped to hold before his eyes the pinpoint tip of the clean wood. He approved of his work and of the progress on their project. "We'll catch something good. I just know we will."

Reuker had heard all the confidence before, when they had excitedly planned it. It was to be a pit, with stakes, like in the Tarzan movies. They would camouflage it and would be sure to catch something big: a deer maybe, or even a bear.

Since the raccoon with the broken legs, they had found other animals and had taken them to the Hole. Once they had lured a dog out to the falls with them. That was the easiest catch of all and, like the others, had its turn on the tether, and then ended up at the bottom of the crevice behind the falls. It was a game for Billy, a vicious assertion of a power and a will that would be shunted aside by any creature able to defend itself. But it was something more than a game for Reuker. It was a time of renewal, a time for cleansing. A time when all the inadequacies that leeched to his body were gloriously and simply washed away. Washed away by the eternal waters.

"Okay. That's good enough," Billy announced.

Reuker leaned with relief on his shovel. He swatted at some minuscule, hovering bugs that had found the hole, and then he prepared to climb out. The sandy-orange soil was held in place by the roots, and it was one of these roots near the surface that he grabbed and used to pull himself up.

Then Billy jumped into the hole and began planting his stakes. He had ten of them, and each one he placed equidistant from the others in a grid that covered the floor of the pit. He sank them about a foot into the dirt, leaving their tips two feet from the surface. He climbed out, and they covered the hole with thin branches, then scattered dead leaves on them.

By the time they were done, it was so dark they could barely see at all. Billy began to lead Reuker back toward town, and at first there was no question to his step. But once the trees that stood near the pit dissolved into darkness, and there was nothing on which to set his course, Billy grew progressively tentative.

"It looks different at night," was all Billy could say.

To Reuker it all looked the same.

Suddenly Billy headed in a new direction. Reuker had no choice but to follow, and he found it difficult keeping up with him. Billy was panting, he could hear, and walking faster. He would stumble and one time he almost fell, but he did not slow down. Reuker couldn't tell if he knew where he was going, or if he was just plain scared, gripped by the first stages of panic.

After walking for far longer than it seemed it should have been necessary, they could see a glow through the trees ahead. It was the lights of the town, and they headed toward it. Billy started to chatter when he first saw the lights, and by the time they reached the streets he was talking in his nonstop way, telling Reuker there had been nothing to worry about and he knew exactly where they were all along.

When they reached home, Billy's father was sitting at the head of the dining room table, waiting for his dinner. He didn't say anything to Billy when he saw him. Instead, he called out to the kitchen, "They're home."

There was a clatter of dishes, and Reuker started up the stairs with Billy just behind him, when Billy's mother came out of the kitchen. "Where were you?" she said crossly.

"In the woods."

"I know that. But you were out there much too long."

"We couldn't help it. We had some stuff to do."

A buzzer sounded in the kitchen, and she glanced back toward it, then up at Reuker on the steps. To Billy she said, "Hurry and get ready. And make sure you're clean." She turned toward the kitchen, then over her shoulder she called, "And tell Karen if she soiled her blouse she's in trouble."

Billy smiled at Reuker, and they scampered up the steps. He hoped she had soiled her blouse, and he delighted in the thought of telling her she was going to be in for it. But she wasn't up there.

They washed and came down to the table. It was close to nine o'clock; only a little late for their normal dinner hour. During the summer Billy's dad worked from eight until eight, making up for the lax hours during the winter. And the family adjusted to his hours.

At the table Rebecca Stilkes sat hunch-shouldered at the corner opposite Billy's father. Next to her was an empty chair where Karen usually sat, and across from her sat Billy and her son, Reuker.

Rebecca never talked much in the house, especially when Billy's dad was around. Even as she took their food and their shelter, she appeared resentful, harboring a secret hate for having to take it, as if it were her sister's fault.

As if to emphasize her disassociation from the house, Rebecca did none of the work, and it was Billy's mother who brought in the last dish from the kitchen. She sat next to Rebecca and opposite her husband. She served herself, then Rebecca, then passed the dish to the boys. When she served Rebecca from the second dish, she noticed Karen was not there. Immediately she glared in the direction of the stairs. "Where's Karen?" she demanded of Billy.

"I don't know."

She finished serving herself, then stalked to the bottom of the steps. "If you're trying to clean that blouse," she called angrily up the stairs, "it's too late. Now get down here."

"She's not up there, Mom," Billy took special glee in telling her.

"Didn't she come in with you?"

"No. Why would she?"

"Why? Because she was with you all day in the woods."

Billy's jaw dropped. His eyebrows furrowed as he glanced at Reuker, then he said, "No, she wasn't."

"She wasn't out there?" She glared at Reuker.

"No, Aunt Trudy."

She didn't trust Reuker, and her stare hardened with suspicion. "She said she was going to be, and I saw her leave."

Billy answered. "We never saw her all day."

She looked at her son, and gradually her expression changed as she believed him. Her lower lip began to quiver, and she brought her fingertips lightly upon it, as if to steady the twitch. "My God," she whispered, "it's nine o'clock."

Trudy rushed to the buffet in the hall where the phone was, and she dialed one of the neighbors. Her voice came back to the dining room in shrill phrases and frantic snatches of conversation. ". . . haven't seen . . . what about . . . sure?" She dialed another number. ". . . Did Sissy play . . . I haven't . . . Could you? . . ."

At the table Billy's father was eating his dinner as if nothing had happened. Gradually the others started to eat, but in silence, listening to Trudy get more frantic with every call. Billy and Reuker cast worried glances at each other, but afraid to say anything.

The phone slammed down, and Billy's mother burst back into the room. In a near-crazed state she shrieked at her son, "What did you do with her?"

"Nothing," Billy said, terrified, green peas slipping from the corner of his mouth.

"It was him, then," she cried.

Reuker pulled back from the table, afraid. Billy answered for him. "No, Mom, we never saw her."

She finally believed him and, with horror creased across her face, rushed back to the phone and called the police. "I've checked, I've called, she's not here. She has to be out there somewhere, in the woods. . . . Oh Lord, she'll die if you don't find her."

Billy dropped his fork to the table and gaped with terror at Reuker. Had she followed them, without being seen? Reuker sensed the question and could only shake his head. They left the table and ran upstairs to Billy's bedroom.

"We've got to go check," Billy argued.

"But what good will it do?"

"If she . . . if she is, and the police find her, they'll come right to us. We have no choice."

Reuker agreed, then they picked up their flashlights and sneaked out of the house. They were just about ready to hop the fence in the back to the alley when Billy stopped and thought. "We'd better bring the shovel," he said, then quietly opened the garage door and retrieved it from where they placed it only a short time before. A clump of orangish dirt still clung to its blade.

Dodging overturned garbage cans and stumbling over hardened mud ruts, they made their way through the alleys to the edge of town. As they passed the tree line, their flashlights burrowed into the black like water falling into mud. It was as if the night were solid and their waving bands of light pushed it back to the limits of the beam, only to allow the dark substance to ooze back into the cavity after they had passed.

They walked tentatively, slowly, silently. It was not the woods of their playground, but the woods of a nightmare. Jagged branches long robbed of sun hung like dead fingers in their line of sight, reaching out to touch them with their brittle sharpness. Lacy ferns lost their innocence, and instead their unbroken canopy appeared the moving, slithering skin of a reptile too large to imagine.

Everything had lost its color, and to Billy and Reuker objects appeared only in shades of gray, or black. It was a hellish place, a place of death, a place where dread turned real and fears came easily to the surface.

With each breath Billy sucked in air through his nose, then exhaled in a quavering rush through his mouth. They had been in the woods long enough to have reached the pit, yet they were moving very much slower than they would during the day. So they would continue, he thought.

But as they progressed deeper into the woods, he became less certain, and his light cast jerking arcs first to one side, then the other. Each tree was different, each marking unique, but to Billy they seemed more and more alike. Imperfect columns so uniformly different that the distinction lost meaning.

Behind him Reuker sensed the uncertainty. His cousin walked even slower now, and like him, Reuker flashed his light in all directions, looking for any sign of familiarity, for any disturbance of the ground. It seemed a hopeless search, and it was that thought that made him break the silence. "Maybe we should split up. We'd cover more ground."

"No!" Billy turned abruptly around.

"But it all looks the same. We'll never find it."

"You're staying with me." Then realizing his fear was showing in his voice, Billy added, "You'd get lost in a minute, and then what would I do? I'd have to find you, too."

Reuker looked away, then tensed. "What's that?"

Billy looked where Reuker pointed, and at first he didn't know what he meant. Then he saw the distant flash of light. "Turn it off. Your light," he said urgently.

In the total darkness they could see it better, the shifting, bobbing glow in the distance. "They're looking for her," Reuker whispered.

"Or us. Come on, let's go." Billy covered the lens of his flashlight with his hand and turned it on, allowing only a fingerwidth of light to escape. They felt their way forward, intent more on the ground in front of them than looking for the pit. They closed to within fifteen feet of it before Reuker realized what it was. He grabbed Billy's arm and pointed.

Billy spread his fingers over the lens wider and when he did, the hole they dug was clearly outlined by the mounded dirt along its edges. Billy felt an imediate sense of relief, and it took a few seconds for him to realize that something was wrong. The camouflage! The sticks were scattered, some pointing like frayed wire into the air, and where the leaves should have been was only blackness. Something had crashed through!

Billy couldn't move. Seized with a dread that locked his joints and stole his breath, he just stood there, his face pale, the light shining on the hole. Reuker moved past him and walked to the edge. He flicked on his own light and shone it down. Billy watched as Reuker stood, unmoving, looking into the pit. He showed no emotion.

"What is it?" Billy wheezed. Reuker did not answer but remained where he was, staring as if he had retreated into his own world. Slowly Billy picked his way up next to him. When he looked down, the first thing he thought of was that his sister's blouse was dirty. Why did she leave it out here? But in the manner of true horror's slow creep, what he saw gradually took root. The horror moved through his limbs, throughout his body, until its clutch was so severe, so deadening, his mind could no longer deny what was below his feet, in the pit.

Billy staggered back, and an inarticulate moan gushed

from deep in his chest. He stumbled and fell heavily to the ground, where he sat with his arms propping him up. The sounds he made were a staccato expulsion of terror intermixed with gasps for breath. The effect of what he saw worsened, wrenching his stomach with its horror until he could control the impulse no more. He rolled to his side and vomited into the dirt. And then again.

The wretching continued until there was nothing more to vomit, until his throat was seared with the burning feel of the acids and the taste of bile thickened in his mouth. Then he rocked to his back and lay in a daze.

After Reuker was sure Billy had stilled, he came over to him. "We have to hide her before they come." His voice was calm. He waited for Billy to say something, and when he didn't, he said again, louder, but still without emotion, "We have to hide her. Before they come."

Billy looked up at Reuker, then as the new horror occurred to him, his eyes opened wide, and he became instantly more alert. He jumped up and looked in the direction they had seen the lights. There was a fleeting sense of relief as he didn't see them. But they were still there and coming closer. His eyes darted back to Reuker. "We'll bury her."

"We can't."

"That's why we brought the shovel. We're all set."

"They're coming this way. They'll find her for sure. They'll get dogs and sniff her out for sure."

Billy swallowed, then glanced again at the distant glow. "Then what'll we do?"

"We have to take her somewhere else. Where they'll never find her."

The thought of touching her terrified Billy.

"I'll take her. You just fill in the pit."

Billy visibly untensed. "Where would you go?"

Reuker looked at him as if the answer was obvious. "To the Hole. I'll drop her in the crevice behind the falls."

Billy tried to consider the plan, but his mind flitted as his eyes did, from the pit to the woods to Reuker. Finally he agreed. "Okay."

Reuker turned and quickly paced back to the pit, then without hesitating, he put his hand on the lip and dropped down. Billy's eyes gaped wide, and he found he had to turn away. He listened as Reuker struggled, then he heard him climbing out. "Now make it look good," Reuker said, and Billy only nodded. He couldn't bring himself to look at him, and he fought the image in his mind of what Reuker was doing.

Billy didn't turn until he could no longer hear Reuker's footsteps cracking twigs that littered the ground. The first few spadefuls of dirt fell into the hole with some effort, but as he continued, he grew faster until he was frantically shoveling the dirt back into the hole. He grew sweaty and hot but would stop only to glance back into the woods. The glow was now distinct beams, as the searchers were getting closer.

Reuker's load was heavy, and the effort made him feel light-headed. He was making steady progress toward the river, but the searchers seemed to be moving even faster. They were gaining on him.

He was not using his light. He was afraid it would be seen, as their distant glow had first been seen, and so he pushed his way through the shifting ferns, gambling, hoping that unseen obstacles wouldn't thwart him. The commotion in the woods behind him grew louder—or was it the fears within him that surged out of control?

A voice! He thought he heard a voice. Reuker spun around, and with the weight on his shoulders, almost toppled over. The lights were still far enough away, but there were voices. He was sure of it. Distant, unintelligible, but the voices of the men on the search. They were closing in, and the feeling he had of being trapped worsened. It was a suffocating feeling that seemed to steal the breath from his lungs. And as it did, it was as if the woods itself conspired to smother him.

Reuker staggered, then fell forward, landing heavily in a tuft of pine needles. Brown and brittle, they jabbed into his knees and the fleshy heel of his hand. Despite the pain he made no effort to pull himself up. Instead, he stayed where he was, gasping for breath, fighting a whimper that wheezed in his throat.

As he slumped on the ground, everything whirled about him. Even the persistent sound of the searchers seemed to be coming from another direction. The composite sound of the voices was but a rhythmless disturbance in the air where no one noise was distinct on its own. Reuker raised his eyes and looked in the direction he had been going, the direction he thought he was going. The noise was coming from there. He stood quickly and listened. It was coming from both directions! He looked back and he could see the light; forward, there was none.

A rippling surge of panic gave him new strength, and he hoisted his load and moved on. The descriptionless rustling of the air grew louder, until it drowned the noises that pursued him. Reuker pushed on, stumbling stiff-legged over the uneven surface. His breath came in short, rapid bursts. With each spurted his anticipation. The rustling ahead shattered the heaviness of the air; its crisp, rushing sound swept away the suffocation.

The sight of the river lifted the weight of what he was carrying. Reuker didn't pause as he splashed into the water and headed upstream. A ribbon of the night sky was exposed by the slash of the river through the forest, and its dim glow lit his way. Stars shimmered in pooled water that was silky black, and where the water foamed white, it seemed to have its own luminescence.

The chill of the icy river numbed his feet, and in the dark with the water rushing like the wind, it was as if he were floating, floating unencumbered through a void where to touch meant nothing and imagination turned real. It was like the void of a dream, the dreams of his mother's suggestion. In the trees, in the darkness, hovered the demons she had warned were ever-present, ever-watchful for a chance to spit their acid saliva onto his skin. Reuker could barely distinguish the shapes, but with eyes of fire there was no mistaking they were there. Like dogs straining at the ends of their leads, the demons were held at the banks, kept at bay by the rushing purity of the waters.

Reuker neared the falls, and its pounding tumult drowned out the snarling of the beasts on the shore. He was caught in the cadence of the falls, intent on the grotto behind, on the cleansing that waited. The dark wall of the cliff face loomed ahead, directing its pulsing waves of vibration toward Reuker. He started up the cascade, the rhythm of the splashing on the rocks becoming his own rhythm, the jittering action of the water his own nervousness.

His breath was little more than wretching gasps as he pushed himself up the twisting course, but he would not rest. He could not rest. He was under the power of the falls, the insistent drumming of water on stone methodically, rhythmically pounding its message into him. It was an exhilarating message, promising release from everything that haunted him. It was a release that came only by following the rituals of his invention.

With the spiritual ecstasy of the enchanted growing within, Reuker moved closer, numbed by the cold and deafened by the roar of the water. It would be like no other time in the grotto, under its dangling roots. Already it was better. The feelings more intense. The throbbing pulse of his blood faster. He knew it would be purer, the cleansing more complete, the sacrament richer.

At the edge of the falls he was nearly in another world. Then he plunged through the wall of water, and that other world's grasp on him was complete.

Billy was on his hands and knees, frantically scraping forest debris over the newly filled-in pit. Even in the dark the patch of fresh orange soil was like a beacon calling attention to the spot. Billy struggled to camouflage it, before it was too late. Before the men reached him.

They had been past him and then back again in their zigzag search pattern, one time not more than a hundred yards from where he crouched silently on the ground. He had heard their voices, calling out for his sister, and to each other, and he even recognized who some of them were.

Billy uprooted a fern, then sank its stiff stem and tear-shaped root into dirt over the pit. He transplanted four more ferns before he was satisfied their three-lobed fronds covered what his camouflage couldn't hide. Then Billy left the spot and began to slink into the darkness of the woods. Though no darker than the site of the pit, at least with the time he was there familiarity had lent vision.

All he wanted was to get away from that spot, avoid the men, and hide. Hide someplace where he could be sure of no discovery, where the fatigue could seep out of him, the fear dissolve into sleep. So he hurried toward the Hole.

He traveled without his light, the shovel slung from one

weary arm. The sweat of the dig cooled on his back, shrouding his fear with icy dread. It wasn't until he reached the bottom of the cascades that he began to lose that fear. He was nearly safe, and the evidence was surely disposed of by now in the yawning black crevice behind the falls. Suddenly he felt like laughing, so total was his relief.

He made his way up the rock-strewn waterway and gradually became soaked with the spray of the falls. It felt invigorating, and this time he did laugh; it was a gleeful expulsion of the tension that had gripped him for hours. As he plunged through the falls into the grotto behind, all the worry of what was going to happen to him if they found out what he had done was wondrously lifted off his mind.

Inside, the eyes cleared and the scene before him he instantly recognized from before, but it was somehow unreal. Something within him denied what he saw, yet even in disbelief he was left stunned. His giddy relief froze, and very gradually it began to change. It changed into something horrible. The laughing release he had felt turned rotten, and he screamed. He recoiled from Reuker, and his scream sounded above even the fury of the falls. It tore into Reuker's ears, echoing louder with increasing volume.

And it echoed through time, playing itself with equal terror in Reuker's memory nineteen years later, as he lay on the floor of his cell.

The door opened and two guards strode in. "Come on, get up," one of them said, then without waiting for him to move on his own, they pulled him to his feet and cuffed his hands behind his back.

He was confused and frightened, and Billy's terror became his. He began to tremble, and the nervousness quavered in his voice as he asked where they were taking him.

"To Huxley," said the guard with the great bulk. "You're going to see your shrink."

Whatever purity that lingered from the cleansing in his dream vanished. He was being led into the very lair of the evil that had brought him all his pain.

20

It has been like this before. The man with the wiry hair and the round glasses leaning against the desk, or pacing through the room, and the gaunt, hunched figure staring with his skeletal face toward the floor, sometimes with his hands between his thighs, sometimes rocking ever so slightly back and forth. It was doctor and patient, interrogator and prisoner. The instruments of therapy, and torture, were the same. The instruments were words, words that circled the slumped, seated figure, trailing streams of evil, binding him within a putrid cocoon.

It had *appeared* this way before, but it wasn't the same. The difference was within each man. Inside one were a certainty, a drive, a compulsion, the taste of accomplishment after the sweat has been spent. In the other were a despair, a sense of damnation, the feeling that every touch, every word of the inquisitor left a burning, festering wound that could only spread and grow worse.

Huxley could see he was no closer to bringing Stilkes out than he had been before. He tried a new tack. "We don't have much time, you know." He let the change of pace sink in, before he went on. "You know why? Because you've been accused of murder."

Reuker looked at him. The only change was a furrowing of the eyebrows, but to Huxley, it was all the reaction he needed.

"They say it happened last night."

Reuker became still; he closed his eyes and thought. The violence of last night he remembered. He was in this very room when the *shooting* occurred, with himself a mere passenger of his racing thoughts. He remembered the prone figure lying motionless on the floor, and for a nervous blink of the eyes he felt what Huxley said was true. But his memory pushed on, and he realized that it was this man, this very doctor, who had been the one on the floor. It had been he who had pushed him into the violence of his thoughts, the need to escape from an atmosphere heavy with the black stain of evil.

Reuker remembered last night. The round eyes made

rounder by the gold-frame glasses had loomed closer, threatening him with an evil only Reuker could perceive. He tried anything to keep him back; he would have said what the man wished, if only he had known what it was. The man had continued to press, and as Reuker thought of last night's encounter, of how he dreaded this man as the pure must dread the stained, he realized that today would be another test. Was the murder accusation a trick? It must be, for the accuser was the alibi. Reuker would play his game. He opened his eyes and looked at Huxley and said with a rare calm, "You know it wasn't me."

"Yes, *I* know. But *they* don't." Huxley paused to let his ominous tone work its effect. He watched Reuker, in the silence; he watched as the powers of thought skewered the man's face. His expression showed an inward reflection he had been unable to command under the drugs.

Reuker felt the first dull throb in his head, deep behind his eyes. It was a distant throb, a muted blip of pressure, like a cloth-swathed hammer's blow reverberating from some remote place on a track. The steel carried the pulse to the center of his head, where finally it reached him in a single, muffled wave. As if riding that wave, Reuker raised himself in his chair, then gripped the arms, and settled back down. Though he became still, he could feel an unsteadiness beginning to vibrate within him. He was being warned that, like before, it would be a struggle to keep the doctor back, to protect himself from the evil aura about him.

To Reuker, it mattered not what had happened the night before, or what they thought he had done. What mattered was to insulate himself against the suffocating uncleanliness of this room, this man, his questions. Whatever it took, he would try to give it. As the tortured seeks to appease the interrogator, Reuker said, "You can tell them. You can tell them for me that I didn't kill anyone."

"Ah, but why would they believe me?"

"Because you're one of them."

"I am no more one of them, than you are one with the other prisoners. We are different, Reuker. You in your way, me in mine." Huxley had paused in his pacing and stood just a few feet away, leering at Reuker. His smile was an imitation of friendship, but those feelings were foreign to Huxley and he appeared as though mocking him.

Reuker shuddered. He was not like him, he thought. Huxley was trying to pull him closer, to establish some kind of affinity between them, but he would resist. He must resist. The only alternative was to succumb to the burning malevolence that infected the very air about him.

Huxley watched as Stilkes shook and nervously looked away from him. Anxious, he stepped closer. He had touched him, he felt. He could see he was breaking through Reuker's shell. He moved to cement the link. "I can prove it wasn't you who did what they say."

Reuker kept his eyes away from the doctor, but in his mind his visage lingered. Creases splayed from the corners of his insincere smile, and his skin had the flakiness of the winter's cold. The dark lines cutting through his parched white face lent the appearance of a demon, one of the fire-eyed creatures of Reuker's haunting. He grimaced and pulled himself tighter into a ball. But the image persisted. He saw the pulsing of Huxley's jugular protruding obscenely down the side of his tendon-stretched neck, and with each pulse he felt the rhythm enter his own body, coursing through his own nerves. "I will stay pure!" The words shrieked through Reuker's mind, and he opened his eyes and looked with fright to Huxley. Had his thoughts leaked into speech?

They hadn't. Huxey's face loomed closer. "I *can* prove it," he assured again. "And the proof lies in your illness."

Stilkes began to shake in tight spasms. The ache in his head throbbed again, slightly more painful—the hammer's blow louder—than the first. Then he said, "I, I don't . . ." and the words choked in his throat. He wanted to say he didn't care, that whatever proof he had to give he didn't want. He wanted nothing from him at all. But forces within had disabled him. He felt helpless, as if falling more under this man's spell. He had all the controls, Reuker realized, and he was reeling him, slowly, relentlessly, into his world.

Huxley was an impatient man—the vice of the gifted whose arrogance has little tolerance for the weakness of others—and his impatience was heightened by the time restrictions he knew were working against him. He couldn't wait for Stilkes to emerge slowly, to gravitate to the logic on his own and then come to the conclusions Huxley had already formulated for him. He would have to push him, Huxley realized, and push him hard. "You couldn't have killed the guard, because you don't kill without a reason. And your reason doesn't fit this crime."

Does he understand the cleansing? The thought spiked true panic through his mind. Could he control his dreams as he controlled his freedom? They were his only refuge from the evil of the institution. The helplessness he had felt expanded into something larger, something more encompassing, something he could do little to control. He felt the despair of the lost. How could he repel him any longer?

"You always had a reason before, didn't you? There was a design behind your killing those women. A design that was logical and precise. And not at all as bad as the others made it appear."

The throb fast became an undulating wave of continuous, pulsing pressure. Reuker grabbed his head with both hands and squeezed. Yet the pain persisted.

Reuker was close to seeing the truth, Huxley could see. He had to push harder. He had to build his case piece by piece so its logic could no longer be repressed by innate taboos active even in the degenerate personality of Reuker Stilkes. "Just think back, Reuker, to when you were in Alkmaar living with your mother in that house on the gravel road. You listen, and I'll help you remember."

Huxley eased a chair close to Stilkes and sat down. Their knees nearly touching, he continued in a soft, hypnotic tone, "You didn't go to school like the other kids, because your mother kept you at home. There were no friends and probably no one you knew to play with out where you lived. There were no brothers, no sisters, no father. Just Rebecca. She was the only one, every day, every week, every month. She was your only contact to the world and you saw through her."

Reuker shivered and tried to pull himself deeper into the chair. Yet the upholstery was ungiving, and the voice continued and the hammer blows grew closer along the track.

As Stilkes pulled back, Huxley leaned forward. And his voice grew louder, more forceful. "And there was something else. Like everything, it came from her. She started it when you were probably too young to understand. It was just a game, and in a world with so few games you latched onto it. It was one thing that you did together that made you smile, and you clung to those brief moments of happiness with everything you had. She was your eyes, she was your thoughts, and she was your pleasure."

As Huxley's voice came in painful waves, Reuker looked at him with growing confusion. He heard yet he did not understand. It was like the old confusion that had presented such anxiety before. It had always grown worse when he was at the mercy of events beyond his comprehension. But then there had always been release. Release from the doubts and frustrations and aches was the fogging effects of the chemicals. Now there was no dampener. The mounting uncertainties were left to whirl sickeningly in his mind. They were left to weave their collapsing web of evil about him.

Huxley pushed harder. "You can remember, I can see it in your eyes. You told me of it yesterday. You would stand before her, and she, her legs open . . ."

The rhythm of the pounding steel in his head was almost deafening. Yet he still heard. There was no escaping it.

". . . waiting for you. And then, just as you were becoming a man, when you had questions about yourself and your body and the uncertainties were at their strongest, she left. She deserted you, never to look back."

Reuker sat there stunned, in part by the pain, in part by the obscurities he spun. He tried to understand, he wanted to understand, if only to stop the pain, to keep him back. But Huxley spoke in words impossible to decipher. What was it he meant, his mind cried in desperation. *What did he mean?*

A nervous heat prickled across Huxley's skin. It was doubt that flickered in his mind, the feeling that perhaps he was pushing too hard, that Stilkes be allowed to face his inner motivations in an atmosphere freer of the tension that was building. The memory of the blow he received the night before flashed through his head, but then it was gone as fast as it had appeared. Then the doubt evaporated with the realization that there was so little time. Stilkes would be lost to Hagan and the psychotropics, and whatever he had accomplished with him would be gone.

The lapse lasted only a few seconds before Huxley continued the assault. And in the alternating fire and calm of an interrogator, he spoke more softly. "The subconscious is a strange thing. It doesn't always respond to logic, and sometimes it is a creature totally of your emotions. When Rebecca left you it didn't matter that she didn't choose to leave, only that she did leave you, alone. Worse than that. The love you felt for her was thrown back in your face. Your love for her during those years was the sum total of every scrap of affection a human being can possess. For you, she was the only outlet. There was no other family, there were no other friends. Whatever sexual feelings you were evolving for women were inextricably wound in with every other feeling you had for her. The bond of mother, and lover, was all-consuming. There was nothing else. And then it ended. It ended because she deserted you. She died on you. It was her own cigarette that started the fire, and you were left without support, with nowhere for your love to focus."

Huxley's tempo had gradually increased. It was machinelike, his voice. Nonstop. Insistent. Overpowering. Reuker's eyes remained shut, but the tenacity lessened. He felt weakened. Amid the throbbing, the confusion, the ache, a phrase was repeated in his mind. It pulsed larger, brighter, louder, until it was all he could hear. *His mother's lover.* He searched for understanding. He thought of Rebecca and the men who would come to their house. He remembered standing in the hallway and watching them, together, on the bed, rolling and struggling against each other. The room stank of sweat and decay and whisky, and as Reuker remembered, it was as if the odor came again, over the years, to make him recoil in revulsion. It was a soiled room, a room of decadence and filth and evil. He felt all those things again, at this moment; they were present in this room, in this office.

As the feeling deepened, he listened more to what Huxley was saying. He could not escape the message, and slowly it drummed into him, deeper, fuller, until finally he realized what he meant. It was himself, Reuker Stilkes, who was the lover. It was him wallowing in her stench and decay, the doctor was saying. It was himself, as a child, that was the foul-smelling creature sharing the bed with Rebecca.

Reuker's face involuntarily began to tremble, and from his throat warbled a pathetic gasp. The suggestion itself broke through whatever defenses he had, and toward him surged the sin, the impurities, the evil he had so desperately been trying to keep away. It seized him, and smothered him, and took the breath from his lungs. Reuker groaned in his terror, but still the voice continued.

"This love you had began to change. With no outlet, with it thrust with such finality right back at you, there was no alternative but for it to change. And it did, slowly at first, then picking up momentum as something inside you realized it was the only way to answer the painful urges within you." Huxley had fallen again into his hypnotic cadence, his own emotions carrying him along as he tried to channel them to push Reuker, to force the destruction of his subconscious barriers. "It became hate. Your love changed so completely that all that remained was the fire of your emotions. As is so terribly common to the human experience, the vast reservoir of single-minded feelings you had changed to a resentment at least as strong as the love had been."

Reuker tried to deny the accusations, but his voice was but a hoarse whisper. So drained was he that speech escaped him.

"The hate was a burning, festering wound that dominated your life since the moment her desertion changed you. You wanted to strike back, but you couldn't. She was dead. So you channeled this hate onto the others and you killed and killed and killed. But deep inside, you knew it wasn't her, and the hate was never released."

A sick emptiness churned deep within Reuker. He thought of the killings, and he thought of the cleansing, how each had been necessary, how each had served to rid the accumulations of the evil that surrounded him. And now the devil before him was tearing at the sacrament, trying to touch even that with his horrors. He shook his head and was able to gasp, "No." It was a tired sound, a defeated plea, and then he repeated it. "No!" He shook, and the word came again, slightly louder, still without force.

"It's true, Reuker," Huxley said as he grasped him solidly at the shoulders. "You see her death as a desertion.

You needed her so desperately and by her own carelessness she was gone."

Suddenly, in his mind, he saw the fire, and he saw her hand reaching out of the flames. As he did then, he watched, and he felt its heat, growing hotter, searing his own skin as it consumed hers.

The thought in Huxley's mind was a frantic demand: Only if the patient acknowledged his true motivation for killing would his psyche be released from its ceaseless inner demand for vengeance. Only then would his rage flame out. He continued to press. "The relationship you had is not a shameful thing . . ."

Reuker burned from the heat of the fire, from the touch of the thickening air, from the image of sin and uncleanliness Huxley was forcing upon him.

". . . You must understand that it wasn't. That impulse was as old as the human race and was one of the first subconscious urges charted by psychiatric science. Your special love, your unique bond to Rebecca, you must not be afraid to acknowledge."

"I hated her!" Reuker screamed. The words erupted in his mind, and for a moment after he heard them he wasn't sure if he had spoken, or if he heard them only within the violence of his thoughts. But he could see in Huxley's face that he had heard them too. And he found that his speech came easily, propelled by the horror of his thoughts. "She was filth. She was a decayed and rotting corpse long before the fire consumed her. She spoke of being clean, of seeing and diverting the evil that pounded on our doors, that reached out at us with the bent fingers of every person that touched us. She said she was my filter to the impurities that surround us, that hover in the air, that cling to skin leaving only a blackened cinder if they are not removed. But she lied! She went willingly into the arms of the devil and it was her evil that contaminated me, that left its mark on my soul." Then in a gravelly-voiced rage he said again, *"I hated her!"*

Huxley was limp. He was aware that the two guards had burst through the door at Reuker's first scream, but they quickly dissolved into the background as he had sat and listened to Stilkes.

It was going all wrong, he thought. It wasn't supposed to be like this. A sinking despair gripped him tightly about the stomach. "You're wrong," he managed to gasp feebly, his voice devoid of conviction. "It just doesn't fit."

"I killed her," he shouted. Then again, *"I killed her!"*—each word pronounced as if a separate statement of fact.

"No, you couldn't have. The fire. She died in the fire started by her own cigarette."

"I poured her liquor over her bed, then I lit it. She was too drunk to move. She could see what I was doing, but she couldn't get up. Then as the fire burned I stood in the doorway and watched. She screamed for me to help her, but I just stood there. I watched her evil lose its grasp on me. The flames destroyed it as they destroyed her. I stayed for as long as I could bear the heat, until her reaching hand dropped to her lap, and then I ran outside. They said later it was an accident, that her cigarette started a fire in alcohol she spilled. *But she never smoked.* No one ever thought that her own son could have done that, but no one ever saw her inner contamination as I did."

Huxley was stunned. The mind he had charted so carefully was in reality an entity so foreign it was beyond his comprehension. It was the same as if a friend he had known for years suddenly became a different person altogether. He didn't speak to the guards, and they not to him as they firmly gripped Stilkes by the arms and led him into the hallway.

21

The handcuffs slapped on his wrists. Reuker winced as Arnie Johnson's hand caught him squarely in the back, pushing him forward. Jack Cooke's hand was lightly clasped around his arm, more to lead than to constrain.

It had been *like* a *shooting,* but it was not quite the same. Images from the past and ideas from the present had thrashed together in his mind, like the branches of a willow in a gale. Yet this time he was not a victim of the flow, an observer without a role. He was central to the event, and he found himself participating. The words had gushed from some deep wellspring of spiritual fervor, and he had succeeded in fending off, for the moment at least, the assault of Huxley's evil.

The tensions and fears that had burst from him in that room, though now silent, still raced in his mind. He was acutely more aware of everything about him, from the hard feel of the thin carpeting in the hallway to the gruff panting of the fat guard behind him. His perceptions had intensified with the *shooting,* and his entire self was one raw nerve reacting to the slightest stimulus.

The locking mechanism tumbled in the door, and below them opened the stairway to the tunnels. Reuker was nudged forward, and with his arms awkwardly secured behind his back, he felt for an instant as though he would tumble headfirst down the stairs. He didn't, and an anxious quiver of fear was ignited within him. He had no choice but to descend the molded concrete steps into the scant light of the tunnels, into the stale air of the perpetual underground, into the depths of Scales.

The men congregated nervously in the lounge. They had been searched and their rooms ransacked, but in each was the realization that this was only the beginning. There remained a satisfaction that one of the MCAs had fallen, but a price would have to be paid. Their minds reared with cruel defects and nurtured now by artificial impulses, they were easy targets for paranoia.

On the floor above them, another thirty captives were tensed by the same anxiety. And in B-Barracks and C-Barracks the atmosphere was no different. It was as if the same broad storm front was settling over each site.

The guards could feel the tension of the men and did nothing to ease it. They wanted them to be off balance, not to know what to expect, to be afraid. It was the only weapon they had, and they were bitter. Bitter at the murder of Wells, at the inmates and their collective guilt, at the system that allowed it to happen—the same system that would do nothing to punish the crime.

In A-Barracks, Eric Creegan looked out from his glass cage, secure behind a locked door, secure in the thought that the crime would not go unpunished. And the killer would not suffer alone. Like conspirators, they all shared in the principal's success, so as accomplices, they would share the penalty.

Creegan's thoughts could not have been plainer if he announced them through the tinny speaker above the glass window that looked into the lounge. The harshness of his glare, the grim set of his jaw conveyed his contempt as it buried into the men the surety of his vengeance.

Hector Irons had done time in every kind of prison and had seen that stare before and perhaps more than any knew what it meant. Though he was afraid, he didn't show it. He had learned early that prisons feed on intimidation and prey on the weak. His eyes the color of granite, he stared back across the glass threshold into the eyes of the guard.

Herman Breitsmann's hand was slick with sweat and grease from running it through his hair. He lacked Irons's control, and he shook visibly, his yellow nubs of teeth chattering like an off-key wind chime. Next to him Squirrel was silent, but restive. Eddie Hyland was the only one who dared talk in a normal voice, but even in him, visible only in the twitch at the corners of his smirk, was the shared anxiety.

For Dennis Ringly there was a special torment. It was the waiting. He knew the other prisoners knew he killed Wells, and he was surprised the investigators had yet to come for him. But they would, he realized. It was only a matter of time. And it was that time that was a weapon, held to his gut, threatening to tear him wide open at any moment.

Ringly could feel no comfort from the other men and did his best to keep his distance. With nothing to do but wait, he found himself moving aimlessly from one corner of the room to another. Always, his hand rested at his waistband. Every few moments he squeezed, feeling for the razor whip as a miser checks for his purse. It was still there, ready to withdraw.

The air itself carried a vibrating nervousness, each man a single pebble in a pond. The ripples created stray tremors, some at odds with the rest, some adding to the crest and trough. Graphed, they would be fine ink-lines rising then falling in erratic arches. Yet within this ravel there was a uniformity; it was as if the tremors were seeking the same rhythm.

The walls of the tunnel were the rock of the island. It was dark stone, jagged, and it absorbed the light into its face, or trapped it on its many edges. It made for darkness that hung in the air as if it were something solid that had to be forged through. Reuker could feel the darkness brush across his body. He could feel its ragged fabric drag its sticky threads across his cheeks. His arms secured behind him, he was helpless to wave it away.

The thought of Huxley could not be torn from his mind. He was haunted by his face hovering just in front of him, as it had in the room. As the face shifted, reflections of light glinted in his glasses, and they became not reflections, but tongues of fire. Like in his dreams, it was the face of a demon.

Huxley's accusation stuck to him like the crusty skeletons of wind-whipped insects. He pictured himself and Rebecca, together as Huxley said they had been together, and it so sickened him he closed his eyes to try to block the vision. He stumbled against the wall. Then he felt the hand at his back, roughly knocking him forward.

The vision did not leave. It worked its sordid black magic on him. Reuker shuddered, and the shudder became an inarticulate whimper in the back of his throat. The devil had been in her, had controlled her, had guided her every action, her every touch. And she had almost succeeded in corrupting his cleanliness, in converting his body to the vessel of filth and decay that was hers.

She had failed though, because he had ended the attempt, decisively. But now, suddenly, she was back. He could feel her presence, and she was clawing for him. And Huxley. Together their evil swirled about him, faster, always faster, creating such a draw that it sucked the oxygen from him. He had to draw deeper for his breath, his chest was forced to pump harder. This time there was nothing he could do. He saw no way to end it. There was no fire of his own to ignite.

The spiraling evil was a whirlwind of blackness that

grew tighter, spun closer to his skin until it touched him. Reuker gasped in shock and pain and collapsed to one knee. The impact on the tile was hard and unbroken, yet it was a pain he could not feel. It was eclipsed by a terror that burst over him, in him, around him; the terror ignited his skin as if it were set ablaze with a splash of alcohol. The sudden, burning horror came from inside his head, from what he realized: *it was in him*. For the first time, *the evil was inside*.

One of the guards pulled him to his feet, and he felt a solid push in the middle of his back. Then they resumed walking through the dark corridor.

The hammer blows along the rail moved to the center of his chest. His heart pounded the rhythm of terror, and his lungs surged for the air that was escaping him. Ahead of them and behind, the footfalls of the three men cracked like the discharge of a small-caliber weapon, and it was this sound that crackled throughout his nerves.

He was dying. The evil had succeeded at last. In his agony there was room for despair.

The tunnel spur they had angled into ended at the molded concrete staircase that led to A-Barracks. Reuker was nudged from behind, and he began to climb. He moved slowly, his feet scuffing on the cement with the sluggish motion of the condemned ascending the scaffold. Yet within, the rhythm of forces was relentless. Through his veins flowed his dread of what was happening to him. The steady pulse drummed its message into him, and he could feel it in his chest, in his wrists, in his neck. The blood rushing through his temples had the sound of wind, and on that wind he heard a whisper, a haunting memory of a voice that reached from across the years. "He will feed on your life until there is nothing left but a pitted and blackened soul fit only for the eternal fire. You must scrape the contamination from your skin, wipe it clean before it burns right into you."

The door opened, and the brightness rushed over them. From the depths of the tunnel, it was a shock to Reuker's eyes, and he teetered on the uppermost step, before being pushed through the threshold.

Huxley sat at the kitchen table in his apartment, his back curved with the weight of his fallen assumptions. He had been so sure, so positive in his analysis that when Stilkes had erupted, Huxley first thought that the man had gone irretrievably insane. His own conviction was that strong—that at first it was stronger than the truth. But the truth was in Reuker's eyes and in the force of his manner, and even Huxley could not deny it.

He had watched in stunned silence as the MCAs had taken Stilkes from his office and back to A-Barracks. His diagnosis had been classic psychology, yet it crumbled into nonsense with his revelations. Huxley tried to understand what tormented world Stilkes had spoken of, but he could fathom no coherence to what he had said. He tried to visualize that world, a world of demons and decay and evil, and what he saw frightened him. It was a world that to understand would take long hours of probing, listening, waiting. It was a world he would not have a chance to enter.

Huxley had left his office and walked with his private despair back to the staff building. The door to his quarters he left open, lost as he was in his thoughts. Sitting alone at the table, he was in a daze. Yet through the unreality of his mood, he felt more than heard distant scratching, like rat's claws in a cellar. It was a disquieting sensation, and as he sat there, the feeling alone seemed to bring back at least some of his clarity of mind. For one of the rare times in his life he looked beyond the narrow limits of what he was pushing himself toward. It was the rage he had seen in Stilkes that made him feel that way; and it was this force that had awakened the personal demons within Stilkes. They were demons from his past, Huxley now knew, that for some peculiar reasons had driven him to kill before, and would surely drive him to kill again.

The hallway opened into the lounge, and as Reuker was led into it, the others stared at him. If it was quiet before, it was now as still as a crypt.

He could feel their eyes, the focus of their vision like the hot cone under a magnifying glass. The pinpoint of fire burned into him as a sudden rush of flame burrows through ash.

The rhythm of terror that had so overwhelmed him became the core of a new strength. It was the strength of desperation, the power of the damned.

The pain he felt was gone. The burning sensations were extinguished.

The handcuffs were off, and his arms were freed. Then everything around him began to move faster. Reuker turned around, his eyes sweeping across the room. It wasn't that the others were moving faster. He was! He moved as if weightless and they as if images projected from a reel slowed by rusted spindles.

His fingers interlocked, and he swung his arms toward the white-shirted, green-trousered devil closest to him. His fist arced like a bony pendulum swinging with the force of a clock spring wound tight for so long, and now suddenly released.

Jack Cooke was caught by surprise. The blow struck him at the side of his face, and he staggered to the side and collapsed to his knees. Stunned, he could barely hold himself steady.

The guard had fallen, and Reuker quickly turned toward the other. He could feel the energy vibrating through his system, powering him to motion faster than he thought possible. He was *shooting*. It was like the other times—the suspension of temporal laws, and the rush of shapes and ideas past him—only this time he saw it all. He could feel it. And he was master of it! The fat guard swung at him, but to Reuker the move was an awkward lunge of a lumbering ox. He could see it coming, and he easily deflected the blow. He struck back with his fists and pushed toward him; the guard was staggered.

Behind the glass Creegan leaped from his seat when Stilkes's doubled fist had first struck Jack. It froze him momentarily with disbelief, and his open mouth gape was the only reaction he was capable of. He thought it a fit, a crazy man's seizure, like they had seen so many times over the years. But then he felt the rage, incumbent within him from the events of the last day, and all the bitterness he felt toward the system, toward the inmates, his anger over Wells's murder, and at Reuker Stilkes, came rushing over him, and he reached for the door and grappled with the lock. This was his chance to make them pay.

He burst from the guard's booth and charged toward Arnie and Reuker. The thought of lifting the protective plastic cover over the yellow alarm signal never entered his mind. There was only one of him, and two of them.

Even alone, Creegan felt sure, he could handle him.

The other inmates were slow to react. The scuffle had caught them all off guard, and in a collective action all stepped back. But like the single thinking unit they were, they surged forward again, as a chest must expand after an exhale of shock.

Ringly more than any felt the violence. It threatened him, and he knew that his waiting was nearly over. He could be the next target, and he wouldn't survive. There would be no forgiveness for the killing of a guard; no trial, no plea of insanity, no verdict of Guilty but Mentally Ill. Inside his head the certainty of the threat triggered the beginning of a reaction he could do little to control. And with each step he fell further under its spell. "It's happening!" someone whispered behind him, and everyone knew what it meant. From Ringly's waist sprang the thin metal strip.

Reuker had brushed aside Arnie's clumsy attempts to strike him and flailed away at his head. His fingers raked across his face when Creegan reached him from behind. Creegan struck him between the shoulder blades, and Reuker lunged forward into Arnie. He pushed back and whirled to face him, and as he did, he felt the guard's hands at his throat. They sank into his neck, and for an awful moment his entire body was seized with the lack of breath. The blackness threatened to overcome him, the dull throb at the back of his head erupted with its familiar pain, when suddenly Creegan was snatched away from him.

Ringly had him by the throat. His razor whip was wrapped around Creegan's neck, and he pulled with all the massive strength he possessed. The edge sank into his skin, and almost instantaneously Creegan had a collar of blood.

Arnie gasped in horror as he watched Creegan frantically try to grip the wire around his neck. His eyes bulged, and his face puffed red, as if it were going to burst.

Hector Irons was the first to join in. He crashed into Arnie and knocked him from his feet. Then as the guard raised his hands to his face to protect himself, Irons slammed his fist into his soft belly, then immediately reached for the keys in the man's pockets. They were tethered to his belt by a snakelike chain, and this he tore loose with one solid tug.

The sight of the keys in his hands was like an electric prod to the others. Adrenaline more powerful than the artificial chemicals that pulsed in their veins unleashed a surge of emotion. Their destiny was their own. At last!

Some of the men broke for their cells to break apart the chair legs that concealed their knives, or to rip ventilation covers off their brackets and retrieve their handcrafted weapons that had eluded the detection of the guards. Some of the others ripped razor whips from their waistbands, while the rest surged around the stricken Creegan and the fat guard, now wallowing in fear at their feet.

Jack had fallen toward the booth, and as the violence broke around him, he was aware of the noise, but the painful throb in his head robbed him of the ability to think. He could barely maintain his balance as in his ears cracked the echo of Stilkes's blow to his face. Then as the combination intensified and shifted to other areas of the room, around Creegan and Arnie Johnson, his head cleared, and he was able to glance around him.

The door to the guard's booth was open, Jack could see, and he lunged for it. With the sudden motion the dizziness returned, and he slumped at the entrance. He looked toward the console of controls. The microphone on its pedestal wavered like a snake coiled to strike and the controls below it dissolved into a confusion of color. He shook his head, as if to shake free the dizziness, and then he let go of the door jamb and fell toward the counter.

The square release cover for the emergency alarm, hinged to the counter at the back, was down. Clumsily his fingers groped for it. His hand seemed not his own as it wavered in front of him. It was like watching a mechanical arm inside a sterilized compartment, and trying for the first time to get it to react to commands. He struggled to control it, to bring it to the hinged box. Gradually the cloud inside his head lifted, almost as if Jack's struggle had burned it away. The emergency lid snapped open.

In the control center where any alarm would first alert the compound of a problem, two men were on duty. Robin Pettaway sat within the semicircle of the television screens, and Jay Sachs stood with coffee in hand just on the other side of the screens. They would spell each other on the tedious task of keeping an eye on the flicking black-and-white images relayed to them from 160 cameras within the facility. Sachs's job at the moment was to monitor the radio and act as switchboard operator for any telephone calls coming in or going out of the island.

Pettaway had his feet stretched up onto the counter at one end of the semicircle. The four screens he faced were permanently trained on security cameras within his own building, while the other twelve alternated on scenes throughout the facility. Each screen would hold one view for ten seconds, then jump to another.

Sachs rested his elbows on the top of the electronic display. "I wasn't surprised. I mean I was, but not that it was Wells."

Pettaway nodded. "He was a shit."

Over Pettaway's left shoulder the third screen from the other end showed a dimly lit tunnel. No one was walking in it. The screen flickered, and another shot appeared. It was of a sewerlike stairway leading up from the tunnels. A white overlay at the bottom of the screen identified it as the entrance to A-Barracks.

"What the hell was he doing in there in the middle of the night?"

The screen changed again. A-BARRACKS—FIRST FLOOR LOUNGE, the overlay read.

"It's almost as if he was looking for something. Looking for an edge over one of them. Setting it up, maybe."

The screen over Pettaway's left shoulder showed the frenzied action in the lounge. The inmates had surged around one of the guards who was on the ground. His keys were wrenched from his belt. It was a strange scene, the silence adding to the ghostliness of the images.

"That would be like him. I mean, I'm no friend of any of the loons . . ."

One of the guards slumped dead, garroted by an invisible wire. Because the screen was black and white, the color at his neck did not resemble blood. It would've looked phony to someone used to the special effects of television.

". . . but I try to keep my distance. Wells, he baited them . . ."

Several of the men whipped odd, flexible items from their waistbands. They were thin and barely visible in the picture. Belts? Ropes? Over the tiny screen, no one would have been able to tell, even if he had been watching closely.

". . . And now, he's made it bad for all of us."

The third screen from the end abruptly changed. It was a lounge, just like the one that had been on the screen, but there was no commotion. The men sat idly, nervously about the room. The overlay identified it as the second floor of A-Barracks.

"I wish to hell the shithead had done his job right. If he had, none of this would have happened."

Jack reached for the yellow alarm signal. The sharp pain in his face remained, yet his head had cleared. The vision in his left eye was blurred, but from tears the ducts had released, not from any dizziness. The button was half-depressed when suddenly his arm jerked away. He neither saw nor felt anything, but the force of his arm being pulled from the console.

And then he felt the pain at his wrist. A slim metal band was wrapped around it and as he watched, it was yanked clear and where it had caught him a thin line of blood appeared. His watch crystal was broken and the leather band sliced cleanly through, and it fell to the floor.

One of the inmates stood at the doorway, and his arm slung back, the metal whip snapping in the air. Jack lunged forward and caught him squarely in the chest before he could swing again.

"Stop him!" the man cried, and Jack looked toward the others. Then he turned and broke past the guard's booth and into the hall. Through the noise of the commotion behind him, Jack could hear one sound that was distinct from the rest. It seemed the only purposeful movement. It was the sound of pursuit.

As he ran, he had to fight to grasp his keys. Damn these locks! The words sprang angrily in his head. Every day every crossing through a door meant the keys had to be used. How many times a day? Fifty? A hundred? A thousand? Jack had gotten used to the inconvenience, but the years of dislike for it and the inhibitions it meant for his own freedom came rushing over him like a wall of water through an earthen damn.

The key found its mark and so did the pursuer. As the door opened a crack, Jack was tackled and along with his attacker caromed off the wall and slid a few feet down the corridor. Jack spun and twisted the man to the side. Though he had no trouble outmuscling him, he could not break free. He clung to Jack like a vine to an oak.

It was Eddie Hyland, perhaps the only one in the confusion who had not taken his eyes off Jack Cooke the entire time, and now that some manner of freedom was theirs, the only one who cared about where Jack was going. He had his own reasons. "She's mine now," he breathed, his face close to Jack's. "We're taking charge here, and then she'll be mine forever."

Eddie's was a sweaty face with sparsely stubbled chin and a kind of sickly sweetness to it. There was a weakness about his face, yet the eyes blazed with his passions. One was a mere slit because of the swollen discolored lump high on his cheek caused by Jack's assault. It was purplish and seemed to have a pulse of its own.

Jack pushed him off and jumped up then rushed through the door into the tunnels. As he ran down the stairs, Hyland's shriek carried after him. "I'm coming for her, Jack Cooke. Tell her I'm coming for her."

When the men saw Reuker Stilkes erupt in his frenzy, the individual caldrons where anxieties had melded with anger breached their barriers and ran together. The collected hates and fears of all swirled into a common storm, a storm that broke as suddenly as a summer gale. There was little pattern to how each acted, and even less order to each one's thinking. The common fire cycloned above them fanning the individual flames. They moved blindly at first, their only thought to strike back, to take over, to seize the freedom that was suddenly theirs. Then, as fire seeks new tinder to stay alive, they sought others of their kind.

With Eric Creegan's keys, a contingent raced up the stairs to the second floor. Hector Irons shouted at the rest to follow him into the tunnels. Almost all of them knew the layout as well as the staff, and indeed all did know where the weapons room was.

Stilkes watched as they left, then his eyes scanned the room. Arnie was a whimpering mass of flesh moaning in one corner, while in another a daytime television show broadcast its own brand of pain. Creegan lay dead where Ringly had let him slip to the floor.

Reuker seemed to be looking for something. The nervous energy was still alive within him. Unlike before, once the *shooting* was over, he did not feel drained and confused. It was almost as if the racing madness had not ended, as if he were still in the grip of forces that tried to push him forward, to erase the stain of the evil that was on him and in him. He wanted something to happen, but he just didn't know what had to be done.

Somewhere within him a flicker of knowledge was alive that would tell him what to do. He couldn't yet feel it. But it was there.

Jack was at the central hub of the tunnel network when he heard shouts and pounding of footsteps coming down the stairs ricochet through the stone and tile and concrete passage. The thought to race first to the control center never entered his mind. He had to reach Marion before Hyland did, before any of them did. She was part of him, and the institution was not. He had been a foreigner there since the first day he walked inside, and there was little drive to save it while risking all that he cared for, all that meant anything to him.

It was not a conscious decision to ignore alerting the control center. In fact, if he had thought of it, he would have figured they had already caught it on the cameras, and the alarm had sounded in the other barracks, and guards were rushing to A-Barracks to quell the disturbance and seal it off, and in B- and C-Barracks the other residents had been ordered into their cells. All just as it was supposed to happen. But Jack didn't take the time to consider it. There was only one operative fact that mattered to him, and it demanded an immediate response.

He rushed up the concrete tube leading to the staff building. Another door; again the key. He pushed through, then secured it behind him. He dashed down another hall and into the kitchen. Marion was at a sink, with Ricky next to her and sitting on the counter. Jack was astonished to see him, and his fear sounded like anger. "What's he doing here?"

She looked at him in surprise. Then her eyes flashed her anger, that in a second told Jack to be quiet. Don't hurt the child's feelings. He has so little to do here on the island. Then she said simply, "He wanted to come with me today."

Jack moved by her to the window and looked out into the yard. It appeared as calm as ever.

Only after he had turned away from her did the blossoming discoloration at the side of his face strike home. And now, his rushing to the window. In the moment it took for what she was observing to course through her, she sensed what had happened. "What is it, Jack? Is it the residents?"

The *residents*. She never lost her respect for them. "Yeah. It's them," he said as he turned from the window.

"Is it a breakout?" Ricky sounded more excited than scared.

"They've got my floor. And I think some may be heading here." He didn't mention Eddie's name, and he didn't want Marion to think it. But he could tell she knew. Her eyes anxiously on him, he said, "We'll find a safe place for you to ride this thing out. On the other side of the building, so if need be you can get to the outside." Like the Administration Building, the staff apartments straddled the perimeter of the compound with their outside wall beyond the barrier fencing.

"It'll have to be upstairs," Marion said. "The bottom windows have the steel screens."

Marion's and Ricky's parkas hung on pegs in the hallway to the pantry, and below them on the floor were their felt-lined boots. They gathered their outside gear and made for the exit.

As they stepped into the corridor, a siren broke in the building with the shattering effect of an explosive charge. They could hear the reverberations of the alarm come from the outside as well. If they had not been scared before, they were genuinely frightened now. The system meant to localize any alarm so as not to shock the rest of the Facility and perhaps even precipitate outbreaks of violence elsewhere. So if one floor had a problem, the alarm would signal in the other floor of the same barracks and in the control center. The operator of the TV banks would tune in to the disturbance, close that section off, and signal for more guards if it looked like it was needed. A general alarm throughout the Facility signaled a major problem that had pushed past its containment point and threatened the entire compound.

The siren came in waves, and with each new pulse the sound spiraled deeper into them. Jack thought, then ushered them back inside the kitchen. He strode to the phone, then touched the three number code for A-Barracks, the second floor. There was no answer. Then he tried the control center atop the three-story tower. It rang longer than it should before it was answered.

There was nothing said as the receiver was lifted, as if someone were listening to see who it was. In the background he could hear the heavy clang of metal on metal and shouts of men. "This is Jack Cooke. What's happening there?"

"They're here!" The radio operator was no longer tentative. "And they're trying to get in. You have to come and bring the others."

"What's the status in the barracks?"

"We're losing it," his voice was near panic. "You've got to hurry!"

"What about the guns?"

"They haven't gotten to them yet. Please, hurry."

"I'll do what I can." Jack hung up the phone, and they hurried into the hall.

The stairs to the second level were in the middle of the rectangular building, the same place where the staircase led up from the tunnels. They walked quickly but silently to the stairs. Jack leaned around the doorjamb and saw that the door to the tunnel was still secure. Then he ushered Marion and Ricky upstairs.

They tried the first of the apartment doors, but it was locked. As Marion pounded on the door, and Jack went to the next, Ricky ran ahead to where he saw an umbrella of light in the corridor from one of the apartments. "Dad. Mom. Here's one."

The siren had only made Huxley's headache worse. He reacted in no way to it other than standing and moving to the window. When he heard the boy's voice, he turned to look, his blank expression a mirror of his thoughts.

When Jack and Marion appeared at the door, he gave them a puzzled look. They were like a refugee family with clothes in hand, standing at the doorstep of the wealthy. As they stepped inside, he turned to face them. "What are you doing?" he demanded.

"Don't you hear that?" Jack said, meaning the alarm.

Huxley looked as if he were about to say "So what?" but Jack brushed by him to the window. "We have to have a way out, if we need it."

"You're not opening that," Huxley said.

Jack looked at him, and finally he recognized that blank stare. He saw it all the time, but usually not on people like Huxley. It was the same blank stare of the residents. He turned to him, gripped him firmly by the shoulders, and with direct eye contact talked slowly and distinctly. "The prisoners have rioted and are trying to take over the place. They just might succeed, and I'm going to make sure my family will be safe, if the worst happens."

Huxley nodded. "Of course. We have to be ready." It was all so unreal to him. The alarm, the confusion, the specter of violence. In a way it was what he dealt with all the time. But it was always only talk. Other people's suffering. Violence that had already happened in a safe and distant past. The loss of direction he felt when Stilkes had been taken from his office deepened.

The window had two vertical panels of glass; one side was hinged to open inward, while the other was fixed. Coagulated grease made the crank turn with difficulty, but it opened. The outer window was frozen shut. Jack resisted breaking it since it would already be a tight squeeze through the half panel, and jagged edges of glass would make it hazardous. He pounded the frame with his fist, and the ice seal cracked. With his fingertips gripping the narrow metal edge, he inched it to the left behind the fixed side's storm. The screen permanently fixed to the frame cut easily with a kitchen knife, and Jack pushed it free.

With the escape path cleared, Jack cranked the inner window closed. "Where's your room keys?"

Huxley fished them from his pocket and handed them to Jack.

Jack turned on the TV monitor built into the wall. He switched to the channel that was fed the security monitor for the building. It was a split screen, with one-half a shot of the tunnel leading to the building, the other a panorama of the yard from their ground-level camera. "Ricky. If you see them coming, any of them, I want you to lead your mother out the window. You got that?"

"Wait a minute," Marion interrupted.

Jack ignored her. "Try to get to Phil and Emma's. Understand?"

"Yes. Don't worry about us."

Marion grabbed his arm. "You're staying here, with us."

"I can't."

"But why?" She was nearly frantic.

"Because they need my help."

Marion had always given of herself for others, and Jack's logic was unarguable. She felt a pang the selfless may feel before accepting yet another hardship, then she released his arm and steeled herself with her special resolve.

Jack turned to Ricky. "Remember what I told you, and don't open this door for anyone but me."

He seemed close to tears. "Dad. Come back. Please."

For just a second the look of determination softened in Jack's face. Marion knew he did not need anything to weaken him at this point, so when his hand came to her cheek, she said nothing and closed her eyes so he wouldn't see her fear.

He closed the door behind him, and as he did, the alarm that had become just part of the background, ceased. There was an awkward moment as the three stood there in the new silence, feeling their own different levels of helplessness.

Marion turned to the TV monitor and watched until she saw Jack appear in the tunnel, moving away from the steps and the camera. His black-and-white image in the dim light looked ghostly, and as he disappeared from the screen Marion felt a sinking loneliness spread throughout her.

From the first floor of A-Barracks the rebellion had spread. When they burst into the second-floor lounge, the other residents were as surprised as the three guards. With their fears and uncertainties piqued by the shakedown, they expected only worse to come. But they quickly realized it was others from below, and a sense of relief catapulted them into trying to seize the moment.

The men had charged into the room with their razor whips and overpowered the two guards who were on the floor with little trouble. The others congregated excitedly around. Inside the glass booth a third MCA unhinged the safety box over the alarm and slapped the yellow button. The signal was immediately conveyed to the guard booth just below them, and to the control center. Before he could get on the phone to speak directly with the control center, the inmates had burst into his sanctuary using keys wrenched from the guards in the lounge.

When the alarm sounded in the control center, Robin Pettaway was still sitting with his feet on the console. The alarm was a persistent yet relatively quiet beep-beep-beep; it was not a sound that would startle someone into action. It was accompanied by a single flashing red light on a board where a number of other lights were unlit.

Pettaway stared at the light as if he didn't have the faintest notion of what it was. Then he glanced over to Jay Sachs, who was looking at the board.

"Where's it coming from?" Jay said.

Pettaway swung his feet to the floor and stood up so he could better read the identifying label. "It's from A-Barracks, the second floor." He was reacting slowly, partly from the surprise, partly because nothing had ever happened when he was on watch. Then as an old car at last will sputter to life, he turned to the television monitor in front of him.

He set himself before the controls, then punched several codes into the computer keyboard, overriding one of the monitors. It was a slowly sweeping scene of a residents' lounge. There seemed nothing out of the ordinary. The pool table wasn't in use, and the men seemed to be doing nothing. Perhaps it was unusual the way they stood or sat or shuffed nervously, but nothing wrong.

"You've got the wrong one." Jay Sachs had walked up behind him. "That's B."

Robin Pettaway punched a new code into the computer, and the screen flickered, then a different scene materialized. It was the lounge in the second floor of A-Barracks.

"Holy shit!"

It was difficult to discern what was happening. There seemed to be movement in every direction, and Pettaway's and Sachs's eyes flitted from one figure to the next without following any one individual closely. It was a melee among the prisoners, they thought. Why they were fighting they didn't know.

Sachs hurried over to the communications network and tried to contact the guard's booth. There was no response. Then he tried the first floor, to send them upstairs. Again, the buzzing continued unanswered. "They're not supposed to be out of that booth."

Pettaway glanced at him with an expression that seemed to say, Do you really expect them to follow regulations all the time?

"Get the first floor on the screen," Sachs said, coming over again to stand behind Pettaway.

The screen flickered for a moment before the downstairs lounge of A-Barracks appeared. A feeling as empty as the room suddenly contorted itself within their stomachs. "Where the hell are they?" Pettaway began to punch another code into the computer, for the camera in the first-floor hallway, when Sachs stopped him.

"What's that?"

Pettaway halted the sweep of the camera. Near the wall a white-shirted, dark-trousered figure lay prone. The black-and-white monitor did not reveal the color of the stain that discolored the man's collar and had spread across his shoulders. It didn't look like blood, and the men were slow to comprehend.

The screen flickered back to the second floor. They saw the confusion clearer this time. The men were not fighting among themselves but had overwhelmed the MCAs. Each was pinned with his arms now held behind his back. They hadn't noticed in their first brief glimpse a single weapon, but now it seemed all of the inmates possessed some manner of knife, metal strap or bludgeon.

Pettaway's fingers were now nimble on the keyboard, and he brought a shot of the first-floor hallway leading to the tunnel. The door was open and unguarded.

Sachs was just a fraction of a second behind Pettaway in activating the automatic barricade system for A-Barracks. The electronic locks of the doors to the yard were overridden so no key could open them. And at the bottom of the tubular staircase that led to the tunnel a barred gate came out of matching slots on both sides of the wall and met and locked in the middle.

But by the time A-Barracks was sealed off, about forty of its sixty occupants had escaped into the tunnels.

There were no appointed leaders of the rioters, and at the beginning there was no plan. But quickly some gravitated to leadership, and despite the surging madness—indeed they seemed never clearer—they knew what had to be done to neutralize the threat to themselves.

Hector Irons had two objectives, and with the strategic thinking of a commanding officer, he split his forces. One group he led to the tubular staircase of the three-story control center. The master key opened the door at the top of the steps, and they were inside.

To the left of Pettaway and Sachs the monitors that were continuously trained on their own building chronicled the assault. If they hadn't been so intent on watching the combined four floors of B- and C-Barracks as the men there were locked in their cells, they would have seen Irons and his group dash up the stairs from the first floor to the second, then to the third. If they had seen them, they could have activated the electronic override locking system for their building as well, keeping them at a lower level.

But they didn't see them until they burst through the door on their level. Irons rushed to the key lock at the left of the first barred gate.

Sachs screamed, "The lock," and he lunged for the control panel. He activated the override, but the first door's circuit was already broken. It was opening in its torturously slow manner. Irons squeezed through and inserted the key in the next lock, but it had no effect.

"Open it," Irons shouted, the tendons stretched in taut white lines at his neck.

Pettaway moved quickly to the board where the solitary light of the A-Barracks alarm still flashed. He threw a switch and every light instantly came on, and in every building and on outside speakers the alarm blared. It was so loud where they were it shocked them all—both inside and outside the bars—into silence. But the moment was fleeting.

When the door reached its broadest extent, the override locked it where it was. The rest of the men surged forward, and for an awful moment Pettaway feared that the press of their bodies would knock the gate down. There were more than a dozen of them—fifteen, maybe twenty—but as he watched them press against the bars, the brief irrational thought vanished. The gate would hold.

Irons screamed for them to open it, but Pettaway and Sachs merely stepped farther back. They wanted to retreat, but there was nowhere to go, and seemingly nothing to do but watch.

One of the inmates lifted his arm and flung his crudely crafted blade at them. It flew past and clanged noisily at the far side of the room. The move had proved harmless, but it nudged Sachs into action. He turned to the communications network. All the lines coming in were lit, and he began answering them, calling for help.

Angrily Irons shouted, "We've got the place. There's nothing you can do." The frustration of his control of the Facility within sight but out of grasp was maddening.

Pettaway tried to buy time. The bars had never been tested, and though they seemed safe inside, the sight of the bedraggled platoon of armed convicts gnashing at the barricade did little to make him feel at ease. "You're not in control of the Facility and you won't be. Both B- and C-Barracks are locked up tight and that other officer is sending for help right now."

"There's more of us right here than they'll be able to send."

"But think of what you're doing. With their guns, you can't hope to have a chance. You and the others will be hurt, some killed. Needlessly." As he spoke, he could see Irons's lips curl at the corners in a smile that suggested he was privileged with information unknown to Pettaway. It was an unnerving sensation the watch operator felt.

"You've got your eyes all over. You check the weapons room. Tell us what you see."

Pettaway looked into his eyes and saw, not madness and irrationality, but an intelligence that startled him. The knot within him twisted suddenly tighter, and he moved to the bank of TV monitors. He punched in the code for the weapons room, safely carved into the rock below the MCA Barracks. When the entrance flashed on the screen, Pettaway staggered backward. The hall was filled with convicts.

"You open this gate now, and you and your friend won't be hurt, needlessly."

As Irons laughed, Pettaway shouted to Sachs. "Get Suomi." Sachs looked at him, wanting to disbelieve they were that close to losing. "Forget that and get Suomi."

Sachs dropped the phone and shoved his chair away from the island communications system. He flicked the switch on the radio transmitter and gripped the microphone. He called for the mainland contact for the Facility, then paused a few seconds, then signaled again. It was a routine either he or someone else had followed twice a day since the Facility accepted its first residents. But this time it was different. For the first time there was a significance to the routine.

PART II

THE ISLAND

22

Ike Suomi weighed 225 pounds and stood six feet four. He was as hard as a linebacker in his prime, yet he carried his strength as a hunter carries his stealth.

But the most distinctive characteristic about him, if one of his friends were asked to describe him, was his independence. He would call it freedom. Freedom from what other people expected of you. Freedom from the many hooks civilization hid among its temptations. The regular hours of a regular job, the demands of a family, the requisites necessary for attaining financial goals were all hooks that could work into a man and pull him into a world of someone else's design, and someone else's rewards. "Stay clear of the hooks," he'd say. "Don't take the bait, and you'll stay clean."

Attached to his belt, a beeper signaled him with its unhurried call. It was activated by the radio signal coming from Scales Psychiatric Facility twenty-six miles due north over the water. Because it was under his heavy parka and because of the sound of the waves, he didn't hear it at first. But he felt its minute electronic vibrations tickling at his side. When he listened, he could hear its muffled beep, beep, beep persistently jostling against him, like a steady breeze fluttering dune grass against a sunbather's naked skin.

He rolled his glove back and looked at his watch, its face on the underside of his wrist. It was 3:30. A good half hour before the scheduled call from the island.

Suomi pulled his glove all the way off, then opened his parka from the bottom zipper, just enough to be able to reach the beeper. He felt for the recessed button, then pushed it, and the tone was cut short in midbeep. Then he zipped his coat and put his glove back on. He made no effort to get up but instead looked around behind him to check for the golden retriever, then turned back to the lake.

Suomi liked the shoreline in winter better than any other season. It was so white, and clean, and pure. And there was nothing—not the sun, not the offshore breeze, not the churning of powerboats far offshore—that was there to lessen the power and the might of the lake. The water that at its murkiest allowed clear sight to the bottom at several leagues seemed never clearer than during winter. In the airborne ice crystals shimmered a rainbow, as one would in the spray of a waterfall. Even the sounds could hold him there for as long as he could endure the cold. He heard music in the give-and-take of water in the air pockets under the shelf, and in some places where it wore through, a blowhole would occasionally spurt in a rush of air like the Hawaiian surf pounding a lava coast.

He felt the beeper buzz again—an itch that would not go away. He shut it off, then to his dog complained, "Shit, Spud. They call late, they call early. Time doesn't matter to them." The dog was sitting behind Suomi protected by both the boulder and the man's formidable windbreak. It looked up from its patient pose, head on paws. "But it matters to us, doesn't it, boy." The dog did not disagree, and Suomi reached back and scratched behind its ears with his fat-fingered gloves. Then he returned to his icy solitude.

The only safety precaution clearly beyond the reach of the Scales inmates sat by itself on the ice looking out over the water.

From the tunnel leading away from the staff building Jack headed for the gun room. All the tunnels intersected in the middle, but some had connecting passages between buildings closer to each other than to the central point. Not all were connected in this direct fashion; the plans for a more complete network were scaled down as costs rose.

To get from the staff building to the gun room, though both were located on the southwest side of the compound, Jack had to go to the central hub of the tunnel network, then work his way back. The hub was not round with the tunnels' evenly spaced spokes branching out, but rather a tunnel itself, 125 feet long with the intersecting spurs connecting at various locations.

Jack knew some of the inmates were in the tunnels, and some had found their way to the control center, but according to Jay Sachs the gun room was safe. But why hadn't the other MCAs gotten there already, and with that uncontested firepower brought everything under control? The question went unasked, intent as he was on making it himself to the secure room under the guards' barracks.

He could hear the sounds of commotion, but no voices were distinct. It was just a collective babble that rolled through the stone-and-tile halls like the noises from a locker room in an empty stadium. At the hub, the sound seemed to echo from each of the tunnels. As he disappeared into the corridor leading to the MCA Barracks, he had no reason to think that the noise was not just as loud in the other tunnels.

The gun room was at the end of a hall that branched off from the tunnel near its staircase to the barracks above. The hall had one bend in it before reaching the double-barred gates that, like the system at the control center, could not be opened at the same time. It was in this leg of the L that Irons's other platoon was camped. They hadn't been able to get inside, so they stood just around the corner, out of range of the lone MCA who was there.

Jack came to a stop, his back against the cold stone wall of the tunnel, his hands spread flat against it as well. Though he couldn't see them, he perceived the situation. It was a standoff, with guns safe from the inmates, but with them controlling the only entrance. Whoever was inside would never be able to shoot his way through the horde, Jack realized. He would have to get enough men to overpower the inmates. He could hear someone talking about starting a fire at the entrance. He had to act fast.

The staff barracks was just up the steps, and with the twenty to thirty men from last night's shift who should still be there, most asleep when this thing started, they could secure the room. But why hadn't they responded already to the alarm? With no answer to the question, Jack inched closer to the open passage leading to where the inmates waited. His key for the door at the top of the staircase he readied, then he lunged across the opening.

"One of the guards!"

He was seen! The frustrated rage of the men had a new focus. They were after him. Jack was at the top of the steps when the first appeared at the bottom. What he saw almost paralyzed him where he was. It was an inmate, followed by another, with the deadly razor whip wrapped around one hand.

The key turned, and he pushed. But the door did not budge! Jack crashed his shoulder against the barricade, and it was as if his key had had no effect. They had blocked it on the other side! The bastards had locked themselves in. "Open!" he screamed, but it was too late. The brunt of the whip's blow slashed against the concrete.

Jack whirled and grabbed his wrist, preventing him from striking again. But there was another, just behind him, and two more after that. His arms were pulled back and he felt a sharp pain in his stomach. It felt as though he had been stabbed. Oh, my God, he thought, then tried to shout, "They're killing me!" to the men behind the door, but he was doubled over with the blow, and his shout was more a failing cry.

It hadn't been a knife but an iron bar. A crowbar. Something from the VSB. Had they been there already? Then he felt himself being pulled down, hands grappling for a piece of him everywhere. They had him, and he could not resist the forces pulling him back down the steps.

It was unfair, so goddamn unfair. He had been safe. Yet he had come back. And the bastards had locked him out! They were saving their own necks. Why, why did he come back? The anguish threatened to take over his reason, and he tried to block it out.

With the steps carved out of the curving walls of the tubular passage, there was room for only two men side by side. Next to him, his step always a fraction of a second ahead of his, was Herman Breitsmann, his hand gripped on Jack's shirt. Behind was another whose impatient push he could feel. And below were two more of his captors.

Flushed with rage and success that made Jack shudder, Breitsmann suddenly turned to him and breathed, "You will pay. You'll see. You'll all pay. You and the Pillkillers will suffer as we have." His foul breath made Jack recoil, and through his snarl the brown scum on his teeth glistened with saliva. "We've been your toy and you've kept us here without reason for your games. Like Hitler did to the Jews."

It was an irrationality that was useless to confront. Pausing there, halfway between the surface and what was below, Jack felt a trembling heat ignite throughout him. It was as if tiny wind-flicked flames had suddenly fired in every muscle, in every nerve. It was terror, he felt. Terror of Breitsmann's madness, of the twisted, demented rationality that had been unleashed throughout Scales. It was a force, he suddenly felt, that had been waiting to erupt. Logic and sanity operate within limits. But madness recognizes no bounds.

He was being pushed again, down into their world. Jack's head snapped back, and above him, its cold one-eyed stare unblinking, was one of the cameras. They were watching him. The bastards in the building whose entrance he had pounded at were staring at their monitors relieved that the horde had turned back from their threshold.

The madness touched him. Jack felt a rage pulse with the fire of his terror. He was pushed harder from behind, and Breitsmann to his side stumbled and, for just a second, loosened his grip. Jack reacted fast. He knocked Breitsmann into the curved wall, then leaped forward onto the backs of the two inmates in front. The impact carried all three into the air, and they sailed the five remaining steps to the tile floor.

They landed hard and Jack immediately rolled off. He seized the iron bar and wrenched it from the man's grasp. Jack sprang to his feet, and as one of the inmates struggled to rise, Jack crashed the bar into his skull, shattering it like an eggshell. Then he sprinted ahead, past the passage to the weapons storage, and down the tunnel.

It was 150 feet to the central hub, with its spokes veering off in a confusing array of directions, and Jack was halfway there before he heard the sounds of pursuit. He didn't look to see how many; he just ran with all the reserve of energy he possessed. Yet it wasn't limitless. His muscles burned with the effort, and the dull pain in his stomach where the bar struck him throbbed. With mere seconds to think, all the important considerations seemed to flash simultaneously through his mind. He would never reach the door to the staff barracks before his pursuers reached the hub. He would lead them right to Marion and Ricky. He'd run off elsewhere. But where?

It was then he left the tunnel leading directly to the MCA Barracks and entered the connecting area in the center. On the floor, like a mammoth spider, was the shadow of the overhead network of pipes and cables. He looked up, and the plan cemented in his mind. He bolted around the corner and into the tunnel leading to the staff building. He slid the bar through his belt, then leaped upward and grabbed one of the pipes. He pulled himself higher, yet his legs still dangled in the air. Behind him, he could hear the steps pounding rapid-fire on the tile. The noise tapped the fear into him, and Jack swung one leg up to the pipes. As the sound broke into the hub, just a dozen feet away, Jack raised his other leg up to the narrow gap between the pipes and the ceiling.

"Damn!" one of them exclaimed.

Jack lay on his back on the steampipe, largest of them all. His shoulder blades arched backward as he gripped the pipe with whatever edge he could use. Though it was padded with insulation, he could feel the warmth passing beneath him, and the heat of his exertion broke over him as well. He felt drained, as if he couldn't move, as if he would lack the strength to stay on his perch.

The charge had ceased, and Jack imagined them standing there, confronted by the yawning openings leading off in different directions. They would be frantically checking each passage. Would they see the shadow as he saw it?

The spreading bruise at his stomach had a deadening sensation for his entire midsection, and inside he felt increasingly sick. Jack breathed deeply, then very carefully brought his knees up until they touched the ceiling. He was trying to stop the convulsions that gripped his stomach, that threatened an illness that would betray him. The sickness radiated a burning sensation throughout him, and he could feel the sweat collecting on already damp skin. He fought to control himself, to mobilize every ounce of reserve he could.

He could feel the vibration of the footsteps, and sense the heavy breaths of his pursuers. The pulsing in his ears seemed to block out parts of their speech, so all he could hear were partial phrases. ". . . don't know," "Couldn't have . . . ," ". . . any other way?" They were searching, and it was apparent they had not thought of the possibility he was above. Jack could not see that one of the men was ignoring the other four and was very carefully scanning the network of overhead pipes in the hub. Dennis Ringly knew something about the tunnels and the pipes the others did not.

* * *

"Huxley, I know you're in there. I heard your voice. Open it." Lummer pounded heavily on the door.

Ricky looked, round-eyed, toward his mother. For the first time since Jack left, her eyes were taken off the monitor. At the furthest limit of the camera's range, she had seen a shape. She felt for sure it was Jack, though her sight could not confirm it. Then the figure, a shadowy blur moving so fast the monitor tracked the image, jumped to something above and pulled himself out of view. The pipes above? She knew they were there, but in all the miles she must have walked beneath them, she had never looked at them closely. Then she realized why he must have had to try to hide, and as the realization bored into her, moving her closer to the screen, a flurry of activity appeared just beyond its reach. It was a flickering of light coming from the distance, like someone, a number of people, moving where the tunnels intersected.

It was then that Lummer began pounding on the door. His voice was panicky, and he sounded so alone, and frightened. Ricky started toward the door.

"Your father said not to," she warned, but made no move to stop him, as if deferring to his judgment.

"Are you alone?" Ricky called through the door.

"Yes, yes. I'm alone. Please, open the door!"

"Don't do it," Huxley said. "He's lying."

Ricky turned toward the door and started to unlock it. Huxley bounded across the room reaching Ricky just as the knob was turning. "Don't!" But it was too late.

The door crashed open, and Lummer fell inside. From the force, Ricky expected others, but there was no one else. As he slammed it shut, all eyes were on Lummer or him. No one was watching the monitor where, on the side of the split screen trained on the outside entrance, someone had reached the door and was letting himself inside. It was one of the inmates, and he was alone. His hat covered part of his face, and the angle of the camera would have made it hard to identify him, but if Marion had been watching, she would have recognized who it was.

Dr. Neil Lummer stood with his back propped against the wall, huge spasms of fear pounding within his chest. He looked at the others watching him, then said, "They're taking over." He said it as if to infect the others with his fear, or perhaps to justify his own. The stares did not alter.

"They'll be here soon, you can be sure of that. The guards aren't doing a damn thing."

"My husband went back into those tunnels, alone. He'll . . ." Marion suddenly choked and couldn't go on. She turned away, her eyes tightly shut.

"He's coming back," Ricky said. "And when he does we got a plan. We'll be busting out."

"Where?"

"The window. We're going to escape to the outside."

Lummer pushed himself away from the wall and stepped to the window. Outside it appeared cold and bleak, with a lifelessness that stood as a challenge to anyone who dared test its harshness. If ever he had stood on the coast of a polar sea, this is what he imagined it would look like. They would never survive out there, he thought.

As the prospects narrowed, Lummer felt a creeping despair. But as a child might deal with hopelessness, he struck out at another, at the cause of his hopelessness. "It's his fault," he said, still looking out the window.

Ricky glanced at Huxley. He did not understand.

Lummer turned from the window. "It was *him* who started it. He is responsible for all of this the same as if he gave them the keys and pointed the way to the guns." Lummer moved away from the window and stalked toward Huxley. "He knew more about the *criminal mind* than anyone here. He took away our fragile control because somewhere within his great intellect he had the power over madness. Oh, yes. He really thought that. He thought that because he had ground to break, because he had a place to carve out for himself in the vast history of psychiatry." Standing directly before him, Lummer then shouted, spewing tiny droplets of spray in Huxley's face. "He put all of our lives in jeopardy because of his own stupid, selfish plans."

Huxley's left darted like a puncher's jab, and he slapped Lummer across the face. Lummer didn't flinch, and his head barely reacted to the blow. He simply grabbed his chin with his hand and stared into Huxley's eyes.

Ricky stepped toward them and took Lummer's arm. "You'll need a coat. And boots. And other warm gear." He tugged at his arm. "Come on. Let's get to your apartment and collect what's needed."

Marion wheeled and shouted, "Don't go out there."

"Dad needs the gear too. I'll have to find some for him."

Throughout the exchange Marion's eyes had been taken from the screen. At least for a few moments she was spared from having to watch the gut-wrenching tension there.

Jack rolled to his stomach and began inching his way toward the stairs. The pipe was fifteen inches in diameter and came in lengths of twenty feet. The ends were flat flanges pressed together with a sealer between and joined with four bolts. The flanges were not covered by insulating material, and the metal was hot. Flanking the steampipe were smaller pipes—water, sewage—and cables—electricity, communications, locking control. The steampipe was suspended from the ceiling by U-brackets sunk into the rock. When he came to one of the suspension brackets, Jack had to roll to his side to squeeze through.

A grating sound of metal over rock spiked into his thoughts. The pipe sagged, and for just a moment, for the missing beat of his heart, he was weightless. Ahead of him a small cloud of stone dust emanated from where the U-bracket was attached to the ceiling. The pipe had dropped less than an inch, but to Jack it felt as though he had fallen much farther.

He steadied himself, then looked behind. As best he could tell no one was in the tunnel below him. Then he looked forward five feet to where the bracket was attached to the ceiling. At each side he could see a short extension of clean metal where it had just pulled free.

He began to creep forward again, his eyes intent on the bracket. The metal creaked, and a tiny rivulet of stone dust spilled out. Jack caught his breath as if that would stop the spill. As he watched, the stream dribbled to nothing, and without the visual evidence of the instability of the pipe's anchor, he moved on.

Behind him, at the hub, Dennis Ringly held the dulled, weighted end of the razor whip in his palm, so that it looped at the ready from his hand. He had directed the others to check the pipes above in the tunnels, and they had. First the tunnel to the Administration Building, then the VSB, then the control center. The men were in a position to take the Facility, and they were determined one loose end was not going to remain free to knot up the attempt. The shouts were coming back to Ringly that they had not seen him yet, and their calls were ricocheting in the hub and reaching out into all the spurs. Jack could hear their progress. He did not have much time.

He pushed on, and with every move the pipe sagged lower, the bracket showed a fraction more of its shiny surface. One of the pipe joints was just beyond the brace, and it was hot, not scalding, but hot. Like a stove pan's edge on simmer.

Jack was on his side, squeezing through the bracket. Stone dust was spilling on him in a steady stream. He grunted as he tried to pull himself forward, and as if in negative response, the steel groaned as the brace slipped lower. Jack breathed in short gulps of air, as if looking for any edge to limit his weight, to keep himself as still as possible. He reached blindly ahead and grabbed the hot flanges. It was a long moment before the heat registered, and he cursed as he let it go.

The burning of his hand hurt more as a reminder of his other pain, the dull throbbing in his stomach from the bar and at the side of his face where he had been struck by Reuker Stilkes. Jack brought his hand back and draped it lightly across his chest. His eyes closed as he tried to steady his breathing, as he tried to bring control to the twitching nerves and muscles that were losing their desire. It was as if he had already lost. He was trapped, he would be found, and Lord knows what they would do with him. But at least, Jack thought, at least he had not led them to Marion and Ricky. They were safe.

Whether he really believed it or not, he felt sure that they would be able to hold out until help at last arrived. That thought was the only comfort he had.

"Shit!" Suomi tore his glove off and reached in to the small electronic box at his side. He pushed the button, and the irritating beeping ceased. But as he did, he realized it was like trying to swat a midnight gnat buzzing in his ear. The effort was useless. The noise would always come back.

Suomi yanked the beeper from his belt and for just a second felt like throwing it beyond the ice line into the water. But he thought better of the impulse, and he activated the response signal. It would tell the transmitter their signal was received, and he would respond as soon as he reached his radio.

Ike slipped the box into the cavernous pocket of his coat and stood up from the ice-encased boulder. Hundreds of tiny ice crystals—the wind-blown wave spray that had been caught in the folds of his parka—were unleashed and avalanched to the ground. The golden retriever got up slowly, as if the cold had numbed its joints, then shook the collected ice from itself.

"Let's go, Spud. They've ruined it for us anyway." And with that Ike Suomi began to pick his way over his old tracks sunk deep in the snow that led back toward the tree line and his cabin.

The rough-ground metal point of the steel bar dug into the wall, sending tiny chips of the block to the floor and cement dust into a growing cloud. A trench had been chiseled into the cement blocks where they butted against a steel frame, and at least two homemade knives were hacking away at the trench, gouging it deeper. The frame was rectangular, one foot wide and two feet high. It framed a flat metal plate with no keyhole and no readily apparent way to open it. It was set into the wall next to the inner iron gate that sealed the control center from Hector Irons and the other inmates.

Irons had noticed it was just to the left of the locking mechanism of the door, and he had tried to force the plate off. He dented it but did not loosen it in the least. Then he had started to hack at the wall, and the others had joined him. The cement blocks lacked the resilience of fire-baked bricks, and they chipped and disintegrated easily. It would not take much longer before the entire frame would be chiseled free and they could wrench it from the wall.

On the other side of the bars Jay Sachs continued his feverish calls into the microphone. His voice was frantic; though nearly hoarse, it had a high-pitched, desperate ring to it.

"Where the hell is he?" Pettaway shouted, pulling his eyes away from the monitor showing the entrance to the gun room.

"I don't know, goddamn it, I don't know." He gripped the microphone and depressed the bar for the hundredth time. "Mainland base, this is Scales. Do you read? This is urgent. Do you read?" He released the bar and the speakers spit out their static-y snarl.

"Come on, come on," Pettaway pleaded.

"This is Sachs, damn it. Can't you hear? We're in trouble. Answer me!"

Again, the static was uninterrupted by Suomi's voice.

Could somehow they have gotten to him? It was impossible, Sachs quickly realized. He was falling victim to his terror. "Mainland, come in. This is Scales. Please!" He released the bar and glanced toward the men just outside. He didn't know what the hell they were doing, yet he still feared their plans. He was not privy to the design plans for Scales, and he had never given that metal plate or what was behind it a second thought. Could it lead them into here? Could they chisel their way right through the wall?

Sachs let a tremulous gasp seep from his chest. They had always told him the place was impregnable, and he repeated to himself the reassurances he had heard. They were safe, he reasoned, but reason is a meek combatant to fear. The safety he wanted to believe in did nothing to make him feel secure.

The bracket snapped. It wrenched loose from the rock ceiling, and the U-shaped prongs sounded a deep tone, like the tines of a giant tuning fork. The entire length of steampipe sagged under its and Jack's weight, and the sound of metal against metal sent a shrill noise echoing throughout the tunnel network. It was the ear-shattering shriek of heavy metal pushed to its tensile limits. For two of the four bolts at the flange, the stress point was surpassed. They snapped in half as if they were merely brittle twigs of a dead tree.

For an awful moment Jack lost all feeling of support. Then he tried to move, to get away, but he couldn't. He was trapped. Pinned between the prongs of the bracket.

Jack tried to twist to his stomach, but he was held fast. His hands reached forward to the flange. The heat he did not feel as he gripped it and pulled with all his strength. At the bottom of the flange, where the two bolts had snapped, the sealant stretched like warm taffy, and steam started to whistle through the holes that were opening.

In his chest a whimper died as Jack refused to succumb to the strain. Then slowly he could feel himself moving.

He was breaking free! His hips slid past the pincer-hold of the bracket, and he was loose. As the claustrophobic fingers unclenched around his mind, the other fears came rushing back. He started to propel himself forward, but when he was squarely over the flange, the metal groaned, and it sagged, and another of the connecting bolts snapped. More steam began to billow from the tear in its joint. They would be coming, he realized, within seconds. He glanced forward to the stairs and realized he would never make it that far. He had to try to keep them back, if only to give Marion and Ricky time. Time to get out through the window. They would see it all on the monitor and be warned.

Jack passed to the far side of the flange and doubled his body around. From his belt he pulled the crowbar.

When the pipe broke at the hub of the tunnel network, the echo of the cracking rock and the steel had resounded from every open passage only a fraction of a second after it had erupted from the corridor leading to the staff apartments. Ringly's men abandoned their search and dashed back to the center. Stunned by the noise, they were ready to bolt back to the gun room. What the hell was that sound? Were the tunnels collapsing upon them?

The fears rebounded over them all, and it was Ringly who was first to pull out of it. It was the pipe overhead, he realized. It had collapsed. "You'll see him now. The pipe must be down," he shouted, then charged to one of the tunnel entrances that branched off from where he was. It was clear. He went to the next, the other four men staying with him.

"Oh, my God," Marion breathed. On the TV screen she saw the pipe sag and a man's leg drop into view. It dangled onscreen for only a second before it was lifted out of sight. For the first time the picture had sound, for the terrible noise rumbled through the steampipes to the radiator covered by the square metal grating by the window in Huxley's room.

She resisted the impulse to cover her eyes, then she felt Ricky at her side. On the screen the violence, the drama, the danger were before her, and somehow it did not seem real. It was TV. Like any other of the weekly fare. It would be over soon, the credits would roll, and all would be the same as before. No one hurt, no one injured.

The irrationality began to spin in her head. It threatened to whirl her away, but inside, deep within herself, she was still in control. She knew it was not fake. The entire story was real. And it was Jack who was there, in the tunnel. It was Jack who was trying to get back to her. Why didn't he come down, why didn't he just run to them? Because they were looking for him, she realized. Because they must be only just beyond the range of the camera.

She wavered where she stood, and her breath gushed from her chest like the steam she saw escaping from that pipe. She felt faint, she was losing strength.

But she did not fall. She was held by strong arms. They were guiding her to a chair. "Sit here, Mom. It'll be okay. You'll see."

Marion sat down and looked into Ricky's face. It was like looking at Jack at his strongest, when she was at her most vulnerable. It was as if the boy had suddenly become the man, as if Jack had suddenly entered Ricky. Marion tensed. It was as if one life had been snuffed out and another took its place, as if Jack had died and was reborn in Ricky.

"Oooh, nooo," she moaned, and whatever reserve she had drained totally away, and her head collapsed into her hands. And she sobbed a widow's grief.

Reuker Stilkes knelt on the floor in the middle of the lounge in A-Barracks and stared at the red that gushed from Eric Creegan's neck. He had settled there shortly after the others had escaped. It was his nervous energy that brought him there, before the dead body; it was the madness within he listened to.

The blood formed a large pool on the floor, and it was already beginning to gel. Reuker sat back on his ankles and stared at it, at the cleansing liquid, the eternal waters. The whimpering incoherence of the fat guard somewhere within the room came in even waves, it had the brushing sound of wind, of water splashing on a rock. Reuker listened, and he heard the falls, he heard the rhythmic rush of the water catapulting off the V-ledge somewhere above him, then creating its own breeze as it fell toward the cascades.

It was what was needed, he realized. Yet it wasn't. The

blood before him was dilute. It was impure. It was little more than meaningless slime coagulating on the floor.

He turned his head from it, then stood, then strode to the far corner of the room, behind the pool table, then around it and aimlessly toward the window. Inside, something was eating him away. It was restlessness. It was the despair. It was the frustration. It was the evil! The evil that burned within him, that scorched his soul the same as it pitted and rotted his skin. It was the stain that had been placed there by the doctor, by the man with the halo of hair and the round glasses.

Reuker grabbed his head and shouted. He screamed his rage, his fear, his terror to the walls, to the corpse, to the whimpering guard, to the demons within. "Nooo," his cry echoed. He spun around in place, his hand still clenched over his ears, his elbows tight to his body.

But it was no good. The pain in his head only became worse. The itching, wretching nervousness could not be calmed. He was dying! He was unclean! He was soiled with the grime and stench of Huxley.

It was Huxley who had driven him to this point. It was Huxley who now tore at his guts, trying to wrench his bowels from his body's cavity. He thought of the man's evil, of the suggestion of himself, with Rebecca, touching her, and her evil touching him. The picture pulsed in his mind, and as it did, it seemed to become real. The evil of it all *was* real. It was inside him. The horror of Rebecca's sins was real and *it was in him*!

Reuker's arms exploded away from his face with the force of his horror, with the force of the revulsion that gripped him. He had to be cleansed. The acid touch of Huxley, of Rebecca, of the thoughts that rotted within him had to be washed clear.

Fragments of past cleansings flashed through his mind. The animals, the young girl, the women. He could almost feel the blood on his skin, washing him, clearing away the sins, the touch of the impure. Yet this time the dreams would not be enough. He needed to feel the waters, the red eternal waters. He had to bathe in it, he had to revel in it, he had to drink it.

Within him was awakened an evil so hideous the horrors of his past were engulfed and overcome by its black glow. The evil within was not from the touch of Huxley, or the memory of Rebecca. It was the evil of Reuker Stilkes.

Jack wedged the flat edge of the crowbar into the sealant between the steampipe's connecting flanges. There was one bolt to go. He pushed on the bar first with just his arms, then with his shoulder pressed against it. The metal creaked and groaned, but it did not break. His face grew oily-wet from perspiration, from the hot steam leaking through the taffy-pulls of the sealant.

Jack pulled back on the bar, then pushed forward again. The point worked its way in deeper, only a fraction of an inch, but still deeper. It was a better hold. He pushed the bar with all his strength, until he felt as though his muscles would lock in a painful cramp, until he felt the ache in his back, as if his vertebrae were compressing together.

The joint still held, so he pulled back and forced the point in farther; it took a deeper bite. Then he pushed again, and the last bolt snapped, the metal piece ricocheting off the rock like a bullet. As it broke, the pipe sagged more and the steam spewed out along the rim of the flanges in directionless plumes. But it did not break.

"Down here!"

Jack heard the call, then the rush of footsteps. He was hot. The steam was billowing around him, soaking his shirt, burning him. He wheezed for breath, but it was only hot air that rushed into his lungs, scalding his throat, his chest.

He rolled to his back and tried to bring his legs up so he could push off the ceiling, to force the pipe down. But it was too cramped. There wasn't room for his legs to coil about him. He reached to the ceiling with his hands and pushed, and the metal only groaned. The footsteps were closer. He looked, and through the haze of the steam he could see them twenty-five feet, twenty feet away.

Jack quickly reversed himself, his stomach to the pipe, his face above the escaping steam. He closed his eyes and looped his arms around the bare metal at the end of the pipe. He screamed as it burned his arms, but he didn't let go.

He rolled to the side and let himself fall below the pipe. He saw a figure just in front of him and heard the whiplike whoosh of the razor-metal slicing through the air. It missed, and he kept falling, falling, yet the pipe was in his arms. It came with him! With a shattering crash it broke loose, and the end he was on drooped into the corridor. Hot steam blasted from it with the roar and a rush of a long dormant geyser. Tiny droplets of scalding water were carried with the steam into the faces of the men who had been running down the hall, and even over the roar of the air Jack could hear their cries.

He let himself drop to the floor and rolled clear. He sprang to his feet and dashed the rest of the way to the stairs, then up the tubular passage to the door. The key! The goddamn key! His arms were red with the fire of the pipe, and his fingers were numb. They could not feel the keys. They could feel nothing! But they were there, and he felt them against his thigh.

He fisted his hands together and squeezed, to force feeling back into his fingers, to chase the numbness. The steam was following him up the stairs, collecting at the top like a searing, burning storm cloud. Jack coughed, then gagged. He reached again for the ring of keys and this time was able to pull it from his pocket.

The master key slipped into the door, and it opened. He fell inside, then slammed it behind him. He paused only a moment, not enough time even to catch his breath, then he dashed up the stairs to the second floor.

The moment he was in the staff building's first-floor hall he did not look to either side, intent as he was on the stairs in front of him, on his wife and son upstairs in the apartment. If he had looked, he would have seen the willowy, stoop-shouldered form of Eddie Hyland rush out of the kitchen into the hall to see what the noise was.

Hyland stopped dead when he saw Jack, then as Jack disappeared up the stairs, Eddie realized that's where she was. That's where he was hiding her.

He ran back to the kitchen and straight to the shadowboard. He pulled a meat cleaver from its perch. It had a blade as wide as two hatchets and was honed to bone-splitting sharpness. He tested the grip and the weight, then broke back into the hall.

At the stairway he became more careful, abandoning his charge to creep stealthily up the steps. He did not want to give his presence away.

Outside the last gate to the control center, the group of inmates led by Hector Irons stood waiting as an angler fish waits for its prey to come within reach. It was an incongruous scene of calm between two antagonists, like the battlefield stories of the Confederate and the Yankee meeting in the calm between the hail of grapeshot. Except that here there was no mutual respect and no talk of similar backgrounds and shared heritage. There was only hatred, or fear.

The men had been taking turns gouging at the steel frame in the wall. The trench circled it completely, and at places they could reach their fingers behind it. It was loose, but still it held. They continued chipping and hacking, and Sachs continued his calls to the mainland.

"Let's try it," said Irons, and the knives stopped chiseling. As many as could get near reached their hands into the groove, their fingers groping for a hold behind the frame.

"Pull!" Irons shouted, and they did. It gave but not all the way. "Pull!" and the men grunted in unison like galley slaves.

"Goddamn it, Suomi. Answer!"

The cement cracked, and the frame jerked from the wall and crashed to the floor. The edge, studded with jagged cement pieces, fell on the man closest to it and cracked his ankle. The others were impervious to his cries, and Irons pushed by to the hole in the wall.

There were a number of circuits, a number of wires, leading from—or to—the control center. Some cables were as thick as three fingers held together and protected with thick, gray rubber sheath. Others were multicolored and as thin as twenty-gauge wire. Irons put his head to the side to see if he could tell which carried the electronic signal to the locking mechanism just to the right of the plate. It was too dark, too far.

He felt a nervous heat tickle his sides, and he felt the old dryness in his throat. He was aware of the others watching him, waiting. Then he noticed it. The tape. The colored tape embossed with letters and wrapped around the wires. Irons laughed and turned to the others. "They left us a map," and they laughed with him.

Electricity. Communications. Island telephone. Video. Locking override. This last cable ended at a flat metal circuit, where sixteen smaller wires spiraled out of it and led to the top of the circuit. Each was fixed to the metal plate, ran across it, and then was twined together with the others at the resumption of the mother cable. Irons bowed his head closer. He read the identifying tabs. Cell—A, B, C. Tunnel—A, B, C. Hall—A, B, C. VSB. Admin. Con Cen. Med. Plant. MCA. And Staff.

He weaved his crude blade through the wires and selected Con Cen. With a flick of the wrist he snapped it clean. There was the slightest of sparks, and simultaneous with the break in the circuit an alarm sounded. Unlike the other, it did not echo throughout the Facility and outside its walls. It blared only within the control center.

Irons was first surprised at the siren, then he laughed and looked around at the others. Wasn't that smart, he thought. They rigged it with an alarm. And then he laughed even harder.

The circuitry from the labeled alarm cable was similar to the locking override. He slipped his blade behind the wires, and this time was not as selective. He tore them all loose.

The latch on the gate was down, but there was no longer any override. He took the batch of keys he had torn from Arnie's belt and began to fit them one by one into the lock. The first was the master key, and that did not work.

Pettaway was by the window, frantically looking out to the yard for any sign that someone was coming. Any sign of hope. And his mind frantically raced through possibilities of escape. But the windows were bulletproof glass and cemented into their frames.

"Mainland, come in please. Mainland. This is Scales. Come in." Sachs was talking fast, his words were running together. His hand ached from gripping the microphone bar. Contact. That's all he needed, was contact, before they were through, before they had the island. He felt so alone, so isolated, so deserted. The worst terror seemed possible: They would never know! Like some backwoods hermit who wasn't found until the spring thaw. And by then it would be too late, his bones already gnawed by ravenous scavengers. Oh God, what horrors would they commit? "Suomi! Answer. This is Scales. Come in!"

Twenty-six miles away Spud pawed at the cabin door. The dog had porpoised through the snow and had reached the shelter before Ike was out of the thick trees.

The dog whined impatiently as Suomi finally came to the door. He brushed the snow off his legs, then stomped his feet as clean as he could. When he went inside, the speaker was spitting like a cat in heat.

"Mainland, come in. This is Scales." There was a pause, and the speaker went dead. Then, "For Christ's sake, Suomi, answer."

What the hell were they mad about? They were the ones wrong on the time. Unhurriedly Suomi took off his hat, gloves, parka. Then he unlaced his boots.

"Come in Mainland. Anyone, on this frequency. Please respond. Come in!"

The voice sounded excited. Suomi's eyebrows furrowed in thought. Then the call came again. He listened to the tone, to the urgency in the voice. It wasn't normally like that. It had never been like that.

His boots he lined carefully on the mat, then walked in his thick-stockinged feet toward his radio transmitter.

"Mainland. This is Scales. Come in!"

Or was it the interference that pitched his voice high? Was it the static that caused it to sound abnormal? But there was always interference on this band, and always static. Or were they just as angry as he was? Was *his* watch wrong? A flash of discomfort flickered over his skin, and he quickly glanced at the wall clock. No. They were early.

The power was on, and he was seated before the console. When the latest blaring transmission stopped, Suomi flicked a switch and spoke into his mike. "Scales. This is the Mainland Base. I read you. Over."

Suomi flicked the switch and listened. The only sound he heard from the speaker was static. "This is Mainland Base, calling Scales. Come in, please."

There was more static, and Suomi felt the anger coming back. What the hell were they trying to pull? He was about to flick the switch to transmit and call one more time, when a voice came through the speaker.

"This is Scales." The static lasted a few more beats beyond the words, and nothing else was said. Or were they saying something else? In the background? Before Suomi could hone his hearing to the minute sounds, the transmission ended.

He slammed the switch. "Is that all you got to say?" Then he listened. There was no response. He called again. "You were early, damn it. So quit trying to jack me around."

"Sorry," came the response. "We thought you weren't there."

Suomi could barely hear over the static, and to him the voice was strangely distant, as if the speaker's mouth was too far from the mike, or his voice had suddenly gone feeble. Or was it a different voice? "I wasn't *here*. I was outside. I wasn't *supposed* to be here until four."

"You're right. You're right. I'm sorry."

His anger lessened, but he wasn't going to let it all slip by that easily. He said, "I'm just a contact. A con—tact. Not an employee. I can't tie up my whole day for you guys. So please, next call keep it on the mark. And every time after that."

"When is the next time?" The question came fast.

"Jesus. What's with you guys?" He felt like signing off, but then again, he wanted the next call when he was expecting it. "Nine tonight. Like it says on the sheet."

At the radio console in the Scales Control Center, Irons spied a sheet of paper taped to the metal cabinet. It had three columns, the first a date and the second two were times. Uppercase letters at the top read: EMERGENCY FALL-BACK SYSTEM—CONTACT SCHEDUEL [the misspelling was uncorrected]. The first date was January 1. Irons ran his finger along the columns to the twenty-first. Every time in the latter two columns until then was crossed off. After the twenty-first the two times were 16:00 and 21:00. He gripped the bar on the microphone. "Okay. I got it. Just wanted to be sure. And then seven tomorrow morning, right?"

"How the hell should I know? Do you think I've got the schedule memorized?"

"Sorry I messed up. It won't happen again."

The static-y assurance calmed Suomi a little. He was impatient of others, especially when it infringed on his time, but he was a good man, an honest man, a compassionate man. He wasn't one to hold a grudge. And besides, the relationship he had built with the voices from Scales over the years was a good one whose only cross words were normally just good-natured jibing aimed at breaking the routine. And with Suomi, friendships didn't die easy.

Suomi signed off, and after he did, on the island Hector Irons took a second look at the sheet. The times were listed through the end of February.

"Hey. Lookit this." The inmate was standing in the semicircle of TV monitors, his eyes dancing excitedly from screen to screen. Irons moved toward him. "Look at them. They're scared, really scared." He meant the MCAs in B- and C-Barracks.

The cameras showed that it was a lockdown. Irons turned from the screens and strode over to where Pettaway was pinned with his arms twisted behind his back, near the window. He grabbed him by the collar and arm and pulled him toward the monitors. "I want you to open them. The cells."

"I can't. Not from here."

"You're lying," said Irons. Then he took his wrist and jacked it up his back higher.

Pettaway grimaced with pain, and across the room as Sachs flinched, he was struck in the chest just below the shoulder blade.

"There's no way. It's controlled by the guards, in the booths."

"Then what's the locking override?"

Pettaway's eyes bulged. He sputtered, looking for words, then he groaned as Irons increased the pressure on his arm.

"Here it is! Here it is! The locking override."

Irons looked toward the battery of controls, then dragged Pettaway to them. "Open them," he said.

"But these are only for the tower. This tower. And you're already in."

The inmate who saw the controls said, "That's just shit. It's more than that. It controls the whole fuckin' place."

"No, it doesn't," Pettaway gasped, and as soon as the words left him Irons spun him around and gripped him by the throat.

Irons's fingers dug in around the windpipe. "It's for the whole place."

This time Pettaway nodded and was able only to whisper his answer, "Yes."

"Open them up."

"I, I can't."

Irons pulled his knife, rough and jagged from chipping the cement, and pushed Pettaway against the wall. Then he pressed the point of the cold steel against his jugular.

Pettaway could feel the roughness of the blade pinching him, pulling at the thin layer of neck skin. Tiny hairs were snagged by the jagged metal and pulled. It hurt, but it would be nothing if, if . . .

"Open it!"

Pettaway nodded, and the knife slowly lowered. He turned to the computer keyboard and punched in a lettered code. When it flashed on the screen, he pushed INPUT. Then he typed five more characters, then again INPUT.

"Ah hey!" someone yelled at the TV bank. "They're opening."

And they were. All of the cell doors were unlocked, first in B-Barracks, then in C. The men in the cells heard the solid thunks of their individual locks, and they came out. Some tentatively, some bursting out as soon as they realized what was happening. They had heard the alarms and had felt the same tensions. And now they responded with the same rage.

The few guards on each of the floors were easily overpowered. Some were in the observation cubicles, and a few managed to retreat into them. The men in the control center laughed as they watched the others set upon the booths, trying to bash their way in. One of the phones rang, and Irons answered it.

"They're out in here," one of the guards, unseen on the monitors, shouted. "The sons of bitches have busted out!"

Irons laughed, then said, "The sons of bitches are here too. And they've won!"

The receiver in his ear was silent, and Irons imagined the horror the guard must suddenly feel. Then he could hear the door crash open and the receiver fall.

Jack dashed down the hall to Huxley's apartment and pounded on the door. "Marion, it's me. Open up."

The door flung open, and before he could step inside, Marion was in his arms. Her face was streaked with tears, and her fingers locked around his sides and dug into his back. "Jack, Jack, Jack," she repeated over and over. It was all she could say.

Jack stood half in, half out of the door, his back exposed to the hall. Something told him to push her inside, to blockade the door, to rush them to the window. But at that moment he felt the same as she, about being in each other's arms and touching, just touching. The emotions he had denied—the feeling he would never see her again—broke in a cold, feverish shaking throughout his chest and arms and legs.

Standing there with her head pressed against his shoulder and her body squeezed against him, he felt as though he had been lifted to another world. His scalded forearms were soothed, the blow at the head forgotten. At his back were the violence and horror of the institution, and it would always remain that way. For the first time since he saw the scope of the breakout, he felt they were going to make it. Oh, God, please let that be so.

He tried to take a step, to move out of the hall, but Marion did not budge. "We've got to go," he said, but still she clung to him with the vise grip of someone who would never let go. Jack was still partly in the hall, his back unprotected. "Marion," he said, bringing his hand to her chin and gently moving her face away from him so they could see each other eye to eye. "Marion, it isn't over. They'll be here, soon. We have to leave, like we planned." Jack was intent on her expression, and he didn't hear the footsteps approaching down the carpeted hall. She stared at him for a long while, her eyes locked on his with the same tenacity of her fingers at his back.

"Come on, Mom. We don't have much time." Ricky touched her arm.

She smiled tentatively at first, then the quaver vanished, and her cheeks became full and her teeth showed bright.

They stepped inside and locked the door. "I found these," Ricky said, and Jack took the coat and insulated gloves. They looked like they would fit, as did the felt-lined boots. The boots appeared new, as if requisitioned for the Scales winter, but then the wearer had only rarely gone outside.

"You'll freeze out there," Lummer said.

"You'll die in here."

Lummer grabbed Jack's shoulder. "They don't know we're here. We'll be safe. Safety in numbers, you know."

Jack stared at him coldly. "I'm taking my family out. You do what you want."

"But you're going out to certain death. Where will you go? Where will you hide?"

Jack glanced out the window toward the barren, frozen seascape. He did not know.

"To the caves," Ricky said. "We'll hide in the ice caves."

Marion felt an awful catch in her throat. She had spent her life on Lake Superior's shores and knew of the shifting ice chunks, the slush-filled holes, the icy death of the water. She caught Jack's eye, then realized there was little alternative.

"We'll find shelter in the caves," Jack confirmed. "Then we'll wait, at least until dark."

"For what?"

For the help from the mainland, for the revolt to collapse, for the chance to walk under cover of darkness around the Facility and across the ice to the town. Jack didn't know what they'd be waiting for. All he knew was that they had to get out of there, and fast.

The boots were a little snug, but the felt would compress. He reached for his parka. Ricky and Marion were nearly ready. On the TV monitor the half-screen trained on the tunnel was a churning, foggy blur. How long it would be before the pressure died, or they came across the yard, he didn't know.

Huxley watched the three getting ready, and what they were going to do seemed unreal. Since Stilkes had left his office, he felt everything was unreal, like he was half-sick, half-senseless—a being at the center of a zone buffered from, but not quite cut off from, the outside. Then as they moved to the window, it suddenly became all too real—the fact he was going to be left behind. He broke for his closet and his parka dangling from a hook just inside the door.

As Jack opened the window, Ricky nudged Lummer. It was only then that he began to get ready for the cold.

Below the window the snow was drifted in a mound that almost reached the sill of the first-floor windows. Ricky climbed into the open slot so his feet rested on the ledge, then without hesitation he jumped into the drift. It was like landing in a feathery bale.

Marion was next, and she hesitated briefly before leaping from the window. Then Lummer and Huxley, and two blankets torn from Huxey's bed. For Jack it was a tight squeeze through the narrow aperture, and he had to let himself fall off balance into the snow. When he was dusted off, Ricky began to lead them directly out onto the ice shelf, the tortured expanse of shifting solid blocks and supportless pockets.

From one of the second-floor windows of the staff building a sunken-chested, oily- and stubble-faced inmate watched them as they pushed their way through the thick snow toward and onto the crusted ice. He watched with a mixture of desire and hatred, of lust and domination. Eddie Hyland was moved by his desire to ravage the woman, but even more so was he moved by an unconscious drive he knew only as hatred for the man: It was his need to humiliate him.

As he watched them escape from the Facility, Eddie felt not frustrated, but good. The satisfaction of his needs prickled under his skin, just beyond his touch. Scales was theirs. Marion and Jack had nowhere to go.

The ice shelf near the shore was as solid as rock, and the mounds of early winter's ice jams were rounded and deep with oversnow. The caves were closer to the outer edge, where they had yet to settle or collapse of their own weight.

With each crunching step on the crystalline surface, Jack felt the relief spread. It was over. Scales Psychiatric Facility was behind him. They had escaped from the immediate dangers, and from the hold the Facility had over their lives.

It was this latter escape that pumped the relief to his inner core of uncertainty and fear. From the very first day within the fences he had felt out of place; he had sensed the malevolence of the grounds, the people, the atmosphere. But now it was all behind him.

At that point Jack had no way of knowing that the worst of his stay on Scales was just beginning.

23

Philip and Emma Tardif had never heard the siren at the Facility, and when it first came on, they didn't know what it was. They lived across the cove and on a hill above Gulletston, and from that distance it sounded like the echoed call of a hundred thousand gulls swooping down onto a beach littered with dead alewives.

"What do you suppose it is?" Emma stood in the middle of the room, her eyes studying the ceiling as if the mystery sound came from the rafters.

"I don't know," Philip said, and he didn't. But he did know it came from across the cove. He pulled on his hat and coat and stepped outside. From the porch he could look down over the town—over the mostly abandoned houses and shops that used to be the town—and out across the iced harbor. The Facility looked as stark and lifeless as it always did. There was nothing unusual about it—no plumes of smoke or scattering troops in the yard or men breaking through the fences. Just the sound was out of place. Its shrillness was dulled by the snow, by the cold, by the distance, and from where he stood the siren sounded like a deep moan, as if the island itself were crying out in agony.

The door opened and shut, and Emma came out of the house behind him. She brought the binoculars, and with them she scanned slowly over the Facility. "I don't know what I'm looking for," she said.

"You won't see anything, but something's happening over there. Inside." Philip turned and went back into the house. He pulled off his gloves and hat and dropped them on a chair as he went for the phone. He dialed the control center, the same as he would for a line to the mainland, and he waited. It was still ringing when Emma came inside and followed him to the kitchen. She looked at him expectantly, but all he could do was shake his head. He broke the connection and dialed again, and again it rang unanswered. Ten, eleven, twelve rings.

"If there is a disturbance, the men on the phones would be too busy with that to bother about us."

Philip cradled the phone slowly, thinking as he did. "They would be busy all right."

"That's all it could be, couldn't it? Just a disturbance?"

From a life in the wilderness, he thought like a wild animal. Sometimes the hunter, sometimes the prey. Always in control. Always analytical. He realized the alarm wouldn't have sounded unless it was something big. It was more than a mere disturbance, a fistfight between inmates, a fire in a cell. His expression conveyed his concern to Emma.

"There are more of *them,* than the guards, aren't there?"

"Yes."

"Could they do it? Take control of the place?"

"They say not a chance." Emma showed a sign of relief. "But that's what worries me. That's what has always worried me. There's always a chance for anything."

Philip glanced out the window toward the Facility, then turned back toward Emma. "You stay on the phone. Keep it up until you can get through. And call Marion. See if she's home, if she knows anything. And Tom, too."

Philip took the binoculars from her, picked up his hat and gloves, and went back outside. From the porch he studied each building of the compound, like a field commander on maneuvers. But he wasn't a soldier, he was a retired DNR ranger. And he didn't command a regiment. He had a sixty-one-year-old wife to protect.

Staring out across the barren snowscape of wind-tufted drifts, he felt suddenly terribly isolated and vulnerable. And afraid. If only they had a sign; if only they knew what was happening. He lowered the binoculars for a broader look, and he noticed some figures rushing from the Administration Building, the entrance to the Facility. He trained the glasses on them.

Even with the binoculars they were too far to distinguish faces, to discern expressions. But he could tell that the first two, with coats flapping unzipped, were running away. And the others—there were three others, all coatless—were chasing.

Philip watched as the two ran down the embankment to the ice. The first tripped, and the other somersaulted over him. Then they were up and moving again, onto the frozen harbor. He watched as they made their way farther out onto the ice: at this distance their movement was a crawl. But the others were gaining.

They caught them in the middle. Philip watched as the two twisted on the ground, their arms trying to shield themselves, while the others lashed at them again and again. A wire? An iron bar? A club? He couldn't tell. He lowered the glasses and watched the scene unfold.

The three were merciless in their beating. They continued, relentlessly, slashing forward with their arms. Philip felt sick, frightened, dizzy. There was no need to raise the glasses. When the three left them to go back toward the Administration Building, he could tell they were dead. Without the magnification, the two bodies side by side could just as easily be the lifeless carcass of a moose killed on a frozen inland lake. But the wolves, at least, had a reason for their savagery.

Philip went back inside. Emma moved the mouthpiece of the phone below her chin. "There's still no answer. And nothing at Jack and Marion's. Tom said he doesn't know and doesn't care what's happening over there." She managed a smile.

"Come on, we're going to the cabin. Let's get ready."

"The cabin! Why?"

"You organize the food. Take whatever we can carry comfortably."

In fifteen minutes they were ready. Philip had a heavy canvas pack that narrowed at his shoulders, allowing free movement of his arms. It was a small pack and needed no frame. Emma filled it with two canteens of water, eight cans of food—stew and fruit—a chunk of frozen beef, spaghetti she broke in half, powdered juice and milk, and coffee. In her worn coat pockets she stuffed two bananas and three large bars of chocolate.

Emma remembered that the boy had gone with Marion today, and she was worried. She tried calling again, but there was no answer. Then she called old Tom. "I don't care. They've chased everybody else off this island, and I'll be damned if they chase me out of my home."

Emma then dialed the control center and, finally, they answered. She said they were across the bay and heard the siren and asked what was happening. She listened, and her face went white, and the receiver slipped from her fingers and crashed to the floor. "They've taken over. They've got the control center." Her lips began to tremble, and she glanced toward the front window.

Philip took her arm and led her to the back door. Outside, they lashed on their snowshoes and began the long, slow climb. It was already getting dark.

They were into the trees before Philip noticed the siren no longer sounded. "The alarm's off," he said.

"It's been off for a while." Emma sounded defeated, tired, already struggling for breath. "He said they"—she took another step, another wheeze—"were coming for us." Again a heavy breath. "Could they follow us up there?"

"We'll be safe at the cabin. There's not a chance they could find us."

Marion could hear the slosh of water somewhere beneath their feet. With each new splash it became louder. And the surface was unsteady. She could feel it rise and settle, rise and settle, as the humps of leveled waves spent their last energy.

"Ricky. Are you sure you can find it?"

"There's lots of them. All over."

"But where?"

"They're close to the edge. That's where the best ones are."

The icescape of the frozen apron that extended into Lake Superior off the coast of Scales was a fractured expanse of jagged peaks and sloping crevices drifted with snow. Ice chunks blown by the waves would collect along the shore and freeze solid at night, only to be faulted upward within a few days by the force of the lake. New ice chunks would collect at the new ice line, the process continued, and the ice shelf crept outward. Over time the mounds settled, but until then they remained unstable. And they tended to shift, keeping open the crevices between them.

They were walking single file, Ricky in the lead, followed by Marion, then Drs. Huxley and Lummer. Finally, Jack. He had been glancing over his shoulder back at Scales every several steps, but there was no one there. No one pursuing them. They were safe.

The footing grew steadily more treacherous. The ice mounds were steeper, the troughs between less stable. Just ahead of them Ricky could see the telltale slush of an open sluice to the lake. He pointed it out to his mother, then angled away from it, his eyes looking ahead for the angular slabs of ice that had yet to settle. Where two had buckled at odds with each other, they would find their cave.

The surface was no longer crusted snow but a layer of compressed ice crystals—frozen droplets of spray blown inland during times of high winds. It crunched noisily as Ricky started down one of the rounded mounds. Because of the crunching, and because of the slightness of movement, neither Ricky nor Marion noticed that the mound reacted to each step. The total weight of the massive pile of ice and snow was close to three tons, but balanced as it was along the ice faults, and floating above what its waterline would be if it floated free, it was sensitive to minute shifts in its equilibrium. With Huxley, then Lummer moving carefully across it, the mound sagged even lower.

It was still bright, but already it was below zero. The cold made their knees stiffer, their muscles less limber. It was harder to maintain their balance.

The mound rose on an unseen water swell, and under thick snow a crack in the fault spread an inch, two inches apart, then came together again as the mound sank in the gentle trough. Jack stepped on the mound and it sank even deeper. The next swell approached silently under the floating mantle of ice, and as it reached the three men, the mound began to rise, faster than before. Huxley wavered in midstep, then lunged forward off the mound. The ice sprang higher, and Lummer fell to his back. The fracture at its base cracked wider, its brittle report like a volley of rifle fire. Jack staggered, then fell to all fours.

Lummer screamed, "Help!" as he started to slide. He grabbed blindly at Jack, clasping him around the arm at the elbow. His slide stopped, and he twisted quickly to his stomach and pulled on Jack. Jack fell off balance and slipped to his side, sliding below Lummer. He tried to grab at the surface, at Lummer, at anything, but there was nothing to hold. And Lummer was pushing, trying to clamber to the top.

Water rushed in at the fracture, filling the trough between the mounds. It was clear and cold, and Jack could see a jagged line of black down the middle where it opened to the lake below. He was sliding, slowly, agonizingly toward it.

Ricky was at the edge of the next mound, coming back. "Stay there!" Jack screamed. The soles of his boot dug frantically at the ice, his fingers gouged into the loose crystals, but still he slid, as if it all was in slow motion. And then in the same unhurried pace, the swell passed and the mound sank and the crack closed.

The trapped puddle of water came higher, to his leg. He was sinking into it. Deepening gouges trailed from where his slide started to his fingers. Finally they held.

Lummer had reached the top and was draped across the summit of the mound. Jack was stable, and as the next wave began to roll underneath, he shifted to his stomach. His right leg he kept dry as the water receded.

He tried to inch upward, but it was as though his muscles were locked. Again it started to sink, and water rushed in. It touched his left leg, then submerged it. He could feel the cold reaching into his boot, soaking through the felt.

Ricky skirted the fracture, then leaped onto the mound. He dropped to his stomach and grabbed onto Lummer, draping his feet toward his father.

Jack grabbed Ricky's leg and began to pull himself upward.

"Let go," Lummer screamed. "We'll all go down."

But Ricky held fast. Jack moved slowly, carefully until he was above the waterline, until he could grip the ice surface with his feet.

He brought himself to all fours, then was able to crawl beyond the fracture. Jack stood and carefully stepped off the mound. Ricky and Lummer followed.

It was Huxley who spotted the slitlike aperture of the cave on the lee side of the faulted mound and led them to shelter. Inside, there was room for all five of them to huddle together. Lit with the translucent glow of daylight refracted through ice, it was a protected hollow several feet long and four feet high at the peak. Hoarfrost had crystallized everywhere in the cave, creating a cushiony, crinkling latticework of ribbony ice, and when it broke, it tinkled like fine crystal. It was warmer under the ice, and with the five bodies it became warmer still.

Marion wrapped Jack in Huxley's wool blanket and massaged his left leg. His flesh was icy, and through her hands, up her arms, the chill seeped into her. Jack asked the others to wring out his clothes and the boot liner, and they did, as best they could.

But Huxley felt it was futile. It was a long shot for all of them, and for Jack, his leg submerged in the ice water, it was hopeless. The leg would never come back to body temperature in this ice cave, and it would continue to draw heat from the body. Eventually he would lapse into unconsciousness, then suffer cardiac arrest.

"That's enough, Marion. Let me have the clothes."

"But, Dad, they're wet."

"Better wet than frozen."

"You're not going to make it," Huxley said. "The clothes will freeze anyway, then your leg, then you."

"I'll be fine. You just give 'em to me. We're not going to be here much longer anyway. As soon as it's dark enough, we'll head across the cove to the town. I'll get warm there."

"We can't move over this stuff in the dark." Lummer had been facing the wall of the cave and now turned toward Jack. "We were almost killed when we *could* see. It'd be suicide to try it at night."

Marion was on her knees, working on Jack's leg, and she spun to face Lummer. "I hope you stay here. God, do I hope that." She spoke with an anger Jack had never seen, an anger bred of fear and worry and desperation. An anger fueled by the cowardice of Lummer, by the chill that was sapping the life from her husband. Like Huxley, she knew Jack couldn't survive long in the cold.

Lummer turned back to his wall, and Jack pulled on his thermal underwear, his pants, sock, then boot. They were wet, and cold, but his body temperature would keep them warm. At least for a while, as long as the clothes didn't freeze. As long as his body produced enough heat to keep them from freezing.

Across the ice, and in their own subsurface cavern, the new masters of Scales were lighting a fire. It was a fire of paper and cloth and mattress stuffing, and it was ignited in the L-shaped tunnel spur below the MCA Barracks.

Locked alone inside the weapons room was Barry Knudsen. He had been there since the start of the uprising with nowhere to go, waiting for the help that never came. He knew the control center was gone, and if there was a way for him to escape now, he would do it and leave the guns for the inmates. It wasn't his island, nor his building, and the other MCAs weren't his people. They had shown that when he pleaded with them on the phone to come down and help. But they said no, it was impossible, there were too many of them, the only chance they had, the Facility had, was to wait them out, wait for help from the mainland.

Barry sat on the floor, his back wedged into the far corner of the room, his view of the barred entrance blocked by an overturned desk. The room wasn't very large, but its firepower was awesome. Gun racks along the wall carried forty standard-issue .300-caliber rifles with scopes, ten 12-gauge shotguns, and twenty-five .38-caliber sidearms. Many of the guards had their own weapons, for hunting or protection—something they were comfortable with—and these were required to be kept secured with the others as well. If they weren't carrying them, the inmates couldn't get them, the thinking was.

Barry wasn't holding one of the guns. Over time, he thought less and less of what he would do if they appeared around the corner, if they figured a way to break in. He was thinking of his wife and his child. Barry was only twenty-four and had thought himself lucky to be offered a job within the Corrections system during times of reduced budgets. And after his training, and he was assigned to Scales, he didn't much mind. It would be for only a short while, they had said, then they would rotate him out.

Elizabeth wanted to come to the island with him and take one of the staff apartments, but Barry was afraid. It wasn't that he foresaw what had happened today, but he feared exposing her to the sights and sounds of a prison. So she took an apartment in Grand Marais, and every two weeks Barry would hitch a ride with the mail plane or a supply plane and fly over. Each time they said they'd call only once in between to save the fares, but each time apart they broke that vow.

Sitting there by himself, afraid, he wondered if he would ever see her again. Pangs of loneliness settled heavier upon him, and after a while he felt as though he had already lost her, as if she had just died. Though the danger was to him, the sense of loss was the same.

Then finally something happened that drew him out of his melancholic stupor. It was a fire. He smelled traces of the smoke first, then he could hear it. He peered around the edge of the desk, and he could see the light of the blaze flickering on the black walls of the tunnel. As he watched, it grew brighter, the shadows jumping faster. The smoke billowed along the ceiling to the turn in the tunnel, where it curled downward and was drawn out. Then the shouts started again, like when the inmates had first arrived.

They had hoped to smoke him out, but the draft of the tunnel network behind them was pulling the smoke the wrong way, into their faces. "We've got to block it off. The opening." But it was too thick, and they had to back off. The fire burned hot and fast.

Please God, just let me live. Make them let me live! The prayer was a product of his panic, of the realization that it was only a matter of time before they got in, like they had in the control center. Somewhere within the irrational corners of his mind he thought it would be good if they had the guns. He would die cleaner, faster, without pain. But then they would be an armed fortress. If help did come, they would be able to resist, to prolong the siege, to fight off what Barry realized was their only hope.

He sprang up from the floor. The ammunition. The guns will be no good without the bullets! A hysteria of sorts gripped him, and he began pulling cabinet doors open and grabbing boxes of ammunition. There were thousands of rounds, hundreds of boxes of rounds.

He tore the lids off and with pliers began crimping the end of the brass shell casings, one by one. He worked fast, a feverish energy pushing him on. But there were so many. So many to render inoperative. If only he had thought of it earlier.

From the barracks the inmates retrieved blankets, sheets, and then the beds themselves. Fighting the billowing ash and heat, they rushed the bedframes to the opening of the tunnel spur, with the blankets draped over them. They leaned them against the passage and staggered back, their lungs filled with soot and smoke. But it worked. The draft was cut and the smoke blocked.

Barry could see there was a change. The smoke billowed into the turn in the tunnel, collected there, then began rolling in toward him. It was a wall as dark and solid as the basalt of the tunnels themselves. He looked at the boxes and scattered loose shells that littered the floor. He had destroyed dozens of boxes, but there were hundreds left.

His hand ached from the pliers, but he worked faster. The smoke billowed through the bars and into his refuge. Barry glanced again toward the entrance. Nervous energy rocked through him, making him sweat, causing his body to shake. The pliers slipped and crashed to the floor. He looked about the room. In the corner was a metal cart on wheels. He rushed to it and rolled it to the pile of ammunition boxes he had on the table. The air was murkier, rapidly turning heavy. His eyes began to water. Barry began to shovel the boxes onto the cart. Some spilled to the floor, but most held. Then he went to the cabinets. More boxes. Shotgun shells. The sidearms. He reached in and pulled the boxes off the shelves, tumbling them into the cart, onto the floor.

But the smoke was getting worse. The overhead light was a hazy blur. His eyes he could barely keep open. He hacked a cough and gasped for breath, but what he inhaled was worse. It doubled him over, and he collapsed to the floor, on his knees. His face nearly touched the tile, and he retched and gasped and fought for breath. Along the floor there was more oxygen, and he gulped in the air.

The cold metal of the cart was slipping in his hands as he gripped it, as he began to push it toward the barred gate. His keys he pulled from his pocket, then felt for the lock. His eyes were mere slits, seeing only shadows in the billowing, thickening haze. The first gate began to open, in its slow, mechanized draw. Barry hacked again, and again, his throat raw and burning. And the fire touched his lungs. He could feel it inside.

Finally the gate cleared wide enough. Then he pushed through to the next. It was hotter, the smoke denser. He was holding his breath, saving his air, resisting the tortured gasps that seared his throat.

His fingers guided the key to the lock, and again, slowly, the gate rumbled in its track to the side. It was open, but Barry couldn't move. His temples pounded, and the heat rushed throughout his head, his every nerve.

He fell to the floor, and the cart rolled forward. He covered his mouth with his shirt and breathed. He had no choice but to breathe, to accept the air heavy with smoke and ash and heat. Square in the middle of his forehead an ache stabbed like a driven nail. The oxygen was weak, but it was enough. Barry, now almost totally blind, pushed the cart forward. The hall seemed to stretch forever. Then he felt the fire, its direct heat to his right, and the cart hit the wall. He looked, and he saw the flames, the sharp yellow spikes of light, and he stepped toward them, with the cart. He pushed right into the flames, into the soft mush of cotton and ash and paper, pulling the cart with him. He overturned the cart, and with the effort he fell forward through the flames. He was past the fire!

The synthetic fabric of his pants leg melted to his skin, his hair singed to ash on his forehead, but the pain was secondary. It was the air, the lack of breath that seized him, that racked his body with pain, that screamed in his mind.

On his hands and knees he crawled, he scrambled down the corridor. It couldn't be this far, it shouldn't be this far! Just a few steps. That's all it took. A few steps.

He didn't see the blankets until his head butted into them. He tried to push through, but they were solid. Something solid was behind them. Oh God, let me live! He clawed at the cloth barricade. The blankets, the sheets wavered at his touch. They seemed to tease his fingers, seemed to tangle around his wrists, to mock his attempt to break free.

He felt the metal through the cloth, and he gripped it. He pulled himself to his feet. Then behind him the first of the shells exploded, and its load ricocheted off the rock, splintering into a thousand fragments of lead. Then a shotgun shell exploded, and stray pellets peppered his back. He pushed forward, and the barricade gave way. It collapsed to the floor, and Barry fell through on top of it. The smoke shifted and billowed out into the tunnels, pulled by the draft. It's not fair, he thought. He had made it free, and still the cloud pursued him.

But in the moment the air was clear he had gulped the oxygen and had felt it surge into his chest. He pushed over the frames onto the tile, the cold tile, and then down the hall. It got clearer, the breaths came easier, he moved faster. But at the hub they were waiting for him; they seized him and, like the others, dragged him to one of the cells. Inside, he collapsed on the floor.

Back in the tunnel, in the tunnel spur leading to the Facility's weapons cache, the fire received greedily the cardboard boxes and the powder. The casings exploded, some ricocheting bullets to the walls, others mangling their load with the unchambered explosion. The bursts of powder continued long after the flames died, and it wasn't until the next day that anyone was able to step into that hall.

In the tunnel Reuker could smell smoke. He could see it. The air was thickening, as he had imagined it before; it was turning solid with the burning evil of the island, with the rotting stench of its impurities.

Reuker followed the same path he had followed earlier, to the Medical Building. The door at the top of the tubular staircase was only slightly ajar, so the haze collected there, in milky layers. As he pushed his way through, the layers of smoke swirled around him and followed him, an angry tempest buffeted by his rage, captured within his draft.

Stepping into the corridor, he gagged on the air, then expelled the phlegm from his throat onto the green carpeting. He forced himself to move on, down the hall, toward the room. The door was closed, it was locked. A fluttering nervousness trembled in his throat. He could sense the evil growing stronger, he could picture it becoming tangible, a burning black cloud that stole the oxygen from the air. He was in there, Reuker felt certain. Huxley was there!

He crashed his shoulder against the door, and it flung open. Reuker stumbled inside, the raging forces within nearly knocking him to the floor. He regained his balance and looked toward the desk, then spun toward the side, looking throughout the room. It was empty. He was gone.

Yet his presence lingered. It was all around, in the air, in the furniture, in the walls, and it was leeching onto him, sucking his life from him. He felt the revulsion, the fear, the hate he had felt before, in this room, but this time it was all very different. He didn't cringe into himself, he didn't try to escape the haunting visions, he didn't hope for the veil of drugs to dim the fires within. Because now the forces didn't paralyze, they gave him strength. His hatred and revulsion were all he had to keep the evil away, to keep it from devouring him, to keep himself alive until he could find him, until the cleansing.

Stilkes swept his arm across the desk, spilling papers, books, objects to the floor. Then he vaulted over it and yanked on a drawer, but it was locked; they were all locked. The madness flared in his eyes, and he flipped the desk to its back.

Twin file cabinets were in the corner, and Reuker clawed at the drawers, pulling them out, dumping their contents.

The steel cabinets became porcelain, the cement walls, tile—dirty, rust-stained tile. It was the other room, it was this room, they were the same. The evil was the same.

He saw the doctor, his hair ringing his head, round glasses blackening with shadows. His eye sockets were round, deep, dark. As if surrounded in scaly, withered skin. They were the eyes that had guided bony fingers to his shoulders, pushing him into the water, that flamed righteous fire while scouring him with sins, that had connived with emotion while betraying him to their own evil. Those eyes were his, the same eyes that had glared with accusation, that in some demented vision had seen Reuker with Rebecca, reveling in her vileness, drinking of her filth. The horror was strong, it clung to him and in him, like oil in rags, and it burned. It would continue to burn, the flames would grow ravenous, until his blood—only *his* blood—doused the fire, until Huxley's eternal fluids ran across Reuker's skin, scraping away the impurities, cleansing him of all the evils that threatened to consume him whole.

Papers and files littered every square inch of the floor. The cabinets themselves were dented and overturned. Stilkes was exhausted and hot, and his head ached with the driving force of his compulsion. And from the exertion, his chest heaved. It was hard to breathe, like the other times, like all the other times.

He stumbled into the hall to escape the suffocation. Aimlessly he moved forward, but still the smothering forces gripped his chest, squeezed his chest, squeezed his lungs. He had to get out of there. To the tunnel.

He made it to the entrance to the stairs, then grasping the side of the door swung into the opening. The smoke and steam were drifting lazily upward, into his face. He could feel the hot, moist breath, the suspended ash carried on visible currents of air. He coughed and backed away, then turned and ran. Blindly he forged ahead. Away from the suffocation.

Another door. He opened it and pushed through. The

cold smacked into his chest with such an impact that it staggered him. It stole what breath he had, and it froze his lungs. He couldn't breathe, he couldn't even gasp for the air. The wetness that glazed his cheeks, that dampened his clothes instantly began to ice.

He turned back to the door. It was closed! He dropped to his knees and reached for it. His fingers clawed at the edge, at the knob, fighting for a hold. Then it opened. Crusted snow had jammed along the bottom edge, and the door had not locked. He fell inside, then rolled to his back. His legs worked against the rug and pushed him forward. He moaned, then rolled to his side, into the wall.

It was there he rested, it was there the inner turbulence drained into unconsciousness. His body twisted by fatigue, his brain racked with secret agonies, he slept.

Hagan sat huddled on the floor in the corner of the small, white-walled cubicle. Nervously his eyes twittered about the confines of the room, then came to rest, as they always did, back on the door, on the barred opening near the top of the door. He sat there and pondered.

The imponderable had happened. The defenses had collapsed. The system had failed.

Eventually they had come for him. It was long after the alarm had sounded, then ceased, long after the control room was seized, and after the weapons room was neutralized. Everything that was critical to the Facility was dealt with first; everything that was important. And then they had come for him, toward the very end. That's what Hagan thought of as he sat curled into the corner of the locked cell. It was well staged, he thought. They had better plans than the designers of the Facility had.

Yet it hadn't been planned. It happened. The inmates were observers of the routine, exploiters of weakness. After the men in B- and C-Barracks were released and the MCAs on duty overpowered and the gun room set under siege, they systematically prowled through every building, rounding up every guard, every employee, every non-prisoner, and as the darkness outside became total, brought them to the detention barracks and locked them in the cells. It was an unimaginable achievement, with unimpeachable glory.

The only building they had not yet penetrated, on this first day of the takeover, was the MCA Barracks. But they would, sooner or later. There was nowhere for the guards to go, nothing with which to resist.

Four men had died. Creegan was the first, then two on the ice, and one in C-Barracks. There were injuries on both sides.

After the initial release of tension, after Scales swung inescapably into their hands, there was a collective sense of accomplishment—and much more. There was a rapturous delight, an exuberant expulsion of restrictions, demands, deprivations. It was a carnival, and in their celebration they relished their freedom, the control they assumed, the confinement of their captors.

Hagan realized that when the emotions ebbed, when the carnival died, the old fears and hates and neuroses would reappear. And the call for vengeance would be strong.

24

It was cold, a cold that kills. A cold that drives beast to shelter and man to hearth. It was a cold that could fracture rock and turn the air itself to ice. There was no escaping its reach: there was only endurance. Moose stood under pines, hare burrowed into snow, and the island became still, as if its twin ridges of basaltic mass clenched together, like a wolf curling nose to tail.

From the Arctic the cold had come straight across Canada to Lake Superior. It was a dome of air so heavy it pressed outward from its center at least 700 miles in all directions. It was a high-pressure system guided by an upper atmosphere loft—the jet stream—that dipped low into the North American continent.

The upper atmospheric pattern had been established in the first week of January, and one after another, Arctic air masses had been pulled down the chute, chilling the air, the water, the entire Great Lakes basin. But with this dome of cold there was a change. The system was blocked. It did not pass on.

Along the northeast coast of the United States the previous high sat stationary, jammed against the Appalachian spine and the rocks of Maine like the Superior ice off the shore of Scales. Storms that had originated in the Carolinas were moving southwesterly, following the coastline north, keeping the stacked-up highs where they were. These low-pressure systems spinning out of the South could last for a few days, a week, maybe longer. And until the pattern broke, the Arctic air mass over Lake Superior had nowhere to move.

The air above Scales Psychiatric Facility, above the settlement of Gulletston, above the faulted ice line that circled the island, was 18 degrees below zero.

In their cave the temperature was 25 degrees. It was well past darkness, and for what must have been the tenth time, Jack pulled his glove back to look at his watch. But like the nine times before, it wasn't there. The razor whip had sliced it neatly from his wrist, and each time Jack looked he thought how lucky he was the tanned leather, instead of his skin, had absorbed the blow. A thin flap of white flesh where the whip had touched his wrist showed how easily it cut.

The blanket was spread flat, and all five had a piece of it. The air in the insulated cavern would warm with their body heat, and so that wasn't the chief worry. It was the snow and ice below that would drain their body warmth, slowly, inexorably, until trembling skin gave way to fever. Marion kept Jack's left leg close to hers.

"It's time we leave." Like his moist breath, Jack's words hovered in the air, undisturbed, unchallenged.

Lummer had been near sleep, as much made inactive by the cold as his fatigue, and to the suggestion was slow in comprehending.

Huxley was cramped, cold, tired, but he felt safe. He glanced out the narrow crack to the blackness beyond, and it looked even colder. "Maybe we should stay. At least till morning."

Jack would have ignored him, but he saw in Marion's face the same question. "We'd be like seals on an ice floe in the daylight. They'd see us and if they wanted would pick us off with rifles without even leaving the shore."

"Then we could stay here."

"For how long?"

"Until help arrived."

"Or until we froze, or the ice shifts, or these slabs collapse on our heads?"

Marion rolled to her knees and stretched her back straight. "No. We leave now."

She was the first to crawl through the narrow slit in the ice to the outside, and initially it was a relief just to stand up. But the cold was bitter, a bitterness that she could feel through her clothes. Her skin felt as though enveloped in a shrinking sheet of icy cellophane, and soon her every thought was of the cold, her every moment dictated by it.

Huxley was surprised at how bright it seemed, out there on the snow. "They'll see us anyway," he said.

But they couldn't. The reflected light of Scales, of unseen stars created a midnight glow that was a poor imitation of day. It was a black-and-white world with nothing in between. There was either shadow or snow. No objects, no definition, no color.

When Jack looked at Scales from just outside the lip of their sanctuary, the ever-present yellow light flickered as it hovered above the Facility. Was it the mercury vapor itself shuddering in the cold? Did layer upon layer of frigid air refract the light? Or was it a reflection of the fire storm that had cycloned through the barracks, every inmate in the barracks scorching through drugged exteriors, releasing a torture and a tumult that had smoldered like coals under ash since the bricks and mortar and tunnels had come to Scale Island?

It didn't matter, of course. Nothing about that place would ever matter again to him. Once this was over.

They began winding their way around and over the ice mounds, leery of shadows and alert for shifting footholds. Jack took the lead, followed by Marion, Ricky, Huxley, then Lummer. They were maybe a half mile from shore and would have to cover that distance, plus get around the spit of rock Scales sat upon, then traverse the flat ice of the cove before reaching Gulletston. A walk of a mile, perhaps a mile and a half. Tardif's house was up the slope above the town, and they would shelter there.

Jack angled closer toward shore but still kept his distance. He wanted to be away from the ice line and its instability, while staying within the old humps of ice and their shadowy protection. But the wind ignored the shadows and the mounds and pricked at their backs like icy needles.

Jack's pants leg crinkled with every move, leaving white lines at each fold in the fabric. His leg was a sieve through which his body's heat drained from him, feeding the ravenous cold. He could last an hour, he felt certain. There was no need for concern.

Moving carefully forward, between the mounds, Jack glanced toward the shore. The yellow light still shimmered above the compound, the expanse between them was still devoid of life.

They pressed on, silently, shoulders hunching forward, heads bowing toward the ice. Soon it didn't seem to matter to Jack, to any of them, if some wayward eyes chanced on the moving figures far out on the ice shelf—so consuming was the cold, so heavy was the air pressing on their thoughts. It was all they could think of, all they could endure.

Whoever heard the distant whirring first did not mention it. It seemed an inconsequential buzz, an irritating backdrop to the pain of the cold. But then, eventually, all became aware of the waxing and waning of the whir, and in time it became little more than an adjunct of the whistling of the wind across the nylon-shelled hoods of their coats.

It was the wind that taunted their ears with its mysteries. It was the wind that made their legs burn with the cold. It was the wind that brought the chill through every seam, between every gap, to lap with frigid tongues at their skin. And it was the wind that plunged its frozen pylons deep into their chests.

Jack trudged on, and the others followed. When the land rise of the peninsula was cleared, Jack did not notice. He pushed on, swinging wider, playing it safe. And he did not notice the others had stopped in their tracks until Marion's voice overtook him.

"My God." It was more a whisper than a cry, but it carried the impact of a scream.

Jack turned to look at her, at Ricky, at the two doctors.

"Oh, my God." It was a plaintive moan, a wheezed sigh of desperation.

Lummer's shoulders sank, and he let himself drop to the ice, his knees grinding into the gritty surface.

Jack turned to face the cove, the settlement on the other side of the cove. Recognition brought a feeling of despair. It had been obvious, but he had not seen it. He had not understood. And for that failure, he felt foolish.

The flickering yellow light he had seen in the sky had been fire. Not of an imaginary maelstrom, but from a real, raging inferno. With the fire hidden behind the tip of Scales, behind the structure within the fences, he had been unable to see the destruction itself—only its wavering glow in the sky above. But now it was all too clear.

The scattered buildings of the old community were aflame. From the distance over the ice each was like a separate bonfire on a beach, a gathering of tribes for forgotten rituals. Even as they watched, another fire appeared, first as a tiny flicker, then rapidly flashing into a blaze. The building's old, dry clapboard frame sucked the fire into it like a sponge water. It must have been the last they had reached, sitting as it was high on the hill, the last structure to be purged. Marion and Ricky knew as well as Jack that there was only one house that high on the hill.

Then from near the flames a single white light split away, racing down the slope. It bounced and rocked, sending jerky slashes of light through the night sky. And faintly, ever so faintly, they could hear the distant whir, the mystifying adjunct of the wind.

"It was stupid to have left the cave," Huxley said. "We were warm. Safe. We could have held out."

There was a hope, a slim hope that Philip and Emma had seen what was coming and had gotten out. They would have had only one place to go.

Jack watched as the headlight of the snowmobile was joined by two others near the embankment. They maneuvered at an angle down the steep drop, and when they reached the flat ice cover of the harbor, the lights lurched forward and the whirring buzzed loud again. They sped in single file toward the opposite shore, then three-quarters of the way, the second swung inland and the last swung outward. They circled in wide crazy loops, then sped toward each other, veering off at the last moment. They had much to celebrate, Jack thought. They had accomplished so much.

He turned to Ricky. "How's the trail to the cabin?"

Ricky pulled his eyes from the spectacle on the bay and looked at his father. "It's deep, Dad."

"Could we make it?"

"Without snowshoes—" Ricky stopped. He sensed from his father they had only one choice, there was only one answer from him he wanted. "—it would be slow. Hard. But we could do it."

"We'd better start," Marion said.

"Where? Where are you going?"

"To the top of that ridge."

To Huxley, the ridge, this island, even the land just beyond the settlement had always been a different world. Remote. Inaccessible. Forbidding. He stared at the dark silhouette that hulked over their end of the island from five miles away. He could just as easily have been looking at the moon.

Jack began to walk again, skirting farther to the northwest, aiming to circle Gulletston before turning inland to hike up to the cabin. Lummer passed Huxley, and they had all moved thirty yards before Huxley started to follow. He had no choice.

In the snow flats of the north woods subzero winds chiseled the surface into knifelike ridges. The prehistoric Indians called them *shenigata*, cat's teeth, because they were so white and hard and needle-sharp. At the opening to Gulletston Bay the winter winds were funneled by the twin points of land into a blowing chute that carved the surface into *shenigata*. The corrugated ridges did not give to the pressure of footsteps and were a difficult surface to traverse.

Beyond the cove's entrance the snowmobiles continued their erratic swings, their near-misses, their dangerous play. Jack kept an eye on them. The men on those machines seemed wrapped in their own world, consumed with their own spirits, but Jack and his family were exposed on ice, the faulted mounds behind them. If a wayward beam of a headlight cast in their direction, if the driver had a momentary lapse of perception, he would see their shadows. He would signal the others. They would chase them out on the ice.

Then, as if Jack's fears froze into some awful reality,

one of the snowmobiles, in the midst of another wide-sweeping arc, suddenly turned straight, and its headlight shone directly out to the lake, directly toward Jack and the rest. Its beam reached out toward them, seeking to capture them within its glow. Jack stopped and watched. The machine did not bend. It was coming straight for them.

Jack looked out toward the lake. The *shenigata* twisted in its low ridges like snakelike curls out into the darkness. Beyond his scope of vision he could hear the slap of the water on the ice line. Forward, it was still a quarter mile until they were beyond the Gulletston point. There was nowhere to hide. But in the teeth of the *shenigata*.

The headlight screamed through the darkness. The engine's roar grew louder. It was almost drowning out the wind-carried sound of the waves. "Get down," Jack shouted, and they fell to the snow, into the fangs of the cat.

They ground themselves into the ice pack, each one lying flat in the corrugated grooves of the *shenigata*. Jack could see Ricky behind him, in the same groove. Marion in another. If they hadn't been seen already, they should be safe. They were hidden. But still the machine approached. Turn, Jack prayed. Turn away. And then he saw Huxley. He was still standing, still walking, about fifty feet from where they lay in the *shenigata*.

Jack shouted at him to get down, to drop into the linear shadows of the ice. But Huxley didn't seem to understand. He didn't seem to be aware of the sprocketed growl of the treaded beast bearing down on them. He stopped and stared at Jack, bewildered.

"Get down!"

It was as if the cold had numbed his brain. He stood and stared, wavering in the cold. The rocking, jerking spear of light from the snowmobile flashed across the ice where Huxley stood, and for a second he was bathed in its harsh glow. He turned and squinted at the glare, then the light bounced with the feel of the terrain and shone back toward Jack and the others.

Jack lowered his head close to the ice, and he felt its chill touch his cheek. It was dry cold, and where his skin touched it, there was no melt. Instead it felt like tiny knives jabbing into his face, grating at his cheeks. He grimaced with the stabbing sensation.

"Dad. Dad. He's still coming!" Ricky was terrified. He couldn't help but watch, his head an irregular bump in the sleek shadows of the *shenigata*.

Jack twisted to look back at him, then said to keep down, they'd see.

"But they already do. They're coming!"

Jack looked up again, and the light was near the narrowest part between the two points. Just a few hundred feet. Only a few seconds at this rate. Jack looked toward Marion. Should they break for the ice line, lure it out where he could not follow, to the hidden cracks between the mounds? He looked again at the light, and as he did it swerved to the southeast, then the east. The engine revved shrilly as the snowmobile banked in a wide turn. Above the roar, above the distant crash of the waves, they heard the wild shout of the rider, like a horseman at a rodeo. He completed the loop at the bay's entrance and headed back into the cove.

Was he going for the others? Jack struggled to his feet. "Let's go. We have to make it beyond the point, before he comes back." Marion and Ricky climbed out of the grooves, then walked past him. Lummer staggered to his feet. "Hurry."

Huxley saw them rise, and he began walking again, faster. Jack hurried on, past Lummer, up to Marion. It was difficult, almost impossible, to hurry over the slippery, slant-edged footing of the *shenigata*. Marion stumbled stiff-legged over the snow ridges, her leading foot slipping, twisting with practically every step. It was tiring, high-stepping over each crest, but she struggled to keep the pace. If only for Ricky and Jack. To get beyond the Gulletston point.

They were running, or as close as they could come to that. The four were close together, and Huxley was gaining. To his right, Jack could see the snowmobiles circling.

Marion fell. The bladelike edge of a ridge crashed across her midsection, another opened a gash in her forehead. Jack picked her up by the back of the coat and, holding her, forced her to continue moving, to continue trudging forward.

"Go on, Ricky. Keep on!"

Her legs tripped over the teeth of the surface, but Jack held her up. She was dazed; her eyes she struggled to keep open. "Oh, Jack," she moaned. She wanted to lie down, to be left behind. She wanted to grasp her head and hold the stifling throb. But he wouldn't let her. Jack pushed her on. "Please," she managed to gasp. "I can't."

Huxley caught them and looped an arm around her back. Together they half-carried, half-dragged her. For the first time since they left the cave Jack felt warm. But it was a dangerous warmth. Sweat was forming under his arms, down his back, across his forehead.

They passed the entrance to the harbor, and from their angle it appeared that the dark band of the Gulletston point connected with the extended finger of land on the opposite shore. The lights of the machines vanished, and the noise of their engines dropped off as if a great door slammed shut. Instantly the wash of the water at the ice line became louder, and the snowmobiles reverted to the distant whir they were before. And the whir became the wind, the persistent, undying wind.

They slowed, and Marion grew steady. She felt her forehead, and the blood had already begun to freeze, matting in her eyebrow. Huxley looked at the gash, his fingers expertly feeling the skin. "It'll be all right. You'll need a plastic surgeon, though, to take out the scar. When we get back."

She smiled, and they moved on, past the town, past its flaming bonfires, and angled toward shore. The wind was light, compared to what it could be, but its steady, driving force hit like a thousand arrows, each sharper than the last. The temperature, in still air, was 22 degrees below zero. In air that cold the skin, even under wraps, seems to shrink on its frame, pulling tight over bones that turn brittle as dried twigs. And it tingles with a feverish chill, sometimes hot, sometimes cold.

After passing Gulletston point there was a sense of victory, but the elation lasted only until the reality of the weather took hold. It was oppressive, and its weight bent their shoulders and chilled their thoughts. Within each settled a gloom.

Jack looked straight up the coast of the island. The vast white apron of ice stretched farther than he could see. It dissolved into the blackness, a blackness that nipped at the edges—water to one side, the forbidding dark mass of the island to the other. The apron was a pale, lifeless tongue lapping at nothing, gaining no nourishment. And that's where they were heading. Into the desolate infertility of the blackness.

They reached the shore, and along the bank snow had drifted. It was dry and light, and at its deepest they sank to waist-level. When they were atop the first rise of the rocky shore, the snow was compacted by the wind, and it was easier, for a time.

As they fell farther behind the line of spruce, the wind became increasingly blunted, until they could feel it no more. But without the wind, the snow was weightless fluff that drew deep each plodding step. It was easier to follow another's tracks, and so they walked single file. Jack led first, until he could barely hoist his feet out of the snow, until finally he realized it would be best for all if fresh legs took over.

Marion took the lead but tired soon. Ricky insisted on taking a turn, and because he didn't sink quite as far, seemed to last the longest. By the time Huxley took the lead, the slope had increased. He trudged on, as best he could, slogging through the drift.

Huxley's scarf across his chin was frozen solid from his breath, and where it touched his face, his skin was numb. But inside, he burned. He sweated with the effort necessary for each step. His inner clothes were damp, and where the cold reached the dampness, his skin shivered. The extremes clashed, and in his head feverish blood swirled in a sickening rush. He became dizzy, and a winded moan escaped from his chest. But still he pushed on, and the dizziness grew worse. Until, finally, he fell face first into the snow.

The fine crystals scratched his face, the drift clogged in his mouth, and he was trapped, unable to move, as if in quicksand. He felt hands at his back pulling at his coat, and he tried to push, but his arms simply sank through the drift.

When they pulled him up, Huxley didn't open his eyes. He made no effort to brush the snow from his face. He just sat there and whimpered.

Despite the cold, Jack realized they would have to stop. Twenty yards farther ahead, he could see where the steep-pitched branches of two side-by-side spruce trees tented together. It wouldn't be the protection of the ice cave, but it would give shelter, for a while. They moved toward it.

"Dad. Here's the trail. And it's been traveled tonight."

The trail was not a packed walkway but simply the most direct route from Gulletston to the top of the ridge. Jack could see a four-inch-deep trough the width of someone on snowshoes, extending up the slope. The snow would be compressed slightly more than where untrod and fractionally easier to forge through. It would make the ascent easier.

It was a fitful time, a restive time. It was at least as much a struggle battling the cold, trying to achieve comfort, as it was slogging through the drift. The gaps in the snow-laden branches vented whatever heat the five bodies produced, and it wasn't long before the heat of exertion turned icy.

They were tired, and sleep seemed the most precious of luxuries, yet the cold was always there, an ungentle mistress, prodding with chilled fingers, shaking with its solid grip. But it was a vigilant mistress, for to fall asleep would be to succumb without a struggle to the cold.

They sat huddled, shivering, drifting off into drowsiness for a minute, several minutes, before shaking alert with a start, looking wildly about in shock, until the sleepy veil lifted and they remembered where they were. It would be so easy, Jack thought, just to sit there on the snow and close their eyes and wait for the cold to dull them until they could not feel it, until they drifted off to sleep. There would be no more struggle, no more pain—just a blissful surrender. Then once more his head snapped, and he jerked alert. He was sitting with his back to Huxley's, with Marion to his side. He tried to roll forward to his knees, but it was as if every joint were locked, every muscle frozen. He groaned with the effort, but he just couldn't move. He settled back and breathed hard. Just a moment to rest, he thought. Then to move, and rouse the others, and climb out. Just a moment to rest.

His consciousness was rapidly drifting away.

Marion touched Jack on the leg. Then she nudged him. He didn't respond. "Jack," she said, and he moved, looked at her. "It's time we go. We can't stay here."

He nodded and looked the other way. But he made no effort to move. She rolled to her knees and gripped his leg, but only when she touched him at the shoulder did he look toward her, his eyes glassy. She squeezed her hand on his left leg hard, and he gave no indication he felt it. She took her glove off and touched it. "Oh, my God," she breathed. His leg was a cold, lifeless lump.

"Jack," she said loudly, and the others stirred. "We're moving on now. We have to start moving before we all freeze."

There were moans of protest, but Marion did not let them settle back down. She kept at them until they were again standing outside and moving along the trail.

They made slow but steady progress. To talk was an effort, and so each fell into private thoughts. After a while, the march developed a cadence, and the structure of their steps somehow made it easier. And most importantly, the time passed faster.

Jack refused to alter his pace. He refused to stop and gape through the breaks in the trees down the slope toward the fires of Gulletston and the unnatural glow of Scales. At first he had, but each view appeared the same, as if they had covered no ground at all. So he just looked down, at the snow, at the white cold.

It was a dead place, a spiritless place, where shrouded trees bent low to the ground in weary exhaustion, their burden bowing their limbs and bending their spines. In the preternatural midnight illumination of the snow country everything cast the same glow—there was no resolution to features, no depth to the scene. There were only black and white, shadow and snow, each shade masking contour and shape. It was a lifeless, imageless world. A world too far from the sun. A world with air alien to existence, where cold burned and sweat meant freezing.

The temperature continued to drop. And Jack knew, they all knew, there would be no break until dawn.

Inside the old iron stove embers glowed with red heat, and the room was warm. It had been a long, difficult hike, especially for Emma. It was the first time in fifteen years she had been to the cabin in winter, and never had she, nor Philip, made the trek in the kind of cold that was out there tonight. Just keeping warm had a way of draining the body's strength away, leaving little energy for the difficult effort required to scale the ridge with snowshoes.

She slept soundly, victim of a fatigue she hadn't felt in decades. Philip was also tired, but his fatigue was a pain that made it difficult to sleep. He alternated through a series of fitful unconscious turns on the narrow cot, and periods of quiet wakefulness. He seemed more at rest when awake and so he lay there, listening to the occasional spark of the wood, and thinking of the fire he had seen as they had ascended the ridge. He didn't think of the loss, only how thankful he was they had left when they did.

Earlier he had listened to the wind whistling past the old building's cracks and pelting the windows with crystals of snow, but over time the wind died, and a rare calm came to the crest of the ridge. It was an eerie stillness, the kind that creates sounds where there are none and gives flight to imagination.

When he heard the crunch of crusted snow giving way, Philip thought it was only his tired imagination. But it continued, growing louder, maintaining its steady pace, until, unmistakably, he realized something was there. The first thing he thought of was that it was a wolf pack prowling in hunger into virgin territory. But the movement was too slow, too lumbering for wolves.

The cot squeaked as he climbed out of bed. At the window he scraped a layer of ice from the glass with his fingernails and peered outside. The tree line appeared hazy, as though in a cloud. Ice fog hung in the air. Then in the fog, in the floating crystals of ice, a figure began to take shape. It moved not clearly into view but rather grew progressively more solid, as though materializing from the hazy substance itself. Other figures took shape in the mist, behind the first. He watched and hoped it was Jack and Marion and Ricky. It must be the Cookes, he thought. No one else knew this place.

But the shapes kept appearing, and as they did, an agonizing thought gripped him with a chill as frigid as the air outside. If the authorities had reasserted control, the figures could be escaped inmates seeking desperately to maintain their freedom. They could have seen the fresh tracks and followed them.

Philip felt Emma's arm wrapping around his back. "Who is it?" she asked, peering out the glazed window.

"I can't tell yet."

She rubbed the glass and looked closer. They were mere shadows in the mist, stiff beings lumbering through air so cold it froze. "It's the boy!" Seeing him, she realized who it was.

Emma went to the door and flung it open. "Ricky! Marion!" she called, and the line stopped.

Plodding purposefully forward, they had barely noticed the crusting of the snow, the leveling of the rise. So intent were they on their pain, on the cold, on the need to keep moving, step after step.

The voice cut through the crisp air, and they halted, stunned. Then they saw the cabin. Marion tried to call out, but her voice cracked weakly in her throat. Her mouth was as dry as if she were coming off desert sands after a day without water.

"You've made it," Emma cried. "You're safe now!"

Unable to move faster, they could only stumble clumsily forward. When their feet touched the solid wood surface, it felt as though tiny bones in their ankles would give way and crack. It felt as though each step vibrated up brittle legs, through knees too stiff to absorb the shock. And then the warmth.

Philip lit a kerosene lamp and set it on a table in the center of the room. Emma recoiled. "Dear God!" she muttered, and then Marion fell into her arms. She held her, then pushed her back to look into her face.

Her breath had condensed on her hood, her chin, her eyebrows, creating gnarled lumps of crusted ice. Bloodless cuts split her lips, and minute cracks ribboned across parched skin. Round spots of stark white flesh were on her cheeks, the hoary mark of frostbite.

Emma touched her palms to Marion's face, and her warmth flowed into her. The heat brought tiny pinpricks of feeling, and in time, as the skin thawed, it would bring a painful burning.

For all of them the cold would burn. For all, the pain was just beginning.

25

In his dream there was nothing he could do to keep warm. He stood by the fire, then wrapped himself in blankets, but it only got worse. He curled tighter into himself, until the cold at last awakened him. Quickly he realized what was dream and what was not imagination. Even in the darkness he could see his breath, and his feet and nose and ears were icy.

Ike Suomi lay there watching the tiny clouds of vapor condense and wishing he didn't have to get up. But he had no choice. The fire would have to be relit.

His bed was in a loft with a log railing and staircase. The wood floor was cold under his feet as he hurried down into the living room. He opened the door of the wood-burning stove and was surprised to see the logs still glowing with red heat. Standing right next to it he could barely feel the warmth, and he shivered. He crossed his arms, then chafed himself, looking up at the ceiling, out the windows, as if he could see the cold itself pressing in on him. Through the structure it seeped, hanging in the air like a dead cloud, weighing everything down, collapsing the heat of the fire further and further into the embers. The Arctic air snatched the warmth directly from the stove as a desert wind sucks moisture from the morning ground. It evaporated and was gone.

Suomi wedged two more logs into the iron box, then opened the air vents at the bottom so the fire would burn hotter and faster. He took a flashlight and shone it through a window on an outside thermometer. "Jesus." The gradation went as low as 30 degrees below zero, and Suomi could see that the alcohol was below that. It had been cold this winter, and each winter, Suomi thought, seemed to be worse than the last. It made it hard to work, to sleep, to move outside. Keeping warm was a daily struggle, and always, just beyond the door's threshold, hovered the danger of the cold. A stalled engine, or an icy road, or any of a hundred everyday emergencies could mean death. A man could not survive long in that cold, Suomi knew.

He climbed back to the loft and into bed. Spud was

curled into a tight, furry ball on a rug on the floor and had not budged all the while Ike was up.

The sheets had chilled, and Suomi shivered. It took a few minutes before the bed warmed, and a few more before he fell asleep again.

It was nearly an hour and a half later that static spitting from the radio speaker awakened him. Groggily he shifted under the covers. The cabin had warmed, and he was in a deeper sleep than before. But the static bursts remained constant. Suomi looked at the clock. It was exactly 7:00 A.M. He flipped the blankets back and climbed out of bed.

The metal of the radio was cold to his touch. He flicked the switch to transmit, then tried to rub warmth into his hands. "Scales, this is Mainland Base. I read you. Over."

The static crinkled in the air. "It's seven o'clock, and this is today's first call."

Suomi laughed. "You don't have to sound so official about it. And for Chrissakes if you're ever going to be late, these early morning calls are the time for it."

Suomi switched to receive and listened. The static snarled without interruption for a long moment. To Spud he said, "They must be pissed at me."

Then the voice came across. "Just wanted to let you know all is okay over here. No disturbances. Over."

Suomi tensed. A rigid chill stiffened his spine. "What was that?"

"All is okay. No, I repeat, no disturbances."

Why the hell did he have to say that? The call itself told him everything was fine, as usual. They signed off, and Suomi sat there in the cold, thinking. It was their most basic rule, unwritten and unstated. The island never said how things were at the Facility, and he never asked. To talk about it was to put the suggestion in the air where it could crystallize into something real. It wouldn't happen that way, of course. They were not superstitious men. But like many nonsuperstitious men, they saw no reason to change the routine.

Suomi got up from the chair and climbed back to the loft. He felt as though still half-asleep, as though the disturbing thoughts were dreamy intrusions that would disappear with full consciousness.

He climbed back into bed, and as he did, he thought about the voice through the speaker. Like last night's call, and the afternoon before, it sounded far off. Remote.

There was something lacking, something different about it. It seemed flat, dead. There was no warmth to it. Like it had the fire, the Arctic cold had snatched the warmth from the voice as well.

Suomi lay in bed staring at the ceiling. He was not dreaming. He was wide awake.

The new masters of Scales arose slowly. They had slept in the lounges, in the cafeterias, in the hallways—wherever they had dropped the night before. It had been a day and night of emotional extremes, and when fatigue at last caught up with them, its grip was total.

There had been a release of great energy, an expulsion of nervous tensions and overpowering hates and numbing fears. Well into the evening rumors erupted spontaneously of counterattacks by guards, of helicopters dropping men out of the sky, of townspeople assembling on the ground beyond Scales with high-powered rifles and telescopic sights. Each rumor spread like the fire of rebellion had earlier spread, and each brought sudden surges of panic. But each was untrue, and after each there was an even greater release of tension and a revival of a festive, almost juvenile mood.

The Medical Building was trashed and the pharmacy left in a shambles. The carnival lasted until early morning as they reveled in their new roles of keepers, rather than the kept, intoxicated by their freedom.

The aged homes and clapboard buildings across the bay took their turn as targets of rage. They had stood mockingly out of reach beyond the fences since each inmate's first day of incarceration at Scales. They were always there, always free, reminders of their own lack of freedom. The deserted houses were the closest, most tangible objects of a blind society that had dumped them in this godforsaken place and left them to die.

For some, they saw the destruction of Gulletston as the neutralization of a threat to their control. Only two old men were found, and they were brought back to the prison and locked up with the rest.

The morning after left a hangover from the euphoria of clouded, confused heads. And they were cold and uncomfortable sprawled on couches, thin carpeted floors, or vinyl-backed chairs. As they assembled in the cafeteria, a jittery uncertainty moved through the body of men.

Conversations nervously sought the same energy of the night before, but each attempt fell flat. There were more questions than answers.

Eventually they turned to someone to lead, and Hector Irons's voice boomed louder than any. "The first and most important fact is that we have succeeded."

"That's right!" a voice shouted, joined by a chorus of assent.

Irons continued. "We have won control of Scales. We have taken every building but one, and that will be ours soon. They didn't fight last night, and they won't today. Especially when we have the rifles." Another chorus of shouts. Confidence was building.

"But we can't make any mistakes. We got to be careful. We have to cover all the angles. We're just an island, and when they across the water find out about us, it's over. So we have to organize. We have to run this place so at least from the outside it looks the same. If there's a flight due, we meet it. If a call comes in, we take it. We can make this thing last a long time, if—"

"Forever!" someone shouted. Then a different voice. "We don't need the outside. We got Scales. It's ours and it will always be ours!"

Irons let the irrationality sweep through the room on the upraised voices of the men. He knew, and if they didn't they would soon realize, their hold was limited. All they had was time, and that's what Irons wanted to preserve. Time.

The room was cold. The entire Facility was cold, with the decrease in pressure because of the break in the pipe. Irons wanted to figure out the heating system and, at last, secure the weapons. He shouted to restore order, to begin the process of organization. The voices trailed off.

Though he succeeded in leveling the voices, with the focusing of attention came the precision of dissent. "What are we going to do with them?" The question came from the middle of the crowded room, but it just as easily could have come from them all. Failing anxieties and celebrations had given way to a night of memories of past treatment, of past fears. Anger and ideas of retribution were now in the air.

"We're not going to do anything with them," Irons said.

"We're going to treat them as they treated us!"

"What good is revenge?"

"We're not talking revenge. We're talking justice."

After another chorus of shouts a different voice hovered above the noise. "As long as they're alive, there's always the chance they will find a way to retake the Facility. They know this place better than us. We've got to eliminate them!"

Irons raised his arms to quiet the room. "It is essential all outside appearances remain the same. And we'll need their help to run this thing, from heating the buildings to securing food. And any number of other things that will come up that we can't even imagine right now."

"How do you know they'll cooperate?"

Irons smiled. "If they don't, then maybe that will be the time for a little justice." They all laughed, and he knew he had them with him. "We're in control now, and they're not a threat to us. We control them all."

"That's not true." Eddie Hyland shouted from the far corner of the room. As he pushed his chair back noisily and stood, the others turned toward him. "We don't have them all. I know because I saw them get away with my own eyes. There were five of them, and they jumped out of the second floor of the staff apartments."

Where the doctors lived! The thought flashed through nearly 180 minds like a razor through putty. It was the doctors, the psychiatrists, who were most at fault for their being here. It was the psychiatrists who had coaxed words from them with understanding nods and promises to help, then turned their backs on them and testified in hearings, twisting what they had said, drawing conclusions that ensured their being irretrievably labeled criminally insane and cast aside like refuse to an area unfit for human life. And their brand of treachery and torture did not end there. It followed them to their prison, doping them with poisons that turned them into something they were not, that polluted their faculties and dried the very spit in their mouths. Every day was an agony, every swallow raw torture.

A grim, determined loathing gripped every man in that room. A silence as deep as the empty growl within their chests hung in the air. It remained until a skeletal-framed man with deep sunken eyes took the floor and moved slowly toward Hyland. The man's manner of rage was feared by even them, and Hyland glanced apprehensively to the side.

Stilkes stopped a table-length from him and asked in a voice that carried throughout the room, "Was it them? Was it the doctors?"

They all waited. Hyland nodded. "Yeah. They were there. The two shrinks. Huxley and Lummer."

"Damn!" The expression came from a seated figure, his lips twitching with spasms of drug side effects.

"Where did they go?" Irons called out. Many eyes shifted back toward him.

"Out on the ice. Straight out from the shore. I watched until I couldn't see them anymore."

"Then I think the problem is solved. They couldn't survive out there. And with the town destroyed, they had nowhere to go."

"How do you know?" Hyland's face flushed with his passions. "Have you been into the woods the other side of Lake Siskiwit? Have you been behind even that first bank of trees beyond the town? They could be there. They could be anywhere. And as long as they're out there, we're in danger. As long as they're out there, we have the risk that they can make contact to the mainland."

"I say they're dead. Frozen stiff." It was a voice from the other side of the room, and with it came a torrent of feeling, from all over.

As Irons bent down to listen to Ringly, he was bothered by the nagging prospect of five people outside their control, doing what he didn't know. Around him stormed the latest anxieties. It was a democracy without order, a mob without unanimity.

In the middle of it all, Reuker Stilkes stood in silent agony. Inside he ached with the fire, the black fire that fed on the evil that was on him and in him, an evil that would decay his body while there was still breath in his lungs. But it was from this very decay that he drew strength. It was a firming of resolve. Pushing through the men toward the door, scattered fragments of their debates flowed like the wind past his ears. In his sight, in his mind hovered a misty figure of rounded eyes, dark eyes, of haloed hair. The figure beckoned with its release, tempted with the cleansing it offered.

Reuker heard the man at the front of the room declare they would search for the missing people. With them would be the shrouded figure.

Since the first eruption in the A-Barracks lounge the

men had been carried along by buffeting spirals of adrenaline too powerful even for the mind drugs of Scales. But adrenaline wanes, and drugs are artificial. Not a single inmate had taken any medication in the seventeen hours of mutiny, and chemical controls of psychoses that had been in remission were becoming more dilute by the hour.

Louis Poiret's airplane was kept in an unheated tin hangar with its engine block plugged into an electric socket. Even with the juice flowing through it all night, it still took every trick, every bit of mechanical knowledge, every coaxing word of flattery to get the thing to kick over. After it cranked fitfully to life, Louis loaded his sacks of mail and slid the metal doors open.

It wasn't until he was well over the lake that the warmth from the engine began to cycle over his legs, unstiffening his knees and ankles. But no matter how much hot air the tiny fan forced into the cabin, the cold that seeped in through cracks, that radiated through the metal, captured and eventually crushed each kernel of warmth like a braggart's grip on an aluminum can.

There was little headwind for the plane to labor against. The air was crisp and clear with a gray ceiling at 4,000 feet. Far below, Poiret could see on the surface of the water broad, slowly bobbing swells, gentle expansions of relief from the savage January winds. It was so cold in the interior of this stationary high-pressure system, to Poiret it seemed that the wind itself had been smothered by the frigid weight pressing down from above.

In the distance he could see Scales. On the horizon it appeared a dirty-white, humpbacked aberration, incongruously afloat in a sea of black. It was a low-slung iceberg with an eastern shelf like a flat blade held at water's edge. As the plane came closer, sharper distinctions between dark and light on the island grew more apparent, as vegetation, rock, or buildings peeked from under the mantle of white. But to Poiret, the distinctions would remain a bit blurred, a bit hazy, no matter how close he approached.

He had always bragged in his younger days, as he ferried fishermen into the northern Ontario wilderness lakes, that he could spot trout-rich waters from 500 feet, and have their lines in the midst of them within ten minutes. He said he had the eyes of an eagle, but even eagles get old. But as he would never give up his flying, he would never give up on the fiction of his youth.

Poiret radioed ahead that he would be dropping the mail in about fifteen minutes. While he waited for the connection from the control center, he glanced at his watch. It was five after two. He signaled again, and still no answer. Then he began to bank to the right to circle around the southeast tip of the island for a direct approach to Lake Siskiwit.

Then Scales responded to his aircraft.

"Hate to wake you guys up so early this afternoon, but I'll be dropping your mail on Sisky."

"We read you."

"Tell Chesser it'd better be cinnamon today." The coffee had better have brandy.

There was a static-y pause, then, "The message will be relayed."

Poiret laughed. Must be a new one. They're afraid the air waves are bugged.

He came in low over the lake, Siskiwit in his sights. To the left were the concrete blocked structures of Scales, and beyond that the cove. On the other side, to Poiret's eyes, the town was little more than dark against white.

The small craft sailed over the tops of the spruces and cedars, and then its skis touched the snow with a clean swish like a pontoon on water. It glided to a stop near the far shore of the finger lake, and then he brought it around and ready to take off again. He jumped out onto the snow and pulled a canvas mail sack from a side panel.

He looked to the narrow opening through the trees. "Damn. Don't make me wait. Not today." He chafed his hands over his arms, then maneuvered the bag with his feet from the plane. Maybe the rookie got it wrong, he thought. Maybe Chesser didn't get the word at all. He glanced into the cabin and thought of calling again, then decided not to. One minute, he decided to wait, then he'd tell them from the air their mail was on the ice, and if they wanted to deliver theirs, they could swim it over.

"Oh, Mary, Mother of God. Is it cold!" He convinced himself not to wait even a minute. But as he opened the door and swung his foot up to the step, he heard the sputtering of a two-cycle engine whining above his plane's steady idle.

He looked, and from the narrow trail at the other end

of the lake a snowmobile emerged and carefully treaded its way from bank to surface. He watched as the black-and-yellow, shark-nosed snout of the machine came directly toward him, gliding over the snow like a missile in a cloudy sky, aiming its death load directly at his aircraft.

It was different, he could tell. The snowmobile drove tentatively at times, avoiding snow bluffs it should blow through, and the crotchety grinding of missed gears carried ahead of it in the crisp air. It wasn't Chesser.

He couldn't tell who it was. He wore a wool hat under his parka hood and a scarf wrapped lengthwise over his mouth and ears. Only his teared eyes were uncovered. It pulled up next to the plane. "Who are you?" Poiret called.

"I work here." He spoke defiantly, as if it were Poiret's fault this duty was thrust upon him.

He was a chip-on-his-shoulder type, and immediately Poiret disliked him. "Wouldn't expect you out here if you didn't." Poiret didn't back away from a challenge.

The man climbed off his machine, all the while his eyes trained on Poiret's.

"Where's Chesser?"

"Couldn't come today. Is that the mail?"

Poiret looked down at the canvas sack, then narrowed his gaze on the courier's cocky, youthful, shit-sure eyes. "It ain't a creel of muskies."

He waited for Poiret to hand him the sack, but when the pilot didn't make a move, he had to stoop down by his feet and pick up the mail bag.

"Where's yours?"

The courier didn't answer. He stepped back to the snowmobile and straddled the seat. He revved the engine, then stared cold and hard at Poiret.

The intensity of the look stabbed into the pilot, and he could feel its chill sink deep into him. For a second he saw something wild, mean, unpredictable in the eyes, and it startled him. But he recovered in a blink of his own eyes. "Chesser brings coffee," he said. "Good idea if you're doing his job, you do it right."

The machine jerked into gear and circled past the plane and headed back toward the trail. "The son of a bitch," Poiret said, then thought he wouldn't have sipped brandy with him even if it had been offered.

It wasn't until he was in the cockpit and flying over the interior of the island heading southwest for Marquette that he felt the shiver from that last look from the courier. His eyes had flared with some indefinable anger, and it was only now as he played it back in his mind that he recognized what it was. It was a madness. It was a look of impulse and insanity, a crazy, frightening expression of violence and hate.

Poiret had always felt that living inside that place, that working at Scales couldn't help but affect a person. But as the gentle swells of the inland sea opened up below him, he wondered if it had been only the Facility that had touched that man with madness.

26

To step outside after looking through chain-link fences for so long brought a rush of emotions. It eclipsed even the sting of the cold.

Eddie Hyland led a troop of men through the Administration Building and around to the coastal side of Scales. They followed the ice shelf out to the first row of rounded ice mounds, where Eddie had seen Jack and the others going the day before. They didn't walk much farther. At the first feel of the surface shifting beneath their feet, they stopped. Eddie climbed onto the faulted ice and scanned out toward the water and saw nothing. He thought, and as he did he turned slowly, his eyes following the ice ridges in their more or less parallel layout to the shore. From where he stood the rise of land and the Facility blocked Gulletston, but he was sure that was the direction they headed.

He came off the mound and with the others began heading along the coast toward the cove, the town, and the island beyond.

When Eddie had first come out of the Administration Building, another group had headed in the opposite direction, following the shore of the harbor. They found Jack and Marion's cabin at the deepest extent, but it was cold inside with no fire. No one had been there for some time. They moved on, walking toward the gutted and blackened remains of Gulletston.

Inside Scales, for some, anxieties replaced boredom. For others, an expectant energy continued to spark through their nerves. But for all there was one unalterable fact: Life on this first day of freedom was not that much different.

While others stood or paced in the A-Barracks lounge, waiting for what they didn't know, Hector Irons sat huddled in a corner with Dennis Ringly and Richard Smith. Their shoulders were hunched forward—their postures an effective barricade—and their voices they kept low.

"This isn't going to last," Irons said. "I'm surprised it has lasted so long already. I mean, they don't even know what's happened over here."

Ringly nodded. "So what are you saying?"

"I'm saying we got a golden chance to get off of here. Before the whole world finds out, or before these crazies tell them."

"Who's chance is it? Everybody?"

"Hell no. Just us. Us three. The rest of them think as long as we keep answering the phone and keep the guards locked up this island will be theirs forever. And if they believe that, they belong here."

"Where would we go?"

"Where would we go!" Irons was incredulous. "We'd go home, we'd go back to civilization, back to living again. Man, don't you see? We got a chance to really make something for ourselves from this little riot here."

"Yeah, I see," Smith said, excited. "We got a good chance."

Irons looked at him and smiled, then peered over at Ringly. That's why he liked Smith around. He was always ready to agree. But it was Ringly he really needed. He would need his talents to help get them off the island.

"It sounds like a good chance to get killed. How we going to cross that water?"

He had him. Irons grinned. "We'll find a way. Given a little time, we'll find a way."

At that very moment a small airplane was just leaving Scales behind and flying out over Lake Superior. None of the three had been in the control center when Louis Poiret had radioed ahead, and none was aware that the mail plane had landed, had been met, and had lifted off. And at that moment none of them realized Louis Poiret would be back.

Ringly leaned back and smiled. At last, he would be leaving Scales.

The cabin was warm and moist. A large oval pot filled with melted snow was steaming on the iron stove. Philip had disassembled the bent-ash furniture and suspended the narrow strips of wood over the pot from a loose net of fishline he hung from the ceiling. With a better steamer, a hotter fire, a more constant source of water, the ash would be ready to rebend and shape into snowshoe frames in two hours. But the wood was old and dry, the pot not as large as he would like, and as a result it was taking twice as long as normal.

By the time their five guests had warmed, had tea, and had bedded down, it had been near dawn. Philip and Emma slept for a few hours, then got up and began preparing for the descent back to Gulletston. Whether it was today or tomorrow or the next day, they would need snowshoes for the journey and dry clothes and whatever edge over the bitter cold they could get.

Emma had taken the two wolf pelts from the wall and cut them into four-inch strips. Then she began sewing the strips to the rims of the hoods. A parka ruff of wolf fur wouldn't collect ice from warm breath condensing against it, and would prevent facial frostbite like Marion had.

While Philip waited for the ash to steam, he separated the rawhide lacing—the babiche—then soaked it in warm water to make it flexible. As it later dried on the frame, it would shrink and pull taut.

It was after two o'clock before the first of them got up. Lummer had been awake for a half hour, staring at the dark-stained, hand-chiseled log rafters and listening to Philip and Emma work. The night before seemed years away; two days before, a different world. It had been a safe world, where his living was planned and his financial future secure. The Department paid a good wage—not as much as he could make in private practice, but he didn't have the headaches and hours of private practice either. He had been at Scales for four and a half years, much longer than he had thought he could stand, but he had actually come to like it there. A few more years, he had thought, and he'd leave. With his pension, a staff position at a hospital, or working with the courts, he'd have the best of both worlds.

But things had changed. Scales had changed. Whatever happened, he knew he could never go back there. And it was this anxiety over the future, over the disruption that had come to his life, that kept him nervously staring at the ceiling. Finally he flung back the moosehide cover and arose from his bed on the floor.

"You feeling better?" Philip whispered.

Lummer looked at him with a faraway gaze, then looked past him to the ice-encrusted windows. "Yeah. I'm alive." He walked past the stove to the window. "I wasn't so sure about that last night." Philip didn't answer. There was a long, silent pause, with the only sound the bubbling of the water in the pot. "There were times I was so cold, it was like my head was numb. As numb as my feet and my hands. I couldn't think. I didn't want to think."

"It's better to be like that, when you're out there. You think about the cold, and it only gets worse."

Lummer stared at the window, his vision fogged by the moisture that collected on it, then froze into a clear but crinkled layer of ice. He thought of what he had been forced to endure, and the changes that would come. "You know, it's a shame. All this trouble, all this pain, because of one guy. Because one guy thought he knew more than me, than the system, than anybody else who had spent a hell of a lot more time than him working with the kind of crazy at Scales."

There was another pause. Then Tardif said, "I don't follow you."

Lummer turned from the window. "This whole thing is the fault of Huxley. You realize that? You lost your house, I lost my job and damn near my life, because of him." Tardif just looked over at him, through the steam. "Maybe you don't understand, so I'll tell you. You see, those inmates down there were kept in check, locked up, under control, not because of the fences, or their cells, but by medicines. Drugs. Antipsychotics. That's about all we could do. The best we could hope for was to keep them under control, from killing each other, or us. It worked fine, until Huxley changed the rules. And when that happened, it was only a matter of time before the whole thing came unglued."

"Does it matter now?"

"Yeah, it matters. It matters that he know how it has affected everybody. It matters that he know that once he gets out of this thing, if he gets out of it alive, that he's through. He's finished in psychiatry. He won't practice again, anywhere."

"I think you'd better stop thinking like that, and start thinking about getting out of here in one piece. We need each other, and we'll have to rely on each other."

Huxley was awake and listening. He felt alone, empty. He swung from caring only about survival, to not caring about anything. If only he hadn't been rushed, he thought. If only he had had more time with Stilkes, it would have been different, he would have gotten through to him. It would have worked out. But now, all that didn't matter. It was his failure they would care about. He knew government departments well enough to know that they would look for someone to point the finger at, and he would be the one. Lummer was probably right. After that there would be nowhere for him to go.

Emma cooked a pound of spaghetti and heated a powdered mix with melted snow for a thin sauce. She found some canned biscuits in the cupboard and heated those on the stove, the steam giving them a little needed moisture. By three o'clock she was finished, and the others were rising.

Jack was weak and moved very slowly. His face was swollen where Reuker's doubled fist struck him, and his forearms were red and blistered from the hot steel of the steampipe. But it was the pain he could not feel that troubled him the most. His foot was like a wooden stump, and only when he brought his weight on it could he feel anything at all: a wretched, tearing ache from the center of his instep; but there was no feeling at all from the skin. He was afraid to peel his sock back and look at his toes. So he sat with the others, and he ate. He was famished, but such was the effort of chewing that he didn't finish his share.

They talked of walking back down the ridge, of the new

snowshoes they would have, of the help that would surely be coming soon from the mainland, of the aircraft they would see. They talked of anything but the cold and the trek up the night before. For the most part Lummer was quiet, eating fast, not looking at any of them. Huxley asked only one question: What if there were no airplanes?

Philip answered him. "Then we survive up here as best we can until help does arrive."

He believes what Lummer told him, Huxley could tell. He saw it in Tardif's eyes. He could decipher it in his manner. He glanced quickly at the others, and they seemed intent on other things. But they would believe him. In time, they would all believe him.

Huxley spread his collar wide. It seemed so very close in there, with the steam filling the dense air. And there was no place to hide. When he finished his food, Huxley slipped on his parka and stepped outside.

He walked away from the cabin and looked out over the sloping edge of Blackstone Ridge toward the mainland twenty-six miles away. He couldn't see it. The sky was too white and the lake was too black, and where they came together on the horizon there was a contrasting blur. The water was like black ceramic, smooth and reflective, even of the dull white light of the winter sky.

Huxley moved around the end of the cabin and stared out into the interior of Scales. He had never seen so much nothing before. To him it was a dead scene, a forbidden vista of a land with no life, of cold, unforgiving rock and snow and ice. It was an expanse of pine and spruce, of leafless aspen and birch, maple, beech, and oak. Stands of grayed, barkless trunks marked patches of dead forest where beaver dams drowned hardwoods, eventually to leave pits of muck and mire.

He saw no beauty in the wilderness. Only desolation, loneliness, and failure. As he stared into this desolation, he thought of a summer when he was a kid and had gone to summer camp. Some older kids had put him in a canoe without a paddle and shoved him out from shore. It was a small, calm lake, and he drifted to the middle. They left him and the sky darkened and a thunderstorm came. The noise grew louder and louder, cracking through the trees, echoing across the water, until the storm was directly overhead and lightning bolts were striking all around—the trees on the shore and even the water. He lay flat in the canoe, too terrified to cry, and covered his ears with his hands. The storm clouds passed as quickly as they came, and eventually the canoe drifted to shore. The counselors found him at night, still on the bottom of the canoe, his hands still clasped to his head.

He was sent home from camp, and he left with an abiding hatred for the woods, the wilderness. Those feelings, as he grew older, turned to indifference. To Huxley there was nothing inherently beautiful about a sunset, a tree, a craggy cliff. It was just the way things were.

But at that moment, staring out at Scales, he felt not the least indifferent about its wilderness. He felt the same as he did as a child, in that canoe. And only now, after all those years, did he realize his feelings back then were more than just hatred. There was also a deep and terrible fear.

Inside the cabin Philip stoked the fire higher. Ricky had to dig through drifts for the logs and then brush off as much snow as he could. Smoke poured straight up through the chimney pipe as the fire roared.

Five miles to the southeast Eddie Hyland stood on the bank by Scales Psychiatric Facility pier, and stared at the great rising mass of the island. Much more than he could see was hidden from view, as if the island were a polar berg rising out of the salt sea. They must have slipped by the town in the dark and gone inland. Somewhere, up there, they were hiding.

Eddie gazed out over the white landscape, searching, thinking, all the while a frustrated urge churning in his gut. His eyes swept across the horizon. Then he stopped, blinked in the glare, and looked closer. Above the snow and against the clouds there was a dark streak, a dirty smudge against the white background. It rose vertically from the ridge, or just beyond the ridge. He watched it, and as he did, he noticed that the dark stain did not shift with the clouds but stayed in the same position. Eddie smiled. It was smoke. Smoke from *their* fire.

At the same time Eddie made his sighting, across the cove behind the burned-out shell of the Tardif house, two inmates discovered snowshoe tracks leading straight toward the ridge.

Eddie tried to move fast, but the cold had locked his knees. They were within sight, within reach, and a feverish anticipation rippled through him. He would assemble the men and be off soon, and reach the camp during the night. In the dark they wouldn't be seen until it was too late.

27

Marion and Ricky shared a cot, and Emma slept on the other. The men lay on rugs and moosehide on the floor, with coats as blankets. Embers glowed red-hot within the old stove, but from more than a few feet away the heat was minimal.

The Arctic air was a silent invader pressing in on the building, chilling the walls themselves from the outside in, then capturing and crushing the warmth given off by the stove. There was no wind, no noise, no hint of its deadly assault. And even if the invader had betrayed its stalk, it is unlikely those inside would have heard. They were that fatigued by the cold, by their ordeal, by the meager food.

Jack lay curled on the floor, near the cot with Marion and Ricky. He was cold, yet sweat formed on his brow, under his arms. He was running. In his dream he was running down a hall. A tunnel. It was in the subterranean labyrinth of Scales. There was a dull, throbbing pain in his stomach, an empty pounding that threatened to stop him in his tracks and double him over with sickness. But he kept on, running faster, his muscles in his thighs straining, his feet aching with the pounding pressure. The tunnel was endless. It was a long, dark tube with no end in sight. It curved, but around each bend it stretched out again with no limit to its reach, with no door at the far side. He wanted to stop, to give up, to give in to the convulsive pangs in his stomach, but he couldn't. He couldn't because of the echoing noise in the tunnel, the pounding of feet, many feet, behind him, following him, threatening to overtake him. Jack gasped for breath, he fought off the deep yearning of his lungs, his legs to give up, to yield to the inevitable. When would it end? When would the tunnel end? Something would have to happen. Something was going to break.

And then it did. There was an explosion, a great rending crash, a fracturing of metal so sharp it was like plate glass shattering from a powerful impact. The tunnel flashed brilliantly in his mind, and then it was gone, and for a long, confusing moment he drifted, shocked by the concussion of the blast. Then his dream leaped ahead, and he was on the pipe. It had just cracked open, and the shriek of the breaking metal resounded in his ears.

"Jack, Jack. They're here!"

The words boomed out of the echo. It hadn't been like this before. He curled and tried to bring his arms to the side of his face.

"Jack! They're outside."

It was Marion! Lord, God, please don't let her be here in the tunnel. The pounding footsteps, the following shouts. They would get her!

"Please, Jack. Wake up. They're out there."

He felt himself rolling to his side. Then to his back. His arms were tugged away from his face. "Marion!" She was a blur. Everything was a blur. There was movement all around. Feet over wood, not tile. It was cold, not hot.

"Jack, Jack. Listen to me." Marion gripped his wrists, her spittle spewing into his face. "It's the residents. They've found us."

She came clearer. The dream fell away. The sudden confusion crystallized into something real, close, and terrifying.

"Brace the door." It was Philip Tardif, shouting directions to Huxley.

Jack looked and saw them propping a bench from the table against the door. To the right was the window. The glass was gone! The shattering explosion in his dream had been the window. It had been smashed in.

Jack jumped to his feet and lunged toward the window, but at the first step on his dead foot he collapsed. He struggled up to his knee and looked toward the window. It was a jagged-toothed hole, gaping open to the blackness beyond. It shrieked in silent horror, baring frost-rimed teeth in a frozen snarl.

Jack grabbed the iron poker from the stove and using it as a prop pushed himself up. He limped to the window and looked out. A shape against the night snow was just a few feet away. Jack flinched. But it was only the post, at the corner of the porch. He stepped closer, and as he did, he could feel the cold. There was no wind, but the air streamed inside through the open glass, and he could feel its force across his chest. It bit like a hundred tiny mouths, a voracious, penetrating army of invisible, sharp-jawed slugs. He had to pull away, and he fell back against the wall to his side.

"What is it?" Philip asked, his own back braced to the wall next to the door.

The image was like a photographic negative. The ground, the trees, everywhere the snow was blank. Images showed as shadows. Jack closed his eyes and took a deep breath. There was no one there. "I didn't see anybody. At least by the cabin."

"They could have thrown something. It could have been a gunshot." Lummer moved closer to the barricaded door.

"A shot I would have heard," Philip said. "And nothing came through."

Jack looked at the sill, then the floor. He stepped close again and looked outside. It appeared as though as much glass was outside as in. As if it simply shattered, without a force, and pieces of glass fell straight down.

"Take away the bench," Jack said. He pulled the felt boots on, then his coat. With the poker in hand he stepped outside. The drifts below the window were unbroken. No one had come near it. He looked over the open summit of the ridge, and there was no evidence that anything was there, or had been there. He went back inside.

"It was the cold," Philip said. "The air's so cold it just plain and simple shattered that glass."

Ricky suggested they use the kitchen cupboard doors to block off the hole. They did, then covered the other windows that hadn't broken in the same fashion.

When they were finished, it was like a cave inside. Not even the night glow of the snow was able to filter inside. The cabin was now blind; protected against the sudden draft of cold, but unseeing of outside dangers. It left them all with a jittering uneasiness.

The large, wide-treaded Sno-Cat sputtered to life, then clattered off the concrete floor of the garage outside into the daylight glaring off the snow. A small cabin sat between the treads, and a flat bed extended from the cabin to the rear of the vehicle. The entire apparatus was low to the ground for good gravity.

Inside there were four men, and in the back four more sat with their backs against the rear wall of the cabin. Each held a rifle, its butt against the bed and its muzzle in the air. Below them vibrated the powerful engine of the machine.

The Sno-Cat jerked and halted as it neared the embankment, then descended into the iced cove, and it wasn't until it crossed halfway across the flat surface that the operator felt in control.

From inside the cab Eddie Hyland tried to steady his binoculars as he peered toward the summit of the ridge. The smoke streak was fainter, but it was still there.

Eddie had wanted to go the day before when he had first sighted the dirty smudge on the horizon, but the others said it was too late and would be too dark. So they waited, and it took until late morning before the Sno-Cat rumbled across the frozen harbor.

At the far side of the cove they took the rising embankment too fast and almost bounced the outside riders off. They held on and laughed, and the vehicle climbed up to Gulletston. It maneuvered through the blackened skeletons of the buildings, past the Tardif house, and onto the same path of the snowshoes. The trail dived straight into the woods, straight toward the smoke at the top of the ridge.

The single-engine Aeronis Champion banked in a wide arc to the east, then came back in a straight approach for the Lake Siskiwit runway. Poiret was quiet and cold and holding a grudge from the day before. If it was the same courier from yesterday, he was ready for a fight. Words, fists, anything. The place may have driven him a bit crazy, but Poiret looked at himself as a bit crazy too. Everybody who was his own man in the north country had to be. But that didn't give anyone license to treat a man the way the guy on the snowmobile had treated him yesterday. People relied on people up here, Poiret thought, and if he didn't accept that, then maybe he'd better be taught the local practices.

By the time the plane roared over the treetops, Poiret was ready to take on even Chesser. At least fill him with what he thought of his replacement.

He came down hard on the ice, and the sudden jar brought him back to what he was doing. The trees raced by his cockpit in a blur. It was too fast. Much too fast. The skis whistled, and the craft threatened to turn. If it did, the plane would flip and crack a wing.

"Slow down, baby." But the plane raced on. His anger had gripped him and surged through him into his plane, and he hadn't been thinking. He had been careless. Foolish. The thoughts sped through his mind, fogging what he should do. Raise the flaps, give it power and leap over the far end of the lake? By the time the thought occurred to him, it was too late. He'd never make it above the trees.

Poiret pulled on the lever holding the flaps down, and he could feel the strain. He could hear the angry rushing of the wind. The shore was rapidly coming closer.

He steered just a fraction off center, and the plane moved with a jerk, almost tumbling out of control, tail over fuselage. But he held it on course, and the skis angled into deeper snow. It was light, fluffy, not packed by his daily touchdowns. The plane sank a few inches, and the snow gripped harder. Then it slowed and finally came to a halt.

Poiret sat unmoving in his chair, feeling the nervous trembling in his arms, in his legs. If he had been standing, he would have fallen. He swallowed, then felt a trembling sigh escape from deep in his throat. He rubbed a hand from his eyebrows straight back over his forehead and across his scalp. Whether it was the gesture, or the passage of time, he gradually relaxed.

There was enough room in front to taxi the plane around and ready it for liftoff. The engine roared noisily, but he didn't budge. A little more power, and he was able to break the hold of the snow. The craft rocked awkwardly over the uneven surface until it was positioned in the center, facing the southeast. Again the engine died down.

It was only after making his turn that he noticed no one was there. There was no snowmobile racing to meet him from the trail to Scales—no one anywhere. He was too shaky to be mad. He didn't have it in him for even a mild curse.

Poiret looked at his watch and saw that it was a few minutes after eleven. Just when he always arrived. He hadn't radioed ahead because he was right on schedule, and that meant Chesser would be waiting. But he wasn't.

Poiret hit the latch and climbed out of the cockpit onto the snow. He opened the horizontal cargo door and dumped the canvas mail sack on the ice. He kicked it once to knock it off the runway, then climbed back into his plane.

"Risk my damn life for a sack of paper and not even a cup of coffee for it. To hell with you."

He revved the engine, and in a few moments the plane crept into forward motion. By the time it had gained airlift speed, Poiret was back to normal. Airborne, he banked hard left to cross the island and head toward Marquette. As he passed over the long rise to the twin ridges, he glanced down and saw the large red snow tractor of the Facility. It was halfway to the summit and puffing labored clouds of exhaust into the air.

He wondered briefly what the hell they were up to, but then he shook the question from his mind. He looked forward, first at his gauges, then the air space ahead. He couldn't care less what they were doing. He couldn't afford to let what they did down there work again on his mind.

Inside each of them was a wildness, a hunger, a sense of desperation. Things had changed, and to survive they had to react to the changes. The relationships between them had built over the years until the group as a whole settled into its own personality. A personality that reacted to the ebb and flow of the seasons, of new faces, but remained relatively stable. Only in times of great stress was that personality, that order of things, in danger of cracking, wolf by wolf.

It was cold and the snow was deep, and if the pack wasn't crossing crusted lake ice or following a moose trail, the movement was slow and laborious. It was a time that demanded more food for energy, but the winter had been hard on their prey as well. The pack numbered eight wolves, trimmed by three since the fall. A yearling and an old female had succumbed to starvation, and another yearling had its skull shattered by the powerful kick of a male moose in its prime that the pack in desperation had tried to bring down.

Their territory of almost a hundred square miles was not supporting them, and so they tested its boundaries. Two other packs controlled the northern extent of Blackstone and Greenstone ridges and the land between, so it was natural that they push to the southeast, to the great barrier where the ridges met.

As they left the familiar signs and scent markings that mapped their territory, the pack became uneasy. The alpha male inspected for scent marks at least every minute, then left his own on a tree trunk, brush, or protruding rock. The other males marked it as well.

They began to angle up the northern ridge toward its crest, where the wolves knew they would find firmer snow. Halfway up the rise the alpha male sensed the marking of another wolf. It was near the base of an aspen, and the wolf circled it three times, reading it carefully, fixing the time it was left. It wasn't new, and the pack pushed on. The other wolves sensed the foreign marking, and immediately there came the feeling that they were interlopers—encroaching on another's territory. It meant they felt defensive, an attitude that in a fight could take the edge off their aggressiveness and turn the results against them. Instinctively, the pack realized this, and as a whole they felt weaker, more vulnerable, more desperate.

With each find of a new scent marking, the alpha male became increasingly aware of a distinctive factor about the marks. Always it was the same. There was only one scent. The alpha male grew more confident, until at last it was positive: there was only one wolf in the new territory. They would not be challenged.

But to the other wolves, what the alpha sensed was not apparent. When they reached the wind-crusted snow at the summit, one of the males, younger by two years, challenged the leader. But the alpha was strong, and the growling, snapping confrontation turned in its favor. Neither wolf suffered injury, and the rank was preserved, but the hold was more tenuous than before.

When the pack began to move again, the challenger was at the rear of the column. Both it and the alpha were weaker for the efforts they expended. It was clear adequate supply of prey had to be found to prevent the total disintegration of the order and the inevitable deaths of the individual wolves.

A few miles to the southeast, in front of the cabin, Philip Tardif stood still in the cold and listened. The chugging of the diesel was like the distant moan of a generator hidden deep within the bowels of a large building. It was a constant rumble that he could feel as much as hear. The low vibrations carried in the crisp, still air with the ease of light passing through space. There was no wind to interfere with the sound waves, no rustling branches to overwhelm it, no particles of dirt or dust in the air to absorb it.

Philip's binoculars hung from his neck. The view down the ridge was blocked by the forest. So he just stood and listened, trying to read the noise, trying to determine if it was getting closer.

Inside the cabin, slants of light sneaked in along the cracks in the shutters.

"Will we make it out of this alive?" Ricky spoke with the directness of youth. He didn't understand the totality of death that threatened. If he did, he would have blocked the question from his mind, as the adults had done.

Emma was sitting with him at the table. "Of course we're going to get out of this thing. We'll walk right on down when it's all okay down there." Ricky's expression didn't change. "You come up here all the time with that old man of mine and don't seem to have any trouble. What's the difference now?"

Ricky looked around the room, at Lummer lying on a cot, at Huxley peering out through a crack in the covered window, at his father lying down, his wrist at his forehead and a knotted look of pain frozen on his face. "It is not the same, Emma." It was not the flippant contradiction of an elder by a child. Rather, it was a straightforward statement of fact.

Emma took his hands in hers. "You're right. It isn't the same. But we need to be strong. And most important of all is to be strong in our thoughts. Do you know what I mean?"

Ricky didn't answer. They both looked quickly toward the door as a cracking burst of noise resonated from outside. An explosion of rifle fire ripped through the air like a mountain thunderclap. Steps pounded on the snow-covered porch outside, then the door flung open and Philip came through.

"They're on their way up the ridge. They've got that snow tractor and are coming straight for us."

"How could they?" Emma said. "How could they know we're here?"

"Maybe the smoke. Maybe they saw us. I don't know."

Jack said, "Why would they even care? They've got the Facility."

"Because of him!" Lummer shouted, pointing at Huxley. His fears gushed out of him. "This all started because of him, and now they're after us because he's here."

"Shut up, Lummer," Jack said. "You don't know what you're talking about."

"Ask him. Ask *him* about transference, about prodding dormant hates and fears from sick minds. About how it can transform, become directed against someone else. Become so strong it is all that matters. Until they'd do anything, *anything* to get at him."

Jack stepped close to Lummer, speaking directly in his face. "It doesn't matter what he did down there at Scales. What matters is we're up here alone, and they're coming for us."

"But don't you understand? It is him they are after, not us." His meaning was clear, and it hung for a long, silent moment in the cabin.

But it wasn't just him, Jack thought. A scene flashed through his mind, a scene of bedlam and noise and stark, racing terror. He remembered running down the hall, away from the lounge, from the inmates rioting in the lounge. He remembered the pursuit, the struggle with Eddie Hyland, then breaking free and escaping into the tunnels. And most of all, he remembered Eddie's shrieking threat: "I'm coming for her, Jack Cooke. Tell her I'm coming for her."

The gunfire exploded in rapid bursts. It was erratic fire, the reports of more than one rifle.

"I warned you," Lummer shrieked, shaking with hysterical spasms of fear. "I warned you," he said again, his voice trailing off to hoarseness. Then he fell to his knees, sobbing, his hands to his face.

The display seemed to have a calming effect on the rest

of them. "We're going to have to get ready to leave here," Philip said. There was no disagreement. No asking where, or how. His words were accepted with a rugged determination.

"How long do we have?"

"I don't think they're more than halfway up. And the trail only gets thicker." To Jack, Philip asked, "Do you think that tractor can make it?"

"It's powerful. It might be able to run right over some of those trees."

"Yeah, but not all of them. Not coming uphill." Philip was thinking, planning. Feeling more at ease. "If they're stopped soon, I don't think they'd have it in them to make it the rest of the way on foot. Not in this cold."

But they all knew there was no way to be sure. There was a jittery, anxious feeling in the room, like cornered prey waiting for the final stalk, wondering whether to break for it, or stay put.

"But they'll be back, for sure at least by morning. If we can wait till then, we'll have the day to work with and be able to head out Greenstone a safe ways, and dig in."

"And if they continue coming now?"

"Then we leave in the dark."

There was little reaction against the plan. Anything, to elude the wild, mad hunger of the hunters.

Diesel fumes spilled into the hot cab. Reuker had opened his coat and leaned back in his seat. It was crowded, and he was shoulder to shoulder with another inmate, another body in the narrow back seat of the Sno-Cat. The edges of the side window were iced, and Reuker rested his face against the glass for its coolness.

He gasped for breath, and the hot, thick air provided little relief. He gagged, then coughed, then crossed his arms across his stomach and squeezed. He squeezed to stop the churning sickness, to still the trembling nerves, to keep his body from disintegrating into separate, decaying pieces of the whole.

His teeth chattered as though shivering, and he leaned forward, bringing his forehead nearly to his knees. Not now, not here, he prayed inwardly. Keep it from burning, keep it from destroying. Keep the evil from killing.

He stretched back, unclenching himself, but there was no relief to the horrors within. There was no end to the intensity. There was no longer the release by the drugs or by his dreams. No release, except for the cleansing.

Reuker lurched forward again and this time could not hold the sickness. He vomited into his lap, down his legs, onto the floor.

"Jesus Christ!" the man next to him shouted, trying to pull back.

The driver reacted to the odor by jerking the vehicle forward. On the back deck one of the inmates rolled off the side and his rifle discharged, sending an errant shot into the trees. The treads halted, and the machine rocked forward.

The four men on the outside had grown colder, stiffer, sitting there without movement and forced to grip the cold steel of the Sno-Cat and hang on as it had wended its way through thickening woods. It wasn't as they expected, and no longer were they filled with the fire of tracking down the doctors, of preventing their contacting the mainland. When the Sno-Cat jerked and the one fell off, the others came suddenly alert. Alert to the cold, the numbness of their hands, the slowness of their ascent. The shot rang out, and the machine stopped.

They stood and gripped their weapons as if waiting for the woods to react with a volley of its own rifle fire. There was none, but at least they could move, at least they could stretch.

Eddie Hyland swung the door open and climbed onto the tread. One of the men on the back jumped off to help the other, and he sank up to his waist. He turned and looked back, and the others laughed. For one, quick moment, the good feelings returned. Something was happening, and the eventless sitting was broken.

In the woods, beyond a bent cedar, there was a scurried movement. One of the men on the deck caught it out of the corner of his eye, and he raised his rifle and fired. Snow puffed into the air where his slug burrowed harmlessly into the ground.

Then again, the movement. It was a hare, zigzagging through the trees. Another shot, another miss. Then the second rifleman on the tractor bed saw the animal and fired. The two in the snow joined, firing blindly into the woods. Their shots reported through the air like the cracking of a glacial crevasse yielding to the forces of spring.

At the first shot the hare was no more than twenty-five

feet from the edge of the tread. It was in sight until it disappeared into a snowbank sixty feet into the trees. Not a single shot came close, but the men didn't care. They didn't even think of the need to conserve ammunition. They felt the power kicking against their shoulders, the heat spitting from their metal rods. They felt the thrill of action, a surge of excitement from the loud explosions at their command. After at least a dozen rounds had been fired, the guns fell quiet. But ringing in their ears, pounding in their chests, the gunfire echoed.

Hyland looked back over the path they had followed. They had strayed from the tracks of the snowshoes as the trail had narrowed, and behind them was now a jig-jag path through the woods. Some of the smaller trunks had toppled beneath the treads, while others were gashed where the Sno-Cat had swung too close.

The driver came out for air and with Hyland surveyed what was in front of them. It grew steeper, denser, and there was no clear view of the summit. It was still a long way to go.

They had no choice. They climbed back in the cab, and when the others resumed their positions in the back, the driver brought the Sno-Cat to life. Maneuvering through the trees had lent him a skill he had not started with, and he ably turned it around, reversing one tread while putting the other in a forward gear. The vehicle spun almost in place, then began down the rise.

As it made steady progress, within Eddie, within Reuker, and to some extent within all of them, frustrated urges ate at their guts as if acid had touched their inner tissue. It was a frustration that wouldn't go away, a frustration that would breed new resolve.

28

A million prisms were suspended in the air like glass dust hanging in the stillness, each glinting its own silver light. It was ice fog, and it appeared only when it was very cold and very still. The hanging crystals looked brittle, sharp, and the cold seemed to cut the skin as if the ice were indeed broken glass.

It was shortly after dawn, and the seven occupants of the cabin were walking out the northwest branch of the mighty wishbone spine of Scales. Philip chose Greenstone because the crest was more level, easier to walk over.

They had been up late preparing the snowshoes, rushing the drying process, making bindings from strips of the moosehide. Emma carefully wrapped their remaining food and emptied the cabinets of the few tins that had been cached there. They would need more food, especially exposed to the cold, and Philip brought all the fishline and hooks he could find. The line would make snares for small game, and if they could chisel through the ice of inland lakes, they'd be able to catch fish. One of the canteens he filled with kerosene.

Jack and Ricky and Lummer and Huxley had taken turns until late at night, watching and listening for signs of change—gunfire, aircraft, anything—down at Scales. The only thing they saw was a fire at the inland extent of the cove. They had found Jack and Marion's cabin hidden among the spruce and with senseless anger had burned it to the ground. It was an anger that would bring them back for another assault on the ridge.

Walking along the wind-tufted crest, the group carried their snowshoes lashed to their backs. Occasionally they sank through the crust, but the snow was too uneven—a choppy lake frozen in midgale—for the shoes to be manageable. But their necessity would come.

Their breath froze in plumes of frosty crystals as soon as it was exhaled, and the tiny ice flecks joined the glittering fog, drifting and dispersing into the frozen air. After nearly an hour Emma was wheezing, and with each deep breath the cold rushed into her chest. They all had been slowed to her pace, and now they rested, because of her.

Philip sat next to her on a snow-covered rock, and she rested her head on his shoulder.

"I'm trying to be strong," she whispered to her husband. "If only for the boy. If only to keep his spirits up."

"You'll be fine, Emma. We won't go much farther. I know a place where we'll be all right."

"I'm sorry I'm holding you back."

"You've never held me back. Without you, there wouldn't be much use for going on."

Emma breathed easier. Such a good man, she thought. Such a good man.

"Dad." Ricky had wandered ahead and was now coming back. "Look at this."

Jack took the mottled gray and black fur in his hand. "Where was it?"

"Just lying on the ground."

"In the open?"

"Yeah."

The wolf must have been by just recently. "Did you notice any prints? How many there were?"

Ricky thought. "No. I guess I didn't. But there's only one. We saw him last time, right, Philip?"

"It could be the same one," Philip said.

"It has to be." Ricky was excited. "He's the only one I've ever seen up here." He had thought of the wolf often since coming so close, since observing its majesty, its primitive grace. It was as if the gaze of the wolf had bewitched him and lingered in his mind, calling for him to return. And Ricky wanted nothing more than to see him again.

As they resumed the walk, the ice fog had settled, leaving a glistening layer of dry, white powder on the ground. Ricky was alive with excitement. The cold he barely felt, the threat of the inmates was out of his thoughts. He thought only of seeing the wolf—*his* wolf—again. Its eyes had locked on his as if it had wanted to communicate, as if it wanted to bridge the gap that separated beast from man. Ricky had sensed the meaning in the gaze but had failed to connect. He did not know the language. He had not had the time. But the wolf was patient. It would come back. It would teach him.

Raised in the wilderness, a child of nature's games, Ricky's imagination was beholden to fantasies bred of his environment. In that respect, he was no different from any other youth.

With the trees rising closer to the summit, the surface was less crusted from the winds. They stopped to put on their snowshoes, then continued on, in the shuffle-stepped waddle made necessary by the shoes.

Ricky walked in front, gradually widening the gap between himself and the others who walked at Emma's pace. Marion was behind him and over time thought less of the gap and the wolves and more of the aching muscles in her thighs. More than anything, her head was bowed, and she was looking bleakly at the snow. She was not watching her son.

On the inland side of the ridge Ricky could see he was nearing the conical natural tepees of a spruce stand. As he came closer, he studied it carefully. It was dense, a good place for a wolf to hide. Under the umbrella of the drooping branches it couldn't be seen. A dozen wolves couldn't be seen. Ricky felt his heart quicken.

The excitement within turned into something alive, kinetic, driven by its own commands. It was a tingling sensation with its own heat, its own direction. And it began to guide him, to lure him, to dominate him. He moved toward the trees.

Just like the last time, he thought. It was what the wolf liked. Protection from the cold, protection from its enemies, and camouflage from its prey.

He angled from the center line of the ridge toward the spruce. Behind him no one noticed. The gap was wide.

Ricky moved carefully, slowly. His chest heaved, not with exertion but from excitement. From trying to hold himself back. He could feel the wolf. It was here. It was almost as if he had gained the animal's senses, as if he could read the air with his nostrils.

Closer he walked, his gangling steps side-slipping him forward at an agonizing pace. He was looking for movement, listening for sounds, alert for frozen puffs of breath. But it was still. Deathly still. And because of that, he at first did not notice the wolf. Its muzzle rested on the snow, its teeth clenched with the quiet tenacity of a death grip.

He huffed audibly. The snow swished forward with each shuffle-step, tumbling a few feet down the incline in miniature waves of frozen spume. Ricky swallowed hard, feeling only a dry, raspy pain in his throat. He glanced around, into the shadowed tents, beyond the trees, down the slope. There was no movement, no sound, no wolf.

Only when he stopped did the scene stop moving with him. Only then did he begin to see the details. Only then did he see the eyes.

That was what he saw first. The wolf's eyes. Twin, shiny black disks amid the snow, each glinting the brightness of the cloudy sky.

Its head was on the ground, its snout pointed like a dagger directly at him. Its canines extended out over its lower lip like cold saber-toothed ivory of a prehistoric beast. Yet to Ricky the silent snarl and the clenched teeth were not wicked. They were not threatening. He saw only the smooth purity, the ivory's innocence.

An emptiness spread from his chest to his limbs, bringing a numbness as it moved. He was in awe of the animal, and carefully he stepped forward. His eyes locked on the wolf's, and he saw its intelligence. It was trying to communicate, but Ricky did not understand. He moved closer.

When Marion looked up she didn't see Ricky. A flash of panic was muted because of the numbness, because of the aches. She stopped and looked into the distance, then from one side to the other. Ricky was near the trees to the left.

"Oh, my God," she muttered. Just beyond him, where he was walking, she could see the outline of the wolf's head. Its gray, black, white fur was a distinctive contrast with the snow. It was an unbelievable scene, and it took her mind a moment to comprehend. Then she screamed, "Ricky." She lunged after him. "Ricky. Don't!"

But he did not hear, or he didn't want to hear. Or he was unable to sense anything but what was before him.

Don't run. Please don't run, he thought. Don't let it happen like the last time.

The wolf stayed where it was, unmoving, its head perched on a mound of snow, its body hidden behind it. It remained immobile, as if transfixed on the sight before it, on the boy struggling toward it.

Jack didn't see the wolf, but he saw Ricky off to the side and Marion jerking awkwardly toward him. He followed, and with each heavy pressure on his left foot he could feel sharp stabs of pain rocketing up his leg. But he did not relent.

"Ricky. Don't go near it," Marion cried.

Philip realized it was the wolf and joined Marion's cry. He shouted for Ricky to stay back. To get away. The wolf was dangerous.

It wasn't dangerous, Ricky thought. It was peaceful, placid, waiting for him. Its gaze did not break as Ricky came closer. He could see beyond its head to its coiled body. He could see its, its—

Ricky gasped. The wolf did not budge. Its eyes did not blink. There was no breath, no plumes of icy vapor coming from its muzzle. It had registered, but he hadn't thought. He hadn't figured what it meant.

Marion came from behind Ricky and grabbed his shoulders. She pulled him into her chest, her arms looped around him.

"He's dead, Mom. He's dead."

She looked to the wolf, its face so alive, its eyes so alert. But that was all there was. Just its head. And a mangled mat of fur and pieces of bone. Except for its head that perched grotesquely on the snow mound, the wolf had been devoured. The snow beyond it was trampled and stained.

To Philip it looked like a moose kill. The messy remains of a wolf pack's recent meal. Yet it was different. It was different because he had never seen a wolf fall prey to its own kind.

"They're not cannibals, are they?" Jack had never seen such a thing either.

"No. They may kill an intruder, a lone stray in their territory, but they don't go after them for food. And as long as I've hiked this ridge, I've never known a pack to claim this as their territory."

To Huxley the explanation was simple. "They must have been hungry."

"Starving. To do that." Philip looked beyond the remains of the wolf to the pattern of trampled snow. There were the imprints of many wolves. An entire pack.

"So what's the big deal?" Lummer said. "The wolf's dead. Let's go on."

Philip eyed Lummer, trying to understand him. He had met people like him all his life, and in one respect they were all the same. They couldn't see the simplest things about the animals, about the wilderness, that were so obvious. And they wouldn't listen even if told. He looked away, toward the woods where the wolves must have retreated, and said only, "It's just not something they do."

Lummer's expression did not change. He glanced at Jack, at Ricky, then turned and trudged back up to the pathway of the ridge.

Ricky looked at Philip. He understood. "They don't go after people either. Do they?"

"No. They don't."

Ricky looked back to the wolf, at its frozen stare that a few moments before he had sensed was an attempt at communication. He had not understood the language. But now he realized what its message had been: The madness of Scales has touched the wolves. It is a madness that can cause your own species to do this.

It was a warning that tumbled over within him, again and again, as he walked up to the ridge. He remembered what Emma had said to him yesterday when they were sitting at the table, and he came to understand why she had seemed so intent on any edge, whether real or illusory, to fend off death. For the first time he understood its totality.

The distant whir had been so slight, and increasing at such a gradual magnitude, that no one noticed the sound until the first snowmobile reached the summit of the two ridges. Jack turned and listened, staring back in the direction of the cabin. In rapid succession machine after machine roared up over the rise, their chattering engines carrying well in the clear, crisp air.

"How many snowmobiles do they have down there?" Philip asked.

"There's twelve of them."

"Could the inmates learn to run those things?" Philip had never touched one, had never considered owning one.

"It's easier than riding a bike."

The snowmobiles swarmed around the cabin, and in the distance the hacking clatter sounded like a gathering of locusts, their raspy legs of chitin grating against skeletal bodies while countless stiff wings frantically flailed against each other. It was an uncomfortable sound, a sound that worked on all of them standing out on Greenstone. It burrowed under parkas, crept along the skin, bringing a chill unrelated to the cold.

"How far do we have?"

Philip gritted his teeth together, thinking. "We should-'ve been there by now, I'd have guessed. It's just so damn slow in winter."

"So it can't be far."

"Not too. But we'd better get going."

When Philip turned around, he saw Emma leaning against one of the gnarled, stunted oaks, her head and shoulders bowed forward. "Em?" She didn't turn. She appeared to be rocking back and forth, very slightly. He walked closer, and as he did, he could hear her breath, wheezing in and out. "Emma!" he said and hurried to her.

She held her left hand to her chest, her right balancing her along the tree. Her eyes were closed, and her lungs worked furiously for air. Philip took her shoulder and turned her toward him. She moved but did not look up. She couldn't look up, consumed as she was in racking gasps for breath.

Jack came up beside Philip, then called to Huxley.

Emma slumped until she was in a half crouch, held up only by her husband.

"Let her down," Huxley said, then he knelt beside her. "Is there pain in the chest?" he asked, but she didn't respond.

Huxley tried to lay her flat, but Emma resisted. It was harder to breathe that way. Huxley took her chin and forced her to look at him. "Is there a pain in your chest?" She opened her eyes and stared, as if thinking. Finally she shook her head no. "Can you feel my hands?" He touched her on her left hand, then moved up her arm. She could feel him. Then the same with her right arm.

In the distance the engine noise of the snowmobiles disrupted the air, sending waves of nervous sounds toward them. Inside, Emma could sense the jittering effect of the ragged waves. Her skin trembled.

"It's not her heart," Huxley said. "It's the anxiety. Everything is adding up. The cold, the exertion. Her fear."

"What do we do?"

"Just hold her. And wait."

Philip slid closer, then cradled her head on his lap. Already Emma's breathing seemed more controlled, no longer wild, howling gasps. "It's going to be all right.

You're going to be fine," he said, then took off a glove and placed his hand on her forehead. Both hand and scalp were cold, as cold as death, and for one unpleasant moment their eyes locked as the same thought occurred to each.

Philip brought his hand down to her cheek and touched her face gently. Her chest still rose and fell in deep breaths, but the rapid spasms abated. Looking down on her, her face so still, so white, so lifeless, he thought of how real the possibility of death was. He had to close his eyes and turn his head away to chase the feeling.

Lummer watched from several paces away. He was growing more nervous, standing in the cold, waiting, listening to the distant engines. He stepped to the side of the ridge and looked back toward the cabin. He could not get a clear view, but as he peered in that direction, he noticed a difference in the sound of the snowmobiles. They were no longer sputtering impatiently but were revving with power. They were on the move again.

Emma brought her hand to Philip's and squeezed. He looked down to her and caught a smile. "It won't be so bad if I don't make it."

"Don't talk like that. You're going to make it through and we'll build a new house and things will be the same as they've always been."

"Tell me you'll go on, if I don't." He was going to interrupt, but she shushed him with a squeeze. "They need you, you know. No matter what happens to me, you have to lead them through. Especially the boy. Don't let him get cheated out of living."

"They're coming!" Lummer cried. "We've got to get moving."

Philip looked up, then listened. The snowmobiles were in motion and were coming out Greenstone. The inmates had made the same decision they had to follow the easier path.

Lummer moved closer to Philip and Emma on the snow. "Come on."

"We can't go just yet. A few minutes at least."

"You led us out here. You can't just give us up because she can't go on."

Philip's eyes raged, and if he hadn't been cradling Emma's head, he would have gone after him. Jack grabbed Lummer's coat from behind and pulled him around.

"We're waiting for her. Until she's ready to move, we're not moving. If we have to we'll dig into the snow right here."

"What's wrong with you? Do you want your kid and wife to die just because the old lady's ready to give out?"

Jack twisted his grip of Lummer's coat at the collar and dragged him away from Emma. As he did, Emma let go of Philip's hand. "He's right, you know. It's silly to risk everybody, for one."

"I promise I'll carry on after you, if that's what you want me to say. I promise I'll do whatever I can to help them. To help the boy. But I'll be damned if I'm going to give up on you and let you die. Don't ask me to do that. Please don't ask that."

"Then let me up. I can go."

"A few minutes. Just lie there without talking for just a few minutes. Then we'll go."

"But you don't have—"

Philip covered her mouth with his hand. "They've got four miles over crusted, irregular snow. They won't move fast, and when they hit the drifts, they'll sink and go even slower. We've got at least an hour."

Emma didn't fight him. She closed her eyes and rested.

Lummer pulled free of Jack's choke hold and shouted to Tardif. "You tell me where we're heading. Where it'll be safe, and I'll go."

Philip ignored him, staring down at Emma, gently caressing her cheeks.

"You won't find it," Ricky said. "Just give her a chance, and then we'll be off."

Lummer had no choice. He paced, then finally squatted over his snowshoes and tried to cuddle himself against the cold.

By the time they were ready to move again, the cold had seeped through their clothes and chilled skin kept warm by the exertion of the hike. Jack's leg was little more than a dead stump, good only for balance and support. A tenuous balance, at that. But he kept up, limping along at Emma's pace.

They settled quickly into the silence of the trail, fighting their own fatigue, hunger, cold, and all the while thinking of just one more step. And behind them, overtaking them, was the sound. The omnipresent grinding of the two-cylinder engines, whining their own struggles into the chill air. The snowmobiles revved unevenly as they fought the corrugated icescape carved by earlier winds. It had made walking difficult, but now it was saving them. It lent them time.

The ridge wound to the right, then rose up a steep rock bulge. To the left, the inland side, the ridge was stepped with a series of precipitous drops, like giant stairs leading to the valley below.

Philip was leading with the rest behind him single file. He angled left from the center of the ridge close to the uppermost spruce. He stopped and turned around. "Ricky. Stay in the track and take Drs. Huxley and Lummer up to the top of that knot. At the top where it's exposed, it'll be crusted over. Go at least that far, then double back to here. When you see our trail, you'll know what to do. Your Dad and I will be digging in below the second drop."

As the three of them passed by to lay the false trail, Philip took off his snowshoes and told the others to do the same. He tossed his down the slope beyond the second row of trees. Then he jumped from the trail, landing in the deep drift next to the drooping branches of the first spruce. From there to the trail the snow was unbroken.

Emma went next, falling more than jumping from the elevated spot down to where Philip waited. She was unhurt and just made it beyond the closest branch that dusted against the snow surface. She landed six feet from the trail. Marion and Jack followed. Philip then reached a snowshoe as high as he could and batted the heavily laden branches, causing snow to slide free and whump to the ground.

From the trail coming up the ridge, the break in the snow to the left could not be seen. As one came back, the depression looked like the impact of heavy snow from the tree. Beyond that, the trail would be obscured by the scattered stand of spruce.

They lashed on their snowshoes and began making their way down the slope. The sound of the pursuing snowmobiles had grown louder, but they were still a distance away. More than ample time for Ricky and the others to break the trail to the crusted ice and return. Philip felt sure of that, or he wouldn't have sent them.

"You guys are spoiling me." Suomi tried to be lighthearted, but it was forced. Something had gone out of their conversation in the last few days, and he was uncomfortable about it. The voice from Scales had become so cold, so distant, so perfunctory. At first he thought he had caused it. But it was clear that it was the voice on Scales that had changed. Maybe he'd been there too long, Suomi thought. The isolation, the winter, the crazies finally got to him. He just didn't know.

The words came at him through the speaker intermixed with the usual static-y snarl of the radio. "What do you mean?" The tone was flat. Emotionless.

"You're on time, man. Four days in a row now you haven't missed. You shooting for some kind of record?"

"We're just doing what we're supposed to do. What the schedule says." There seemed just a hint of a challenge.

"Yeah. I know."

"Things are okay here. No problems." It was how he signed off, everytime.

Suomi tensed, thinking fast. "Listen. What's with the status of the zealots?" He switched to receive and waited to hear the voice laugh, then say something about the pagans on the mainland, or the spirit of John Gullets watching over them, or even just a simple, "Fine, but we're looking forward to spring."

But there was no such response. The static crackled uninterrupted for a long moment, and Ike could almost sense the confusion at the other end. Finally, "We didn't read you. Please repeat."

"Oh, doesn't matter. I just like to hear myself talk." But it did matter. It was a small thing, a simple thing, his calling them zealots. It was the kind of friendly banter that went on between people who worked together. The kind of thing somebody familiar with the routine would not have missed. Suomi continued, "Listen, I got to talk to Hagan. Message from Lansing. Can you get him to the tower?"

"Something urgent?"

"You know how they are in Lansing."

"I'll tell him."

They signed off, and Suomi rocked back in his chair, balancing on the rear two legs. Spud eyed him from his spot near the fireplace, his ears flat to his head. The dog sensed something wrong and began to whine.

Suomi ignored him, trying to think of something he could do, some way he could stifle that uncomfortable twinge that kept nipping at his thoughts.

The chair dropped heavily to the floor, and he checked a number in a slim phone book. He dialed the airport at Grand Marais and asked for Louis Poiret.

"He's on the run to Scales. Probably there right now."

"Tell me. He been going every day?"

"Yep. Same as usual."

"Has he said anything about the island? Anything different about it."

"Not to me. Course, I'm not always here when he is. Why?"

"I don't really know, to be honest. I'd like to talk to Louis, though."

"He'll be at the Black Bear tonight, if you want him."

"You sure?"

"If it's Saturday he'll be there. I can't imagine anything that would keep him away."

Suomi thanked him and hung up. It was 2:30, and out the window he could see a trace of snow in the air. If the sky didn't open all the way up by evening, he decided he'd make a trip into town.

As he sat quietly in the chair, Spud walked over and rested his head in his lap. The dog cried softly.

On the island Hector Irons sat with his eyes riveted on the tight mesh steel of the microphone head. His hand was still gripped around its base. He was thinking, trying to analyze the voice from the mainland. Why did he want Hagan? Did he know?

Each specified hour on the schedule, Irons had radioed his report to Suomi. There had been no hitches up to now. It had all gone smoothly. Irons pushed his chair from the counter with an angry shove. But it couldn't last forever, he realized. He had known that from the beginning, but somehow he had begun falling into the trap. Seduced by the feeling of leadership, by his mastery over Scales, he had begun to think only of the present, relishing it to the exclusion of his good sense, preferring to ignore what inevitably would come, preferring to believe in the illusion the rest of them clung to.

Sitting there in the control center, staring at the silent microphone, Irons had caught himself. Suddenly he saw his error. And he realized he did not have much time. It didn't matter what the voice on the mainland knew or didn't know. He would know it all, sooner or later. What was important was to escape the island. He and Ringly. Together they would find a way.

He stood up and began walking through the room, past the bank of monitors, toward the double-barred gates. If the others knew what he wanted, they would stop him, as they tried to stop the doctors. So convinced were they by their fantasy.

Buzzing in the sky beyond the thick plate windows, the mail plane circled the southeast tip of the island, preparing for its run into Siskiwit. It was an easily discernible dark speck against the clouds.

Irons left the room to Ross Nyze. His cell had been in C-Barracks, and he had come to the mutiny late. He knew radios and electronics, and because of that, he was left on watch in the control center.

It was different being up there, without the noise, without the activity of the other people around him. He didn't like it at first, but soon he preferred it there, all alone. He was able to watch the monitors through their silent eyes and follow anything, anywhere, within the Facility. He watched as the residents armed themselves with guns, then picked through the shelves for the ammunition not destroyed by the fire. He watched as the guards from the MCA Barracks chose not to resist the armed men and opened their door and were led through the tunnels to the locked cells of the former inmates.

It was a marvelous seat, high above it all, observing but not being touched. He had a cot brought to the control center, and he settled in as the touchstone of the new Scales to the outside world. But with the responsibility came a gnawing tension. At the beginning he didn't recognize it for what it was. It grew on him, though, and soon he was feeling things he hadn't felt in a long while, since before coming to the institution, since before the drugs began.

He was glad to be rid of the medicines, the dryness of throat they brought, the lack of clarity to his thinking. But with this freedom came the tensions, the concerns he had known before, the nervous tingling that worked its tensile fingers deep inside where they met and knotted and twisted tighter and tighter until he doubled over with the pain, until he crashed from wall to wall within the control center, until he felt like grabbing his face within his palms and squeezing harder, firmer, until it all ended. Until he could feel no more.

Alone in the tower, he thought increasingly of his family, how it had been back then. The demands, the responsibilities, the increasing weight placed on his shoulders had grown heavier until he couldn't work at his job anymore, until he couldn't stand the baby's cries. The sight of his wife's face mocked him with its serenity, taunted him with his failed love. The pressure was unbearable until, at last, he ended it. He struck out to stop the pressure, to bring an end to the increasing demands, to thwart the responsibilities that were never satisfied.

He had ended it all and had come to Scales. He never thought of his family in the years since then, until now, until the past few days. It was the first time since then that he felt the old feelings returning. And Ross Nyze was worried that, like before, the tensions would continue to grow worse.

He sat on his cot and stared at the radio across the room. He dreaded its spitting call, coming when he was alone, demanding that he respond. He worried that he wouldn't be able to keep his control, that he wouldn't be able to protect their secret. He worried that the forces he couldn't control within would make him fail.

The top of the bulge along the ridge was crusted, just as Philip said it would be. Having extended the track to the hard surface, Ricky, Huxley, and Lummer turned to retrace their steps. The men on machines would have to cross the wind-carved *shenigata* along the open crest before they realized the track was false. And by then they would be well on their way to the shelter.

Distances were deceptive in the blank terrain of the snow, and it had taken them longer to reach the top of the rise than they had thought. As they descended, the ratchety noise seemed appreciably louder.

Lummer noticed the difference, and he forged past Ricky. He became captive to the sound: the grinding roar entered his head, it fueled his lungs. As the engines raced, his body responded. Faster, harder he moved.

Behind him, Ricky and Huxley tried to run as well. The same dictates of the racing engines had entered them and exerted their control. They felt the same urgency, the same fear. Ricky's smaller stride, his weaker legs were causing him to fall behind.

The surface grew softer. Where it leveled and curved to the left, Ricky could see the spot where Philip had left the trail. It seemed so far. He glanced up the ridge, into the teeth of the sound that whipped like a chain saw over a metal fence, and he saw them! A glint of metal, or glass. A flash of color between the trees. Could they see him?

Ricky pushed on, slipping, sliding, falling down the slope. Lummer was well ahead, Huxley in between. Muscles that had been sore and tired now screamed with pain. They seemed ready to lock, to give up, to fail him. But he kept moving. Down the slope, toward the stand of spruce, toward the trail to shelter. Frigid air gushed through his raw throat.

The wolf. Ricky thought of the wolf, he thought of its gaze staring at him from the snow-heaped mound. He thought what it had tried to communicate. He thought of its warning.

The ground became level. He was near the side trail, where Huxley was, but Huxley was just standing there, not moving. "Go on," Ricky gasped, but Huxley waited. When he reached him, he saw why.

Lummer had tromped from the ridge directly over and down the hump that led to Philip's camouflaged trail. A six-inch-deep trough led directly to where they had gone. A clear blaze to their position. All the effort to the bulge and back, for nothing.

The sound of the snowmobiles careened through the narrow passage of trees that aligned the summit of the ridge. It rushed at them with its powerful impact, pounding at Ricky, telling him to move, to get off the ridge.

He dropped to the ground, then began to unlash the moosehide straps of his snowshoes. They were stiff, caked with snow and ice. And his fingers were cold, hard to bend. Huxley struggled with his, and finally they were off. Ricky said to fill it in. To fill the trench in. With snow only from the trail. Using his webbed shoe as a shovel, he scooped a mound of snow, then dumped it in the depression Lummer left. Huxley did the same. They worked frantically, digging the snow, filling the trough, recovering his tracks.

Gradually it filled in. The trough became level with the

surface, but it was still painfully clear the snow had been broken. They leaped beyond it to the ground below, next to the spruce. Ricky looked back at the scar that pointed directly at them. Under the flat sky there were no shadows, and it was somewhat better than before. But still it was obvious, if they were looking for it. If they slowed down and searched for the camouflaged trail, it would be as clear as a footprint cast in ice.

"Get down!" Huxley cried.

The rapidly firing two-cycle engines burst from the curve of the ridge. They were single file, following the trail packed by the snowshoes. Through the breaks in the needles and the gaps in the clumps of hanging snow, they could see the first of the machines. Just the flash of its color, the outline of its riders.

Huxley dropped to the snow and pulled in close to the tree. Ricky fell beside him, and together they lay flat to the surface. The cold pressed in against Ricky's face. His cheeks, hot with fear, with the exertion, melted the snow where it touched him.

The noise growled over to them, just beyond the tree, along the center of the ridge. The hammering of pistons and the screeching whine of metal on metal became so loud it hurt. Then with a whoosh the first of them was past. Then the second. And a third machine roared, then died. The reverberating sound of the engines pounded in Ricky's head. It was all he could hear, all he could think about. The noise was relentless, the throbbing at his temples ached with the pressure, the pressure of the rasping, hacking engines.

Six times the roar increased, then died. After the sixth, there were no more, and Ricky raised his head. None of them had stopped. They had all raced by the tree, the scar in the unbroken snow, intent as they were on the unambiguous trail in front of them.

As they moved away, the engine noise deepened, and he could hear the sound of treads biting the surface, then churning it into a roostertail of compressed chunks of snow. Rapidly he could hear them moving up the rise to the bald.

They pushed themselves up, and Ricky told Huxley to go on. "I'm going to sweep it smooth. I'll be right behind."

Huxley left as Ricky pushed through to the trunk of one

of the spruce away from the ridge. Tiny twigs scratched at his face as he grasped one of the branches. He bent it away from him, then back, then away again. The bark split, and the branch snapped. When it broke free, Ricky tumbled backward and fell into the snow.

Propelled by his fears, by the urgency of covering the tracks, Ricky struggled to his feet and dragged the branch toward the trail. He reached the broad, frondlike branch up to where they had jumped from, to the beginning of Lummer's trench, and drew it gently over the snow. From side to side, then toward him he swept the broom of short, dense needles.

The broken snow became smoother. It was much better than before. Not perfect, but it would take a close eye to notice the snow was any different there than anyplace else along the trail.

Ricky pulled back, sweeping carefully as he did. Inside, the panic had vanished. He was feeling better, his plan was working; the trail would be covered, and he'd be long on his way down to the shelter Philip and his dad were preparing. But through the glow, still nagging at him somewhere, was the fear. Despite it all, something was wrong. As he backed closer to the cover of the spruce, the feeling grew worse. It gnawed at him, as if there were something he overlooked. He thought but could think of nothing.

Then he noticed it. The noise! The machines were returning. Ricky peered up the grade, and, sure enough, the first of the snowmobiles was already coming back. How could it be? They couldn't possibly have made it across the bald and back already. And then he realized, there could be only one reason: they had seen him.

Inside, the terror blossomed. Ricky backed away, and the branch fell from his hands. He felt drained, without strength to resist, without will to escape. He was tired, so very tired, and his thoughts came harder. He staggered backward, unable to think, barely able to move. Nearly paralyzed with fear.

Louis Poiret guided his small craft over the tops of the trees toward Lake Siskiwit. From overhead, the evergreens appeared earthbound spikes, a spiny coat of protection for Scales. The skis came close to the last of the pointed tips before the white slash of the lake opened up beneath him.

He settled the airplane straight and center, and it glided toward the far shore. Yesterday's near-disaster sobered him to how little room there was for error, and how critical it was to maintain a clear head. The plane's skis whistled over the snow, slowing gradually, until the craft lost its grace and rocked unevenly along. He pulled it up and taxied it around in place.

Poiret adjusted his scarf before climbing down to the frozen surface. The dirty, off-white color of the heavy canvas mail sack made it difficult to pick it out against the snow, and Poiret noticed it only by its shape. It looked like a bulldozed clump of highway snow, except that there were no bulldozers and no highway. He walked closer until he was sure. It was the sack he had left the day before, now stiff and glazed with a thin layer of frost.

He looked quickly toward the trees, in the direction of Scales, and his temper broke like a fever across his skin. He plodded angrily back to the plane and retrieved today's mail sack, then brought it over to the first and dropped it on the ice.

After climbing into the cockpit, he radioed the control center. "What the hell's going on over there?" he bellowed, giving no reason for his anger.

In the control center Ross Nyze froze, as if a rigid spear of ice lanced his spine. The angry call screamed at him from the speaker, demanding that he respond. What was it that the voice knew? What was it about his own voice that betrayed the secret?

"Answer me, damn it."

Nyze felt the tension knot in his stomach. It was something real, something of its own substance, a substance that was foul and demented and that tore at his insides, wrenching him further from what little stability he still had. His voice trembled as he spoke. "There's nothing wrong here. It's the same as always."

"Then why the hell is the mail sitting out here on the ice?"

Nyze didn't know what to say. The confusion began to mount, piling fear upon fear. "I, I don't know what you mean."

"I've just landed on the lake with today's mail, and I find yesterday's still here, untouched."

Through the confusion a thought flashed clearly through Nyze's head: Call Irons. Get him up here. Or send him to meet the plane.

"Now once it's inside those walls, I don't care what you do with it. Burn it, eat it, or give it to the crazies and let 'em cut paper dolls. But just don't get me in trouble. This is the *U.S. Mail* you're talking about."

Nyze hadn't yet called Irons. He was paralyzed. "What do you want?"

"Jee-sus Christ. Have the loonies taken over the funny farm? What the hell do you expect I want? Get a machine out here to pick these bags up."

He pulled the phone closer to him, then said into the microphone, "I'll send somebody out now. You wait." Things were falling into place. His mind was working fast. He picked up the phone.

"No, I'm not going to wait. My contract says I don't have to and I'm not."

"It'll be just a minute."

"Good. You'll find the bags at the end of the runway. As for me, I'm gone." Poiret listened as the voice from the control center came again. It sounded odd, almost as if he were frightened, and not just of him. He listened, and as he did a disquieting sensation crawled across his skin. He shivered, and somewhere deep inside a thought began to form. It pecked uncomfortably at his solid view of things, at his belief in things simple and orderly and unchanging. He thought and began to get a feel that maybe it wasn't as simple as it always seemed. That maybe the order wasn't as it appeared.

Poiret looked in the direction of Scales, but he saw only trees. The leafless aspen and birch and oak scattered among the spruce could have all been dead trunks, reminders of the life that once flourished. And only in spring, when the buds did not come, would it be clear that the forest had died.

He looked toward his instruments and fired the engine. The thoughts were becoming too irrational. The imponderables threatened his simple order, and he chose to block them out. The airplane began to move along the glazed runway, slowly at first, then gathering momentum.

It was as the Indians had believed, Poiret thought. The island was evil, and it affected all who walked upon it.

* * *

His fingers had gone white around the phone. He hadn't been able to call. He had only the presence of mind to deal with the voice on the radio, to fend it off, to limit its intrusive demands. Nyze felt as though he were spinning, faster, out of control. A burning rawness touched his throat, the taste of bile rising. It was like before, and he was scared. The feeling was like it had been when he was home before the police, the courts, coming to Scales. He didn't want it to be like that. He didn't want it to end like it did before.

The radio contact was broken, and the voice was leaving him alone. The immediate crisis was passed. He had succeeded in protecting the secret. But he was only slightly relieved. He worried about falling apart like he had four years ago. He sat there in horror of the disintegration he had suffered, when it had felt like his body had been torn into pieces and trod upon by a thousand hooves, when there seemed nothing he could do but collapse into himself and scream.

The antipsychotic drugs that for four years had kept that horror from building were now but a lingering trace in his veins. As he sat there alone in the control center, fighting the images of the past, the last thing on his mind was to tell someone to go out to Lake Siskiwit and get the mail.

As Poiret's aircraft banked toward the mainland, the canvas sacks remained where he left them, unattended and forgotten.

29

A snowmobile in the wilderness is a crude deception—a child molester as a teacher, a thief as a magistrate. It is an obscene fraud on what makes the wild unique, a vulgar imposition of sound and smell on a fragile terrain at its most vulnerable. It brings to the quiet and the unspoiled a machine belching noxious filth where purity is naive prey, and peace a helpless innocent.

It is the sound that kills. The sound that destroys all that is quiet, all that is serene. From its ratchety sputter to its angry, screeching wail, the machine disrupts and destroys the stillness and the beauty. Its sound shatters the air, as if the sky were ice and the snowmobile a brick from an anonymous cretin of the alleys.

Bathed in its horrid sound, trees turn ugly and snow appears little more than the flaking grit of some great, roaring, unwashed beast. The wilderness itself is changed. The noise hurts. The machines are evil.

Ricky gripped his gloved hands over his ears as tightly as he could. But the sound found its way through and burrowed deep inside his skull. Close to where he lay, the snowmobiles growled.

He had plowed into the snow at the base of a spruce when he heard the pursuers returning. The branches brushed against his side, and a dusting of snow covered him where he had swept it over himself. He lay still, clenched against the cold, against the harsh sounds of the machines.

In his mind Ricky could see the broken snow off the main trail; it was an obvious spur leading to their escape route, leading directly to him. He was scared, and the image of the scattered remains of the wolf came to him, and he saw death.

The screech of the first machine arrived, and its howl turned Ricky's fear to terror. They were here! The beasts had come to devour him.

Eddie Hyland had piloted the lead snowmobile since they had left Scales. At the beginning, the tracks of the Sno-Cat made a fast trail, but where the large tractor had turned back, their pace slackened. Uphill, through deep snow, they could barely keep the machines moving. At times they bogged down completely and Eddie and his rider had to jump off and push theirs along.

At the top of the ridge they had found a warm cabin and knew they couldn't be far behind. Greenstone appeared the obvious route, and so they headed in that direction. Footprints showed they were correct.

The hard-packed crest was initially fast, but ribs of wind-carved ice slowed them to a grinding, jarring pace. Where the trees came closer to the summit, the surface was soft again. It was slow but better than the irregular, hard ridges.

When Eddie reached the top of the bald, the *shenigata* were the worst they had seen. They tried to make progress, but it was difficult. His arms were stiff from gripping the bars for four and a half hours, and his entire body vibrated from the power of the engine. Nearly deafened by the noise, they decided to head back to the cabin and wait until morning.

So the six machines turned around and began heading back over the trail they had just laid. It was deep and well grooved, and Eddie did not need to keep his eyes as intent on the trail as before. He glanced repeatedly off to the side, his gaze drawn by the stark wilderness, by its deathly stillness. There seemed no movement, no sign of life anywhere.

The slope down from the ridge was steep, and at times their snowshoes had skied. It was a struggle to keep them from sliding, especially for Jack, walking on a leg without feeling.

Philip led them around the points where the ledges slanted out from the slope and through the thickening trees to the bottom of the second ledge. The first was a sheer drop of about twenty feet, the second nearly twice that. Philip was sure he'd find deep, compacted drift blown from the ridge and settled in the lee of the cliff, and he was right.

For the cave, he selected a site where the drift was at least ten feet deep. It was hard work digging into the snow with the small, six-inch blade of the stove shovel from the cabin, and Jack and Philip took turns working on the entrance. As they toiled, Marion sat huddled with Emma on the moosehide and wrapped in blankets. The temperature was dropping fast.

By the time the cavern was large enough for both men to climb inside and gouge at the snow walls, Lummer was nearing the shelter. Huxley wasn't far behind.

Huxley told of the snow Lummer broke leading to the concealed spur. He told how they had filled it in, and how Ricky was sweeping it smooth.

"How far back were the inmates?" Jack asked.

"They had already passed us. They went right by, on

up the slope where the trail led."

"And you left him?"

"He told me to go on. He said he'd be right behind."

Jack looked in the direction of the summit and tried to judge the direction of the sound. He stood shivering with the cold, the sweat of his labor chilling rapidly.

"They had a long ways to go. No way couldn't the boy be done and coming down." Huxley was nervous, trying to justify himself. "It didn't make sense for two to be there. It was a one-man job."

"So you left the boy to do it." Marion's voice was weak, but its soft edge was ragged with anger.

"Ricky!" Jack called, then waited. There was no response. Because of the trees he couldn't see too far back along the trail. He listened to the echoing roar of the snowmobiles, and though he couldn't be sure, it seemed they were heading back.

Jack hurriedly lashed on his snowshoes, zipped his coat, and pulled over his hood. "Be careful," Marion called as he began to retrace the path. He was barely aware she had called to him, his concentration single-mindedly on his son.

He tended to think of Ricky as older than he was. Especially since this all began. But he was just eleven years old, for Christ's sake. It wasn't fair that he be the one they find. That he have to sacrifice himself for them. It just wasn't fair!

Reuker Stilkes had lurched and jerked behind the other five snow machines at the beginning, but he mastered the simple controls early. Pushed on by his compulsion, by the horror that ate at him, by the lure of the blood's absolution, he had guided his machine into the stark wilderness of Arctic temperatures.

The feelings raging inside were eventually cooled by the weather, by the wind of motion that nipped his face like a swarm of biting insects. The cold and fatigue beat him down until all he could do was react to the pitch and roll of his machine, and keep pace with those in front. He rode alone, while three of the other five snowmobiles carried two riders.

When they turned to go back, Reuker lagged behind. The constant pressure of maintaining the chase was broken, and he looked at where he was with a different perspective. Atop the bald, all was white, pure, the complete absence of the darkness that had settled within him. The air he breathed became clear of the exhaust of the machines he had been following, and he inhaled deeply. It was cold, but it soothed the inner fire.

Stilkes put the snowmobile in gear and guided the skis into the tracks of the others. His mind drifted from those in front of him, to his own world, to a vision of himself running across a blank expanse. The vision had come and gone during the long day, but never had it been as vivid as it was now.

The only break in the white void he was in was a black-caped figure. Its back was to him, and it was running as well. He was chasing it! Though the face was away from him, he could see it. He could see the halolike rim of black hair, the round, dark eyes. It was neither male nor female, neither human nor beast. But it was living and moving, and it had touched him. In the past it had touched him and left its stain, a poisonous mark that ulcerated his skin, that bored deep into him.

The pain of that touch became fresh in his mind, and in the vision he ran faster, pushed himself as hard as it was possible. His lungs screamed for breath as the air gushed through his throat. He was burning, in his vision he was burning, but the relief was within sight. The caped vessel grew no farther away, and within the vessel he knew pulsed the fluids of his cleansing, the waters that would rinse the stain from his body, that would douse the flames of consumption and bring life back to his chest. He would reach it. He must reach it. Or he would die.

Reuker Stilkes came to the bottom of the rise. He plunged into the depths of the trail, dredged deep through the thick snow by the multiple passes of the snowmobiles. The edge of the snow trench came to his waist, and suddenly Reuker had the sensation of sinking into the whiteness that surrounded him. The vision of the caped figure and the chase vanished, and around him all he saw was an undefiled landscape of purity. It was a hint of what it would be like for him, once the evil had been cleansed.

The burning within drew back to a flicker, and he savored the soothing chill. He drank in the scene of untainted whiteness, and as he did, he felt close to it. Not part of it, but close.

It was a sign, Reuker knew. A sign that the rotting,

acidic brew within would be diluted. It would be rinsed from him, and, at last, he would be cleansed.

His grip on the throttle eased. The tread rotated slower. Finally, the snow machine stopped.

Ricky's every muscle was as taut as the dried leather of his snowshoes. He lay flat on his face in the snow, afraid to move, yet unable to stifle the shiver that vibrated through him.

The noise of the first machine roared so loudly it rocked in his skull, battering his frantic thoughts into stray beams of panic shooting out in all directions. He gritted his teeth, and a tremulous moan, a cry of terror, escaped from his chest.

Then it was past. The first of the snowmobiles was past. His heart froze as he expected it to stop, to veer off the trail, to rush onto the spur. But it didn't. And the second roared, then shot past. He pulled his hands from his ears and heard the distinctive whoosh of the tread biting the snow, a sound like wind through a slatted fence, then the deep engine sound as it was gone.

He felt a sudden rush of his blood through his temples, into his face. It brought warmth, hope. A confusion of feelings. Then in rapid succession the roar of more engines, followed by the whoosh of the treads and the rush of tailing air. The sounds all blended into one, into one loud screeching wail, until the final torrent of air was gone, until the receding engines melded into a single deep groan.

Ricky was too shaken to move. Instead, he lay there, listening to the pounding echo in his ears, letting his breath flow in and out in trembling waves.

It had all happened so fast he had not counted the snow machines. On the first pass, on their way up to the bald, there had been the sound of six distinct vehicles. If he had separated the sounds of their retreat, if he had not been a victim of his terror, he would have realized not all of the snowmobiles had returned. Only five had passed him. And in the distance he would have realized the retreating groan of the engines he heard was the dying call of only those five.

Reuker Stilkes cut the engine, and its idling hum died. He sat alone, straddling the bench seat, staring at the great heaps of white all around him. The snow was so thick, so immaculate, so unspoiled that for one brief instant he could almost forget the decay that had transformed his own organism into the rotting carrier of another's evil. The effect was that powerful.

Stilkes was captivated by the white world around him. With the snow high along the trench, and the trees laden with their burden, he felt as though he were sinking into it. Into a vast scene of purity. It was an unbroken expanse, from ground to sky, like in his vision. Only he wasn't racing across it. He was calm.

Ricky lay still as he listened to the sound rapidly grow more distant. As it did, he became more aware of his discomfort, of the cold. His nerves released from the trauma, they shook with the knowledge of how close it had been. Whether it was because of that knowledge, or the lack of food, he felt light-headed, and in his stomach he felt a sickness beginning to take hold.

He brushed the snow from around his neck and head, then pushed himself up to all fours. He was stiff, and his muscles ached with the movement. He gathered his strength, then stood and brushed the snow from him as best he could. Then he looked between the trees where he had been sweeping.

They hadn't noticed the break in the snow. He didn't understand why they hadn't, because to him it appeared so obvious. He looked at the sky, and already a few flakes were falling. Just a few inches, and it would be disguised. Ricky was ready to turn and begin the trek down the ridge when he decided to finish what he had started. It would take just a minute to finish sweeping it smooth, and then even the most meager of snowfalls would make the scar indistinguishable.

Ricky grabbed the wide, fan-tailed branch and stepped up between the trees, then beyond them into the open. He began to brush the surface, side to side, covering the last evidence of their tracks.

His eyes may have absently glanced toward the rise, but in any case, he didn't notice the silhouette of a man's head and upper body rising above the snowmobile tread. He just didn't look close enough.

Stilkes heard the brushing of the branch in the still air.

It was distinct from the low rumble of the receding machines, and barely noticeable. But its delicate, light swish came to him like a breeze, or the first blow of rain in a storm.

He searched the blank void, and as he did, he saw something move, 150 feet away. He saw the swishing movement of the fan-tailed branch. The cape? The question rocked through his calm and steeled his muscles. He watched carefully, and then he saw it. The figure. He saw it moving in time with the sweep of the cape.

Reuker dismounted his vehicle and stepped in front of it. He stayed in the trench, where the snow was compacted, and walked toward the figure. He didn't move fast. It hadn't seen him.

Ricky was stepping backward into the trees as he swept. In the corner of his eye, it appeared that the hanging spruce branches moved as he did, back and forth. The movement was the same with each stroke.

Ricky pulled deeper into the trees. The scarred snow was nearly undetectable, except for a careful search. He was feeling satisfied that despite everything else, it was going well. He was feeling better.

But within his rising emotions, there was the seed of new fear. It coiled there, like a snake in the rushes, and Ricky sensed its presence. The seed took root, and he stopped his own motion. But there was still movement. To his left. Between the ragged edges of the branch ends. It was a shape. A darkness over snow.

Ricky took a step forward and looked. He saw the man, and beyond him the top of the windshield and the flank of the treaded beast, lying in wait, hidden in the snow. He was moving slowly, steadily. He couldn't tell facial detail from that distance, but he could tell the eyes were fixed on him. They were like black holes in his face, empty sockets hiding dark intent.

A panicky flash threatened to take control, to render him unable to think, unable to move. But Ricky fought it. He backed away, and when he did the tails of his snowshoes dived into the snow. He stumbled, almost falling, but it broke his near-trance. Ricky dropped the spruce branch, then pulled the wood tails free and turned around. As he did, the man began to run. How was that possible? Across the snow, how could he move so fast? Ricky began to clomp forward, trying to run but able to effect only an awkward waddle.

Reuker saw the figure pull back, and the warning pealed like a brass bell in his mind: Don't let it escape. Like the vision, it would try to run into the void. But it wasn't a vision. It was real, and there was a difference. He could stop the figure. He could bring it down.

Stilkes pulled off a glove and tore open the Velcro closure over his pocket. Inside he felt the cold steel. It was a .38 caliber revolver. Standard Corrections issue.

The figure turned, and Reuker broke into a run. As he ran, he pulled the pistol from his pocket and clutched it tightly in his swinging arm. The figure had disappeared between the trees. Reuker moved quickly along the track until he reached the area where he had seen it, off to the side.

The figure had disappeared into the trees, but Reuker could see the trail. It wound away from the clearing and down the slope. He saw it all in just a few seconds, then he took a long step off the track and immediately sank to his calf. The snow gripped him solid, but Reuker forced another step, then he dropped down an embankment along the edge, sinking to his thighs.

He struggled to pull himself free, straining with his leg muscles. The feeling from the vision was real. *It* was escaping. The figure would beat him again.

With the adrenaline surge of the rising panic, Reuker stomped forward. As the trail steepened, he could use the snow for his advantage, letting it catch and soften his long strides, like a mountaineer running down scree.

The trail leveled again and straightened. And there, ahead, was the figure. Reuker raised his weapon hurriedly and pulled hard on the trigger.

At the explosion of powder, Ricky dodged to the right behind cover, following the trail. But he knew there would be nowhere to hide. He tried to think what to do, how to escape, but each thought ended with the same horror: There was no escape.

The despair hit Ricky hard in the chest, snuffing his wind, threatening his resolve. But still his legs moved, his wide-framed shoes shuffling clumsily forward. Please, please, please, he prayed. Don't let this happen. The thoughts rocked crazily in his head. He thought of how effortlessly the man had crossed the snow; he thought of how he must be gaining. He thought of his father, and he wished like he never wished before that he would see him. That somehow, he would be there. "Please, Dad," he whimpered, the words barely distinguishable from his panting, wheezing moans of terror.

Jack had heard the gunshot, and he looked above him at the sound. It was a single shot, and as he waited to hear another, he felt a sense of dread rush over him. Was that his son? Had Ricky just died?

Jack forced himself to move faster, stomping along the trail in his snowshoes. He fought the snow, he fought the steepness of the slope. Let them take me, Lord. Let them take me. The agonized plea bounded answerless in his mind. He pushed himself harder. Pain streaked through his frozen foot as if with each step he buried a saber deeper up the length of his leg, but he refused to slacken his pace. There was only one imperative that guided him.

Ricky realized with horror he was leading the gunman directly to the others, to the shelter. He broke off the trail and headed to the right. He was moving onto a ledge, the first of the giant steps to the valley below. With new purpose Ricky found new strength. He would lead him as far from the trail as he could. Lead him away from the others.

Reuker continued his pace along the tracks, between the trees, pushing himself always harder. Sinking deeper the faster he went. Until finally the slope was too steep, he was moving too fast, and he fell.

He fell on his backside and began to slide. He dug his hands in behind him to stop himself. When he did, he pushed upward immediately to continue the chase.

The snow puffed into the air with his frantic steps. It seemed so light, so harmless. Yet it grabbed with such power at his legs. Reuker lurched against the drag of the snow, then fell again, face forward. He tried to scramble to his knees, but each hand sank deep into the snow. He floundered like a fish on the beach. The prospects grew bleaker, he grew more frantic. He fought the fluff until finally he could raise himself to his knees.

He wiped the snow from his face, and as his eyes cleared, he saw movement through the trees. He raised the pistol, but as fast as it appeared, the figure was gone. Obscured. Reuker rose and continued to follow the track.

Ricky moved close to the top of the cliff. He looked for bare rock, for a cave, a crack, a cleft he could drop down into and hide. A crevice in the rock. He knew they existed in the old basalt. He had seen them before. If there was another, he would seek refuge.

His heart pounded with the glimmer of hope, with the demands of his exertion. His throat was raw from the dry air, his mouth moistureless, and each breath brought burning pain.

The ledge was clearer of trees than the slope. Reuker had a cleaner view of the figure. And it was closer. He could see it. But it was different. It was not the figure of his vision. It was not the black-caped repositor of the evil, the sexless creature that had touched him with its decay.

Reuker moved closer, numbed of thought and feeling. The figure was close to the brink of the ledge. It had slowed, seemingly without any place to go. Reuker moved steadily, plowing through the snow, cutting off the retreat.

Ricky turned. He was there! He was so much closer, as if he had suddenly materialized from the thin air. Please, Daddy, don't let him shoot me. Don't let him do it.

Reuker came even with the figure. He could see his face, his eyes, a shock of hair. It wasn't the face of death and decay he had thought. It wasn't a face with a massive ring of hair, or eyes that gleamed a glossy black, round and deep and nearly hidden within a grotesque visage. It was a young face, a smooth face. It was the face of a boy. A boy with a pillowy, parka-padded body. Reuker raised the weapon and aimed it at him, and as he did, he stared deep into the youthful face, as if he saw something other than what was before him.

Ricky gasped as he stared into the man's face. It was a face of extremes, of light and dark, of sharp features and deep holes. It was a ghastly face that seemed to accentuate all the hate and violence that was possible in one man.

The eyes were set in a black pit, and at the bottom of the holes, as he stepped closer, Ricky could see the eyes, round and wide. They were staring, thinking, anticipating. There was a wildness about them, a piercing intelligence that froze him in his place. They were the eyes of the wolf.

In the man's eyes Ricky saw the same intensity of the wolf, the same untamed grace. But unlike the wolf, there was something else. And it made him shudder. He saw in the eyes the creature's madness, an insanity so deep it plunged through all order, all purpose, all reason. He saw a monstrous visage of something neither human nor animal, but of something that shouldn't exist, of a creature only a sleeping imagination could conjure from the depths of subconscious horror.

Ricky was captured within the gaze. He was not entranced, as he had been with the wolf, but paralyzed with fear.

Reuker had seen that same look before. It was another face, a young face, and it stared at him with the same expression of fright and revulsion. Karen was there at the Hole, and Reuker had felt totally and wondrously cleansed. Like the waters that fell with crashing fury onto the rock, like the purity the sacrament had promised. He had been filled with the richness of the cleansing and had sensed spiritual ecstasy. It had been a new experience, the best experience, until Billy had come. Until Billy had pushed his way through the curtain of water and had screamed and recoiled in horror from him.

Reuker's mind was a timeless-scape of images and ideas. Past was present and present past. Through it all ran a single constant. The constant of the burning pain. The taunts, the deadening ache at the back of his neck, the acidic slime on his skin, the decay within. It was all part of the same evil that had always tormented him, that had always lurked in the fiery eyes of demons stretching out for him, that had always threatened to destroy him.

Reuker saw Billy, and he saw the hate in his eyes, he felt the revulsion of his cousin's heart. And in this new vision Billy had changed, since that night at the Hole, with Karen. He was a few years older, but he had the same pudgy face, the same pillowy body.

He spoke with a vehemence that cut deep. "I don't want you here. My mother don't want you here." Billy's voice cracked with his emotion. "How could you even think of living here after you killed my sister."

"But it was your idea to dig the pit. And to bury the stakes."

"That's a lie. You killed her at the Hole."

Reuker felt helpless, having to disagree with a lie so full of its own resolve. Like he always had, Billy changed things to suit himself. In his mind, as he stood near the snow-covered ledge, frozen in time, he could see it, and the youth in his past realized it. But he answered Billy in his dream with the same panic he had felt back then. His chest sunk, as he wheezed a feeble, "No."

Billy stepped forward and pushed Reuker in his bony chest, knocking him backward. "Don't ever say things about me like that again, or you'll regret it."

"Why haven't you told on me then? Why have you kept it a secret?"

Billy's cheeks grew redder, and his face appeared even more bloated, as if it would burst. "I hate you, I hate you, I hate you," he shrieked. "You killed your mother, you burned her alive. I don't care what they said. I know you did it. You're a devil, Reuker Stilkes. You're a devil. And you can't stay here. They can't make us keep you. Ain't no law says relatives got to take you in. You can go to hell, for all I care. You're a devil."

Standing in the snow, his weapon raised and pointed at the parka-clad youth in front of him, Reuker could see his cousin's mottled face shaking with rage and hate. He could see it all, and the event flashed through his memory in a few seconds, in the time it took for the boy to slide back two steps. The memory was more a feeling than distinct thoughts, and in that instant he felt Billy's horrible revulsion, that unjustified rejection. He hated him! Reuker hated the fat-faced demon, the carrier of the evil.

Ricky caught his breath and closed his eyes. He saw him readying to fire.

Reuker's hand was as cold as the steel of the gun in his palm. Unmelted snow clung to the back of his hand. He held the pistol at eye level, fully extended from his body. His aim was accurate. Carefully he squeezed the trigger.

Through closed lids Ricky could see the flash. The explosion ripped through his hearing, cracking in his head, and suddenly he was falling, falling. He had left the ground and felt as though floating, slowly, downward. There was no pain. No feeling of any kind. Only a sense of timelessness. Timelessness to his fall, to his wait for what was to come. And then it began to fade. The white world grew dim, gray, and then it was gone.

Jack looked to the cliff at the sound of the gunshot. "Oh, dear God, they've killed my boy!"

He had reached the first tier when the gun fired, and was directly even from where he saw Ricky land. Jack began to run in the hopping, side-to-side waddle of the snowshoes. Intent on his son, he didn't think of any other danger. The fact that the gunman must still be there, above on the ledge, didn't even occur to him.

He stomped over the unbroken snow, sinking several inches into the light fluff even with the shoes. It was slow, but he worked hard. His lungs beat furiously, pumping frigid air deep inside. His inner clothes were wet with his sweat from digging the cave, from his climb, from his sudden surge of terror.

Like the bottom of the cliff where they dug the shelter, at the bottom of this first tier the snow had drifted. He couldn't see Ricky. Only the depression where he had sunk into the snow. Jack plowed into the drift, flailing the white stuff with wide frantic sweeps of his arms. And then he saw him.

Ricky's eyes were closed and his face lifeless, and the sight brought a sudden emptiness to his chest, as if pummeled there with the full weight of a felled log. The emptiness was a stupefying mix of grief, guilt, sorrow.

Somewhere above, the gunman wavered with gun still in hand. Jack was unconcerned. He knelt in the snow and burrowed to Ricky's level. The boy seemed so at peace, his body tightly wrapped in cottony drift. As if he were comfortable. As if he were relieved it was over. But it wasn't right! Through the numbing paralysis that gripped him, Jack felt a hot pang of grief bore deep inside him, flaring hotter as it sank. Why, why, *why,* he agonized. Why Ricky? For what cause, for what sins?

Oblivious to any gunman above on the ledge, Jack pulled the boy to his lap, his hand groping his body for the wound. To plug it, to caress it, to make it better. But no wound was apparent. There was no blood. Jack pushed the hood back and tilted his head. The jugular still throbbed. "Ricky," he whispered, almost disbelieving. "Ricky, listen to me. I'm here now." He touched his cheek and rubbed him.

Ricky's eyelids fluttered, then they opened. "Dad," he said, and the white world rushed in on him. The gun. The explosion. The terror. "He's still there. Up on the ledge."

Jack spun around and looked up the cliff. His body shielded his son. But there was no one there. No gunman taking aim.

The gunman was kneeling in the snow at the spot where he had fired. Reuker's hands were grappling at his face.

He brought snow to his eye, to the cinder-scorched orb that burned with pain.

The gun barrel had been jammed solid with snow and had split wide open along the top from the pressure of the impacted bullet, as if the steel had been soft modeling clay. The exploding cartridge had recoiled the firing pin, showering burning bits of black powder and fire from the end of the chamber. Each speck of ignited powder that touched his face seared tiny black burns into his skin. There were burns across the top of his hand, melt holes in his parka, and the powder had touched his right eye.

At the explosion of the cartridge Reuker howled in startled fear and pain and collapsed to the snow. He couldn't see! His wrist felt broken from the snap of the gun. His face burned not with some imaginary horror, but with real fire. He was burning alive! He held his face. He brought snow to it. His left eye was watering. He became vaguely aware he could sense light through that eye. But he couldn't keep it open. So intense were the pain and the burning that both eyes reflexively shut tight.

As the snow worked its chilling effect and the burning numbed, Reuker was able to open his left eye a crack. His right eye was sightless. He started to feel his way back along the trail. Where his individual trough met the tracks of the others he had to climb upward. He had to scramble in parts up steep drops, slipping and sliding and falling back.

As he did, his mind was a roiling caldron of flashing images, of blaring sounds, of confused, timeless emotions that were in total control of his body. He saw the boy, the caped figure, the swirl of hair, the slamming door, the round glasses, the stark office, the eyes of fire; he listened to the relentless questions, the unspeakable suggestions of the doctor, the muffled slosh of water over his head; he felt the deadening pain that slammed at the back of his neck.

He thought of his own death. He could see his death. He knew he was dying. But it wasn't death he feared. It was the festering evil within. It was the horror that had seized him, the detestable rotting decay that filled his body with impurities, that filled his nostrils with its stench, that gripped his very soul in gnarled, scabbed talons of undilute evil.

He struggled back to the ridge, back to the machine,

his body torn by the injury, by the cold. He had to preserve his decaying vessel long enough for the sacrament. For the black acts of his cleansing. More than ever he needed its fulfillment.

30

The deep-treaded snow tires of Suomi's jeep crunched over the hard pack of the Black Bear Inn parking lot. He pulled into an open space and, holding his unzipped coat closed with one hand, ran to the building. Inside, aged cigarette smoke had infiltrated the cloth, the wood—seemingly even the glasses and the brass footrail of the bar—and it created a palpable odor that hung like a brown mist in the air, obscuring and dimming vision.

He saw Poiret at a table with two other men. "Louis," he said, walking toward him.

Poiret looked up. "Ike!" he cried with the loud vigor induced by a half dozen glasses of beer.

Suomi nodded at the other two, Jim and Danny Richard, father and son. Then to Poiret, "Mind if I join you?"

"You got any of your friends here?"

Suomi's eyebrows wrinkled together.

"He means the guys from Scales," Danny explained.

Suomi looked back to Poiret. He felt a hot tickling flutter across his chest. He slipped his coat off and sat down. "That's what I wanted to talk to you about."

"What the hell's going on over there?" Poiret shouted. The Richards smiled at each other, and an unspoken message passed between them.

Suomi leaned forward, his forearms resting on the edge of the table. "What do you mean?"

"Those sons of pricks don't know the first thing about

living around here, about how a man treats a man in the north woods.'' Earlier in the day, as he sat in his plane on Lake Siskiwit and talked to Scales over the radio, he had felt more than simple anger. There had been an uncertain, disquieting feeling as he listened to the man from the tower, as he stared into the lifeless forest. He had blocked those thoughts then because they threatened his simple order, and now, because of the alcohol, could feel only the anger. ''You'd think they'd've learned, would've picked up the ways. But they haven't, and I guess it's not surprising. They earn their city money and stay over there on that rock as if *we're* the ones that brought the nuthouse to *them*. And the only jobs they have, they don't do right, and then they expect us to do their work for them.'' His voice turned raspy from the drink, the smoke, the night-long talking. He swallowed a deep draw of his beer and settled back in his chair. ''Well, you can't piss in the river and drink it too.''

All of Suomi's uneasy feelings were alive with a creeping, undefined suspicion. What the hell has happened over there? ''Have you talked with anybody inside?''

''There's something they gotta learn,'' he said, gearing himself up. ''They can put their money in the mattress and not spend it over here. They can look down their noses at the real people of the Lake, they can take turns porkin' each other in the ass. They can do whatever the hell they want, but there's one thing you just don't do. *You don't fuck with the U.S. Mail.*''

Jim Richard snorted. His friend Louis Poiret was in good form tonight.

Poiret's eyes bulged from his face, and he pointed a finger at Richard as if it had been he who had ridden out on that snowmobile two days before and stared at him from behind the scarf. ''I'll tell you one thing. If they jack me around tomorrow, it'll be the last time Louis Poiret brings them anything.''

''And since when does the *U.S. Mail*''—he emphasized it the same way Poiret did—''get delivered on Sunday?''

''Aw, shit,'' Poiret said. He eyed them contemptuously, then pushed his chair away and walked toward the bar. As he did, the Richards, father and son, laughed.

Suomi followed him. As Poiret settled onto a stool, he touched him on the arm. ''I've been thinking something's not right over there the last few days—''

"The last few days?" Poiret said, as if his feelings for Scales had never been any different.

"What exactly did you see over there?"

Poiret swiveled toward Suomi and stared closely at his face, trying to read if he was serious, or baiting him like the Richards. Suomi's expression didn't break, and after a silent moment Poiret turned back to the bar. "Two days ago they send out a shit-sure bastard I never seen before, and the way he looks at me you would'a thought he would just as soon slit my throat as talk to me. Then yesterday, they don't send anybody, and when I came in today I find the damn mail sack still there. Sitting on the snow. Can you believe that?"

Suomi sat on the stool next to Poiret, and his eyes drifted absently to the row of cheap liquors on the counter behind the bar. There was so much to consider, so little to go on. Was he being realistic in his developing theory—a scenario that had tumbled erratically into focus, each bounding crash bringing more substance to the thought. It seemed so incredible, so unarguably out of the question. Yet somehow, it seemed to be the only logical explanation.

If he had taken the time to sort through the possibilities, he would probably have decided he was jumping too far too fast. But at that moment the sickening swirl of what could be dizzied him to any thoughtful analysis. It suddenly seemed so real. So glaringly possible.

Suomi left Poiret at the bar and picked up his coat from where he left it at the table. He didn't know the answers, but he was determined to find out.

He left the Black Bear Inn and hurried out to his jeep.

The cavern Philip and Jack had hewn out of the snowbank was as protected from the elements as any natural formation in granite or limestone could offer. The ceiling was at least twelve inches thick, and under that amount of insulation the air temperature would be 50 to 60 degrees warmer than outside. With the body heat and the kerosene lamp, the temperature inside the shelter had risen above freezing, while outside it was approaching 30 degrees below zero. The ceiling was arched, igloo-style, so that moisture condensing would follow the curve and run to the side, rather than drip onto them. Three ventilation holes were spaced along the length of the cave above the sleeping shelf. At the foot of the shelf a spillway for colder air led to the tunnel entrance, now blocked with a chunk of snow.

Despite the closed entrance, a faint but distinct odor permeated the wall from the outside and seemed to settle in the spillway. It had been in the air the entire day, but Philip had ignored it. Looking over at Jack in the glow of the kerosene lamp reflected off the white ceiling, he could see that Jack recognized the smell and knew what it would mean when they left their cave and pushed inland.

They had stretched the two moosehides over the snow shelf for an insulating cover, and would share the three wool blankets when they lay down to try to sleep. At the moment they were sharing a meal. Their food store had dwindled to two sixteen-ounce cans of stew, a can of sliced peaches and one of mixed fruit, coffee, and a bar and a half of the chocolate.

One of the cans of stew was opened, and it was passed from hand to hand slowly, carefully, like the precious life-sustaining substance it was. Then Emma opened a can of mixed fruit chunks in a thick, sugary syrup. It was the syrup and its sugar that their systems eagerly accepted.

A wolf's howl broke into the still air outside, and the haunting tone hung like driftless smoke in the cave. Its tone abruptly changed, and its harmonics were joined by a second wolf, then a third. Marion stared at the tunnel entrance as if hypnotized by the howls.

Jack nudged her with the can of fruit. She smiled, then took it from him.

The melodic calls of the wolves worked their chilling effect on Lummer. "Goddamn," he blurted. "What are they doing?"

"There's nothing you can do about them," Philip said. "And there's nothing they can do about us, in here. You'd be best to ignore them."

Jack could tell he spoke without conviction, with something else on his mind. "It's the peat fire you're worried about, isn't it?"

Philip was brought out of his thoughts. He looked at Jack, nodded. "Yeah. It's the peat fire."

"What, what do you mean? What fire?" Lummer said.

"That smell. Notice it?"

Lummer looked off toward the entrance, as if trying to see the odor.

Huxley maneuvered to face Tardif. "Yes," he said. "I have."

"What is it?" Lummer wasn't sure if he could smell it or not.

"That's the peat. It's the stuff that makes up most of the soil in the valley between the ridges, and it's on fire."

Lummer looked from Philip to Jack, then back to Philip. "What do you mean it's on fire. How can dirt be on fire?"

"The ground is not just dirt. It's the accumulated decay of plants and animals for thousands of years, pressed together. It's the same stuff as coal, but not as old. It hasn't yet been turned to rock by age and vast pressures. But it's got the same chemical makeup as coal, and the same flammability." Philip had turned to Ricky and Marion and Emma. He wanted them to understand what they faced, to be aware of the dangers.

"Did the inmates start it?"

"No, it's been burning under the snow since last fall. Last summer maybe. Getting wider and deeper all the time. There's probably pockets of it scattered all over, wherever the peat was driest."

"Is this some kind of joke?" Lummer grabbed Philip's shoulder so he would look at him. "That's it, isn't it. You're telling us this as a kind of game, to keep our minds off something. The wolves. The cold." He laughed nervously, releasing his grip. "A fire under the ice. That's crazy."

In the dim, yellowish glow of the flame on the chiseled ceiling of the snow roof, Philip could see Ricky's intent expression, Marion's hand tightly gripping Jack's. "The danger is this. As the peat burns, it does two things. It turns the hard ground to ash, and it slowly melts the oversnow, sculpting small caverns just like this one. In other words, it destroys the surface support, and if you try to walk across it, you'll fall through."

"You mean you couldn't even tell if it was right in front of you?" Ricky asked.

"Since the snow melts from inside out, you won't notice anything until it melts a hole to the surface. But with the snow we get here, there's always more to keep it covered."

"How deep would the fire go?"

"Could be a few feet. Could be thirty feet."

"So there isn't any way to tell you're about to walk into one of these, these pits of fire?"

"The smell, maybe. Wherever the fire is, that strong, acrid, almost medicinelike smell will be there."

Lummer could finally discern the odor, and there was something faintly familiar about it. "I've smelled that before."

"It's the same aroma as Scotch whisky. The Scots use the peat for fuel, and they boil their whisky with it in open vats, so it absorbs that flavor. The Irish use peat for fuel in making their whisky too, but in closed vats that keep the taste of the peat from absorbing into the liquids."

Lummer dropped his feet into the trench at the base of the shelf and stood. He tried to pace but there was so little room he could only shuffle one foot in front of the other, then turn around. A nervous delirium was showing itself in his eyes. "This is crazy. A fire under snow that smells like Scotch. Wolves howling their heads off outside. Maybe I'm dreaming this. Maybe the cold has finally gotten to my head and driven *me* crazy. Maybe I'll wake up and I'll be back in my room"—his voice cracked—"and this whole thing will be some awful nightmare."

"You're wasting your energy, and your warmth," Jack said. "Get back on the shelf and cover up."

Lummer halted and stared at Jack. His chin drooped, and he breathed slow, steady breaths.

"Tomorrow we're going to have to head inland," Philip said. "They know where the trail spur is, but we'll have a couple hours on them in the morning. We got a good chance to make it where it's hard to track us, but I wanted you all to know about the peat fires. About what it is we'll be facing out there."

Lummer climbed back to the sleeping shelf, and all seven of them lay down and waited and hoped for sleep to come fast. They felt the cold, and they thought of the fire, and for some, it wasn't difficult to imagine the fire as some kind of relief. They would be warm, the cold would be cheated, the pain would be over.

For Lummer, there was no such relief, even in fantasy. He thought of the agonizing, slow progress they had made over the course of the day. The laborious trudging through the snow, the corrugated ice surface, the waiting for Emma Tardif. And most of all, he thought of the relentless pursuit by the inmates of Scales Psychiatric Facility.

Over the years he had learned to fear his patients. He saw what they were capable of doing, he saw the misshapen ideas that sparked randomly in their minds. It was a cerebral territory better left unexplored, he had decided, and had always been able, with the drugs, to keep it that way.

But now things were different, and they were coming for him. As he lay there, he shivered with the thought of tomorrow, of another day like today. He imagined what it would be like, moving slowly through the thick snow, muscles aching with the fatigue, and all the while the sound of the machines chasing, searching, tracking them down. They would try to move faster, but they would be held back, like they were today by the old woman. Tied to her pace, they didn't have a chance. If only she weren't here, Lummer thought. If only they were free to move at their own pace, there would at least be the possibility they could get far enough into the interior that the machines could not find them.

Lummer twisted, his brain churning with the prospect of tomorrow, with the burden of the old woman. Faced with the dangers, with his fears of the patients, he couldn't bring under control the thoughts that were keeping him awake, that were making the discomfort of the cold all the worse. Like any mind that dips into the irrational, Lummer sought easy solutions. He sought simple and visible targets to blame. And at this moment, as he lay on the bed of ice, the danger increasingly became centered in Emma Tardif. It was she that would cause them all to die.

Scale Island was a part of the same county as Grand Marais, but the sheriff's office had little to do with it. That's the way it had always been, even before the Facility. It used to be that if something happened that required the law and couldn't be settled by the islanders themselves, they would bring the offender to the mainland, and the sheriff would take it from there. Since Scales had been built and most of the people from Gulletston had left, there had been even less contact. Despite that, the sheriff's office is where Ike Suomi went first.

The deputy said that Don Dobbins wasn't there, so Ike drove straight to the sheriff's house. He was at home, playing canasta with his wife and her sister and husband.

Mrs. Dobbins opened the door for him, and Ike stepped just inside. Stale cigarette smoke from the bar clung to his clothes, and the odor quickly dispersed throughout the living room. Ike apologized for interrupting, then asked if he could talk to the sheriff in private. Dobbins motioned for him to step back onto the porch, enclosed by glass but unheated. Suomi told him his suspicions.

"So why come to me about all this?"

"There's nobody to contact in Lansing, on a Saturday night. You know that."

"If you ask me, Ike, I'd say you're afraid of sounding like a damn fool to those people down there, and you want me to check it out for you."

"Of course I want to know for sure, before I do anything with the state. I've got to know exactly what's happened, if anything. That's my job."

"Well, it sounds to me like they got a new guy in the radio booth who's duty-conscious. That's all. And he doesn't know all your little habits and the inside stuff that goes on between you and the other guys that has been going on for so long."

"But they would have told me. And they sure as hell would have told him how things were done."

Dobbins crossed his right arm across his chest, and rested the other elbow in his hand. His left hand pensively stroked his chin. It was cold on the porch. "Did you ever think there may have been an emergency? Maybe your normal contact's sick, or he flew home unexpectedly?"

"I know, Don. There could be a number of explanations. But it's more than that. I can't put my finger on it, but I got a feeling something's not right over there. That something bad has happened, and for whatever reason—either Scales doesn't want me to know, or they're being prevented somehow—they're keeping it a secret."

"You don't expect me to do something crazy like hire a plane and fly over there in the middle of winter just on a bad feeling you have?" Dobbins's gaze narrowed. "Or maybe it was something you had at the Black Bear?"

"I went there for one reason, and that was to talk to Poiret. What I've said didn't just pop out of my head after a few drinks."

"No, probably not."

"And what happened to Poiret supports the fact something odd is going on over there. They just wouldn't leave the mail on the ice."

"You said Poiret said it was a new guy. So he screwed up. He forgot."

"Maybe, but there's a pattern. The guy on the radio, and the one who met Poiret. Both seem different, like they don't know what's going on, and for the mail pickup, he's got it all wrong. It all adds up."

"To what?"

"To maybe the inmates have taken over the prison. Cut off everything, running it on their own, doing who knows what with the people over there."

Dobbins laughed. "An Israeli commando team couldn't get away with that, all without anybody knowing."

"They're so isolated over there. Anything could happen, and if it broke right, no one would know."

The sheriff shook his head, then chafed his arms against the cold. "Have you ever been over there?"

"Yes."

"I have too. One time. After they opened it, they took me over and I got a tour of the place. If you've been there, you should know, probably better than me. They've got the best security system I've ever seen. They've got a small amount of convicts, by prison standards. They keep them in different buildings, and even within each building they are kept in smaller groups. They have the highest staff to inmate ratio of any prison in the state, and they've got so many electronic monitors that they can keep every single person in that place on TV more than Ed McMahon, if they want. And to back it all up, they've got you. Face it, Ike. It just couldn't happen. There's probably not a prison in the entire United States where the inmates have taken over completely, and kept it secret at that."

"I know all that. I've been thinking about it all day. But I just can't get away from the feeling that something's happened over there. Things aren't like they're supposed to be."

"Listen. We're not talking about a gang of streetwise, hardened criminals. We're talking about a bunch of crazies. And from what I saw of them and that dope they give 'em, they couldn't take over the Grand Marais County Jail, much less a well-fortified prison like Scales."

"Sheriff," Ike said, gripping his arm. "We've got to check it out. At the least."

"*You* got to check it out. You call Lansing, if you think it's so bad." He tried to step back. "You're not going to get me to shoot at shadows."

"I'm just asking that you go over to Scales. With some of your men, maybe. And check it out."

"My cars don't have wings and there's a reason for that. That island is not my territory. I don't care what the dotted line on the map says. Scales is the state's problem." Dobbins turned and placed his hand on the doorknob. Then he paused, his head tilted toward the floor. When he spoke again, his voice was quieter, more under control. "I'm not going to turn my back on somebody if they need help, wherever they are." He turned back to face Suomi. "I just can't afford to waste time flying off on a wild goose chase. If the state bought me a plane and paid me for a pilot, I'd send him over that island every day. But until then, and until there's something definite, like word from Scales itself that they have a problem, I'm not going to worry about it. I don't have the resources to let me worry about it."

The door opened behind the sheriff, and Mrs. Dobbins looked out, her face full of concern. "Is there something wrong, Don?"

"No, no. Nothing to worry about."

"You'd better get inside then. It's cold."

"In a minute, honey." The door closed, and to Ike he said, "Lookit. I don't mean to come down hard, and if there was really something going on, I'd help you however I could. But from what you've told me, I think your conclusions have taken a long jump ahead of the facts. Go home, think it over, and tomorrow talk to—What's the director's name? Hagan?—talk to Hagan and I bet he'll have all the answers for you."

The sheriff patted him on the arm, then went inside. When Suomi got home, Spud was curled up on the floor by the iron fireplace. The dog didn't get up to greet him and didn't move as Ike sat at the table, his coat still on, staring across the room at the radio.

"It's hard to believe that there are people that used to live like this all winter long. In worse conditions even, in the Arctic." Lummer was addressing no one in particular. He was talking to the darkness. "The Eskimos have survived for thousands of years like that and they can do it because of their experiences, and the customs they evolved. They had harsh ways of life to deal with the harsh environment. If they didn't, they wouldn't have survived."

It was quiet inside the cave, except for Lummer. He didn't know why, but listening to him brought Jack a sense of discomfort. As if he were leading into something dangerous.

"Frequently, I've read, that if a girl is born during bad times, they'd put her out on the ice to let her freeze. They realized they were all on the edge and having an extra mouth to feed might mean there wouldn't be quite enough for everybody else. She couldn't contribute for a good many years, and they knew they couldn't afford to support her. So if there was no husband for her, they'd let her die."

To most of the others, Lummer's talk was little more than incoherent babble from a man too weak to hold his fears inside. Philip turned to his side, trying to ignore him. Jack listened, nervous, wondering what he was leading up to. Emma lay back, tired, thinking of the Eskimos Lummer spoke of, about the harsh customs they were forced to follow.

"Sometimes others in the group got that way. As helpless as infants. They would get old, and if it was a woman, her teeth were only nubs and she couldn't chew mukluks soft anymore. Or she was slow and couldn't keep pace. She kept them from making the hunts. She held the group back from keeping pace with the caribou, or the seals. She became a danger and an encumbrance to all of them. Being a nomadic people, they had to stay on the move to stay alive."

"Go to sleep," Jack said. "That kind of talk doesn't help."

Lummer ignored him and went on talking. "You know what they'd do? The old folks who couldn't pull their weight, who were a burden on the others—"

"Shut up, Lummer."

He spoke faster, getting excited. "—who couldn't keep pace and slowed the group down?"

There was a silent pause, full of a static tension. Lummer let the question hang in the air; he let its suggestive meaning wrap around their thoughts, around Emma's thoughts; he waited to let it burrow into her mind.

Then he started again, in a soft, unhurried voice. "The old folks would just disappear one night. They'd go off by themselves and go sit on the ice, take off their parka, and die. Just like the infants had died."

Philip pushed the blanket away and scrambled off the shelf to the trench. "Don't listen to him, Emma," he said, and he began to feel his way along the cold wall toward the end of the cave, where Lummer was.

"For the good of the others, they'd go off and freeze to death."

Tardif felt for Lummer's feet. Lummer tried to pull them back, but not fast enough. "Hey, what's wrong with you? Get away!"

Motivated by an incomparable anger, Philip dragged Lummer toward him. His once solid muscles, made leaner by age, were like steel.

"Let go of me," Lummer shouted, frantic.

In the darkness Tardif could feel the slight, eely body twisting, pulling, trying to escape. He grabbed him by the chest and with hands like vises pulled him into the air, then crashed him down to the hard surface. He cried out, and Tardif slugged at the noise, striking him with a glancing blow that deflected to the shelf. The solid thud hurt his hand, but it didn't do anything to stop him, to quiet the fire that had been ignited.

Marion felt for the lamp. A match. The kerosene wick flamed to life, and the dim reflective glow came back to the cave. Shadows pocketed the uneven gouges of the ceiling.

"Philip! You're going to get hurt." Emma was on her knees on the moosehide, her heart pounding with her fear.

Tardif didn't listen. He couldn't listen, consumed as he was with his anger. Lummer was pushing himself up with his elbows when Philip crashed a fist into him. Lummer groaned and fell dazed back to the ice. Philip grabbed him by the collar and swung him around, bashing him hard against the outer wall.

"Don't! Please don't." Emma was frantic, near hysteria. "Don't, don't, don't," she shrieked.

The wall was solid, but above his head a new shadow opened in a long crack in the ceiling. Lummer quickly regained his senses. He tried to twist out of the man's grasp, but Tardif only gripped tighter, Lummer's collar beginning to choke him. Lummer felt the hard-pack wall give a little at his back. He tried to say, "Stop. The cave is collapsing," but he could only croak in a hoarse, incoherent wheeze.

"We've shared our food, we've given you shelter, we've saved your life," Philip said, his teeth tightly clenched. "And you answer that with trying to kill."

Lummer tried to shake his head no but could only move it a fraction of an inch in both directions. Tardif gripped him harder at the sign of resistance, pushing him harder into the wall. Lummer looked frantically above him. The ceiling was cracking.

"Your weapon is your knowledge, your doctor's learning of how a mind works. You know how to play on it, to twist it, to appeal to a sense of sacrifice that is so alien to your own feeling that I'm surprised you could recognize it in someone else. You're an evil man, the most wretched example of a human being I've ever come across. And you're going to die, Lummer. You're going to freeze out there on the ice because you're not staying in here with us."

"No, Philip. Please let him go." Emma started to crawl on her knees toward them.

"You're getting out of here. You're on your own from now on. Your own food you can find, your own shelter you can dig."

Lummer's eyes were wide, terrified. He looked toward Emma, then back to Philip.

Jack was sitting at the far side of the cave, his arms around Marion and Ricky. They watched, not taking part. Huxley, who had been lying next to Lummer, had pulled back to the inner wall and now sat there with his back braced against it. Nervously he eyed the ceiling above Tardif.

Emma put her hand on Philip's shoulder and tugged. "You can't force him outside. You just can't kill him."

"He'll have every chance we have to survive. If he doesn't, that's not our fault."

Emma put her arms around her husband from behind and hugged him. She was crying, her head tilted down, tears running across her cheeks. "Please, Phil. Let him go. I'm all right. I'm not listening to him. He's not going to hurt anybody."

Tardif twisted his grip harder, and Lummer's eyes flared again. He gagged, trying to breathe.

"If we don't make it out of this alive, I don't want his blood on your hands." Emma was pleading, and to Ricky, it was the first sign of weakness on her part, of her feeling that they indeed would not survive. He thought of what she had said to him, in the cabin, about how important it was to be strong in their thoughts, and as he did, he couldn't help but think she had given up. She expected to die.

Ricky felt empty inside, a hollow sorrow that was like a hunger. He felt that maybe she was right. If she had given up, she would not survive. He put his head against his father's chest and cried a tearless cry.

Philip gradually relaxed his grip, and Lummer slumped to the floor of the trench. As Tardif climbed back onto the shelf, Lummer stayed where he was, watching in a kind of drugged horror. The light went out, and in the quiet he crawled back to his slot on the sleeping platform.

All were thinking; all sensed a little of Emma's desperation. As for Emma herself, she thought of her husband and Marion and the boy. Especially the boy. It was so unfair he should be trapped in with all this. It was so unfair he be cheated out of his life. The others, at least, had had a chance. Especially her, and Philip.

She felt sad for Ricky, and the sadness translated into a woeful, vacuous sensation. She thought of Lummer, and of the customs of the Eskimos. She thought of the courage it must have taken. How it was the only way for them, in their situation.

Emma was still awake, many minutes later, after all of them had apparently fallen asleep, succumbing like hibernating beasts to a cold stupor. She felt strange, distant, as if some of the life had gone from her already.

With suspicion shrouded by doubt, a sense of guilt tempered by uncertainty, Suomi slouched by himself on the couch, his feet raised to the coffee table, his hands interlocked at the back of his head.

He thought of what the sheriff had said, and he thought of the logistics of the scheme that would have faced the inmates. The more he logically analyzed it, the more he realized it just couldn't have been done. Dobbins was right about the guy on the radio. He was new, dutiful, didn't know the ropes. And then there was Poiret. He was as crotchety and cantankerous as they come. It wasn't surprising he could make an enemy real fast, especially one of the state people from down below who didn't want to be there in the first place and who didn't particularly take to Poiret's vision of how people act in the North. And of course, it stretched credibility past the breaking point to figure a disorganized band of mentally impaired inmates drugged beyond reality could have engineered such a feat.

He was coming back to the same conclusions he had drawn before, but like before, he could not rid himself of that creeping, uncomfortable twinge that was centered not in his intellect, but in his gut. No matter the logic, the questions remained.

Could Hagan be trying to hide something? Something that happened out there, and he's trying to keep it from Lansing? Suomi was aware of the Senate visit and the appropriations procedure. The guys in the radio room bitched about it all the time. Maybe Hagan wanted to keep whatever was going on, or had happened, under wraps until the money issue was decided. That would be like Hagan, he thought.

But the ultimate question remained the same. What kind of disruption could it have been that was so serious that he found it necessary to keep secret? What could have caused the changes out on Scales so apparent to Poiret and him? And could it have gotten out of control—Hagan's scheme—leading to what Suomi feared in the first place?

His concerns had come full circle, and his head ached with the constant analysis, rearranging of facts, the plumbing to the depths of his emotions. His mind on a mental carousel, he was dizzied and tired. He would find no answers, he realized, by agonizing any longer.

Tomorrow. All he could do was wait until tomorrow.

The scent the wolves were attracted to was tinged with danger, but more and more it became unmistakably the scent of prey.

Seated on their haunches, their muzzles coned toward the starless sky, they howled their hunger, their kinship, their claim to new territory. Each of them would hold a steady note, then drop lower, or suddenly rise in pitch, and by the accumulated harmonics of the pack, it sounded like there were many more wolves than there actually were.

Their howls wavered in the still, heavy air like the haunting chords of an organ in a stone-columned cathedral. Their song penetrated the snow walls of the cave, and to ears fighting for sleep, seemed the sound of laughter, of a taunting impatience that was sure of its final success.

The wolves were the voice of the wilderness, saying in melodic clarity that it would win in the end. As the cold continued, as the fire spread, the rock-spined strength of Scales could only grow stronger.

31

The fire burned fast and hot, and after the men in the cabin had fallen asleep, the coals gradually receded. The cold pressed in from outside, and on the floor, on the cots, with only sheets and their clothing protecting them, the men unconsciously curled into themselves.

Eddie Hyland's obsession became his dream. And in his dream Marion smiled at him. It was the same smile he had seen so many times before, in the kitchen. But this time there was something more to her smile, a suggestive glint of piquant mystery, a hint that delicate fantasies played on her mind. She was inviting him to step closer, she was inviting him to touch her. He could see it all in that smile, in the pulse of her breast against her shirt, in the graceful movement of her hand, its light brush against her thigh.

Eddie did step closer, and as he did the sonorous wail of a tortured voice wafted in the air from some unseen cavity. It was more a whimper than a cry, the sound of defeat rather than protest. He turned from Marion, and he saw Jack, his face crossed by the vertical slants of iron bars. The guard was in a cage, a white-walled cage with a door solid except for a tiny rectangular opening, and it was at this opening that Jack's face was pressed.

The rise and fall of the wail was music for the seduction, and it grew in intensity as he approached. It entered him, and on its mournful tones he could feel Jack's pain and resignation. The music filled him, becoming part of his lust. It grew stronger, louder, until it eclipsed that lust, until it became the rhythm of his body's moves, the pulse of his blood, the pounding driving force at his temples. It was all that he could hear. It was all that he could feel. Then suddenly it sang with a resonant percussion. A thumping power. A sound that hurts.

Eddie Hyland awakened to a cold room of almost total darkness. Torn from his obsession, he was in a daze. For a few lung-seizing moments he panicked. He didn't know where he was. He couldn't explain the driving forces that still rippled through him.

Gradually he saw, and he remembered. There was one more heavy thump as the last of the logs was dropped to the wood floor. Then the inmate stooped to the iron stove and opened the grate. He had awakened to the dying fire and had gone outside to retrieve wood from the porch.

By the time the fire was stoked and the iron stove hot, it was getting lighter outside.

Emma was the first to awaken. She had slept little during the night, kept awake by a despair deeper than what she saw as her impending death. Indeed, she had accepted that. She knew she wouldn't last much longer in the cold, in the wilderness. So her despair was for the others, for her husband, for the boy. She was making it harder for them, she realized. Each mouthful of food she had, took the nourishment from their mouths. Each step she made, slowed their escape from the machines.

She rolled to her back and stared at the domed ceiling of their cave. It was opalescent with the early light and to Emma appeared like the murky white of the normal Scales winter sky.

She looked at the others, and no one else moved. Philip's eyes were closed. It was deathly still. Slowly she slipped from under the wool blanket and slid her feet to the trench. She sat there, unmoving, trying to collect her thoughts, trying to still the pounding tumult in her chest.

A dullness of thought seemed to settle over her. Reason mixed with fear, making her nerves come alive, tingling in confused anxiety, vibrating with a singular impulse. She pushed herself to her feet and began to move toward the exit. But the nagging uncertainty persisted.

There was something else, she knew, but could not identify. She saw the light beams around the edges of the snow chunk. They were the only glare in the cave. The only source of direct light.

The air holes! She looked to the domed ceiling, at the three vents spaced evenly across. There was no light streaking in. They were blocked.

Emma seized a branch that had been brought inside to keep the air holes clear, and pushed it through the first of the vents. Crystalline powder drifted downward out of the bottom of the hole, dropping with the weight of feathers onto Philip's face. He did not budge. Blocked by a light snow, the carbon dioxide had collected in the cave, Emma realized. She reamed the other vents, and her commotion caused Jack and Ricky to stir. She dropped into the spillway and pushed the blockage out of the way.

Huxley woke groggily, with barely enough strength to prop himself to his elbows. "My head," he rasped, feeling the pain, sensing the dullness in his body.

Jack rolled to Marion and shook her. She moaned but did not awaken. "Honey, can you hear me?"

The voice was far off. Muffled. She tried to listen but couldn't understand. Marion struggled to hear and gradually realized it was Jack talking. She tried to answer, but the sound from her throat was the same as his voice. Far away and distorted. She felt herself being moved, and she opened her eyes. Everything was a blur. She saw Jack, Ricky. They were touching her, pulling her. She was going down to the floor, to the spillway. Then came the light, and the cold. And the air. Oh God, the air. She breathed, and it filled her lungs. It filled her body, and gradually clarity came to her sight. Feeling came to her arms, her face, her head. As the murky dullness receded, she could feel the pain grow stronger. It jabbed like a thousand needles in her forehead, it throbbed like the beating of a club at the back of her neck. The more she breathed, the clearer came her vision, and the more it all hurt.

She turned her head and saw Jack coming from the cave

entrance, pulling Philip behind him. Emma came and knelt beside him, rubbing his shoulders, his hands, his face. Then from the hole in the cave came Huxley, pulling Lummer, and Ricky behind.

They revived quickly, but the headaches lingered for all. The only comfort was the silence, and the thought of what that silence meant.

When Philip had regained his strength, he stood and looked in the direction of the ridge. "It's still quiet," he said. "They haven't started out yet."

Ricky looked where the older man did. "That gives us time?"

"It gives us a chance. A chance to get away from here and head inland." Philip turned toward the cave, then the others followed him back inside.

The most critical function of winter survival was food. Food to fuel the body's furnace, to compensate for rapid heat loss. Food to maintain the body's critical core temperature, a temperature that if it dropped would lead to loss of speech, hallucinations, unconsciousness, then death. Though starvation could be survived for longer than a month, hypothermia was a deadlier foe. It would provide a much quicker and surer kill.

The half can of fruit and syrup was a meager breakfast, and it was rationed carefully. When finished, they set off. It was their fourth day since the takeover, since Jack led them out of the Facility and onto the ice. The snow had diminished to an occasional flurry, more often than not dislodged from the trees rather than new snowfall from the sky.

The night's accumulation was less than two inches. Just enough to take the hard edge off the trail they had plowed, making their track harder to follow from the ridge to the cave, but not enough to disguise it altogether.

As they trekked farther down the ridge into the interior, deeper into the land of beaver dams and pockets of peat, the stillness remained.

"Maybe they won't be coming," Ricky said.

"Maybe," Philip replied.

But Huxley knew better. He knew the depths of the horror that motivated Reuker Stilkes; he had glimpsed the madness that conquered all reason. It had a power and a strength of its own, a power and a strength greater than the cold, the wilderness, the limits of physical pain.

And Jack had seen Hyland's obsession, a sexless lust more vicious than passionate, fueled by an inexplicable torment that shrieked for release, that would drive him to risk everything to satisfy his urges.

For both Dr. Michael Huxley and Jack Cooke, the realization was grimly kept: The machines would be back. They knew that the pursuit would continue at all costs.

Reuker's sightless eye cast blankly through the cabin. He sat by himself on the backless bench at the table, aloof from the others in the room. His madness was a brand that scared the mad, that kept them at a distance.

The only constant was the burning. His eye was red and yellow, pus festered from the raw wound. Around his eye the skin was peppered with black dots from the powder—a backfire that still burned. But he had grown used to the discomfort just as he had before. As he always had before.

The thoughts that recurred in the impatient, patternless flashes in his mind were of a fat-faced boy, of death, desecration, and of a final cleansing.

Stilkes had a queer aura about him, the others perceived, and they tried to stay out of it. If drawn close, if they gazed into that eye, they would see the horror that churned within him.

Two snowmobiles roared to life and headed back toward Scales. Eddie Hyland came inside and for an instant was caught by Reuker's gaze. As he turned from him and went over by the stove to warm up, he felt touched by some awful decay, an inner rot that bubbled out through his torn eye.

He had sent the two snowmobiles back for food, more fuel, and blankets. The cabin was now their base, and they would need the supplies to support the chase and capture of the fugitives. Whether today, or tomorrow, or the next day, they would be caught.

For the rest of the men, the carnival atmosphere had lifted, the exuberance of the early chase had turned to something sober. It had settled into a steely determination. It was their mission to prevent the escape of the doctors, to protect their new hold over Scales.

They discussed whether there was another community on the island the doctors were heading toward, an outpost from which they could contact the mainland. None of the men knew for sure, but of one thing they were certain: The doctors had a plan to hurt them. They always had in the past. They were always in control.

For the present there was little to do but stay warm and wait. And fight the effect of the vast uncertainties their freedom had wrought.

Why hadn't Hagan gotten back to him? Or had he tried when Suomi was out? Like before, the confounding circuit of indecision and uncertainty was still there. But when the call came in at 11:00 A.M., Suomi was ready for it.

"I told you I have to speak with him," he said. "Where is he?"

The static snarled at him like an angry viper. He had to wait for his answer, and eventually it came. "He said he'd get back to you on Monday."

"I have to talk to him now."

"Nothing Lansing says can't wait until Monday."

He was right, Suomi knew. But he pressed. "That's not your decision."

"It wasn't my decision. It was Hagan's."

Suomi swallowed hard. "It's not Hagan's decision either."

The viper coiled, spitting its venom through the speaker. Then the voice came again. "He's my boss. What do you want me to do? If he doesn't want to disturb his Sunday, it's not up to me to tell him differently."

It was Suomi who was now silent, letting his transmission hiss its static-y snarl.

"For Christ's sake, he's not going anywhere. Give him a break." Then the voice changed. It was abrupt, harsh, final. "He'll call tomorrow."

Suomi let the connection die. It did make sense, he thought. Whatever message or reply Lansing could conceivably want could wait until office hours in the state capitol. But there was something about the voice that didn't make sense—apart from all his other misgivings. There was something about the hard, calculating tone of the voice that bothered him.

He sat quietly, pondering his next step, formulating what he could say to Lansing. In the midst of his thinking, the phone rang. The loud jangle startled him, and his nerves jittered nervously to life. He stared at it, making no move to answer. The unhurried ring beckoned, four times, five times, but he resisted its call. For some strange reason, the same trepidation he felt for Scales entered him regarding the phone.

The track from the snow cave at the base of the ledge down into the island's valley was steep and slow, but Philip read the terrain like he knew it intimately, though it had been probably twenty years since he was this far inland during winter. The constant downward angle of the descent, and the sinking into untrod snow, made the muscles along the tops of their thighs sear with an ache that streaked from knee to waist. They were the same muscles reacting to the identical strain, step after step, yard after yard. Each new pace was a struggle, each upward thrust of the leg a painful, burning ordeal.

They rested frequently, and at one stop Emma began to cry. At first she kept it to herself, under control, but gradually the convulsive sobs overcame her.

Philip wrapped his arm around her back, and she leaned into him. "Dear, it's hard now. But we'll last this thing out." She tried to stop the crying, but her attempt failed with short, moist gasps. "Don't worry, Em. You've got so much strength there isn't anything you can't endure. I know more about your reserve than you do."

She looked at him, tears glistening in her eyes, and tried to smile.

"Believe me, old lady. You'll last this thing out longer than any of us."

The crying received new impetus, and she began to shake her head. Her voice came between chokes, raspy and weak. "I, I can't, I—"

"Don't talk. We'll rest, then move on, when you're ready."

"My legs. Philip. It's my legs."

"I know, Em. I know."

"No," she said, louder, with an anger more at her own legs than at him. "You don't know. I can't move them. I can't move them anymore!"

He stared dumbly at her, then his lack of comprehension turned to disbelief, then denial. "You can. You're tired."

She turned away, ashamed of her sobbing. Her legs were trembling. The muscles were so overworn they con-tracted and stretched uncontrollably, unable to respond anymore to the message of the nerves.

Philip placed his hands on her thigh and felt the rippling of the muscles; it was her body's abject surrender to the fatigue. And yet she had held out this long, he thought, until she collapsed. "We'll carry you then."

"No! Philip, you can't." She sounded frantic, desperate for their own safety.

"We will."

"We'll need a couple saplings," Jack said. "For a sled."

Philip looked at him and nodded. "Some aspen. Or birch."

"Please don't," Emma protested.

Marion knelt next to her and began to massage her thighs in long, kneading strokes. "We're in this together," she said, "and none of us can give up. If one does, we all will."

"But the machines," she cried. It was the first time any of them had mentioned the snowmobiles since they had heard them again, about an hour ago.

"Damn the machines. We'll fight them with sticks and icicles if we have to."

Emma was too weak to protest anymore. She settled to her back on the snow and let Marion work on her legs.

It took fifteen minutes just to chop the saplings, only three inches in diameter, as Jack and Philip took turns using the stove shovel as a hatchet.

All the while the noise of pursuit carried in the abnormal stillness of the frigid, Arctic high. The call of the machines howled from ridge across treetops into the labyrinth of snow-clogged trails and passages, down to the seven fighting to ignore the presence of the snowmobiles.

They worked fast, but it was a half hour before they were ready to move again. From the direction of the sound, it was apparent the snowmobiles were making good time racing out Greenstone Ridge. And they should, for the trail was packed, and the inmates knew the way.

Emma was fixed on the litter, her snowshoes attached with fishline lengthwise between the poles, and Jack and Philip were the first to pull it. They gripped the front ends of the poles and dragged the litter behind them. Eventually they reached the bottom of the rise to the ridge. From that point on, the ground alternately rose and fell, mirroring the same sharp features of the basaltic, scalelike terrain beneath their feet.

The forest was thick in parts, sparse in others, and where the hardwoods dominated, seemed little more than an open expanse of dead trunks. And over all permeated the strong odor of peat.

They followed one of the many moose trails for a while before Philip broke away from it, following a sense of direction two decades old. They changed positions to stay fresh, Philip dropping back with Marion, Jack and Ricky breaking trail, and Huxley and Lummer dragging the litter. Marion kept an eye on Jack, as she had been doing for some time, watching as he grew more laggard in his step, slower in his pace. He had been limping, and now he seemed to be dragging his left foot. She mentioned it to Philip, but all he said was that it is easier to walk on a frozen foot than a thawed one.

She shuddered, looking away from Jack, away from his dead limb dragging behind him. Then she stared down at the snow and thought of her own pain. Always another step, another struggle. Always more snow.

"Have you ever been to Minong?" Philip asked.

Marion swallowed, shaking the desperation. "Never," she croaked.

"Not even in summer?"

"You mean the mines?"

"Yes."

She shook her head.

"It can't be much farther," he said. "That's where we'll shelter."

As she settled back into the rhythm of the hike, the true horror became again the distant clatter of the snowmobile engines. Coming closer, searching the spur, racing to catch up to them.

The noise ground a gritty reproach in Huxley's mind, reminding him of his failure, crying out to all who listened his incompetence.

Huxley breathed hard, and fast. The litter dragging in the snow seemed heavier. The ends of the poles seemed to be clutching at the surface, fighting all his efforts. His chest pumped the cold air deep inside, and with the rapidity of breath came a dizziness. He felt suddenly lightheaded, and taking sustenance from this airy confusion, his thoughts began to tumble one over the other.

They had been preparing to take him away! Take Stilkes away from him and back to the drugs. Back to the Prolixin. Close off his mind forever. He had had no choice but to press him. There had been so little time. Oh Christ, if there only had been more time to talk, to listen, to guide, to build confidences. It may have all been different.

As he gasped for breath, he suffered from a delusion, a delusion of evil turning into substance and enveloping him. Could it be true, Huxley thought, that Stilkes's world was reality and his own something less?

His mind blanked white with the dizziness, with the tension. But through it all there was a noise. Louder and closer than before. A cracking report that spiked through the collapsing veil around him. And then the litter sagged. The other pole had been dropped, and he held it alone. He pushed on, dragging it himself, gasping with the exertion. Gagging on the smell. The strong, acrid odor that gushed from the bowels of the earth.

"Stop!"

The word shrieked through the echoing, conflicting noises in his head. And he heard Emma crying out on the litter behind him. Something had happened, something was different. In front of him. Just ahead.

Slowly his vision caught up with his thoughts, with the racing delusions, and he saw. Like a time-delayed reply, he saw one of the trees before him start to fall. It plunged into the snow, and suddenly a huge cavity opened up. The snow hissed as it fell to the coals below.

"Stop him," Emma screamed, fastened onto her stretcher.

Jack had jumped off to the side when the tree began to fall and he looked back at Huxley and Emma with horror. Huxley was glassy-eyed, appearing as though in another world, and he continued to struggle directly for the fire pit pulling the litter with him. Jack tried to scramble toward him, but his snowshoes dragged and anchored in the thick drift. He spun to his back and fought to free his legs. But his left foot was like dead weight. He reached and lifted it out with his hands, then rolled on his back bringing his feet into the air.

Huxley struggled forward, confused and oblivious to the screams. The cavity was near. The hissing, spitting evil had opened before him. He stepped closer to look, to peer at this great mystery, to look into Reuker Stilkes's world.

"Stop him!" Emma shrieked.

Huxley teetered on the edge. Jack brought his shoes flat to the snow and pushed himself up, then struggled toward Huxley. When he neared the edge, the snow began to give way, avalanching into the pit. A dusty plume of ash spouted into the air, then the snow began to hiss. Coals, exposed to the oxygen, glowed suddenly brighter. Tiny flames burst into life.

Jack grabbed Huxley's arm and pulled him to the side. The litter dropped, and Jack and Huxley tumbled to the snow. Philip and Marion reached the back of the litter and took the poles, pulling it away from the brink of the pit.

Huxley tried to prop himself up, but his arms sank into the snow.

"Hold it," Jack said. "Don't force it."

But Huxley had at last realized the peril and now frantically tried to push himself away from the cavity. His movements dislodged a chunk of snow, and it broke away from the edge like a calving glacier and plunged into the fire and ash. Jack tried to hold him still, but he continued to struggle. A new crack began to appear in the snow below Jack's waist.

Huxley broke from Jack's grasp and scrambled over him away from the edge. Jack turned to his stomach, and as he did he felt the snow move, and he moved with it, a few inches, toward the pit.

"Dad. Grab the poles." When Emma had been taken out of the litter, Ricky slid it toward his father. Jack grabbed the end and pulled. The effort seemed to stabilize the snow, and the crack widened no more. "Stay still," Ricky said. Then he and Philip carefully dragged Jack away from the brink.

Jack pushed himself quickly to his feet and looked back toward the pit. The snow edge precariously hung in place, ready to split and fall into the fire with only a little more force. He stepped farther away, and as he did, the crack opened even more, dropping slivers of the snow. The fire hissed with a sinister cunning, eating steadily farther into its hidden fuel.

"I think I can make it now, on my own," Emma said.

Jack looked toward her, then said, "Let us know if you can't."

She nodded, then they began to hurry away from the open cavity, propelled by a nervous energy common to them all. Jack took the lead, and at first he tested the firmness of the snow with a pole every few steps.

But that was taking too much time, and time was again critical. The noise of the machines had dropped because the inmates were no longer on the ridge. They had come to the trail spur and had turned inland.

Jack forged ahead, the others stretched out in a line behind him. He relied only on his sight and smell to warn him of any other pockets of fire under the ice. It was a misguided trust, for the smell of burning peat was everywhere.

The eight wolves padded along the trail cut through the snow. They moved quietly, effortlessly, each paw rising then dropping in a single fluid motion, each step part of an overall grace and economy of movement.

Though they moved without visible hesitation, inside each wolf was a feeling that they treaded where they shouldn't, that a danger lay ahead of them on the trail.

The alpha male was in the lead. The others continued to follow because he was the leader, but the strains were there. With only one recent kill as nourishment for the entire pack, they were starving.

The animals they followed were traveling together, like a herd. For a time the track became a moose trail, and the scents mixed together, blending the scent of the animals with the scent of the wolves' main source of food.

As the animals they tracked plunged deeper into the woods, farther from the ridge, from the southeast end of the island, they became more and more part of the wilderness, part of the natural cycle of hunting, food, and survival.

Gradually, the scent was losing its dangerousness. The longer the wolves followed, the more the animals became removed from any category of instinctual fear. And the more they became just like any other prey.

It was afternoon when Ike Suomi dialed the operator and asked her to cut in on a busy signal at the Lansing number. He told her it was an emergency.

A short time before he had received a call from Elizabeth Knudsen in Grand Marais. She was worried—more than that—nearly hysterical, about her husband. He was one of the MCAs, she had said, and because he could be with her only every other weekend, they would talk frequently on the phone. She said he hadn't called and she had been trying to get him for three days but had been unable to talk to him.

"He worked with the guns there," she said. "Could there have been an accident?"

Suomi paused. Another piece clicking into place.

She began to cry, her words moist with her worry and sadness. "Why won't they let me talk to my husband? Why?"

Suomi said he didn't know, but he would find out for her. Her trembling voice seemed reluctant to give up the connection, but when she did, Suomi checked a number he had taped to the bottom of the phone, an emergency number in Lansing he had never used before, and immediately dialed it. It rang once, then was answered, and he heard the whir of a machine beginning. It was a tape recording.

The recording gave the home phone number of a deputy-assistant in the Corrections Department. When the operator interrupted the busy signal, Suomi could hear the women's voices on the line. The receiver crashed to the table when the operator said it was an emergency.

William Lilly, twenty-nine years old, Bachelor of Arts in Sociology and Criminal Justice from Michigan State University, hurried to the phone.

Suomi came on strong, saying there was a major problem at Scales.

"Oh, dear God, oh, dear God," he mumbled.

Suomi filled him in on what he knew and what he suspected.

There was a long pause, and Suomi thought he could hear the nervous flipping of pages. Finally, "But what did you hear from them? From the people at Scales?"

"I didn't hear anything from them! They can't make contact because the inmates control the radio, the telephone lines, and probably everything else."

"Okay, why don't you give me the number up there. No, never mind. I should have it here. Yes, I've got it. I'll call."

"Scales?"

"Yes. I'm going to talk to—"

"What good is that going to do?"

"It just might save a lot of time. And money."

"It won't save a thing because you won't get through to anybody that will mean anything."

His voice suddenly squeaked higher. "And it might just save your butt."

"Call the department head. Your immediate supervisor. The governor. Whatever your procedures call for. I don't know what's happened on Scales, but we owe it to those people over there to do our best to find out."

"I said I was going to call. I'll call Scales. If I get any problems, I'll get back with you. Okay?"

Suomi closed his eyes, clenching the receiver until his knuckles went white. "Ask for Hagan," he said, resigned. "He's the director there, you know."

There was a pause and more pages flipping. "Yes. Dr. Peter Hagan. I'll talk to him."

There was nothing else he could say. Suomi was tired, almost drained. He went outside with Spud down to the lake and stood on the shore staring out toward the island beyond the horizon. It was bitterly cold, and the pounding of the waves was not the comfort he had sought. Rather, they were the continuous drumbeats of a warning, an ominous, persistent percussion of dwindling hope.

The machines were down to five. One had not returned from the supply trip to Scales, and by the time the other one did, it was late morning. The inmates then set out, retracing their trail out Greenstone until they came to the spur, where the doctors and the others from the institution had left the ridge.

They guided their machines down the steep incline. Many times they became bogged down in the deep snow and had to get off and push, but gradually they drove inland. Sometimes the machines fanned out, pursuing what appeared to be diverging trails, but always the track proved false and they had to route back to find each other. They hurried, racing the clock, the impending darkness.

The noise of their rapidly firing engines traveled before them to the Minong Mines. The mines were surface gouges, like shafts laid on their sides with the top edge exposed to the air. They were on sites where prehistoric peoples hacked pure copper from the ground, and where nineteenth-century miners chiseled the deep-cut vertical gorges in the rock, following the faulted veins of the copper. As Tardif had expected, deep snow had drifted along one side of the narrow trough, like it had below the second tier rising to the ridge, and in this snow he dug their shelter. This time, all the men took turns digging out the cave, and it was finished within an hour.

One of the trees at the bottom of the mine had outgrown its wind protection and had been blown over. Its trunk had braced against the top of the opposite wall, and as it continued to grow over the years, it had curved upward seeking the light.

The angled trunk created a tunnel that was a natural barricade near the northern entrance to the mine. At this V, Tardif stretched nylon fishline, several times back and forth, from the trunk at one side to a tree on the other. Then he cut short pieces of the line, tied fishhooks to them, and then began fixing them in a dangling curtain across the entrance to their sanctuary. Against the white backdrop of the snow the line was nearly invisible.

The other end of the mine trough opened up 150 feet away to Lake Minong, a half mile long and no wider than 200 yards at the maximum extent. Jack and Ricky trudged out nearly to the center, and with the small iron stove shovel began to dig toward the water.

The top layer of snow was soft powder and was tossed easily to the side. Below that, older snow, compacted by the weight above, was more of a struggle to remove. They dug in a circle, about three feet in diameter, at first staying outside its circumference. When the hole was two feet deep, the snow became firmer still, and to dig one of them had to step to the bottom.

Ricky took his turn, chopping at snow that was now frozen by pressure and melted into crusty chunks. He was hungry, and since the fruit in the morning, all any of them had had to eat was a piece of the chocolate bars, for energy. All that remained of their food cache was a can of stew for tonight, a can of peaches, and a sliver of chocolate for each. It was the lack of nourishment and the prospect of finding food that combined within Ricky, creating a dizzying mix of desperation and hope.

He sat back on his haunches, leaning against the wall of snow. "We're going to eat tonight, aren't we, Dad? We'll catch fish, and eat as much as we want?"

"We will, Son. We will." Jack dropped down into the

hole and got beside Ricky. "I've heard there's so many fish in these lakes, do you know what they do sometimes, just to get out of the crowds?"

Ricky looked gullible and wide-eyed, the yearning pain in his stomach suddenly forgotten. "No, what?"

"They jump right up onto the beach. For a little air."

Ricky laughed. "Big ones?"

"There's only big ones here. If there's been one fish-hook in this lake in the last five years, I'd be surprised."

"And they're mighty hungry, I bet. During the winter."

"I'd say they would be."

"They might even go for this," Ricky said, fingering his father's lure, fashioned from his brass belt-buckle.

Jack laughed. "Even that."

"It doesn't look like a fish."

"It's *not* a fish. It's a *lure*. All it has to do is be shiny."

"I don't know, Dad. It looks kind'a fakey to me."

"They'll come to the light shaft of this hole to see what's going on. Then as soon as they catch a glint of the lure, they'll strike. Trout, bass, perch, walleye. You name it, we'll catch it."

"Dad? One more thing."

"What?"

He held the shovel out. "It's your turn."

At a depth of three feet, marble-sized chunks of clear ice were fixed together by the snow, like stones cemented with a primitive mortar. It was nearly solid, and Jack chopped at the ice with the blade of the shovel. He worked hard, as fast as he dared, but despite the precautions he could feel the sweat collecting on his skin, soaking into his innermost layer of clothes. It was moisture that would cool and chill him all the more when the work was finished and his exertion over. The sweat could kill him, he knew, and he tried to measure his efforts more carefully.

But the ice grew firmer, and he was forced to chop harder, and eventually they reached the solid ice of the lake itself.

Jack rested while Ricky cleared the last layer of firn from the surface of the lake. The ice seemed black and hard—made of the same stuff as the shovel itself—as if forged by a cruel hand that manufactured obstacles for their attempts at survival, that watched with a callous disregard for their safety. It was the hand of Scales, an appendage of the ancient serpent, of the wilderness, of the cold.

As they worked, Tardif continued weaving his fishhook trap, and Marion and Dr. Huxley collected firewood. Ground litter was impossible to reach, and so they had to prune the dead branches still clinging to the trees. Marion had followed Jack and Ricky, and she scavenged near the shore.

Huxley had gone the other way, and when he had come to where Philip was stringing his trap, though he dipped under the line, the doctor didn't realize what Tardif was doing. He was thinking of his failure; it was consuming him.

Hallucinations can be induced by lack of food, or by dropping body temperature. For Huxley, the fall into unreality was not that far off.

Lummer was alone with Emma in the snow cave. He began to talk to her, quietly, of the Eskimos. Of their customs. He spoke of the selflessness of the old who chose to freeze to death rather than be a continued burden to the others. It was better for one to die, they felt, and the rest survive than for all to die. And that's what it came down to, he said, in some circumstances. One or all. And it came down to selflessness. And courage.

Emma sat on the edge of the sleeping shelf warming the last can of stew over the kerosene lamp. She was tired and drained. She had forced herself by the power of her will to walk after climbing from the sledge. But it had been a struggle, and she knew she would not be able to do it much more.

She was hearing Lummer and his soft, suggestive voice, but she was thinking of other things. She stared past the can balancing over the flame at the blank wall of the cave. She was thinking of Ricky, and of another boy. A boy younger than Ricky. He was little more than an infant. He had been the only child she and Philip had been able to have, and he had died. She never conceived again.

It had been so wrong, she thought as she had many years ago, that he had not lived. It was so unfair he had not had a chance at life.

Emma was morose, feeling the same pain and sorrow she had known four decades ago, sensing that same unfairness, the unfairness that the youth have to suffer for the crimes of adults. Through it all, Lummer's voice wavered like the manipulative roll of an illusionist's finger.

"I hear it's not painful at all," Lummer's words droned on. "The cold quickly numbs the body, and unconsciousness comes fast. It's just like falling asleep."

Emma listened, lost in her own world of sorrow, of injustices past and present.

Outside, another of the party was rapidly falling into a private world haunted by images from the past. Huxley followed the slant of the ground out of the narrow trench of the mine.

"Don't go too far," Philip shouted. "Watch your prints."

The words rifled past Huxley without striking home. He forged his way off the trail toward an oak and snapped off a branch long dead and no more than an inch in diameter. He broke it in half to make it easy to carry, then reached for another branch.

More time. If only there had been more time. Huxley broke the branch, then trudged to another tree, farther from the mine, closer to the grinding echo of the snowmobiles.

His body became powered by forces other than the meager nourishment they had so niggardly rationed, by forces that had gradually tightened around him and now were strangling his reason, his perception, his grasp of reality.

The fire of his obsession broke out in hot sweat under his arms, down the middle of his back, around the yoke of his neck. It flared behind his eyes, searing an imprint into his brain. Stilkes was in the chair in his office, and the rage in his face struck Huxley hard. It was the night of the killing in the VSB, when Stilkes had knocked him out and run from his office. Because of his loss of consciousness, Huxley had never been able to remember those last few seconds before he was struck, but by some power, now he was able to see the tormented horror rising out of the chair, lunging toward him, his eyes fired with hate and his face contorted into otherworldly designs.

As he had after that very first session with Reuker Stilkes, Huxley was repulsed by the man, by the aura that enveloped the man, that settled in him and around him an imaginary yet palpable stench of decay and rot. And like after that first session, Huxley was intrigued. He was captivated. He was drawn to the mystery, the awful horror that lay hidden inside the man's puzzling interior. The feelings were the same as before, except that now, calm analysis had turned to raving fear, and curiosity to obsession.

If only there had been more time. If only he could have another chance. If only he could speak with him again, tell Reuker he had been wrong, and that now he could see his error.

Propelled by his fantasies, blinded by the glare of intellectual exuberance, Huxley chased the visions in his mind. Sweat streamed down his body as he strained on a branch. The bark split like the dried peel of old fruit, but the branch held. As he pulled, then bent it the other way, he could hear the call of the machines. He pulled harder, and his breaths came in erratic gasps until at last his actions were taken over by what had stolen his mind. The machines called. Reuker Stilkes was searching for him.

He gave up on the branch, on the search for firewood, and began walking. He couldn't think of what he should do, only to move on, as fast as he could.

He reached the track they had trenched through the snow on their way down, and he began to follow it, back toward the ridge, toward the howling wail of the beasts, toward the sprocketed whir of spinning chains, toward the deep-throated moan of distant engines. The noise beckoned him with its constancy, it enticed him with its nearness, it tantalized him with its mystery. He felt the sound touching him, entwining around his back, pulling him.

Huxley was running, as best he could on the oversize shoes. The pounding of his blood behind his eyes, by his ears, became one with the rhythmic sound of the snowmobiles' pistons. His body's own sounds became the call of the machines, and together they boomed louder, more insistent.

Something ahead of him was moving. Through the trees he was aware of shapes, of movement. The machines were there, he thought, and he heard them. Rushing faster, he traveled along the packed trail.

But where? The movement had been there, he was sure. Or was it his own movement that caused the trees to come to life? Huxley slowed, then came to a halt. The sounds were still there. In his ears he could hear the rasping growl of the machines.

"Reuker," he gasped through a parched throat. "It's me, Dr. Huxley." No voice responded.

The movement came again! The dizziness robbed him of clarity, but he could tell something was there, and it was moving fast, close to the ground.

The noise suddenly roared louder, crashing through the illusion he had built and grasping firmly, at last, his sense of reality.

Huxley staggered under the weight of his fear, of his desperation, of his utter loss of control.

To Jack, the machines sounded as if they were more distant, as if they were retreating. But he paid little attention to the noise, consumed as he was by the ungiving layer of solid ice below him. It never gave more than the tiny chips, never split or cracked or opened up wider no matter his efforts. Just the arduous chipping, splintering, disintegrating to powder.

The end of the handle bent and rounded, growing useless as a pick. He switched back to the blade of the shovel and continued to hack away at the ice. Below him, it was a full two feet thick.

If it was only the lack of food, they would be able to survive, maybe for weeks without irreversible damage. They could put up with the headaches and hunger and endure the weakness, if it was only a lack of food they faced. But it was the cold that sneaked in behind their defenses and killed. Like a bayonet to a wounded soldier, hypothermia would find easy victims.

The echo of the pinging blade became a steady note hovering in the snow pit. The sound rang in Jack's ears, rising in pitch, making him work harder. The blade was curling at the end, beginning to split along one side. But he kept banging it against the ice.

It rose, then fell, and then it snapped. The shaft above the blade snapped, and Jack collapsed over the crater. The sharp edge of the jagged metal tore through his glove, scraping his hand. He rolled to his back and buried his hands into his stomach. As Ricky maneuvered over by him, his ears continued to ring, but it was not the echo of the blade lingering in the air. It was the distant hum of the machines.

Huxley spun around in place, looking in every direction. The terror seemed to ice him to the spot—he couldn't take a step. He couldn't think, only observe and fight for clarity of vision, for some manner of understanding, for the reining in of his disbelief.

Though it seemed an eternity he was frozen in place, in actuality it was mere seconds. A few beats of his heart before he started to run, before he began plunging into the white world. He ran without plan, without any idea of where he was going, how he was going to get away.

His mind could not distinguish hallucination from reality. The only thing that remained constant was the growling of the beasts, the gnashing, snarling sound he had been following, the lure of his patient's calls for him. The sound had become something solid, something of this world, this wilderness, something of substance and power and intelligence. They were Reuker's demons, and they were machines of death.

The straps around one foot tore loose, and the shoe snagged on the snow. Huxley pulled out of it and continued running, but things were different. The trees had changed. He hoped he was nearing the mine, but he couldn't be sure. It was all coming at him so fast, and there was so much he didn't know, so much he couldn't grasp. He tried to call out, but his lungs could spare no breath.

There was no mine, no trench, no slanting trees. Had he run the wrong way? Had he dashed into them?

All Huxley's lifelong fears and hates of the wilderness came rushing out of the past and overtook him. His fright had a purity of its own, a stark, unshackled force that careened rampant through every nerve, through every charged part of his body. It was the deadened panic of a boy, set adrift in a canoe with lightning crashing all around; it was the split-second shock of Reuker's contorted face bursting out of the chair toward him; it was the appalling realization that Stilkes's evil had become real and had taken shape.

Through the red flare of his terror, amid the confusion and disarray of a mind succumbed to fear, he could feel the slope of the ground descending. The mine, he hoped, he prayed. He ran harder, pushing himself, calling on the dying surge of his adrenaline. It must be the mine, he thought, but it was different. He followed the trail as it tunneled through the trees, and as he bent his head he felt a stabbing, tearing pain.

It was more than his fear; it was real and it seemed to come from all over his body at once. It stopped him in his tracks, and he staggered back, unable to move forward.

He felt a strong tug and again went backward. He fought the pull, but it twisted harder, exerting unyielding pressure. And suddenly the pain was localized. As it increased, he could feel the tightness, the penetrating, daggerlike incision of the tools into the fat of his thigh. And he could hear the noise, the vicious snarling of the beasts.

The pressure relented, but only for an instant. Before he could sway forward, the jabbing, viselike grip took hold again, wrenching him backward, rending the flesh of his buttocks as if it were the meat of a carnivore.

Huxley fell onto his back, and the beasts were at once all around. The horror and the pain took shape in his chest. It fought, then overcame the rushing, panting, gasping throes of exertion that had stilled his voice. It was expelled through his throat, and at last he could release it to the outside, he could release his agony to the air.

His voice was the language of fear—a call of pain and terror and unintelligible sounds, an echo from the raging of his mind, an unfathomable reflection of incoherent thoughts and images made unknowable by that fear. All this was embodied in his scream, and then the wolf had him by the neck.

Huxley's cry strangled in his throat. There was a heavy sucking sound, like air rushing to fill a vacuum, and then the sound stopped, replaced by a frantic, thrashing struggle.

Philip heard the scream and immediately turned and began following the track toward Huxley. He was at once shocked and perplexed by the cry of terror—the snowmobiles for some time had been growing more distant, he had thought. The inmates had apparently given up for the day in the face of approaching darkness and had turned back. But why the scream? Could it have been a trap, like it had for Ricky the day before? Without pausing to reflect on the danger, Tardif shuffled forward at his measured, seemingly unhurried pace toward the scream.

He was the only one to hear it. The scream did not penetrate the snow cave of their shelter, nor did it carry as far as Marion near the lake. And out beyond her, Jack and Ricky had given up on the ice. As they lashed their snowshoes onto their boots, Tardif neared a rise where the trail twisted around the naked branches of a sun-starved spruce. The noise from just ahead was frightening, and though he recognized what it was, Philip refused to believe what he heard until he saw it himself.

The brittle twigs scratched his glove as he carefully pushed his way through the trees. At once he saw the movement, the blur of grayish fur near the bottom of the depression. He stepped closer, his legs seemingly no longer under his control. The only thing he felt was a dread that clenched with numbing fingers at his very core.

Three of the wolves were bobbing, maneuvering, stabbing their jaws forward at what lay on the snow, then twisting and jerking their heads until pulling free. When any of the others approached they were met with a teeth-bared snarl that drove them back, to circle and try again. To get their share, they had to be quick.

Philip moved cautiously along the trail. So far he hadn't been noticed, and he was propelled by a need to be sure. Finally, he was close enough to see, and Philip was held by the scene, transfixed by its sound, frozen in place by the mind-numbing realization that what he saw was a man being wrenched apart and devoured by wild animals. He stood there, watching this primeval scene, without regard to his own safety, until at last the largest of the wolves stepped back from the carcass.

As soon as it did, the other wolves descended upon the meat, and their combined sound created an umbrella of predatory fever that effectively sealed whatever was near inside its arc of horror. The noise brought Philip out of his trance, and he sensed a quickening of his pulse as he watched the largest of the wolves amble forward along the packed trail, directly toward where he stood.

Philip lifted one of the shoes from the snow and began to turn in the opposite direction. At his first movement the wolf snapped alert, looking toward him. Philip froze and stared at the wolf, waiting for its move. The predator's ears were perked straight, its muzzle angled toward the snow, its hackles raised, and its eyes fixed in a deadly gaze directly on him.

Its eyes locked Tardif's own, and he sensed its cunning, beastly intelligence. He completed turning himself around, moving as evenly as he could. As he did, he noticed the wolf's head rise slightly, its front left leg cocked as if it were ready to spring. Behind it one of the other wolves had had its fill and taken a position behind the leader. Both of them were unflinching in their gaze.

Philip gently raised his shoes and slid them forward. He could feel his heart beating, he could hear the pulse in his temples. He inched along the trail, toward the hump of the slight rise, then into the dead branches of the spruce.

As he left the sight of the kill, Tardif glanced back at the lead wolf. It was still in position, cocked yet remaining where it was. Its fierce and fearless stare—its brazen challenge—chilled Tardif to the bone, and the shiver it inspired stayed with him until long after the fire was blazing down in the trench of the mine.

The temperature dipped to many degrees below zero, as it had every night, and the smoke from the fire rose straight into the domed sky. Though the warmth of the flames could barely dent the heavy mantle of cold, the intensity from very close brought a relief and a pleasure they hadn't felt for days.

Emma sat back, away from the fire, as if the heat were something corporeal and to absorb it was to steal it from the others. She was moved closer, but when she looked into the flames she saw not comfort, but weakness; she felt not warmth, but a dank chill of cowardice.

Philip sat next to her but the demands on his mind were so great he could give her little attention. Earlier, after the last of the canned meat was served and the fire was being prepared—long enough for the wolves to finish—Philip led Jack to the sight. It was the least the wilderness required—a decent burial.

But when they reached the trampled, stained snow, there was nothing to inter. Every scrap of flesh and bone and sinew had been totally consumed. The wolves had devoured him whole. Even the babiche of his snowshoes had been eaten.

As they stood and stared at the ground, Philip had an awful sensation that they were being watched, that the wolves had dissolved into the grayness of twilight and hung back just out of sight. He felt they were there, keeping them in their senses, evaluating new prey. But regardless of the suspicion, he couldn't take his eyes off the shredded nylon of Huxley's coat.

Despite the grisly scene, it was far less disturbing than the memory of the carnivores wrenching the body limb from limb. It caused a discomfort in his stomach, and the feeling worsened as they walked back to the cave. He had never felt that way about the wilderness. He had never before feared it.

Emma could sense her husband's mood as he sat next to her by the fire. She knew of his fear, but like him, the demands on her were too great to allow her to give comfort.

Rather than being warmed by the fire, she was chilled. And cold burns, Emma thought. It burns for only a short while, and then the numbness comes. When that happens, pain is no longer to be feared. It's just like falling asleep.

She thought of the infant, and other young lives cheated by circumstance out of the joys of living. And if ever there were a child who deserved his chance more, it was Ricky. Emma's thoughts became a prayer, and she prayed that he survive. If there is any justice in God's plan, he will live.

Emma moved slowly, following the others into the snow cave. As she took her place on the shelf, she was at peace, and the chill of the cave did not bother her.

32

The Arctic weather cell was a dome of cold that arched high over the Great Lakes basin. It hovered there, as if the lubricant that greased the normal flow of air had turned to ice and held the dome fast.

On that Sunday night, after the fourth full day of the stationary weather system, a solitary figure knelt with bare knees on the snow of Scale Island. The cold had numbed the skin where it touched the ground, and exposed flesh was turning chalky white. The mark of the frostbite started on the cheeks, the tip of the nose, the backs of the hands, the rounded areas of fat—the buttocks, the thighs, the calves—and it dabbed its sterile brush along the back, which was curved inward against the cold. The small white circles grew, and where they met one another, the skin formed a crevice. There it cracked, and though in places a thin line of blood colored the crevice, more often than not the capillaries under the skin had already been destroyed and could carry no blood to the surface.

Breath was erratic and was never unaccompanied by a moan, a shrill whistle that ended with a moist, rattling sound in the throat. Each breath was progressively more difficult, becoming more a wheeze than the act of taking air. But since there was no more power to the lungs, there was little effort behind the body's struggle for oxygen. Slowly the figure was dying.

There was no body movement, and the face was contorted in an agonized expression—the look of someone asleep and caught within a wakeless nightmare. Because of the lack of movement, the frozen look of horror, it was impossible to discern if there was any thought left in the brain, if there was any awareness that life was slipping away. All that was apparent was that the figure had long since given up on retaining that last spark of life.

It had begun earlier, when Arnie Johnson was taken from his cell. He had been held there since the beginning of the mutiny, and over time he had sensed an increasingly aimless desperation among the inmates. They had the Facility, but they didn't know what to do with it; they had their freedom, but they were still imprisoned on Scales. The medicines were wearing off, and the fulcrum of mental stability was swinging far out of kilter.

They came more often to his cell to scream epithets, to spit through the bars, or most unnerving of all, to tell him in a calm tone of voice of their hate for him. After four days of continuing biochemical degeneration, something snapped, and when it did, it was only natural that the rage that spread like a contagion through the men in

A-Barracks was directed toward Arnie Johnson, the fat guard. He was the closest symbol of all they despised and feared and blamed for their condition.

They hauled him from his cell and dragged him to the lounge area, a dozen hands reaching for a piece of him. He was terrified, and he was crying, the tears streaming over his cheeks. His clothes were tearing under the grasping fingers. The inmates were shouting, fighting, in some manner of indecision over where their rage would take them. The fear pounded so loud in Arnie's head that he didn't hear the argument. All he could do was plead for his life. "Please, leave me alone. Don't hurt me. Please." He moaned, his words interrupted only by his sniveling sobs.

Then as if the mob came suddenly of one mind, an idea spread like fire over droughted savannah. They began to tear his clothes, ripping them from his body, and he was buffeted among them like a stricken rag doll.

Then he was moving again, railroaded along the corridor, a dozen hands pulling, pinching, squeezing his fat flesh. At the end of the corridor they stopped. The door opened.

"Nooo," he screamed, and before the echo of his cry died, he was outside and the door slammed shut. He was flat on his chest, and he scrambled quickly to his knees, then stood and turned back toward the door, toward the small window in the door.

The full impact of the subzero cold struck hard. For a moment he was seized with panic as he couldn't breathe, and it was this panic that propelled him forward again.

He clawed at the window, at the ice that rimed the glass, and inside he could tell someone was doing the same thing. When it cleared, he saw a face, a wild, grinning face, then another, as the first was pushed out of the way. They were craning their necks to see him.

He stumbled back from the door. He turned and looked around the yard, toward the other buildings. He thought of running to another door, of pounding to be let inside, but with each new step the soles of his feet felt as though being cut to shreds. Walking on the snow was like walking on broken glass.

He turned back to A-Barracks. Surely they weren't going to let him stay out there. The fun would wear thin, and they would let him in. They wouldn't let him freeze.

No one could be so cruel, so insane as to commit such an act. He would wait.

The glass iced again, but through the blur he could still see the heads taking turns to watch. "Please, open," he whimpered, taking a step toward the door.

His closed fists rested against the steel, and the whimper grew louder. Fed by a churning realization that they might not let him in, the whimper became a shout. Then a scream as panic took control. He pounded his fists on the door, crying out for them to open it, to let him inside, not to let him die.

Then at last he heard the bolt tumbling in the door. It was the sound of salvation, and his panic broke. "They're letting me in. Oh, thank God, they're letting me in," he jabbered to himself.

The door cracked then swung open, and he stepped forward. But someone slammed him in the chest, and he was staggered. A great gush of steam cut the air like misty knives flailing and flickering in mad confusion. And then he felt it. He felt the sting of the water. They had doused him with water!

It felt like a thousand needles pricking his skin, and where the water ran over him, it burned like boiling oil. An instant after the impact, he heard a laugh, then the door slamming shut.

Erupting from his throat was a scream of agony, of horror, and it echoed off the silent brick of the yard. An unintelligible stream of syllables whipped through the air, an accurate reflection of the incoherency inside his head.

The water froze rapidly, and it stung his skin. With the energy of his scream spent, Arnie chafed at his body, brushing off the thin layer of ice. The cold was unbearable; it stifled his movement, his thinking, then finally his breathing. Arnie collapsed again, but this time he could do nothing about the cutting cold that impaled itself through his knees.

The frostbite came, and eventually the white patches grew together. His body gave its heat to Scales, and in the end, he died as Jeremy Willet had died.

Marion shook her husband's shoulder. "Jack, wake up." He stirred, his eyes fluttering open. "Wake up," she said again, a crisp tone of urgency to her voice.

He woke with the aching expression of a night hard

spent. Marion was talking, and he could hear, but in that first haze his mind could not comprehend. He tried to shake himself alert.

"They're gone. Phil and Emma aren't in the cave."

Jack was on one side of the shelf, Lummer on the other. In the middle, where the Tardifs should be, the blanket was flat. "What happened?"

"I don't know. When I woke they were gone."

Jack looked toward the snow block in the spillway. It was in place. He looked toward Lummer, and he could see the doctor was on his side, staring at him. The expression showed lack of wonder, as if he knew, as if he concealed some private mystery. Jack flipped the covers off himself and hurriedly climbed from the shelf.

He jimmied the block from side to side until he could push it from the opening. Then he crawled outside, followed by Marion. Inside, Ricky was rustling.

"Phil," Jack shouted, the ice fog swirling in curling clouds of vapor, buffeted by his breath.

He called Emma's name, then Philip's again, but still there was no reply. They wouldn't have gone the way of the wolves, so he turned toward the lake. He followed the tracks of the snowshoes, his boots sinking deeper than the trough, and he eyed the ground ahead with a kind of reluctance. When he saw them, the shock was not any less because it was what he expected.

Shrouded by the fog, they looked like twin humps of snow. Jack crept closer, his eyes fixed on Philip and Emma, an unsteady dread nearly locking his movement. She was faced toward him; he away. He stared at her face through the mist, through the floating ice crystals, until he realized its pallor wasn't just because of the ice fog. He was stunned.

Marion pushed by him and walked toward the Tardifs. Jack could sense fear in the trembling of her breath. He started after her, his gaze frozen on the slumped figures. They looked the same—two humps of snow affixed by the cold to the earth below—but they weren't. There was a difference. Jack quickened his step, keeping pace with Marion.

It was Philip. He seemed to be moving, bobbing slowly from the waist. When he reached him, Jack could see that he was crying and that the tears had turned to ice and dangled from his chin like tiny stalactites. He seemed oblivious to the cold, to Jack and Marion, to everything but the solid, frozen lump before him.

Emma's coat was folded next to her on the snow, and her gloves were atop that. Her eyelids were iced together, and a rim of frost circled her mouth and trailed down her chin like an old man's fuzzy beard. Though her face had captured and now held in permanent relief a haggard pain, it conveyed a certain serenity. She looked at peace, squatting as she was in the snow, Eskimo style.

"She didn't deserve this," Philip rasped. "She was a good woman. Such a good woman."

Marion started to cry and slowly let herself kneel next to Tardif. She gripped his arm, as much to gain support as to lend it.

"Why did you do it? Why, Emma?" he said to his wife's dead ears. "Why did you have to do this? Why couldn't you have turned to me? I wouldn't have let you die."

Jack felt a painful lump knot in his throat, and he had to turn away from Emma, from Philip's pathetic lament. As he did he felt a flaring of hatred for Lummer, for the man whose suggestion had touched this fatal response in a noble woman. But his hatred quickly grew complicated by a peculiar sense of guilt he could not understand. He felt shamed, and because of it he could do nothing but stand there and listen to Philip and his anguish.

It was Tardif's place to seek redress, Jack thought. Yet Philip was to seek none, either because so great was his grief that it eclipsed all anger, or so empty was the feeling inside that vengeance offered little satisfaction. Philip said nothing when they went back to the cave, nor later, after the ice fog had fallen and the sky was getting brighter.

And Lummer said nothing as he waited for them to get started, to put as much distance as they could between themselves and the ridge. Already he could hear the faint sound of the machines traveling out of Greenstone. He was anxious to leave, but because of the old woman's death, they were not to move for some time.

Philip was determined to protect her from the wolves. Whatever it took, he would bury her where they could not do to her what they had done to Huxley.

He walked slowly through the trench until he located a crevice in the rock wall. It was on the side opposite the high drift, and it was concealed behind a sheet of ice formed by water washing down from above.

He began to chip at the sheet with the stove shovel handle as a chisel. As he did, Lummer approached, and said, "We could bury her in the snow cave. We won't be using it again."

Philip turned and stared at Lummer, his chisel poised in his hands like a broken sword. Lummer stepped back.

Then Philip turned quickly back to the curtain of ice and slammed the pick into it. His hands rested on the iron for a moment, and he said to Lummer, "The wolves would dig her out of the cave."

Lummer stood as if waiting for him to say more, but when he wrenched the pick from the ice and resumed chopping, Lummer turned and moved hesitantly away. Jack joined Tardif, and with the old man's knife chipped at the vertical slants of ice from the opposite side of the cleft.

As the sound of metal into ice settled into a rhythm, Lummer settled into a vigil, listening in tense silence to the chipping of the ice, and to the snowmobiles and their constant clattering noise, never changing, never veering.

Lummer was neither religious nor superstitious, but as he waited for Jack and Philip to do their job, he sensed what only could be described as a premonition. He was unnerved by the sensation, and though he tried to ignore it, to label it false, he could not rid himself of the feeling that what he feared would at last come true. Today he would come face to face with the virulent malice of the inmates from Scales.

The men in the cabin were rested and eager to get started. The day before expectations had soared a number of times as they thought the group from the institution was within their grasp. But each time those expectations proved groundless, and eventually they had to turn back because of the early nightfall.

Yesterday, after they had reached the bottom of the ridge, the track had become increasingly difficult to follow. Two inches of new snow did not hide the trail, but it did make it difficult to determine if it was made by man, or animal. They followed false leads—some old animal trails, some mistaken turns in the trees—and sometimes they were routed back to their own tracks. And through it all, they had to struggle against the grasping hold the thick snow had on their machines. But today, leaving early and with a full day to work with, Eddie Hyland felt sure they would be able to run them down. There was no new snow, and he had a plan.

They would always head southwest, straight into the island's interior, toward the opposite ridge. That's where he felt they were heading. To the opposite shore. Where they were unsure, they would split one machine off until they were all fanned out, if necessary, and then keep in contact by the sound of the engines. The signal to come was gunfire. Though two more men had quit the chase, racing back to Scales with one of the machines, there were still six men and four snowmobiles.

Eddie Hyland took the lead from the cabin, racing out the well-worn track along Greenstone Ridge. He guided his machine and his rider down the steep descent, following their path from the day before, and when they reached level ground, they switched. Eddie sat behind so he could concentrate on the trail, the woods, or anything around them, rather than on the driving itself.

They had reached the bottom of the ridge so fast, all the men held their confidence. They were inwardly jubilant over the prospect of quickly bringing the pursuit to a close, of keeping their island secure. For Eddie, with his peculiar mixture of lust and violence, of passion and revenge, he was thinking of his moment, at last, with Marion and Jack. The dreams had come again early in the morning, and again Marion lured him with her willingness, and Jack whimpered in pathetic futility. She would be willing, he thought, and more importantly, Jack would witness it all. He would suffer this final outrage, and then he would die.

On the last of the four machines, Reuker Stilkes traveled alone. His good eye watered from the wind of motion, and the other, blinded by the blast of the gun, stung from the bite of the cold.

Like the others, Reuker felt the people on foot were within their reach. In his tormented vision, he saw the caped figure, the pillowy boy, the black-haloed face. They were one and the same. They were of the same evil. And he saw fear in them. At last, they suffered from what they had wrought. At last, his haunting would come to a close.

Suomi's call from Scales came in on time Monday

morning, and as he expected, there was no Hagan. He didn't press it until the very end, when finally he asked if his message had been relayed to the director.

"I told him." The radio speaker turned static-y, and no other explanation was offered.

"Where is he?" Suomi asked.

"He said he'd call Lansing directly. He may already have, for all I know."

The conversation was over. During the brief contact each of them said only what had to be said. It was a battle of wits, one against the other; Suomi seeking information, Scales concealing it. And for Suomi, it was the clearest affirmation that something was terribly amiss.

Yet what could he do about it, sitting alone in his isolated cabin on the shores of Lake Superior? The authorities, both at the local and state levels, did not share his convictions. So it was up to him, Suomi realized, to prove to the authorities they were wrong. He sat thinking for several minutes, weighing his options, and they all led to a single imperative. He had to get to the island.

Suomi dialed the airfield and asked for Poiret.

"He's left already," Finny Kuula said. "Should be just about there with the mail."

"Can you raise him? Bring him back?"

"What for?"

"I want him to take me to the island."

Finny laughed. "You know what he'd say. He'd say 'I'm no goddamn taxi and don't fuck with the U.S. Mail.'"

Suomi shifted tensely, looking at the clock on the wall. "When's he going to be back?"

"Well, he's got to fly to Marquette after Scales. Then back to here. Same as always. I'd say he'll be here by two-thirty or three. Depends on how much talking he does at his stops."

"Do you have anything you can rent me?"

"You? You haven't flown for years. I wouldn't rent you my grandfather's biplane."

"Do you still have your piper?"

"Yep."

"And the skis. Are they on?"

"Well, sure."

"Then let me charter it, and you can fly me over."

"Hell, no. My plane's not going over that lake in winter.

You know as well as I a storm can kick out of a white sky in ten minutes, and then that's it. No sir, the Piper stays over dry land until spring and the golden hook-danglers come. That's my business and I can't risk it for nothing."

"Listen, Finny. It's important to the people over there I get to the island. There's some trouble, and I have to check it out."

"So call the sheriff."

Suomi closed his eyes, fighting to control the heavy breath of exasperation. "He doesn't have a plane. You know that."

"Well, I guess you're out of luck, Ike. Unless you can talk Poiret into it later on. Maybe he'll take you there tomorrow. He's the only one around here crazy enough to fly that lake in winter."

Suomi felt as though there were a conspiracy. At every turn he was blocked. Resigned to having to wait, he said, "What time did you say Poiret would be back? Two to two-thirty?"

"Two-thirty to three."

Suomi asked to have him call, and after hanging up he stood staring at the phone, then the radio, trying to think of something—anything—he could do. But like so often in the past few days he was left with nothing to do but wait.

Louis Poiret's aircraft cut cleanly through the currentless air. It was easy flying, and for Poiret that meant it was a bore.

"Jesus, I wish this weather'd break," he said to himself. The air was as still and lifeless as the inside gloom of a closed mausoleum. For the past several days it had been more than just still. It was as if something dying were settling over the land, as if the life were being suffocated out of it.

It was a morbid thought, and Poiret suddenly laughed out loud at himself. Acting like a kid on Halloween, he thought.

The plane was halfway between the mainland and the island, and looking back Poiret could see only a blurry stripe where the snow-covered shoreline was. It was a white line against the gray of the sky, rapidly fading from view, as if it were no longer there. And ahead, Scales held its own mantled camouflage as if it were hiding, as if the island had something to conceal.

Marion and Ricky dug in the snow where it was sculpted shallow by the same forces that drifted it deep on the other side of the trench. They collected loose rocks that had fallen from the stone face and piled up over the years, by kicking them free from the mortar of snow that bonded them together. Reluctantly Lummer helped them scavenge for the rocks. It was the only way to get them moving, to resume their flight from that infernal noise.

Working together, they caused a pile of stone to collect near the cleft. They were the bricks that would wall Emma inside the crypt.

The Apaches buried their dead that way, Philip had said. That's what made him think of providing for Emma in this fashion. "When they're placed in the rock and sealed off by the boulders, the belief is they become part of the mountain. They gain its strength, its stature, and most of all, its permanence."

Jack twisted the blade of his knife, and another chunk of ice broke free and fell to the ground. The flat sorrow of Tardif's voice moved him, and he said what he could. "She'll always be here, Phil. Part of this place. Just as you are part of the island."

Philip paused. "I don't know if I want her to be a part of Scales. At one time I would have thought so. But now"—he let his voice hang, then it dropped—"I don't know. This is such a bad place. It's changed so much."

Jack agreed but said nothing.

"At least she'll be safe from the wolves. That's all I can ask."

Philip's sense of loss seemed to become more profound as time elapsed. The realization she would never be there with him to share his laughs, to prompt his stories, to comfort his pain, to provide him love, to accept his *love*, to *live* with him—indeed, she was his life—this realization became clearer, and as it did, its impact was devastating.

Scales was a remote place, a place that if it were to be survived, had to be shared, as he and Emma had shared for forty-three years. They had lived the land and the inland sea, hiking its trails and camping on its shores. They had seen from the ridge the sun turn crimson at the lake's edge, and they had seen it from the valley silhouette the spindly trunks of innumerable trees both east and west. They had snacked on thimbleberries, had watched the mating of red foxes, and had themselves made love in the forest on a spongy bed of pine. They had watched the island stay the same, and had watched it at last change. All of this was done together. One life. Inseparable.

With the cavity nearly hewn out of the ice exposing a narrow crevice in the stone—a grotto behind a frozen waterfall—Philip decided it didn't matter if Emma was left in the rock to be forever a part of Scales. It only mattered that they were together.

The machine plowed powerfully through the trench splaying loose snow to the side and kicking up a roostertail of tread-compacted snow chunks in its wake. It bounded through dips like a dolphin in surf.

Eddie Hyland held his face slightly off center so he could look around his driver. Benny Nichols was a tall man, and large, and straddling the seat behind him on the snowmobile, Hyland found it difficult to see. And he desperately wanted to keep his eyes on the trail ahead. They were close, he could feel it, and he could do little about restraining his excitement, nor did he try. Today would be the last of the chase.

They were alone, the other machines having sidled off one by one in other tracks and other leads. The four snowmobiles were spread out, all of them plunging deeper into the thick interior of the 300-square-mile island. Though Marion and Jack could be anywhere, Eddie felt sure they were ahead of him, having laid the track he followed. He couldn't give a reason for that feeling; it was just something he knew. He had tried yesterday to read the trails and had failed. So now he went with his intuition, and his plan to head always southwest, toward the opposite ridge.

The skis dropped into a depression, then suddenly were shot skyward and the machine left the surface. Weightless for a second, Eddie floated upward from his seat. When the crash came, he rocked sideways, almost falling off. He grabbed the driver's coat and righted himself. Nichols looked over his shoulder, and Eddie could hear his roaring laughter above the sound of the engine.

Eddie laughed too, more as a nervous reflex than a great burst of exuberance. He quickly felt the large box pocket of his parka. The revolver was still there, the Velcro closure was still tight.

With his hand tightly gripping Benny's coat, he again peered around him to see the trail ahead. It rushed at him in a blur, indistinct both because of the speed and the bouncing of the machine. A dying spruce angled across the track ahead, and in the moment they saw it, they had time only to duck, and the branches whipped across their heads.

Nichols was laughing, enjoying the feel of the machine, the power he held at his command. He leaned into a curve taking it fast. As the snowmobile curved to the right, Eddie saw another trail branching off from the trench they followed. It was shallow, yet instinctively he reacted. "Stop," he shouted. The machine kept its pace. Eddie tugged hard on the coat, screaming in his ear, "Stop. Now."

Nichols let the throttle spin back to idle. The machine slowed, then came to a halt. "We missed it," Hyland said.

"We couldn't have. We're following the same track."

Eddie climbed off the back of the vehicle and started to retrace their path. "I'm going to check." He walked fast, trusting his hunch. He came to the fork, and the spur was less of a depression than the trail Nichols had followed. Hyland could see it cut directly into the trees, as if it deliberately meant to be concealed.

Nichols came up behind him. "We had it right. It's the trail we've been following for the last hour."

"Yeah. And maybe the trail they had followed, until here. A moose wouldn't have pushed its way into that thicket."

Nichols looked at the dense matting of low-hanging branches. Then he studied the path itself. "Hey, look at this," he said. "This ain't no human print, snowshoe or not."

Eddie bent down closer. The only discernible markings in the new snow of the spur were overlapping pawprints, most obliterated by later footfalls. He stared long and hard at the prints, unable to give in to the feeling he had inside. The most recent passage was by animals, but were they the only things that had passed that way?

Eddie stood and looked up the trail past the snowmobile. It was old, rounded, like so many of the other stale moose trails they had followed the last two days. But this one, this spur with the pawprints, seemed different. Eddie couldn't explain why, but the feeling persisted, growing stronger the longer he stood there and pondered.

He turned and started toward the machine. "We're coming back," he said. "That's the way they went."

They maneuvered the snowmobile in a tight circle, struggling through the drift, and brought it back to the spur. Cautiously Nichols guided it through the dense matting of branches, before gradually increasing his speed.

Hyland had no doubt. They were on the track of Marion and Jack Cooke, whose trail lay hidden under the indecipherable prints of some unknown beast. He saw through their subterfuge. They would not escape.

The single-engine Aeronis Champion cast its efficient noise in a wide arc as Poiret banked cleanly around the tip of Scale Island. He manipulated the small aircraft into position for its descent to the runway of Lake Siskiwit, then he brought it down.

The skis touched, and the plane glided toward the far shore. When it came to a stop, Poiret looked over his shoulder at the road-cut to Scales. There was no machine rushing out to meet him.

Poiret brought the plane around, positioning it where he usually did for takeoff. The engine idled to an even purr, and he climbed out onto the ice. "Come on, Chesser," he said to himself. "Don't make me wait out here." He was doing his best to forget about what happened last week. He was denying to himself there had been a problem, that there may be a problem today. He was just late, Poiret told himself, and would be coming through at any moment. But as he stood there in the utter stillness of Lake Siskiwit, the only noise the gentle hum of his own aircraft, there was no sound of an approaching snowmobile.

He turned and opened the storage compartment and pulled the mail sack out and let it swing to the ground. The door slammed shut, and he turned back toward the lake. A touch of the old anger nipped at the edge of his control.

"Damn it now. Come on."

He stepped away from the plane, dragging the sack with him. His eyes were cemented on the cut in the trees at the opposite end of the lake. He was watching for the flash of color, listening for the sounds, so at first he did not notice them. He did not notice the lumps on the snow.

He took another angry step forward, then stood solidly watching and waiting. "I can't take much of this, damn it. I've bent over backwards for—" Poiret stopped in mid-sentence. His eyes flared, and he let the sack slip from his fingers.

Before him on the ice, their canvas bent over like supplicating sinners, were the two mail bags. He was frozen in astonishment and outrage. The dirty canvas was glazed with a thin layer of ice, and where the ice fog had settled, it sparkled in the white light.

Poiret stomped forward and kicked one of the bags. The canvas crinkled, white lines spreading across it like cracks in glass, and it sailed only a few feet away.

"Those sons of bitches," he barked, then turned toward the plane. He shut the engine down, then snatched the sack of today's delivery and swung it over his shoulder, then began walking the length of the lake.

The repressed anger was boiling out of him now. He was a pilot, for Christ's sakes, not a goddamn delivery boy. And it was up to Scales to meet him at the runway.

His job was a trust, he always felt, with people on both sides of the water depending on him. It just wasn't right that the Corrections people in charge here didn't share that trust. At least, it wasn't right they should screw it up so it looked like his fault. And that's what they'd do when the complaints started: Blame it on him!

Those bastards, Poiret thought. "Well, I'm bringing it in myself and dumping it straight on your desk. Then try and deny I didn't get it here, as my contract says." Poiret's voice was gravelly tough, made staccato by his rapid breaths. Conditioned by long solo flights, his thoughts frequently turned oral, especially when his anger was taking control. Nearing the shore, he shouted, "You just don't fuck with the U.S. Mail!" There was no reply, no echo. His words died quickly in the heavily mantled woods.

Poiret followed the rut of an old snowmobile track up the embankment and into the narrow swath cut between the trees. He followed the hard-packed trail of the Sno-Cat as it wended deeper into the forest. Soon he couldn't see the plane, then the lake, then nothing but the silent columns of leafless trunks and the stoic evergreens. And the snow.

His sky was without barrier, and it was the sudden contrast that made him feel enclosed, that made him think of the voice on the radio he talked to on Saturday.

The voice had seemed unsure, as if he had been frightened, as if succumbing to private fears that could exist and grow only in a mind locked by isolation, in a mind numbed by the barrenness of the Scales winter. Poiret felt a twinge of that same disquiet he had felt on Saturday when he sat in his plane listening to that voice. He was used to dealing with absolutes, with rights and wrongs, with situations that announced themselves clearly. But the feeling that now pricked at his tough hide threw that simple outlook into chaos.

He had shaken it off on Saturday, but the feeling was too strong for him to do that now. Poiret's charge had slowed, but he was undeterred. Whatever the hell was going on inside those walls, he decided, he would find out for himself. And he'd find out even if it meant breaking down the director's office door with his bare hands.

The dead forest yielded Poiret a view of the Facility. It proved no relief. Scales was an unbreathing mound of stone and steel, more lifeless than the forest itself.

At the top of the cleft Jack and Philip had broken through to the hollow. It was a vertical crevice sunk into the side of the wall narrowing as it extended inward six feet. Whether formed by ancient forces, or the blasting of the nineteenth-century miners, what was left was a well-kept enclosure, a perfect crypt.

Neither Jack nor Philip had been thinking about the sputtering cry of the snowmobiles. It was such a constant, it seemed at times just to blend into the background, into the sound of metal chipping ice, of rock being dropped upon rock.

It wasn't until the yellowish curtain of ice was penetrated near the top that they paused to listen. There was something different about the sound of the machine. Over time, they seemed to acquire a knack for reading the noise, for sensing what was happening with the driver. And now they could tell the approach was steady, unyielding, like a predator that had found the scent. And it was louder.

As they listened, they could tell that each of them sensed the change. "They're coming," Philip said tonelessly.

"We have to finish," Jack said, looking down the trench toward Emma's body, wrapped in one of the moosehides. He started toward her.

"You take Marion and Ricky and go on. I'll stay."

"Keep on that ice," Jack called, ignoring the suggestion. Frozen solid in her squatting position, she made an awkward bundle, but Jack was able to carry her back to the cleft. The opening was widening faster as Philip chopped at the exposed edge with his pick.

Jack tried to save time by pounding with his hands on the ice, trying to break away enough so Emma could be squeezed inside, so they would have room to create a wedged rock wall as a barricade. The ice gave with the pressure, but it didn't break.

The snowmobile was closing fast. They were on the right track, he was sure. They were coming!

For the first time Jack began to think of how to react to them when they came. There was a chance, he thought, and as that thought took hold, Jack became a part of a plan, carried along by it, by what he envisioned would happen, by what he would have to do. A feverish energy surged through his veins. If he could stop the first one and get his weapon, there would be a chance.

He tried to determine if it was only one machine, or several; if they were still spread out, or on a single trail.

He could hear no other sounds from different directions. The closest machine drowned everything else out.

Jack gripped the knife and dug its blade into the ice. He levered it, then pushed against the ice with his shoulder. It cracked, but still it held. He tried again, his muscles fueled by the urgency, his fear fed by an adrenaline that pulsed in his system.

The sound attacked his hearing, and as it did, his sensile awareness heightened. There wasn't much time! He pushed harder, and with the roar of an avalanche a great piece of the ice wall shattered, and Jack tumbled into the crevice. Inside the echo of the machine seemed even louder. Even closer. The walls of rock seemed as if they were closing in. A claustrophobic tingle fluttered the length of his spine. He felt Philip tugging at his waist, and then he was free. Philip told him again to leave, that he would finish. But Jack didn't bother to reply. He picked up the moosehide-wrapped bundle and with Philip eased it into the rock.

* * *

The speed they traveled created a rushing excitement, an electric charge that sparked acuity to every sense, to every thought.

Eddie no longer ducked his head through the low-hanging branches. He let the fine stiffness of the needles scratch across his face. He let himself become part of the flow of the wind, with the branches weaving and bobbing and brushing over him.

Benny Nichols's lock on the throttle seemed infected with the stuff of Hyland's lust. He was captivated by the power, by the prospect of an end to the search. Like no time before, during the chase, had he felt as strong. He now believed Eddie. They were on the right trail, he could sense it.

The snowmobile was on a gradual descent, just part of the natural contour of the valley, when a flash of color caught Eddie's eye. He tensed. It was the fabric of a jacket. Nichols noticed it a fraction of a second later, and immediately the machine began to slow down.

Eddie looked into the woods to either side, before them, up into the trees. There was no movement. No other signs of color.

As they approached they could see that the clothing was shredded and strewn about the matted area. And the snow was splattered and stained. Eddie didn't think what the scene had been. It didn't bother him what must have happened, what manner of beast could have accomplished what he saw. He viewed it only as a sign—the absolute proof—that they had been here. That they were near.

"Go, go," Eddie shouted, pounding Nichols with the flat of his hands. The driver's sense of power, of violence unspent, surged again and the machine lurched forward. He guided it up an incline, toward a knob covered by snow, and beyond that they could see a thickness of trees.

Jack and Philip worked frantically with the rocks. A line of them was wedged across the bottom of the cleft, braced solidly against the stone walls. They started the next layer, sizing the rocks, twisting them in their hands to find the right contour, then fitting them in like a primitive mason.

As Jack wedged a narrow chip of rock between two larger ones, there was a sudden explosion of sound. It seemed to come from the lake, from the forest, from the crevice itself, so booming was its impact. Like a concussion, there was momentary disorientation. Jack grabbed his ears, looking wildly at Tardif.

"It's the inmates!" the older man cried.

The noise had erupted like a low-flying jet suddenly soaring over a hill. Unprotected by the muffling of rock and vast distances of snow-covered forest, the engine noise was unmistakably near. It was the sound of Scales, and it was getting closer.

Jack pulled himself to his feet. He looked toward Marion, halfway down the trench between himself and the lake. "Run!" he shouted. "Take Ricky and run toward the lake."

She stood there staring at him, as though struck dumb by the noise, as though questioning what he was going to do.

"Take him and run! Now!"

Finally she reacted and turned Ricky toward the lake. He wanted to run the other way, toward his father, but she wouldn't let him. She forced him around and pushed him forward. Over his shoulder Ricky stole one more glance at his father, and as he hurried out of the trench toward the lake, the glimpse froze in his mind as if he knew he would long recall that look, as if it would be the last glance he would have to savor of his father.

Jack told Philip to follow them, to see that they were safe. Then he left him and started toward the forest entrance of the trench, toward the noise, toward the approach of the inmates.

As he had planned, he would have a chance, if only he could get to the first one. If only he could seize his weapon.

Jack was without his snowshoes, but the pathway was well trampled. He clenched his knife with a grasp that nearly strangled his hand's circulation. He plodded forward, wading into the teeth of the sound, and as he did, his mind was haunted by a vision, and a warning.

He thought of Eddie Hyland, and he pictured his oily, sweaty, stubbled face leering at him with contempt, with vengeance, with his brand of madness and lust. And he could hear him, in his mind he could hear his last curse, his last oath of revenge. "I'm coming for her, Jack Cooke. Tell her I'm coming for her."

Jack pushed himself as he had never pushed himself before. His body racked by pain and injury and deprivation, he was powered by his adrenaline, by his love and fear for Marion, by his disgust and revulsion for the little man and what he wanted to do to her, to him, to anything that was good and pure and out of his reach.

Jack saw where one of the tree trunks ahead angled from one side of the mine to the other creating a V they would have to come through. That's where he would stop them, he decided. That's where he would stage his ambush.

The initial blast of noise that had boomed in the mine had come from the snowmobile. When Benny Nichols and Eddie Hyland reached the top of the rise that ascended from the stained, clothes-strewn patch of white, they hit a tight knob of snow and were suddenly airborne. Nichols drifted backward, and his hand twisted, revving the engine. The RPM needle shot to the maximum, and the resulting roar erupted from their machine with the force of an explosion. Then they came down, crashing through branches as they did. The ragged, prickling sensation of the needles felt good as they brushed across Eddie's face. The feeling tantalized him, it piqued his expectation. The machine rushed onward.

The trail was easily seen. Tear-shaped footprints were clearly observable. There was no mistake. They were near their camp, and Eddie felt sure—more hope than knowledge—they were still there, hiding.

The machine raged across the trail, swerving around trees, its tread tearing at the snow. The footprints led straight down an incline, a gorge, a canyon, a cut in the rock. This is it. Where they hid. Protected from the outside, this was their refuge.

A crazed, happy, frothing delirium had taken hold of Hyland. It was a throbbing pressure inside his skull, a red-hot spike of flame that flared down his spine, a wild, uncontrollable hysteria. He was part of its command, he was prisoner to its fictions. She beckoned for him, she waited for him, she cried out for him. Just ahead.

The machine raced downward, descending farther into the narrow cut, dropping deeper into this open wound of Scales. Eddie could feel the machine's power vibrating between his thighs, and his lust and hate and unfathomable needs reacted to the stimulation. They swirled into an indecipherable mash, and at the vortex, at the very center of Eddie Hyland's madness, was an implacable determination: There was nothing to stop him. Nothing!

The machine raced at near full throttle, expertly weaving between the stunted trees. To either side, the rock walls enclosed them in the miniature canyon. The engine noise was amplified by the echo, the roar nearing the limits of aural endurance. Ahead, more trees. More low branches.

The machine's metallic snout dove unrelenting into the tunnel of branches, into the V of the slanting trunk. As it did, Nichols's head snapped back, his skull cracking into Eddie's teeth. In almost the same instant, Benny's body slammed flush into his chest, the force knocking the wind from him, and Eddie was aware of a sudden weightlessness. They were in the air, and for a second Nichols was stretched parallel to the ground. The machine had gone out from under them and careened riderless somewhere ahead. Then they fell, Nichols under the overlapping branches, and Eddie behind him in the snow.

Hyland was dazed and his teeth and jaw numb from the collision with Nichols's head. His vision was a swirl as he wheezed for breath, as he fought for consciousness, as he moved without direction on his hands and knees. Then he rolled over, coming to rest in a semi-reclining position.

His sight became a wobbly set of images, as everything he saw turned to rubber. One of the images had movement of its own, independent of his incapacity. He tried to focus, to cement his attention on it.

It was Nichols, he was sure, twisting onto his stomach, slowly rising to his feet. Eddie tried to speak, but his voice was an incoherent gargle. Finally, the shape was able to stand, and Eddie could hear a low, mournful sound, a pitiful wail that was far less the sound of a man than it was a haunting whisper of a creature condemned to some unspeakable half life where pain and horror became the only constant, and misery the single truth. The eerie moan signaled a surrender of humanity to a world not of conventional bearing that offered only subhuman existence.

The sound filled him with dread, and the feeling served to bring his eyes to some manner of clarity. He watched as the figure pivoted unsteadily. Slowly it came to face him. It looked like Nichols, but—

"Oh, my God." Eddie Hyland's vision and his realization merged. "My God," he breathed, the words vented from some deep wellspring of revulsion. He began to shake, his head began to rock from side to side. "No, no, no. My God, no," he cried.

Nichols took a step forward. "Oh, dear Jesus, they've ripped your face off." His whimper turned to a wavering shout of disbelief. "They've ripped your face off!"

The fishhooks of Philip's trapline had caught Nichols in his upper lip and the middle of his cheeks, and had torn his skin straight back over the top of his head with the precision of a medical examiner peeling the scalp during an autopsy.

His eyeballs bulged round and seemed to hyperextend from his face. They stared straight ahead, glared, showing only that he was stunned, unaware, half-dead.

It was a monstrous sight, and Hyland found himself gagging on his vomit. Yet he couldn't look away from the apparition before him, a hellish creature, a horror fomented by some new demented drug. Its teeth and gums were exposed in a sardonic grin. Red muscle and tissue glistened with internal moisture. And through it all came a gurgling noise like water percolating in an air hose.

"Oh God," he could only say as he stared transfixed by its appearance. Then it took a halting step toward him. "No!" Eddie screamed, but the creature didn't listen. It took another step. Eddie tried to scramble up, but he was trapped in the snow. "No, no, please God. Take it back." But the apparition staggered toward him.

Hyland was frantic. He could hear the raspy hacking for breath, he could see the awkward motion, the arms tented at its sides, gloved fingers that groped at nothing, that reached for him. Eddie tried to push himself up, but his hands sank into the soft fluff. The revolver, he thought. In his pocket.

The Velcro ripped open, and he grabbed for his gun. It was lengthwise in the pocket, and his gloved hand was bulky. It was a struggle to try to get it out. "Stay back," he screamed, but it kept on, its death gaze unflinching, its energy coming from the realm of the dead.

Eddie pulled the pistol free and waved it at the creature. "Stay back," he cried. Once more he warned. Then without waiting he squeezed the weapon with the force of the horror that had seized control of him. The cartridge exploded, and his wrist jerked, and the missile careened wildly off the rock wall. Quickly, his finger flinched, and he fired again, and again he missed.

For the first time some manner of expression came to the bared eyes, and the teeth opened wider in a gasp. The winded sound wheezing from its throat turned to a hurried rush of air as it struggled harder, toward him. Eddie fired again, and the creature was spun in its tracks. It was struck in the shoulder and momentarily halted. But the wound seemed to give it new strength, a new urgency, and it took a long faltering step toward him.

The revolver rang again, and the slug struck it square, and the creature wobbled, then staggered on stiffened knees. The entire body shuddered as it fought to resist the impact of the bullet. The gun shook in Eddie's hand, and when he shot a fifth time, the creature doubled over, hit in the stomach. He squeezed the trigger again, and abruptly the faceless apparition was flung bolt upright.

Staring into the hideous mask, the skeletal grin of bared teeth and veined orbs protruding from the skull, Eddie succumbed totally to his hysteria. He squeezed the trigger, again and again, rapid-fire, but the only sound was the metallic click of the hammer as it struck the chambered, empty shells. The creature still stood, though wavering unsteadily.

Eddie's terror finally allowed him to grasp a splinter of rational thought. He had his chance to get away. He began to fight against the grasping hold the snow held on him.

The arms of the creature stopped their convulsive shudder, and they drooped to its side. The shoulders slumped, and it collapsed to the ground, falling slowly as if it were still fighting for life. When it came to rest, the limbs were buckled awkwardly underneath it.

Eddie's breath trembled in a great gush of relief. At last he found the balance to push himself up, and it was several seconds before he was able to tear his eyes off the fallen creature and look toward the movement, toward the slanting trunk and the hanging branches. There was another figure walking toward him. It was all unclear. His mind was confused. Benny?

No, Christ, no. It was the guard. My God, it was the guard. How could it be?

Eddie turned square toward Jack, his eyes widening with disbelief. Slowly the realization turned solid. In a reflex move he raised the pistol and pulled the trigger, over and over, only to hear the hollow click of empty brass. He was coming at him, and Eddie twisted the gun to use as a club.

Jack lunged with the knife and Eddie swatted him in the arm and knocked the knife to the ground. Before he could reach for it, Eddie jumped at him, and they both dropped to the snow.

They grappled with each other, flailing blindly with their hands, reaching for a grip, trying to strike, to strangle, to injure however they could. Eddie had dropped the empty pistol when he fell on top of Jack and tried to pin the guard with his weight. He held the advantage not in size, but in energy reserves. Despite the adrenaline surge, Jack was weak, and as they wrestled, it was all he could do to defend himself.

Their wrestling carried them over the snow as they pushed and rolled. The snow caked in the folds of their clothes and clung to their hair. Jack's face turned sideways, and Eddie ground it into the gritty surface. The cold and the crystals cut like glass. He jammed his elbow into Eddie's chest and knocked him off.

Then they were back at each other, face to face, arms locked in arms. Jack could feel a surprising strength ripple through Eddie's body. He was lithe, athletic, and it was all he could do to match him. At another time, not drained by injury and ordeal, Jack would be able to overpower him. But now he lacked that extra reserve, and in Eddie's face he could see Eddie had a little more.

The stubbled cheeks shone a gleaming red, as much from some inchoate ferocity as from his exertion. It was a febrile rage that burned in Eddie's face, and it radiated a murderous, lecherous villainy. It was the same malevolent loathing he had seen that day in the hallway when Eddie, a beaten pulp on the floor, had grasped Jack's shirt with an agility he was surprised he still controlled and vowed he would get to Marion, someday, at any cost. It was the same madness Jack had sensed at the moment of the takeover as he escaped into the tunnels with Eddie's curse echoing all around him in the rock tube. It seemed so long ago, with all that had intervened, but the look in Eddie's face made it all rush back, and made the danger seem never more imminent.

Jack tried to lever his shoulder against the snow to bring

himself up, to twist from Eddie's hold. He fought with his greatest effort for Marion, to prevent this beast from approaching her, from getting anywhere near her. He lost all concern for his own survival. Whatever happened, this Eddie Hyland must die.

Eddie resisted, and he could feel himself winning. Their arms broke free, and Jack struck him in the head. But it was a glancing blow, without effect. Eddie pitched his flattened hands hard into the guard's chest, just below his neck. Jack's head snapped back, and Eddie rolled. He came back and kneed him in the stomach. The moment was his. He had him! It was a sweet moment, of revenge and power and domination.

Eddie looked past the guard to where the knife lay in the snow. He started toward it, but Jack had him by the waist.

With a monumental effort Jack spun him back to the ground, beside him. They both started to scramble, trying to push themselves up. Jack's legs were twisted. His frozen left limb was like an anchor, cementing him in place. He couldn't move as fast as Eddie.

Hyland was to his feet while Jack was on all fours. He kicked him in the side, and Jack went down again. Eddie swung his foot again, even harder. Jack caught the boot and twisted. The inmate flipped in the air and fell flat on his face.

Jack rolled again to his knees and was able to climb off the frozen, sharp-edged surface. As he did, Eddie scrambled forward on his knees, then stood and faced Jack.

He held the knife. Goddamn, he had the knife. And in his face Jack could see the glint of a smile. He had the advantage, and he knew it. He sensed Jack's weakness; he sensed the battle was near its culmination.

Eddie's lips curled like the underbelly of a snake. "Where is she, Jack Cooke?" he asked.

Jack watched him, trying to concentrate just on the knife, trying not to fall into the trap.

"I've come for her. Surely she knows I've been coming."

The knife, and only the knife, he thought as it flexed in the other man's hand.

"She's just up there, isn't she?"

"You're not getting near her."

"Oh," he laughed. "The noble husband. You forget,

Noble Husband, she wants me. She's wanted me for a long time."

Jack moved sideways as Eddie did, keeping him in front. The knife was held in the same position, away from the body.

"You're not protecting her. You're protecting yourself. You're protecting yourself from seeing me with her."

Jack took his eyes off the knife and cemented them on Eddie's eyes.

"You can't stand the thought of what it'll be like. The only thing you hate worse than your failure with her is admitting it, is having to face that failure, of watching someone else satisfy her as you only could dream to do."

Jack stepped forward, and the knife came up.

"Come on, come on," he taunted, beckoning him with his other hand.

Jack settled into his hunched position. That's what he wants, he thought. Just relax. He'll come. And watch the knife.

Eddie broke into a harsh laugh. It was a sound ragged with derision and disdain. He held no respect for his quarry, and that, Jack thought, was the leveling factor. He would have only one chance to use it against him. "Whatever happens, you're stopping here. I don't even care if your friends pass, but you're not getting close to Marion."

Eddie smiled, stepping closer, moving in. "She's calling me, Noble Husband. Can't you hear?"

Jack tried to stay limber, ready for his move. "You're not getting by," he said.

"You going to stop me?" He sidled closer, within range. "You're dead, Jack. You're not stopping anybody."

The knife. Concentrate on the knife.

Eddie's hand ripped forward, slashing at his chest. Jack bent away, sucking in his lungs. Then he came at him. Eddie lunged with the knife, but it appeared in slow motion. Jack saw it all. He caught his hand at the wrist and pulled him forward, twisting his arm at the same time.

Eddie howled as he was spun past Jack, and his arm was yanked up his back. The knife came loose. Jack balanced on his bad leg and kicked Eddie square in the middle of the back, and he was vaulted forward, toward the trees. Off balance, he fell.

Eddie sailed toward the ground, but he didn't reach it. His scream was cut short, dissolving into a gargling, gasping sound. His head snapped back and his entire body bounced as if he were a marionette on elastic lines. Jack recoiled from the sight, the sound.

Eddie's neck had snagged on the fishline. Three hooks had torn with the weight of his fall into his skin. His arms flailed impotently, reaching for the ground, for support to ease the pull. His fingers could barely touch, and as he struggled, the barbs took a sterner hold, tearing at life-critical veins.

Jack could only watch in horror. The rapid bubbling noise in Eddie's throat grew sluggish as if his blood were becoming less viscous, choking off his breathing. He gagged and coughed, and in time he drowned in his own blood. It was over.

Jack didn't stay to watch, to revel, to drink of his relief. The noise of the other machines was still in the air, and now that he listened, they seemed to be converging. Drawn to the gunfire, they were pulling together. Following the signal.

Jack climbed under the sagging line and walked back up the trench, past Eddie's snowmobile that had sputtered out, past their cave, and finally to the cleft. Philip was still there, but only in the physical sense of the word. He was kneeling by the rock wall, now half-built, and crying. Jack stopped and felt a knot tighten in his throat, not for Emma, but for Philip. At last he had his private moment of sorrow, when the events swirling around him passed him by. It was like it should have been, and Jack was not going to interrupt.

He walked toward the lake and called for Marion. In a few minutes she and Ricky appeared, followed by Lummer. He told them briefly what happened and then said, "You and Ricky will take the snowmobile, and we'll follow behind."

"I'm staying with you," Ricky declared.

"You're going on the snowmobile with your mother, and if we can, we'll squeeze Philip on as well."

"What about the gun?" Marion said.

"It was out of ammunition," then he paused, thinking. "But they must be carrying more. I'll have to check." He said it with a reluctant catch in his voice. The thought of searching those two bodies was not a pleasant one.

"I'll go, Dad. I'll get the gun."

"No." It was an angry command, and it startled Ricky. Then Jack's voice became softer, "You help Philip with the stone, and, Marion, I think you'd better go to him too. He needs something."

Lummer said he'd go with Jack, and he followed him through the mine to the slanted trunk, then under the fish-line. As Jack went for the revolver lying in the snow Lummer went to Hyland still dangling by his neck from the line and in his left coat pocket found a box of shells. "Let me see the pistol," he said.

Jack hesitated, eyeing Lummer critically. Lummer wasn't returning the gaze. Instead, he stared away from his face down at the gun in Jack's hand. In the distance the sound of the snowmobiles had merged, and Jack could tell they were following the track of Eddie Hyland. The moment of indecision passed, and Jack handed him the revolver. "Come on," he said. "Let's get back to the others."

"You go on. I'll check the other guy for weapons."

Jack looked at the body lying crumpled on the snow, then said okay and turned to rejoin Philip. When he reached the cleft, Philip had collected himself and now was hurrying to finish his job. Ricky was handing him the stones, and Philip was wedging them into place. There wasn't much of a gap left to fill.

Jack joined them, working with Philip, cementing the wall in faster between them. Jack had only worked in two rocks when he heard the snowmobile engine roar, then sputter and die. He turned and saw Lummer astraddle the machine, trying to get it started. "Not yet," he shouted. "Keep that thing off."

But Lummer didn't even look in his direction. He fired the motor again, and it roared to life. He twisted the throttle hard—too hard—and it screeched a deafening howl that ricocheted from wall to wall of the narrow trench. Jack yelled at Lummer, but he couldn't even hear himself over the roar.

Lummer jerked it into gear, and the tread lurched the machine forward. At first Jack's reaction had been one of anger, that Lummer stupidly was firing up the engine too early, giving the inmates a beacon to follow before they were ready to leave. But then it struck him. He's leaving. My God, he's taking the machine for himself!

Lummer spurted along the foot trail toward the lake. It revved high, and when he shifted out of first gear, the machine momentarily glided without power. Jack turned from the cleft and stepped toward the middle of the mine. When the gears caught, Lummer jerked forward and the machine gained speed rapidly.

"Jack, watch out!" Marion cried. But he was too intent on Lummer to listen. The son of a bitch, he thought. He's not getting out of here.

Jack stood directly in Lummer's path, but the doctor didn't slow down. The bastard curled low over the handlebars, maintaining his speed. Jack steeled himself for the chance to leap on the driver. Just as he had planned it before, for Eddie.

"Jack! Please!" Marion shrieked.

Lummer weaved the machine to the side, banking off the steep drift. Jack lunged, falling on Lummer's back, then rolling off. He hit the padded rear of the bench seat, felt the upraised back cushion smack into his side, and then he was in the air.

The snowmobile jerked back into the trail and continued toward the lake. Jack hit the snow, rolled, and brought himself to his feet in one motion. He looked toward the machine, clenching his fists in angry futility.

Lummer shifted without a hitch into the next gear, and his snowmobile shot out of the mine trench and onto the surface of the frozen lake. Left in his wake, Jack could only watch in disbelief, in anger, in utter frustration. He should have known what Lummer was going to do. *He should have known.*

"Jack. We've got to hurry." Marion was at his side.

The machine's ugly sputter, its ratchety hacking, trailed behind as if the sound had taken the shape of thorny vines twisting and slashing and cutting at him. The noise decreased as Lummer pulled away, until the sound whined a high-pitched lament, a feeble apology, an empty expression of regret.

"We've done all right on our own so far. We'll do all right now." Philip's voice was strong and convincing. There was no trace of his emotional breakdown. He was as he had always been.

Jack did not even try to disguise his defeat, his resignation. He had felt with Eddie Hyland gone things would change. He had unconsciously allowed himself to feel that the danger from the inmates had passed, that it was Scales alone that they would have to battle to survive, and survive they would.

But that unspoken confidence had crashed. Staring at Philip, he had the look of a long-distance runner who had run and run but could run no more. The finish line had been suddenly snatched away.

In the distance he could hear the sound of the inmates, getting closer, pushing what now seemed their inevitable meeting up earlier. Why go on, why fight it, push to the limits and endure the pain when in the end it didn't make any difference?

It was a bitter feeling, Jack felt, a sense of being cheated, a sense of losing after the ultimate sacrifices had been paid. It just wasn't fair.

33

"He took the revolver," Jack said.

"It wouldn't help. They outgun us anyway." Philip watched his friend in suspense. They needed him, if they were to have a chance.

"I'll get the shoes," Ricky said. "We'll be ready to go in a few minutes."

Jack looked up toward Tardif. He nodded, his eyes telling him the weakness had passed. Philip smiled, then turned back to the wall. A few more stones, and it was finished. Emma was gone, absorbed into Scales, and for the moment at least, there was no emotion from Philip.

They began to strap on their snowshoes. Marion was ready first, and she looked back toward the opposite end of the gorge. She didn't have a clear view of the two bodies, but she thought of them, lying there in the snow.

Somehow it just didn't seem right. "What about them? The two back on the snow?"

Jack stopped what he was doing, but it was Philip who answered. "They'll slow up the wolves."

They fell into single file, following the tracks of Lummer's snowmobile out of the mine, onto the lake, and directly across its flat expanse. In the open, the sound of pursuit seemed clearer, stronger, and more resolved. There could be no lagging behind. No stopping to rest. The last can of fruit had been eaten for breakfast, and outside of a couple chocolate squares, there was no more food. No more source of heat to ward off the cold.

Lake Minong received its name from the Algonquin word for the wild blueberries, a ground-hugging bush that dominated the flats south of the lake. It was a wide-open area, and walking across it they would be exposed and vulnerable. For a while, they would be able to be seen from the far shore of the lake where the mine was. Their only real chance was to move fast, to cross the flats and make it to the safety of the dense woods. There they could buy more time. Another night.

But it was the bogs that the blueberries thrived upon. It was the widest peat field on the island, and it stretched down the center of the valley like the stripe on a skunk's back.

The acrid, whiskylike odor was strong when they reached the shore. They paused there, reading the land, the scent in the air, planning what to do. "We'll follow the tread of the snowmobile," Philip said at last.

Jack followed the track with his eyes until it disappeared beyond a gentle rise 150 yards away. Then he glanced back toward the narrow cut in the rock on the opposite shore. "If we stick to that trail, it'll lead the others directly to us."

"They'll see us eventually anyway, if they come over here. The worst thing facing us right now is the fires. At least we can be sure that if the snowmobile made it, we can too."

The logic was inescapable, and they resumed their trek. They followed the track Lummer left behind, moving always deeper onto the mantle of the peat.

Ike Suomi stood at the window in his living room, staring out at the absolute peace that enveloped his house. It was what he liked about living in the North; it was why he chose to build where he did. But it was a lonely place. The isolation at times had its effect on him, especially in winter when there was little work to be had.

Since he lived alone, his self-doubt had no adversary but himself. And at times, that was the weakest of competition.

There was a scratching at the door, an impatient, gnawing sound, Spud's insistent demand. The dog whined, a kind of singsong lament that ended in a loud bark. Suomi left his window and opened the door for him. Spud hadn't been out long, but the cold was too severe. He curled on the floor next to the iron fireplace and began licking his paws.

Suomi was tense. It was after twelve o'clock, and he hadn't eaten a thing. He couldn't eat, he couldn't do anything but think about the island, about Scales, about Poiret. When's he going to call? He wasn't due until later, but Suomi couldn't wait. He had a suspicion, just one of many, but it worried him. Poiret wouldn't put up for long with the treatment he had received over there. He wouldn't take it one more day. Suomi dialed the airfield.

It was a long ring. Finny answered, winded and irritated.

"This is Suomi. Any word from Poiret?"

"He's got a couple hours yet. I told you that."

"I know, I just thought maybe he got back early. Listen, any contact with him at all?"

"No."

"Could you try to raise him?"

"Hey, I'm busy. And you know damn well I'm not going to ask him to give you a hop to Scales." Finny was talking fast, his voice rising. "No, sir. I get enough of his bad side as it is."

Suomi relented. "Have him call then, when he gets in."

"Yeah, yeah."

"It's important."

"Okay. I will. All right?"

Suomi said okay and hung up. He was left alone in the quiet, with nothing to do but wait. And think about what was happening over on that island.

The flats had their gentle rises and dips over and in between snow-covered spines of rock that stretched laterally through the valley. There were sparse stands of trees that thrived on the peat, then died when a new beaver dam saturated the soil, drowning the roots. The middle stripe of the island, the broadest and deepest expanse of the peat, was open and flat only in comparison to the rest of Scales. But to Philip Tardif, it could have been a barren tundra because there was no place to hide, and no good place for shelter. And it was burning.

Over the packed trail of the snowmobile their feet did not sink into the surface at all, and they were able to move fast. The only time they stopped was to tighten the babiche. The moosehide lacing of the snowshoes fashioned in the cabin had stretched until it was like walking on a miniature trampoline. Philip wove some twigs between the babiche, stretching it taut.

As they finished relashing the shoes to their feet, Jack studied the trail as it wound along and over humps of snow, skirting as much as possible pockets of peat that were cupped in the hollows of the rock. "Where do you think he's going?"

"He doesn't know," Philip said. "He's just going."

"At least he's trying to stay on the high ground."

"Ready," Ricky said, and they resumed their walk. The cold made the air as dry as the Sahara, and the canteen was passed frequently. Jack scooped up handfuls of snow to conserve the water for the others.

The trail rose over a hummock, and to the northwest toward the splaying end of Scales, there was an open view of a meadow. They were all struck by the sight, by the open scars that blemished the white plain. There were three craters, open lesions to the raw wounds below, each with black ash sullying the lip.

The fire was no longer hiding from them. It was an unnerving sight, and imaginations conjured the horror of one of these craters opening suddenly below their feet. The fire was smoldering everywhere, devouring the island.

There was no smoke from the craters. There was only the smell, that oily, acrid odor that tingled like a sulfuric cloud inside the nostrils.

They pushed on, following the safety of the treaded track, moving at an agonizing pace toward Blackstone Ridge. The last of the food, the chocolate cubes, they divided and shared. Each savored the sweet, thick taste as long as he or she could.

The trail rolled and weaved, pushing always farther across the treacherous mantle of snow. The pathway ahead came to a straight stretch, and Jack tried to read it. In the mono-light he could see no contours, and it was hard to tell if the snow ahead was flat or rising. He could tell only that the trail seemed to end, as it would disappearing over a hill. And yet there appeared to be no hill.

As he continued his approach, Jack fell out of the rhythm of the trail. The others noted what he did as they came closer. Finally Jack stopped them where they were. "Stay here," he said, moving on himself.

"Be careful, Jack," Philip warned.

He walked carefully, his feet losing their trust of the solid feel below him. He became aware of the snow's most minute give, and his knees became less steady because of it.

For the first time, he noticed that there was no sound. The trailing whine of Lummer's machine no longer polluted the air, and he realized it hadn't for some time.

There was a hole in the surface, he could see for sure, and the track of the snowmobile led directly into it. It was a jagged tear about fifteen feet long and no more than four feet wide. It appeared that when it collapsed beneath him, the machine sailed forward, lengthening the slit in the snow.

The closer Jack came, the more he was aware of a new sound. It carried a constant tone, not unlike the distant buzz they had been following, but it had a quality that was distinct. It was a weaker, more haunting sound. It was the sound of pain and it was this tone that hovered above the hole like carrion birds soaring in lazy circles.

Jack inched closer to the rim. The nose of the snowmobile was buried in ash up to the windshield, and the rest of the machine was nearly submerged. The bench seat angled upward, and part of the tail was exposed. Lying parallel to the seat was Dr. Neil Lummer. He was halfway between lying flat and on his side. His left arm was exposed, and his face was just barely protruding from the ash, his chin thrust forward like a man neck deep in water. He appeared as though buried in black snow, drift that rather than falling from the air came up from the underside of Scales.

Lummer was the source of the haunting, wavering sound. He was moaning, and his voice was coarse and raspy from maintaining his constant pitch for so long. His eyes fluttered, then suddenly locked on Jack, and he stared in shock, as if he didn't believe what he saw.

Jack was as still, but his stillness was one of indecision, and guilt. He felt a peculiar need to help the man, not for Lummer's sake, but for his. Something in Lummer Jack shared, and it shamed him. By all rights he should turn away, leave him to the fate he chose, but that whisper of shame kept him where he was.

"Help me," Lummer rasped. His face was sweaty and streaked black with ash that melted like snow on his skin.

"Jack?" Marion had approached to within twenty feet.

"Stay back," he said quickly.

"Look to the edges, under the lip," Philip said. "Can we go around it?"

Jack neither checked to see if he could determine the spread of the fire nor responded to Philip. "He's still alive," is all he said.

The way he said it, it sounded as though he were going to rescue him. "Jack," Marion force-whispered in disbelief. "You can't mean to risk yourself!"

He had killed once already, Jack thought. No matter it was in self-defense, no matter the man had some unspeakable horror in mind for Marion. Killing does something to the soul of a just man. It makes him regret the deed no matter how just the act. The regret had weighed on him during the walk from Minong. Not the who or why, just the simple fact of the killing. It was easy to say it had been right. It was another thing to try to alter that sick feeling in his gut over which he commanded no easy control.

"Ooh," Lummer moaned. "Please, please help me." There was no acknowledgment of what he had done, no expression of regret, not because he wouldn't if he thought it would help him, but because so overwhelming was the suffering that he could think of only one thing: getting out. Ending the pain. The burning. The slow roasting of his flesh.

One of the blankets was wrapped like a gunbelt over Jack's shoulder. He lifted it over his head, then lay on his belly and inched his face over the edge of the pit. The stench came immediately stronger, as though something solid filled his nasal cavities, increasing the pressure in his forehead. It was the acrid, oily smell of the peat, but there was also the smell of burning rubber, and then over that something else. It was an undefinable odor, a sweet yet charred smell.

Jack felt hands grasping his feet. Below him, Lummer tried to move, but by struggling only sank farther, kicking up ash and making him choke.

Jack flung the end of the rolled blanket toward him. Lummer's eyes gaped as he struggled to reach the lifeline. He rolled, coughing, bringing his right arm up from beneath him. It was raw and black, appearing as though his skin had turned inside out. The nylon had melted into shriveled veins that ribboned over his burnt flesh.

Lummer couldn't reach the blanket, and his hand groped blindly for anything solid to prevent him from sinking. He grabbed the handlebars and pulled. But it was of no help. The entire machine tilted, then rolled toward him. Lummer screamed in his hoarse way, his hand pulling harder, riding over the top of the snowmobile desperately trying to keep above it. He coughed as a cloud of ash thickened in the subterranean chamber.

Jack started to call for him to reach again for the blanket, but the ash choked in his throat as well, his words dying in a spasm of hacking coughs.

Lummer had rolled to his back, and all that was visible were his face and his right arm, groping for a hold on the machine. But still it turned.

There was a new smell. Through the ash Jack distinguished a sharp, piercing odor. The fear struck before the realization of what it was.

He turned back toward Marion and Philip and Ricky. "Get back," he shouted. "Gas!"

The three hit the snow and covered their faces. As they did, an explosion erupted from the pit with a deafening blast. The deep yellow and black of a gasoline fireball rocketed skyward. It was a billowing, seething mass of fire, the flames held tight to the ball by the draft. Even with their eyes shielded, the flare was a red glow. The ground shook, and the tumultuous crash of the explosion seemed centered directly inside their skulls, so loud and devastating was its force. They were stunned.

Marion propped herself up on her elbows. She could see Jack curled on his side, his knees bent to his chest in a fetal position. Beyond him a black column rose straight from the narrow slit in the snow. It mushroomed over them, darkening the sky. She looked behind her toward

Ricky. He was climbing to his feet with a stunned look. Philip was sitting, with his hands a half foot in front of his face. She couldn't hear him, yet she could read his lips. "My eyes," he was saying. "Help him," she said to Ricky, yet the sound seemed only vibrations in her throat.

Then she turned back toward her husband. He hadn't moved. "Jack," she screamed, but it was like yelling in a vacuum. There was no sound to her ears. The blast reverberated in her head, drowning out all hearing.

She struggled to her feet and moved to Jack. His features were clenched, the skin at the corners of his eyes wrinkled in tight folds. It was as if he recoiled from a continuing explosion, grimacing to the echo of it in his head. She grabbed his shoulders and tried to pull him out of his clench. He resisted the force, fighting to keep himself in a ball.

Already the ash was drifting down upon them. Marion coughed. The air was getting thick. She tugged hard on his shoulder, rolling him to his back. But it wasn't until he had to wheeze for breath that he opened his eyes.

She couldn't hear herself, and she doubted if he could hear her, but Marion cried out his name anyway. She told him to get up. The ash!

He could only stare at her in shock. He began to gag, and as if infected with the same convulsions, Marion began to shake with gasps for air. She gave up on trying to break through to him. They would suffocate, right there on the snow. She had to pull him out.

Marion grabbed Jack by the ankle and began to pull. His clench had relaxed, but the racking coughs for breath provided their own resistance. Marion felt it too, in her lungs, the desperate need for air. She dragged Jack away from the brink of the pit, sliding him on his back in the snowmobile trench. Ash poured upon them like some awful, defiled snow. It thickened in her nose, collected in her mouth. Fine particles of soot filled her lungs. She coughed, feeling lightheaded, ready to lose consciousness.

Over her shoulder she could see Ricky leading Philip out of the cloud. With him as a beacon, as encouragement, she staggered backward, dragging Jack. Her throat was raw, but gradually she could feel the chiller air. It was getting clearer. Easier to breathe. Her lungs pumped furiously for relief.

The cloud grew less dense. Jack's convulsions stopped fighting her.

"Mom." She could see the word form in Ricky's mouth. He came to her and took one of Jack's legs. Quickly they dragged him further from the pit, from the settling cloud of ash.

Reuker heard the roar crackle in the crisp air, and he turned just in time to see the fireball boil up out of the forest. At the height of its leap the ball suddenly opened, spilling its fire in all directions, then it turned black as it flamed out. The roar became muted, an angry rumble as if bits and pieces of it had snagged on the tips of trees and were being released at gradual intervals.

It was a stunning sight, an awesome spectacle of power and fury that bolted Reuker to immobility. It was a display of incarnate evil he had seen many times in his dreams, he had often felt in the hot, swirling, acidic air around him. It was at last turning solid, coming out of the murky depths where shadows tempted only to flicker into night when he came close.

It was a sign. A sign directed to him alone. Despite its show of force, it was an indication of weakness, a childish tantrum belching toward the sky. Framed by the pervasive color of the snow, the evil was but a tiny blemish.

In the cloud he saw the haloed face, the round-rimmed eyes, the fat-faced boy. In its smoke and ash he saw all the disparate faces of the evil that had haunted and tortured him, had seared his flesh, had pounded at the back of his neck until he lost consciousness, had eaten directly into his core. As the cloud mushroomed, all the elements churned and billowed and mixed together.

Though he had seen its fire, the full force of its burning effect, he had not felt it. At least at this moment he felt strong, and excited. A bubbling euphoria percolated in his veins, bringing a rapturous lightness to his head. He sensed that the time was near.

They were there. Vulnerable. Waiting for him.

When they were clear of the cloud, Marion sat heavily on the snow. She brought handfuls of it to her face, wiping the grit from her eyes. She took snow in her mouth then spit black saliva. Jack rolled to his knees and balanced on all fours, clearing his throat and mouth as well. The roar in Marion's ears diminished until she could hear a croaking echo. "Philip can't see," Ricky said.

"You help your father," Marion told him, then she went to Tardif. She cleaned his face and held snow over his eyes. As the burning relented, he brushed the snow away. Slowly his sight returned, but he had to squint as if a bright sun were glaring off the icescape.

Twenty minutes passed before they were able to shake the effects of the concussion. They remained shaky, but there was no time to recover, and this was not the place. They had to get off the flats and find shelter.

"Are they still coming?" Jack asked Ricky.

"I can't tell, Dad. My ears—"

It was the same for all of them. There was a sourceless buzz that made it impossible to tell if the sound of the machine still hovered in the distance. But logic told them it must.

Philip stood and looked in the direction they had come, his hand shading his eyes. "Do you think they found their friends?"

"They must have, if they were on the same track."

"Maybe then that stopped them."

"Maybe," Jack said, but his tone declared he couldn't believe that. The inmates had come too far to give up.

The cold was settling in them, and it was beginning to snow. They had to move. Jack fashioned a staff from a branch and took the lead, plunging it into the snow in front of him as he went. It made their earlier trek seem a fast-paced jaunt, but they had no choice. The peat was under every step.

Ike Suomi couldn't get out of his mind what Poiret had said at the Black Bear Inn on Saturday. His reaction to the changes at Scales was simple and direct. He was angry, and Poiret was the type of man who knew only one response to a challenge: confrontation. If he saw the mailbags still on the snow, Suomi figured, Poiret would have done something about it on his own. And that would have been at least an hour and a half ago. It was now shortly after two.

Ike again dialed the airfield. Finny's voice was short and clipped when he answered. Suomi asked, "How can

I get in contact with the people Poiret deals with at the airport in Marquette?"

"What for?"

"I thought maybe I could catch Poiret there."

There was a pause, then, "Haven't you heard?"

"Heard? Heard what? I was waiting to hear from you."

"I'm sorry, you're right. It's just been so hectic here."

"Why? What's happened?" Suomi felt a sudden spiking of dread, a queer feeling of prophecies come true.

"He's gone down."

Suomi was stunned. He couldn't speak.

"He was overdue at Marquette, and they called Scales, and it was reported he had actually been in and out early. The radio contact said he watched the plane head west over the lake. And that means only one place he could be."

Reacting against the initial shock, Suomi's mind came alive. He was thinking fast, assembling suspicion with fact. "No last word from Poiret? No last call?"

"No, nothing but what they got from Scales."

"What could have happened to make him lose it?"

"The weather looks like it's going to break, so the Coast Guard thinks he was caught in a sudden squall. Me, I say the damn cold just froze his engine solid in midstroke, and he plunked straight down like a rock."

"Is anything being done?"

"Hell, yes. The Coast Guard's putting their tub on the prowl, and their one chopper is already in the air covering the lane between Scales and Marquette. I'm going up myself, in a bit. I've called around but just about everybody's plane is on blocks. I did get MacGregor in the Soo, God bless him. You can always count on the Canucks."

Suomi spoke evenly, trying to control the rising passion in his voice. "Now listen to me, Finny. You're going to be looking in the wrong place. He didn't go down in the lake. He never left Scales."

"You think so, eh?"

"Damn it, Finny. They're searching in the wrong place."

"What's good enough for the Coast Guard's good enough for me. There's just nobody we can spare to check Scales. It's three hours' flying time from Grayling's air base and its helicopters, and by then it would be too dark. If Poiret's got a chance, we have to find him now."

"Look on the island!" Suomi shouted, but he wasn't sure if his last call was heard. The receiver went dead.

Caught within the frantic rush of his own thoughts, Suomi dialed the sheriff. When he got Dobbins on the line, he started where he left off with Finny. He was too loud, and talked too fast, but damn it, they just wouldn't listen.

Dobbins reacted to Suomi by talking slower, calmer, in an exaggerated, folksy manner. He was used to dealing with excited people in his job, and he knew his words had to soothe as much as inform. "As a matter of fact, Ike, I was just talking to Lansing, about the plane crash. I thought about what you said the other day, so I asked them about it. I asked if there was anything wrong up there, on the island. They said nope, not a thing."

Suomi listened. It was no use trying to convince him. His mind was set.

Dobbins continued his comfortable manner. "You're seeing the devil in every shadow, Ike. Why don't we both just relax a bit and give the Coast Guard a chance to do its job."

"How long before they give up? Before they decide to check Scales?"

"Oh, I don't know. The *Edmund Fitzgerald* went down in those waters and it took them five years to find her. And that was a thousand-foot ship."

After they hung up, Suomi's frustration gave way to anger. There was one more place to call. It was time to end the charade.

He switched on the power for the radio, and immediately the empty-aired static sparked in the speakers. He switched to transmit, and the electronic snarl evaporated. "Scales, this is Mainland. Do you read? Over."

He waited and listened, and the hissing, crackling static filled the room, surrounded him, then seemed to enter him directly. His nerves sparked with the same erratic clicks and snaps of the open channel, and it all fed his anger.

The vehemence was undisguised in his voice. "Scales. This is Mainland. Come in."

The three snowmobiles had raced through the forest, past the red snow, through low-hanging branches brushed clean of clinging drift. The machines strained like dogs on a hunt that had finally detected the scent. They streaked down the embankment into the Minong Mines, following the tracks of Eddie Hyland.

Their moment of discovery, of victory, was quickly dashed at the sight of the bodies. For Reuker Stilkes, vibrant memories flooded him of other faces, of other bare-eyed stares of penultimate terror. His own blood at the sight he felt quicken. Benny's corpse was the clearest indication his sacrament was not out of reach. It was a demon's face, the same as the crook-fingered creatures of Rebecca's haunting.

Reuker left the others to their sicknesses, their dread, their trembling hysterics, and he walked under the fish-line, past the snow cave to the shore of Lake Minong. It was while he was standing there that he saw the fireball. It was his sign that the cleansing was at hand.

Before him was a world of cold, not fire; of perfection, unmarred by the devil's stain. He was close to entering that world, letting himself dissolve into its goodness the same as the smoke and fire dissolved into the atmosphere.

But he was not yet in that world. He remained outside, his cleansing remaining but an elusive promise. And it burned, like always, it burned.

The mushroom cloud had settled, and Reuker's burgeoning sense that his fulfillment had already begun settled as well. He felt the sting of the frigid air pricking his face. His eye burned, and he turned and walked back into the mine. The others had moved near the shelter dug into the drift, leaving the two bodies where they were, one still snagged on the hooks, the other crumpled on the snow.

They argued over what to do, and finally, recognizing the evening pall that threatened, they decided to settle in for the night. They had come prepared for that, having found the first cave the day before.

There was still an hour, maybe two, of enough light to travel, but there was little stomach for it. The who and why of the chase lagged in significance to the grisly discovery at the mine. For some, the fire of revenge had gone out. For Reuker Stilkes, his own fire never burned hotter.

Ross Nyze was alone in the control center at Scales. The radio speakers whooshed with a far-off wind sound, the words like barbs on a whip.

"Scales. This is Mainland. Come in."

Nyze felt the sting of the lash, the unyielding nature of the demand. The jittering uncertainty he had known before, years before, came suddenly alive, crackling through his nerves, sparking a conflicting array of signals, of emotions, of feelings. It was the same uncertainty, the same nervous tension that had been reawakened a few days before, after the mutiny began, since he had found himself in the control center as the touchstone of the new Scales to the mainland.

Four years before, the pressure of the family, the job, the constant demands, the failing responsibilities, inched him inexorably closer to his own destruction, until he did the only thing he could that would save him. It had been a horrible experience of pain and mental agony until he had struck back at the responsibilities, at the source of the responsibilities.

In the radio room he was the sole contact to the outside. The entire mutiny depended on him. When Marquette had called earlier, and asked about the mail plane, he had listened to what they wanted and had been able to fend them off. He told them the plane had left, he had watched it sky above the trees and bank westward. They said they were going to begin a search of the route his craft would have followed. They signed off, he had succeeded, but the nervousness continued to build. What do they know? And now came the disembodied voice again, with new demands, with a more blatant insistence.

Nyze felt a rawness in his throat—acid rising from a tormented stomach. It was not his choice to assume this role. It had been thrust upon him by the others, the inmates, the new masters of Scales.

Damn them! Damn them all. Why did they lay him bare to the agony that would surely come from the relentless demands? What manner of sadistic pleasure did they derive by placing him here, vulnerable to the pain, the wrenching, twisting torture that contorted his gut as it throbbed with merciless blows in his head? Why were they trying to kill him?

"Scales! This is Mainland. Answer, damn it!"

The voice wouldn't go away. It had kept coming at him, lashing his bare soul for a seeming eternity. He had to stop it. His hand trembled with a vibration that shook his entire arm. He guided it toward the microphone, to its cold, columnar steel.

"Respond, damn you. I'm telling you to acknowledge."

He squeezed the bar, and the static broke. The channel was open.

Suomi listened, and several seconds passed before the voice crackled through the static at his end. It was a howl from a crypt, a moan from a derelict building. It was his response, clear and according to procedure, but somehow carrying the unmistakable tone of madness.

It silenced him momentarily, but Suomi recovered. "I don't know who you are or how you have accomplished what you have. But I know what has happened, and I am coming."

Suomi listened, and the air was dead of voice. The silence was the most certain of confirmations he could have heard. He transmitted again. "You'll pay. If anyone has been hurt, so help me you'll pay."

Suomi listened to the static, waiting for the voice, for a denial, for anything. But there was only silence, the eerie melody of the static. It was a formless sound, and as he listened, it gathered substance and structure of its own, as if becoming a living entity with its own purpose and intelligence. It was as if a force had been set in motion and now couldn't be stopped.

Ross Nyze grabbed his head with both hands, trying to crush the cacophony of noise that pounded in his brain. They know! The people on the outside know what has happened. They have discovered the secret through him.

The beating tumult of psychic pain pushed Nyze closer to a state of mind he had felt only once before. And like that time, four years earlier, he wanted to die, he wanted to bring the agony to an end.

Nyze picked up the rifle that was leaning in a corner of the room. He chambered a round, then walked through the double-barred gate, to the stairs, then down the three flights to the tunnel.

Ash had marred the snow fully 300 feet from the explosion crater. That much ash meant to Philip it had been a deep fire that had smoldered and eaten the peat for many months, more than enough time for other underground fires to spread to virtually any part of the vale.

With Jack testing the snow with the staff, their progress

was slow. But eventually they made it out of the flats, the stripe of mostly open country that stretched down the center of the island, and into the dense uplands. They followed a moose trail as it coursed over a hidden vein of rock, and where there appeared to be a protected gully with drifted snow, they decided to make camp.

The gully wasn't the perfect natural protection of the mine, and the snow hadn't collected as neatly in a large, mounded pile. It was sculpted from above by the wind and below by the contour of the rock, and it was deeper in some places than others. They had to dig two caves, with the sleeping bench in each sideways to the rock.

Jack was exhausted and settled in one of the caves to rest. While Marion and Ricky collected dead branches for a fire, Philip followed the moose trail away from the gully. With fishline and hooks he was going to make a snare and set it for small game.

He came to a clearing and started across it, his eyes peeled for the signs of rabbit or fox. He was alone, and there was no one else to point out to him the disturbance in the snow, to warn him of what appeared to be a sinkhole in the surface. As he neared, he first saw the prints. They were large canines, and the prints had left the snow trampled in a circular pattern. The pack had come from the opposite side of the clearing, Philip could see.

It was then he noticed the sinkhole. A fire pit? He approached closer, tentatively sliding his snowshoes forward before putting his entire weight on them. About a foot below the snow was a half-devoured moose carcass. Tardif brushed off the dusting of snow that had been falling. He saw that most of the exposed meat had been wrenched from the carcass, but underneath the meat was relatively untouched. The kill was fresh, and he knew that the wolves would be back. He would have to work fast.

He had carried the two parts of the broken shovel, and holding the blade he cleared away the snow from around the rump of the animal. He dug a trench around its rear quarters and began to scoop out the snow from underneath its groundside haunch. Even half devoured, the beast was too heavy to lift. His only hope was to hack off, twist off, a chunk of its meat.

With the shaft of the shovel he picked at the snow/ice conglomerate. It chipped easily, but it was a slow task, and he tired. The sweat accumulated under his jacket, and he unzipped his collar. He should rest, he should limit the perspiration, but the anticipation of the food, for himself and the others, was strong. He worked faster, oblivious to the dangerous moistening of his clothes, chopping at the ice, hurrying to complete his task before the pack returned.

The bottom hind leg was free, and Philip grabbed it around its back-jointed knee and pulled. It remained firm. He tried again, jerking at the leg, putting his weight behind the effort. Finally the entire haunch moved, then it cracked where the thigh had moved in the creature's natural gait.

Along this break in the meat, Philip began to saw with his knife. He was in an awkward position, below the surface of the snow, and because of that did not see the movement in the trees at the other side of the clearing.

His breath came in bursts of exertion as he forced the blade deeper, guiding it into the fold of the animal. When he reached the bone, he began to carve around the joint.

The wolves closed in. Philip dropped his knife onto the snow and stood at the rear of the moose. The meat was cut to the bone, and he began to twist the leg, to break it from the thigh joint. It was a massive animal, but he worked on it, twisting it back and forth, gradually breaking the hold of the cartilage, until at last the haunch cracked free.

Philip thumped the meaty thigh on the snow and sat next to it to rest. As he sat there, he studied the tracks in the snow, and he thought of how it resembled the trampled area around the spot where Huxley had been attacked and devoured. He felt a chill waft down his open throat where the cold penetrated to sweat-soaked clothes. The wolves were fanning out to circle around him when he first became aware they were there.

Tardif turned rigid as he stared at the pack. Were they real, or was this a haunting from his vision of Huxley's death? Slowly he rose, and the scene did not change. The wolves were real; and they were preparing to attack. They had come to protect their kill.

Keeping his eye on the wolves, Philip slipped his knife and the shovel blade into his pocket. Then he hoisted the moose thigh and slung it over his shoulder. In his right hand he carried the smoke-blackened iron shaft. He started to back away from the moose.

With a snarl from the largest male the pack quickened its pace and closed the circle around him. Tardif paused, weighing the situation, then he turned in the direction of the shelter and took a step forward. The largest of the wolves stood in his path and gave no ground. Its ears flattened to the sides, and its lips curled upward baring its teeth in an angry snarl.

The wolf's eyes locked on Philip's, and it was the same cunning, the same intelligence he had perceived in the gaze of the wolf at Huxley's kill. It was a different wolf and another pack, to be sure, but they shared a communion of spirit that shone with frightening clarity in its eyes. Their commonality of motive this singleness of fierce expression, was the reflection of their one imperative: survival. He was prey, and he had violated their kill. To survive, the wolves had to defend their food to the death.

As the quiet sound of paws on snow approached from behind, Philip was locked on the wolf's stare. He saw anger and rage, but not madness. The wolf was in complete control.

Ross Nyze emerged from the dim light and stark shadows of the tunnel spur and stepped into the connecting hub of the subterranean network. His eyes were the mirrors of an automaton, powered by violence, guided by something far outside the realm of rationality.

An echo of footsteps clicked in the hub. Nyze looked nervously from one gaping tunnel entrance to another. The clacking of heels on hardened floor betrayed no direction—it seemed to be coming from everywhere. Nyze ran to near the center, then spun around. The sound of walking stopped, and a voice called.

Nyze narrowed the direction and turned to face it, stepping back against a wall. He brought the rifle to the ready and braced it against his waist. The echo resumed.

From one of the tunnel spurs two men appeared. Nyze aimed and fired, dropping one of the men. The blast cracked off the rock, sounding like a full platoon's volley of rifle fire. The other inmate stared in shock and disbelief at Nyze, then to his friend.

The rifle was chambered, and the inmate turned to run, but as he did he was spun around on his heels by the impact of the second bullet. He fell to the floor, and Nyze approached, firing point-blank into the writhing form.

He felt a glimmer of hope, a tiny pulse of returned power. The confusing array of images and sounds vying for dominance within his mind momentarily abated. The confusion was still there, but it was settling, becoming more solid. Through it all an urgent demand beat with precision: Survive!

Nyze moved as if instinctively guided toward one of the tunnels. It was a familiar path he had been led through many times before. At the end of the corridor was the tubular staircase, and he ascended it two steps at a time. He burst through the door into another hall. To the left he turned. His muscles were steeled by that driving impulse within, but his lungs could not deny the effects of his exertion, his excitement. They pounded in his chest, calling furiously for air.

The hall opened into a broad, well-lit room with a pool table, a TV, scattered chairs. There were other people—a number of other people. He had to survive!

One man saw Nyze and started to get up from his chair. Bracing himself against the wall, Nyze fired, and the figure was knocked backward over the chair by the impact of the bullet. He chambered the rifle and aimed at another and fired. A second inmate dropped.

There was an outbreak of confusion, of men moving in all directions. Nyze fired again, but the shot ricocheted in a puff of cement dust. The bolt of the rifle slid expertly forward then back again, but the report of a different weapon came before he could squeeze the trigger. Nyze was slammed against the wall. Another shot, another strike. From a different direction another gun fired, and in seconds a fusillade of fire was directed toward him. His body buffeted against the wall, defying gravity by the force of the bullets, until finally he slumped to the floor.

The moment of terror lingered though the gunfire had died. Each man clutched his weapon wondering why. What was Nyze's purpose? Or was he responding in his own way to urges all of them had felt, and feared? Would it happen again, with somebody else in this room? Each man looked into himself and wondered if it would be he, unable to defuse the increasing deterioration in his mind, a state all of them knew well.

As Ross Nyze's blank eyes stared lifelessly at the ceiling, there was a common feeling that spread on unspoken whispers throughout the room: Their world was falling around them.

In the wolf's eyes, if detached from the outward countenance of beastly rage, there was an emotionless neutrality to its gaze. It was a creature of one instinct, of survival, and for that end it was an efficient machine.

Philip shifted the load of the moose haunch on his shoulders, then took a step forward. The wolf's gravelly snarl flared into a full growl. Philip answered. "I'm coming through. Just back out of my way and let me pass."

The wolf gave no ground. Tardif started walking forward, each step a carefully gauged maneuver. "You've got the moose, or an islandful to choose from. You won't miss this piece of meat." He talked soothingly, as much directed at himself as the wolves.

The alpha male in front of him began to sidewind back and forth. Out of the corner of his eye Philip saw one of the others dart toward him. He turned and yelled, "Back," waving the iron shovel handle at it with just enough bravado to reinforce instinctual fears. The wolf retreated. Philip continued to walk forward, the pack now moving with him, but closing in steadily, testing him.

He heard a heaviness of paws behind, and he spun about. A wolf was charging. He clubbed it across the side, and it pulled back. Another was on him from the other side. Its jaws clamped on his thigh, and its legs angled back as it tugged. Tardif swung down with his full strength, catching the beast square on the skull. It yelped, collapsed, then stumbled out of his range.

Philip shouted an inarticulate cry, the war holler of a battle-crazed infantryman, and he thumped forward with all the speed he could muster. The alpha male scooted to the side, and Philip was out of the circle. He continued running and yelling until he reached the edge of the clearing, where he stopped and looked back.

The wolves stood and watched, some with teeth still bared, others suddenly placid. The alpha glanced at the moose kill, then back toward Philip. Their cache was protected. It gazed at Philip with an undefeated, challenging stare. It appeared as though thinking, absorbing what had happened. It had learned from the encounter, and the knowledge would help it the next time.

The scavenger turned with his load of meat and left the

wolves. He moved to rejoin the other intruders, foreigners in this structured world where reasoned savagery is the law, and wanton compulsion a thing unknown.

34

The meat thawed slowly over the fire, and as sections of it warmed, Philip sliced them off and began cooking each individually. Ricky never dreamed moose could taste so good. For all of them, it was one of the finest meals they ever had.

They split into pairs and crawled into the two snow caves, each sleeping shelf covered by half of the remaining moosehide from the cabin. There was one blanket to share in each shelter, and that plus the ten-inch walls would keep the sleeping bearable. Though the air inside was above freezing, the body was still called upon to produce greater than normal heat to maintain constant temperature, and the meat had been a critical replenishment of their reserves.

Marion and Jack were lying on their sides facing each other. A length of her blond hair curled from under her hood and snaked across her cheek. Jack pulled off his glove and gently tucked the wispy strands of hair under the wolf ruff, then he allowed himself to touch her cheek, luxuriating in its softness.

She kissed his fingertips, then curled her head into his shoulder. "Are you afraid?" she whispered in the language of the bedroom. She felt Jack's head nod, then she continued. "I'm worried that after all this we've been through, after all the suffering, we might end up the same as if we hadn't taken a step outside the Facility." Jack's arms looped around her back. It was a comforting hold she was slipping into. "That wouldn't be right, after all this."

Jack hugged her to his chest. As he thought of their chances, Emma's sacrifice came to mind, and he was unable to say anything of comfort to Marion. Laying on the bed of ice, with his wife in his arms, he was as though suspended in time. He felt a strong mix of love and shame.

"Will all of this have been worth it?"

"You will survive this thing, Marion. You and Ricky. I promise you that."

"And you?" she said, pulling her head back. "You believe you will, don't you?"

Jack squeezed her tightly, bringing her face to his shoulder.

She waited for him to answer, but he did not. She sensed the insecurity in his grip. "Honey, what's wrong?"

It took a few moments for him to be able to put it into words. And when he did, the feelings gushed from him. "I tried to tell myself that the reason I felt guilty about Emma was because I let an older lady sacrifice her life for me. But that's not the real reason." Marion tried to bend back, to look into his face, but Jack squeezed tighter. "When you woke me up this morning and said she was gone, I was . . . I was glad." He said it as though with disbelief, a disbelief that had come only later, upon reflection. "My first thought was we'd move faster. We'd be safer. I felt if she was dead it would make it easier on us, on you, on Ricky."

Marion felt the emotion beginning to convulse in his chest. She let the silence linger, then said, "You can't be blamed for what you think. Thoughts like that are unconscious and come to all of us. We're all concerned at the bottom for ourselves. What is important is you didn't act on those thoughts. You discarded them. You helped her and you wanted her to live. That was a conscious act, not an uncontrolled flicker in your mind."

Jack became calmer, not because of her comfort, but as if icy realization froze his emotions. "You don't understand. When Lummer had talked of the Eskimos, I was silent, and I kept thinking that he was right. I thought that because of her we did run a greater risk of being caught by the inmates."

"But you pulled her on the litter till you were ready to drop. You did everything you could to help her."

"But I didn't *tell* her. I didn't say to her, 'I want you

to live. We need you. We love you.' And I think I worked hard only to show her what a burden she was."

"Oh, Jack. Oh Jack, Jack, Jack. You're so wrong. You're the most caring man there is and ever was. The most loving, the most selfless. And only because you are that way you torture yourself now. Your grief comes out as guilt, but that's all it is. Grief.

"We are all sad for Emma, and for Philip. But there was nothing any of us could have done to change things." Marion had forced her head back from Jack and now was propped on an arm looking intently down at him. "*Please* believe that."

Jack absorbed what she said, thinking silently. It was the inmates who had sparked the revolt, it was the system that created the situation, and it was Eddie Hyland and the others with their own, hidden obsessions who had pursued them to near-exhaustion.

"It was Emma's decision to go out onto the ice, and it took courage to make that decision. To say she felt unwanted and did it out of despair denies and disparages the courage she possessed. It was her decision, and she was a saint. Don't render her or her death any less than that."

In the opalescent glow of the snow cave, edges became indistinct creating the impression of shape rather than the image itself. It was an artist's light, and in that medium Jack sensed the intensity of her expression, and he sensed the truth in what she said. "She was a brave woman," Jack said.

Marion settled into his arms, dissolving into a blur as she came close. "I love you," she said.

"And I love you."

Several minutes passed before Marion brought her mouth to his. Their lips brushed, and an electric tingle ignited a dormant flame. They came together in a lengthy kiss, and the initial spark became a steadier source of heat. It thawed memories frozen by the ordeal, the constant state of danger, by a pervasive dread that overwhelmed all other feelings. Even the expression of their love had been subordinated to the fears and concerns and anxieties. Now with the kiss, with the gentle affirmation of their devotion, their love had found its release.

The embrace wound tighter, and it was a wondrous feeling, lying there, bodies meshed, minds unburdened. Forgotten during the wilderness trek—and even before, since the night Eddie Hyland caused something to come between them—had been how easy it was to peel away tensions by losing themselves in each other's arms. But that awareness came rushing back as Jack's kiss searched the softness of her face, tasting the salt of her sweat, feeling the cleft of her eyes.

Under the wool blanket, in their down jackets, in the insulated cave, they were warm, and within each a special heat kindled the warmth higher. Passion is a potent force of its own, oblivious to events, unflinching to dangers and consequences. They succumbed to its powerful draw.

Marion touched Jack gently, almost shyly, "Can we manage?"

It was difficult, side by side and stingy with removal of clothes, but they managed. There was no rush, no urgency, and at last, Jack was inside her.

They rested, and in the dim glow Jack could see her eyes wide on his; her face radiated innocence. She said, "Did we do it?"

It was what the eighteen-year-old girl she had been had asked him that night on the Grand Sable Dunes under the northern lights. Then, it had been an earnest question that revealed her selfless hope for his fulfillment, as much as it did her inexperience. Now, it was a reminder of that first time, of a commitment that had never wavered over their fourteen years.

As they moved against each other, slowly, deliberately, the corner of Jack's eye moistened, and he felt a tear roll across his cheek. There were joy and contentment, to be sure, but in addition to that there was a sadness, a feeling that it was all coming to an end. It was as if he realized this was the last time they would ever make love.

In the morning the sky was blue for the first time in days, and Jack forgot about the sad premonition from the night before. But at the time there had been a certain belief in the truth of the realization, and this truth would hang in the air as the ice fog had hung every other morning but this one.

The sun had yet to rise above Greenstone, and the valley was a shadowed bowl, as if the darkness were heavier than air and had sunk into and filled the depression. Still, it was clear and crisp.

Ricky built a fire in the gully. "Some Bullwinkle?" he

said to his father, holding out a chunk of meat.

Jack smiled. "Yeah. I'll take some of that moose."

"I've got a good feeling today," Marion said. "I think things are going to break right for us. Something has to be happening back at the Facility by now, and sooner or later those residents chasing us are going to give up."

Philip laughed. "That's the kind of talk I like to hear. Let's hope you're right. We'll get to Blackstone Ridge today and once we do, I've got a plan. You folks are going to head right up it—it's steeper than Greenstone, and their machines can't handle it—while I'm going to make a track north."

"By yourself?" Marion asked.

"No." Jack was emphatic. "We can't let you do that."

"Listen. I'll be able to lead them to somewhere they'll never get out. That land gets wilder out there, if you can believe it, and I know it like the back of my hand."

"There's no need for that, Philip," Marion said. "We've outrun them and we'll continue to stay out front. We can all be saved."

"Saved? For what? Emma was—" Philip looked quickly away from Marion, toward the snow, as if the bitterness that had leaked out was something he should be ashamed of. He reassumed control, and his voice became friendly, reassuring. "Oh, I'll survive this thing. You can be sure of that. Matter of fact, I'll be better off without you guys, gimpy leg"—he indicated Jack—"and all. Ricky, have you learned enough to take care of your parents?"

"Yes."

"Good. I'll check you on that on the mainland."

Ricky looked nervously to his father. He didn't know how to react, but he did know he didn't want Philip to leave them.

"We can't let you do that, Philip," Jack said. "We'll all head up Blackstone."

"If I do, we'll all be like sitting ducks on the clear face to a guy with a good rifle. We'll need something to throw them off, and that something is me."

"We'll just have to take our chances, together, as we have. That's the only way."

Philip stared noncommittally, the look of a man holding the high card. It was up to him, not Jack, to decide when to play it. He stood. "Maybe today's the day they've given up. Maybe we won't hear the machines following our trail."

Jack could tell Philip didn't believe that. But there was nothing else to be said, at least for now. They gathered the moosehide halves, the blankets, divided the meat, then they strapped on their snowshoes.

There was a few inches of new snow, and when the sun rose above the ridge, the many-faceted light fluff sparkled like a field of cut gems. It wasn't until they'd been ploughing through it for an hour that they heard the far-off whine that had become so familiar. By this time Jack had long forgotten his premonition from the night before. He was thinking of Philip and how he wasn't going to let him sacrifice himself as Emma had.

They walked in single file, taking turns breaking trail, with Jack in the lead followed by Tardif, Marion, and then Ricky. They were moving into a rugged upland that in summertime would reveal protruding slants of the ancient basalt, cocked at the 45-degree angle of the Lake Superior syncline. There were trees, but the terrain couldn't support the dense forest as it existed elsewhere on the island.

They came to one of the bowls cradled amid low-slung spines of rock. A winter-dry streambed was at the high end, and to their right was where a succession of prehistoric beaver dams had blocked the runoff. Mosses and organic debris had collected in the pond, eventually to leave a dry pocket of peat after the beavers gave up the area, letting the water run its natural course.

Under the snow the peat was on fire, eating with the minute crawl of its slow combustion downward and to the sides. Its pattern of burn created overhanging shelves that eventually would topple into the cavity below. But the shelves could last a long while, kept in place partly by the four-inch layer of duff. It was a tough layer of soil, matted with roots that even without underneath support could resist collapse from pressure above.

Jack led them along the edge of the flat area. The center of it was open without a single tree. If they had studied the surface, they may have noticed elongated rumples in the snow where tree trunks had collapsed through earlier cover. But none of them noticed that, and with the endless snow of Scales, any holes had long been covered and the scars rounded off.

The compression of the snow and the springy lacing of

the shoes created a cushionlike effect to their walk. With every step there was a little give, and Jack had come to expect it. So when he led the others into the bowl, and the snow gave a little under his feet, he did not notice anything different.

Behind him Philip didn't notice it either, even though it became a little more pronounced. The snow had compressed under their weight, leaving the duff to absorb most of the pressure. Marion followed.

She looked to her right over the flat, protected area, and it appeared so beautiful, so peaceful. She was still filled with her earlier optimism about this day being a turning point in their struggle. There was still the acrid smell, but that was everywhere. There was no smoke because peat fires burn so slow, and with almost total combustion, they give off none. Her feet slid forward, one after the other. It had been a long trek, but Marion was confident it was coming to an end.

The ground under her seemed to give. It wasn't the slow compression of the snow, but rather the weightless drop of failing support. It dropped a few inches so suddenly, it caused her body to lurch. When her next step landed, she sank even farther. She looked to her feet and saw a fissure opening in the snow. She was frozen with disbelief as the snow split silently wider. Then the ramifications came clear. "Ricky. Get back!" It was the first thing she thought to say, and the last, before the snow, the duff, gave completely away and she became weightless, falling with the snow, becoming part of it, drifting downward, yielding to the darkness of the subterranean cavity.

The white turned black as a cloud of ash erupted around her. It was in her face, her mouth, her eyes. Marion coughed, gagging on the swirling, particulate mass. Her eyes stung and were involuntarily kept tightly shut. The ash broke her fall like a cushion, but it greedily drew her into itself. Marion flailed with her arms, but there was nothing of substance to grasp, to stop her descent. It was like quicksand.

Quicksand! She spread her arms and legs flat, as she should do if she had fallen into mire. She came to rest at last, and tried to open her mouth, but her face was covered with the ash, and she gagged on it. She brought a hand to her face and brushed her mouth clear, then her eyes.

She was at the bottom of a pit, ten feet below the surface. To her left she could see that a great mass of snow had been pulled down with her, opening a hole twenty-five feet across. A tree slanted across the sky above her, and Jack was leaning against it. He was calling to her; so was Ricky it appeared. But she couldn't hear. Their words were drowned by the roar.

It was an angry hiss, the sound of a scalding tempest brewing around her. The snow sizzled on the coals sending up a billowing cloud of steam. The fire was so hot the snow instantly vaporized, keeping the dousing effects of water to a minimum.

Jack recoiled from a sudden belch of noxious fumes when he first leaned over the pit. A tamarack, its taproot eaten by the fire and held upright only by the snow and the layer of duff, leaned precariously over the chasm. It was too deep to reach a blanket. He would have to go down.

Jack leaned against the tree and was able to topple it the rest of the way. A tamarack was the only pine to lose its needles in winter, and the trunk fell with a heavy whoosh. Its tip buried into the ash, and its trunk angled back to the lip of the pit.

Breaking the moosehide straps of the snowshoes, Jack tore out of them and began to shinny head first into the hole. It was a skeletal trunk of jagged limbs and sharp twigs, and the entire tree nose-dived deeper into the ash as Jack progressed. The steam wet his brow, and in it were carried suspended particles of grit and ash. The grime collected in his face, and he coughed, trying to clear his mouth. For a second he lost sight of Marion, then his sense of bearings. And the fumes—the gas—caused his mind to flutter with a light-headed dizziness, with a diminishing grasp of reality. It caused him to turn rigid on his rickety perch.

"Dad. You're okay. Keep going," he heard Ricky call to him. So he moved, blindly, downward. It was a boiling inferno he was inching into, and at its core lay Marion. Oh, dear God, why? It was a question that had come frequently over the past few days. Why them? What manner of sin had brought these horrors upon them?

A twig jabbed into the corner of his eye. He swung his arm and cracked the twig away, and even with that motion he could feel the bounce of the entire tree.

It was true, he thought. The disquieting feeling he had

sensed the night before, that awful prickling of dread that told him the tenderness they shared would be lost, that everything was coming to an end, this festering premonition of death was true.

At least it ended for the two of them at the same time. There would be no sorrow, none of Philip's agony. This realization was more a feeling than a distinct thought. His mind was swirling with too many thoughts, with too many images from the past to alight with any sagacity on any one idea.

But the feeling was there, and he took comfort in it. And Ricky would survive. With Philip, he would survive. "Marion," he called.

He heard her say, "Yes." It was more a gasp than a response, and it was followed by a retching cough. Then at last he could see her. She was buried in the ash except for her face, and that was blackened and smudged with soot.

She saw him, he could tell, and their eyes locked. Despite the failing hold on his consciousness, in that brief exchange he felt a lifetime of love. To glimpse each other at this moment was a reprieve. It was a gift. He felt not defeated, but fortunate. All because of being given that look.

He felt certain it would be their last.

Reuker Stilkes was alone. The treaded beast he straddled was the sole machine that had traversed Lake Minong. The other inmates had gone home, victims of a dread that had haunted them throughout the night, of biochemical imbalances that churned a fetid brew within their tormented skulls. Only Reuker was driven by forces beyond the reach of natural phenomena that affected even the minds of the mentally disturbed.

When he set out across the lake, in the furrow of Lummer's snowmobile, his gas tank was still half full. It was enough to take him the entire length of the island three times, though it was a security that mattered little to him. His only concern was the trail, the demons ahead, the fireball that had been in the sky.

Stilkes crossed the flat stripe down the center of the island as if guided by some demented providence, an unholy guardian of craft and person. The burning evil that threatened him had become his ally, keeping him from the island's living ulcers. It was an alliance he would deny, as he pursued his own special purity.

He followed the snowmobile furrow to the crater, then continued in the less distinctive furrow left by the passage of the snowshoed feet. As the trees thickened and the terrain changed, the trail became harder to follow. The three inches of new snow had rounded and disguised the track, so divergent moose trails looked no different from the trail he had been following. He drove slower, sometimes reversing himself, but always returning to the southwest heading, toward the rising face of the ridge.

A sense of expectation began to deepen, as it had before, coming to him at random times like the cross wind-besieged surf of a Great Lakes bay.

There was a design to their pattern of escape. As he pondered that design, trying to see through to its key, the words of the haloed priestess rang in his ears in the familiar, hissing cadence of her voice. "Evil has a clever master. It is wrought with deception and guided by trickery. To best it you must follow my lead, you must see with my eyes, you must . . ." The voice trailed off into oblivion, for the priestess was unholy, and had herself assumed a mantle of deception. Reuker had only himself to guide him.

And yet the warning lingered, and he concentrated on the trickery. He tried to see through to their design. For the first time in years he tried to plan himself. Like it had been in the past, when he had stalked the vessels, he had chosen the time and the place and the manner. He had been in control then, and now, using a cognitive process dormant for seven years, he tried for that same control.

The machine dipped into a gully. Immediately apparent were the charred remains of the campfire. It was a black stain against the white; it was their sign.

Around the fire and leading from the gully the tracks were fresh.

The jeep glided to a stop along the shoulder of the highway. The plow moraine of crusty snow and ice was above the roof of the four-wheel-drive vehicle, and higher than the driver's head after he got out. He swung the door until it made contact with the latch, then pressured it closed. He walked along the shoulder until he came to a drive. It was a narrower gully of snow, carved by the massive steel blades of the plow. He walked into it.

Scrub pines lined both sides; their scraggly branches and bark that peeled like dried scabs made the forest appear more dead than alive. Where the trees abruptly ended, Suomi cautiously climbed the embankment so he could peer over the top.

The airstrip was an oblong white scar amid the jack pine. There were no lights, but instead colored disks were on poles along each side. Some were buried by the snow, but most were not. A wind sock hung from another pole, its bottom touching the snow.

On the far side of the runway were two hangars. One was corrugated dull gray steel, while the other was flat aluminum panels painted alternately red and white. The snow was cleared only in front of the striped hangar.

Directly opposite the two buildings, on Suomi's side of the open field, was a clapboard frame house. It was too far to distinguish anything inside, but he could see a flash of light and dark at one of the windows, as if someone were moving about the room.

Suomi backed off and went to where the trees began. He scaled the embankment and began to cross the end of the airstrip under cover of the pines. He sank in the soft, wind-protected fluff up to his thighs, and moving through it was like wading in mud-thickened water.

When he finally reached the other side, he approached the newer hangar from the back. The only entrance concealed from the house was blocked by the drift. He had no choice but to stage his break-in through the wide aircraft doors facing the house.

He followed the wall to the front of the metal structure, then peered across the field. Suomi could feel a tightness in his chest. The time had come. There was no other way.

He slipped a screwdriver from his pocket and broke from his cover to the center of the broad, sliding doors. He forced the screwdriver under the padlocked latch and struck the handle with the palm of his hand. The metal snapped loose with a crack that rang in the cold stillness.

Suomi was startled by how loud it was, and he turned quickly to look at the house. Nothing had changed.

He grabbed the vertical bar handle and tugged on the door. He slipped through the slit, then brought the yawning opening closed. Feeling the heavy rush of his heart, he leaned back against the door for a moment to calm himself.

Before him was Finny Kuula's plane. It was a four-passenger Piper, the kind of craft Suomi had flown before. But it had been years, and a flutter of panic came suddenly to his stomach. He pushed himself away from his metal brace and stepped to the plane, where he pulled himself into the cockpit and settled in the seat. He sat there and studied the controls, resting his hands on the wheel, then the throttle. He adjusted the tail rudder and looked over his shoulder to see if it moved unobstructed. As he became more familiar with the controls, the rising sense of nervousness over his ability to fly dissipated.

He climbed back to the floor and pulled the airplane as close to the hangar doors as he could. Unmelted snow from Finny's flight the day before slickened the concrete floor.

He opened the hangar exit a slit and looked over toward the house. Satisfied no one was watching, he pulled hard on the metal edge, and the door began to slide open. It rattled and groaned and grew progressively harder to move until it wouldn't budge at all. Suomi glanced at the house, then stooped outside to the leading edge of the door. The night's snow was packed in the runner preventing the door from sliding. Quickly he dropped to his knees and began shoveling it clear with his hands. He had no choice but to leave the door open, and as he brushed the snow clear, he couldn't withhold a nervous glance over his shoulder across the field. There was a flicker of light at the window. Had he seen?

He went to the other side and cleared that runner, then Ed: "went" back inside the hangar. This time the doors opened all the way, but not without an agonizing screech of unoiled friction points.

Suomi hurried into the cockpit and punched the ignition switch. There was a low moan as the engine tried to kick over, then silence as it failed. Sweat was quickly forming under his arms and down the middle of his back. When he tried the ignition again, he eyes were focused directly on the door to the house.

The engine turned over, emitting a throaty growl, but it failed to catch. He tried again. "Come on, come on," he said, tapping the control panel absently with his left hand.

Across the way the door flung open, and Finny stepped out onto the porch. He stood there for a second staring in disbelief, then he disappeared back inside, slamming the door. The engine coughed, sputtered, then died.

He would be coming. There wasn't much time. Suomi tried the ignition again, and the engine hacked and coughed, gasping for life. Suomi kept his hand on the throttle, feeding it gas, cutting back when it sputtered. It held.

He began to rev the engine and tried to kick the plane into motion. But it didn't move. The house door opened, and Finny burst outside, hat on and coat flapping behind him. In his hands he carried his rifle. The motor revved higher, the noise an unbelievable racket clanging inside the hollow building.

Finally it lurched forward, and Suomi guided it toward the center of the runway, directly toward the approaching Finny. The plane jerked around as he reached the middle, and Suomi aimed his craft down the center of the airstrip.

Finny had approached to within twenty-five feet of the plane and could see who was inside. But he didn't care. No one was stealing his plane. He dropped to one knee and raised the butt of the rifle to his shoulder. As the plane slowly began to move forward, he took careful aim.

Suomi opened the throttle full. The plane creaked forward, gathering momentum.

Finny clenched the gun solidly, but in the end he could not bring himself to fire. Damn it all, he thought. The son of a bitch would just crash it up if he got hit. Finny slowly stood and watched as his plane lurched and bounced over the snow.

Then suddenly the craft was airborne, and Suomi was pulling above the trees. In about a minute he was at the shoreline, and Finny's voice howled over the radio that was bracketed on top of the control panel. "Damn you, Suomi. Bring my plane back. You're gonna get yourself killed. And you're going to wreck whatever chance Poiret has. I was going to check the coast from here to Marquette this morning. If he's on land anywhere, that's where he is."

The plane soared over Lake Superior, climbing steadily higher.

"Damn it, Suomi. You'll never make it back from that island."

Suomi switched the radio off and left the Upper Peninsular land mass behind him. The propeller noise was drafted quickly into his wake, and he was left with the rush of the wind. It was a soothing sound, a gentle sound, and at last something was being done. The troublesome uncertainties bred of inaction and not knowing were giving way to a new spirit. He was in control. And he was going to unmask the impostors.

He was to the island in less than half an hour, then he steered his craft along the coastline of Scales, past the Facility, the entrance to the harbor, and then past Gulletston.

Suomi banked out toward the lake, then circled for a direct pass over the Facility. Low to the surface, it came up fast on him. The concertina-topped fences flashed by, then the open yards, and then he had to pull up to go over the rising bank of land and its trees.

He flew over Lake Siskiwit, then circled for another pass of the institution. Barely a hundred feet above the tower, he could see the entire area clearly. No one was outside. There was no sign of an ongoing disturbance. Nothing appeared out of the ordinary.

Suomi made a wide turn to the southeast. He could tell nothing from the air. He was going to have to bring it down.

"Jack! Grab the shoe." It was Philip, from the brink of the pit. "The shoe, Jack. Grab it!"

He looked from Marion back toward the rim of the pit. Philip had lashed Jack's snowshoes together at the ends and was swinging one out toward him. He stared, remaining disoriented. The rush of the fumes, of throat-clogging ash, of the blinding steam had conspired to weaken him, to fuddle his thinking.

"Take the shoe, Dad," Ricky cried. "For Mom. For her to hold."

Of course. For Marion. To haul her out of the pit. He reached back woodenly as though he lacked all coordination, as though any sense of balance had deserted him.

The lower snowshoe swung near him on its hinge, crashed against his knuckles, then swung out of reach. But he had to try again. He reached, and the hinged, moose-laced frame caught in his fingers. Philip released his end, and the ladder swung to Jack.

The coals still spit steam in angry defiance, but the tempest was decreasing. It was coming clear, and with it came a clarity of purpose. And the realization that the abating steam meant whatever dampening effect the snow had on the fire was being lost.

Jack squeezed between two branches and continued his slow crawl down the tamarack.

Marion moaned as though losing consciousness, and her head began to slide sideways. When her mouth touched the ash, she coughed and fought to right herself. Panicky, she flopped her arms, but that only worked her in deeper.

"Don't move," Jack shouted. "Just try to keep your balance. I'm going to pull you out of there."

Her eyes fluttered, and she nodded. Jack had only a few feet to go before he would be at his closest to where she lay. A thick limb protruded directly skyward in front of him. He reached his right hand around and beyond it, then transferred the snowshoes to the leading hand. Then he brought his left arm around the same side and began to snake his body past the branch.

He felt the tree shimmy with the shifting weight. It had moved only a fraction, but it had rolled toward the side he was on.

He tried to control his breathing, as if the tremors of his unsteady breath would topple him into the fire.

"Dad, keep going. You can make it."

Jack inched his fingers along the trunk, sliding his body past the limb. The tree seemed to sense his movement, and it began to roll. Jack crawled faster, fighting the pull of gravity, racing the shifting trunk. As he abandoned the delicacy of his movement, the roll of the tree gathered momentum.

Suddenly his legs were swinging free, and he was falling. Toward the ash, the fire.

"No!" he heard Marion cry out in anguish from below.

He swung one hand around the trunk and grabbed it from the other side. When the tree came to rest, Jack was dangling straight down, his boots in ash to his ankles. He pulled himself up until his head touched the tree, and then he tried to swing an elbow over the top. But it was a nine-inch trunk, and he couldn't reach that far. He had to let himself hang to give himself time to regain his strength.

The tree tip suddenly dived deeper into the ash, and

Jack's leg sank a few more inches. He looked and saw Philip at the very end, ready to descend. "It won't hold," Jack said to him. "If you try it, we'll both go down."

Philip hesitated, nodded okay, and backed off. Jack slowly pulled himself back to the trunk then swung one leg over the tree. It remained stable, and he climbed back on top.

The snowshoes had snagged in twigs, and he freed them, then inched farther down the trunk. When he was near Marion, he lay flat against the tree and dangled the snow-shoe ladder beneath him.

She reached but missed it, and as she did, she turned to her side. Jack could see beyond her the red glare of embers burning faster with the luxury of so much oxygen.

"Try again. You'll reach it this time." As he pulled it back to swing it forward, Marion's face suddenly contorted into a mask of pain and shock. She screamed, "The fire!" It was a cry filled with torment and horror. The hidden fire had reached her!

The frame dropped into the ash right near her face, but she didn't appear to see it. "The frame, Marion. Grab the frame," Jack shouted. She showed no recognition and could only cry out in agony. Jack yelled louder. "The frame is by your shoulder. Take it in your hand."

Her eyes were wide with panic and fear. She searched madly for it, but as she did, she sank deeper into the ash. When her hand at last found the frame, her face was buried. Her fingers twined through the laces.

Jack pulled, and she yanked upward. Her body convulsed with coughing as she spit the ash from her mouth. Jack pulled, but Marion was worse than dead weight, her convulsions trying to wrench the frame from Jack's hands.

Where the treetop was buried in the ash, a flame suddenly burst into life.

Jack reached the lower of the snowshoes. Hand over hand he raised Marion higher, out of the ash. Still choking, she could do nothing but hang on. Halfway down the frame, he was only inches from her wrist. The fire at the tip quickly spread to the dry, needleless twigs, and Jack could feel its heat.

He grabbed her wrist, then let go of the snowshoes, and they fell into the ash. He pulled with a reserve of strength he didn't know he possessed. She came higher, until he had her under the shoulder. She reached to his coat and grabbed hold, and with her climbing and Jack pulling, she was able to scramble up on top of him. He remained steady as she shinnied backward, then turned around.

When Jack raised himself, he was staring into a raging bonfire. It was destroying their bridge, traveling along the upward slant toward them. He twisted his body around, swinging one knee up to the top of the tree. Carefully he pulled the other leg up and began to crawl after Marion back toward the surface.

When Marion reached the lip of the pit, Philip grasped her arm and helped her onto the snow. Jack was behind, squeezing between the branches, racing the fire. But the flames greedily consumed the wood. Near the tip, where it disappeared into the coals, the trunk suddenly snapped, and the rest of the tree dropped, vectoring more steeply toward its base still at the surface.

As the tree sank into the embers, he caught a glimpse of Marion's face, frozen in horror. There would be no lingering farewell.

Then he reached for the spindly branches and began to climb. He scaled the tree in reverse, moving up toward its lower branches.

The ravenous tips of the flames first touched his left leg, the limb frozen of feeling since it had plunged into the icy water a seeming eternity ago. It was fortunate because he didn't feel the heat, the pain. All he could think of was to climb. Closer to the surface, to Marion, and to Philip and Ricky. They were calling for him, reaching for him, until at last he felt their grip.

Philip had one hand, Marion the other. He kicked off the tamarack and was slid onto the snow. Instantly Ricky was smothering his leg with snow, and the fire was out. It never had a chance to spread.

There was no time to relax. "We're still on the edge of the shelf," Philip said. "We've got to move." He was the first up off the snow and began breaking trail. Ricky was right behind him, leaving his mother and father, without snowshoes, to follow in their padded tracks.

Tardif led them along the side of one of the rock spines, then up and over it and on toward Blackstone. He was relentless in his march, moving fast, keeping the pace near what they could bear.

Finally Marion cried out to stop. Her legs sinking into

the drift, her thighs burned with the exertion. And her arm burned from the coals. "I have to rest. Please, stop."

"Not yet," Philip cried. "If the machines were close, they'll be drawn to that fire and its smoke. We have no choice but to keep on."

And they did, pushing their way through the snow, winding through trees, diving deeper into the ceaseless wilderness. It was a time for unconscious control, for lapsing into an automatic state of locomotion, of trying not to think of the pain, the searing call for breath, the weakening reserve of energy. It was a time for one thing only: a time for not giving in, after so much had been suffered.

They forged through the drift, Marion barely noticing when Philip reached a padded moose trail. There was no relief because it only meant that Philip could move faster.

The heavy boots padded tirelessly over the white surface. They were without snowshoes, but because the trail was well packed, they didn't sink up to their thighs in drift. Around and above, a canopy of leafless oak and snow-draped spruce and balsam shielded them from sight. And in a short while, even the fences and buildings of Scales were out of view. Ahead, through the narrow slash in the forest, lay the landing strip of Lake Siskiwit.

Irons carried his pistol in hand, and next to him Ringly's own gun was in his pocket. Trailing them was Richard Smith, a rifle clasped firmly in his outstretched hands. They had moved quickly at the first sight of the airplane and had slipped unnoticed out through the Facility's main entrance. Irons knew the others would find out soon enough about the plane and head out to the airstrip. If they did, he would be as much a target as the intruder.

He had missed his first opportunity to escape the island because he had not been in the Administration Building when the pilot of the mail plane had appeared. Those who had met him saw the pilot and the plane as a threat, and they raced out to the lake and disabled and camouflaged his craft. Irons was disappointed, but he prepared himself for the next plane that sooner or later he knew would surely come.

He realized that their hold over the Facility wouldn't last. Indeed, the forces of despair and innate anxieties threatened to bring down the mutiny even before the outside found them out. He felt certain that the aircraft that had just buzzed the Facility offered his final chance to escape Scales.

Suomi circled for a pass over the length of Lake Siskiwit. The runway, he could see, was narrow and short, and surrounded by trees. He would literally have to drop out of the sky and get his skis on the ice in a hurry. There wasn't much room for error.

He didn't see Poiret's plane, and on his second pass he looked closer. But from the air, staring down at the blank whiteness of the lake surface, he could discern no shadows. He couldn't see the tracks of the skis that led from the end of the runway toward the shore and into the woods.

It seemed so quiet, so peaceful, and there was no sign of the mail plane. Could he have been wrong?

Suomi completed his bank off the southeast tip of the island, and he aligned his plane with the landing strip. He was bringing it down:

The ground rush of the mounded apron became a blur. Then he was above the pines, and it appeared the land had suddenly leaped up to meet him, as if the spiny points of balsam and fir, of spruce and pine were arrows targeted for his craft.

Then the last trees passed just a few feet beneath his skis, and the runway opened up below him. Suomi brought the plane down fast, and it bounced when it first touched the surface. When it settled back on the ice, Suomi cut the power and pulled hard on the flaps.

The wind rushed in a torrent over his craft, and though it slowed, gradually, it seemed to Suomi to be moving faster. It was the effect of being on the ground, he knew, but still he was victim to the illusion.

The runway was a slick track, and the plane seemed to glide like a toboggan going downhill. Suomi felt the tension pull tighter in his chest as the far end of the lake loomed closer. And just beyond the shore was a solid line of trees, black columns that would pulverize the thin metal and fiberglass of his plane.

The skis began to whine at a decreased decibel as the aircraft slowed, but it was still too fast. The plane's flaps were straining for a bite of the air, to grasp a sterner hold.

The rush of the wind diminished. Out the side windows the trunks of trees came gradually out of their indistinct blur until, at last, the aircraft came to rest.

He was nearly at the end of the runway and barely had enough space to taxi the airplane around. When he did, and it was positioned back in the center of the runway ready for lift-off, he climbed out of the cockpit and dropped onto the packed snow. He started to walk toward the far end of the finger lake and the path to the Facility.

Except for the scrunching of the snow under his feet, it was quiet. Everything was white and dreamlike, the bright sun causing a glare that made objects imprecise. It was as though things were lost in a fog, and Suomi had to squint to protect his eyes.

As he moved farther from his plane, deeper into the glare, he sensed an eerie foreboding drumming on muted skins inside his head. There were no sounds of animals, no sounds of the wilderness, no sounds of any kind. It was as though the forest waited and watched, as if it braced for a violent upheaval only it could foresee.

After he had moved about a hundred feet from the plane, Suomi thought he saw movement ahead, where the path entered the lake. He stopped and cupped his hand over his eyes and gazed toward the far shore. He saw nothing, and his inability to determine what had indeed been moving unfettered a gnawing sense of trepidation he had struggled to keep under control. If there was someone there, why would he hide?

It wasn't until he began to creep forward that he saw them. When he stopped again, they came out into the open and stood on the bank. Something just wasn't right, Suomi thought. They weren't welcoming; they weren't offering assistance. They were studying him, as a stalker observes its quarry. Was this how it happened to Poiret?

Cautiously, the three men proceeded down onto the lake surface, and even from that distance Suomi could swear not one of the figures took his eyes off him. They followed packed snow to the center of the runway and began walking toward him.

Suomi knew it wasn't right, but where was Poiret's plane? This was the only place he could have landed, and if he had never left, the plane would still be here.

Suomi scanned quickly the shore in front, then behind him. There was no aircraft. Then he looked back toward his plane, and when he did, he noticed the curving tracks in the snow. They began about halfway between himself and his plane, and curved in a gentle arch to the shore. The bank was low there; the brush was thick.

My God! The plane was there. The fuselage was pulled between the trees and the wings had been battered off. Brush and tree limbs were piled on it and around it, and covering everything was a vast camouflaging sheet of snow.

Suomi looked quickly back toward the three men. They stopped, as if sensing his discovery. He glanced over his shoulder to judge the distance to his plane. He could make it there ahead of them without trouble. As long as the engine fired, he would be safe. As long as they carried no weapons.

Suomi turned and began to hurry back toward the Piper. As he accommodated his footing to the slick surface, he was able to run. He could hear the garbled cry of one of the men calling after him. It was not the query of someone who didn't understand, but a command to halt. He didn't turn to look back. All that mattered was getting to the aircraft in front of him.

The first gunshot rang out when he was still several paces from the plane, and the second as he was climbing inside. The aim was far off the mark, and he heard only the report, not where the bullet struck.

He adjusted the throttle, set the controls. He switched the ignition, and the engine turned over and came unhurriedly, unexcitedly to life. The plane jerked into motion and began to inch forward.

The men were almost at the center point of the lake, halfway to where he was. They stopped their charge, and one of them braced a rifle against his shoulder. The other two appeared to hold handguns.

The rifle bearer recoiled, and even above the sound of the engine Suomi could hear the whiplike crack of the exploding gunpowder. The plane was gathering momentum, moving directly toward them. In that, he had no choice.

There were more shots flying high as the target came toward them. Then suddenly, there was the sound of a bullet striking metal. Then again, the same sound. Suomi slid lower in his seat, peering above the controls just enough to see. Would he feel it if he was struck? Or would it be so sudden there would be no pain? The questions bounced crazily in his mind. The throttle was open full, and the plane fairly bounded over the ice. And still they fired.

The windshield received its first strike, and the glass shattered with the impact. Suomi struck his fist through it so he could see, and tiny cubes of glass showered into his face. Cold air pierced like a knife's edge. The metal and fiberglass rang with the sounds of impacting rounds. He was almost upon them, and still they held their ground, firing point-blank.

Bullets that penetrated the cabin crashed at the back wall, through the side windows, into the padded seat next to him. Then suddenly there was the flash of a shadow, and the side of his face was torn with a searing blow. He had been struck! His vision went blurry, and his grip on the control faltered for a second, and the plane veered. He fought to bring it back in track, to bring clarity to his sight.

At last they had found their mark. But it hadn't penetrated; it had been a glancing blow. And then his thoughts caught up with what he had seen, and he realized that it hadn't been a bullet, but a piece of the windshield anchor dislodged by the force of the wind.

The three men dived to the side, and he was past them. But still they fired, and he could hear the shots striking the fuselage, the wings.

The velocity wasn't enough, and yet the wall of timber ahead rushed toward him. There was nothing he could do but hold it steady, to grasp the controls with his iron grip. But he was running out of space.

He adjusted the flaps for lift, and the plane leaped from the ice as if catapulted from the surface. Then the engine coughed as though it were going to stall, and Suomi could feel it dip. He eased on the upward angle, and the plane steadied itself. Slowly it was climbing.

It rose at an agonizing rate, and the few seconds that elapsed from lift-off to the shore seemed an eternity. He wasn't going to make it!

There was a tug at the underside of the craft as a ski snagged on a bough of balsam. It caught in an angled rod, and as the plane continued to glide upward, following the rise of the ground below, it brushed across the tips of other trees, dislodging a cloud of snow dust that trailed behind the airplane. Then suddenly Suomi was free. The plane soared above the evergreens as the land descended toward the lake. The branch rapped against the underbelly of the fuselage, and then it was torn loose by the rush of the wind, and it floated back to the surface.

He was aware of the smell of fuel immediately after clearing the rise, and he checked the gauge. The needle was fluttering, but there was no way he could tell how fast it was spilling.

As he crossed the Lake Superior shore, Suomi banked toward the south and continued his climb. He took the radio transmitter in his hand and flicked the power on. But there was none. He manipulated the switch, then slammed the radio with the flat of his hand.

It gave not a flicker of response.

35

Marion had been able to keep up with Philip's pace, but only at a sacrifice. Her energy was rapidly depleted, until at last she collapsed. As she lay on the ground, her legs trembled as the muscles gave way to involuntary spasms. She whimpered in defeat, her will to continue the struggle fading fast.

"Take Ricky," she gasped. The peace of just giving up seemed so appealing. "You go on."

"We're going to rest here," Jack said. "You'll be all right with a little rest."

"But the machines?" Their interminable, rasping groan carried in the crispness. Through the multitude of rock gulleys and the innumerable canyons between the trees, the sound came. It could have been a hundred machines. It could be only one.

"We have no choice. None of us can keep this up forever. We have to rest." Jack was not far from collapsing himself.

Philip had walked on ahead. He called from where the trail crested on a rise. "Can you make it this far, Marion?" She looked in his direction. "We'll be better up here."

She looked at Jack, nodded, then struggled to stand. He helped her, and with her arm over his shoulder they came to where Philip was. The old moose trail they had been following continued on a parallel course with Blackstone, following the giant striations of the bedrock, and farther ahead they could see it loop back toward the interior.

"Up there," Philip said, pointing.

They were next to a hump of rock that formed a ten-foot barrier along the trail. Where Philip pointed a break in the wall angled back in the direction they had come. It was a natural stairway in the crevice, and they climbed it to the higher ground above.

"They can't bring their machines up this," Philip said.

"But they can go around, and back."

"It gives us time, Ricky. Another few minutes of time."

They moved away from the edge and against a snowbank. Jack spread out half the moosehide, and with Marion and Ricky he sat down. They cut pieces of the meat they carried and ate. As Philip chewed his portion, he stood on the edge of the rock barrier and studied the moose trail below them as it curved off into the interior.

Marion was almost too tired to eat and was the first to give up on it. She took a drink from the canteen, then lay flat on the hide with her head cradled in Jack's lap. Ricky was curled next to her, and Jack spread the blanket over them. The sun beat directly down from the cloudless sky, and for what the temperature had been, it seemed warm. It was above 20 degrees.

It did not take long for Jack to yield to the same fatigue that overtook Marion. The toll of the ordeal had been high, and his body's machine simply lacked the reserve to stay awake. And there was no need. The rest would help. The sound of the approaching snowmobiles seemed to lessen, and it even took on a rhythmic, soothing tone. Urging him to sleep.

He was aware Philip had been crouching in the snow watching him. Through the descending veil that draped like a dense mist over his thoughts, he heard Philip's voice.

"It has to be this way, Jack."

The voice came to him as would the sight of an apparition in the fog. It was there, but somehow unreal, somehow not touching his sense of reality. Jack had slumped so he was bent over Marion, and in reply to the voice he only nodded.

"I'll be fine. You remember that. And remember where your greatest obligations lie."

Jack was asleep, and what Philip was telling him didn't make sense until he awoke. Almost thirty minutes had slipped by before he was awakened by Ricky.

"Dad. He's gone. Philip's gone!"

He awoke to the same blurred thinking that had been with him as he had fallen asleep.

"Philip is gone!" Ricky shouted again.

And then it came rushing in on him. Philip studying the moose trail. Watching him. What he said. Jack moved to the edge where they had climbed the natural staircase. The snow-covered track that continued past where they were was no longer smooth and untrampled. It showed clearly that someone had passed over it. It showed clearly that Philip had done what he said he was going to do: lay a false track to lead the inmates back into the interior.

Marion stood next to him. All three knew the choices they had. They were above the foot trail and could continue southward, toward the ridge, or they could go inland after Philip. By himself, the woodsman might survive, Jack thought. But Marion wouldn't. Nor Ricky. Nor would he himself. As he stood there and pondered, there really was only one choice, as Philip had known there would be. His greatest obligation was to his wife and son.

They bundled up the moosehide and blanket and headed toward Blackstone. Jack wore Ricky's snowshoes and broke trail. Always the land was inclining upward, until at last they were at the foot of a massive ridge that rose at a steady angle.

For the most part the stunted trees formed a veritable ladder with unequally spaced rungs up the 120-degree slant of the slope. They climbed slowly and rested, so the fear of collapsing was not an imminent one. Yet it was a constant battle.

From where they began the climb, to the crest, was a vertical rise of 450 feet. The steepest part was two-thirds of the way to the top, and at this section no trees could take root. It was the bare face of the ridge, with wind-crusted snow clinging to it like a leathery sheath of scales to a reptile's side. When they reached it, they rested.

"Don't look up," Jack said. "Just concentrate on where you are. On your grip of the ice." Marion nodded, yet her eyes could not be torn from what they would have to climb. "We'll be safe once we reach the trees. At that point we're almost to the top."

Safety, Marion thought. At least for a day. Maybe two. Would the pursuit last that long? When would the siege of the Facility begin? Kneeling on the edge of Blackstone, the dominant feature in a primeval three-billion-year-old land, it was easy to feel forgotten. Cast aside by the rest of the world. Left to freeze and die without notice.

"Let's begin." Jack went first, kicking his foot through the crust of the snow, then putting his weight on the one foot as he stepped up.

Marion and Ricky followed their own line so the hand- and footholds would be stronger and to avoid sharp ice chunks bouncing into their faces. "Be sure of the hold before you put your weight on it," Jack said. "There's no danger that way."

And there wasn't, as long as they went slowly, testing every grip, every toehold. And Marion did, at first, as she scaled the open face. Left hand, right foot, right hand, left foot. Inching upward, moving toward the halfway point, making agonizing progress. It was difficult, like everything else had been, and her breaths came in wheezes. Her hands through the gloves felt numb, plunging into the snow. Her fingers hurt from cracking the crust, and her sense of touch became less sure. But still she pushed on, keeping pace, scaling the white sheet of ice.

She fell into the routine of the movements, and a kind of dizziness came to her. It was a call for more oxygen, a command that her lungs work harder. And they did, her chest expanding and contracting, stretching her parka taut.

"Marion. Slow down."

Her left foot pulled out of its hold and kicked at the snow. The crust cracked, but her boot didn't sink in. It was bare rock, just below the surface. Her weight was already shifting, in the routine motion of her climb. Her toes scraped frantically for a hold, but it was rock. Solid, unyielding rock.

Instinctively she let herself fall toward the inclined surface. It was a reaction of panic, and it was a mistake. She began to slide.

Her fingers clawed at the surface, but that could not stop her.

Jack was calling frantically, in horror, but his voice was lost on the wind, on the rush of the wind by her ears, the rapid pulse of the blood in her temples. She was sliding in full contact with the surface, but when she hit the first tree, it was like it had been a free-fall for the full fifteen feet of her drop.

Her feet hit first and slipped off, and she careened past the tree. Her arms grasped for the trunk, but the force of her weight was too severe. Another tree, and where her arms hit they instantly numbed with the blow. It rolled her sideways, and then suddenly she came to a jarring halt. A tree caught her in the stomach and she was doubled over it.

The wind left her, and she retched for air. The others, she thought, and managed to look. Jack was inching downward. "Stay—"—she forced herself to gasp, but it carried no farther than the trees. Her lungs wheezed, and on a great expulsion of air she cried, "Stay there!"

Jack looked down at her.

"Okay," she gasped. "Okay."

Jack held his position and watched her from above. He told Ricky to keep on, to move to the upper tree line, while he waited. It was a few minutes before Marion uncoupled herself from the crook of the tree. It took that long to catch her breath, to regain any semblance of strength.

It would be easier to give up. To stay where she was. But she knew if she did, Jack would come down for her. And what of Ricky?

She struggled to pull herself to the next tree, then to the uppermost rung of the ladder. The sheer face stretched out before her, and she began the climb again. One foot at a time, alternated with each hand grip. Her entire body seemed a wobbly mass of nerve and unresponsive muscle, and the dizziness returned, but she managed to continue, holding her grip. Pushing herself upward.

Jack could do nothing but offer encouragement, but his

voice was what carried her forward. It swirled in her mind, dulling the competing impulses of pain and fatigue. "You can make it," he said. "We'll all make it. Just a little farther. One step at a time."

Her head throbbed, but she kept moving, her raspy throat kept cycling the dry chill air, and she came closer to where she had slipped. It was as if she were controlled by some outside force, by an instinct to survive that went beyond simple will to live.

Propelled by this inexplicable force, she crept higher. Just above, Jack waited, and above him, Ricky was nearing the tree line and the easier gradient. Against the bald white face of Blackstone, they were clearly discernible—black shadows against a blank screen.

The course the snowmobile laid grew progressively erratic. The trail that led from the gully and the remains of the campfire had been clear, and Stilkes had felt that at last the scent was unshakable. But the sun was bright and growing brighter as it neared its zenith, and the strain on his one good eye was great. The glare obliterated shadows and converted the rumpled track of freshly trod snow into the same blank whiteness that was everywhere.

It wasn't long before Reuker had lost the advantage he had. He circled and was led astray by false leads, and it came to be that even in the shade the glare pursued him. The powder burns on his right eye became matched by a fire in his left. There was a gritty feel in the eye, as if sand were under his lid, and it hurt. The cleansing seemed a distant promise, a taunt from an unsympathetic god. Yet the promise was all he had. His only hope, his only chance.

He guided the machine up a rise. As he neared the crest, the whiteness flared even brighter, and he was forced to close his eyes. But the glare did not vanish. Then suddenly the snowmobile cracked into an object, and Reuker was sailing free. He had driven straight into a sapling, its slender trunk having dissolved into the glare.

The machine careened to a halt, and Reuker plunged a few yards from it into the deep drift. He was buried, and he scrambled frantically, pushing with his arms, trying to force himself out of the snow. But it was weightless fluff, and he only foundered.

The chill entered him through his face where it touched

the snow, and though he continued to struggle, he came to notice the relief the cold brought. The rawness of his eye was eased, and gradually his fight against the snow lessened, until he lay still, letting it work its soothing effect.

After a few minutes Reuker stirred and was able to pull himself out of the drift. Then he forged his way back to his machine and sat on the bench seat.

He slumped over his knees, holding a compress of snow to his eyes. A vibrating nervousness fluttered in his stomach—the unsteady residue of panic—but he was under control. And as the pain of the glare dimmed, the control assumed a greater hold.

Like he had just prior to finding the campfire, and like he had years before as he planned his sacrament and stalked his vessel, Reuker began to think, to plan, to deduce. It was a deception, as the haloed priestess had said. The trails were lies. Their movement was neither circuitous nor random. They had a destination.

Reuker took his hands away from his face and brushed the snow clear. He squinted, and he could see without pain. The only feature that lay ahead was a ridge, as it had during the entire pursuit in the interior. With a calm deduction foreign to a Prolixin-enslaved mind, Stilkes understood their plan. He knew what their evasion would entail.

He stood next to his machine, then climbed atop it, his feet planted squarely on the cushioned bench. They would scale the ridge, hoping to strand the snowmobiles at the foot of its precipitous rise. Their plan was as simple as it was obvious.

Reuker scanned the face of Blackstone, a little more than a mile distant. At first he wasn't sure there was any movement at all, but as he stood atop the snowmobile and squinted and stared, he became certain. He could see the silhouettes of the three climbers clearly outlined against the white face of the ridge.

His eye traced their prospective path to the top, then he followed the crest of Blackstone to the northwest. The ridge gradually declined—the sloping back of the serpent in middive—and he could see that the farther out it stretched, the less steep it became.

Reuker climbed from his perch and straddled the bench seat. He restarted the engine and shifted into gear. No longer dependent on perceived nuances of the trail, he was no longer prey to the deceptions. He was able to unleash the power of the treaded beast, and he drove it fast. He settled onto a longitudinal spine of rock that paralleled Blackstone, and it became his throughway. Rapidly left behind were the false leads that had deceived and tormented and very nearly blinded him. And left completely undiscovered was the carefully laid track of Philip Tardif.

Marion breathed heavily. Only one more step and she could reach the tree line, she could grip the solid feel of the trunk. But the muscles that stretched along the backs of her calves were beginning to tremble, and her feet that were jammed into the ice vibrated up and down like a diver holding his balance while gathering poise for a back flip.

"Just take your time," Jack said. He was a few feet to the right of her. "Rest if you want."

Marion nodded, then let herself lean forward until she lay flat against the sloping surface. She rested, and Jack rested with her. "Just a little more," he said. "Just a little more."

When she began again, she was stronger and able to reach the trees. She grasped the first trunk and dislodged snow, which trickled down into her face. She brushed it away, pulled herself farther up, making new toeholds for her feet. Then she was in the trees.

Ricky was waiting, balanced between a tree and the slope. He smiled, and as he did, that awful, gnawing tension that had become almost like a natural biological function began to lift. It began to lift for all of them. Jack put his hand on Marion's shoulder, saying, "It's not much farther to the crest."

"And it gets easier as we go on," Ricky said.

Marion looked up to Ricky, then beyond him. "We'll be safe up there?"

Jack's fingers squeezed reassurance. "I doubt their machines could scale this cliff. I think we're free of them now."

"And maybe they'll give up?"

"Maybe. Or maybe they'll go back the way they came, back to the cabin, and out Blackstone. But that'll give us a couple days, and from up there we'll be able to see them coming."

"What about Philip?" Ricky said.

"I think he was right when he said he'd be better without us. If they follow his trail, they'll never catch him."

"Let's go," Marion said. "I'm tired of hanging like a bat to the side of this cliff."

Ricky laughed, and they resumed their climb, from trunk to trunk, rung to rung. The gradient lessened until they were able to walk upright, and at last they reached the crest. The trees were sparse and the view unencumbered. It was a majestic scene, and they looked out over their island, where they had traversed. From above, it seemed tame. Like a land different from the one that had challenged and fought and very nearly defeated them.

It was Ricky who noticed it first, and he tugged on his father's arm. He pointed, and Jack looked where his finger aimed. What he saw changed everything, and the tension that had deserted him at the tree line came back. It was as if it had never been gone.

Reuker Stilkes was racing out his thoroughfare, his spine of rock that was Blackstone Ridge in miniature. To lessen the glare, he had wrapped a cloth around his eyes and had cut a slit for his left eye. Peering through it was like peeking through a tiny hole in a wall, or through a crack in a box that encased him. He was in one world, everything else in another.

He was looking from the shadows out into a landscape of whiteness and purity, a world as immaculate and clean as the water of a wilderness stream tumbling airborne over a precipice. The waterfall was visible in his mind, as it always had been, to some extent, since that summer of the first cleansing.

It had been a long time since the sacrament, such a long time, and for Reuker the stench of his own decay was strong.

They were there, the same tormentors were ahead of him, and still they played their taunts, they dangled their lures. But it was they, Reuker had vowed, who would be his vessels. His source of eternal waters for the sacrament, for the cleansing.

The machine's engine shrieked as it was revved to its mechanical limits. When he hit the slightest mound of snow or submerged obstacle, he was airborne, then dropping in a cloud of drift back to the surface.

Propelled by his otherworldly mix of revenge and religion, of soiled virtue and sacrament, Reuker clung with a tenacity bred of madness to the handlebars of the snowmobile. The wind lashed his face with its icy chill, then rushed in an unending torrent past his ears. The sound of the wind was a whistling echo, a fluttering of pages, the passage of time.

Dreams pulsed in flashes of color, and each though it lasted but a few seconds was seen and absorbed by Stilkes. He was not lost in the past experiences, as he had been so many times before when he welcomed their release. Rather, the dreams became part of the present. His memory became one with what was happening around him. The real world blended with fantasy in a way that was neither real nor fantasy, neither truth nor illusion. It was a blend that for Stilkes was fact, as defined and literal as reality was to the sane, as the wilderness was to the wolf.

The flitting images appeared and vanished in time with the rushing spin of the treaded machine, in time with the beating nervousness in his chest. Feeling the tensions of the pursuit and of a race against the deterioration that was consuming him, he saw an earlier time, and an earlier pursuit.

Then, like now, the building evil had driven him to his sacrament. It had been in the city, and it was a cold and rainy night. He remembered stalking and capturing the vessel, and he remembered her fighting him, clawing at his eyes, kicking, scratching, pummeling him with her hands, her elbows, her knees, her feet. As he remembered, he saw clearly. He forced her up the concrete steps, through the old door. His hand was over her mouth, his other arm around her chest from behind.

Still she struggled and kicked, her feet straining against the staircase he pushed her up. She was strong, much stronger than he had imagined, and it took his every reserve to hold her. Then he felt the pain in his hand as she bit him, and she screamed. It was an ungodly noise, a shrieking reverberation that tremoloed up and down every flight of the old hotel. A door opened and slammed. Reuker struck her hard in the back of the head, and the scream halted. To the second floor, then the third. She resisted but was nearly in a daze.

He opened the door to his room. He had left it unlocked. He dragged her inside, and as he closed the door behind him, she came again to life. She screamed, flailing with her arms at his head, his shoulders, his chest.

Stilkes stood there stunned, accepting the blows, covering himself with his arms. Slowly he maneuvered away from the door, and as he did, she lunged for it. Reuker grabbed her shoulder and spun her around, then clubbed her across the face. She turned groggy and slumped to the floor. And as she did, he suddenly felt a great flush of energy and strength. He became almost like her, a limp body more unconscious than alert.

But he had to resist the temptation. The taloned grip of the evil was increasing. He tore a strip from the stained sheet and stuffed it in her mouth. Then he worked fast, before she regained her strength. His own strength he pushed to the limit. There wasn't much time. She groaned, her eyes fluttering.

Reuker secured her hands behind her back, then looped a rope under her arms, then over the upper bar of the bedframe he had earlier set on end on chairs in the high-ceilinged room. She was dead weight, and he strained to raise her, and only slowly did she rise, until at last her feet dangled off the floor.

He tied the rope, then stumbled backward and fell heavily onto the mattress. It was flat on the floor, buttressed up against the wall, and Reuker sat there, reclining against the curving mattress. He was so tired, so much pain. He had to rest. He had to have his strength for the sacrament.

Reuker wanted to move, but he couldn't. He remained where he was, staring at her, at the vessel, his lungs pounding within his bony chest.

The man's uniform was like the others in the room, except that his shirt was white and on his collar was a single gold bar. He used the boxy black phone and dialed the three-digit number for Homicide. Detective Sergeant Aaron Simpson answered.

"Aaron, this is Hayes at the second precinct. Is McDaniel there with you?"

"Yeah."

"Good. I think we may have something on your boy. We just got a call about a guy in the Corridor forcing a

woman into an old hotel. Real violent. Sounds like it might be him."

Simpson signaled McDaniel, who came quickly to his desk. It was cold and rainy. The pattern fit. It was the call they had been waiting for. Simpson asked where it was.

"Off Cass on Pennborough. An old, seedy place."

Simpson repeated the location aloud, and McDaniel nodded.

"We know it. We'll be there."

"I've got one car on the way. The guy's supposed to be on the third floor."

When Simpson hung up the phone, McDaniel was already out the door and on his way to the elevator.

Reuker leaned forward, resting his hands on his knees. The woman was alert, and her eyes wide and fixed on his. He had calmed, and now felt an expectant prickling that enlivened his skin, that brought erect the tiny hairs on the back of his neck. He pulled himself to his feet and began to strip off his clothes. He began to prepare for the sacrament, for the ritual cleansing that would bring purity back to his soul, life back to the seared flesh of his body.

As he dropped his shirt to the floor, the vessel's eyes grew broader still. They were filled with a terror that comprehended nothing but the steely black stare of the man before her. When she saw the knife slip from its sheath, she began to twitch like a tarpon on a line, and she tried to scream. It came out as an unintelligible noise, a muffled sound distinct only in its horror.

Reuker felt a nervous tremor in his chest as he stepped forward. It was the tension of the supplicant, the anxiety of the faithful. "Anything touched by Satan will be his. Those who live under him have his powers, and their touch will leave your soul pitted and blackened and fit only for the eternal fires. The same flames that lap at you now you will feel forever. Forever!"

The voice he heard was clear and loud, and it commanded him. He moved closer, and the terror of the vessel electrified the air. He could hear the gushing voice of the haloed priestess still hissing in the air in its strange and whispered manner. As he had always remembered it, her voice whistled like a kettle on a fire, and as he approached, as he listened, the whining shriek grew louder.

The woman was twitching desperately and now looking

away from him toward the window. As if there were some other terror. As if there were some other hope! Reuker looked, and at last he realized the sound was not Rebecca's haunting whisper. It was a siren. A shrieking call of a police vehicle spun louder and louder in his mind, in the room, in the narrow canyon of decrepit brick and stone of the street. Reuker ran to the window and looked down. A police car with a flashing blue light screeched to a stop. Two officers jumped out. A man in a tattered robe met them, then pointed up. He was pointing at him.

He fell away from the window and braced his back against the wall. He stared at the vessel, and she cried out in her muffled way. He heard the stairs pounding under the rushing steps of the police.

Reuker twisted to the window, then tried to open it. It rose an inch, then wedged itself solidly in the runners. He slipped his fingers in the gap and tugged harder on the old wood, frantically struggling for release. But it stayed jammed. The steps pounded louder, closer.

With his knife he shattered the glass, then swept his forearm over the shards that remained stuck in the putty. The pain was incidental to the black veil that was descending upon him, that was smothering him in a scalding sarcophagus of fiery liquids.

He pushed through to the fire escape, then began running down the steps. The cold steel of the grated stairs dug into his bare flesh, but he didn't slow down. He had no choice. It was cold and burned at the same time, and sitting astraddle the snow machine, having succumbed to the rhythm of the tumultuous roar of the beast he guided, Stilkes could feel again that same pain. He could feel again the tortured agony of the steel grate cutting into the soles of his feet as he pounded down the iron steps. The pain from then was now. The tension of his pursuit was then. He was a timeless creature without a hold on any place or any era.

At the bottom of the fire escape he dropped to the pavement. His bones were brittle in the cold, and the fall seemed to snap something in his ankles, in his knees. But he could not sit and massage away the pain. There was no time.

He started to run down the street and hadn't gone more than a few paces when a second car with a flashing light fishtailed around the corner at the end of the block. He retreated in the other direction, his bare feet slapping on the wet cement, the rain coursing over his naked shoulders and running down his back.

Simpson slammed the brakes, and the car skidded sideways to a halt next to the marked car. He and McDaniel sprang from the vehicle. "Did you see somebody up there? In the lights?"

Before Simpson could answer, they heard a voice shout from above. "He's down there, and he's got a knife."

McDaniel broke toward where they had seen the flash of movement in the headlights. His chest filled with phlegm, and a cough rattled in his throat, but he would not be stopped by it. They were so close. This was their chance.

Past the third door there was a passage between buildings. Too narrow for cars, it wasn't an alley but a walkway to the rear of the buildings, to the back exits. They turned into the black crevice. It was strewn with glass and stank of garbage.

Reuker heard the scuffing of shoes, the echo of pounding steps in the narrow cut between the sheer walls. His legs continued moving as if powered by a force unconnected with himself. His knees felt the jarring of each step, but his feet, his legs had gone numb.

He spun around the building's corner and into the alley. A yawning cavern beckoned. Water from the gutterless roof fell in a ragged curtain over its entrance. He hesitated only a moment, then plunged through the cold water to the darkness beyond. To the dank grotto behind the falls.

McDaniel came around the corner and stopped dead. Simpson was right behind. They looked both ways, and against the light at either end of the alley they saw no movement. No one running. They became quiet and listened.

He was here. Somewhere, he was in the darkness. Their own breath rushed heavy in the stillness, but on top of it, there was the sound of another person breathing. They could hear the air whistling through his nose, and even in the sound of his breathing there was the sound of madness.

In their pause Simpson was able to fish his light from his pocket and turn it on. The beam flashed into the shadows, and tiny, silent creatures scurried from its cone. McDaniel kicked a garbage can lid, and a rat squealed.

The light played on the doors. They were closed. They started to walk forward, weapons drawn, alert for any movement. The rear of a building that fronted the next street had an entrance that was down two steps and indented into the wall. McDaniel nudged his partner, and they approached cautiously.

As they stood safely clear, the light flickered into the dark pit. At the back, flush against a door, stood a being on the brink of humanity's furthest domain. Both detectives were frozen by the sight of the apparition, and they could do little but stare with a collective sense of disbelief and revulsion.

Through the sheet of water his misshapen features seemed distorted all the more. He was more a skeleton than a living person, his face more a pattern of pits and black cavities than even a killer's face should appear. It was a visage torn from the scriptures of the most fanatical sect, the incarnate horror of the most virulent zealot. The creature standing before them was possessed of a madness outside the darkest element of their imaginations.

Even motionless they could sense a savage bent to his mind, an air of evil to his presence. It seemed an inner malice that answered to no reason, that was tempered by no compassion. An atmosphere hung about him the two detectives had to force themselves to enter.

The light was a focused beam, like the brightness that shone in through the slit in the cloth. He was nearly blinded, caught in its glare. But he could hear the voices, the low measured voices, and the careful steps over the broken glass that littered the rock floor.

Reuker braced himself against the wall behind him, as if he were trying to forge a secret passage. The voices, the light came closer.

And then they were at this sides. He could feel their touch. He stiffened, and he felt himself moving. They were maneuvering him around. His hands were drawn together behind his back, and there was a cold, brittle feel. The sharp-clawed talons latched tightly around his wrists. Reuker shivered, and his body lost its tautness, and he felt as though he were caving in. It was with a sense of frustration and despair that he nearly collapsed. His sacrament was torn from him, his cleansing was but a thing of his desire, slipping rapidly from what had been rightfully his. And as it did, he was lapsing deeper into their world. Into their world of pain and suffering and a malevolence so overpowering it consumed everything within its black glow.

He remembered—on his machine racing through the Scales wilderness, he remembered—how that all-consuming evil had over time increased its hold, its suffocating grasp of his soul. He remembered the tiny barred cell they had taken him to that night that stank of filth and the residue of the unclean. He remembered the questions of the police, then later the psychiatrists—each interrogator spinning webs of trickery and deceit, adding to the smothering effect of the dank cloud that clung to him, that grew in density with each passing day. He remembered, and felt the presence of, the courts, the procession of faces, the glares of the crook-fingered demons. He remembered the later confinements, the transfer between facilities, until, finally on the island, he could no longer think. The black cloud was so pervasive it smothered him completely. It was difficult to walk, to speak, to swallow. He had become a breathing organism only, an adjunct to the greater forces that had come to dominate his world.

His fingers locked on the steering mechanism of the snowmobile with a tenacity born of past horrors and of his fear that it all could happen again. Stilkes felt threatened by that same frustration that had gripped him the night he was captured. He feared losing the sacrament he so desperately needed.

The path he followed had angled closer to the ridge. Blackstone was less than half as high as it had been, and its gentle slope presented little more challenge than much of the terrain he had covered in the past few days.

Powered by the terror of his failing chance at the cleansing, by the memory of all those years of fire and pain, by the feel of the accumulated grit and grime that tainted him, he steered off the spine of rock and onto Blackstone Ridge.

The engine roared as he reversed his direction and began heading back toward the figures he had seen clinging to the face of the rock.

They were his vessels, and he was unalterably seized with the necessity of their destruction. And in this destruction would be his renewal.

36

From their crestline aerie, Jack surveyed the open vista below them. The tension he felt when Ricky first pointed it out to him had taken deeper root with the indecision. Suddenly there was a new and dangerous option to consider.

Looking out over Lake Superior, they saw not the usual ragged streamers of foam from breaking waves, not the patternless, continually shifting white lines that appeared the edge of frayed linen. Instead, they saw the reflective glint of the sun off ice. It wasn't the ice of crusted snow, nor the battered and faulted apron that lined the shore. It was a smooth expanse of black glass that stretched as far as they could see.

The frozen lake surface was marred only by the recent snow that collected in crescent drifts like new sand over desert mud. It was an unbroken bridge that appeared to reach clear to the mainland, an alluring temptation to end their ordeal. Yet the risk of an icy death was clear.

"I think we should do it." Ricky was excited and confident. He was hostage to the youthful inability to estimate danger. For him, the choice was obvious.

"We wouldn't reach land until well after dark," Jack said.

"We made it up to the cabin in the middle of the night, and that was a lot harder. This is just plain flat."

Jack shifted away from Ricky to look at Marion. She nodded. The boy was right. That trek on the first night was through thick snow, up an incline. It was more difficult.

Jack paced closer to the edge of the crest, as if a few extra feet would provide a clearer view. "There's got to be open patches of water out there. And how thick can that ice be?"

"The moose made it across. And the wolves. That's how they got here. Over an ice bridge from the mainland, Philip told me. If it could support them, it could support us."

"But that was a different bridge and a different time." Though outwardly he disagreed, inside he felt the same impulse. He was falling victim to that same heady intoxication made of hope and impatience. The alternative was to wait atop Blackstone for another day, another two days, another week. How long, he couldn't be sure, just as he couldn't be sure how long they would survive exposure to the elements.

He turned and looked to Marion. She was ready, he could tell. And at last, for himself the lure of an end to the deprivation, the cold, the pursuit by the inmates, proved too strong to resist. He succumbed to the promise. "Okay," he said, his eyes locked on Marion's. "Let's try it."

She smiled. "It makes sense to at least go down to the ice, to check it."

"Yeah. At least to do that."

The slope of Blackstone down to the shore was a world apart from the precipitous inland rise to the crest. Yet it was steep enough so they could move fast, taking long strides and letting the snow cushion each step. They fell into their own rhythm, and it was a pleasure to move so effortlessly. Things were finally changing for them, they all sensed. The ordeal had lost its harshness, and they were close to beating everything that had been thrown up against them.

Like so many times before, hope outdistanced reality. They were blind to the fact that the danger was never more imminent than at any time since they had escaped the fences and brick of Scales.

They reached the crusty surface of the apron and walked straight out onto it. It was solid, and their footing remained steady even when they came to the faulted mounds of uplifted ice. There were no lake-borne swells rolling underneath, and because of that no sound of water sloshing in protected caves. Prickling against the bare skin of their faces was the hint of a breeze trying to reach them around the windbreak of the island.

A few miles north, on the other side of Blackstone, Philip pushed through heavy drift. He had followed the sound of the machine as it rocketed past him, toward the sloping end of the ridge, and he realized what had happened. He abandoned the track he was laying and headed toward Blackstone. If Tardif had stayed with Jack and Marion, he would have felt the breeze that now touched their faces, and he would have known what that meant. He would have been able to warn them.

Jack stood on the last of the mounds looking down at the beginning span of their bridge. There was a margin of new snow that had blown off the slick surface and caught at the edge of the apron, and beyond that was the ice. Clear, smooth, and delicate.

"It makes sense I go first," Ricky said.

Jack smiled and rubbed his hand across the top of Ricky's head. "Since when did you start thinking your old man always made sense?"

"I'm lighter, though."

"Yes, that's true. So you'll wait here until I say to follow." Jack didn't wait for an answer. He climbed from the apron down to the collected pile of soft snow. The footing was solid. He stepped a few paces to the edge of the new ice line. It was as clear as glass, and looking down at it was like looking through a window. Air bubbles trapped under the surface were the only things that assured him that indeed the water was covered with a layer of ice.

He pushed one foot forward, gradually shifting his weight. Alert for the sounds of cracking ice, he heard none. He stepped fully onto the ice, then walked away from the margin of loose snow. Tiny air bubbles scurried from under his feet from the pressure of his weight, but the ice held secure. He looked back to Marion and Ricky. "We'll be all right. It's good and strong."

They followed him onto the frozen surface of Lake Superior, and together they started toward the mainland. They had moved only a hundred feet from the edge of the apron when Jack stopped suddenly. He was startled and involuntarily reacted to what he saw before him, below the ice.

It was a submerged rock monolith that jutted straight out of the black depths below. Under the water the stone appeared yellowish and could be seen only when almost directly overhead. It was an eerie sight, this bare rock arm reaching out for him, and it made him feel as though he were floating unprotected above a deep chasm. He had to look away to chase the fluttering sense of vertigo, and as they moved past the rock monolith, the unsteadiness lingered.

The sensation produced a chill, a cold prickling along the skin that was intensified by the wind. The breeze was coming from the northwest, paralleling the shore of Scales, and its sting grew as they left behind the protection of the land.

Since the night before, the Arctic high-pressure system that had been sitting over the Great Lakes basin was on the move. It had brought an uncommon stillness that had calmed the great lake, and an extreme cold that allowed the ice bridge to form. But now it was all changing. The pattern of stacked weather cells was unblocked by the end of the series of low-pressure systems spinning out of the Carolinas.

Northwest of the island, in the vast expanse of Lake Superior, great swells had been called up from the surface. Near the farthest extent of the frozen channel at the tip of Scales, where open lake water met thin ice, waves were beginning to erode the edge of the bridge.

The fragile shell was shattering. The ice bridge was breaking apart.

Jack estimated they had moved about two miles from the shore. The sun had passed its midday height, and he figured they had only a few hours of daylight left. From where they were, if they could make steady progress, the mainland was still five to six hours away. But if the sky stayed clear, the stars would give them enough light to see.

The vibrations where they walked were too minute to be noticed. Jack had no way of knowing that the bridge would not last into the night.

Stilkes at first did not see them out on the ice, but he saw the tracks they had left in the snow. He stopped and climbed off his machine, and standing atop the crest of Blackstone he could see the broken trail as it led straight down to the lake. He strained against the glare of the ice until at last he saw them—three tiny figures moving toward the distant band of dark on the horizon.

The complex swirl of thought and dream blared loud a frantic warning: They were escaping. The cleansing would be lost.

Reuker remounted the snowmobile and nudged it into motion. The trail they had left on foot was too steep, and he had to drive along the ridge for several minutes before he found where he could angle down toward the shore. The delay only increased his anxiety.

The tension from his capture was fresh, and the turbulent emotions of then were part of him. He felt the muscle fatigue of the struggle with the vessel, of forcing her up the steps, to the room. The fear of that capture, of being overcome by the evil, vibrated in tremors of terror from the base of his back to his neck.

He fought to control the machine as it surged powerfully through the deep drift. He struggled to keep it moving, and at times he had to travel cross-hill until he found where the gradient decreased. It was a monumental struggle, but there was nothing to cause him to relent. The horrors that faced him, that chased him, fueled his inner drive.

An hour passed from the time he first sighted the figures until he reached the shore. They were six miles out, and he couldn't discern their shapes on the horizon, but he knew they were out there.

The tread bit greedily into the crisp snow of the apron. He guided his machine through the mounded slants of faulted ice, and he neared the flat open expanse of the surface where there were no obstacles. Where there was nothing to deter him.

The constant drumming of his frostbitten foot on the hard surface sent needles of pain up the center of Jack's leg. It grew worse with every step, and he feared that he wouldn't be able to keep the pace. It would be him that dragged them all down.

The frozen membrane they walked across was not as it had appeared, a single smooth sheet of ice. It was ribboned with a patternless network of long cracks that had opened and refrozen a number of times as the ice shelf had established itself. The cracks created a series of jagged shards cut from a larger plate, each irregular section varying from a few hundred feet across to no more than a few yards.

As they walked, the ice made low groaning sounds as it stretched and gave under their weight. It was an eerie noise that traveled along the fault lines, and at first they thought it was the sound of jets just beyond the horizon. But the phantom planes never appeared, and they grew accustomed to the sound and soon tired of looking for the nonexistent source.

They accepted the sound as an aural mirage, and because of that, when the helicopters appeared far to the southeast, they did not perceive them. The UH-1s were miles away on a course from Grand Marais directly to the Scales Psychiatric Facility, and they were staying low to the surface to avoid being seen. It would have taken a studied eye to discern them against the horizon. The concussion of the blades sent silent waves Jack and Marion and Ricky could feel more than hear, but to them the concussion was nothing more than an adjunct to the phantoms.

But the sound of Reuker's snowmobile carrying across the ice was different. It was a grating, insistent sound, the shriek of unfitted metal. It had bedeviled them for days, in the wilderness, and as that horrid, high-pitched whine battled the wind to reach their ears, the memory of the sound tipped a disquieting apprehension. It was like a haunting that refused to leave them in peace.

Jack looked around but could see nothing.

"Could the sound carry all the way from the ridge?" Marion asked.

"I don't know. I doubt it. Do you think it's really them?"

Marion nodded. Jack squinted, trying to pick out any movement coming toward them. His eye moved to the side of the ridge, to the crest, but it was too far now to pick out anything that small. He turned and said they had to continue moving. He had planned to rest soon; to give his foot a chance to cease, for only a few minutes at least, the jabbing pain. But there seemed a new urgency, and though he didn't see the machines, he had an awful feeling that they were there, that the new sounds were not phantoms.

They continued the trek over the frozen wastes, single file, Ricky in the lead, Jack at the rear. Wisps of ground-hugging snow curled across the ice, billowing into whirlpools of white crystal around their feet, then being caught by the air as their feet moved. The wind was increasing, and as it did, it was lifting the snow, layer by microscopic layer, from the crescent drifts, and carrying it along the surface, only to deposit it at the next drift.

As he watched the motion of the snow, Jack was coming to an uncomfortable realization. If the bridge was a gift of the cold and stillness of the last week, it would be a victim of the wind. The thought rekindled the mix of fear within him, and he looked anxiously to his right, to the northwest, into the teeth of the wind. There seemed an unsteadiness in the air, a change that was rapidly brewing. Jack moved faster, his pace hurrying Marion and Ricky in front of him.

All the while the ratchety screech of the machine was getting louder, until at last, even without looking, he knew they must be there. Pursuing them. Across the ice.

When he turned and looked back, it was without shock, without surprise, that he saw the vehicle gliding across the ice. It was rocketing straight toward them at its full throttle. There appeared to be only one, but at that distance, of at least a mile, he couldn't be sure.

He turned to Marion. "Take Ricky to the next drift and lie flat behind it."

"But what about you?"

"Like in the *shenigata*, Marion. We don't have any time to argue."

Indeed, there was none. The snowmobile was approaching rapidly. As she hurried ahead to seek what little protection the crescent of snow offered, Jack began to move away from them toward the southeast. He ran as fast as he was able, as fast as the slick surface would allow. The pain jabbing up his leg reached into his chest, then spiked with a furious thrust directly into his head. His mind seemed ready to rupture from the piercing, throbbing ache, from the strain of his frantic rush to get away from his wife and son.

Through the pain, the pounding rush of blood through his temples, he could hear a prayer whispering, then shouting within his thoughts. "Don't let them use their guns too soon. Not until I've led them away. Please, please, please. Save them. Save Marion and Ricky."

The unspoken words turned to ideas, to feelings, and then he began to lose coherence to his thoughts. He was powered only by his emotion, by his desire that they live, that somehow they be spared. He ran faster, the hard feel of the ice jarring him with every step. The sound of the machine was like a weapon, thrashing out at him, seeking to envelop him, to bring him down.

Reuker crouched to avoid the stinging bite of the wind. Unencumbered by deep drift, by the obstacles of the Scales interior, he was racing across the ice at forty miles per hour. The vessel was in his sights. No matter there was only one, and that there had appeared more figures before. The urgency of the cleansing was all that mattered.

And inside he felt a euphoric tension sparking through every nerve. The despair was rapidly falling away. The frustration of so many years, the despair of the failed sacrament, was lifting. The death the burning residue sought to bring upon him would be staved off. He would defeat the evil of the haloed priestess, the round-eyed figure that had come to him again at Scales. He would survive the destructive touch of her acolytes of darkness, of the tiled room, of the greedy touch of all who sought to consume his purity, his innocence, his devotion. He would be cleansed. Reuker felt the climax was near. He would be cleansed!

Jack stumbled awkwardly forward. He was losing the ability to carry himself on, so great was the gasping call for breath in his lungs, so painful was the raw burning of frigid air in his throat. The sound was deafening, as if it were nearly upon him, as if its source were struggling to enter his own mind, as if it were going to explode in a tumultuous final blast directly within his own skull. And still, he thought of their guns. Not yet. Not yet, he prayed.

But at last the powerful report came. It cracked through the air with the impact of a hundred rifles. The sound staggered him, and Jack lost all sense of balance, thinking only of Marion and Ricky. He managed to look back, as he was falling, back toward where they had been, toward where his wife and son had taken refuge in the slight mound of the drift.

He didn't see them. They were hidden. Everything was happening in the fraction of a second, but he had forced himself to look in their direction, and he forced the realization into his mind: They would be safe. They were hidden.

Jack's shoulder crashed to the ice, and he began to slide. The crackling, explosive sound continued to erupt all around him. It was a continuing volley of gunfire, a ceaseless crackling of charges that only seemed to grow in power.

Reuker became enveloped by the crisp, shattering tone. Past merged with present, and illusion with reality. He was on the brink of his dreams, on the verge of entering his sinless world of purity and sacrament. The sound and the sensation were so great he lost sensory awareness and became numb. And as he did, he fell. He fell into his world, his dreams, into his release.

Jack at last stopped his slide, and he remained where he was, clutching at the clutchless surface. He was afraid to move, even to begin to search for his wounds. But as he lay there, the resounding crash became an echo, and then it was gone. Carried away by the wind. Slowly he rolled to his side, then pushed himself to his knees. He looked in the direction the machine had been, but it was no longer there. It had vanished.

Jack raised himself to his feet and stared at where the pursuer had been. Had it been a haunting? The sound of his terror? The delusion of his ordeal? He swallowed in an attempt to still the tremor of his heart, to call upon an answer for the imponderable.

The water was as smooth and black as the ice, and only when he noticed the ripples did Jack perceive the difference. And then he understood.

Reuker Stilkes had crashed through the fragile surface and had plunged into the depths of the lake.

"Jack!" Marion's voice was made shrill by the wind. They were over 300 feet away, but he could still hear. "The ice! It's breaking."

Beyond them, in the distance, he could see what appeared to be swells looming above the surface of the bridge. The rising mounds of water were a few miles off, but it was the glint of the sun that gave them away. He started toward Marion and Ricky, and they toward him. As he walked, he sensed an emptiness, a strange feeling of loss he could not explain.

His eyes were drawn to the sight of his family. He felt compelled not to look away, as if every moment he could see them was something he would later treasure. His sense of rationality had been overwhelmed by the ordeal, and what came to him, as he approached Marion and Ricky, he felt was a premonition. It was a disquieting vision that nipped horribly at all that mattered to him.

He began to hurry, trying to close the gap between them, before whatever it was occurred. Before it was too late.

The rising swells were littered with chunks of ice like flotsam from an ocean catastrophe. The edge of the bridge was crumbling, and as it did, the shock of water and ice slamming into it sent vibrations throughout the shelf. The strain increased along the frozen and refrozen faults.

A grinding sound like cracking rock rumbled along with the wind, and the noise joined with the jittering, shaky feeling within Jack. The air was coming alive with the distant shattering of ice, and underlying it all was the groan of deep stress.

Marion and Ricky heard it too and were scared. It was an unseen enemy coming at them from where they couldn't tell.

They had approached to within fifty feet of each other, and Jack could see the fear on her face. The frozen edge of two massive slabs of ice angled from the northwest to the southeast between them. When it began to open, the leading edge of the crevasse moved with the speed of a galloping horse.

There was a loud and continuing snap that grew in intensity as echo magnified upon echo. Jack shouted for them not to approach any farther, while he continued to move. The crack followed the former opening, and its leading point was like a stiletto's tip. It pierced through the ice, rapidly slicing into the bridge that linked them to a common fate. Jack ran, but he was not fast enough. The crack traveled along the edge of the plates and divided their piece of the bridge in two.

As the point of the knife raced ahead, the tailing edge widened, inch by inch. It was a bottomless chasm opening before his eyes. The edges sank, and water spilled over them and lapped onto the ice. Marion staggered backward away from the opening, away from Jack. Her fingers crooked in frozen horror as they lightly brushed against her lips, to stifle a cry, to cease a winded gush of breath.

The edges of the plates rebounded, and the water slid back toward the chasm. It was getting wider by the second. Jack ran toward it. There was only one option. To leap to the other side.

It was slick near the edge, and when he jumped his feet slipped and seemed to give way beneath him. The crack had split to a width of five feet and Jack's effort was more a dive than a leap. He landed on his belly and slid on the ice away from the opening.

Ricky grabbed him under the arm before he stopped sliding and dragged him farther away from the crack. Jack had to shout to stop him. Then Marion was there, helping him to his feet.

The distant rumble of where the bridge met the lake had become a constant. Jack could hear it, but he refused to consider the gathering evidence that this fragile link to survival was doomed. To face reality at this point could lead to only one logic: to give up. So for Jack there was nothing to do but continue, to try to outrace the crumbling bridge.

They resumed heading for the mainland, but at an angle. They moved to the east, away from the direction of the wind, as much as toward the south and the land. There was nothing to do but move fast, to run from the danger.

Though he could deny reality, he could not invent a nonexistent hope. If it existed anyplace, it was not within his province.

The brown-and-green-splotched Air National Guard spotter plane circled above the Scales Psychiatric Facility. Ike Suomi had been the logical one to lead the squadron of helicopters to the island, and for once the state officials listened to logic.

Eight helicopters had made the trip from Grayling with their National Guard flight crews, and at Grand Marais they picked up an assault team of prison guards from Marquette and state police drawn from northern Michigan posts.

They came in low to the Facility and dropped down directly into the yard and just outside the perimeter by the entrance to the Administration Building. The resistance they met was minimal. It was as if the inmates wanted it to end, as if they welcomed a release from the psychic torment their mutiny had reawakened within them.

From his vantage point soaring high overhead, Suomi could see the lines of men being led out into the open under guard. He was in contact with Colonel Thompson, commander of the assault force, and when he received assurance that everything was under control, he signed off and swept his craft in a wide arc to head back to the mainland. As he flew toward the wishbone crest where Blackstone met Greenstone Ridge, Suomi was filled with a great sense of relief, and he let the plane fly. He relaxed the banking motion and soared over the ridge, and the vast interior opened below him.

It was a spectacular vista of primitive beauty. And

above all, it was open and free and untouched by the things that had tainted the southeast tip of this wilderness. It was a scene that complemented the feeling Ike savored, and only reluctantly did he bank to the south to resume his course for Grand Marais.

He was several miles out over the ice sheet when the tension returned. Far to his right he could see the breakup of the ice, and in front of it, by not more than a mile, he saw movement across the surface. There was something down there. There was some manner of creature stranded on the crumbling bridge.

Suomi swung into the wind. Quickly he realized there was more than one creature, and his first thought was that they were wolves heading for the mainland deserting a hunting ground made barren by the heavy snows and cold.

But as he grew closer, a trembling unsteadiness took root deep within his mind. Though within moments he could see the creatures were not wolves, he was reluctant to admit just exactly what they were. He refused to believe it until he was almost on top of them and their identity was without question.

The plane flew directly over the three figures, and they were waving at him. And one had been a child! Before he banked completely around, he was over the churning surface of open water where sharp slabs of broken ice were being tossed like featherweight debris.

When he saw the extent of the destruction, Suomi realized they didn't have a prayer. If they weren't rescued now, they had no chance to survive.

The spotter plane was a single-engine craft with an overhead wing. It was designed for lightness and stealth, Suomi considered. Would the ice support it? There seemed no time for anything else.

On the slick surface it would take a long runway to stop, so he gave himself a distance of three times what he felt the plane would normally require. Then he banked hard into the wind and began to bring it down.

When the skis first touched, they slapped with a bang on the hard surface, and the entire craft bounded into the air. Suomi feared the skis would be snapped off. He brought it back down, easier, and this time the plane settled onto his runway. The ice held, but there was a grinding, crackling noise of metal against ice.

With so little friction, he could sense no decrease in

speed. Blowing crystals of surface snow swirled at him and by him as if propelled by a blizzard wind. Though air rushed in a deafening roar over the downturned flaps of the craft, still the plane shot across the ice as if powered by an auxiliary engine that kept its own throttle.

The plane was on the edge of control as Suomi felt a tendency to skid to the side. He had to fight it, to struggle to keep it from twirling into a tailspin and tumbling out of control.

Gradually the plane lost velocity. He was winning. Suomi could see the three figures in front and to the right. Then suddenly his neck snapped back, and for an awful moment he was weightless.

The plane had crashed through the surface. Dear Jesus, it's going through!

His instincts reacted faster than he could think, and he gave the engine full throttle. He adjusted the flaps.

The airplane skidded over the cracking surface, over the water itself, and Suomi could do nothing but hang on and hope it wouldn't suddenly catch and dive straight into the ice. Behind him a giant tear was opening in the fragile shelf. The skis were shattering the surface as if it were nothing more than brittle plastic.

His arms shook from the strain of holding the controls. The entire craft vibrated from the forces that were assaulting it, that were trying to draw it down. But he maintained the speed. It was just enough to keep the plane skimming over the surface.

A garbled shout rumbled involuntarily deep in his throat. It was a raspy, churning scream that encompassed his fears, his strengths, his deepest hope. "Stay up, damn you," he cried, a coherence returning. "Stay up!"

The plane skated over the ice. Slowly it gathered power, and as it did, the craft seemed to increase in velocity. Suddenly it jumped, and for just a second, one glorious heart-soaring second, the skis left the surface.

Faster. More speed he needed. The ice was no longer cracking beneath him. The weight of the plane was sailing too fast over it to cause it to break.

Suomi thrust the flaps up, and the plane leaped into the air. It soared skyward, over the shelf, beyond the shattering border of the bridge, over the bobbing, crashing field of floating ice.

From the surface Jack watched as the tiny craft banked

in a tight turn and began to fly toward Scales. "We have to keep moving. He'll be back."

The swells of the lake had chewed to within a half mile of where they stood. All along the front, long spikes of opening cracks radiated out from the advancing edge. Jack and Marion and Ricky ran ahead of them.

They were destined to lose the race. But that no longer mattered. They needed time. They needed to stay ahead of the collapsing sheet long enough for the plane to return with other help, with a life raft, with what Jack couldn't fathom. He lacked the capacity to reason it out. He was guided strictly by emotion, by a resurgent hope, by a feeling that the ordeal was coming to an end. That his family, despite it all, was going to survive.

Suomi was shouting into the radio as soon as he leveled his craft. He tipped his wings as a signal to the people below that he wasn't deserting them. Surely they must realize that.

"Colonel Thompson," he yelled again. "Damn it, what's going on? Answer!"

Finally the radio crackled in response. It was a young voice, the voice of a reservist. "He's gone inside, sir. He's in the Administration Building of the Facility."

"Who are you?"

"Lieutenant Baker, sir."

"Are you the pilot?"

"Yes."

"There are three people out on the ice shelf about ten miles west of the Facility, and maybe seven south of the island. You got that?"

"Yes."

"They need help, and they need it now. Get your chopper in the air as fast as you can and head southwest. When you see the spotter plane, I'll lead you to them."

There was silence on the airwaves. Suomi waited for the confirmation. At last, the voice came. "Sir, I'm sorry but we can't do that. We were ordered to stay right here, at the entrance to the Facility."

"Damn you," Suomi shouted. "There are three people trapped on ice that's breaking up all around them. If you don't come, they're going to die."

The voice was nervous, rising in pitch. "We'll try to locate Colonel Thompson inside. We'll tell him and get his permission."

Suomi fought to control himself. The words rumbled from his throat like a vehement snarl. "There's no time for that. There's no time for anything." His tenuous control broke. "Goddamn it. Get that thing in the air."

Lieutenant Baker looked to the air corpsman next to him, the only other person in the helicopter. He was even younger than Baker, and his eyes were wide and his face a blank sheet of nervous indecision. From inside the Facility Baker could hear no gunfire, no sign that all wasn't going smoothly. Then he signaled Suomi. "Okay. We're coming."

From the beginning, from the first paper-thin slick of ice over the calm channel, the bridge had been a transient feature, an improbable link between archipelago and mainland. To the open lake, smoothness and peace were an aberrant condition, while violence and power were the rule. The rapid breakup of the ice was neither a thing of evil, nor the arbitrary tantrum of a neglected beast. The lake was merely reclaiming its own.

The sheets of ice rose and fell with the swells, and as they did, the four-inch-thick edges slammed into each other with the force of their own weight, with the force of gravity, with the force of the shifting weather systems. The ice exploded in shattering impact after impact, flinging knifelike shards of crystalline shrapnel in all directions.

The noise was a series of blasts as the crust crackled and broke along its brittle edge. Jack was running, always running, from the moment Reuker's doubled fist had struck him in the side of the face and the mutiny began. And like then, the destruction was on his heels. A force too powerful to confront, and like the drug-repressed madness of the inmates, a force beyond his ability to calm.

Marion and Ricky were shepherded in front of him, and seemed to be moving faster than he was. He was losing ground. They were inching ahead. His leg throbbed with an ache that pounded in every nerve, that seemed to pulse through every vein. The sound of the crashing surf rolled toward him like an avalanche in free-fall. It buried him and smothered him with the frenetic destructive fury of the waves.

He could feel the tiny crystals of frozen spray smattering against his back. He could sense the awakening fury in the water a few inches beneath his feet. And then he began to move, not under his own power but with the ice itself.

A huge sheet of ice a hundred yards deep broke free from the shelf, and it drew back on the swells. Then it slammed forward, and they all fell to the ice. Beneath them, enormous stresses were being absorbed by the sheet of ice, and the entire thing was ready to disintegrate.

Suomi had met the helicopter and had banked back into the wind. The minutes dragged on; there was no release for the tension. He sensed the gut-wrenching inadequacy of being witness to a tragedy he couldn't prevent.

Slowly the leading front of the bridge came closer. He could see the swells, the mounting power of the lake, but it was too far to distinguish any figures on the ice. It seemed his plane at times hovered in the air, as if it struggled against a headwind that equaled the thrust of his propeller.

But gradually he neared the crumbling ice line. He dived lower, his eyes frantically scanning the solid shelf of ice, then the shifting slabs, but there were no figures. And then he was past the ice line and over the turbulent sea.

Suomi looked out the fogged side window toward the island. Could he have flown too close to the land? Were they farther out? He banked to the left and came back to the border of water and ice. Before him as far as he could see stretched the glasslike field that fractured and splintered before his very eyes.

"Were they this close to the edge?" the voice from the helicopter asked.

"Yes, damn it. They were on the edge. They were down there, somewhere."

Ahead Suomi saw a narrow furrow in the ice sheet. It was where his skis had broken through. Yet it was only a fraction of the length it had been before. The lake had progressed that far.

He searched the unbroken sheet, but there was no sign of them. The radio spit an anxious cry: "To your right, sir. There they are!"

Suomi looked just in time to see them, on a huge shifting plate. It was crumbling along the sea edge, and throughout the plate he could see where white fracture lines were building in response to the stresses. The entire sheet was ready to shatter!

The helicopter came no lower than fifty feet. Even at that altitude, with the strength of the wind, the entire craft could be dashed into the water before the pilot had time to correct.

The corpsman swung the broad side-door open, and a blast of cold nearly catapulted the helicopter around. He kicked the harness out, and the winch began to lower it.

Down on the ice they watched as the life-saving yoke came toward them. Unhurriedly it sank, as if there were no rush, as if this were a practice exercise on a grassy field.

"Come on, come on," Jack pleaded. Marion clutched Ricky tightly to her, praying inwardly for it to arrive, for the boy at least to be saved.

The harness swung in wider arcs the longer the line became. And the helicopter was having difficulty stabilizing its position. When the harness at last was near the surface, it was swinging back and forth in wild, blustery sweeps. Jack waved his hands ineffectually at it once, twice, without even touching it. Then the helicopter began to swing around above them. Jack lunged and grabbed the harness. Marion helped him push it over Ricky's shoulders and the boy looped his arms over the padded sling.

Jack waved, and Ricky began to rise. As they watched, there was a shattering explosion of ice and water, and the entire sheet they balanced on pitched forward. It was breaking up!

The edge was crumbling along the border where it battered against the as yet solid bridge. As the chasm opened and filled with chunks of ice, the sheet felt the effects of the draw and push of the lake, of the rise and fall of the swells.

They could not maintain their balance, and they fell to the surface. Jack could hear the tortured moan of the ice, he could sense the growing pressures.

The foaming surf of the open water was no more than fifty feet from them. It appeared a volcanic sea, rolling and pitching and spewing steam into the air. But the steam was spray, and the rocks were ice, and the lava was water so frigid it could stop the beating of a healthy heart in minutes.

Ricky was inside, and the winch at its nonurgent pace

was lowering the harness. Jack and Marion clutched each other in their arms. Her eyes were fixed above, as if denying the danger. Jack looked from the harness to the crumbling edge and back to the harness. Water was spilling over the flat surface and sloshing toward them, then withdrawing as the sheet responded to the roll of the lake. Each new advance came closer until, finally, the water was splashing against their legs, first from one side, then from the other, from the widening chasm along the inside edge.

When the line reached them, they were barely able to stand. The surface was that slick, that unsteady. Jack grabbed the sling and had to force it over Marion's head. She fought against him, screaming that he go first. But he was stronger, and she relented, realizing the enemy was time.

She was lifted from the surface and rose at an agonizing pace toward the helicopter. Her feet dangled and swung in the air, and the harness dug into her armpits with the added force of the pressure from the winch.

Jack watched her from below. He squinted into the brightness above, directly into the concussion of the whirling blades. He watched her spinning and swaying at the end of the tether, reacting to the whim of the wind, but at last safe from it. The concerns were melting away. An exuberant, joyous sensation began to churn deep within him; it began to still the jittering tangle his nerves had become. He sensed and savored the first tingle of success. And with the feeling came a new strength. The pain seemed absent from his leg, and his weakness from the lack of nutrition was overcome by a surge of hormonal chemicals.

It was as he stood there maintaining his balance on the shifting surface, and as Marion was reaching the gaping side of the helicopter, that the eroded sheet of ice bucked on a swell and splintered into a dozen fragments. Jack was thrown to the surface, and then the slab he was on began to pitch. Jack clawed frantically at the ice, but he was sliding. He couldn't halt himself. He was being driven toward the water.

The raft-sized chunk of ice pitched higher, and Jack was airborne. He was falling, drifting, out of control. Then the feel of weightlessness was replaced by the sluggish grip of the water. He was plunging into it. His legs were spearing into the black depths.

It rushed up his thighs, under his coat, and when it slapped the bare skin of his face, he was stunned by the unimaginable chill. And then he was under.

The silence was sudden, and the sharp reports of cracking ice were muffled and removed and distant. He kicked and fought and stroked toward the surface, but his clothes, his parka, were rapidly absorbing the water. He was being drawn down, burdened with the added weight.

He struggled and groped above him for something to grasp, to pull himself up. The water succeeded in reaching his chest, and the full brunt of its near-freezing temperature at last exerted its full effect. His lungs approached paralysis from the shock, and he found himself fighting to resist the urge to gasp for breath, to suck furiously at air that wasn't there.

When his head broke the surface, the sound of the explosive fury of the ice spiked into his skull.

Jack grabbed onto a rectangular piece no more than ten feet long and four feet across. As he leaned his elbows onto it, his weight caused it to tip, and he began to slip again under the water. He released the ice and kicked and treaded madly with his arms. Then he felt a solid bang at the back of his head, and despite the chill, a hot flash of terror shot through him. Another slab was pushing him toward the ice he had grabbed. He had no choice but to dive, to sink below the depths. He held his breath and went down, and as he did, the two sheets slammed into each other, and where they hit, the edges disintegrated into fist-sized chunks of ice.

He kicked and forced himself through the debris and had to fight to stay at the surface. The ice chunks restricted the movement of his arms. His face bobbed below the water, and each time he broke clear he gasped for a mouthful of air, for a tiny bit of oxygen to fight the paralysis, to keep himself from blacking out, from slipping out of the range of the ice, of the helicopter sling.

The sling was coming lower, but it was difficult to follow. It was swinging like a pendulum, and the water kept rushing into his eyes, blurring his vision, making everything appear distorted. Oh, dear God, bring it down, bring it down!

Then the wavering of the harness disappeared, the helicopter disappeared, as he sank beneath the surface, and the ice chips swallowed the space he left. He had lost feeling in his jaw and had to concentrate to keep his mouth clenched shut. His blood was thickening, carrying less oxygen to his lungs, and he could take only a few seconds submerged before an involuntary spasm would force a desperate gasp for breath, before he would suck the freezing liquid deep into his chest.

Marion spun from the opening and shrieked at the corpsman. "Can't you do anything? He's drowning!"

The corpsman looked toward the pilot, his face mirroring the hysteria that had taken hold of Marion. Baker eased the craft lower, closer to the peaking crests of ice and water.

Jack kicked and brushed his hand awkwardly above himself. He was losing the ability to control his muscles, to move his limbs. But he was possessed of a frantic command to live, to survive, to be with his wife and son.

He broke through the ice, and his throat screeched for air. He fought with whatever strength he had to stay above the surface, to give himself time to breathe.

He was getting dizzier. The shapes he saw, the images he imagined, were in motion. But through it all there was one constant, one swinging, pendulumlike constant. The harness!

Jack raised a wooden limb as the shape swung in its wind-buffeted arc. It cracked off the back of his hand, but he lacked the dexterity to grab it. The sling swung out of his reach, and then back. But again he missed it, and then he dipped below the water. He fought back to the surface, but he continued to rise and fall with the swells, and continued to be jostled by the ice.

He lost sight of the harness and looked frantically about him. Then he looked above and saw the snakelike line, and he followed it down to the water. The harness was bouncing on the surface, the line going slack then taut. Yet in its erratic movements it was bounding closer.

Jack rose on a swell, then as he plunged into the trough, he saw the edges of two massive sheets of ice balancing at the crests of the swells he was between. The lake surface continued its convulsions, and Jack twisted his neck from one slab to the other, watching as the ice was being rocked and pushed by the motion of the water.

The swells rose, and the ice floated closer. Jack fought

a rising sense of panic, but the dire images were impossible to stem: The knife-edges would shear him in half. The anesthesia of the cold wouldn't matter. The end would be sudden and violent.

The frantic rush of thoughts ignited a terror, a terror that deep within his mind Jack saw in great splashes of color, of fiery strokes lashing at his last glimpses of life, stealing from him his only comfort, his diminishing vision of Marion and Ricky, safely in the aircraft.

The corpsman shouted, "The ice is building up fast. We won't be able to take the weight." Spray from the waves was coating the outside of the helicopter with a thickening layer of glaze. It was blowing into the open door, pelting them with stinging crystals.

Jack sank into a trough, and one of the great sheets slid over the top of the swell behind him and banged into the back of his head. The harness popped into the air and dropped near him as he rose with the water. He struggled toward it, to grab the twitching lifeline that jerked with the minutest movement of the helicopter above. His left hand touched it, and it was glazed with ice and slippery, but he was able to hook his elbow through the yoke. Then he struggled to bring around his right shoulder to slip into the harness, but it wouldn't respond.

The line remained slack as Baker risked coming even lower, "Come on, come on. Get into that thing."

The swell began to drop and Jack could feel the ice nudging him from behind. He glanced and saw the other sheet rising on the opposite swell, balancing at the very crest. Then it began to slide. Oh Jesus, it was sliding over the summit. It was sailing straight down the hill of water.

The helicopter pilot saw what Jack saw. He lunged hard on the controls, and his craft leaped skyward.

As the knife-edge of the ice sliced toward him, Jack felt his shoulder being nearly torn from its socket. He was rising, pulling out of the water. And then he was yanked clear. The ice cracked just below his feet and buckled upward as if in a desperate grab for its victim, unfairly snatched from its grip.

Below him Jack could see the boiling caldron of the lake, the turgid brew of ice and spume churning, billowing, leaping in swollen mounds of black water, in freezing fingerlings of spray. Despite the deadened sensation of the cold, deep in his shoulder there was tearing, wrenching pain. His elbow felt as though it were distended, and the sinew, muscle, and flesh were slowly tearing.

He brought his right hand to the harness, but it was slick with ice, and his fingers were not agile enough to grip it. He could only hope to hang on.

The agony from his arm spread and dominated every other feeling within him. It was a dulling veil settling over his consciousness. The light was dimming.

The wind chill was below zero. The outer layer of his clothes was already frozen. Ice crinkled along the folds of his face. It stiffened his hair, nearly cementing shut his eyelids.

The path of hypothermia was accelerated. His mind was slipping into darkness, into a dizzy swirl of failing thought and sickness. He was on the edge of consciousness.

The winch felt not the emotions that acted on the actors. It neither slowed nor speeded, it neither succumbed to tension nor was fired by adrenaline. It merely continued to turn in the same unhurried manner, slowly, unflinchingly recoiling the line, drawing the harness closer to the ship.

The lake below became a blurry whirl of nondistinctive shapes and colors. Jack was losing even the sound, the sense of its destructive fury. The noise from above became louder, deeper, sending waves of concussion throughout him.

The wind blew him beneath the helicopter, and Lieutenant Baker rotated to bring him out, to enable him to reach the open side. Jack's arm banged against the landing bar and went numb. The pendulum was swinging in the opposite direction. The corpsman struggled to reach the line, seeking to pull it back.

"He's slipping, he's slipping," the corpsman cried. "Bring it around."

Baker fought to maintain the craft's stability in the wind and slowly began to rotate again. The winch had inched him higher.

His eyes were iced shut. He was blacking out. And then, suddenly, the blackness became total. The pressure on his shoulder eased, and the sensation was as though he were weightless. As if he were falling. He waited for the crash to the ice, for the feel of the cold rushing over him. It would feel almost warm. It would thaw the ice crusted to him, and he would sink. He would drift into peace. The ordeal would be over.

Yet the release of the ice, the water did not come. He was inside. He fought to keep his hold of the harness, but there were hands pulling at his arm, trying to break it free. Finally it was torn from him, and then the feel of the wind ceased as the door slammed shut.

His coat was being torn off. His boots removed. The helicopter was rising higher above the sea, then at last it abandoned its stationary hover and proceeded ahead fast.

The touch of others was soothing. The voices comforted. Yet despite it all, hidden within the new security was a nagging last detail. It prevented him from ending the struggle, from accepting his deserved release. He tried to force it out, but he lacked the power. His mouth opened, but he could not utter a sound.

A raw expulsion of breath wheezed through his throat. A shape bent close to listen. He could sense Marion's face near him. He tried to speak, and his voice at best was a hoarse whisper. One word, that's all he tried. Over and over, until it at last formed on his lips. Until it at last took shape from the tortured sounds of wind escaping from his lungs. "Philip, Philip," he was saying.

And through the descending fog he could hear her voice. He could hear it come in soothing waves, lapping at his ears with the feel of a gentle warmth washing over him. He reacted to the sound, to the warmth, as if it was her bare arms wrapping around his back and pulling his chest close to hers. "They've been told," she was saying. "We're flying toward Blackstone to find Philip."

He surrendered willingly the last of his resistance and accepted the quiet urges of the warmth. He relaxed and allowed his head to be propped up and a hot liquid poured into his mouth. It burned, but he couldn't imagine a better feeling. He couldn't imagine a more glorious sensation to plunge deep into his throat, his chest, his stomach, sending ripples of life and warmth throughout his body. He was being wrapped within a wool blanket, and he could feel Ricky and marion in their own blankets snuggling close against him. Jack alternated between a semiconscious state and his eager wish to enjoy the moment. He wanted to savor the taste of what survival meant; he wanted to contemplate the joys that waited, the prospect of a life unencumbered by an anxiety that had become as much a function of his living as the act of inhaling oxygen or pumping blood.

He could not as yet resume control of his muscles, and so he had to content himself with the meager awareness of what was happening around him, with the knowledge that the door had opened, the winch was lowering, then rising, with the wondrous sounds of his family, and of Philip Tardif. He sensed the victory, and he felt their joy, and cradled within its soft caresses he succumbed not to unconsciousness, but to sleep.

The helicopter roared, and the entire craft shook. Its vibrations worked a delicate massage, and the rhythm of movement, of the power of the rotors, signaled a final break with the angry forces of Scales.

The dread within Jack had died. His peace had returned. The final twinge of discomfort the island, the inmates, the institution itself had held over him, vanished.

He and his family would never again breach the shoreline of the basaltic archipelago.

EPILOGUE

Grains of wind-carried sand pricked her cheek. Long blond strands of hair played gently on the warm breeze, tangling in a fine mesh across her face. Marion swept it from her eyes and leaned closer to Jack.

They stood at the crest of the Grand Sable Dunes near Grand Marais and stared out across the lake toward Scale Island. Philip was a few yards away, at the very edge of the dune where it began to slope sharply, and behind him stood Ricky.

The water was deep blue, decorated with tattered ribbons of white froth. From above, it appeared columns of soggy lint on serge. They were too far up to hear the waves breaking on the shore, and because of that the lake lent a certain tranquillity to the atmosphere. There was an easy rhythm to the waves, a casual give-and-take that extended beyond the wash of the water. Soft, rounded hills of muted sand-hues absorbed the August sun, and delicate wisps of dune grass brushed in the breeze with the sound of a harpist's breath against her strings.

They had come because it was Philip and Emma's anniversary. But it was not a graveside vigil. Six and a half months had passed since they left Scales, and they had lived through the grief and accepted her loss.

"It would have been forty-four years," Philip said. It was a simple statement of fact, bereft of sadness. Ricky looked to his mother, worried, as if torn with lack of anything to say. Marion just shook her head. We're here to listen, she could have been saying.

"They were all good years," Philip continued, and indeed they were, for all of them, the times they had known her.

Standing there on the crest of the dune, Emma's tomb

a distant sight, they all felt enriched by her sacrifice. There was a strength from her memory, as if a part of her vigor would always be alive within them. Within each there was a quiet joy, a sense of pride for having known her.

Jack wrapped his arm around Marion, and he squeezed her to his side. Almost fifteen years earlier, at this same place, they had lain together on the sand. It had been down near the shore, at night, and the northern lights had streaked the sky with curtains of shimmering illumination.

Now they watched as dark plumes of smoke rose from Scales, coloring the horizon with a grimy curtain of black soot. When released from the mantle of snow, the peat fires had ignited the forests of the interior. The island had been burning for three months, and there had been no attempt to douse the flames. Where the fires raged, the island was being left to burn right down to its ancient rocky core.

The Department of Corrections had abandoned the island. The inmates had been moved to other facilities, the guards transferred. Hagan had retired. The brick buildings they left behind were already stained and darkened by the ash and soot from the fires. It was as if they were being absorbed into the black, basaltic rock of the island itself. In time, the metamorphosis would be complete, and the Facility would be inextricably fused with the tradition of the land.

Philip turned, then said to Ricky, "She's glad you're here." He smiled and brought his hand to the top of his head and gently tousled his hair. "If she could tell us anything now, she'd say she's glad the boy was here."

Ricky smiled, and he turned with Philip, and then they all began to walk away from the crest of the dune. They were a family now, the four of them, bound together by a kinship stronger than blood. They shared the same house, and they would be moving together soon to Isle Royale.

Jack had taken a job with the National Park Service, and Isle Royale was a wilderness island-park 150 miles northwest of Scales near the Minnesota-Ontario shore. They were to live at the ranger station on the north coast, a remote outpost far removed from the Rock Harbor headquarters.

"What's it going to be like at Isle Royale?" Ricky

asked. His anticipation was shared by all of them. Life was finally going to settle into something new, and the past would be entrenched only in memory.

Philip laughed. "I've told you. Your father's told you. We could tell you a hundred times and you'd still ask."

"Dad? What's it like?"

"It's a lot like Scales. The same kinds of trees, rocks, animals. Everything."

"It's part of the same geologic formation," Philip said. "There's a long rock spine called the Niagara escarpment that goes from upper New York all the way to Canada. It's along the edge of the body of land that the North American continent grew up around. Scale Island is part of it, and so is Isle Royale."

"Will they let it change, like Scales?"

"It never has, and it never will. The National Park people have the good sense to keep it as a wilderness. To keep it as it's always been."

Ike Suomi waited for them in his jeep a few hundred feet from the crest. He was parked in the middle of a faint trail that followed a twisting path through the mounds and dips of the shifting dunes.

As they approached, Jack's limp was barely noticeable. He lost only a part of his left foot to frostbite, and the doctors said that after a while, there would be no limp at all.

As they left the dune, they talked and planned and anticipated the move to the island wilderness, to a land that was as much a part of them as their blood and bone and tissue.

They would live there together, as a family, and together would enjoy its peace and beauty. Except in winter. No one was allowed on the island then, and come every October they would have to shift bases to the mainland and Hancock on the Keweenaw Peninsula.

They would not challenge the forces of winter. The island would be left to the wolves and the moose and the cold and the snow. It would be left to the might and whim of Lake Superior.